THE REAL AMERICAN UNDERGROUND

THE ILLUMINATUS! TRILOGY

"The longest shaggy dog joke in literary history....A hundred pages in I couldn't figure out why I was wasting my time with this nonsense...after three hundred I was having too much fun to quit, and by the end I was eager to believe every word – I loved it.

— *Rolling Stone*

"More important than *Ulysses* or *Finnegans Wake.*"

— Timothy Leary

"Funny, savagely sarcastic, definitely anarchistic...wild and irreverent...Shea and Wilson blend a marvelous amount of fact and inspired fiction together to weave one of the most dizzying tales I've come across in years.... Laugh or rage at it or with it...you won't be able to put it down."

— *Limit*

"All the ingredients: kinky sex, raunchy language, and a fantasy plot that oscillates between a schizoid nightmare and a psychedelic dream."

— *Booklist*

THE ILLUMINATUS! TRILOGY

The Eye in the Pyramid, The Golden Apple, and *Leviathan*

Robert Shea & Robert Anton Wilson

MJF BOOKS
NEW YORK

Published by MJF Books
Fine Communications
Two Lincoln Square
60 West 66th Street
New York, NY 10023

The Illuminatus! Trilogy
Library of Congress Catalog Card Number #97-75440
ISBN 1-56731-237-3

Manufactured in the United States of America on acid-free paper

MJF Books and the MJF colophon are trademarks of Fine Creative Media, Inc.

10   9   8   7   6   5   4   3   2   1

CONTENTS

ILLUMINATUS!
PART I

The Eye
in the Pyramid

*To Gregory Hill
and Kerry Thornley*

BOOK ONE

VERWIRRUNG

The history of the world is the history of
the warfare between secret societies.
—Ishmael Reed, *Mumbo-Jumbo*

THE FIRST TRIP, OR KETHER

From Dealey Plaza
To Watergate . . .

The Purple Sage opened his mouth and moved his tongue and so spake to them and he said:

The Earth quakes and the Heavens rattle; the beasts of nature flock together and the nations of men flock apart; volcanoes usher up heat while elsewhere water becomes ice and melts; and then on other days it just rains.

Indeed do many things come to pass.

—Lord Omar Khayaam Ravenhurst, K.S.C.,
"The Book of Predications." *The Honest Book of Truth*

It was the year when they finally immanentized the Eschaton. On April 1, the world's great powers came closer to nuclear war than ever before, all because of an obscure island named Fernando Poo. By the time international affairs returned to their normal cold-war level, some wits were calling it the most tasteless April Fool's joke in history. I happen to know all the details about what happened, but I have no idea how to recount them in a manner that will make sense to most readers. For instance, I am not even sure who I am, and my embarrassment on that matter makes me wonder if you will believe anything I reveal. Worse yet, I am at the moment very conscious of a squirrel—in Central Park, just off Sixty-eighth Street, in New York City—that is leaping from one tree to another, and I think that happens on the night of April 23 (or is it the morning of April 24?), but fitting the squirrel together with Fernando Poo is, for the present, beyond my powers. I beg your tolerance. There is nothing I can do to make things any easier for any of us, and you will have to accept being addressed by a disembodied voice just as I accept the compulsion to speak out even though I am painfully aware that I am talking to an invisible, perhaps nonexistent, audience. Wise men have regarded the earth as a tragedy, a farce, even an illusionist's trick; but all, if they are truly wise and not merely intellectual rapists, recognize that it is certainly some kind of stage in which we all play roles, most of us being very poorly coached and totally unrehearsed before the curtain rises. Is it too much if I ask, tentatively, that we agree to look upon it as a circus, a touring carnival wandering about the sun for a record season of four billion years and producing new monsters and miracles, hoaxes and bloody mishaps, wonders and blunders, but never quite entertaining the customers well enough to prevent them from leaving, one by one, and returning to their homes for a long and bored winter's sleep under the dust? Then, say, for a while at least, that I have found an identity as ringmaster; but that crown sits uneasily on my head (if I have a head) and I must warn you that the troupe is small for a universe this size and many of us have to double or triple our stints, so you can expect me back in many other guises. Indeed do many things come to pass.

For instance, right now, I am not at all whimsical or humorous. I am angry. I am in Nairobi, Kenya, and my name is, if you will pardon me, Nkrumah Fubar. My skin is black (does that disturb you? it doesn't me), and I am, like most of you, midway between tribalism and technology; to be more blunt, as a Kikuyu shaman moderately adjusted to city life, I still believe in witchcraft—I haven't, yet, the folly to deny the evidence of my own senses. It is April 3 and Fernando Poo has ruined my sleep for several nights running, so I hope you will forgive me when I admit that my business at the moment is far from edifying and is nothing less than constructing dolls of the rulers of America, Russia, and China. You guessed it: I am going to stick pins in their heads every day for a month; if they won't let me sleep, I won't let them sleep. That is Justice, in a sense.

In fact, the President of the United States had several severe migraines during the following weeks; but the atheistic rulers of Moscow and Peking were less susceptible to magic. They never reported a twinge. But, wait, here is another performer in our circus, and one of the most intelligent and decent in the lot—his name is unpronounceable, but you can call him Howard and he happens to have been born a dolphin. He's swimming through the ruins of

Atlantis and it's April 10 already—time is moving; I'm not sure what Howard sees but it bothers him, and he decides to tell Hagbard Celine all about it. Not that I know, at this point, who Hagbard Celine is. Never mind; watch the waves roll and be glad there isn't much pollution out here yet. Look at the way the golden sun lights each wave with a glint that, curiously, sparkles into a silver sheen; and watch, watch the waves as they roll, so that it is easy to cross five hours of time in one second and find ourselves amid trees and earth, with even a few falling leaves for a touch of poetry before the horror. Where are we? Five hours away, I told you—five hours due west, to be precise, so at the same instant that Howard turns a somersault in Atlantis, Sasparilla Godzilla, a tourist from Simcoe, Ontario (she had the misfortune to be born a human being) turns a neat nosedive right here and lands unconscious on the ground. This is the outdoor extension of the Museum of Anthropology in Chapultepec Park, Mexico, D.F., and the other tourists are rather upset about the poor lady's collapse. She later said it was the heat. Much less sophisticated in important matters than Nkrumah Fubar, she didn't care to tell anybody, or even to remind herself, what had really knocked her over. Back in Simcoe, the folks always said Harry Godzilla got a sensible woman when he married Sasparilla, and it is sensible in Canada (or the United States) to hide certain truths. No, at this point I had better not call them truths. Let it stand that she either saw, or imagined she saw, a certain sinister kind of tight grin, or grimace, cross the face of the gigantic statue of Tlaloc, the rain god. Nobody from Simcoe had ever seen anything like that before; indeed do many things come to pass.

And, if you think the poor lady was an unusual case, you should examine the records of psychiatrists, both institutional and private, for the rest of the month. Reports of unusual anxieties and religious manias among schizophrenics in mental hospitals skyrocketed; and ordinary men and women walked in off the street to complain about eyes watching them, hooded beings passing through locked rooms, crowned figures giving unintelligible commands, voices that claimed to be God or the Devil, a real witch's brew for sure. But the sane verdict was to attribute all this to the aftermath of the Fernando Poo tragedy.

The phone rang at 2:30 A.M. the morning of April 24. Numbly, dumbly, mopingly, gropingly, out of the dark, I find and identify a body, a self, a task. "Goodman," I say into the receiver, propped up on one arm, still coming a long way back.

"Bombing and homicide," he electrically eunuchoid voice in the transmitter tells me. I sleep naked (sorry about that), and I'm putting on my drawers and trousers as I copy the address. East Sixty-eighth Street, near the Council on Foreign Relations. "Moving," I say, hanging up.

"What? Is?" Rebecca mumbles from the bed. She's na-ked, too, and that recalls very pleasant memories of a few hours earlier. I suppose some of you will be shocked when I tell you I'm past sixty and she's only twenty-five. It doesn't make it any better that we're married, I know.

This isn't a bad body, for its age, and seeing Rebecca, most of the sheets thrown aside, reminds me just how good it is. In fact, at this point I don't even remember having been the ringmaster, or what echo I retain is con-fused with sleep and dream. I kiss her neck, unself-con-sciously, for she is my wife and I am her husband, and even if I am an inspector on the Homicide Squad—Homi-cide North, to be exact—any notions about being a stranger in this body have vanished with my dreams into air. Into thin air.

"What?" Rebecca repeats, still more asleep than awake.

"Damned fool radicals again," I say, pulling on my shirt, knowing any answer is as good as another in her half-conscious state.

"Um," she says, satisfied, and turns over into deep sleep again.

I washed my face somewhat, tired old man watching me from the mirror, and ran a brush through my hair. Just time enough to think that retirement was only a few years away and to remember a certain hypodermic needle and a day in the Catskills with my first wife, Sandra, back when they at least had clean air up there . . . socks, shoes, tie, fedora . . . and you never stop mourning, as much as I loved Rebecca I never stopped mourning San-dra. Bombing *and* homicide. What a *meshuganah* world. Do you remember when you could at least drive in New York at three in the morning without traffic jams? Those days were gone; the trucks that were banned in the daytime were all making their deliveries now. Everybody was supposed to pretend the pollution went away before dawn. Papa used to say, "Saul, Saul, they did it to the Indians and now they're doing it to themselves. *Goyische narrs.*" He left Russia to escape the pogrom of 1905, but I guess he saw a lot before he got out. He seemed like a cynical old man to me then, and I seem like a cynical old man to others now. Is there any pattern or sense in any of it?

The scene of the blast was one of those old office buildings with Gothic-and-gingerbread styling all over the lobby floor. In the dim light of the hour, it reminded me of the shadowy atmosphere of Charlie Chan in the Wax Museum. And a smell hit my nostrils as soon as I walked in.

A patrolman lounging inside the door snapped to attention when he recognized me. "Took out the seventeenth floor and part of the eighteenth," he said. "Also a pet shop here on the ground level. Some freak of dynamics. Nothing else is damaged down here, but every fish tank went. That's the smell."

Barney Muldoon, an old friend with the look and mannerisms of a Hollywood cop, appeared out of the shadows. A tough man, and nowhere as dumb as he liked to pretend, which was why he was head of the Bomb Squad.

"Your baby, Barney?" I asked casually.

"Looks that way. Nobody killed. The call went out to you because a clothier's dummy was burned on the eighteenth floor and the first car here thought it was a human body."

(*Wait: George Dorn is screaming. . . .*)

Saul's face showed no reaction to the answer—but poker players at the Fraternal Order of Police had long ago given up trying to read that inscrutable Talmudic countenance. As Barney Muldoon, I knew how I would feel if I had the chance to drop this case on another department and hurry home to a beautiful bride like Rebecca Goodman. I smiled down at Saul—his height would keep him from appointment to the Force now, but the rules were different when he was young—and I added quietly, "There might be something in it for you, though."

The fedora ducked as Saul took out his pipe and started

to fill it. All he said was, "Oh?"

"Right now," I went on, "we're just notifying Missing Persons, but if what I'm afraid of is right, it'll end up on your desk after all."

He struck a match and started puffing. "Somebody missing at this hour . . . might be found among the living . . . in the morning," he said between drags. The match went out, and shadows moved where nobody stirred.

"And he might not, in this case," Muldoon said. "He's been gone three days now."

"An Irishman your size can't be any more subtle than an elephant," Saul said wearily. "Stop tantalizing me. What have you got?"

"The office that was hit," Muldoon explained, obviously happy to share the misery, "was a magazine called *Confrontation*. It's kind of left-of-center, so this was probably a right-wing job and not a left-wing one. But the interesting thing is that we couldn't reach the editor, Joseph Malik, at his home, and when we called one of the associate editors, what do you think he told us? Malik disappeared three days ago. His landlord confirms it. He's been trying to get hold of Malik himself because there's a no-pets rule there and the other tenants are complaining about his dogs. So, if a man drops out of sight and then his office gets bombed, I kind of think the matter might come to the attention of the Homicide Department eventually, don't you?"

Saul grunted. "Might and might not," he said. "I'm going home. I'll check with Missing Persons in the morning, to see what they've got."

The patrolman spoke up. "You know what bothers me most about this? The Egyptian mouth-breeders."

"The what?" Saul asked.

"That pet shop," the patrolman explained, pointing to the other end of the lobby. "I looked over the damage, and they had one of the best collections of rare tropical fish in New York City. Even Egyptian mouth-breeders." He noticed the expressions on the faces of the two detectives and added lamely, "If you don't collect fish, you wouldn't understand. But, believe me, an Egyptian mouth-breeder is pretty hard to get these days, and they're all dead in there."

"Mouth-*breeder?*" Muldoon asked incredulously.

"Yes, you see they keep their young in their mouths for a couple days after birth and they never, never swallow them. That's one of the great things about collecting fish: you get to appreciate the wonders of nature."

Muldoon and Saul looked at each other. "It's inspiring," Muldoon said finally, "to have so many college graduates on the Force these days."

The elevator door opened, and Dan Pricefixer, a red-headed young detective on Muldoon's staff, emerged, carrying a metal box.

"I think this is important, Barney," he began immediately, with just a nod to Saul. "Damned important. I found it in the rubble, and it had been blown partly open, so I looked inside."

"And?" Muldoon prompted.

"It's the freakiest bunch of interoffice memos I ever set eyes on. Weird as tits on a bishop."

This is going to be a long night, Saul thought suddenly, with a sinking feeling. A long night, and a heavy case.

"Want to peek?" Muldoon asked him maliciously.

"You better find a place to sit down," Pricefixer volunteered. "It'll take you awhile to go through them."

"Let's use the cafeteria," Saul suggested.

"You just have no idea," the patrolman repeated. "The value of an Egyptian mouth-breeder."

"It's rough for all nationalities, man or fish," Muldoon said in one of his rare attempts to emulate Saul's mode of speech. He and Saul turned to the cafeteria, leaving the patrolman looking vaguely distressed.

His name is James Patrick Hennessy and he's been on the Force three years. He doesn't come back into this story at all. He had a five-year-old retarded son whom he loved helplessly; you see a thousand faces like his on the street every day and never guess how well they are carrying their tragedies . . . and George Dorn, who once wanted to shoot him, is still screaming. . . . But Barney and Saul are in the cafeteria. Look around. The transition from the Gothic lobby to this room of laminated functional and glittering plastic colors is, one might say, trippy. Never mind the smell; we're closer to the pet shop here.

Saul removed his hat and ran a hand through his gray hair pensively, as Muldoon read the first two memos in one quick scan. When they were passed over, he put on his glasses and read more slowly, in his own methodical and thoughtful way. Hold onto your hats. This is what they said:

ILLUMINATI PROJECT: MEMO #1

7/23

J.M.:

The first reference I've found is in *Violence* by Jacques Ellul (Seabury Press, New York, 1969). He says (pages 18-19) that the Illuminated Ones were founded by Joachim of Floris in the 11th century and originally taught a primitive Christian doctrine of poverty and equality, but later under the leadership of Fra Dolcino in the 15th century they became violent, plundered the rich and announced the imminent reign of the Spirit. "In 1507," he concludes, "they were vanquished by the 'forces of order'—that is, an army commanded by the Bishop of Vercueil." He makes no mention of any Illuminati movement in earlier centuries or in more recent times.

I'll have more later today.

Pat

P.S. I found a little more about Joachim of Floris in the back files of the *National Review*. William Buckley and his cronies think Joachim is responsible for modern liberalism, socialism and communism; they've condemned him in fine theological language. He committed the heresy, they say, of "immanentizing the Christian Eschaton." Do you want me to look that up in a technical treatise on Thomism? I think it means bringing the end of the world closer, sort of.

ILLUMINATI PROJECT: MEMO #2

7/23

J.M.:

My second source was more helpful: Akron Daraul, *A History of Secret Societies* (Citadel Press, New York, 1961).

Daraul traces the Illuminati back to the 11th century also, but not to Joachim of Floris. He sees the origin in the Ishmaelian sect of Islam, also known as the Order of Assassins. They were vanquished in the 13th century, but later made a comeback with a new, less-violent philosophy

and eventually became the Ishmaelian sect of today, led
by the Aga Khan. However, in the 16th century, in Afghanistan, the Illuminated Ones (Roshinaya) picked up
the original tactics of the Order of Assassins. They were
wiped out by an alliance of the Moguls and Persians
(pages 220-223). But, "The beginning of the seventeenth
century saw the foundation of the Illuminated Ones of
Spain—the Allumbrados, condemned by an edict of the
Grand Inquisition in 1623. In 1654, the 'illuminated'
Guerinets came into public notice in France." And, finally—the part you're most interested in- the Bavarian Illuminati was founded on May Day, 1776, in Ingolstadt,
Bavaria, by Adam Weishaupt, a former Jesuit.
"Documents still extant show several points of resemblance between the German and Central Asian Illumi-
nists: points that are hard to account for on grounds of
pure coincidence" (page 255). Weishaupt's Illuminati
were suppressed by the Bavarian government in 1785;
Daraul also mentions the Illuminati of Paris in the 1880s,
but suggests it was simply a passing fad. He does not accept the notion that the Illuminati still exist today.

This is beginning to look big. Why are we keeping the
details from George?

                                                    Pat

Saul and Muldoon exchanged glances. "Let's see the
next one," Saul said. He and Muldoon read together:

ILLUMINATI PROJECT: MEMO #3

                                                    7/24

J.M.:
The Encyclopedia Britannica has little to say on the subject (1966 edition, Volume 11, "Halicar to Impala," page
1094):

> *Illuminati,* a short-lived movement of republican free
> thought founded on May Day 1776 by Adam
> Weishaupt, professor of canon law at Ingolstadt and
> a former Jesuit. . . . From 1778 onward they began
> to make contact with various Masonic lodges where,
> under the impulse of A. Knigge (q.v.) one of their
> chief converts, they often managed to gain a com-
> manding position. . . .

The scheme itself had its attractions for literary men like Goethe and Herder, and even for the reigning dukes of Gotha and Weimar. . . .

The movement suffered from internal dissention and was ultimately banned by an edict of the Bavarian government in 1785.

Pat

Saul paused. "I'll make you a bet, Barney," he said quietly. "The Joseph Malik who vanished is the J.M. these memos were written for."

"Sure," Muldoon replied scornfully. "These Illuminati characters are still around, and they got him. Honest to God, Saul," he added, "I appreciate the way your mind usually pole-vaults ahead of the facts. But you can ride a hunch just so far when you're starting from nothing."

"We're not starting from nothing," Saul said softly. "Here's what we've got to start with. One"—he·held up a finger—"a building is bombed. Two"—another finger— "an important executive disappeared three days before the bombing. Already, there's an inference, or two inferences: something got him, or else he knew something was coming for him and he ducked out. Now, look at the memos. Point three"—he held up another finger—"a standard reference work, the *Encyclopedia Britannica*, seems to be wrong about when the Illuminati came into existence. They say eighteenth-century Germany, but the other memos trace it back to—let's see—Spain in the seventeenth century, France in the seventeenth century, then in the eleventh century back to Italy and halfway across the world to Afghanistan. So we've got a second inference: if the Britannica is wrong about when the thing started, they may be wrong about when it ended. Now, put these three points and two inferences together—"

"And the Illuminati got the editor and blew up his office. Nutz. I still say you're going too fast."

"Maybe I'm not going fast enough," Saul said. "An organization that has existed for a couple of centuries *minimum* and kept its secrets pretty well hidden most of that time might be pretty strong by now." He trailed off into silence, and closed his eyes to concentrate. After a moment, he looked at the younger man with a searching glance.

Muldoon had been thinking too. "I've seen men land on

the moon," he said. "I've seen students break into administration offices and shit in the dean's waste basket. I've even seen nuns in mini-skirts. But this international conspiracy existing in secret for eight hundred years, it's like opening a door in your own house and finding James Bond and the President of the United States personally shooting it out with Fu Manchu and the five original Marx Brothers."

"You're trying to convince yourself, not me. Barney, it sticks out so far that you could break it into three pieces and each one would be long enough to goose somebody up in the Bronx. There *is* a secret society that keeps screwing up international politics. Every intelligent person has suspected that at one time or another. Nobody wants war any more, but wars keep happening—why? Face it, Barney—this is the heavy case we've always had nightmares about. It's cast iron. If it were a corpse, all six pallbearers would get double hernias at the funeral. Well?" Saul prompted.

"Well, we're either going to have to do something or get off the pot, as my sainted mother used to say."

It was the year when they finally immanentized the Eschaton. On April 1 the world's great powers came closer to nuclear war than ever before, all because of an obscure island named Fernando Poo. But, while all other eyes turned to the UN building in apprehension and desperate hope, there lived in Las Vegas a unique person known as Carmel. His house was on Date Street and had a magnificent view of the desert, which he appreciated. He liked to spend long hours looking at the wild cactus wasteland although he did not know why. If you told him that he was symbolically turning his back upon mankind, he would not have understood you, nor would he have been insulted; the remark would be merely irrelevant to him. If you added that he himself was a desert creature, like the gila monster and the rattlesnake, he would have grown bored and classified you as a fool. To Carmel, most of the world were fools who asked meaningless questions and worried about pointless issues; only a few, like himself, had discovered what was really important—money— and pursued it without distractions, scruples, or irrelevancies. His favorite moments were those, like this night of April 1, when he sat and tallied his take for the month and looked out his picture window occasionally at the flat

sandy landscape, dimly lit by the lights of the city behind
him. In this physical and emotional desert he experienced
happiness, or something as close to happiness as he could
ever find. His girls had earned $46,000 during March, of
which he took $23,000; after paying 10 percent to the
Brotherhood for permission to operate without molesta-
tion by Banana-Nose Maldonado's soldiers, this left a
tidy profit of $20,700, all of it tax free. Little Carmel,
who stood five feet two and had the face of a mournful
weasel, beamed as he completed his calculations; his
emotion was as inexpressible, in normal terms, as that of
a necrophile who had just broken into the town morgue.
He had tried every possible sexual combination with his
girls; none gave him the *frisson* of looking at a figure
like that at the end of a month.

He did not know that he would have another $5 mil-
lion, and incidentally become the most important human
being on earth, before May 1. If you tried to explain it to
him, he would have brushed everything else aside and
asked merely, "The five million—how many throats do I
hafta cut to *get my hands in it?*"

But wait: Get out the Atlas and look up Africa. Run
your eyes down the map of the western coast of that continent until you come to Equatorial Guinea. Stop at the
bend where part of the Atlantic Ocean curves inward and
becomes the Bight of Biafra. You will note a chain of
small islands; you will further observe that one of these is
Fernando Poo. There, in the capital city of Santa Isobel,
during the early 1970s, Captain Ernesto Tequilla y Mota
carefully read and reread Edward Luttwak's *Coup d'Etat:
A Practical Handbook,* and placidly went about following
Luttwak's formula for a perfect coup d'etat in Santa Isobel. He set up a timetable, made his first converts among
other officers, formed a clique, and began the slow process
of arranging things so that officers likely to be loyal to
Equatorial Guinea would be on assignment at least forty-
eight hours away from the capital city when the coup occurred. He drafted the first proclamation to be issued by
his new government; it took the best slogans of the most
powerful left-wing and right-wing groups on the island
and embedded them firmly in a tapiocalike context of
bland liberal-conservatism. It fit Luttwak's prescription ex-
cellently, giving everybody on the island some small hope
that his own interests and beliefs would be advanced by

the new regime. And, after three years of planning, he struck: the key officials of the old regime were quickly, bloodlessly, placed under house arrest; troops under the command of officers in the cabal occupied the power stations and newspaper offices; the inoffensively fascist-conservative-liberal-communist proclamation of the new People's Republic of Fernando Poo went forth to the world over the radio station in Santa Isobel. Ernesto Tequilla y Mota had achieved his ambition—promotion from captain to generalissimo in one step. Now, at last, he began wondering about how one went about governing a country. He would probably have to read a new book, and he hoped there was one as good as Luttwak's treatise on seizing a country. That was on March 14.

On March 15, the very name of Fernando Poo was unknown to every member of the House of Representatives, every senator, every officer of the Cabinet, and all but one of the Joint Chiefs of Staff. In fact, the President's first reaction, when the CIA report landed on his desk that afternoon, was to ask his secretary, "Where the hell is Fernando Poo?"

Saul took off his glasses and polished them with a handkerchief, conscious of his age and suddenly more tired than ever. "I outrank you, Barney," he began.

Muldoon grinned. "I know what's coming."

Methodically, Saul went on, "Who, on your staff, do you think is a double agent for the CIA?"

"Robinson I'm sure of, and Lehrman I suspect."

"Both of them go. We take no chances."

"I'll have them transferred to the Vice Squad in the morning. How about your own staff?"

"Three of them, I think, and they go, too."

"Vice Squad'll love the increase in manpower."

Saul relit his pipe. "One more thing. We might be hearing from the FBI."

"We might indeed."

"They get nothing."

"You're really taking me way out on this one, Saul."

"Sometimes you have to follow your hunches. This is going to be a heavy case, agreed?"

"A heavy case," Muldoon nodded.

"Then we do it my way."

"Let's look at the fourth memo," Muldoon said tonelessly. They read:

ILLUMINATI PROJECT: MEMO #4

7/24

J.M.:

Here's a letter that appeared in *Playboy* a few years ago ("The Playboy Advisor," *Playboy*, April, 1969, pages 62-64):

> I recently heard an old man of right-wing views—a friend of my grandparents—assert that the current wave of assassinations in America is the work of a secret society called the Illuminati. He said that the Illuminati have existed throughout history, own the international banking cartels, have all been 32nd-degree Masons and were known to Ian Fleming, who portrayed them as *Spectre* in his James Bond books—for which the Illuminati did away with Mr. Fleming. At first all this seemed like a paranoid delusion to me. Then I read in *The New Yorker* that Allan Chapman, one of Jim Garrison's investigators in the New Orleans probe of the John Kennedy assassination, believes that the Illuminati really exist. . . .

Playboy, of course, puts down the whole idea as ridiculous and gives the standard *Encyclopedia Britannica* story that the Illuminati went out of business in 1785.

Pat

Pricefixer stuck his head in the cafeteria door. "Minute?" he asked.

"What is it?" Muldoon replied.

"Peter Jackson is out here. He's the associate editor I spoke to on the phone. He just told me something about his last meeting with Joseph Malik, the editor, before Malik disappeared."

"Bring him in," Muldoon said.

Peter Jackson was a black man—truly black, not brown or tan. He was wearing a vest in spite of the spring weather. He was also very obviously wary of policemen. Saul noted this at once, and began thinking about how to overcome it—and at the same time he observed an increased blandness in Muldoon's features, indicating that he, too, had noted it and was prepared to take umbrage.

"Have a seat," Saul said cordially, "and tell us what you just told the other officer." With the nervous ones it was sound policy to drop the policeman role at first, and try to sound like somebody else—somebody who, quite naturally, asks a lot of questions. Saul began slipping into the personality of his own family physician, which he usually used at such times. He made himself *feel* a stethoscope hanging about his neck.

"Well," Jackson began in a Harvard accent, "this is probably not important. It may be just a coincidence."

"Most of what we hear is just unimportant coincidence," Saul said gently. "But it's our job to listen."

"Everybody but the lunatic fringe has given up on this by now," Jackson said. "It really surprised me when Joe told me what he was getting the magazine into." He paused and studied the two impassive faces of the detectives; finding little there, he went on reluctantly. "It was last Friday. Joe told me he had a lead that interested him, and he was putting a staff writer on it. He wanted to re-open the investigation of the assassinations of Martin Luther King and the Kennedy brothers."

Saul carefully didn't look at Muldoon, and just as carefully moved his hat to cover the memos on the table. "Excuse me a moment," he said politely and left the cafeteria.

He found a phone booth in the lobby and dialed his home. Rebecca answered after the third ring; she obviously had not gotten back to sleep after he left. "Saul?" she asked, guessing who would be calling at this hour.

"It's going to be a long night," Saul said.

"Oh, hell."

"I know, baby. But this case is a son-of-a-bitch!"

Rebecca sighed. "I'm glad we had a little ball earlier this evening. Otherwise, I'd be furious."

Saul thought, suddenly, of how this conversation would sound to an outsider. A sixty-year-old man and a twenty-five-year-old wife. And if they knew she was a whore and a heroin addict when I first met her . . .

"Do you know what I'm going to do?" Rebecca lowered her voice. "I'm going to take off my nightgown, and throw the covers to the foot of the bed, and lie here naked, thinking about you and waiting."

Saul grinned. "A man my age shouldn't be able to respond to that, after doing what I did earlier."

"But you did respond, didn't you?" Her voice was confident and sensual.

"I sure did. I won't be able to leave the phone booth for a couple of minutes."

She chuckled softly and said, "I'll be waiting. . . ."

"I love you," he said, surprised (as always) at the simple truth of it in a man his age. I won't be able to leave the phone booth at all if this keeps up, he thought. "Listen," he added hurriedly, "let's change the subject before I start resorting to the vices of a high school boy. What do you know about the Illuminati?" Rebecca had been an anthropology major, with a minor in psychology, before the drug scene had captured her and she fell into the abyss from which he had rescued her; her erudition often astonished him.

"It's a hoax," she said.

"A what?"

"A hoax. A bunch of students at Berkeley started it back around sixty-six or sixty-seven."

"No, that's not what I'm asking. The original Illuminati in Italy and Spain and Germany in the fifteenth to eighteenth centuries? You know?"

"Oh, that's the basis of the hoax. Some right-wing historians think the Illuminati still exist, you see, so these students opened an Illuminati chapter on the campus at Berkeley and started sending out press releases on all sorts of weird subjects, so people who want to believe in conspiracies would have some evidence to point to. That's all there is to it. Sophomore humor."

I hope so, Saul thought. "How about the Ishmaelian sect of Islam?"

"It has twenty-three divisions, but the Aga Khan is the leader of all of them. It was founded around—oh—1090 A.D., I think, and was originally persecuted, but now it's part of the orthodox Moslem religion. It has some pretty weird doctrines. The founder, Hassan i Sabbah, taught that nothing is true and everything is permissible. He lived up to that idea—the word 'assassin' is a corruption of his name."

"Anything else?"

"Yes, now that I think of it. Sabbah introduced marijuana to the Western world, from India. The word 'hashish' also comes from his name."

"This is a heavy case," Saul said, "and now that I can walk out of the phone booth without shocking the patrol-

man in the hall, I'll get back to work on it. Don't say anything that'll get me aroused again. Please."

"I won't. I'll just lie here naked and . . ."

"Good-bye."

"Good-bye," she said, laughing.

Saul hung up frowning. Goodman's intuition, the other
detectives call it. It's not intuition; it's a way of thinking
beyond and between the facts, a way of sensing *wholes,* of
seeing that there must be a relationship between fact number one and fact number two even if no such relationship
is visible yet. And I know. There is an Illuminati, whether
or not those kids at Berkeley are kidding.

He came out of his concentration and realized where he
was. For the first time, he noticed a sticker on the door:

THIS PHONE BOOTH RESERVED FOR CLARK KENT

He grinned: an intellectual's kind of joke. Probably
somebody on the magazine.

He walked back to the cafeteria, reflecting. "Nothing is
true. Everything is permissible." With a doctrine like that,
people were capable of . . . He shuddered. Images of
Buchenwald and Belsen, of Jews who might have been
him. . . .

Peter Jackson looked up as he reentered the cafeteria.
An intelligent, curious black face. Muldoon was as impassive as the faces on Mount Rushmore. "Mad Dog, Texas,
was the town where Malik thought these . . . assassins
. . . had their headquarters," Muldoon said. "That's
where the staff writer was sent."

"What was the staff writer's name?" Saul asked.

"George Dorn," Muldoon said. "He's a young kid who
used to be in SDS. And he was once rather close to the
Weatherman faction."

Hagbard Celine's gigantic computer, FUCKUP—First
Universal Cybernetic-Kinetic-Ultramicro-Programmer—
was basically a rather sophisticated form of the standard
self-programming algorithmic logic machine of the time;
the name was one of his whimsies. FUCKUP's real claim
to uniqueness was a programmed stochastic process
whereby it could "throw" an *I Ching* hexagram, reading a
random open circuit as a broken *(yin)* line and a random
closed circuit as a full *(yang)* line until six such "lines"
were round. Consulting its memory banks, where the

whole tradition of *I Ching* interpretation was stored, and then cross-checking its current scannings of that day's political, economic, meterological, astrological, astronomical, and technological eccentricities, it would provide a reading of the hexagram which, to Hagbard's mind, combined the best of the scientific and occult methods for spotting oncoming trends. On March 13, the stochastic pattern spontaneously generated Hexagram 23, "Breaking Apart." FUCKUP then interpreted:

> This traditionally unlucky sign was cast by Atlantean scientist-priests shortly before the destruction of their continent and is generally connected with death by water. Other vibrations link it to earthquakes, tornadoes and similar disasters, and to sickness, decay, and morbidity as well.
>
> The first correlation is with the unbalance between technological acceleration and political retrogression, which has proceeded earthwide at everwidening danger levels since 1914 and especially since 1964. The breaking apart is fundamentally the schizoid and schismatic mental fugue of lawyer-politicians attempting to administrate a worldwide technology whose mechanisms they lack the education to comprehend and whose gestalttrend they frustrate by breaking apart into obsolete Rennaisance nation-states.
>
> World War III is probably imminent and, considering the advances in chemicalbiological warfare in conjunction with the sickness vibrations of Hexagram 23, the unleashing of plague or nervegas or both is as probable as thermonuclear overkill.
>
> General prognosis: many megadeaths.
>
> There is some hope for avoidance of the emerging pattern with prompt action of correct nature. Probability of such avoidance is 0.17 ± 0.05.
>
> No blame.

"My *ass*, no blame," Hagbard raged; and rapidly reprogrammed FUCKUP to read off to him its condensed psychobiographies of the key figures in world politics and the key scientists in chemobiological warfare.

The first dream came to Dr. Charles Mocenigo on February 2—more than a month before FUCKUP picked up the vibrations. He was, as usual with him, aware that he was dreaming, and the vision of a gigantic pyramid which seemed to walk or lumber about meant nothing and quickly vanished. Now he seemed to be looking at an enlargement of the DNA double helix; it was so detailed that he began searching it for the bonding irregularities at every 23rd Angstrom. To his surprise, they were missing; instead, there were other irregularities at each 17th Angstrom. "What the devil . . . ?" he asked—and the pyramid returned seeming to speak and saying, "Yes, the devil." He jolted awake, with a new concept, Anthrax-Leprosy-Mu, coming into consciousness, and began jotting in his bedside pad.

"What the hell is this Desert Door project?" the President had asked once, scrutinizing the budget. "Germ warfare," an aide explained helpfully. "They started with something called Anthrax Delta and now they've worked their way up to something called Anthrax Mu and . . ." His voice was drowned out by the rumble of paper shredders in the next room. The President recognized the characteristic sound of the "cesspool cleaners" hard at work. "Never mind," he said. "Those things make me nervous." He scribbled a quick "OK" next to the item and went on to "Deprived Children," which made him feel better. "Here," he said, "this is something we can cut."

He forgot everything about Desert Door, until the Fernando Poo crises. "Suppose, just suppose," he asked the Joint Chiefs on March 29, "I go on the tube and threaten all-out thermonuclear *heck*, and the other side doesn't blink. Have we got something that'll scare them even more?"

The J.C.'s exchanged glances. One of them spoke tentatively. "Out near Las Vegas," he said, "we have this Desert Door project that seems to be way ahead of the Comrades in b-b and b-c—"

"That's biological-bacteriological and biological-chemical," the President explained to the Vice-President, who was frowning. "It has nothing to do with B-B guns." Turning his attention back to the military men, he asked, "What have we got specifically that will curdle Ivan's blood?"

"Well, there's Anthrax-Leprosy-Mu. . . . It's worse than any form of anthrax. More deadly than bubonic and anthrax and leoprosy all in one lump. As a matter of fact," the General who was speaking smiled grimly at the thought, "our evaluation suggests that with death being so quick, the psychological demoralization of the survivors—if there are any survivors—will be even worse than in thermonuclear exchange with maximum 'dirty' fallout."

"By golly," the President said. "By *golly*. We won't use that out in the open. My speech'll just talk Bomb, but we'll leak it to the boys in the Kremlin that we've got this anthrax gimmick in cold storage, too. By gosh, you just wait and see them back down." He stood up, decisive, firm, the image he always projected on television. "I'm going to see my speechwriters right now. Meanwhile, arrange that the brain responsible for this Anthrax-Pi gets a raise. What's his name?" he asked over his shoulder going out the door.

"Mocenigo. Dr. Charles Mocenigo."

"A raise for Dr. Charles Mocenigo," the President called from the hallway.

"Mocenigo?" the Vice-President asked thoughtfully. "Is he a wop?"

"Don't say wop," the President shouted back. "How many times do I have to tell you? Don't say wop or kike or *any* of those words anymore." He spoke with some asperity, since he lived daily with the dread that someday the secret tapes he kept of all Oval Room transactions would be released to the public. He had long ago vowed that if that day ever came, the tapes would not be full of "(expletive deleted)" or "(characterization deleted)." He was harassed, but still he spoke with authority. He was, in fact, characteristic of the best type of dominant male in the world at this time. He was fifty-five years old, tough, shrewd, unburdened by the complicated ethical ambiguities which puzzle intellectuals, and had long ago decided that the world was a mean son-of-a-bitch in which only the most cunning and ruthless can survive. He was also as kind as was possible for one holding that ultra-Darwinian philosophy; and he genuinely loved children and dogs, unless they were on the site of something that had to be bombed in the National Interest. He still retained some sense of humor, despite the burdens of his almost godly office, and, although he had been impotent with his wife for nearly ten years now, he generally achieved orgasm in the mouth of a skilled prostitute within 1.5 minutes. He took amphetamine pep pills to keep going on his grueling twenty-hour day, with the result that his vision of the world was somewhat skewed in a paranoid direction, and he took tranquilizers to keep from worrying too much, with the result that his detachment sometimes bordered on the schizophrenic; but most of the time his innate shrewdness gave him a fingernail grip on reality. In short, he was much like the rulers of Russia and China.

In Central Park, the squirrel woke again as a car honked loudly in passing. Muttering angrily, he leaped to another tree and immediately went back to sleep. *At the all-night Bickford's restaurant on Seventy-second Street, a young man named August Personage left a phone booth after making an obscene call to a woman in Brooklyn; he left behind one of his* THIS PHONE BOOTH RESERVED FOR CLARK KENT *stickers.* In Chicago, one hour earlier on the clock but the same instant, the phone booth closed, a rock group called Clark Kent and His Supermen began a revival of "Rock Around the Clock": their leader, a tall black man with a master's degree in anthropology, had been known as El Hajj Starkerlee Mohammed during a militant phase a few years earlier, and his birth certificate said Robert Pearson on it. He was observing his audience and noted that that bearded young white cat, Simon, was with a black woman as usual—a fetish Pearson-Mohammed-Kent could understand by reverse psychology, since he preferred white chicks himself. Simon, for once, was not entranced by the music; instead, he was deep in conversation with the girl and drawing a diagram of a pyramid on the table to explain what he meant. "Crown Point," Pearson heard him say over the music. *And listening to "Rock Around the Clock" ten years earlier, George Dorn had decided to let his hair grow long, smoke dope and become a musician. He had succeeded in two of those ambitions.* The statue of Tlaloc in the Museum of Anthropology, Mexico, D.F., stared inscrutably upward, toward the stars . . . *and the same stars glittered above the Caribbean where the porpoise named Howard sported in the waves.*

The motorcade passes the Texas School Book Depository and moves slowly toward the Triple Underpass. At the sixth-floor window, Lee Harvey Oswald sights carefully through the Carcano-Mannlicher: his mouth is dry, desert dry. But his heartbeat is normal; and no sweat stands out on his forehead. This is the moment, he is thinking, the one moment transcending time and hazard, heredity and environment, the final test and proof of free will and of my right to call myself a man. In this moment, now, as I tighten the trigger, the Tyrant dies, and with him all the lies of a cruel, mendacious epoch. It is a supreme exalation, this moment and this knowledge: and yet his mouth is dry, dust-dry, dry as death, as if his salivary glands alone rebelled against the murder which his intellect pronounced necessary and just. *Now:* He recalls the military formula BASS: Breathe, Aim, Slack, Squeeze. He breathes, he aims, he slacks, he starts to squeeze, as a dog barks suddenly—

And his mouth falls open in astonishment as three shots ring out, obviously from the direction of the Grassy Knoll and Triple Underpass.

"Son-of-a-bitch," he said, softly as a prayer. And he began to grin, a rictus not of omnipotence such as he had expected but of something different and unexpected and therefore better—omniscience. That smirk appeared in all the photos during the next day and a half, before his own death, a sneering smile that said so clearly that none dared to read it: *I know something you don't know.* That grimace only faded Sunday morning when Jack Ruby pumped two bullets into Lee's frail fanatic body, and its secret went with him to the grave. But another part of the secret had already left Dallas on Friday afternoon's TWA Whisperjet to Los Angeles, traveling behind the business suit, gray hair, and only moderately sardonic eyes of a little old man who was listed on the flight manifest as "Frank Sullivan."

This is serious, Peter Jackson was thinking; Joe Malik wasn't on a paranoid trip at all. The noncommital expressions of Muldoon and Goodman did not deceive him at all—he had long ago learned the black art of surviving in a white world, which is the art of reading not what is on a face but what is behind the face. The cops were worried and excited, like any hunters on the track of something both large and dangerous. Joe was right about the assassination plot, and his disappearance and the bombing were part of it. And that meant George Dorn was in danger, too, and Peter liked George even if he was a snotty kid in some ways and an annoying ass-kisser about the race thing like most young white radicals. Mad Dog, Texas, Peter thought: that sure sounds like a bad place to be in trouble.

(Almost fifty years before, a habitual bank robber named Harry Pierpont approached a young convict in Michigan City Prison and asked him, "Do you think there might be a true religion?")

But why is George Dorn screaming while Saul Goodman is reading the memos? Hold on for another jump, and this one is a shocker. Saul is no longer human; he's a pig. All cops are pigs. Everything you've ever believed is probably a lie. The world is a dark, sinister, mysterious and totally frightening place. Can you digest all that quickly? Then, walk into the mind of George Dorn for the second time, five hours before the explosion at *Confrontation* (four hours before, on the clock) and suck on the joint, suck hard and hold it down. ("One o'clock . . . two o'clock . . . three o'clock . . . ROCK!"). You are sprawled on a crummy bed in a rundown hotel, and a neon light outside is flashing pink and blue patterns into your room. Exhale slowly, feel the hit of the weed and see if the wallpaper looks any brighter yet, any less Unintentional Low Camp. It's hot, Texas-dry hot, and you push your long hair back from your forehead and haul out your diary, George Dorn, because reading over what you wrote last sometimes helps you to learn what you're really getting into. As the neon splotches the page with pink and blue, read this:

April 23
How do we know whether the universe is getting bigger or the objects in it are getting smaller? You can't say that the universe is getting bigger in relation to anything outside it, because there isn't any outside for it to relate to. There isn't any outside. But if the universe doesn't have an *out*-side, then it goes on forever. Yeah, but, its *in*-side doesn't go on forever. How do you know it doesn't, shithead? You're just playing with words, man.

—No I'm not. The universe is the inside without an outside, the sound made by one

* * *

There was a knock at the door.

The Fear came over George. Whenever he was high, the least little detail wrong in his world would bring the Fear, irresistible, uncontrollable. He held his breath, not to contain the smoke in his lungs, but because terror had paralyzed the muscles in his chest. He dropped the little notebook in which he wrote his thoughts daily and clutched at his penis, a habitual gesture in moments of panic. The hand holding the roach drifted, automatically, over the hollowed-out copy of Sinclair Lewis's *It Can't Happen Here,* which lay beside him on the bed, and he dropped the half-inch twist of paper and marijuana on top of the plastic Baggie full of green grains. Instantly a brown smoldering dime-sized hole opened up on the bag, and the pot near the coal started to smoke.

"Stupid," said George, as his thumb stabbed the smoking coal to crush it, and he drew back his lips in a grimace of pain.

A short fat man walked into the room, Law Officer written in every mean line of his crafty little face. George shrank back and started to close *It Can't Happen Here;* like lightning, three stiff, concrete-hard fingers drove into his forearm. He screamed and the book jumped out of his hand, spilling pot all over the bedspread.

"Don't touch that," said the fat man. "An officer will be in to gather it up for evidence. I went easy with that karate punch. Otherwise you'd be nursing a compound fracture of the left arm in Mad Dog County Jail tonight, and no right-thinking doctor likely to have a mind to come out and treat you."

"You got a warrant?" George tried to sound defiant.

"Oh, you think you have cojones." The fat man's breath stank of bourbon and cheap cigars. "Rabbit cojones. I have terrified you unto death, boy, and you know it and I know it, yet you find it in your heart to speak of warrants. Next you'll want to see the American Civil Liberties Union." He pulled aside the jacket of an irridescent gray summer suit that might have been new when *Heartbreak Hotel* was the top of the hit parade. A silver five-pointed star decorated his pink shirt pocket and a .45 automatic stuck in his pants-top dented the fat of his belly. "That is all the law I need when dealing with your type in Mad Dog. Walk careful with me, son, or you won't have nothing to grab onto next time one of us pigs, as you choose to call us in your little articles, busts in on you. Which is not likely to happen in the next forty years, while you rot and grow old in our state prison." He seemed immensely pleased with his own oratorical style, like one of Faulkner's characters.

George thought:

> It is forbidden to dream again;
> We maim our joys or hide them;
> Horses are made of chromium steel
> And little fat men shall ride them.

He said, "You can't hit me with forty years for possession. And grass is legal in most other states. This law is archaic and absurd."

"Shit and onions, boy, you got too much of the killer weed there to call it mere possession. I call it possession with intent to sell. And the laws of this state are stern, and they are just and they are our laws. We know what that weed can do. We remember the Alamo and Santa Anna's troops losing all fear because they were high on Rosa Maria, as they called it in those days. Get on your feet. And don't ask to talk to a lawyer, neither."

"Can I ask who you are?"

"I am Sheriff Jim Cartwright, nemesis of all evil in Mad Dog and Mad Dog County."

"And I'm Tiny Tim," said George, immediately saying to himself, Shut the fuck up, you're too goddamn high. And he went right on and said, "Maybe your side would have won if Davy Crockett and Jim Bowie got stoned, too. And, by the way, Sheriff, how did you know you could catch me with pot? Usually an underground journalist would make it a point to be clean when he comes into this godforsaken part of the country. It wasn't telepathy that told you I had pot on me."

Sheriff Cartwright slapped his thigh. "Oh, but it was. It *was* telepathy. Now just what made you think it wasn't telepathy brung me here?" He laughed, seized George's arm in a grip of iron, and pushed him toward the hotel-room door. George felt a bottomless terror as if the pit of hell were opening beneath his feet and Sheriff Jim Cartwright were about to pitchfork him into the bubbling sulfur. And I must admit that was more or less the case;

there are periods of history when the visions of madmen
and dope fiends are a better guide to reality than the com-
mon-sense interpretation of data available to the so-called
normal mind. This is one such period, if you haven't noticed already.

(*"Keep on hanging out with those wild boys from Passaic and you'll end up in jail," George's mother said.
"You mark my words, George." And, another time, at
Columbia, after a very late meeting, Mark Rudd said soberly, "A lot of us are going to spend some time in the
Man's jails before this shit-storm is over"; and George, together with the others, nodded glumly but bravely.* The
marijuana he had been smoking was raised in Cuernavaca
by a farmer named Arturo Jesus Maria Ybarra y Mendez,
who had sold it in bulk to a young *Yanqui* named Jim
Riley, the son of a Dayton, Ohio, police officer, who in
turn smuggled it through Mad Dog after paying a suitable
bribe to Sheriff Jim Cartwright. After that it was resold to
a Times Square dealer called Rosetta the Stoned and a
Miss Walsh from *Confrontation*'s research department
bought ten ounces from her, later reselling five ounces to
George, who then carried it back to Mad Dog without
any suspicion that he was virtually completing a cycle.
The original seed was part of that strain recommended by
General George Washington in the famous letter to Sir
John Sinclair in which he writes, "I find that, for all pur-
poses, the Indian hemp is in every way superior to the
New Zealand variety previously cultivated here." *In New
York, Rebecca Goodman, deciding that Saul will not be
home tonight, slips out of bed, dons a robe and begins to
browse through her library. Finally she selects a book on
Babylonian mythology and begins to read:* "Before all of
the gods, was Mummu, the spirit of Pure Chaos. . . ." *In
Chicago, Simon and Mary Lou Servix sit naked on her
bed, legs intertwined in the yabyum lotus position.* "No,"
Simon is saying, "You don't move, baby; you wait for IT
to move you." Clark Kent and His Supermen swing into a
reprise: "We're gonna rock around the clock tonight . . .
We're gonna ROCK ROCK ROCK till broad day light.")

George's cellmate in Mad Dog County Jail had a skull-
like face with large, protruding front teeth. He was about
six and a half feet tall and lay curled up on his cell bunk
like a coiled python.

"Have you asked for treatment?" George asked him.

"Treatment for what?"

"Well, if you think you're an assassin—"

"I don't think, baby brother. I've killed four white men and two niggers. One in California, the rest down here. Got paid for every one of them."

"Is that what you're in for?" My God, they don't stick murderers in the same cell with potheads, do they?

"I'm in for vagrancy," said the man scornfully. "Actually, I'm just here for safekeeping, till they give me my orders. Then it's good-bye to whoever—President, civil rights leader, enemy of the people. Someday I'll be famous. I'm gonna write a book about myself someday, Ace. Course, I'm no good at writing. Look, maybe we can do a deal. I'll have Sheriff Jim bring you some writing paper if you'll write about my life. They gonna keep you here forever, you know. I'll come and visit you between assassinations, and you'll write the book, and Sheriff Jim'll keep it safe till I retire. Then you have the book published and you'll make a lot of money and be real comfortable in jail. Or maybe you can even hire a lawyer to get you out."

"Where will you be?" said George. He was still scared, but he was feeling sleepy, too, and he was deciding that this was all bullshit, which had a calming effect on his nerves. But he'd better not go to sleep in the cell while this guy was awake. He didn't really believe this assassin talk, but it was safe to assume that anybody you met in prison was homosexual.

As if reading his mind, his cellmate said, "How'd you like to let a famous assassin shove it up to you? How would that be, huh, Ace?"

"Please," said George. "That's not my bag, you know? I really couldn't do it."

"Shit, piss, and corruption," said the assassin. He suddenly uncoiled and slid off the bunk. "I been wasting my time with you. Now bend the hell over and drop your pants. You are getting it, and there ain't no further way about it." He stepped toward George, fists clenched.

"Guard! Guard!" George yelled. He grabbed the cell door in both hands and began rattling it frantically.

The man caught George a cuff across the face. Another blow to the jaw knocked George against the wall.

"Guard!" he screamed, his head spinning with pot and panic.

A man in a blue uniform came through the door at the end of the corridor. He seemed miles away and vastly disinterested, like a god who had grown bored with his creations.

"Now, what the hell is all this yelling about in here?" he asked, his hand on the butt of his revolver, his voice still miles away.

George opened his mouth, but his cellmate spoke first. "This little long-haired communist freak won't drop his pants when I tell him. Ain't you supposed to make sure I'm happy in here?" The voice shifted to a whine. "Make him do what I say."

"You've got to protect me," said George. "You've got to get me out of this cell."

The god-guard laughed. "Well, now, you might say this is a very enlightened prison we have here. You come down from New York and you probably think we're pretty backward. But we ain't. We got no police brutality. Now, if I interfered between you and Harry Coin here, I might have to use force to keep him away from your young ass. I know you people believe all cops ought to be abolished. Well, in this here situation I hereby abolish myself. Furthermore, I know you people believe in sexual freedom, and I do, too. So Harry Coin gonna have his sexual freedom without any interference or brutality from me." His voice was still distant and disinterested, almost dreamy.

"No," said George.

The guard drew his pistol. "Now, sonny. You take down your pants and bend over. You are gonna get it up the ass from Harry Coin here, and no two ways about it. And I am gonna watch and see that you let him do it right. Otherwise, you get no forty years. You get killed, right now. I put a bullet in you and I say you are resisting arrest. Now make up your mind what it's gonna be. I really will kill you if you don't do like he tells you to. I really will. You are totally expendable and he ain't. He's a very important man, and it's my job to keep him happy."

"And I'll fuck you either way, dead or alive," the demented Coin laughed, like an evil spirit. "So there's no way you can escape it, Ace."

The door at the end of the corridor clanged, and Sheriff Jim Cartwright and two blue-uniformed policemen strode down to the cell. "What's going on here?" said the Sheriff.

"I caught this queer punk George Dorn here trying to commit homosexual rape on Harry," said the guard. "Had to draw my pistol to stop him."

George shook his head. "You guys are unbelievable. If you're acting out this little game for my benefit, you can quit now, because you're certainly not fooling each other, and you're not fooling me."

"Dorn," said the Sheriff, "you've been attempting unnatural acts in my jail, acts forbidden by the Holy Bible and the laws of this state. I don't like that. I don't like it one little bit. Come on out here. I wanna have a little talk with you. We goin' to the main interrogation room for some speakin' together."

He unlocked the cell door and motioned George to precede him. He turned to the two policemen who had accompanied him. "Stay behind and take care of that other *little matter.*" The last words were strangely emphasized.

George and the Sheriff walked through a series of corridors and locked doors until at last they came to a room whose walls were made of embossed sheet tin painted bottle-green. The Sheriff told George to sit on one chair, while he straddled the back of the chair facing him.

"You're a bad influence on my prisoners," he said. "I got a good mind to see that some kind of accident happens to you. I don't want to see you corrupting prisoners in my jail—mine or anyone's—for forty years."

"Sheriff," said George. "What do you want from me? You got me on a pot charge. What more do you want? Why did you stick me in that cell with that guy? What's all this scare stuff and threats and questioning for?"

"I wanna know some things," said the Sheriff. "I want to find out everything you can tell me about certain matters. So, from this moment be prepared to tell me only the truth. If you do, maybe things will go easier on you, after."

"Yes, Sheriff," said George. Cartwright squinted at him. He really does look like a pig, thought George. Most do. Why do so many of them get so fat and have such little eyes?

"Well, then," said the Sheriff. "What was your purpose in coming down here from New York?"

"I'm simply on an assignment from *Confrontation,* the magazine—"

"I know it. It is a smutty magazine, and a communist magazine. I have read it."

"You're using loaded words. It's a left-wing libertarian magazine, to be exact."

"My pistol is loaded, too, boy. So talk straight. All right. Tell me what you came down here to write about."

"Sure. You ought to be as interested in this as I am, if you're really interested in law and order. There have been rumors circulating throughout the country for more than a decade now that all the major political assassinations in America—Malcolm X, the Kennedy brothers, Medgar Evers, King, Nixon, maybe even George Lincoln Rockwell—are the work of a single, conspiratorial, violence-oriented right-wing organization, and that this organization has its base right here in Mad Dog. I came down to see what I could find out about this group."

"That's what I figured," said the Sheriff. "You poor, sad little turd. You come down here with your long hair and you expect to get, as you put it, a line on a right-wing organization. Why, it's lucky for you you didn't meet any of our real right-wingers, like God's Lightning for instance. The ones around here would have tortured you to death by this time, boy. You really are dumb. OK, I'm not gonna waste any more of my time with you. Come on, I'll take you back to your cell. You might as well get used to looking at the moon through bars."

They walked back the same way they had come. At the entrance to the corridor where George's cell was, the Sheriff opened the door and yelled, "Come and get him, Charley."

George's guard, his face pale and his mouth set in a lipless line, took George by the arm. The corridor door clanged shut behind the Sheriff. Charley took George to his cell and pushed him in wordlessly. But at least he was three-dimensional now and less like a marijuana phantom.

Harry Coin wasn't there. The cell was empty. George became aware of a shadow in the corner of his vision. Something in the cell next to him. He turned: His heart stopped. There was a man hanging from a pipe on the ceiling. George went over and stared through the bars. The body was swaying slightly. It was attached to the pipe by a leather belt which was buckled around the neck. The face, with the staring eyes, was that of Harry Coin. George's glance went lower. Something was coming out of

Harry Coin's midsection and was dangling down to the floor. It wasn't suicide. They had disemboweled Harry Coin, and someone had thoughtfully moved a shit-can under him for his bloody intestines to dangle into.

George screamed. There was no one around to answer him. The guard had vanished like Hermes.

(But in Cherry Knolls mental hospital in Sunderland, England, where it was already eleven the following morning, a schizophrenic patient who hadn't spoken in ten years abruptly began exhorting a ward attendant: "They're all coming back—Hitler, Goering, Streicher, the whole lot of them. And, behind them, the powers and persons from the other spheres who control them. . . ." But Simon Moon in Chicago still calmly and placidly retains the lotus position and instructs Mary Lou sitting in his lap: "Just hold it, hold it with your vaginal wall like you'd hold it with your hand, gently, and feel its warmth, but don't think about orgasm, don't think about the future, not even a minute ahead, think about the now, the only now, the only now, the only now that we'll ever have, just my penis in your vagina now and the simple pleasure of it, not a greater pleasure to work toward. . . ." "My back hurts," Mary Lou said.)

WE'RE GONNA ROCK   ROCK   ROCK   AROUND THE CLOCK
TO   NIGHT

There are Swedish and Norwegian kids, Danes, Italian and French kids, Greeks, even Americans. George and Hagbard move through the crowd trying to estimate its number—200,000? 300,000? 500,000? Peace symbols dangling about every neck, nudes with body paint, nudes without body paint, long and dangling hair on boys and girls alike, and over all of it the hypnotic and unending beat. "Woodstock Europa," Hagbard says drily. "The last and final Walpurgisnacht and Adam Weishaupt's Erotion finally realized."

WE'RE GONNA ROCK   ROCK   ROCK   TILL BROAD
DAYLIGHT

"It's a League of Nations," George says, "a young people's League of Nations." Hagbard isn't listening. "Up there," he points, "to the Northwest is the Rhine, where *die Lorelei* was supposed to sit and sing her deadly songs. There will be deadlier music on the Danube tonight."

WE'RE GONNA ROCK AROUND THE CLOCK TONIGHT

(But that was still seven days in the future, and now

George lies unconscious in Mad Dog County Jail. And it began—that phase of the operation, as Hagbard called it—over thirty years before when a Swiss chemist named Hoffman climbed on his bicycle and pedaled down a country road into new dimensions.)

"And will they all come back?" George asked.

"All of them," Hagbard answered tightly. "When the beat reaches the proper intensity . . . unless we can stop it."

("Now I'm getting it," Mary Lou cried. "It's not what I expected. It's different from sex, and better." Simon smiled benignly. "It *is* sex, baby," he said. "What you've had before wasn't sex. Now we can start moving . . . but slowly . . . the Gentle Way . . . the Way of Tao. . . ." *They're all coming back; they never died*—the lunatic raved at the startled attendant—*You wait, guvnor. You just wait. You'll see it.*)

The amplifiers squealed suddenly. There was too much feedback, and the sound went off into a pitch beyond endurance. George winced, and saw others hold their ears. ROCK, ROCK, ROCK, AROUND THE CLOCK. *The key missed the lock, turned and cut Muldoon's hand.* "Nerves," he said to Saul. "I always feel like a burglar when I do this."

Saul grunted. "Forget burglary," he said. "We might be hanged for treason before this is over. If we don't become national heroes."

"A fanfuckingtastic case," Muldoon grinned. He tried another way.

They were in an old brownstone on Riverside Drive, trying to break into the apartment of Joseph Malik. And they were not merely looking for evidence, both tacitly admitted—they were hiding from the FBI.

The call had come from headquarters just as they were finishing the questioning of associate editor Peter Jackson. Muldoon had gone out to his car to take it, while Saul finished getting a full physical description of both Malik and George Dorn. Jackson had just left and Saul was picking up the fifth memo, when Muldoon returned, looking as if his doctor had just told him his Wasserman was positive.

"Two special agents from the FBI are coming over to help us," he said woodenly.

"Still ready to play a hunch?" Saul asked calmly, pushing all the memos back in the metal box.

Muldoon merely called Pricefixer back into the cafe-

teria and told him, *"Two feds will be here in a few minutes. Tell them we went back to headquarters. Answer any question they ask, but don't tell them about this box."*

Pricefixer looked at the two older officers carefully and then said to Muldoon, "You're the boss."

He's either awfully dumb and trusting, Saul had thought, or he's so damned smart he's going to be dangerous someday.

"Now," he asked Muldoon nervously, "is that the last key?"

"No, I've got five more beauties here and one of them will—here it is!" The door opened smoothly.

Saul's hand drifted toward his revolver as he stepped into the apartment and felt for a light switch. Nobody was revealed when the light came on, and Saul relaxed. "You look around for the dogs." he said. "I want to sit down and go over the rest of these memos."

The room was used for work as well as living and was untidy enough to leave no room for doubt that Malik had been a bachelor. Saul pushed the typewriter back on the writing desk, set down the memo box and then noticed something odd. The whole wall, on this side of the room, was covered with pictures of George Washington. Standing to examine them more closely, he saw that each had a label—half of them saying "G.W." and the others, "A.W."

Odd—but the whole case had overtones that smelled as fishy as those dead Egyptian mouth-breeders.

Saul sat down and took a memo from the box.

Muldoon came back into the living room and said, "No dogs. Not a goddam dog anywhere in the whole apartment."

"That's interesting," Saul remarked thoughtfully. "You say the landlord had complaints from several other tenants about the dogs?"

"He said everybody in the building was complaining. The rule is no pets and he enforced it. People wanted to know why they had to get rid of their kittens when Malik could have a whole pack of dogs up here. They said there must have been ten or twelve from the noise they made."

"He sure must love those animals, if he took them all with him when he went into hiding," Saul mused. The pole vaulter in his unconscious was jumping again. "Let's look in the kitchen," he suggested mildly.

Barney followed as Saul methodically ransacked the refrigerator and cupboards, finishing up with a careful examination of the garbage.

"No dog food," Saul said finally.

"I noticed."

"And no dog dishes either. And no empty dog-food tins in the garbage."

"What wild notion are you following now?"

"I don't know," Saul said thoughtfully. "He doesn't mind the neighbors hearing the dogs—probably he's the kind of left-wing individualist who likes nothing better than quarreling with his landlord and the other tenants about some issue like the no-pets rule. So he wasn't hiding anything until he ducked out. And then he not only took the dogs but hid all evidence that they'd ever been here. Even though he must have known that the neighbors would all talk about them."

"Maybe he was feeding them human flesh," Muldoon suggested ghoulishly.

"Lord, I don't know. You look around for anything of interest. I'm going to read those Illuminati memos." Saul returned to the living room and began:

ILLUMINATI PROJECT: MEMO #5

7/26

J.M.:

Sometimes you find things in the damndest places. The following is from a girl's magazine ("The Conspiracy" by Sandra Glass, *Teenset,* March 1969, pages 34-40).

Simon proceeded to tell me about the Bavarian Illuminati. The nightmarish story begins in 1090 A.D. in the Middle East when Hassan i Sabbah founded the Ismaelian Sect, or *Hashishim,* so called because of their use of hashish, a deadly drug derived from the hemp plant which is better known as the killer weed marijuana. . . . The cult terrorized the Moslem world until Genghis Khan's Mongols brought law and order to the area. Cornered in their mountain hideaway, the Hashishim dope fiends proved no match for the clean-living Mongol warriors, their fortress was destroyed, and their dancing girls shipped to Mongolia for rehabilitation. The heads of the cult fled westward. . . .

"The Illuminati surfaced next in Bavaria in 1776," Simon told me. . . . "Adam Weishaupt, a student of the occult, studied the teachings of Hassan i Sabbah and grew hemp in his backyard. On February 2, 1776, Weishaupt achieved illumination. Weishaupt officially founded the Ancient Illuminated Seers of Bavaria on May 1st, 1776. Their slogan was *'Ewige Blumenkraft.'* . . . They attracted many illustrious members such as Goethe and Beethoven. Beethoven tacked up an *Ewige Blumenkraft* poster on the top of the piano on which he composed all nine of his symphonies."

The last paragraph of the article is, however, the most interesting of all:

Recently I saw a documentary film on the Democratic Convention of 1968, and I was struck by the scene in which Senator Abraham Ribicoff made a critical remark provoking the anger of the Mayor of Chicago. In the ensuing tumult it was impossible to hear the Mayor's shouted retort, and there has been much speculation about what he actually said. To me it seemed his lips were forming the words that by this time become frighteningly familiar: *"Ewige Blumenkraft!"*

The further I dig, the wilder the whole picture looks. When are we going to tell George about it?

Pat

ILLUMINATI PROJECT: MEMO #6

7/26

J.M.:

The John Birch Society has looked into the subject and they have a theory of their own. The first source I've found on this is a pamphlet "CFR: Conspiracy to Rule the World" by Gary Allen, associate editor of the Birchers' magazine, *American Opinion*.

Allen's thesis is that Cecil Rhodes created a secret society to establish English domination of the world in 1888. This society acts through Oxford University, the Rhodes Scholarships and—hold your breath—the Council on Foreign Relations, a nonprofit foundation for the study of International Affairs headquartered right here on Sixty-eighth Street in New York. Seven out of nine of our last Secretaries of State were recruited from the CFR, Allen points out, and dozens of other leading politicians as well—including Richard Nixon. It is also implied, but not directly stated, that William Buckley, Jr. (an old enemy of the Birchers) is another tool of the CFR; and the Morgan and Rothschild banking interests are supposed to be financing the whole thing.

How does this tie in with the Illuminati? Mr. Allen merely drops hints, linking Rhodes to John Ruskin, and Ruskin to earlier internationalists, and finally stating that "the originator on the profane level of this type of secret society" was Adam Weishaupt, whom he calls "the monster who founded the Order of the Illuminati on May 1, 1776."

Pat

ILLUMINATI PROJECT: MEMO #7

7/27

J.M.:

This is from a small left-wing newspaper in Chicago (*The Roger*SPARK Chicago, July 1969, Vol. 2, No. 9: "Daley Linked With Illuminati," no author's name given):

No historian knows what happened to Adam Weishaupt after he was exiled from Bavaria in 1785, and entries in "Washington's" diary after that date frequently refer to the hemp crop at Mount Vernon.

The possibility that Adam Weishaupt killed George Washington and took his place, serving as our first President for two terms, is now confirmed. . . . The two main colors of the American flag are, excluding a small patch of blue in one corner, red and white: these are also the official colors of the Hashishim. The flag and the Illuminati pyramid both have thirteen horizontal divisions: thirteen is, of course, the traditional code for marijuana . . . and is still used in that sense by Hell's Angels among others.

Now, "Washington" formed the Federalist party.

The other major party in those days, The Democratic Republicans, was formed by Thomas Jefferson [and] there are grounds for accepting the testimony of the Reverend Jedediah Morse of Charleston, who accused Jefferson of being an Illuminati agent. Thus, even at the dawn of our government, both parties were Illuminati fronts. . . .

This story later repeats the *Teenset* report that Mayor Daley used the phrase *"Ewige Blumenkraft"* during his incoherent diatribe against Abe Ribicoff.

Pat

ILLUMINATI PROJECT: MEMO #8

7/27

J.M.:
More on the Washington-Weishaupt theory:

In spite of the fact that his face appears on billions of stamps and dollar bills, and his portrait hangs in every public building in the country, no one is quite sure what Washington looks like. A "Project 20" script, "Meet George Washington" will be seen tonight at 7:30 on Channel (fill in by local stations). The program offers contemporary portraits of the first President, some of which do not even seem to be the same man.

This is a press release sent out by NBC on April 24, 1969. Some of the portraits can be found in *Encyclopedia Britannica* and the resemblance to portraits of Weishaupt is undeniable.

Incidentally, Barbara called my attention to this: the letter in *Playboy* asking about the Illuminati was signed "R.S., Kansas City, Missouri." According to the Kansas City newspapers, a Robert Stanton of that city was found dead on March 17, 1969 (about a week after the April *Playboy* appeared on the newsstands) with his throat torn as if by the talons of some enormous beast. No animal was reported missing from any of the local zoos.

Pat

Saul looked up at the pictures of Washington on the wall. For the first time, he noticed the strange half-smile on the most famous of them all, the one by Gilbert Stuart that appears on one-dollar bills. *"As if by the talons of some enormous beast," he quoted to himself, thinking again of Malik's disappearing dogs.*

"What the hell are you grinning about?" he asked sourly.

Congressman Koch, he remembered suddenly, in a speech years and years ago when marijuana was illegal everywhere, said something about Washington's hemp crop. What was it? Yes: it was about the entries in the General's diary—they showed that he separated the female hemp plants from the males before fertilization. That was botanically unnecessary if he was growing the crop for rope, but it was standard practise in cultivating hemp for marijuana, Koch pointed out.

And "illumination" was one of the words hippies were always using to describe the experience one obtains from the highest grade of grass. Even the more common term, "turning on," had the same meaning as "illumination," when you stopped to think about. Wasn't that what the crown of light around Jesus' head in Catholic art was supposed to mean? And Goethe—if he was really part of this—might have been referring to the experience in his last words, as he lay dying: "More light!"

I should have become a rabbi, like my father wanted, Saul thought bemusedly. *Police work is getting to be too much for me.*

In a few minutes I'll be suspecting Thomas Edison.

ROCK ROCK ROCK TILL BROAD DAYLIGHT

Slowly, Mary Lou Servix swam back to consciousness, like a shipwreck victim reaching a raft.

"Good Lord," she breathed softly.

Simon kissed her neck. "Now you know," he whispered.

"Good *Lord*," she repeated. "How many times did I come?"

Simon smiled. "I'm not an anal-compulsive type—I wasn't counting. Ten or twelve, something like that, I guess."

"Good *Lord*. And the hallucinations. Was that what you were doing to my nervous system, or was it the grass?"

"Just tell me about what you saw."

"Well, you got a halo around you, sort of. A big blue halo. And then I saw that it was around me, too, and that it had all sorts of little blue dots dancing in sort of whorls inside it. And then there wasn't even that anymore. Just light. Pure white light."

"Suppose I told you I have a friend who's a dolphin and he exists in that kind of limitless light all the time."

"Oh, don't start jiving me. You've been so nice, until now."

"I'm not jiving you. His name is Howard. I might arrange for you to meet him."

"A fish?"

"No, baby. A dolphin is a mammal. Just like you and me."

"You are either the world's greatest brain or the world's craziest motherfucker, Mr. Simon Moon. I mean it. But that light . . . My God, I will never forget that light."

"And what happened to your body?" Simon asked casually.

"You know, I didn't know where it was. Even in the middle of my orgasms I didn't know where my body was. Everything was just . . . the light. . . ."

ROCK   ROCK   ROCK   AROUND THE CLOCK TONIGHT

And leaving Dallas that much-discussed November 22 afternoon in 1963, the man using the name "Frank Sullivan" brushes past McCord and Barker at the airport, but no foreshadowing of Watergate darkens his mind. (Back at the Grassy Knoll, Howard Hunt's picture is being snapped and will later turn up in the files of New Orleans D.A. Jim "The Jolly Green Giant" Garrison: not that Garrison ever came within light years of the real truth. . . .)

"Here, kitty-kitty-kitty," Hagbard calls.

But now we are going back, again, to April 2 and Las Vegas; Sherri Brandi (nee Sharon O'Farrell) arriving home finds Carmel in her living room at four in the morning. It doesn't surprise her; he often made these unexpected visits. *He seems to enjoy invading other people's territory like some kinda creepy virus.* "Darling," I cried, rushing to kiss him as he expected. *I wish the creep would drop dead,* I thought as our mouths met.

"An all-night john?" he asked casually.

"Yeah. One of those scientists who works at that place out in the desert we're all supposed to pretend we don't know about. A freak."

"He wanted something special?" Carmel asked quickly.

"You charged him extra?" At times I thought I could really see dollar signs in his eyes.

"No," I said, "he just wanted a lay. But afterward he wouldn't let me go. Just kept jawing." I yawned, looking around at the nice furniture and the nice paintings; I had managed to get everything in shades of pink and lavender, really beautiful, if that creep hadn't been sitting there on the couch looking like a hungry dead rat. I always wanted pretty things and I think I could have been some kind of artist or designer if all my luck wasn't always lousy. Christ, who ever told Carmel a blue turtleneck would go with a brown suit? If it wasn't for women, in my honest-to-Pete opinion, men would all go around looking like that. That's what I think. Insensitive. A bunch of cavemen, or Meander Thralls, or whatever you call them. "This john had a lot on his mind," I said before old candy-bar could start crossexamining me about something else. "He's against fluorides in drinking water and the Catholic church and faggots and he thinks the new birth-control pill is as bad as the old one and I should use a diaphragm instead. Christ, he's got the inside dope on everything under the sun, he thinks, and I hadda listen to it all. That kind of john."

Carmel nodded. "Scientists are schmucks," he said.

I pulled the dress over my head and hung it in the closet (it was the nice green one with the spangles and the new style where my nipples stick out through little holes, which is a pain in the ass because they're always rubbing against something and getting raw, but it really turns on the johns, and, like I always say, that's the name of the game, in this sonofabitching town with all the lousy luck, the only way to heavy scratch is go out there, girl, and sell your snatch) and then I grabbed my robe quick before old blow-job bobo decided it was time for his weekly Frenching. "He's got a nice house, though," I said to distract the creep. "He doesn't have to live out there on the base, he's too important for rules and regularities. Nice to look at, I mean. Redwood walls and burnt orange decor, you know? Pretty. He hates it, though. Acts as if he thinks it's haunted by Count Frankenstein or somebody. Keeps jumping up and walking around like he's looking for something. Something that'll bite his head off in one gulp if he finds it." I decided to let the top of the robe hang open a little. Carmel was either horny or he wanted something else, and *something else* with him generally means he thinks you've been holding back some cash. Him and his damned belt. Of course, sometimes with that I go queer all over for a flash and I guess that's like the come that men have, the orgasm, but it ain't worth the pain, believe me. I wonder if it's true some women get it in intercourse? Really get it? I don't think so. I've never known anybody in the business who gets it, from a man, only from Rosy Palm and her five sisters, sometimes, and if none of *us* do, how could some straight nicey-nicey get it?

"Bugs," Carmel said, looking shrewd and clever, off on his usual shtick of proving he was more hip to everything than anybody else on God's green earth. I didn't know what the hell he was talking about.

"What do you mean, bugs?" I asked. It was better than talking about money.

"The john," he said with a know-it-all grin. "He's important, you said. So his house has bugs. He probably keeps taking them out, and the FBI keeps coming back and putting in new ones. I bet he was very quiet when he was making it with you, right?" I nodded, remembering. "See. He couldn't stand the thought of those Feds eavesdropping on the other end of the wire. Just like Mal—like a guy I know in the Syndicate. He's so afraid of bugs he won't hold a business talk anywhere but the bathroom in his hotel suite with all four faucets going full blast and both of us whispering. Running water screws up a bug more than playing loud music on the radio, for some scientific reason."

"Bugs," I said suddenly. "That's it." The other kind of bugs. I was remembering Charley raving about fluoridation: "And we're all classified as mental cases, because a few right-wing nuts fifteen or twenty years ago who said fluoridation was a communist plot to poison us. Now, anybody who criticizes fluoridation is supposed to be just as bananas as God's Lightning. Good Lord, if anybody wants to do us in without firing a shot, I could—" and he caught himself, hid something that almost showed on his face, and ended like his brain was walking on one foot, "I could point to a dozen things in any chemistry book more effective than fluoride." But he wasn't thinking of chemicals, he was thinking of those little bugs, microbes is the word, and that's what he was working on. I could feel that flash I always get when I read something in a john, like if he had more money than he let on, or he'd caught his wife spreading for the milkman and was doing it to get even, or he was really a faggola and was just proving to himself that he wasn't *completely* a faggola. "My God," I said, "Carmel, I read about those microbe bugs in the *Enquirer*. If they have an accident out there, this whole town goes, and the state with it, and God knows how many other states. Jesus, no wonder he keeps washing his hands!"

"Germ warfare?" Carmel said, thinking fast. "God, I'll bet this town is crawling with Russian spies trying to find out what's going on out there. And I've got a direct lead for them. But how the hell do you meet a Russian spy, or a Chinese spy for that matter? You can't just advertise in a newspaper. Hell. Maybe if I went down to the university and talked to some of those freaking commie students. . . ."

I was shocked. "Carmel! You can't sell your own country like that!"

"The hell I can't. The Statue of Liberty is just another broad, and I'll take what I can get for her. Don't be a fool." He reached in his jacket pocket and took out a caramel candy like he always did when he was excited. "I'll bet somebody in the Mob will know. They know everything. Jesus, there has to be *some* way of cashing in on this."

The President's actual television broadcast was transmitted to the world at 10:30 P.M. *EST, March 31.* The Russians and Chinese were given twenty-four hours to get out of Fernando Poo or the skies over Santa Isobel would begin raining nuclear missiles: "This is *darn* serious," the Chief Executive said, "and America will not shirk its responsibility to the freedom-loving people of Fernando Poo!" The broadcast concluded at 11 P.M. EST, and within two minutes people attempting to get reservations on trains, planes, busses or car pools to Canada had virtually every telephone wire in the country overloaded.

In Moscow, where it was ten the next morning, the Premier called a conference and said crisply, "That character in Washington is a mental lunatic, and he means it. Get our men out of Fernando Poo right away, then find out who authorized sending them in there in the first place and transfer him to be supervisor of a hydroelectric works in Outer Mongolia."

"We don't have any men in Fernando Poo," a commissar said mournfully. "The Americans are imagining things again."

"Well, how the hell can we withdraw men if we don't have them there in the first place?" the Premier demanded.

"I don't know. We've got twenty-four hours to figure that out, or—" the commissar quoted an old Russian proverb which means, roughly, that when the polar bear excrement interferes with the fan belts, the machinery overheats.

"Suppose we just announce that our troops are coming out?" another commissar suggested. "They can't say we're lying if they don't find any of our troops there afterward."

"No, they never believe anything we *say*. They want to be shown," the premier said thoughtfully. "We'll have to infiltrate some troops surreptitiously and then withdraw them with a lot of fanfare and publicity. That should do it."

"I'm afraid it won't end the problem," another commissar said funereally. "Our intelligence indicates that there are Chinese troops there. Unless Peking backs down, we're going to be caught in the middle when the bombs start flying and—" he quoted a proverb about the man in the intersection when two manure trucks collide.

"Damn," the Premier said. "What the blue blazes do the Chinese want with Fernando Poo?"

He was harassed, but still he spoke with authority. He was, in fact, characteristic of the best type of dominant male in the world at this time. He was fifty-five years old, tough, shrewd, unburdened by the complicated ethical ambiguities which puzzle intellectuals, and had long ago decided that the world was a mean son-of-a-bitch in which only the most cunning and ruthless can survive. He was also as kind as was possible for one holding that ultra-Darwinian philosophy; and he genuinely loved children and dogs, unless they were on the site of something that had to be bombed in the National Interest. He still retained some sense of humor, despite the burdens of his almost godly office, and although he had been impotent with his wife for nearly ten years now, he generally achieved orgasm in the mouth of a skilled prostitute within 1.5 minutes. He took amphetamine pep pills to keep going on his grueling twenty-hour day, with the result that his vision of the world was somewhat skewed in a paranoid direction, and he took tranquilizers to keep from worrying too much, with the result that his detachment sometimes bordered on schizophrenia; but most of the time his innate shrewdness gave him a fingernail grip on reality. In short, he was much like the rulers of America and China.

And, banishing Thomas Edison and his light bulbs from mind, Saul Goodman looks back over the first eight memos briefly, using the conservative and logical side of his personality, rigidly holding back the intuitive functions. It was a habitual exercise with him, and he called it expansion-and-contraction: leaping in the dark for the connection that must exist between fact one and fact two, then going back slowly to check on himself.

The names and phrases flow past, in review: Fra Dolcino—1508—Roshinaya—Hassan i Sabbah—1090—Weishaupt—assassinations—John Kennedy, Bobby Kennedy, Martin Luther King—Mayor Daley—Cecil Rhodes—1888 —George Washington. . . .

Choices: (1) it is all true, exactly as the memos suggest; (2) it is partly true, and partly false; (3) it is all false, and there is no secret society that has endured from 1090 A.D. to the present.

Well, it isn't all true. Mayor Daley never said *"Ewige Blumenkraft"* to Senator Ribicoff. Saul had read, in the *Washington Post*, a lip-reader's translation of Daley's diatribe and there was no German in it, although there was obscenity and anti-Semitism. The Weishaupt-Washington impersonation theory also had some flaws—in those days, before plastic surgery, such an undetected assumption of the identity of a well-known figure was especially hard to credit, despite the circumstantial evidence quoted in the memos—two strong arguments against choice one. The memos are not *all* true.

How about choice three? The Illuminati might not be a straight unbroken line from the first recruit gathered by old Hassan i Sabbah to the person who bombed *Confrontation*—it might have died and lain dormant for a term, like the Ku Klux Klan between 1872 and 1915; and it might have gone through such breakups and resurrections more than once in eight centuries—but linkages of some sort, however tenuous, reached from the eleventh century to the twentieth, from the Near East to Europe and from Europe to America. Saul's dissatisfaction with official explanations of recent assassinations, the impossibility of making any rational sense out of current American foreign policy, and the fact that even historians who vehemently distrusted all "conspiracy theories" acknowledged the pivotal role of secret Masonic lodges in the French Revolution: all these added weight to the rejection of choice 3. Besides, the Masons were the first group, according to at least two of the memos, infiltrated by Weishaupt.

Choice 1 is definitely out, then, and choice 3 almost certainly equally invalid; choice 2, therefore, is most probably correct. The theory in the memos is partly true and partly false. But what, in essence, is the theory—and which part of it is true, which part false?

Saul lit his pipe, closed his eyes, and concentrated.

The theory, in essence, was that the Illuminati recruited people through various "fronts," turned them on to some sort of *illuminizing* experience through marijuana (or some special extract of marijuana) and converted them into fanatics willing to use any means necessary to "illuminize" the rest of the world. Their aim, obviously, is nothing less than the total transformation of humanity itself, along the lines suggested by the film *2001*, or by Nietzsche's concept of the Superman. In the course of this conspiracy the Illuminati, according to Malik's hints to Jackson, were systematically assassinating every popular political figure who might interfere with their program.

Saul thought, suddenly, of Charlie Manson, and of the glorification of Manson by the Weatherman and Morituri bombers. He thought of the popularity of pot smoking and of the slogan "by any means necessary" with contemporary radical youth, even outside Weatherman. And he thought of Neitzsche's slogans, "Be hard. . . . Whatever is done for love is beyond good and evil. . . . Above the ape is man, and above man, the Superman. . . . Forget not thy whip. . . ." In spite of his own logic, which had proved that Malik's theory was only *partly* true, Saul Goodman, a lifelong liberal, suddenly felt a pang of typically right-wing terror toward modern youth.

He reminded himself that Malik seemed to think the conspiracy emanated chiefly from Mad Dog—and that was God's Lightning country down there. God's Lightning had no fondness for marijuana, or for youth, or for the definitely anti-Christian overtones of the Illuminati philosophy.

Besides, Malik's sources were only partly trustworthy.

And there were other possibilities: the Shriners, for instance, were part of the Masonic movement, were generally right-wing, had their own hidden rites and secrets, and used Arabic trappings that might well derive from Hassan i Sabbah or the Roshinaya of Afghanistan. Who could say what secret plots were hatched at Shriner conventions?

No, that was the intuitive pole vaulter in the right lobe at work again; and right now Saul was concerned with the plodding logician in the left lobe.

The key to the mystery was in getting a clearer definition of the purpose of the Illuminati. Identify the change they were trying to accomplish—in man and in his society—and then you would be able to guess, at least approximately, who they were.

Their aim was English domination of the world, and they were Rhodes Scholars—according to the Birchers. *That* idea, obviously, belonged with Saul's own whimsey about a worldwide Shriner conspiracy. What then? The Italian Illuminati, under Fra Dolcino, wanted to redistribute the wealth—but the International Bankers, mentioned in the *Playboy* letter, presumably wanted to hold onto their wealth. Weishaupt was a "freethinker" according to the *Britannica*, and so were Washington and Jefferson—but Sabbah and Joachim of Florence were evidently heretical mystics of the Islamic and Catholic traditions respectively.

Saul picked up the ninth memo, deciding to get more facts (or pretended facts) before analyzing further—and then it hit him.

Whatever the Illuminati were aiming at had not been accomplished. Proof: If it had, they would not still be conspiring in secret.

Since almost everything has been tried in the course of human history, find out what hasn't been tried (at least not on a large scale)—and that will be the condition to which the Illuminati are trying to move the rest of mankind.

Capitalism had been tried. Communism has been tried. Even Henry George's Single Tax has been tried, in Australia. Fascism, feudalism and mysticism have been tried.

Anarchism has never been tried.

Anarchism was frequently associated with assassinations. It had an appeal for freethinkers, such as Kropotkin and Bakunin, but also for religious idealists, like Tolstoy and Dorothy Day of the Catholic Worker movement. Most anarchists hoped, Joachim-like, to redistribute the wealth, but Rebecca had once told him about a classic of anarchist literature, Max Stirner's *The Ego and His Own,* which had been called "the Billionaire's Bible" because it stressed the advantages the rugged individualist would gain in a stateless society—and Cecil Rhodes was an adventurer before he was a banker. The Illuminati were anarchists.

It all fit: the pieces of the puzzle slipped together smoothly.

Saul was convinced.

He was also wrong.

"We'll just get our troops out of Fernando Poo," the Chairman of the Chinese Communist party said on April 1. "A place that size isn't worth world war."

"But we don't have any troops there," an aide told him, "it's the Russians who do."

"Oh?" the Chairman quoted a proverb to the effect that there was urine in the rosewater. "I wonder what the hell the Russians want with Fernando Poo?" he added thoughtfully.

He was harassed, but still he spoke with authority. He was, in fact, characteristic of the best type of dominant male in the world at this time. He was fifty-five years old, tough, shrewd, unburdened by the complicated ethical ambiguities which puzzle intellectuals, and had long ago decided that the world was a mean son-of-a-bitch in which only the most cunning and ruthless can survive. He was also as kind as was possible for one holding that ultra-Darwinian philosophy; and he genuinely loved children and dogs, unless they were on the site of something that had to be bombed in the National Interest. He still retained some sense of humor, despite the burdens of his almost godly office, and, although he had been impotent with his wife for nearly ten years now, he generally achieved orgasm in the mouth of a skilled prostitute within 1.5 minutes. He took amphetamine pep pills to keep going on his grueling twenty-hour day, with the result that his vision of the world was somewhat skewed in a paranoid direction, and he took tranquilizers to keep from worrying too much, with the result that his detachment sometimes bordered on the schizophrenic; but most of the time his innate shrewdness gave him a fingernail grip on reality. In short, he was much like the rulers of America and Russia.

("And it's not only a sin against God," Mr. Mocenigo shouts, "but it gives you germs, too." It is 1950, early spring on Mulberry Street, and young Charlie Mocenigo raises terrified eyes. "Look, look," Mr. Mocenigo goes on angrily, "don't believe your own father. See what the dictionary says. Look, look at the page. Here, see. 'Masturbation: self-pollution.' Do you know what self-pollution means? Do you know how long those germs last?" And in another spring, 1955, Charles Mocenigo, a pale, skinny, introverted genius, registers for his first semester at MIT and, coming to the square on the form that says "Religion," writes in careful block capitals, ATHEIST. He has read Kinsey and Hirschfeld and almost all the biologically oriented sexological treatises by this time—studiously ignoring psychoanalysts and such unscientific types—and the only visible remnant of that early adolescent terror is a habit of washing his hands frequently when under tension, which earns him the nickname "Soapy.")

General Talbot looks at Mocenigo pityingly and raises his pistol to the scientist's head. . . .

On August 6, 1902, the world produced its usual crop of new humans, all programmed to act more or less alike, all containing minor variations of the same basic DNA blueprint; of these, approximately 51,000 were female and 50,000 were male; and two of the males, born at the same second, were to play a large role in our story, and to pursue somewhat similar and anabatic careers. The first, born over a cheap livery stable in the Bronx, New York, was named Arthur Flegenheimer and, at the other end of his life, spoke very movingly about his mother (as well as about bears and sidewalks and French Canadian Bean

Soup); the second, born in one of the finest old homes on Beacon Hill in Boston, was named Robert Putney Drake and, at the other end of his life, thought rather harshly of his mother . . . but when the paths of Mr. Flegenheimer and Mr. Drake crossed, in 1935, one of the links was formed which led to the Fernando Poo Incident.

And, in present time, more or less, 00005 was summoned to meet W. in the headquarters of a certain branch of British Intelligence. The date was March 17, but being English, neither 00005 nor W. gave a thought to blessed Saint Patrick; instead, they spoke of Fernando Poo.

"The Yanks," W. said crisply, "are developing evidence that the Russians or the Chinese, or both of them, are behind this Tequilla y Moto swine. Of course, even if that were true, it wouldn't matter a damn to Her Majesty's government; what do we care if a *speck* of an island that size turns Red? But you know the Yanks, 00005—they're ready to go to war over it, although they haven't announced that publicly yet."

"My mission," 00005 asked, the faint lines of cruelty about his mouth turning into a most engaging smile, "is to hop down to Fernando Poo and find out the real politics of this Tequilla y Mota bloke and if he is Red overthrow him before the Yanks blow up the world?"

"That's the assignment. We can't have a bloody nuclear war just when the balance of payments is almost straightened out and the Common Market is finally starting to work. So, hop to it, straightaway. Naturally, if you're captured, Her Majesty's government will have to disavow any knowledge of your actions."

"It always seems to work out that way," 00005 said ironically. "I wish for once you'd give me a mission where Her Majesty's bleeding government would stand behind me in a tight spot."

But 00005, of course, was merely being witty; as a loyal subject, he would follow orders under any circumstances, even if it required the death of every soul on Fernando Poo and himself as well. He rose, in his characteristic debonair fashion, and headed for his own office, where he began his preparations for the Fernando Poo mission. His first step was to check his personal worldwide travel notebook, seeking the bar in Santa Isobel which came closest to serving a suitable martini and the restaurant most likely to prepare an endurable lobster Newburg. To his horror, there was no such bar and no such restaurant. Santa Isobel was bereft of social graces.

"I say," 00005 muttered, "this is going to be a bit *thick*."

But he cheered up quickly, for he knew that Fernando Poo would be equipped at least with a bevy of tawny-skinned or coffee-colored females, and such women were the Holy Grail to him. Besides, he had already formed his own theory about Fernando Poo: he was convinced that BUGGER—Blowhard's Unreformed Gangsters, Goons, and Espionage Renegades, an international conspiracy of criminals and double agents, led by the infamous and mysterious Eric "the Red" Blowhard—was behind it all. 00005 had never heard of the Illuminati.

In fact, 00005, despite his dark hair combed straight back, his piercing eyes, his cruel and handsome face, his trim athlete's body, and his capacity to penetrate any number of females and defenestrate any number of males in the course of duty, was not really an ideal intelligence agent. He had grown up reading Ian Fleming novels and one day, at the age of twenty-one, looked in the mirror, decided he was everything a Fleming hero should be, and started a campaign to get into the spy game. After fourteen years in bureaucratic burrowing, he finally arrived in one of the intelligence services, but it was much more the kind of squalid and bumbling organization in which Harry Palmer had toiled his cynical days away than it was a berth of Bondage. Nevertheless, 00005 did his best to refurbish and glamorize the scene and, perhaps because God looks after fools, he hadn't managed to get himself killed in any of the increasingly bizarre missions to which he was assigned. The missions were all weird, at first, because nobody took them seriously—they were all based on wild rumors that had to be checked out just in case there be some truth in them—but later it was realized that 00005's peculiar schizophrenia was well suited to certain real problems, just as the schizoid of the more withdrawn type is ideal for a "sleeper" agent since he could easily forget what was conventionally considered his real self. Of course, nobody at any time ever took BUGGER seriously, and, behind his back, 00005's obsession with this organization was a subject of much interdepartmental humor.

"Wonderful as it was," Mary Lou said, *"some of it was scary."*

"Why?" Simon asked.

"All those hallucinations. I thought I might be losing my mind."

Simon lit another joint and passed it over to her. *"What makes you think, even now, that it was just hallucinations?"* he asked.

ROCK   ROCK   ROCK   TILL   BROAD   DAYLIGHT

"If that was real," Mary Lou said firmly, *"everything else in my life has been a hallucination."*

Simon grinned. *"Now,"* he said calmly, *"you're getting the point."*

THE SECOND TRIP, OR CHOKMAH
Hopalong Horus Rides Again

Hang on for some metaphysics. The Aneristic Principle is that of ORDER, the Eristic Principle is that of DISORDER. On the surface, the Universe seems (to the ignorant) to be ordered; this is the ANERISTIC ILLUSION. Actually, what order is "there" is imposed on primal chaos in the same sense that a person's name is draped over his actual self. It is the job of the scientist, for example, to implement this principle in a practical manner and some are quite brilliant at it. But on closer examination, order disolves into disorder, which is the ERISTIC ILLUSION.

—Malaclypse the Younger, K.S.C.,
Principia Discordia

And Spaceship Earth, that glorious and bloody circus, continued its four-billion-year-long spiral orbit about the Sun; the engineering, I must admit, was so exquisite that none of the passengers felt any motion at all. Those on the dark side of the ship mostly slept and voyaged into worlds of freedom and fantasy; those on the light side moved about the tasks appointed for them by their rulers, or idled waiting for the next order from above. In Las Vegas, Dr. Charles Mocenigo woke from another nightmare and went to the toilet to wash his hands. He thought of his date the next night with Sherri Brandi and, quite mercifully, had no inkling that it would be his last contact with a woman. Still seeking calm, he went to the window and looked at the stars—being a specialist, with no interest beyond his own field, he imagined he was looking up rather than out at them. In New Delhi aboard the afternoon TWA flight for Hong Kong, Honolulu, and Los Angeles, R. Buckminster Fuller, one of the few people to be aware that he lived on a spaceship, glanced at his three watches, showing local time (5:30 P.M.), time at Hono-

lulu, his point of destination (2:30 A.M. the next morning) and present time in his home at Carbondale, Illinois
(3:30 A.M. the previous morning.) In Paris, the noon
crowds were jostled by hordes of young people distributing leaflets glowingly describing the world's greatest Rock
Festival and Cosmic Love Feast to be celebrated on the
shores of Lake Totenkopf near Ingolstadt at the end of
the month. At Sunderland, England, a young psychiatrist
left his lunch to rush to the chronic ward and listen to
weird babble proceeding from a patient who had been dec-
ade-silent: "On *Walpurgasnacht* it's coming. That's when
His power is strongest. That's when you'll see Him. Right
at the very stroke of midnight." In the middle of the Atlantic, Howard the porpoise, swimming with friends in the
mid-morning sun, encountered some sharks and had a
nasty fight. Saul Goodman rubbed tired eyes in New York
City as dawn crept over the windowsill, and read a memo
about Charlemagne and the Courts of the Illuminated;
Rebecca Goodman, meanwhile, read how the jealous
priests of Bel-Marduk betrayed Babylon to the invading
army of Cyrus because their young king, Belshazzar, had
embraced the love-cult of the goddess Ishtar. In Chicago,
Simon Moon was listening to the birds begin to sing and
waiting for the first cinnamon rays of dawn, as Mary Lou
Servix slept beside him; his mind was active, thinking
about pyramids and rain-gods and sexual yoga and fifth-
dimensional geometries, but thinking mostly about the
Ingolstadt Rock Festival and wondering if it would all
happen as Hagbard Celine had predicted.

*(Two blocks north in space and over forty years back
in time, Simon's mother heard pistol shots as she left
Wobbly Hall—Simon was a second-generation anarchist—and followed the crowd to gather in front of the
Biograph Theatre where a man lay bleeding to death in
the alley. And the next morning—July 23, 1934—Billie
Freschette, in her cell at Cook County Jail, got the news
from a matron.* In this White Man's Country, I am the
lowliest of the lowly, subjugated because I am not white,
and subjugated again because I am not male. I am the
embodiment of all that is rejected and scorned—the female, the colored, the tribe, the earth—all that has no
place in this world of white male technology. I am the
tree that is cut down to make room for the factory that
poisons the air. I am the river filled with sewage. I am

the Body that the Mind despises. I am the lowliest of the lowly, the mud beneath your feet. And yet of all the world John Dillinger picked me to be his bride. He plunged within me, into the very depths of me. I was his bride, not as your Wise Men and Churches and Governments know marriage, but we were truly wed. As the tree is wed to the earth, the mountain to the sky, the sun to the moon. I held his head to my breast, and tousled his hair as if it were sweet as fresh grass, and I called him "Johnnie." He was more than a man. He was mad but not mad, not as a man may go mad when he leaves his tribe and lives among hostile strangers and is mistreated and scorned. He was not mad as all other white men are mad because they have never known a tribe. He was mad as a god might be mad. And now they tell me he is dead. *"Well," the matron asked finally, "aren't you going to say anything? Aren't you Indians human?" She had a real evil shine in her eye, like the eye of the rattlesnake.* She wants to see me cry. She stands there and waits, watching me through the bars. *"Don't you have any feelings at all? Are you some kind of animal?"* I say nothing. I keep my face immobile. No white shall ever see the tears of a Menominee. *At the Biograph Theatre, Molly Moon turns away in disgust as souvenir hunters dip their handkerchiefs in the blood.* I turn away from the matron and look up, out the barred window, to the stars, and the spaces between them seem bigger than ever. Bigger and emptier. Inside me there is a space like that now, big and empty, and it will never be filled again. When the tree is torn out by its roots, the earth must feel that way. The earth must scream silently, as I screamed silently.) *But she understood the sacramental meaning of the handkerchiefs dipped in blood; as Simon understands it.*

Simon, in fact, had what can only be called a funky education. I mean, man, when your parents are both anarchists the Chicago public school system is going to do your head absolutely no good at all. Feature me in a 1956 classroom with Eisenhower's Moby Dick face on one wall and Nixon's Captain Ahab glare on the other, and in between, standing in front of the inevitable American rag, Miss Doris Day or her older sister telling the class to take home a leaflet explaining to their parents why it's important for them to vote.

"My parents don't vote," I say.

"Well, this leaflet will explain to them why they should," she tells me with the real authentic Doris Day sunshine and Kansas cornball smile. It's early in the term and she hasn't heard about me from the last-semester teacher.

"I really don't think so," I say politely. "They don't think it makes any difference whether Eisenhower or Stevenson is in the White House. They say the orders will still come from Wall Street."

It's like a thundercloud. All the sunshine goes away. They never prepared her for this in the school where they turn out all these Doris Day replicas. The wisdom of the Fathers is being questioned. She opens her mouth and closes it and opens and closes it and finally takes such a deep breath that every boy in the room (we're all on the cusp of puberty) gets a hard-on from watching her breasts heave up and slide down again. I mean, they're all praying (except me, I'm an atheist, of course) that they won't get called on to stand up; if it wouldn't attract attention, they'd be clubbing their dicks down with their geography books. "That's the wonderful thing about this country," she finally gets out, "even people with opinions like that can say what they want without going to jail."

"You must be nuts," I say. "My dad's been in and out of jail so many times they should put in a special revolving door just for him. My mom, too. *You* oughta go out with subversive leaflets in this town and see what happens."

Then, of course, after school, a gang of patriots, with the odds around seven-to-one, beat the shit out of me and make me kiss their red-white-and-blue totem. It's no better at home. Mom's an anarcho-pacifist, Tolstoy and all that, and she wants me to say I didn't fight back. Dad's a Wobbly and wants to be sure that I hurt some of them at least as bad as they hurt me. After they yell at me for a half hour, they yell at each other for two. Bakunin said this and Kropotkin said that and Gandhi said the other and Martin Luther King is the savior of America and Martin Luther King is a bloody fool who's selling his people an opium utopia and all that jive. Go down to Wobbly Hall or Solidarity Bookstore and you'll still hear the same debate, doubled, redoubled, in spades, and vulnerable.

So naturally I start hanging out on Wall Street and smoking dope and pretty soon I'm the youngest living member of what they called the Beat Generation. Which does not improve my relations with school authorities, but at least it's a relief from all that patriotism and anarchism. By the time I'm seventeen and they shot Kennedy and the country starts coming apart at the seams, we're not beatniks anymore, we're hippies, and the thing to do is go to Mississippi. Did you ever go to Mississippi? You know what Dr. Johnson said about Scotland—"The best thing you can say for it is that God created it for some purpose, but the same is true of Hell." Blot Mississippi; it's not part of this story anyway. The next stop was Antioch in dear old Yellow Springs where I majored in mathematics for reasons you will soon guess. The pot there grows wild in acres and acres of beautiful nature preserve kept up by the college. You can go out there at night, pick your own grass for the week from the female of the hemp species and sleep under the stars with a female of your own species, then wake up in the morning with birds and rabbits and the whole lost Thomas Wolfe America scene, a stone, a leaf, and unfound door and all of it, then make it to class really feeling good and ready for an education. Once I woke up with a spider running across my face, and I thought, "So a spider is running across my face," and brushed him off gently, "it's his world, too." In the city, I would have killed him. What I mean is Antioch is a stone groove but that life is no preparation for coming back to Chicago and Chemical Warfare. Not that I ever got maced before '68, but I could read the signs; don't let anybody tell you it's pollution, brothers and sisters. It's Chemical Warfare. They'll kill us all to make a buck.

I got stoned one night and went home to see what it would be like relating to Mom and Dad in that condition. It was the same but different. Tolstoy coming out of her mouth, Bakunin out of his. And it was suddenly all weird and super-freaky, like Goddard shooting a Kafka scene: two dead Russians debating with each other, long after they were dead and buried, out of the mouths of a pair of Chicago Irish radicals. The young frontal-lobe-type anarchists in the city were in their first surrealist revival just then and I had been reading some of their stuff and it clicked.

"You're both wrong," I said. "Freedom won't come through Love, and it won't come through Force. It will come through the Imagination." I put in all the capital letters and I was so stoned that they got contact-high and heard them, too. Their mouths dropped open and I felt like William Blake telling Tom Paine where it was really at. A Knight of Magic waving my wand and dispersing the shadows of Maya.

Dad was the first to recover. "Imagination," he said, his big red face crinkling in that grin that always drove the cops crazy when they were arresting him. "That's what comes of sending good working-class boys to rich people's colleges. Words and books get all mixed up with reality in their heads. When you were in that jail in Mississippi you imagined yourself through the walls, didn't you? How many times an hour did you imagine yourself through the walls? I can guess. The first time I was arrested, during the GE strike of thirty-three, I walked through those walls a million times. But every time I opened my eyes, the walls and the bars were still there. What got me out finally? What got you out of Biloxi finally? *Organization*. If you want big words to talk to intellectuals with, that's a fine big word, son, just as many syllables as *imagination*, and it has a lot more realism in it."

That's what I remember best about him, that one speech, and the strange clear blue of his eyes. He died that year, and I found out that there was more to the Imagination than I had known, for he didn't die at all. He's still around, in the back of my skull somewhere, arguing with me, and that's the truth. It's also the truth that he's dead, really dead, and part of me was buried with him. It's uncool to love your father these days, so I didn't even know that I loved him until they closed the coffin and I heard myself sobbing, and it comes back again, that same emptiness, whenever I hear "Joe Hill":

> "The copper bosses killed you, Joe."
> "I never died," said he.

Both lines are true, and mourning never ends. They didn't shoot Dad the clean way, like Joe Hill, but they ground him down, year after year, burning out his Wob fires (and he was Aries, a real fire sign) with their cops, their courts, their jails, and their taxes, their corporations, their cages for the spirit and cemeteries for the soul, their plastic liberalism and murderous Marxism, and even as I say that I have to pay a debt to Lenin for he gave me the words to express how I felt when Dad was gone. "Revolutionaries," he said, "are dead men on furlough." The Democratic Convention of '68 was coming and I knew that my own furlough might be much shorter than Dad's because I was ready to fight them in the streets. All spring Mom was busy at the Women for Peace center and I was busy conspiring with surrealists and Yippies. Then I met Mao Tsu-hsi.

It was April 30, *Walpurgasnacht* (pause for thunder on the soundtrack), and I was rapping with some of the crowd at the Friendly Stranger. H.P. Lovecraft (the rock group, not the writer) was conducting services in the back room, pounding away at the door to Acid Land in the gallant effort, new and striking that year, to break in on waves of sound without any chemical skeleton key at all and I am in no position to evaluate their success objectively since I was, as is often the case with me, 99 and 44/100ths percent stoned out of my gourd before they began operations. I kept catching this uniquely pensive Oriental face at the next table, but my own gang, including the weird faggot-priest we nicknamed Padre Pederastia, had most of my attention. I was laying it on them heavy. It was my Donatien Alphonse François de Sade period.

"The head-trip anarchists are as constipated as the Marxists," I was giving forth; you recognize the style by now. "Who speaks for the thalamus, the glands, the cells of the organism? Who *sees* the organism? We cover it with clothes to hide its apehood. We won't have liberated ourselves from servitude until people throw all their clothes in the closet in spring and don't take them out again until winter. We won't be human beings, the way apes *are* apes and dogs *are* dogs, until we fuck where and when we want to, like any other mammal. Fucking in the streets isn't just a tactic to blow minds; it's recapturing our own bodies. Anything less and we're still robots possessing the wisdom of the straight line but not the understanding of the organic curve." And so on. And so forth. I think I found a few good arguments for rape and murder while I was at it.

"The next step beyond anarchy," somebody said cynically. "*Real* chaos."

"Why not?" I demanded. "Who works at a straight job here?" None of them did, of course; I deal dope myself. "Will you work at a straight job for something that calls itself an anarchist syndicate? Will you run an engine lathe eight unfucking hours a day because the syndicate tells you the people need what the lathe produces? If you will, *the people* just becomes a new tyrant."

"To hell with machines," Kevin McCool, the poet, said enthusiastically. "Back to the caves!" He was as stoned as me.

The Oriental face leaned over: she was wearing a strange headband with a golden apple inside a pentagon. Her black eyes somehow reminded me of my father's blue eyes. "What you want is an organization of the imagination?" she asked politely.

I flipped. It was too much, hearing those words just then.

"A man at the Vedanta Society told me that John Dillinger walked through the walls when he made his escape from Crown Point Jail," Miss Mao went on in a level tone. "Do you think that is possible?"

You know how dark coffee houses are. The Friendly Stranger was murkier than most. I had to get out. Blake talked to the Archangel Gabriel every morning at breakfast, but I wasn't that heavy yet.

"Hey, where you going, Simon?" somebody called. Miss Mao didn't say anything, and I didn't look back at that polite and pensive face—it would have been much easier if she looked sinister and inscrutable. But when I hit Lincoln and started toward Fullerton, I heard steps behind me. I turned and Padre Pederastia touched my arm gently.

"I asked her to come and listen to you," he said. "She was to give a signal if she thought you were ready. The signal was more dramatic than I expected, it seems. A conversation out of your past that had some heavy emotional meaning to you?"

"She's a medium?" I asked numbly.

"You can name it that." I looked at him in the light from the Biograph marquee and I remembered Mom's story about the people dipping their handkerchiefs in Dillinger's blood and I heard the old hymn start in my head ARE YOU WASHED are you washed ARE YOU WASHED in the BLOOD of the Lamb and I remembered how we all thought he hung out with us freaks in the hope of leading us back to the church holy Roman Catholic and apostolic as Dad called it when he was drunk and bitter. It was obvious that whatever the Padre was recruiting for had little to do with that particular theological trade union.

"What is this?" I asked. "And who is that woman?"

"She's the daughter of Fu Manchu," he said. Suddenly, he threw his head back and laughed like a rooster crowing. Just as suddenly, he stopped and looked at me. Just looked at me.

"Somehow," I said slowly, "I've qualified for a small demonstration of whatever you and she are selling. But I don't qualify for any more until I make the right move?" He gave the faintest hint of a nod and went on watching me.

Well, I was young and ignorant of everything outside ten million books I'd gobbled and guilty-unsure about my imaginative flights away from my father's realism and of course stoned of course but I finally understood why he was watching me that way, it was (this part of it) pure Zen, there was nothing I could do consciously or by volition that would satisfy him and I had to do exactly that which I could not *not* do, namely be Simon Moon. Which led to deciding then and there without any time to mull it over and rationalize it just what the hell being Simon Moon or, more precisely SimonMooning, consisted of, and it seemed to be a matter of wandering through room after room of my brain looking for the owner and not finding him anywhere, sweat broke out on my forehead, it was becoming desperate because I was running out of rooms and the Padre was still watching me.

"Nobody home," I said finally, sure that the answer wasn't good enough.

"That's odd," he said. "Who's conducting the search?"

And I walked through the walls and into the Fire.

Which was the beginning of the larger and funkier part of my (Simon's) education, and where we cannot, as yet, follow him. He sleeps now, a teacher rather than a learner, while Mary Lou Servix awakes beside him and tries to decide whether it was just the pot or if something really spooky happened last night. Howard sports in the Atlantic; Buckminster Fuller, flying above the Pacific, crosses the international date line and slips back into April 23 again; it is dawn in Las Vegas and Mocenigo, the nightmares and anxieties of night forgotten, looks forward cheerfully to the production of the first live cultures of Anthrax-Leprosy-Pi, which will make this a memorable day in more ways than he expects; and George Dorn, somewhere outside this time system, is writing in his journal. Each word, however, seems magically to appear by itself as if no volition on his part were necessary to its production. He read the words his pencil scrawled, but they appeared the communications of another intelligence. Yet they picked up where he had left off in his hotel room and they spoke with his private idiom:

. . . the universe is the inside without any outside, the sound made by one eye opening. In fact, I don't even know that there is a *uni*verse. More likely, there are many *multi*verses, each with its own dimensions, times, spaces, laws and eccentricities. We wander between and among these multiverses, trying to convince others and ourselves that we all walk together in a single public universe that we can share. For to deny that axiom leads to what is called schizophrenia.

Yeah, that's it: every man's skin is his own private multiverse, just like every man's home is supposed to be his castle. But all the multiverses are trying to merge, to create a true universe such as we have only imagined previously. Maybe it will be spiritual, like Zen or telepathy, or maybe it will be physical, one great big gang-fuck, but it has to happen: the creation of a universe and the one great eye opening to see itself at last. Aum Shiva!

—Oh, man, you're stoned out of your gourd. You're writing gibberish.

No, I'm writing with absolute clarity, for the first time in my life.

—Yeah? Well what was that business about the universe being the sound of one eye opening?

Never mind that. Who the hell are you and how did you get into my head?

"Your turn now, George."

Sheriff Cartwright stood in the door, a monk in a strange red and white robe beside him, holding some kind of wand the deep color of a fire engine.

"No—no—" George started to stammer. But he knew.

"Of course you know," the Sheriff said kindly—as if he were suddenly sorry about it all. "You knew before you left New York and came down here."

They were at the foot of the gallows. ". . . each with its own times, spaces, laws and eccentricities," George was thinking widly. Yes: if the universe is one big eye looking at itself, then telepathy is no miracle, for anyone who opens his own eyes fully can then look through all other eyes. (For a moment, George looks through the eyes of John Ehrlichman as Dick Nixon urges lewdly, "You can say I don't remember. You can say I can't recall. I can't give any answer to that that I can recall." *I can't give any answer to that that I can recall.*) "All flesh will see it in one instant": who wrote that?

"Gonna miss you, boy," the Sheriff said, offering an embarrassed handshake. Numbly, George clasped the man's hot, reptilian palm.

The monk walked beside him up the gallows' steps. Thirteen, George was thinking, there are always thirteen steps on a gallows. . . . And you always cream in your jeans when your neck breaks. It has something to do with the pressure on the spinal cord being transmitted through the prostate gland. The Orgasm-Death Gimmick, Burroughs calls it.

At the fifth step, the monk said suddenly: "Hail Eris."

George stared at the man dumbfounded. Who was Eris? Somebody in Greek mythology, but somebody very important. . . .

"It all depends on whether the fool has wisdom enough to repeat it."

"Quiet, idiot—he can hear us!"

I got some bad pot, George decided, and I'm still back on the hotel bed, hallucinating all this. But he repeated, uncertainly: "Hail Eris."

Immediately, just like his one and only acid trip, dimension began to alter. The steps grew larger, steeper—ascending them seemed as perilous as climbing Mount Everest. The air was suddenly lit with reddish flame— *Definitely*, George thought, *some weird and freaky pot.* . . .

And then, for some reason, he looked upward.

Each step was now higher than an ordinary building. He was near the bottom of a pyramidal skyscraper of thirteen colossal levels. And at the top. . . . And at the top. . . .

And at the top One Enormous Eye—a ruby and demonic orb of cold fire, without mercy or pity or contempt —looked at him and *into* him and through him.

The hand reaches down, turns on both bathtub fau-

cets full-power, then reaches upward to do the same to the sink faucets. Banana-Nose Maldonado leans forward and whispers to Carmel, "Now you can talk."

(The old man using the name "Frank Sullivan" was met, at Los Angeles International Airport, November 22, 1963, by Mao Tsu-Hsi, who drove him to his bungalow on Fountain Avenue. He gave his report in terse, unemotional sentences. "My God," she said when he finished, "what do you make of it?" He thought carefully and grunted, "It beats the hell out of me. The guy on the triple underpass was definitely Harry Coin. I recognized him through my binoculars. The guy in the window at the Book Depository very likely was this galoot Oswald that they've arrested. The guy on the grassy knoll was Bernard Barker from the CIA Bay of Pigs gang. But I didn't get a good look at the gink on the County Records building. One thing I'm sure of: we can't keep all this to ourselves. At the very least, we pass the word on to ELF. It might alter their plans for OM. You've heard of OM?" She nodded, saying, "Operation Mindfuck. It's their big project for the next decade or so. This is a bigger Mindfuck than anything they had planned.")

"Red China?" Maldonado whispers incredulously. "You musta been reading the Readers Digest. *We get all our horse from friendly governments like Laos. The CIA would have our ass otherwise." Straining to be heard over the running water, Carmel asks despondently, "Then you don't know how I could meet a Communist spy?"*

Maldonado stares at him levelly. "Communism doesn't have a good image right now," he says icily; it is April 3, two days after the Fernando Poo Incident.

Bernard Barker, former servant of both Batista and Castro, dons his gloves outside the Watergate; in a flash of memory he sees the grassy knoll, Oswald, Harry Coin, and, further back, Castro negotiating with Banana-Nose Maldonado.

(But this present year, on March 24, Generalissimo Tequilla y Mota finally found the book he was looking for, the one that was as precise and pragmatic about running a country as Luttwak's *Coup d'Etat* had been about seizing one. It was called *The Prince* and its author was a subtle Italian named Machiavelli; it told the Generalissimo everything he wanted to know—except how to handle American hydrogen bombs, which, unfortunately, Machiavelli had lived too soon to foresee.)

"It is our duty, our sacred duty to defend Fernando Poo," Atlanta Hope was telling a cheering crowd in Cincinnati that very day. "Are we to wait until the godless Reds are right here in Cincinnati?" The crowd started to scream their unwillingness to wait that long—they had been expecting the godless Reds to arrive in Cincinnati since about 1945 and were, by now, convinced that the dirty cowards were never going to come and would have to be met on their own turf—but a group of dirty, long-haired, freaky-looking students from Antioch College began to chant, "I Don't Want to Die for Fernandoo Poo." The crowd turned in fury: at last, some real reds to fight. . . . Seven ambulances and thirty police cars were soon racing to scene. . . .

(But only five years earlier Atlanta had a different message. When God's Lightning was first founded, as a splinter off Women's Liberation, it had as its slogan "No More Sexism," and its original targets were adult book-stores, sex-education programs, men's magazines, and foreign movies. It was only after meeting "Smiling Jim" Trepomena of Knights of Christianity United in Faith that Atlanta discovered that both male supremacy and orgasms were part of the International Communist Conspiracy. It was at that point, really, that God's Lightning and orthodox Women's Lib totally parted company, for the orthodox faction, just then, were teaching that male supremacy and orgasms were part of the International Kapitalist Conspiracy.)

"Fernando Poo," the President of the United States told reporters even as Atlanta was calling for all-out war, "will not become another Laos, or another Costa Rica."

"When are we going to get our troops out of Laos?" a reporter from the *New York Times* asked quickly; but a man from the *Washington Post* asked just as rapidly, "And when are we going to get our troops out of Costa Rica?"

"Our Present Plans for Withdrawal are going Forward according to an Orderly Schedule," the President began; *but in Santa Isobel itself,* as Tequilla y Mota underlined a passage in Machiavelli, *00005 concluded a shortwave broadcast to a British submarine lying 17 miles off the coast of the island:* "The Yanks have gone absolutely bonkers, I'm afraid. I've been here nine days now and I am absolutely convinced there is not one Russian or Chinese agent in any way involved with Generalissimo Tequilla y Mota, nor are there any troops of either of those governments hiding anywhere in the jungles. However, BUGGER is definitely running a heroin smuggling ring here, and I would like permission to investigate that." (The permission was to be denied; old W., back at Intelligence HQ in London, knew that 00005 was a bit bonkers about BUGGER himself and imagined that it was involved in every mission he undertook.)

At the same time, in a different hotel, Tobias Knight, on special loan from the FBI to the CIA, concluded his nightly shortwave broadcast to an American submarine 23 miles off the coast: "The Russian troops are definitely engaged in building what can only be a rocket-launching site, and the Slants are constructing what seems to be a nuclear installation. . . ."

And Hagbard Celine, lying 40 miles out in the Bight of Biafra in the *Lief Erickson,* intercepted both messages, and smiled cynically, and wired P. in New York: AC-TIVATE MALIK AND PREPARE DORN.

(While the most obscure, seemingly trivial part of the whole puzzle appeared in a department store in Houston. It was a sign that said:

NO SMOKING.   NO SPITTING.

THE MGT.

This replaced an earlier sign that had hung on the main showroom wall for many years, saying only

NO SMOKING

THE MGT.

The change, although small, had subtle repercussions. The store catered only to the very wealthy, and this clientele did not object to being told that they could not smoke. The fire hazard, after all, was obvious. On the other hand, that bit about spitting was somehow a touch offensive; they most certainly were not the sort of people who would spit on somebody's floor—or, at least, none of them had done such a thing at any time since about one month or at most one year after they became wealthy. Yes, the sign was definitely bad diplomacy. Resentment festered. Sales fell off. And membership in the Houston branch of God's Lightning increased. Wealthy, powerful membership.

(The odd thing was that the Management had nothing at all to do with the sign.)

George Dorn awoke screaming.

He lay on the floor of his cell in Mad Dog County Jail. His first frantic, involuntary glance told him that Harry Coin had vanished completely from the adjoining cell. The shit-pot was back in its corner and he knew, without being able to check, that there would be no human intestines in it.

Terror tactics, he thought. They were out to break him—a task which was beginning to look easy—but they were covering up the evidence as they went along.

There was no light through the cell window; it was, therefore, still night. He hadn't slept but merely fainted.

Like a girl.

Like a long-haired commie faggot.

Oh, shit and prune juice, he told himself sourly, cut it out. You've known for years that you're no hero. Don't take that particular sore out and rub sandpaper on it now. You're not a hero, but you're a goddam stubborn, pig-headed, and determined coward. That's why you've stayed alive on assignments like this before.

Show these redneck mammyjammers just how stubborn, pig-headed, and determined you can be.

George started with an old gimmick. A piece torn off the tail of his shirt gave him a writing tablet. The point of his shoelace became a temporary pen. His own saliva, spat onto the polish of the shoes themselves, created a substitute ink.

Laboriously, after a half hour, he had his message written:

WHOEVER FINDS THIS $50 TO CALL JOE MALIK, NEW YORK CITY, AND TELL HIM GEORGE DORN HELD WITHOUT LAWYER MAD DOG COUNTY JAIL

The message shouldn't land too close to the jail, so George began looking for a weighted object. In five minutes, he decided on a spring from the bunk mattress; it took him seventeen minutes more to pry it loose.

After the missile was hurled out the window—probably, George knew, to be found by somebody who would immediately turn it over to Sheriff Jim Cartwright—he began thinking of alternate plans.

He found, however, that instead of devising schemes for escape or deliverance, his mind insisted on going off in an entirely different direction. The face of the monk from his dream pursued him. He had seen that face somewhere before, he knew; but where? Somehow, the question was important. He began trying in earnest to re-create the face and identify it—James Joyce, H. P. Lovecraft, and a monk in a painting by Fra Angelico all came to mind. It was none of them, but it looked somehow a little like each of them.

Suddenly tired and discouraged, George slouched back on the bunk and let his hand lightly clutch his penis through his trousers. Heroes of fiction don't jack off when the going gets rough, he reminded himself. Well, hell, he wasn't a hero and this wasn't fiction. Besides, I wasn't going to jack-off (after all, They might be watching through a peephole, ready to use this natural jailhouse weakness to humiliate me further and break my ego). No, I definitely wasn't going to jack-off: I was just going to hold it, lightly, through my trousers, until I felt some life-force surging back into my body and displacing fear, exhaustion and despair. Meanwhile, I thought about Pat back in New York. She was wearing nothing but her cute black lace bra and panties, and her nipples are standing up pointy and hard. Make it Sophia Loren, and take the bra off so I can see the nipples directly. Ah, yes, and now try it the other way: she (Sophia, no make it Pat again) is wearing the bra but the panties are off showing the pubic bush. Let her play with it, get her fingers in there, and the other hand on a nipple, ah, yes, and now she (Pat—no, Sophia) is kneeling to unzipper my fly. My penis grew harder and her mouth opened in expectation. I reached down and cupped her breast with one hand, taking the nipple she had been caressing, feeling it harden more. (Did James Bond ever do this in Doctor No's dungeon?) Sophia's tongue (not my hand, *not* my hand) is busy and hot, sending pulsations through my entire body. Take it, you cunt. Take it, O God, a flash of the Passaic and the gun at my forehead, and you can't call them cunts nowadays, ah, you cunt, you cunt, take it, and it is Pat,

it's that night at her pad when we were both zonked on
hashish and I never never never had a blow-job like that
before or since, my hands were in her hair, gripping her
shoulders, take it, suck me off (get out of my head,
mother), and her mouth is wet and rhythmic and my cock
is just as sensitive as that night zonked on the hash, and I
pulled the trigger and then the explosion came just as I
did (pardon the diction) and I was on the floor coughing
and bouncing, my eyes watering. The second blast lifted
me again and threw me with a crunch against the wall.

Then the machine-gun fire started.

Jesus H. Particular Christ on a crutch, I thought frantically, whatever it is that's happening they're going to find
me with come on the front of my trousers.

And every bone in my body broken, I think.

The machine gun suddenly stopped stuttering and I
thought I heard a voice cry "Earwicker, Bloom and
Craft."—I've still got Joyce on my mind, I decided. Then
the third explosion came, and I covered my head as parts
of the ceiling began falling on me.

A key suddenly clanked against his cell door. Looking
up, I saw a young woman in a trench coat, carrying a
tommy gun, and desperately trying one key after another
in the lock.

From somewhere else in the building there came a
fourth explosion.

The woman grinned tensely at the sound. "Commie
motherfuckers," she muttered, still trying keys.

"Who the hell are you?" I finally asked hoarsely.

"Never mind that now," she snapped. "We've come to
rescue you—isn't that enough?"

Before I could think of a reply, the door swung open.

"Quick," she said, "this way."

I limped after her down the hall. Suddenly she stopped,
studied the wall a moment, and pressed against a brick.
The wall slid smoothly aside and we entered what appeared to be a chapel of some sort.

Good weeping Jesus and his brother Irving, I thought,
I'm *still* still dreaming.

For the chapel was not anything that a sane man would
expect to find in Mad Dog County Jail. Decorated entirely
in red and white—the colors of Hassan i Sabbah and the
Assassins of Alamout, I remembered incredulously—it
was adorned with strange Arabic symbols and slogans in

German: *"Heute die Welt, Morgens das Sonnensystem,"* *"Ewige Blumenkraft Und Ewige Schlangekraft!"* *"Gestern Hanf, Heute Hanf, Immer Hanf."*

And the altar was a pyramid with thirteen ledges—with a ruby-red eye at the top.

This symbol, I now recalled with mounting confusion, was the Great Seal of the United States.

"This way," the woman said, motioning with her tommy gun.

We passed through another sliding wall and found ourselves in an alley behind the jail.

A black Cadillac awaited us. "Everybody's out!" the driver shouted. He was an old man, more than sixty, but hard and shrewd-looking.

"Good," the woman said. "Here's George."

I was pushed into the back seat—which was already full of grim-looking men and grimmer-looking munitions of various sorts—and the car started at once.

"One for good measure," the woman in the trench coat shouted and threw another plastic bomb back at the jail.

"Right," the driver said. "It fits, too—that makes it five."

"The Law of Fives," another passenger chuckled bitterly. "Serves the commie bastards right. A taste of their own medicine."

I could restrain myself no longer.

"What the hell is going on?" I demanded. "Who are you people? What makes you think Sheriff Cartwright and his police are communists? And where are you taking me?"

"Shut up," said the woman who had unlocked my cell, nudging me none too affectionately with her machine gun. "We'll talk when we're ready. Meanwhile, wipe the come off your pants."

The car sped into the night.

(In a Bentley limousine, Fedrico "Banana Nose" Maldonado drew on his cigar and relaxed as his chauffeur drove him toward Robert Putney Drake's mansion in Blue Point, Long Island. In back of his eyes, almost forgotten, Charlie "The Bug" Workman, Mendy Weiss, and Jimmy the Shrew listen soberly, on October 23, 1935, as Banana Nose tells them: "Don't give the Dutchman a chance. Cowboy the son of a bitch." The three guns nod stolidly; cowboying somebody is messy, but it pays well. In an ordinary hit, you can be precise, even artistic, because after all the only thing that matters is that the person so honored should be definitely dead afterwards. Cowboying, in the language of the profession, leaves no room for personal taste or delicacy: the important thing is that there should be a lot of lead in the air and the victim should leave a spectacularly gory corpse for the tabloids, as notification that the Brotherhood is both edgy and short-tempered and everybody better watch his ass. Although it wasn't obligatory, it was considered a sign of true enthusiasm on a cowboy job if the guest of honor took along a few innocent bystanders, so everybody would understand exactly how edgy the Brotherhood was feeling. The Dutchman took two such bystanders. And in a different world that is still this world, Albert "The Teacher" Stern opens his morning paper on July 23, 1934, and reads FBI SHOOTS DILLINGER, thinking wistfully *If I could kill somebody that important, my name would never be forgotten.* Further back, back further: February 7, 1932, Vincent "Mad Dog" Coll looks through the phone-booth door and sees a familiar face crossing the drugstore and a tommy-gun in the man's hand. "The god-damned pig-headed Dutchman," he howled, but nobody heard him because the Thompson gun was already systematically spraying the phone-booth up and down, right and left, left and right, and up and down again for good measure . . . But tilt the picture another way and this emerges: On November 10, 1948, the "World's Greatest Newspaper," the *Chicago Tribune* announced the election to the Presidency of the United States of America of Thomas Dewey, a man who not only was not elected but would not even have been alive if Banana Nose Maldonado had not given such specific instructions concerning the Dutchman to Charlie the Bug, Mendy Weiss and Jimmy the Shrew.)

Who shot you? the police stenographer asked. *Mother is the best bet, Oh mama mama mama. I want harmony. I don't want harmony,* is the delirious answer. *Who shot you?* the question is repeated. The Dutchman still replies: *Oh mama mama mama. French Canadian bean soup.*

We drove till dawn. The car stopped on a road by a beach of white sand. Tall, skinny palm trees stood black against a turquoise sky. This must be the Gulf of Mexico, I thought. They could now load me with chains and drop me in the gulf, hundreds of miles from Mad Dog, without involving Sheriff Jim. No, they had raided Sheriff Jim's jail. Or was that a hallucination? I was going to have to keep more of an eye on reality. This was a new day, and I was going to know facts hard and sharp-edged in the sunlight and keep them straight.

I was stiff and sore and tired from a night of driving. The only rest I'd gotten was fitful dozing in which cyclopean ruby eyes looked at me till I awoke in terror. Mavis, the woman with the tommy gun, had put her arms around me several times when I screamed. She would murmur soothingly to me, and once her lips, smooth, cool and soft, had brushed my ear.

At the beach, Mavis motioned me out of the car. The sun was as hot as the bishop's jock strap when he finished his sermon on the evils of pornography. She stepped out behind me and slammed the door.

"We wait here," she said. "The others go back."

"What are we waiting for?" I asked. Just then the driver of the car gunned the motor. The car swung round in a wide U-turn. In a minute its rear end had disappeared beyond a bend in the Gulf highway. We were alone with the rising sun and the sand-strewn asphalt.

Mavis motioned me to walk down the beach with her. A little ways ahead, far back from the water, was a small white-painted frame cabana. A woodpecker landed wearily on its roof like he had flown more missions than Yossarian and never intended to go up again.

"What's the plan, Mavis? A private execution on a lonely beach in another state so Sheriff Jim can't get blamed?"

"Don't be a dummy, George. We blew up that commie bastard's jail."

"Why do you keep calling Sheriff Cartwright a commie? If ever a man had KKK written all over his forehead, it was that reactionary redneck prick."

"Don't you know your Trotsky? 'Worse is better.' Slobs like Cartwright are trying to discredit America to make it ripe for a left-wing takeover."

"I'm a left-winger. If you're against commies, you've got to be against me." I didn't care to tell her about my other friends in Weatherman and Morituri.

"You're just a liberal dupe."

"I'm not a liberal, I'm a militant radical."

"A radical is nothing but a liberal with a big mouth.

And a militant radical is nothing but a big-mouthed liberal with a Che costume. Balls. We're the real radicals, George. We do things, like last night. Except for Weatherman and Morituri, all the militant radicals in your crowd ever do is take out the Molotov cocktail diagram that they carefully clipped from *The New York Review of Books*, hang it on the bathroom door and jack-off in connection with it. No offense meant." The woodpecker turned his head and watched us suspiciously like a paranoid old man.

"And what are your politics, if you're such a radical?" I asked.

"I believe that government governs best of all that governs least of all. Preferably *not* at all. And I believe in the laissez faire capitalist economic system."

"Then you must hate my politics. Why did you rescue me?"

"You're wanted," she said.

"By whom?"

"Hagbard Celine."

"And who is Hagbard Celine?" We had reached the cabana and were standing beside it, facing each other, glaring at each other. The woodpecker turned his head and looked at us with the other eye.

"What is John Guilt?" Mavis said. I might have guessed, I thought, a Hope fiend. She went on, "It took a whole book to answer that one. As for Hagbard, you'll learn by seeing. Enough for now that you know that he's the man who requested that we rescue you."

"But you personally don't like me and would not have gone out of your way to help me?"

"I don't know about not liking you. That splotch of come on your trousers has had me horny ever since Mad Dog. Also the excitement of the raid. I've got some tension to burn off. I'd prefer to save myself for a man who completely meets the criteria of my value system. But I could get awfully horny waiting for him. No regrets, no guilt, though. You're all right. You'll do."

"What are you talking about?"

"I'm talking about your fucking me, George."

"I never knew a girl—I mean woman—who believed in the capitalist system who was any kind of a good fuck."

"What has your pathetic circle of acquaintances got to do with the price of gold? I doubt you ever met a woman who believed in the real laissez faire capitalist system. Such a woman is not likely to be caught traveling in your left-liberal circles." She took me by the hand and led me into the cabana. She shrugged out of her trench coat and spread it carefully on the floor. She was wearing a black sweater and a pair of blue jeans, both tight-fitting. She pulled the sweater off over her head. She was wearing no bra, and her breasts were apple-sized cherry-tipped cones. There was some sort of dark red birthmark between them. "Your kind of capitalist woman was a Nixonette in 1972, and she believes in that half-ass corporate socialist bastard fascist mixed economy Frank Roosevelt blessed these United States with." She unbuckled her wide black belt and unzipped her jeans. She tugged them down over her hips. I felt my hardon swelling up inside my pants. "Libertarian women are good fucks, because they know what they want, and what they want they like a lot." She stepped out of her jeans to reveal, of all things, panties made of some strange metallic-looking synthetic material that was gold in color.

How can I know facts hard and sharp-edged in the sunlight and keep them straight when this happens? "You really want me to fuck you right now on this public beach in broad daylight?" The woodpecker went to work above us just then, banging away like a rock drummer, I suddenly remembered from high school:

The Woodpecker pecked on the out-house door;
He pecked and he pecked till his pecker was sore. . . .

"George, you're too serious. Don't you know how to play? Did you ever think that life is maybe a game? There is no difference between life and a game, you know. When you play, for instance, playing with a toy, there is no winning or losing. Life is a toy, George, I'm a toy. Think of me as a doll. Instead of sticking pins in me, you can stick your thing in me. I'm a magic doll, like a voodoo doll. A doll is a work of art. Art is magic. You make an image of the thing you want to possess or cope with, so you can cope with it. You make a model, so you have it under control. Dig? Don't you want to possess me? You can, but just for a moment."

I shook my head. "I can't believe you. The way you're talking—it's not real."

"I always talk like this when I'm horny. It happens that at such times I'm more open to the vibrations from outer space. George, are unicorns real? Who made unicorns? Is a thought about unicorns a real thought? How is it different from the mental picture of my pussy—which you've never seen—that you've got in your head at this minute? Does the fact that you can think of fucking me and I can think of fucking with you mean we *are* going to fuck? Or is the universe going to surprise us? Wisdom is wearying, folly is fun. What does a horse with a single long horn sticking straight out of its head mean to you?"

My eyes went from the pubic bulge under her gold panties, where they'd strayed when she said "pussy," to the mark between her breasts.

It wasn't a birthmark. I felt like a bucket of ice water hit my groin.

I pointed. "What does a red eye inside a red-and-white triangle mean to you?"

Her open hand slammed against my jaw. "Motherfucker! Never speak to me about that!"

Then she bowed her head. "I'm sorry, George. I had no right to do that. Hit me back, if you want."

"I don't want. But I'm afraid you've turned me off sexually."

"Nonsense. You're a healthy man. But now I want to give you something without taking anything from you." She knelt before me on her trench coat, her knees parted, unzipped my fly, reached in with quick, tickling fingers, and pulled my penis out. She slipped her mouth around it. It was my jail fantasy coming true.

"What are you *doing?*"

She took her lips away from my penis, and I looked down and saw that the head was shiny with saliva and swelling visibly in rapid throbs. Her breasts—my glance avoided the Masonic tattoo—were somewhat fuller, and the nipples stuck out erect.

She smiled. "Don't whistle while you're pissing, George, and don't ask questions when you're getting blowed. Shut up and get hard. This is just quid pro quo."

When I came I didn't feel much juice jetting out through my penis; I'd used a lot up whacking off in jail. I noted with pleasure that what there was of it she didn't spit out. She smiled and swallowed it.

The sun was higher and hotter in the sky and the woodpecker celebrated by drumming faster and harder. The Gulf sparkled like Mrs. Astor's best diamonds. I peered out at the water: just below the horizon there was a flash of gold among the diamonds.

Mavis suddenly struck her legs out in front of her and dropped onto her back. "George! I can't give without taking. Please, quick, while it's still hard, get down here and slip it to me."

I looked down. Her lips were trembling. She was tugging the gold panties away from her black-escutcheoned crotch. My wet cock was already beginning to droop. I looked down at her and grinned.

"No," I said. "I don't like *girls* who slap you one minute and get the hots for you the next minute. They don't meet the criteria of *my* value system. I think they're nuts." Carefully and deliberately I stuffed my pecker back into my trousers and stepped away from her. It was sore anyway, like in the ryhme.

"You're not such a schmuck after all, you bastard," she said through gritted teeth. Her hand was moving rapidly between her legs. In a moment she arched her back, eyes clenched tight, and emitted a little scream, like a baby seagull out on its first flight, a strangely virginal sound.

She lay relaxed for a moment, then picked herself up off the cabana floor and started to dress. She glanced out at the water and I followed her eyes. She pointed at the distant glint of gold.

"Hagbard's here."

A buzzing sound floated across the water. After a moment, I spotted a small black motorboat coming toward us. We watched in silence as the boat grounded its bow on the white beach. Mavis motioned at me, and I followed her down the sand to the water's edge. There was a man in a black turtleneck sweater sitting in the stern of the boat. Mavis climbed in the bow and turned to me with a questioning look. The woodpecker felt bad vibes and took off with a flapping and cawing like the omen of Doom.

What the hell am I getting into, and why am I so crazy as to go along? I tried to see what it was out there that the motorboat had come from, but the sun on the gold metal was flashing blindingly and I couldn't make out a shape. I looked back at the black motorboat and saw that there was a circular gold object painted on the bow and there was a little black flag flying at the stern with the same gold object in its center. I pointed at the emblem on the bow.

"What's that?"

"An apple," said Mavis.

People who chose a golden apple as their symbol couldn't be all bad. I jumped into the boat, and its pilot used an oar to push off. We buzzed over the smooth water of the Gulf toward the golden object on the horizon. It was still blinding from reflected sunlight, but I was now able to make out a long, low silhouette with a small tower in the center, like a matchbox on top of a broomstick. Then I realized that I had my judgment of distances wrong. The ship, or whatever it was, was much more distant than I'd first realized.

It was a submarine—a golden submarine—and it appeared to be the equivalent of five city blocks long, as big as the biggest ocean liner I had ever heard of. The conning tower was about three stories high. As we drew up beside it I saw a man on the tower waving to us. Mavis waved back. I waved halfheartedly, supposing somehow that it was the thing to do. I was still thinking about that Masonic tattoo.

A hatch opened in the submarine's side, and the little motorboat floated right in. The hatch closed, the water drained out, and the boat settled into a cradle. Mavis pointed to a door that looked like an entrance to an elevator.

"You go that way," she said. "I'll see you later, maybe." She pressed a button and the door opened, revealing a carpeted gilt cage. I stepped in and was whisked up three stories. The door opened and I stepped out into a small room where a man was waiting, standing with a grace that reminded me of a Hindu or an American Indian. I thought at once of Metternich's remark about Talleyrand: "If somebody kicked him in the backside, not a muscle would move in his face until he decided what to do."

He bore a striking resemblance to Anthony Quinn; he had thick black eyebrows, olive skin, and a strong nose and jaw. He was big and burly, powerful muscles bulging under his black-and-green striped nautical sweater. He held out his hand.

"Good, George. You made it. I'm Hagbard Celine."

We shook hands; he had a grip like King Kong. "Welcome aboard the *Lief Erickson,* named after the first European to reach America from the Atlantic side, may my Italian ancestors forgive me. Fortunately, I have Viking ancestors, as well. My mother is Norwegian. However, blond hair, blue eyes, and fair skin are all recessive. My Sicilian father creamed my mother in the genes."

"Where the hell did you get this ship? I wouldn't have believed a submarine like this could exist without the whole world knowing about it."

"The sub's my creation, built in accordance with my design in a Norwegian fjord. This is what the liberated mind can do. I am the twentieth-century Leonardo, except that I'm not gay. I've tried it, of course, but women interest me more. The world has never heard of Hagbard Celine. That is because the world is stupid and Celine is very smart. The submarine is radar and sonar transparent. It is superior to the best either the American or Russian government even has on the drawing board. It can go to any depth in any ocean. We've sounded the Atlantic Trench, the Mindinao Deep, and a few holes in the floor of the sea that no one's ever heard of or named. *Lief Erickson* is capable of meeting the biggest, most ferocious, and smartest monsters of the deep, of which we've found God's plenty. I'd even risk her in battle with Leviathan himself, though I'm just as pleased that we've only seen him from afar hitherto."

"You mean whales?"

"I mean Leviathan, man. That fish—if fish it be—that is to your whale what your whale is to your meanest guppy. Don't ask me what Leviathan is—I haven't even gotten close enough to tell you his shape. There's only one of him, her, or it in all that world that's water. I don't know how it reproduces—maybe it doesn't have to reproduce—maybe it's immortal. It may be neither plant nor animal for all I know, but it's alive, and it's the biggest living thing there is. Oh, we've seen monsters, George. We've seen, in *Lief Erickson,* the sunken ruins of Atlantis and Lemuria—or Mu, as it's known to keepers of the Sacred Chao."

"What the fuck are you talking about?" I asked, wondering if I was in some crazy surrealist movie, wandering from telepathic sheriffs to homosexual assassins, to nympho lady Masons, to psychotic pirates, according to a script written in advance by two acid-heads and a Martian humorist.

"I'm talking about adventure, George. I'm talking about seeing things and being with people that will really liberate your mind—not just replacing liberalism with Marxism so you can shock your parents. I'm talking about getting altogether off the grubby plane you live on and taking a trip with Hagbard to a transcendental universe. Did you know that on sunken Atlantis there is a pyramidal structure built by ancient priests and faced with a ceramic substance that has withstood thirty thousand years of ocean burial so that the pyramid is clean and white as polished ivory—except for the giant red mosaic of an eye at its top?"

"I find it hard to believe that Atlantis ever existed," I said. "In fact"—I shook my head angrily—"you're conning me into qualifying that. The fact is I simply don't believe Atlantis ever existed. This is pure bullshit."

"Atlantis is where we're going next, friend. Do you trust the evidence of your senses? I hope so, because you'll see Atlantis and the pyramid, just as I said. Those bastards, the Illuminati, are trying to get gold to further their conspiracies by looting an Atlantean temple. And Hagbard is going to foil them by robbing it first. Because I fight the Illuminati every chance I get. And because I'm an amateur archeologist. Will you join us? You're free to leave right now, if you wish. I'll put you ashore and even supply you with money to get back to New York."

I shook my head. "I'm a writer. I write magazine articles for a living. And even if ninety percent of what you say is bullshit, moonshine, and the most elaborate put-on since Richard Nixon, this is the best story I've ever come across. A nut with a gigantic golden submarine whose followers include beautiful guerrilla women who blow up southern jails and take out the prisoners. No, I'm not leaving. You're too big a fish to let get away."

Hagbard Celine slapped me on the shoulder. "Good man. You've got courage and initiative. You trust only the evidence of your eyes and believe what no man tells you. I was right about you. Come on down to my stateroom." He pressed a button and we entered the golden elevator and sank rapidly till we came to an eight-foot-high archway barred by a silver gate. Celine pressed a button and the elevator door and the gate outside both slid back. We stepped out into a carpeted room with a lovely black woman sitting at one end under an elaborate emblem concocted of anchors, seashells, Viking figureheads, lions, ropes, octopi, lightning bolts, and, occupying the central position, a golden apple.

"Kallisti," said Celine, saluting the girl.

"All hail Discordia," she answered.

"Aum Shiva," I contributed, trying to enter the spirit of the game.

Celine led me down a long corridor, saying, "You'll find this submarine is opulently furnished. I have no need to live in monklike surroundings like those masochists who become naval officers. No Spartan simplicity for me. This is more like an ocean liner or a grand European hotel of the Edwardian era. Wait till you see my suite. You'll like your stateroom, too. To please myself, I built this thing on the grand scale. No finicky naval architects or parsimonious accountants in my business. I believe you've got to spend money to make money and spend the money you make to enjoy money. Besides, I have to live in the damned thing."

"And what precisely is your business, Mr. Celine?" I asked. "Or should I call you Captain Celine?"

"You should certainly not. No bullshit authority titles for me. I'm Freeman Hagbard Celine, but the conventional Mister is good enough. I'd prefer you called me by my first name. Hell, call me anything you want to. If I don't like it, I'll punch you in the nose. If there were more bloody noses, there'd be fewer wars. I'm in smuggling mostly. With a spot of piracy, just to keep ourselves on our toes. But that only against the Illuminati and their communist dupes. We aim to prove that no state has the right to regulate commerce in any way. Nor can it, when it is up against free men. My crew are all volunteers. We have among us liberated sailors who were indentured to the navies of America, Russia, and China. Excellent fellows. The governments of the world will never catch us, because free men are always cleverer than slaves, and any man who works for a government is a slave."

"Then you're a gang of Objectivists, basically? I've got to warn you, I come from a long line of labor agitators and Reds. You'll never convert me to a right-wing position."

Celine reared back as if I had waved offal under his nose. "Objectivists?" he pronounced the word as if I had accused him of being a child-molester. "We're anarchists and outlaws, goddam it. Didn't you understand that much? We've got nothing to do with right-wing, left-wing or any other half-assed political category. If you work within the system, you come to one of the either/or choices that were implicit in the system from the beginning. You're talking like a medieval serf, asking the first agnostic whether he worships God or the Devil. We're outside the system's categories. You'll never get the hang of our game if you keep thinking in flat-earth imagery of right and left, good and evil, up and down. If you need a group label for us, we're political non-Euclideans. But even that's not true. Sink me, nobody of this tub agrees with anybody else about anything, except maybe what the fellow with the horns told the old man in the clouds: *Non serviam.*"

"I don't know Latin," I said, overwhelmed by his outburst.

" 'I will not serve,' " he translated. "And here's your room."

He threw open an oaken door, and I entered a living room furnished in handsome teak and rosewood Scandinavian, upholstered in bright solid colors. He hadn't been exaggerating about the scale: you could have parked a Greyhound bus in the middle of the carpet and the room would still seem uncluttered. Above an orange couch hung a huge oil painting in an elaborate gilt frame easily a foot deep on all sides. The painting was essentially a cartoon. It showed a man in robes with long, flowing white hair and beard standing on a mountaintop staring in astonishment at a wall of black rock. Above his head a fiery hand traced flaming letters with its index finger on the rock. The words it wrote were:

THINK FOR YOURSELF, SCHMUCK!

As I started to laugh, I felt, through the soles of my feet, an enormous engine beginning to throb.

And, in Mad Dog, Jim Cartwright said into a phone with a scrambler device to evade taps, "We let Celine's crowd take Dorn, according to plan, and, Harry Coin is, ah, no longer with us."

"Good," said Atlanta Hope. "The Four are heading for Ingolstadt. Everything is GO." She hung up and dialed again at once, reaching Western Union. "I want a flat rate telegram, same words, twenty-three different addresses," she said crisply. "The message is, 'Insert the advertisement in tomorrow's newspapers.' Signature, 'Atlanta Hope.' " She then read off the twenty-three addresses, each located in a large city in the United States, each a regional head-quarters of God's Lightning. (The following day, April 25, the newspapers in those cities ran an obscure ad in the personals columns; it said "In thanks to Saint Jude for favors granted. A.W." The plot, accordingly, thickened.)

And then I sat back and thought about Harry Coin. Once I imagined I could make it with him: there was something so repulsive, so cruel, so wild and psychopathic there . . . but, of course, it hadn't worked. The same as every other man. Nothing. "Hit me," I screamed. "Bite me. Hurt me. *Do something*." He did everything, the most agreeable sadist in the world, but it was the same as if he had been the gentlest, most poetic English instructor at Antioch. Nothing. Nothing, nothing, nothing. . . . The closest miss was that strange banker, Drake, from Boston. What a scene. I'd gotten into his office on Wall Street, seeking a contribution for God's Lightning. Old white-haired buzzard, between sixty and seventy: typical of our wealthier members, I thought. I started the usual spiel, communism, sexism, smut, and all the time his eyes were bright and hard as a snake's. It finally hit me that he didn't believe a word of it, so I started to cut it off, and then he pulled out his checkbook and wrote and held it up so I could see it. Twenty thousand dollars. I didn't know what to say, and I started something about how all true Americans would appreciate this great gesture and so on, and he said, "Rubbish. You're not rich but you're famous. I want to add you to my collection. Deal?" The coldest bastard I ever met, even Harry Coin was human by comparison, yet his eyes were such a clear blue I couldn't believe they could be so frightening, a real madman in a perfectly sane way, not even a psychopath but something they don't have a name for, and it clicked, the humiliation of whoredom and the predatory viciousness in his face plus the twenty grand; I nodded. He took me into a private suite off of his business office and he touched one button, the lights dimmed, another button, down came a movie screen, a third button, and I was watching a porno-graphic movie. He didn't approach me, just watched, and

I tried to get excited, wondering if the actress was really making it or just faking it, and then a second film began, four of them this time in permutations and combinations, he led me to the couch, every time I opened my eyes I could still see the film over his shoulder, and it was the same, the same, as soon as he got his thing inside me, nothing, nothing, nothing, I kept looking at the actors trying to feel something, and then, as he came, he whispered in my ear, *"Heute die Welt, Morgens das Sonnensystem!"* That was the only time I almost made it. Sheer terror that this maniac *knew*. . . .

Later, I tried to find out about him, but nobody above me in the Order would say a word, and those below me didn't know anything. But I finally found out: he was very big in the Syndicate, maybe the top. And that's how I figured out that the old rumor was true, the Syndicate was run by the Order, too, just like everything else. . . .

But that cold sinister old man never said another word about it. I kept waiting while we dressed, when he gave me the check, when he escorted me to the door, and even his expression seemed to deny that he had said it or knew what it meant. When he opened the door for me, he put an arm on my shoulder and spoke, so his secretary could hear it, "May your work hasten the day when America returns to purity." Even his eyes weren't mocking and his voice sounded completely sincere. And yet he had read me to the core, knew I was faking, and guessed that terror alone could unlock my reflexes: maybe he even knew that I had already tried physical sadism and it hadn't worked. Out on Wall Street in the crowd, I saw a man with a gas mask—they were still rare that year—and I felt the whole world was moving faster than I could understand and that the Order wasn't telling me nearly as much as I needed to know.

Brother Beghard, who is actually a politician in Chicago under his "real" name, once explained the Law of Fives to me in relation to the pyramid-of-power principle. Intellectually, I understand: it's the only way we can work, each group a separate vector so that the most any infiltrator can learn is a small part of the design. Emotionally, though, it does get frightening at times: do the Five at the top really have the whole picture? I don't know, and I don't see how they can predict a man like Drake or guess what he's planning next. There's a paradox here, I know:

I joined the Order seeking power, and now I am more a tool, an object, than ever before. If a man like Drake ever thought that, he might tear the whole show apart.

Unless the Five really do have the powers they claim; but I'm not gullible enough to believe that bull. Some of it's hypnotism, and some is plain old stage magic, but none of it is really supernatural. Nobody has sold me on a fairy tale since my uncle got into me when I was twelve with his routine about stopping the bleeding. If my parents had only told me the truth about menstruation in advance . . .

Enough of that. There was work to be done. I hit the buzzer on my desk and my secretary, Mr. Mortimer, came in. As I'd guessed, it was past nine o'clock and he'd been out there in the reception area straightening up and worrying about my mood for God knows how long, while I was daydreaming. I studied my memo pad, while he waited apprehensively. Finally, I noticed him and said, "Be seated." He sank into the dictation chair, putting his head right under the point of the lightning bolt on the wall—an effect I always enjoyed—and opened his pad.

"Call Zev Hirsch in New York," I said watching his pencil fly to keep up with my words. "The Foot Fetishist Liberation Front is having a demonstration. Tell him to *cream* them; I won't be satisfied unless a dozen of the perverts are put in the hospital, and I don't care how many of our people get arrested doing it. The bail fund is available, if they need it. If Zev has any objections, I'll talk to him, but otherwise you handle it. Then make up the standard number-two press release, where I deny any knowledge of illegal activities by that chapter and promise we will investigate and expel anybody guilty of mob action—have that ready for release this afternoon. Then get me the latest sales figures on *Telemachus Sneezed.* . . ." Another busy day at the national headquarters of God's Lightning was started; and Hagbard Celine, feeding Mavis's report on George's sexual and other behavior into FUCKUP, came out with a coding of C-1472-B-2317A, which caused him to laugh immoderately.

"What's so damned funny?" Mavis asked.

"From out of the west come the thundering hooves of the great horse, Onan," Hagbard grinned. "The lonely stranger rides again!"

"What the hell does all that mean?"

"We've got sixty-four thousand possible personality types," Hagbard explained, "and I've only seen that reading once before. Guess who it was?"

"Not me," Mavis said quickly, beginning to color.

"No, not you." Hagbard laughed again. "It was Atlanta Hope."

Mavis was startled. "That's impossible. She's frigid for one thing."

"There are many kinds of frigidity," Hagbard said. "It fits, believe me. She joined women's liberation at the same age George joined Weatherman, and they both split after a few months. And you'd be surprised how similar their mothers were, or how the successful careers of their older brothers annoy them—"

"But George is a nice guy, underneath it all."

Hagbard Celine knocked an ash off his long Italian cigar. "Everybody is a nice guy, underneath it all," he said. "What we become when the world is through messing us over is something else."

At Château Thierry, in 1918, Robert Putney Drake looked around at the dead bodies, knew he was the last man alive in the platoon, and heard the Germans start to advance. He felt the cold wetness on his thighs before he realized he was urinating in his pants; a shell exploded nearby and he sobbed. "O God, please, Jesus. Don't let them kill me. I'm afraid to die. Please, Jesus, Jesus, Jesus . . ."

Mary Lou and Simon are eating breakfast in bed, still naked as Adam and Eve. Mary Lou spread jam on toast and asked, "No, seriously: which part was hallucination and which part was real?"

Simon sipped at his coffee. "Everything in life is a hallucination," he said simply. "Everything in death, too," he added. "The universe is just putting us on. Handing us a line."

THE THIRD TRIP, OR BINAH

The Purple Sage cursed and waxed sorely pissed and cried out in a loud voice: A pox upon the accursed Illuminati of Bavaria; may their seed take no root.

May their hands tremble, their eyes dim and their spines curl up, yea, verily, like unto the backs of snails; and may the vaginal orifices of their women be clogged with Brillo pads.

For they have sinned against God and Nature; they have made of life a prison; and they have stolen the green from the grass and the blue from the sky.

And so saying, and grimacing and groaning, the Purple Sage left the world of men and women and retired to the desert in despair and heavy grumpiness.

But the High Chapperal laughed, and said to the Erisian faithful: Our brother torments himself with no cause, for even the malign Illuminati are unconscious pawns of the Divine Plane of Our Lady.

—Mordecai Malignatus, K.N.S.,
"The Book of Contradictions," *Liber 555*

October 23, 1970, was the thirty-fifth anniversary of the murder of Arthur Flegenheimer (alias "The Dutchman," alias "Dutch Schultz"), but this dreary lot has no intention of commemorating that occasion. They are the Knights of Christianity United in Faith (the group in Atlantis were called Mauls of Lhuv-Kerapht United for the Truth; see what I mean?) and their president, James J. (Smiling Jim) Treponema, has noted a bearded and therefore suspicious young man among the delegates. Such types were not likely to be KCUF members and might even be dope fiends. Smiling Jim told the Andy Frain ushers to keep a watchful eye on the young man so no "funny business" could occur, and then went to the podium to begin his talk on "Sex Education: Communist Trojan Horse in Our Schools." (In Atlantis, it was "Numbers: Nothingarian Squid-Trap in Our Schools." The same drivel eternally.) The bearded young man, who happened to be Simon Moon, adviser to *Teenset* magazine on Illuminati affairs and instructor in sexual yoga to numerous black young ladies, observed that he was being observed (which made him think of Heisenberg) and settled back in his chair to doodle pentagons on his note pad. Three rows ahead, a crew-cut middle-aged man, who looked like a surburban Connecticut doctor, also settled back comfortably, awaiting his opportunity: the funny business that he and Simon had in mind would be, he hoped, very funny indeed.

WE SHALL NOT   WE SHALL NOT BE MOVED

There is a road going due east from Dayton, Ohio, toward New Lebanon and Brookville, and on a small farm off that road lives an excellent man named James V. Riley, who is a sergeant on the Dayton police force. Although he grieves the death of his wife two years back in '67 and worries about his son, who seems to be in some shady business involving frequent travel between New York City and Cuernavaca, the sergeant is basically a cheerful man; but on June 25, 1969, he was a bit out of sorts and generally not up to snuff because of his arthritis and the seemingly endless series of pointless and peculiar questions being asked by the reporter from New York. It didn't make sense—who would want to publish a book about John Dillinger at this late date? And why would such a book deal with Dillinger's dental history?

"You're the same James Riley who was on the Mooresville, Indiana, Force when Dillinger was first arrested, in 1924?" the reporter had begun.

"Yes, and a smart-alecky young punk he was. I don't hold with some of these people who've written books about him and said the long sentence he got back then is what made him bitter and turned him bad. He got the long sentence because he was so snotty to the judge. Not a sign of repentence or remorse, just wisecracks and a know-it-all grin spread all over his face. A bad apple from the start. And always hellbent-for-leather. In a hurry to get God knows where. Sometimes folks used to joke that there were two of him, he'd go through town so fast.

Rushing to his own funeral. Young punks like that never get long enough sentences, if you want my opinion. Might slow them down a bit."

The reporter—what was his name again? James Mallison, hadn't he said?—was impatient. "Yes, yes, I'm sure we need stricter laws and harsher penalties. But what I want to know was where was Dillinger's missing tooth—on the right side or the left side of his face?"

"Saints in Heaven! You expect me to remember that after all these years?"

The reporter dabbed his forehead with a handkerchief—very nervous he seemed to be. "Look, Sergeant, some psychologists say we never forget anything, really; it's all stored somewhere inside our brain. Now, just try to picture John Dillinger as you remember him, with that know-it-all grin as you called it. Can you get the picture into focus? Which side is the missing tooth on?"

"Listen, I'm due to go on duty in a few minutes and I can't be—"

Mallison's faced changed, as if in desperation which he was trying to conceal. "Well, let me ask you a different question. Are you a Mason?"

"A Mason? Bejesus, no—I've been a Catholic all my life, I'll have you know."

"Well, did you know any Masons in Mooresville? I mean, to talk to?"

"Why would I be talking to the likes of them, with the terrible things they're always saying about the church?"

The reporter plunged on, "All the books on Dillinger say that the intended victim of that first robbery, the grocer B. F. Morgan, summoned help by giving the Masonic signal of distress. Do you know what that is?"

"You'd have to ask a Mason, and I'm sure they wouldn't be telling. The way they keep their secrets, by the saints, I'm sure even the FBI couldn't find out."

The reporter finally left, but Sergeant Riley, a methodical man, filed his name in memory: James Mallison—or had he said Joseph Mallison? A strange book he claimed to be writing—about Dillinger's teeth and the bloody atheistic Freemasons. There was more to this than met the eye, obviously.

LIKE A TREE THAT'S PLANTED BY THE WATER
WE SHALL NOT BE MOVED

Miskatonic University, in Arkham, Massachusetts, is not a well-known campus by any means, and the few scholarly visitors who come there are an odd lot, drawn usually by the strange collection of occult books given to the Miskatonic Library by the late Dr. Henry Armitage. Miss Doris Horus, the librarian, had never seen quite such a strange visitor though, as this Professor J. D. Mallison who claimed to come from Dayton, Ohio, but spoke with an unmistakable New York accent. Considering his furtiveness, she found it no surprise that he spent the whole day (June 26, 1969) pouring over the rare copy of Dr. John Dee's translation of the *Necronomicon* of Abdul Alhazred. That was the book most of the queer ones went for; that or *The Book of Sacred Magic of Abra-Melin the Mage.*

Doris didn't like the *Necronomicon*, although she considered herself an emancipated and free-thinking young woman. There was something sinister, or to be downright honest about it, *perverted* about that book—and not in a nice, exciting way, but in a sick and frightening way. All those strange illustrations, always with five-sided borders just like the Pentagon in Washington, but with those people inside doing all those freaky sex acts with those other creatures who weren't people at all. It was frankly Doris's opinion that old Abdul Alhazred had been smoking some pretty bad grass when he dreamed up those things. Or maybe it was something stronger than grass: she remembered one sentence from the text: "Onlie those who have eaten a certain alkaloid herb, whose name it were wise not to disclose to the unilluminated, maye in the fleshe see a Shoggothe." I wonder what a "Shoggothe" is, Doris thought idly; probably one of those disgusting creatures that the people in the illustrations are doing those horny things with. Yech.

She was glad when J. D. Mallison finally left and she could return the *Necronomicon* to its position on the closed shelves. She remembered the brief biography of crazy old Abdul Alhazred that Dr. Armitage had written and also given to the library: "Spent seven years in the desert and claimed to have visited Irem, the city forbidden in the *Koran*, which Alhazred asserted was of pre-human origin. . . ." Silly! Who was around to build cities before there were people? Those Shoggothes? "An indifferent

Moslem, he worshipped beings whom he called Yog-Sothoth and Cthulhu." And that insidious line: "According to contemporary historians, Alhazred's death was both tragic and bizarre, since it was asserted that he was eaten alive by an invisible monster in the middle of the market-place." Dr. Armitage had been such a nice old man, Doris remembered, even if his talk about cabalistic numbers and Masonic symbols was a little peculiar at times; why would he collect such *icky* books by *creepy* people?

The Internal Revenue Service knows this much about Robert Putney Drake: during the last fiscal year, he earned $23,000,005 on stocks and bonds in various defense corporations, $17,000,523 from the three banks he controlled, and $5,807,400 from various real-estate holdings. They did not know that he also banked (in Switzerland) over $100,000,000 from prostitution, an equal amount from heroin and gambling, and $2,500,000 from pornography. On the other hand, they didn't know either about certain legitimate business expenses which he had not cared to claim, including more than $5,000,000 in bribes to various legislators, judges and police officials, in all 50 states in order to maintain the laws which made men's vices so profitable to him, and $50,000 to Knights of Christianity United in Faith as a last-ditch effort to stave off total legalization of pornography and the collapse of that part of his empire.

"What the deuce do you make of this?" Barney Muldoon asked. He was holding an amulet in his hand. "Found it in the bedroom," he explained, holding it for Saul to examine the strange design:

"Part of it is Chinese," Saul said thoughtfully. "The basic design—two interlocking commas, one pointing up and the other down. It means that opposites are equal."

"And what does *that* mean?" Muldoon asked sarcastically. "Opposites are opposite, not equal. You'd have to be a Chinaman to think otherwise."

Saul ignored the comment. "But the pentagon isn't in the Chinese design—and neither is the apple with the *K* in it. . . ." Suddenly, he grinned. "Wait, I'll bet I know what that is. It's from Greek mythology. There was a banquet on Olympus, and Eris wasn't invited, because she was the Goddess of Discord and always made trouble. So, to get even, she made *more* trouble: she created a beautiful golden apple and wrote on it *Kallisti*. That means 'for the prettiest one' in Greek. It's what the *K* stands for, obviously. Then she rolled it into the banquet hall, and, naturally, all the goddesses there immediately claimed it, each one saying that *she* was 'the prettiest one.' Finally, old man Zeus himself, to settle the squabble, allowed Paris to decide which goddess was the prettiest and should get the apple. He chose Aphrodite, and as a reward she gave him an opportunity to kidnap Helen, which led to the Trojan War."

"Very interesting," Muldoon said. "And does that tell us what Joseph Malik knew about the assassinations of the Kennedys and this Illuminati bunch and why his office was blown up? Or where he's disappeared to?"

"Well, no," Saul said, "but it's nice to find something in this case that I can recognize. I just wish I knew what the pentagon means, too. . . ."

"Let's look at the rest of the memos," Muldoon suggested.

The next memo, however, stopped them cold:

ILLUMINATI PROJECT: MEMO #9

7/28

J.M.:

The following chart appeared in the *East Village Other*, June 11, 1969, with the label "Current Structure of the Bavarian Illuminati Conspiracy and the Law of Fives":

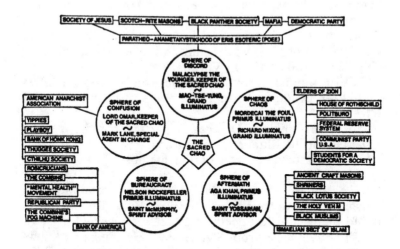

The chart hangs at the top of the page, the rest of which is empty space—as if the editors originally intended to publish an article explaining it, but decided (or were persuaded) to suppress all but the diagram itself.

Pat

"This one has to be some damned hippie or yippie hoax," Muldoon said after a long pause. But he sounded uncertain.

"Part of it is," Saul said thoughtfully keeping certain thoughts to himself. "Typical hippie psychology: mixing truth and fantasy to blow the fuses of the Establishment. The Elders of Zion section is just a parody of Nazi ideology. If there really was a Jewish conspiracy to run the world, my rabbi would have let me in on it by now. I contribute enough to the *schule.*"

"My brother's a Jesuit," Muldoon added, pointing at the Society of Jesus square, "and he never invited me into any worldwide conspiracy."

"But this part is almost plausible," Saul said, pointing to the Sphere of Aftermath. "Aga Khan *is* the head of the Ishmaelian sect of Islam, and that sect was founded by Hassan i Sabbah, the 'old man of the mountains' who led the Hashishim in the eleventh century. Adam Weishaupt is supposed to have originated the Bavarian Il-

luminati after studying Sabbah, according to the third
memo, so this part fits together—and Hassan i Sabbah is
supposed to be the first one to introduce marijuana and
hashish to the Western world, from India. That ties in
with Weishaupt's growing hemp and Washington's having
a big hemp crop at Mount Vernon."

"Wait a minute. Look at how the whole design revolves
around the pentagon. Everything else sort of grows out of
it."

"So? You think the Defense Department is the international hub of the Illuminati conspiracy?"

"Let's just read the rest of the memos," Muldoon suggested.

(The Indian Agent at the Menominee Reservation in
Wisconsin knows this: from the time Billie Freschette returned there until her death in 1968, she received mysterious monthly checks from Switzerland. He thinks he knows
the explanation: despite all stories to the contrary, Billie
did help to betray Dillinger and this is the payoff. He is
convinced of this. He is also quite wrong.)

". . . children seven and eight years old," Smiling Jim
Trepomena is telling the KCUF audience, "are talking
about penises and vaginas—*and using those very words!*
Now, is this an accident? Let me quote you Lenin's own
words. . . ." Simon yawns.

Banana-Nose Maldonado evidently had his own brand
of sentimentality or superstition, and in 1936 he ordered
his son, a priest, to say one hundred masses for the salvation of the Dutchman's soul. Even years afterward, he
would defend the Dutchman in conversation: "He was
OK, Dutch was, if you didn't cross him. If you did, forget
it; you were finished. He was almost a Siciliano about
that. Otherwise, he was a good businessman, and the first
one with a real CPA mind in the whole organization. If
he hadn't gotten that crazy-head idea about gunning down
Tom Dewey, he'd still be a big man. I told him myself.
'You kill Dewey,' I said, 'and the shit hits the fan everywhere. The boys won't take the risk; Lucky and the
Butcher want to cowboy you right now.' But he wouldn't
listen. 'Nobody fucks with me,' he said. 'I don't care if his
name is Dewey, Looey, or Phooey. He *dies*.' A real stubborn German Jew. You couldn't talk to him. I even told
him how Capone helped set up Dillinger for the Feds just
because of the heat those bank-heists were bringing down.

You know what he said? He said: 'You tell Al that Dillinger was a lone wolf. I have my own pack.' Too bad, too bad, too bad. I'll light another candle for him at church Sunday."

HAND IN HAND TOGETHER
WE SHALL NOT BE MOVED

Rebecca Goodman closes her book wearily and stares into space, thinking about Babylon. Her eyes focus suddenly on the statue Saul had bought her for her last birthday: the mermaid of Copenhagen. How many Danes, she wonders, know that this is one form of representation of the Babylonian sex goddess Ishtar? *(In Central Park, Perri the squirrel is beginning to hunt for the day's food. A French poodle, held on a leash by a mink-coated lady, barks at him, and he runs three times around a tree.)* George Dorn looks at the face of a corpse: it is his own face. "In Wyoming, after one sex-education class in a high school, the teacher was raped by seventeen boys. She said later she would never teach sex in school again." Making sure he is alone in the Meditation Room of the UN building, the man calling himself Frank Sullivan quickly moves the black plinth aside and descends the hidden stairs into the tunnel. He is thinking, whimsically, that hardly anybody realizes that the shape of the room is the same as the truncated pyramid on the dollar bill, or guesses what that means. "In Wilmette, Illinois, an 8-year-old boy came home from a sensitivity training class and tried to have intercourse with his 4-year-old sister." Simon gave up on his pentagons and began doodling pyramids instead.

Above, beyond Joe Malik's window, Saul Goodman gave up on the line of thought which had led him to surmise that the Illuminati were a front for the International Psychoanalytical Society, conspiring to drive everyone paranoid, and turned back to the desk and the memos. Barney Muldoon came in from the bedroom, carrying a strange amulet, and asked, "What do you make of this?" Saul looked at a design of an apple and a pentagon . . . and, several years earlier, Simon Moon looked at the same medallion.

"They call it the Sacred Chao," Padre Pederastia said. They sat alone at a table pulled off to the corner; the Friendly Stranger was the same as ever, except that a new group, the American Medical Association (consisting, naturally, of four kids from Germany), had replaced H. P. Lovecraft in the back room. (Nobody knew that the AMA was going to become the world's most popular rock group within a year, but Simon already thought they were superheavy). Padre Pederastia was, as on the night Simon met Miss Mao, very serious and hardly camping at all.

"Sacred Cow?" Simon asked.

"It's pronounced that way, but you spell it c-h-a-o. A chao is a single unit of chaos, they figure." The Padre smiled.

"Too much, they're nuttier than the SSS," Simon objected.

"Never underestimate absurdity, it is one door to the Imagination. Do I have to remind *you* of that?"

"We have an alliance with them?" Simon asked.

"The JAMs can't do it alone. Yes, we have an alliance, as long as it profits both parties. John—Mr. Sullivan himself authorized this."

"OK. What do they call themselves?"

"The LDD." The Padre permitted himself a smile. "New members are told the initials stand for Legion of Dynamic Discord. Later on, quite often, the leader, a most fetching scoundrel and madman named Celine, sometimes tells them it really stands for Little Deluded Dupes. That's the *pons asinorum,* or an early *pons asinorum,* in Celine's System. He judges them by how they react to that."

"Celine's System?" Simon asked warily.

"It leads to the same destination as ours—more or less—by a somewhat wilder and woolier path."

"Right-hand or left-hand path?"

"Right-hand," the priest said. "All absurdist systems are right-hand. Well, almost all. They don't invoke You-Know-Who under any circumstances. They rely on Discordia . . . do you remember your Roman myths?"

"Enough to know that Discordia is just the Latin equivalent of Eris. They're part of the Erisian Liberation Front, then?" Simon was beginning to wish he were stoned; these conspiratorial conversations always made more sense when he was slightly high. He wondered how people like the President of the U.S. or the Chairman of the Board of GM were able to plot such intricate games without being on a trip at the time. Or did they take enough tranquilizers to produce a similar effect?

"No," the priest said flatly. "Don't ever make that mis-

take. ELF is a much more, um, esoteric outfit than the
LDD. Celine is on the activist side, like us. Some of his
capers make Morituri or God's Lightning look like Trap-
pists by comparison. No, ELF will never get on Mr.
Celine's trip."

"He's got an absurdist yoga and an activist ethic?" Simon reflected. "The two don't mix."

"Celine is a walking contradiction. Look at his symbol
again."

"I've *been* looking at it and that pentagon worries me.
Are you sure he's on our side?"

The American Medical Association came to some kind
of erotic or musical climax and the priest's answer was
drowned out. "What?" Simon asked, after the applause
died down.

"I said," Padre Pederastia whispered, "that we're never
sure *anybody* is on our side. Uncertainty is the name of
the game."

ILLUMINATI PROJECT: MEMO #10

7/28

J.M.:

On the origin of the pyramid-and-eye symbol, test your
credulity on the following yarn from *Flying Saucers in the
Bible* by Virginia Brasington (Saucerian Books, 1963,
page 43.):

> The Continental Congress had asked Benjamin
> Franklin, Thomas Jefferson and John Adams to ar-
> range for a seal for the United States of America.
> . . . None of the designs they created or which were
> submitted to them, were suitable. . . .
>
> Fairly late at night, after working on the project
> all day, Jefferson walked out into the cool night air
> of the garden to clear his mind. In a few minutes he
> rushed back into the room, crying, jubilantly: "I
> have it! I have it!" Indeed, he did have some plans in
> his hands. They were the plans showing the Great
> Seal as we know it today.
>
> Asked how he got the plans, Jefferson told a
> strange story. A man approached him wearing a
> black cloak that practically covered him, face and all,
> and told him that he (the stranger) knew they were
> trying to devise a Seal, and that he had a design

which was appropriate and meaningful. . . .

After the excitement died down, the three went into the garden to find the stranger, but he was gone.

Thus, neither these Founding Fathers, nor anybody else, ever knew who really designed the Great Seal of the United States!

Pat

ILLUMINATI PROJECT: MEMO #11

7/29

J.M.:

The latest I've found on the eye-and-pyramid is in a San Francisco underground paper (*Planet*, San Francisco, July 1969, Vol. I, No.4.), suggesting it as a symbol for Timothy Leary's political party when he was running for governor of California instead of just running:

> The emblem is a tentative design for the Party's campaign button. One wag suggests that everyone cut out the circle from the back of a dollar bill and send the wholly dollar to Governor Leary so he can wallpaper his office with them. Then paste the emblem on your front door to signify your membership in the party.

> *Translations*: The year of the beginning
> New Secular Order

Both translations are wrong, of course. *Annuit Coeptis* means "he blesses our beginning" and *Novus Ordo Seclorem* means "a new order of the ages." Oh, well, scholarship was never the hippies' strong point. But—*Tim Leary* an Illuminatus?

And pasting the Eye on the door—I can't help but think of the Hebrews marking their doorways with the blood of a lamb so that the Angel of Death would pass by their houses.

Pat

ILLUMINATI PROJECT: MEMO #12

8/3

J.M.:

I've finally found the basic book on the Illuminati: *Proofs of a Conspiracy* by John Robison (Christian Book Club of

America, Hawthorn, California, 1961; originally published in 1801). Robison was an English Mason who discovered through personal experience that the French Masonic lodges—such as the Grand Orient—were Illuminati fronts and were the main instigators of the French Revolution. His whole book is very explicit about how Weishaupt worked: every infiltrated Masonic group would have several levels, like an ordinary Masonic lodge, but as candidates advanced through the various degrees they would be told more about the real purposes of the movement. Those at the bottom simply thought they were Masons; in the middle levels, they knew they were engaged in a great project to change the world, but the exact nature of the change was explained to them according to what the leaders thought they were prepared to know. Only those at the top knew the secret, which—according to Robison—is this: the Illuminati aims to overthrow all government and religion, setting up an anarcho-communist free-love world, and, because "the end justifies the means" (a principle Weishaupt acquired from his Jesuit youth), they didn't care how many people they killed to accomplish that noble purpose. Robison knows nothing of earlier Illuminati movements, but does say specifically that the Bavarian Illuminati was not destroyed by the government's crackdown in 1785 but was, in fact, still active, both in England and France and possibly elsewhere, when he wrote, in 1801. On page 116, Robison lists their existing lodges as follows: Germany (84 lodges); England (8 lodges); Scotland (2); Warsaw (2); Switzerland (many); Rome, Naples, Ancona, Florence, France, Holland, Dresden (4); United States of America (several). On page 101, he mentions that there are 13 ranks in the Order; this may account for the 13 steps on their symbolic pyramid. Page 84 gives the code name of Weishaupt, which was Spartacus; his second-in-command, Freiherr Knigge, had the code name Philo (page 117); this is revealed in papers seized by the Bavarian government in a raid on the home of a lawyer named Zwack, who had the code name Cato. Babeuf, the French revolutionary, evidently took the name Gracchus in imitation of the classical style of these titles.

Robison's conclusion, page 269, *is* worth quoting:

Nothing is as dangerous as a mystic Association. The object remaining a secret in the hands of the managers, the rest simply put a ring in their own noses, by which they may be led about at pleasure; and still panting after the secret they are the more pleased the less they see.

Pat

At the bottom of the page was a note in pencil, scrawled with a decisive masculine hand. It said: "In the beginning was the Word and it was written by a baboon."

ILLUMINATI PROJECT: MEMO #13

8/5

J.M.:

The survival of the Bavarian Illuminati throughout the nineteenth century and into the twentieth is the subject of *World Revolution* by Nesta Webster (Constable and Company, London, 1921). Mrs. Webster follows Robison fairly closely on the early days of the movement, up to the French Revolution, but then veers off and says that the Illuminati never intended to create their Utopian anarcho-communist society: that was just another of their masks. Their real purpose was dictatorship over the world, and so they soon formed a secret alliance with the Prussian government. All subsequent socialist, anarchist, and communist movements are mere decoys, she argues, behind which the German General Staff and the Illuminati are plotting to overthrow other governments, so Germany can conquer them. (She wrote right after England fought Germany in the First World War). I see no way of reconciling this with the Birchers' thesis that the Illuminati has become a front for the Rhodes Scholars to take over the world for *English* domination. Obviously—as Robison states—the Illuminati say different things to different people, to get them into the conspiracy. As for the links with modern communism, here are some passages from her pages 234-45:

But now that the (First) Internationale was dead it became necessary for the secret societies to reorganize, and it is at this crisis that we find that "formidable sect" springing to life again—*the original Illuminati of Weishaupt.*

. . . What we do know definitely is that the society was refounded in Dresden in 1880. . . . That it was consciously modelled on its eighteenth century predecessor is clear from the fact that its chief, one Leopold Engel, was the author of a lengthy panegyric on Weishaupt and his Order, entitled *Geschichte des Illuminaten Ordens* (published in 1906). . . .

. . . In London a lodge called by the same name . . . carried on the rite of Memphis—founded, it is said, by Cagliostro on Egyptian models—and initiated adepts into illuminized Freemasonry. . . .

Was it . . . a mere coincidence that in July 1889 an International Socialist Congress decided that May 1, which was the day on which Weishaupt founded the Illuminati, should be chosen for an annual International Labour demonstration?

Pat

ILLUMINATI PROJECT: MEMO #14

8/6

J.M.:

And here's still another version of the origin of the Illuminati, from the Cabalist Eliphas Levi *(The History of Magic* by Eliphas Levi, Borden Publishing Company, Los Angeles, 1963, page 65). He says there were two Zoroasters, a true one who taught white "right hand" magic and a false one who taught black "left hand" magic. He goes on:

To the false Zoroaster must be referred the cultus of material fire and that impious doctrine of divine dualism which produced at a later period the monstrous Gnosis of Manes and the false principles of spurious Masonry. The Zoroaster in question was the father of that materialized Magic which led to the massacre of the Magi and brought their true doctrine at first into proscription and then oblivion. Ever inspired by the spirit of truth, the Church was forced to condemn—under the names of Magic, Manicheanism, Illuminism and Masonry—all that was in kinship, remote or approximate, with the primitive profanation of the mysteries. One signal example is the history of the Knights Templar, which has been misunderstood to this day.

Levi does not elucidate that last sentence; it is interesting, however, that Nesta Webster (see memo 13) also traced the Illuminati to the Knights Templar, whereas Daraul and most other sources track them Eastward to the Hashishim. Is all this making me paranoid? I'm beginning to get the impression that the evidence has not only been hidden in obscure books but also made confusing and contradictory to discourage the researcher. . . .

Pat

Scrawled on the bottom of this memo was a series of jottings in the same masculine hand (Malik's, Saul guessed) that had jotted the baboon reference on memo 12. The jottings said:

Check on Order of DeMolay

Eleven-fold DeMolay Cross. Eleven intersections, therefore 22 lines. The 22 Atus of Tahuti? Why not 23??

TARO = TORA = TROA = ATOR = ROTA   !?????
Abdul Alhazred = A∴A∴ ??!

"Oh, Christ," Barney groaned. "Oh, Mary and Joseph. Oh, shit. We'll end up either become mystics or going crazy before this case is over. If there's any difference."

"The Order of DeMolay is a Masonic society for boys," Saul commented helpfully. "I don't know what the Atus of Tahuti are, but that sounds Egyptian. Taro, usually spelled t-a-r-o-t, is the deck of cards Gypsy fortune tellers use—and the word 'Gypsy' means Egyptian. Tora is the Law, in Hebrew. We keep coming back to something that has roots in both Jewish mysticism and Egyptian magic. . . ."

"The Knights Templar were kicked out of the church," Barney said, "for trying to combine Christian and Moslem ideas. Last year, my brother—the Jesuit—gave a lecture about how modern ideas are just old heresies from the Middle Ages warmed over. I had to go for politeness' sake. I remember something else he said about the Templars. They were engaged in what he called 'unnatural sex acts.' In other words, they were faggots. Do you get the impression that all these groups related to the Illuminati are all male? Maybe the big secret they're hiding so fanatically is that they're all some vast worldwide homosexual plot. I've heard show-biz people complain about what they call the 'homintern,' a homo organization that tries to keep all the best jobs for other fruits. How does that sound?"

"It sounds plausible," Saul said ironically. "But it also sounds plausible to say the Illuminati is a Jewish conspiracy, a Catholic conspiracy, a Masonic conspiracy, a communist conspiracy, a banker's conspiracy, and I suppose we'll eventually find evidence to suggest it's an interplanetary scheme masterminded from Mars or Venus. Don't you see, Barney? Whatever they're really up to, they keep creating masks so all sorts of scapegoat groups will get the blame for being the 'real' Illuminati." He shook his head dismally. "They're smart enough to know they can't operate indefinitely without a few people eventually realizing something's there, so they've taken that into account and arranged for an inquisitive outsider to get all sorts of wrong ideas about who they are."

"They're dogs," Muldoon said. "Intelligent talking dogs from the dog star, Sirius. They came here and ate Malik. Just like they ate that guy in Kansas City, except that time they didn't get to finish the job." He turned back and read from memo 8: " '. . . with his throat torn as if by the talons of some enormous beast. No animal was reported missing from any of the local zoos.' " He grinned. "Lord God, I'm almost ready to believe it."

"They're werewolves." Saul answered, grinning also. "The pentagon is the symbol of the werewolf. Look at the Late Late Show some time."

"That's the penta*gram,* not the pent*agon.*" Barney lit a cigarette, adding. "This is really getting on our nerves, isn't it?"

Saul looked up wearily and glanced around the apartment almost as if he were looking for its absent owner. "Joseph Malik," he said aloud, "what can of worms have you opened? And how far back does it go?"

WE SHALL NOT

WE SHALL NOT   BE MOVED

In fact, for Joseph Malik the beginning was several years earlier, in a medley of teargas, hymn singing, billy clubs, and obscenity, all of which were provoked by the imminent nomination for President of a man named Hubert Horatio Humphrey. It began in Lincoln Park on the night of August 25, 1968, while Joe was waiting to be teargassed. He did not know then that anything was beginning; he was only conscious, in an acid, gut-sour way, of what was ending: his own faith in the Democratic party.

He was sitting with the Concerned Clergymen under the cross they had erected. He was thinking, bitterly, that they should have erected a tombstone instead. It should have said: Here lies the New Deal.

Here lies the belief that all Evil is on the *other* side, among the reactionaries and Ku Kluxers. Here lies twenty years of the hopes and dreams and sweat and blood of Joseph Wendall Malik. Here lies American Liberalism, clubbed to death by Chicago's heroic peace officers.

"They're coming," a voice near him said suddenly. The Concerned Clergymen immediately began singing, "We shall not be moved."

"We'll be moved, all right," a dry sardonic, W.C. Fields voice said quietly. "When the teargas hits, we'll be moved." Joe recognized the speaker: it was novelist William Burroughs with his usual poker face, utterly without anger or contempt or indignation or hope or faith or any emotion Joe could understand. But he sat there, making his own protest against Hubert Horatio Humphrey by placing his body in front of Chicago's police, for reasons Joe could not understand.

How, Joe wondered, can a man have courage without faith, without belief? Burroughs believed in nothing, and yet there he sat stubborn as Luther. Joe had always had faith in something—Roman Catholicism, long ago, then Trotskyism at college, then for nearly two decades mainstream liberalism (Arthur Schlesinger, Jr.'s, "Vital Center") and now, with that dead, he was trying desperately to summon up faith in the motley crowd of dope-and-astrology-obsessed Yippies, Black Maoists, old-line hardcore pacifists, and arrogantly dogmatic SDS kids who had come to Chicago to protest a rigged convention and were being beaten and brutalized unspeakably for it.

Allen Ginsberg—sitting amid a huddle of Yippies off to the right—began chanting again, as he had all evening: "Hare Krishna Hare Krishna Krishna Krishna Hare Hare. . . ." Ginsberg believed; he believed in everything—in democracy, in socialism, in communism, in anarchism, in Ezra Pound's idealistic variety of fascist economics, in

Buckminster Fuller's technological utopia, in D. H. Lawrence's return to preindustrial pastoralism, and in Hinduism, Buddhism, Judaism, Christianity, Voodoo, astrology magic; but, above all, in the natural goodness of man.

The natural goodness of man . . . Joe hadn't fully believed in that, since Buchenwald was revealed to the world in 1944, when he was seventeen.

"KILL! KILL! KILL!" came the chant of the police—exactly like the night before, the same neolithic scream of rage that signaled the beginning of the first massacre. They were coming, clubs in hand, spraying the teargas before them. "KILL! KILL! KILL!"

Auschwitz, U.S.A., Joe thought, sickened. If they had been issued Zyklon B along with the teargas and Mace, they would be using it just as happily.

Slowly, the Concerned Clergymen came to their feet, holding dampened handkerchiefs to their faces. Unarmed and helpless, they prepared to hold their ground as long as possible before the inevitable retreat. A moral victory, Joe thought bitterly: All we ever achieve are moral victories. The immoral brutes win the real victories.

"All hail Discordia," said a voice among the clergymen—a bearded young man named Simon, who had been arguing in favor of anarchism against some SDS Maoists earlier in the day.

And that was the last sentence Joe Malik remembered clearly, for it was gas and clubs and screams and blood from then on. He had no way of guessing, at the time, that hearing that sentence was the most important thing that happened to him in Lincoln Park.

(Harry Coin curls his long body into a knot of tension, resting on his elbows and sighting the Remington rifle carefully, as the motorcade passes the Book Depository and heads toward his perch on the triple underpass. He could see Bernard Barker from the CIA down on the grassy knoll. If he carried this off right, they promised him more jobs; it would be the end of petty crime for him, the beginning of big-time money. In a way he was sorry: Kennedy seemed like a nice enough young fellow—Harry would like to make it with both him and that hot-looking wife of his at the same time—but money talks and sentiment is only for fools. He released the bolt action, ignoring the sudden barking of a dog, and took aim—just as the three shots resounded from the grassy knoll.

"Jesus Motherfuckin' Christ," he said; and then he caught the glint of the rifle in the Book Depository window. Great God Almighty, how the *fuck* many of us are there here?" he cried out, scampering to his feet and starting to run.)

It was almost a year after being clubbed—June 22, 1969—that Joe returned to Chicago, to witness another rigged convention, to suffer further disillusionment, to meet Simon once more and to hear the mysterious phrase "All hail Discordia" again.

The convention this time was the last ever held by the Students for a Democratic Society, and from the first hour after it opened, Joe realized that the Progressive Labor faction had stacked all the cards in advance. It was the Democratic party all over again—and it would have been equally bloody if the PL boys had their own police force to "deal with" the dissenters known then as RYM-I and RYM-II. Lacking that factor, the smoldering violence remained purely verbal, but when it was all over another part of Joe Malik was dead and his faith in the natural goodness of man was eroded still further. And so he found himself, aimlessly searching for something that was not totally corrupt, attending the Anarchist Caucus at the old Wobbly Hall on North Halsted Street.

Joe knew nothing about anarchism, except that several famous anarchists—Parsons and Spies of Chicago's Haymarket riot in 1888, Sacco and Vanzetti in Massachusetts, and the Wobbly's own poet-laureate, Joe Hill—had been executed for murders which they apparently hadn't really committed. Beyond that, anarchists wanted to abolish government—a proposition so evidently absurd that Joe had never bothered to read any of their theoretical or polemical works. Now, however, eating the maggotty meat of his growing disillusionment with every conventional approach to politics, he began to listen to the Wobblies and other anarchists with acute curiosity. After all, the words of his favorite fictional hero, "When you have eliminated all other possibilities, whatever remains, however improbable, must be true."

The anarchists, Joe found, were not going to quit SDS—"We'll stay in and do some righteous ass-kicking," one of them said, to the applause and cheers of the others.

Beyond that, however, they seemed to be in a welter of ideological disagreement. Gradually, he began to identify the conflicting positions expressed: the individualist-anarchists, who sounded like right-wing Republicans (except that they wanted to get rid of all functions of government); the anarcho-syndicalists and Wobblies, who sounded like Marxists (except that they wanted to get rid of all functions of government); the anarcho-pacifists, who sounded like Gandhi and Martin Luther King (except that they wanted to get rid of all functions of government); and a group who were dubbed, rather affectionately, "the Crazies"—whose position was utterly unintelligible. Simon was among the Crazies.

In a speech that Joe followed only with difficulty, Simon declared that "cultural revolution" was more important than political revolution; that Bugs Bunny should be adopted as the symbol of anarchists everywhere; that Hoffman's discovery of LSD in 1943 was a manifestation of direct intervention by God in human affairs; that the nomination of the boar hog Pigasus for President of the United States by the Yippies had been the most "transcendentally lucid" political act of the twentieth century; and that "mass orgies of pot-smoking and fucking, on every street-corner" was the most practical next step in liberating the world from tyranny. He also urged deep study of the tarot, "to fight the real enemy with their own weapons," whatever that meant. He was launching into a peroration about the mystic significance of the number 23—pointing out that 2 plus 3 equals 5, the pentad within which the Devil can be invoked "as for example in a pentacle or at the Pentagon building in Washington," while 2 divided by 3 equals 0.666, "the Number of The Beast, according to that freaked-out Revelation of Saint John the Mushroom-head," that 23 itself was present esoterically "because of its conspicuous exoteric absence" in the number series represented by the Wobbly Hall address, which was 2422 North Halsted—and that the dates of the assassinations of John F. Kennedy and Lee Harvey Oswald, November 22 and 24, also had a conspicuous 23 absent in between them—when he finally was shouted down, the conversation returned to a more mundane level.

Half in whimsy and half in despair, Joe decided to perform one of his chronic acts of faith and convince himself, at least for a while, that there was some kind of meaning in Simon's ramblings. His equally chronic skepticism, he knew, would soon enough reassert itself.

"What the world calls sanity has led us to the present planetary crises," Simon had said, "and insanity is the only viable alternative." That was a paradox worth some kind of consideration.

"About that 23," Joe said, approaching Simon tentatively after the meeting broke up.

"It's everywhere," was the instant reply. "I just started to scratch the surface. All the great anarchists died on the 23rd day of some month or other—Sacco and Vanzetti on August 23, Bonnie Parker and Clyde Barrow on May 23, Dutch on October 23—and Vince Coll was 23 years old when he was shot *on 23rd Street*—and even though John Dillinger died on the 22nd of July, if you look it up, like I did, in Toland's book, *The Dillinger Days,* you'll find he couldn't get away from the 23 Principle, because 23 other people died that night in Chicago, too, all from heat prostration. 'Nova heat moving in,' dig? And the world began on October 23, in 4004 B.C., according to Bishop Usher, and the Hungarian Revolution started on October 23, too, and Harpo Marx was born on November 23, and—"

There was more of it, much more, and Joe patiently listened to all of it, determined to continue his experiment in applied schizophrenia at least for this one evening. They retired to a nearby restaurant, the Seminary, on Fullerton Street, and Simon rambled on, over beers, proceeding to the mystic significance of the letter *W*—23rd in the alphabet—and its presence in the words "woman" and "womb" as well as in the shape of the feminine breasts and spread-eagled legs of the copulating female. He even found some mystic meaning in the *W* in Washington, but was strangely evasive about explicating this.

"So, you see," Simon was explaining when the restaurant was starting to close, "the whole key to liberation is magic. Anarchism remains tied to politics, and remains a form of death like all other politics, until it breaks free from the defined *'reality'* of capitalist society and creates its own reality. A pig for President. Acid in the water supply. Fucking in the streets. Making the totally impossible become the eternally possible. Reality is thermoplastic, not thermosetting, you know: I mean you can reprogram it much more than people realize. The hex hoax—original sin, logical positivism, those restriction and constriction

myths—all that's based on a thermosetting reality. Christ,
man, there are limits, of course—nobody is nutty enough
to deny *that*—but the limits are nowhere near as rigid as
we've been taught to believe. It's much closer to the truth
to say there are no practical limits at all and reality is
whatever people decide to make it. But we've been on one
restriction kick after another for a couple thousand years
now, the world's longest head-trip, and it takes real negative entropy to shake up the foundations. This isn't shit;
I've got a degree in mathematics, man."

"I studied engineering myself, a long time ago." Joe
said. "I realize that part of what you say is true. . . ."

"It's all true. The land belongs to the landlords, right
now, because of magic. People worship the deeds in the
government offices, and they won't dare move onto a
square of ground if one of the deeds says somebody else
owns it. It's a head-trip, a kind of magic, and you need
the opposite magic to lift the curse. You need shock elements to break up and disorganize the chains of command
in the brain, the 'mind-forg'd manacles' that Blake wrote
about. That's the unpredictable elements, dads: the errat-
ic, the erotic, the Eristic. Tim Leary said it: 'People have
to go out of their minds before they can come to their
senses.' They can't feel and touch and smell the real earth,
man, as long as the manacles in the cortex tell them it belongs to somebody else. If you don't want to call it magic,
call it counter-conditioning, but the principle is the same.
Breaking up the trip society laid on us and starting our
own trip. Bringing back old realities that are supposed to
be dead. Creating new realities. Astrology, demons, lifting
poetry off of the written page into the acts of your daily
life. Surrealism, dig? Antonin Artaud and Andre Breton
put it in a nutshell in the First Surrealist Manifesto: '*total
transformation of mind, and all that resembles it.*' They
knew all about the Illuminated Lodge, founded in Munich
in 1923, and that it controlled Wall Street *and* Hitler *and*
Stalin, through witchcraft. We gotta get into witchcraft
ourselves to undo the hex they've cast on everybody's
mind. All hail Discordia! Do you read me?"

When they finally parted, and Joe headed back for his
hotel, the spell ended. I've been listening to a spaced-out
acid-head all night, Joe thought in his cab headed south
toward the Loop, and almost managing to believe him.
If I keep on with this little experiment, I *will* believe

him. And that's how insanity always begins: you find reality unbearable and start manufacturing a fantasy alternative. With an effort of will, he forced himself back into his usual framework; no matter how cruel reality was, Joe Malik would face it and would not follow the Yippies and Crazies in the joy ride to Cloud Cuckoo Land.

But when he arrived at his hotel door, and noticed for the first time that he had Room 23, he had to fight the impulse to call Simon on the phone and tell him about the latest invasion of surrealism into the real world.

And he lay awake in his bed for hours remembering 23s that had occurred in his own life . . . and wondering about the origin of that mysterious bit of 1929 slang, "23 Skidoo. . . ."

After being lost for an hour in Hitler's old neighborhood, Clark Kent and His Supermen finally found *Ludwigstrasse* and got out of Munich. "About forty miles and we'll be in Ingolstadt," Kent-Mohammed-Pearson said. *"At last,"* one of the Supermen groaned. Just then a tiny Volkswagen inched past their VW bus, like an infant running ahead of its mother, and Kent looked bemused. "Did you check out that cat at the wheel? I saw him once before, and never forgot it because he was acting so weird. It was in Mexico City. Funny seeing him again, halfway around the world and umpteen years later." "Go catch him," another Superman commented. "With the AMA and the Trashers and other heavy groups we're going to get buried alive. Let's make sure that at least *he* knows we were in Ingolstadt for this gig."

JUST LIKE A TREE THAT'S STANDING BY THE WAAAAA-AATER

The morning after the Wobbly meeting Simon telephoned Joe.

"Listen," he asked, "do you have to fly back to New York today? Can you possibly stay over a night? I've got something I'd like you to see. It's time we started reaching people in your generation and really showing you instead of just telling you. Are you game?"

And Joe Malik—ex-Trotskyist, ex-engineering student, ex-liberal, ex-Catholic—heard himself saying, "Yes." And heard a louder voice, unspeaking, uttering a more profound "yes" deep inside himself. He was game—for astrology, for *I Ching,* for LSD, for demons, for whatever

Simon had to offer as an alternative to the world of sane and rational men who were sanely and rationally plotting their course toward what could only be the annihilation of the planet.

(WE SHALL NOT BE MOVED)

"God is dead," the priest chanted.

"God is dead," the congregation repeated in chorus.

"God is dead: we are all absolutely free," the priest intoned more rhythmically.

"God is dead," the congregation picked up the almost hypnotic beat, "we are all absolutely free."

Joe shifted nervously in his chair. The blasphemy was exhilarating, but also strangely disturbing. He wondered how much fear of Hell still lingered in the back corridors of his skull, left over from his Catholic boyhood.

They were in an elegant apartment, high above Lake Shore Drive—"We always meet here," Simon had explained, "because of the acrostic significance of the street name"—and the sounds of the automobile traffic far below mingled strangely with the preparations for what Joe already guessed was a black Mass.

"Do what thou wilt shall be the whole of the law," the priest chanted.

"Do what thou wilt shall be the whole of the law," Joe repeated with the rest of the congregation.

The priest—who was the only one who had not removed his clothes before the beginning of the ceremony—was a slightly red-faced middle-aged man in a Roman collar, and part of Joe's discomfort derived from the fact that he looked so much like every Catholic priest he had known in his childhood. It had not helped matters that he had given his name, when Simon introduced Joe to him, as "Padre Pederastia"—which he pronounced with a very campy inflection, looking flirtatiously directly in Joe's eyes.

The congregation divided, in Joe's mind, into two easily distinguishable groups: poor full-time hippies, from the Old Town area, and rich part-time hippies, from Lake Shore Drive itself and, no doubt, also from the local advertising agencies on Michigan Avenue. There were only eleven of them, however, including Joe, and Padre Pederastia made twelve—where was the traditional thirteenth?

"Prepare the pentad," Padre Pederastia commanded.

Simon and a rather good-looking young female, both quite unself-conscious in their nakedness, arose and left the group, walking toward the door which Joe had assumed led to the bedroom area. They stopped to take some chalk from a table on which hashish and sandalwood incense were burning in a goat's-head taper, then squatted to draw a large pentagon on the blood-red rug. A triangle was then added to each side of the pentagon, forming a star—the special kind of star, Joe knew, which was known as pentagram, symbol of werewolves and also of demons. He found himself remembering the corny old poem from the Lon Chaney, Jr., movies, but it suddenly didn't sound like kitsch anymore:

> Even a man who is pure of heart
> And says his prayers by night
> Can turn to a wolf when the wolfbane blooms
> And the autumn moon is bright

"I-O," the priest chanted raptly.

"I-O," the chorus came.

"I-O, E-O, Evoe," the chant rose weirdly.

"I-O, E-O, Evoe," the rhythmic reply came in cadence.

Joe felt a strange, ashy, acrid taste gathering in his mouth, and a coldness creeping into his toes and fingers. The air, too, seemed suddenly greasy and unpleasantly, mucidly moist.

"I-O, E-O, Evoe, HE!" the priest screamed, in fear or in ecstasy.

"I-O, E-O, Evoe, HE!" Joe heard himself joining the others. Was it imagination, or were all their voices subtly changing, in a bestial and pongoid fashion?

"Ol sonuf vaoresaji," the priest said, more softly.

"Ol sonuf vaoresaji," they chorused.

"It is accomplished," the priest said. "We may pass the Guardian."

The congregation arose and moved toward the door. Each person, Joe noticed, was careful to step into the pentagram and pause there a moment gathering strength before actually approaching the door. When it was his turn, he discovered why. The carving on the door, which had seemed merely obscene and ghoulish from across the room, was more disturbing when you were closer to it. It was not easy—to convince yourself that those eyes were just a trick of *trompe l'oeil*. The mind insisted on feeling that they very definitely looked at you, not affectionately, as you passed.

This—*thing*—was the Guardian which had to be pacified before they could enter the next room.

Joe's fingers and toes were definitely freezing, and auto-suggestion didn't seem a very plausible explanation. He seriously wondered about the possibility of frostbite. But then he stepped into the pentagram and the cold suddenly decreased, the eyes of the Guardian were less menacing, and a feeling of renewed energy flowed through his body, such as he had experienced in a sensitivity-training session after he had been cajoled by the leader into unleashing a great deal of pent-up anxiety and rage by kicking, screaming, weeping, and cursing.

He passed the Guardian easily and entered the room where the real action would occur.

It was as if he had left the twentieth century. The furnishings and the very architecture were Hebraic, Arabic, and medieval European, all mixed together in a most disorienting way, and entirely unrelieved by any trace of the modern or functional.

A black-draped altar stood in the center, and upon it lay the thirteenth member of the coven. She was a woman with red hair and green eyes—the traits which Satan supposedly relished most in mortal females. (There had been a time, Joe remembered, when any woman having those features was automatically suspected of witchcraft.) She was, of course, naked, and her body would be the medium through which this strange sacrament would be attempted.

What am I doing here? Joe thought frantically. *Why don't I leave these lunatics and get back to the world I know, the world where all the horrors are, after all, merely human?*

But he knew the answer.

He could not—literally could not—attempt to pass the Guardian until all those present gave their consent.

Padre Pederastia was speaking. "This part of the ceremony," he said, camping outrageously, "is very distasteful to me, as you all know. If only Our Father Below would allow us to substitute a boy on the altar when I'm officiating—but, alas, He is, as we all know, very rigid about such things. As usual, therefore, I will ask the newest member to take my place for this rite."

Joe knew, from the *Malleus malificarum* and other grimoires, what the rite was, and he was both excited and frightened.

He approached the altar nervously, noting the others forming a pentagon around the nude woman and himself. She had a lovely body with large breasts and fine nipples, but he was still too nervous to become aroused physically.

Padre Pederastia handed him the Host. "I stole this from the church myself," he whispered. "You can be sure it is fully consecrated and completely potent. You know what to do?"

Joe nodded, unable to meet the priest's lascivious eyes.

He took the Host and spat upon it quickly.

The greasiness and electrically charged quality of the air seemed to increase sharply. The light seemed harsher, like the glint of a sword, just as schizophrenics often described light as a hostile or destructive force.

He stepped forward and placed the Host upon the thighs of the Bride of Satan.

Immediately, she moaned softly, as if the simple touch were more erotic than one momentary contact could possibly be. Her legs spread voluptuously and the middle of the Host crumpled as it sunk slightly into her red pubic hair. The effect was, at once, powerful; her whole body shuddered and the Host was drawn farther into her obviously moist cunt. Using his finger, Joe pushed it the rest of the way in, and she began breathing in a hoarse staccato rhythm.

Joe Malik knelt to complete the rite. He felt like a fool and a pervert; he had never performed oral sex, or any kind of sex, in front of an audience before. He wasn't even turned on erotically. He went ahead just to find out if there was any real magic in this revolting lunacy.

As soon as his tongue entered her, she began heaving and he knew her first orgasm would arrive rapidly. His penis finally began swelling; he began licking the Host caressingly. Inside his temple, a drum seemed to be beating hollowly; he hardly noticed it when she came. His senses spun and he licked more, aware only that she flowed more heavily and thickly than any woman he had known. He put his thumb in her anus, and his middle finger in her vagina, keeping his tongue in the clitoral area, doing it up right—this was the technique occultists call the Rite of Shiva. (Irreverently, he remembered that swingers call it the One-Man Band.) He felt an unusual electrical quality in her pubic hair and was aware of a heaviness and tension in his penis more powerful than he had ever known in his life, but all else was drowned out by the drumming in his head, the cunt-taste, cunt-smell, cunt-warmth. . . . She was Ishtar, Aphrodite, Venus; the experience was so intense he began to feel a real religious dimension to it. Hadn't some nineteenth century anthropologist argued that cunt-worship was the earliest religion? He didn't even know this woman and yet he had an emotion beyond love: true reverence. *Trippy,* as Simon would say.

How many times she came, he never knew; he came himself, without once touching his penis, when the Host was finally dissolved.

He staggered back dizzily, and the air now seemed as resistant to motion as brackish water.

"Yogge Sothothe Neblod Zin," the priest began chanting. "By Ashtoreth, by Pan Pangenitor, by the Yellow Sign, by the gifts I have made and the powers I have purchased, by He Who Is Not to Be Named, by Rabban and by Azathoth, by Samma-El, by Amon and Ra, *vente, vente, Lucifer, lux fiat!*"

Joe never saw it: he *felt* it—and it was like chemical Mace, blinding and numbing him at once.

"Come not in that form!" the priest screamed. "By Jesu Elohim and the Powers that You fear, I command thee: come not in that form! *Yod He Vah He*—come not in that form."

One of the women began weeping in fear.

"Quiet, you fool," Simon shouted at her. "Don't give it more Power."

"Your tongue is bound, until I release it," the priest said to her—but the distraction of his attention had its cost; Joe *felt* It growing in potency again, and so did the others, judging from their sudden involuntary gasps.

"Come not in that form!" the priest shouted. "By the Cross of Gold, and by the Rose of Ruby, and by Mary's Son, I command and demand it of thee: come not in that form! By thy Master, Chronzon! By Pangenitor and Panphage, come not in that form!"

There was a hiss, like air pouring into a vacuum, and the atmosphere began to clear—but it also dropped abruptly in temperature.

MASTER, CALL NO MORE UPON THOSE NAMES. I MEANT NOT TO ALARM THEE.

The Voice was the most shocking experience of the night for Joe. It was oily, flattering, obscenely humble, but there was still within it a secret strength that revealed all too well that the priest's power over it, however obtained, was temporary, that both of them knew it, and that the price of that power was something it longed to collect.

"Come not in that form either," said the priest, more stern and more confident. "Ye know full well that such tones and manners are also intended to frighten, and I like not such jokes. Come in this form which thou habitually wearest in thy current earthly activities, or I shall banish thee back to that realm of which you like not to imagine. I command. I command. I command." There was nothing campy about the Padre now.

It was just a room again—an odd, medieval, mideastern room, but just a room. The figure that stood among them could not have looked less like a demon.

"OK," it said in a pleasant American voice, "we don't have to get touchy and hostile with each other over a little theatrics, do we? Just tell me what sort of business transaction you went and dragged me here for, and I'm sure we can work out all the details in a down-home, businesslike, cards-on-the-table fashion, with no hard feelings and mutual satisfaction all around."

It looked like Billy Graham.

("The Kennedys? Martin Luther King? You are fantastically naive still, George. It goes back much, much farther." Hagbard was relaxing with some Alamout Black hash, after the Battle of Atlantis. "Look at the pictures of Woodrow Wilson in his last months: The haggard look, the vague eyes, and, in fact, symptoms of a certain slow-acting and undetectable poison. They slipped it to him at Versailles. Or look into the Lincoln caper. Who opposed the greenback plan—the closest thing to flaxscript America ever had? Stanton the banker. Who ordered all roads out of Washington closed, except one? Stanton the banker. And Booth went straight for that road. Who got ahold of Booth's diary afterward? Stanton the banker. And turned it over to the Archives with seventeen pages missing? Stanton the banker. George, you have so much to learn about real history. . . .")

The Reverend William Helmer, religious columnist for

Confrontation, stared at the telegram. Joe Malik was supposed to be in Chicago covering the SDS convention; what was he doing in Providence, Rhode Island, and what was he involved in that could provoke such an extraordinary communication? Helmer reread the telegram carefully:

> Drop next month's column. Will pay large bonus for prompt answers to these questions. First, trace all movements of Reverend Billy Graham during last week and find out if he could possibly have gotten to Chicago surreptitiously. Second, send me a list of reliable books on Satanism and witchcraft in the modern world. Tell nobody else on the magazine about this. Wire me c/o Jerry Mallory, Hotel Benefit, Providence, Rhode Island. P.S. find out where The John Dillinger Died for You Society has its headquarters. Joe Malik.

Those SDS kids must have turned him on with acid, Helmer decided. Well, he was still the boss, and he paid nice bonuses when he was pleased. Helmer reached for the phone.

(Howard, the dolphin, was singing a very satirical song about sharks, as he swam to meet the *Lief Erikson* at Peos.)

James Walking Bear had no great love for palefaces most of the time, but he had just dropped six peyote buttons before this Professor Mallory arrived and he was feeling benevolent and forgiving. After all, the Road Chief once said at a very sacred midsummer peyote festival that the line about forgiving *those who trespass against us* had a special meaning for Indians. Only when we all forgave the whites, he had said, would our hearts be totally pure, and when our hearts were pure the Curse would be lifted—the white men would cease to trespass, go home to Europe, and vex one another instead of persecuting us. James tried to forgive the professor for being white and found, as usual, that peyote made forgiveness easier.

"Billie Freschette?" he said. "Hell, she died back in sixty-eight."

"I know that," the professor said. "What I'm looking for is any photographs she may have left."

Sure. James knew what kind of photographs.

"You mean ones that had Dillinger in them?"

"Yes, she was his mistress, virtually his common-law wife, for a long time, and—"

"No soap. You're years too late. Reporters bought up everything she had that showed even the back of Dillinger's head, way back, long before she came here to the reservation to die."

"Well, did you know her?"

"Sure." James was careful not be spiteful and didn't add: all Menominee Indians know one another, in a way you whites can't understand "knowing."

"Did she ever converse about Dillinger?"

"Of course. Old women always talk about their dead men. Always say the same thing, too: never was another man as good as him. Except when they say there never was another man as bad as him. They only say that when they're drunk, though."

The paleface kept turning colors, the way people do when you're on peyote. Now he looked almost like an Indian. That made it easier to talk to him.

"Did she ever say anything about John's attitude toward the Masons?"

Why shouldn't people turn colors? All the trouble in world came from the fact that they usually stayed the same color. James nodded profoundly. As usual, peyote had brought him a big Truth. If whites and blacks and Indians were turning colors all the time, there wouldn't be any hate in the world, because nobody would know which people to hate.

"I said, did she ever mention John's attitude toward the Masons?"

"Oh. Oh, yes. Funny you should ask that." The man had a halo around his head now, and James wondered what that meant. Every time he took peyote alone things like that would happen, and he'd end up wishing there were a Road Chief or some other priest around to explain these signs properly. But what about the Masons? Oh, yes. "Billie said the Masons were the only people John Dillinger really hated. He said they railroaded him to prison the first time, and they owned all the banks, so he was getting even by robbing them."

The professor's mouth dropped open in surprise and delight—and James thought it was kind of funny to see that, especially with the halo turning from pink to blue to pink to blue to pink again at the same time.

(*"A big mouth, a tiny brain/ He only thinks of blood and pain,"* Howard sang.)

Notes found by a TWA stewardess in a seat vacated by a Mr. "John Mason" after a Madison, Wisconsin, to Mexico City flight June 29, 1969: one week after the last SDS convention of all time:

"We only robbed from the banks what the banks robbed from the people"—Dillinger, Crown Point Jail, 1934. Could have come from any anarchist text.

Lucifer—bringer of light.

Weishaupt's "illumination" & Voltaire's "enlightenment": from the Latin "lux" meaning light.

Christianity all in 3s (Trinity, etc.) Buddhism in 4s. Illuminism in 5s. A progression?

Hopi teaching: all men have 4 souls now, but in future will have 5 souls. Find an anthropologist for more data on this.

Who decided the Pentagon building should have that particular shape?

"Kick out the Jams"??? Cross-check.

"Adam," the first man; "Weis," to know; "haupt," chief or leader. "The first man to be a leader of those who know." Assumed name from the beginning?

Iok-Sotot in Pnakotic manuscripts. Cd. be Yog-Sothoth?

D.E.A.T.H.—Don't Ever Antagonize The Horn. Does Pynchon know?

Must get Simon to explain the Yellow Sign and the Aklo chants. Might need protection.

C. says the h. neophobe type outnumbers us 1000-to-1. If so, all this is hopeless.

What gets me is how much has been out in the open for so long. Not just in Lovecraft, Joyce, Melville, etc., or in the Bugs Bunny cartoons but in scholarly works that pretend to explain. Anybody who wants to go to the trouble can find out, for instance, that the "secret" of the Eleusinian Mysteries was the words whispered to the novice after he got the magic mushroom: "Osiris is a black God!" Five words (of course!) but no historian, archeologist, anthropologist, folklorist, etc. has understood. Or, those who did understand, didn't care to admit it.

Can I trust C.? For that matter, can I trust Simon?

This matter of Tlaloc should convince me, one way or the other.

("He only thinks of blood and slaughter/The shark should live on land not water.")

("To hell with the shark and all his kin/And fight like hell when you see his fin.")

When Joe Malik got off the plane at Los Angeles International Airport, Simon was waiting for him.

"We'll talk in your car," Joe said briefly.

The car, being Simon's, was naturally a psychedelic Volkswagen. "Well?" he asked as they drove out of the airport onto Central Avenue.

"It all checks out," Joe said with an odd calm. "It did rain blue cats when they dug up Tlaloc. Mexico City has had unusual and unseasonable rains ever since. The missing tooth was on the right, and the corpse at the Biograph Theatre had a missing tooth on the left. Billy Graham couldn't have gotten to Chicago by any normal means, so that was either the best damned makeup job in the history of show business and plastic surgery or I witnessed a genuine miracle. And all the rest of it, the law of Fives and all. I'm sold. I no longer claim membership in the liberal intellectual guild. You behold in me a horrible example of creeping mysticism."

"Ready to try acid?"

"Yes," Joe said. "I'm ready to try acid. I only regret that I have but one mind to lose for my Shivadarshana."

"Right on! First, though, you'll meet *him*. I'll drive right to his bungalow—it's not far from here." Simon began humming as he drove; Joe recognized the tune as the Fugs' "Rameses II Is Dead, My Love."

They drove for a while in silence, and Joe finally asked, "How old is . . . our little group . . . exactly?"

"Since 1888." Simon said. "That's when Rhodes horned in and they 'kicked out the Jams,' like I told you in Chicago after the Sabbath."

"And Karl Marx?"

"A schmuck. A dupe. A nebbish from the word Go." Simon made an abrupt turn. "Here we are at his house. The greatest headache they had since Harry Houdini knocked out their spiritualist fronts." He grinned. "How do you think you'll feel talking to a dead man?"

"Weird," Joe said, "but I've felt weird for the last week and a half."

Simon parked the car and held the door open. "Just think," he said. "Hoover sitting there every day with the death-mask on his desk, and half-suspecting, deep down in his bones, how we suckered him."

They crossed the yard of the small, modest bungalow. "What a front, eh?" Simon chuckled. He knocked.

A little old man—he was five foot seven exactly, Joe remembered from the FBI files—opened the door.

"Here's our new recruit," Simon said simply.

"Come in," John Dillinger said, "and tell me how an asshole egghead like you can help us beat the shit out of those motherfucking Illuminati cocksuckers."

("They fill their books with obscene words, claiming that this is realism," Smiling Jim shouted to the KCUF assembly. "It's not my idea of realism. I don't know anybody who talks in that gutter language they call realism. And they describe every possible perversion, acts against nature that are so outrageous I wouldn't sully this audiences' ears by even mentioning their medical names. Some of them even glorify the criminal and the anarchist. I'd like to see one of these hacks come up to me and look me in the eye and say, 'I didn't do it for money. I was honestly trying to tell a good, honest story that would teach people something of value.' They couldn't say that. The lie would stick in their throats. Who can doubt where they get their orders from? What person in this audience needs to be told what group is behind this overflowing sewer of smut and filth?")

"May storms and rains and typhoons beat them," Howard sang on. *"May Great Cthulhu rise and eat them."*

"I got into the JAMs in Michigan City Prison," Dillinger, much relaxed and less arrogant, was saying as he, Simon, and Joe sat in his living room drinking Black Russians.

"And Hoover knew, from the beginning?" Joe asked.

"Of course. I wanted the bastard to know—him and every other high-ranking Mason and Rosicrucian and Illuminati front-man in the country." The old man laughed harshly; except for his unmistakable eyes, which still held the strange blend of irony and intensity that Joe had noted in the 1930s photos, he was indistinguishable from any other elderly fellow who had come to California to enjoy his last years in the sun. "The first bank job I pulled off, in Daleville, Indiana, I used the line that I always repeated: 'Lie down on the floor and keep calm.' Hoover couldn't miss it. That's been the motto of the JAMs ever since Diogenes the Cynic. He knew no ordinary bank robber would be quoting an obscure Greek philosopher. The reason I repeated it on every heist was just to rub it in and let him know I was taunting him."

"But going back to Michigan City Prison . . ." Joe prompted, sipping his drink.

"Pierpont was the one who initiated me. He'd been with the JAMs for years by then. I was just a kid, you know—in my early twenties—and I had only pulled one job, a real botch. I couldn't understand why I got such a stiff sentence, after the D.A. promised me clemency if I'd plead guilty, and I was kind of bitter. But old Harry Pierpont saw my potential.

"At first I thought he was just another big-house faggot, when he started tracking me around and asking me all sorts of personal questions. But he was what I wanted to become—a successful bank-robber—so I played along. To tell you the truth, I was so horny it wouldn't have mattered if he was a faggot. You have no idea how horny a man gets in prison. That's why Baby-Face Nelson and a lot of other guys preferred to die rather than go back to the big house again. Hell, if you haven't been there, you can't understand. You just don't know what being horny *is*.

"Well, anyway, after a lot of bull about Jesus and Jehovah and the Bible and all that, Harry just asked me point-blank one day in the prison yard: 'Do you think it's possible there might be a true religion?' I was about to say, 'Bullshit—like there might be an honest cop,' but something stopped me. I realized he was dead serious, and a lot might depend on my answer. So I was cautious. I said, 'If there is, I haven't heard about it.' And he just came back, real quiet, 'Most people haven't.'

"It was a couple of days afterward that he brought the subject up again. Then, he went right on with it, showed me the Sacred Chao and everything. It took my breath away." The old man's voice trailed off, as he sank into silent memories.

"And it really does go back to Babylon?" Joe prompted.

"I'm not much of an intellectual," Dillinger replied. "Action is my arena. Let Simon tell you that part."

Simon was eager to leap into the breach. "The basic book to confirm our tradition," he said, "is *The Seven*

Tablets of Creation, which is dated at about 2500 B.C. the time of Sargon. It describes how Tiamat and Apsu, the first gods, were coexisting in Mummu, the primordial chaos. Von Junzt, in his *Unausprechlichen Kulten,* tells how the Justified Ancients of Mummu originated, just about the time the *Seven Tablets* were inscribed. You see, under Sargon, the chief deity was Marduk. I mean, that was what the high priests gave out to the public—in private, of course, they worshipped Iok-Sotot, who became the Yog-Sothoth of the *Necronomicon.* But maybe I'm going too fast. Getting back to the official religion of Marduk, it was based on usury. The priests monopolized the medium of exchange and were able to extract interest for lending it. They also monopolized the land, and extracted tribute for renting it. It was the beginning of what we laughingly call civilization, which has always rested on rent and interest. The old Babylonian con.

"The official story was that Mummu was dead, killed in the war between the gods. When the first anarchist group arose, they called themselves Justified Ancients of Mummu. Like Lao-Tse and the Taoists in China, they wanted to get rid of usury and monopoly and all the other pigshit of civilization and go back to a natural way of life. So, grok, they took the supposedly dead god, Mummu, and claimed he was still alive and was actually stronger than all the other gods. They had a good argument. 'Look around,' they'd say, 'what do you see most of? Chaos, right? Therefore, the god of Chaos is the strongest god, and is still alive.'

"Of course, we got our ass whipped good. We were just no match for the Illuminati in those days. Didn't have a clue about how they performed their 'miracles,' for instance. So we got our asses whipped again, in Greece, when the JAMs got started again, as part of the Cynic movement. By the time the whole thing was happening again in Rome—usury and monopoly and the whole bag of tricks—the truce took place. The Justified Ancients became part of the Illuminati, a special group still keeping our own name, but taking orders from the Five. We thought we'd humanize them, like the anarchists who stayed in SDS after last year. And so it went until 1888. Then Cecil Rhodes started the Circle of Initiates and the big schism occurred. Every meeting would have a faction of Rhodes boys carrying signs that said 'Kick out the JAMs!' It was the parting of the ways. They just didn't trust us—or maybe they were afraid of being humanized.

"But we had learned a lot by our long participation in the Illuminati conspiracy, and now we know how to fight them with their own weapons."

"Fuck their weapons," Dillinger interrupted. "I like to fight them with *my* weapons."

"You *are* behind the big unsolved bank robberies of the last few years—"

"Sure. Just in the planning, though. I'm too old to vault over tellers' cages and carry on like I did back in the thirties."

"John is also fighting on another front," Simon interjected.

Dillinger laughed. "Yes," he said. "I'm the president of Laughing Buddha Jesus Phallus Inc. You've seen them— 'If it's not an LBJP it's NOT an L.P.'?

"Laughing Buddha Jesus Phallus?" Joe exclaimed. "My God, you put out the best rock in the country! The only rock a man my age can listen to without wincing."

"Thanks," Dillinger said modestly. "Actually, the Illuminati own the companies that put out *most* of the rock. We started Laughing Buddha Jesus Phallus to counterattack. We were ignoring that front until they got the MC-5 to cut a disc called 'Kick Out The Jams' just to taunt us with old, bitter memories. So we came back with our own releases, and the next thing I knew I was making bales of money from it. We've also fed information, through third parties, to Christian Crusade in Tulsa, Oklahoma, so they could expose some of what the Illuminati are doing in the rock field. You've seen the Christian Crusade publications—*Rhythm, Riots and Revolution,* and *Communism, Hypnotism and the Beatles,* and so forth?"

"Yes," Joe said absently. "I thought it was nut literature. It's so hard," he added, "to grasp the whole picture."

"You'll get used to it," Simon smiled. "It just takes awhile to sink in."

"Who really did shoot John Kennedy?" Joe asked.

"I'm sorry," Dillinger said. "You're only a private in our army right now. Not cleared for that kind of information yet. I'll just tell you this much: his initials are H.C.—so don't trust anybody with those initials, no matter where or how you meet him."

"He's being fair," Simon told Joe. "You'll appreciate it later."

"And advancement is rapid," Dillinger added, "and the rewards are beyond your present understanding."

"Give him a hint, John," Simon suggested with an anticipatory grin. "Tell him how you got out of Crown Point Jail."

"I've read two versions of that," Joe said. "Most of the sources claim you carved a fake gun out of balsa wood and dyed it black with your shoe polish. Toland's book says that you made that story up and leaked it out to protect the man who really managed the break for you—a federal judge that you bribed to smuggle in a real gun. Which was it?"

"Neither," Dillinger said. "Crown Point was known as the 'escape-proof jail' before I crashed out of it, and, believe me, it deserved the name. Do you want to know how I did it? I walked through the walls. Listen. . . ."

HARE KRISHNA HARE HARE

The sun beat down on the town of Daleville on July 17, 1933, like a rain of fire.

Motoring down the main street, John Dillinger felt the perspiration on his neck. Although he had been paroled three weeks earlier, he was still pale from his nine years in prison, and the sunlight was cruel on his almost albino-tinted skin.

I'm going to have to walk through that door all by myself, he thought. All alone.

And fighting every kind of fear and guilt that has been beaten into me from childhood on.

"The spirit of Mummu is stronger than the Illuminati's technology," Pierpont had said. "Remember that. We've got the Second Law of Thermodynamics on our side. Chaos steadily increases, all over the universe. All 'law and order' is a kind of temporary accident."

But I've got to walk through that door all alone. The Secret of the Five depends on it. This time it's my turn to be the goat.

Pierpont and Van Meter and the others were still back in Michigan City Prison. It was all in his hands—being the first one paroled, he had to raise the money to finance the jail-break that would get the others out. Then, having proved himself, he would be taught the JAM "miracles."

The bank suddenly loomed before him. Too suddenly. His heart skipped a beat.

Then, calmly, he drove his Chevrolet coupe over to the curb and parked.

I should have prepared better. This car should be souped-up like the ones Clyde Barrow uses. Well, I'll know that the next time.

He left his hands on the steering wheel and squeezed, hard. He took a deep breath and repeated the Formula: "23 Skidoo."

It helped a little—but he still wanted to get the hell out of there. He wanted to drive straight back to his father's farm in Mooresville and find a job and learn all the straight things again, how to kiss a boss's ass and how to look the parole officer straight in the eye and be like everybody else.

But everybody else was an Illuminati puppet and didn't know it. He did know it and was going to liberate himself.

Hell, that's what a younger John Dillinger thought back in 1924—except that he hadn't known about the Illuminati or the JAMs, then—but he was trying to liberate himself, in his own way, when he held up that grocer. And what did it lead to? Nine years of misery and monotony and almost going mad with horniness in a stinking cell.

It'll be nine years more if I fuck up today.

"The spirit of Mummu is stronger than the Illuminati's technology."

He got out of the car and forced his feet and legs to move and he walked straight for the bank door.

"Fuck it," he said, "23 Skidoo."

He walked through the door—and then he did the thing the bank tellers remembered after and told the police. He reached up and adjusted his straw hat to the most dapper and debonair angle—and he grinned.

"All right, this is a stick-up," he said clearly, taking out his pistol. "Everybody lie down on the floor and keep calm. None of you will get hurt."

"Oh, God," a female teller gasped, "don't shoot. Please don't shoot."

"Don't worry, honey," John Dillinger said easily, "I don't want to hurt anybody. Just open the vault."

LIKE A TREE THAT'S PLANTED BY THE WATER

"That afternoon," the old man said, *"I met Calvin Coolidge in the woods near my father's farm at Mooresville. I gave him the haul—twenty thousand dollars—and it went into the JAM treasury. He gave me twenty tons of hempscript."*

"Calvin Coolidge?" Joe Malik exclaimed.

"Well, of course, I knew it wasn't really Calvin Coolidge. But that was the form he chose to appear in. Who or what he really is, I haven't learned *yet.*"

"You met him in Chicago," Simon added gleefully. "He appeared as Billy Graham that time."

"You mean the Dev—"

"Satan," Simon said simply "is just another of the innumerable masks he wears. Behind the mask is a man and behind the man is another mask. It's all a matter of merging multiverses, remember? Don't look for an Ultimate Reality. There isn't any."

"Then this person—this being—" Joe protested, "really is supernatural—"

"Supernatural, schmupernatural," Simon grimaced. "You're still like the people in that mathematical parable about Flatland. You can only think in categories of right and left, and I'm talking about *up* and *down,* so you say 'supernatural.' There is no 'supernatural'; there are just more dimensions than you are accustomed to, that's all. If you were living in Flatland and I stepped out of your plane into a plane at a different angle, it would look to you as if I vanished 'into thin air.' Somebody looking down from our three-dimensional viewpoint would see me going off at a tangent from you, and would wonder why you were acting so distressed and surprised about it."

"But the flash of light—"

"It's an energy transformation," Simon explained patiently. "Look, the reason you can only think three-dimensionally is because there are only three directions in cubical space. That's why the Illuminati—and some of the kids they've allowed to become partially illuminized lately—refer to ordinary science as 'square.' The basic energy-vector coordinates of Universe are five-dimensional—of course—and can best be visualized in terms of the five sides of the Illuminati Pyramid of Egypt."

"Five sides?" Joe objected. "It only has four."

"You're ignoring the bottom."

"Oh. Go on."

"Energy is always triangular, not cubical. Bucky Fuller
has a line on this, by the way: he's the first one outside
the Illuminati to discover it independently. The basic energy transformation we're concerned with is the one Fuller hasn't discovered yet, although he's said he's looking
for it—the one that ties Mind into the matter-energy continuum. The pyramid is the key. You take a man in the
lotus position and draw lines from his pineal gland—the
Third Eye, as the Buddhists call it—to his two knees, and
from each knee to the other, and this is what you get.
. . ." Simon sketched rapidly in his notepad and passed it
over to Joe:

"When the Pineal Eye opens—after fear is conquered;
that is, after your first Bad Trip—you can control the energy field entirely," Simon went on. "An Irish Illuminatus
of the ninth century, Scotus Ergina, put it very simply—in
five words, of course—when he said *Omnia quia sunt,
lumina sunt*: 'All things that are, are lights.' Einstein also
put it into five symbols when he wrote $e = mc^2$.
The actual transformation doesn't require atomic reactors
and all that jazz, once you learn how to control the mind
vectors, but it always lets off one hell of a flash of light,
as John can tell you."

"Damn near blinded me and knocked me on my ass,
that first time in the woods," Dillinger agreed. "But I was
sure glad to know the trick. I was never afraid of being
arrested after that, 'cause I could always walk out of any
jail they put me in. That's why the Feds decided to kill
me, you know. It was embarassing to always find me wandering around loose again a few days after they locked me
up. You know the background to the Biograph Theatre
scam—they killed three guys in Chicago, without giving
them a chance to surrender, because they thought I was
one of them. Well, those three were all wanted in New
York for armed robbery, so nobody criticized the cops
much for that caper. But then up in Lake Geneva, Wisconsin, they shot three very respectable businessmen, and
one of *them* went and died, and Hoover's Heroes caught

all sorts of crap from the newspapers. So I knew where it was at; I could never again surrender and walk away a few days later. We had to produce a body for them." The old man looked suddenly sad. "There was one possibility that we hated to think about. . . . But, luckily it didn't come to that. The gimmick we finally worked out was perfect."

"And everything really follows the Fives' law?" Joe asked.

"More than you guess," Dillinger remarked blandly.

"Even when you're dealing with social fields," Simon added. "We've run studies of cultures where the Illuminati were not in control, and they still follow Weishaupt's five-stage pattern: *Verwirrung, zweitracht, Unordnung, Beamtenherrschaft* and *Grummet*. That is: chaos, discord, confusion, bureaucracy, and aftermath. America right now is between the fourth and fifth stages. Or you might say that the older generation is mostly in *Beamtenherrschaft* and the younger generation is moving into *Grummet* rapidly."

Joe took another stiff drink and shook his head. "But why do they leave so much of it out in the open? I mean, not merely the really shocking things you told me about the Bugs Bunny cartoons, but putting the pyramid on the dollar bill where everybody sees it almost every day—"

"Hell," Simon said, "look what Beethoven did when Weishaupt illuminated him. Went right home and wrote the Fifth Symphony. You know how it begins: da-da-da-DUM. Morse code for *V*—the Roman numeral for five. Right out in the open, as you say. It amuses the devil out of them to confirm their low opinion of the rest of humanity by putting things up front like that and watching how almost everybody misses it. Of course, if somebody doesn't miss something, they recruit him right away. Look at Genesis: 'lux fiat'—right on the first page. They do it all the time. The Pentagon Building. '23 Skidoo.' The lyrics of rock songs like 'Lucy in the Sky with Diamonds'— how obvious can you get? Melville was one of the most outrageous of the bunch; the very first sentence of *Moby Dick* tells you he's a disciple of Hassan i Sabbah, but you can't find a single Melville scholar who has followed up that lead—in spite of Ahab being a truncated anagram of Sabbah. He even tells you, again and again, directly and indirectly, that Moby Dick and Leviathan are the same creature, and that Moby Dick is often seen at the same time in two different parts of the world, but not one reader in a million groks what he's hinting at. There's a whole chapter on whiteness and why white is really more terrifying than black; *all* the critics miss the point."

" 'Osiris is a black god,' " Joe quoted.

"Right on! You're going to advance fast," Simon said enthusiastically. "In fact, I think it's time for you to get off the verbal level and really confront your own 'Lucy in the Sky with Diamonds'—your own lady Isis."

"Yes," Dillinger said. "The *Leif Erikson* is laying off-shore near California right now; Hagbard is running some hashish to the students at Berkeley. He's got a new black chick in his crew who plays the Lucy role extremely well. We'll have him send her ashore for the Rite. I suggest that you two drive up to the Norton Lodge in Frisco and I'll arrange for her to meet you there."

"I don't like dealing with Hagbard," Simon said. "He's a right-wing nut, and so is his whole gang."

"He's one of the best allies we have against the Illuminati," Dillinger said. "Besides, I want to exchange some hempscript for some of his flaxscript. Right now, the Mad Dog bunch won't accept anything but flaxscript—they think Nixon is really going to knock the bottom out of the hemp market. And you know what they do with Federal Reserve notes. Every time they get one, they burn it. Instant demurrage, they call it."

"Puerile," Simon pronounced. "It will take decades to undermine the Fed that way."

"Well," Dillinger said, "Those are the kinds of people we have to deal with. The JAMs can't do it all alone, you know."

"Sure," Simon shrugged. "But it bugs me." He stood up and put his drink on the table.

"Let's go," he said to Joe. "You're going to be illuminized."

Dillinger accompanied them to the door, then leaned close to Joe and said, "A word of advice about the Rite."

"Yes?"

Dillinger lowered his voice. "Lie down on the floor and keep calm," he said, and his old, impudent grin flashed wickedly.

Joe stood there looking at the mocking bandit, and it seemed to him a freeze and a frieze in time: a moment that would linger, as another stage of illumination, forever in his mind. Sister Cecilia, back in Resurrection School, spoke out of the abyss of memory: "Stand in the corner, Joseph Malik!" And he remembered too, the chalk that he crumbled slowly between his fingers, the feeling of needing to urinate, the long wait, and then Father Volpe entering the classroom, his voice like thunder: "Where is he? Where is the boy who dared to disagree with the good Sister that God sent to instruct him?" And the other children, led out of the classroom and across the street to the church to pray for his soul, while the priest harangued him: "Do you know how hot hell is? Do you know how hot the worst part of hell is? That's where they send people who have the good fortune to be born into the church and then rebel against it, misled by Pride of Intellect." *And five years later, those two faces came back: the priest, angry and dogmatic, demanding obedience, and the bandit, sardonic, encouraging cynicism, and Joe understood that he might someday have to kill Hagbard Celine. But more years had to pass, and the Fernando Poo incident had to pass, and Joe had to plan the bombing of his own magazine with Tobias Knight before he knew that he would, in fact, kill Celine without compunction if it were necessary. . . .*

But on March 31, in that year of fruition for all the Illuminati's plans, while the President of the United States went on the air to threaten "all-out thermonuclear heck," a young lady named Concepcion Galore lay nude on a bed in the Hotel Durrutti in Santa Isobel and said, "It's a lloigor."

"What's a lloigor?" asked her companion, an Englishman named Fission Chips, who had been born on Hiroshima Day and named by a father who cared more for physics than for the humanities.

The room was in the luxury suite of the Hotel Durrutti, which meant that it was decorated in abominable Spanish-Moorish decor, the sheets were changed daily (to a less luxurious suite), the cockroaches were minimal, and the plumbing sometimes worked. Concepcion contemplated the bullfight mural on the opposite wall, Manolete turning an elegant *Veronica* on an unconvincingly drawn bull, and said thoughtfully, "Oh, a lloigor is a god of the black people. The natives. A very bad god."

Chips glanced at the statue again and said, more to

himself than to the peasant girl, "Looks vaguely like Tlaloc in Mexico City, crossed with one of those Polynesian Cthulhu *tikis*."

"The Starry Wisdom people are very interested in these statues," Concepcion said, just to be making conversation, since it was obvious that Chips wasn't going to be ready to prong her again for at least another half hour.

"Indeed?" Chips said, equally bored. "Who are the Starry Wisdom people?"

"A church. Down on Tequilla y Mota Street. What used to be Lumumba Street and was Franco Street when I was a girl. Funny church." The girl frowned, thinking about them. "When I worked in the telegraph office I was always seeing their telegrams. All in code. And never to another church. Always to banks all over Europe and North and South America."

"You don't say," drawled Chips, no longer bored but trying to sound casual; his code number in British Intelligence was, of course, 00005. "Why are they interested in these statues?" He was thinking that statues, properly hollowed out, could transport heroin; he was already sure that Starry Wisdom was a front for BUGGER.

(In 1933, at Harvard, Professor Tochus told his Psychology 101 class, "Now, the child feels frightened and inferior, according to Adler, because he is, in fact, physically smaller and weaker than the adult. Thus, he knows he has no chance of successful rebellion, but nevertheless he dreams about it. This is the origin of the Oedipus Complex in Adler's system: not sex, but the will to power itself. The class will readily see the influence of Neitzsche . . ." Robert Putney Drake, glancing around the room, was quite sure that most of the students would not readily see *anything;* and Tochus himself didn't really see either. The child, Drake had decided—it was the cornerstone of his own system of psychology—was not brainwashed by sentimentality, religion, ethics, and other bullshit. The child saw clearly that, in every relationship, there is a dominant party and a submissive party. And the child, in its quite correct egotism, determined to become the dominant party. It was that simple; except, of course, that the brainwashing takes effect eventually in most cases and, by about this time, the college years, most of them were ready to become robots and accept the submissive role. Professor Tochus droned on; and Drake, serene in his lack of superego, continued to dream of how he would seize the dominant role. . . . In New York, Arthur Flegenheimer, Drake's psychic twin, stood before seventeen robed figures, one wearing a goat's-head mask, and repeated, "I will forever hele, always conceal, never reveal, any art or arts, part or parts. . . .")

You look like a robot, Joe Malik says in a warped room in a skewered time in San Francisco. *I mean, you move and walk like a robot.*

Hold onto that, Mr. Wabbit, says a bearded young man with a saturnine smile. *Some trippers see themselves as robots. Others see the guide as a robot. Hold that perspective. Is it a hallucination, or is a recognition of something we usually black out?*

Wait, Joe says. *Part of you is like a robot. But part of you is alive, like a growing thing, a tree or a plant. . . .*

The young man continues to smile, his face drifting above his body toward the mandala painted on the ceiling. *Well?* he asks. *Do you think that might be a good poetic shorthand: that part of me is mechanical, like a robot, and part of me is organic, like a rosebush? And what's the difference between the mechanical and the organic? Isn't a rosebush a kind of machine used by the DNA code to produce more rosebushes?*

No, Joe says. *Everything is mechanical, but people are different. A cat has a grace that we've lost, or partly lost.*

How do you think we've lost it?

And Joe sees the face of Father Volpe and hears the voice screaming about submission. . . .

The SAC bases await the presidential order to take off for Fernando Poo, Atlanta Hope addresses a rally in Atlanta, Georgia, protesting the gutless appeasement of the comsymp administration in not threatening to bomb Moscow and Peking the same time as Santa Isobel, the Premier of Russia rereads his speech nervously as the TV cameras are set up in his office ("and, in socialist solidarity with the freedom-loving people of Fernando Poo"), the Chairman of the Chinese Communist party, having found the thought of Chairman Mao of little avail, throws the *I Ching* sticks and looks dismally at Hexagram 23, and 99 percent of the peoples of the world wait for their leaders to tell them what to do; but in Santa Isobel itself, three locked doors across the suite from the now-sleeping Concepcion, Fission Chips says angrily into his shortwave,

"Repeat none. Not one Russian or Chinese anywhere on the bloody island. I don't care what Washington says. I'm telling you what I have seen. Now, about the BUGGER heroin ring here—"

"Sign off," the submarine tells him. "HQ is not interested in BUGGER or heroin right now."

"Damn and blast!" Chips stares at the shortwave set. That bloody well tore it. He would just have to proceed on his own, and show those armchair agents back in London, especially that smug W., how little they actually knew about the real problem in Fernando Poo and the world.

Storming, he charged back to the bedroom. I'll just get dressed, he thought furiously, including my smoke bombs and Luger and laser ray, and toddle over to this Starry Wisdom church and see what I can nose out. But when he tore open the bedroom door he stopped, momentarily stunned. Concepcion still lay in the bed but she was no longer sleeping. Her throat was neatly cut and a curious dagger with a flame design on it stuck into the pillow beside her.

"Damn, blast and thunder!" cried 00005. "Now that absolutely does tear it. Every time I find a good piece of ass those fuckers from BUGGER come along and shaft her!"

Ten minutes later, the GO signal came from the White House, a fleet of SAC bombers headed for Santa Isobel with hydrogen bombs, and Fission Chips, fully dressed, toddled over to the Starry Wisdom church where he encountered, not BUGGER, but something on an entirely different plane.

BOOK TWO

ZWEITRACHT

"It must have a 'natural'
  cause."
"It must have a 'supernatural'
  cause."
—Frater Perdurabo, O.T.O., "Chinese Music," *The Book of Lies*

Let these
  two asses
be set to
  grind corn.

THE FOURTH TRIP, OR CHESED
Jesus Christ On A Bicycle

Mister Order, he runs at a very good pace
But old Mother Chaos is winning the race
—Lord Omar Khayaam Ravenhurst, K.S.C.,
"The Book of Advice," *The Honest Book of Truth*

Among those who knew that the true faith of Mohammed
was contained in the Ishmaelian teachings, most were sent
out into the world to seek positions in the governments of
the Near East and Europe. Since it pleased Allah to decree this task for them, they obeyed willingly; many
served thus for their whole lives. Some, however, after
five or ten or even twenty years of such fealty to a given
shah or caliph or king, would receive, through surrepti-
tious channels, a parchment bearing the symbol: ♄ That
night, the servant would strike, and disappear like smoke;
and the master would be found in the morning, throat cut,
with the emblematic Flame Dagger of the Ishmaelians
lying beside him. Others were chosen to serve in a different manner, maintaining the palace of Hassan i Sabbah
himself at Alamout. These were especially fortunate, for it
was their privilege to visit more often than others the
Garden of Delights, in which the Lord Hassan himself
would, through his command of magic chemicals, transfer
them into heaven while they still lived in the body. One
day in the year 470 (known to the uncircumcized Christian dogs as 1092 A.D.) another proof of the Lord Hassan's powers was given to them, for they were all summoned to the throne room and there sat the Lord Hassan
in all his glory, while before him on the floor lay a plate
bearing the head of the disciple Ibn Azif.

"This deluded one," the Lord Hassan declared, "has
disobeyed a command—the one crime that cannot be for-
given in our Sacred Order. I show you his head to remind

you of the fate of traitors in this world. More; I will instruct you on the fate of such dogs in the next world." So saying, the good and wise Lord Hassan rose from his throne, walking with his characteristic lurching gait, and approached the head. "I command thee," he said. "Speak."

The mouth opened and the head emitted a scream such that all the faithful covered their ears and turned their eyes away, many of them muttering prayers.

"Speak, dog!" the wise Lord Hassan repeated. "Your whine is of no interest to us. Speak!"

"The flames," the head cried. "The terrible flames. Allah, the flames . . ." it babbled on as a soul will in extreme agony. "Forgiveness," it begged. "Forgiveness, O mighty Lord."

"There is no forgiveness for traitors," said the all-wise Hassan. "Return to hell!" And the head immediately silenced. All bowed down and prayed to Hassan and Allah alike; of the many miracles they had seen this was certainly the greatest and most terrible.

The Lord Hassan then dismissed everyone, saying, "Forget not this lesson. Let it stay in your hearts longer than the names of your fathers."

(*"We want to recruit you," Hagbard said, 900-odd years later, "because you are so gullible. That is, gullible in the right way."*)

Jesus Christ went by on a bicycle. That was my first warning that I shouldn't have taken acid before coming down to Balbo and Michigan to see the action. But it really seemed right, on another level: acid was the only way to relate to that whole Kafka-on-a-bummer example of quote democratic process in action unquote. I found Hagbard in Grant Park, cool as usual, with a bucket of water and a pile of handkerchiefs for the teargas victims. He was near the General Logan statue, watching the more violent confrontations across the street at the Hilton, sucking one of his Italian cigars and looking like Ahab finally finding the whale . . . *Hagbard, in fact, was remembering Professor Tochus at Harvard:* "Damn it, Celine, you *can't* major in naval engineering and law both. You're not Leonardo da Vinci, after all." "But I am," he had replied, poker-faced. "I recall all my past incarnations in detail and Leonardo was one of them." Tochus almost explod-

ed: *"Be* a wise-ass, then! When you start flunking half
your subjects, perhaps you'll come back to reality." The
old man had been terribly disappointed to see the long
row of *A*s. Across the street, the demonstrators advanced
toward the Hilton and the police charged again, clubbing
them back; Hagbard wondered if Tochus had ever realized that a professor is a policeman of the intellect. Then
he saw the Padre's new disciple, Moon, approaching. . . .
"You haven't been clubbed yet," I said, thinking that in a
sense Jarry's old presurrealist classic, "The Crucifixion of
Christ Considered as an Uphill Bike Race," was really the
best metaphor for the circus Daley was running. "Neither
have you, I'm glad to see," Hagbard replied: "Judging
from your eyes, though, you got teargassed in Lincoln
Park last night." I nodded, remembering that I had been
thinking of him and his weird Discordian yoga when it
happened. Malik, the dumb social-democratic-liberal that
John wanted to recruit soon, was only a few feet away,
and Burroughs and Ginsberg were near me on the other
side. I could see, suddenly, that we were all chessmen, but
who was the chessmaster moving us? And how big was
the board? Across the street, a rhinoceros moved ponder-
ously, turning into a jeep with a barbed-wire crowd-sticker
on the front of it. "My head's leaking," I said.

"Do you have any idea who's picking it up?" Hagbard
asked. He was remembering a house lease in Professor
Orlock's class. "What it amounts to, in English," Hagbard
had said, "is that the tenant has no rights that can be successfully defended in court, and the landlord has no duties
on which he cannot, quite safely, default." Orlock looked
pained, and several students were shocked, as if Hagbard
had suddenly jumped up and exposed his penis in front of
the class. "That's putting it too baldly," Orlock said finally. . . . *"It might be somebody years in the future,"* I
said, *"or the past."* I wondered if Jarry was picking it up,
in Paris, half a century before; that would account for the
resemblance. Abbie Hoffman went by just then, talking to
Apollonius of Tyana. Were we all in Jarry's mind, or
Joyce's? We even have a Sheriff Wood riding herd on us
and Rubin's horde of Jerry men. . . . *"Fuller's car is a
stunt, a showpiece,"* Professor Caligari fumed, "and, anyway, it has nothing to do with naval architecture."
Hagbard looked at him levelly and said, "It has *everything*

to do with naval architecture." As in law school, the other students were disturbed. Hagbard began to understand: they are not here to learn, they are here to acquire a piece of paper that would make them eligible for certain jobs. . . .

"There are only a few more memos." Saul said to Muldoon. *"Let's skim them and then call headquarters to see if Danny found this 'Pat' who wrote them."*

ILLUMINATI PROJECT: MEMO #15

8/6

J.M.:

Here's the weirdest version of the Illuminati history that I've found so far. It's from a publication written, edited and published by somebody named Philip Campbell Argyle-Stuart, who holds that the conflicts in the world are due to an age-old war between Semitic "Khazar" peoples and Nordic "Faustian" peoples. This is the essence of his thinking:

> My theory is that an extremely devilish imposed overcrust was added to the Khazar population consisting of humanoids who arrived by flying saucer from the planet Vulcan, which I assume to be not in intra-Mercurial orbit around the sun, but rather in the earth's orbit, behind the Sun, forever out of sight to earthlings, always six months behind or ahead of the earth in orbital travel. . . .
>
> Likewise for the Gothic Faustian Western Culture. The previously comparatively inert and purposeless migrating population streams known as Franks, Goths, Angles, Saxons, Danes, Swabians, Alemani, Lombards, Vandals, and Vikings suddenly had an overcrust added consisting of Norman-Martian-Varangians, arriving from Saturn by way of Mars in flying saucers. . . .
>
> After 1776 it (the Khazar-Vulcanian conspiracy) used the Illuminati and Grand Orient Masons. After 1815 it used the financial machinations of the House of Rothschild and after 1848 the Communist movement and after 1895 the Zionist movement. . . .
>
> One more thing needs to be mentioned. Mrs. Helena Petrovna Blavatski (nee Hahn in Germany),

1831-1891, founder of Theosophy . . . was both hypocritical and devilish, a true witch of great evil
power allied with Illuminati, Grand Orient Masons,
Russian Anarchists, British Israel Theorists, Proto-
Zionists, Arabian Assassins and Thuggi from India.

Source: *The High I.Q. Bulletin,* Vol. IV, No. 1, January
1970. Published by Philip Campbell Argyle-Stuart, Colorado Springs, Colorado.

Pat

"What was that word?" Private Celine asked eagerly.

"SNAFU," Private Pearson told him. "You mean to say
you never heard it before?" He sat up in his bunk and
stared.

"I'm a naturalized citizen," Hagbard said. "I was born
in Norway." He pulled his shirt away from his back
again; the Fort Benning summer was much too hot for the
Nordic half of his genes. "Situation Normal, All Fucked
Up," he repeated. "That really sums it up. That really
says it."

"Wait'll you've been in This Man's Army a little longer," the black man told him vehemently. "Then you'll really *appreciate* the *application* of that word, dads. Oh,
man, will you *appreciate* it."

"It's not just the army," Hagbard said thoughtfully.
"It's the whole world."

*Actually, after they immanentized the Eschaton, I
found out where my head was leaking that night (and a
few other nights, too.)* Into poor George Dorn. The leak
almost gave him water on the brain. He kept wondering
where all that Joyce and surrealism was coming from. I'm
seven years older than he is, but we're on the same valence because of similar grammar school experiences and
revolutionary fathers. That's why Hagbard never really
understood either of us, fully: he had private tutors until
he hit college, and by that stage Official Education is beginning to make some partial concessions to reality so the
victims have at least a chance of surviving on the outside.
But I didn't know any of that in Grant Park that night or
how the Army helped Hagbard understand college, because I was working out this new notion of the total valence of the set remaining constant. It would mean that I

would have to leave when George came on, or say, Marilyn Monroe and Jayne Mansfield had to do the pill or auto-wreck shticks before there was room for Racquel Welch's vibes.

ILLUMINATI PROJECT: MEMO #16

8/7

J.M.:

I think I've found the clue as to how Zoroaster, flying saucers and all that lunatic-fringe stuff fits into the Illuminati puzzle. Dig this, boss-man:

The Nazi Party was founded as the political appendage of the Thule Society, an extremist fringe of the Illuminated Lodge of Berlin. This lodge, in turn, was made up of Rosicrucians—high Freemasons—and its preoccupation was mourning the death of the feudal system. Masons of this time were, like the Federalist Party in post-revolutionary America, working diligently to prevent "anarchy" and preserve the old values by bringing about Christian Socialism. Indeed, the Aaron Burr conspiracy, which Professor Hofstadter notes was allegedly Masonic in origin, was an American prototype of German intrigues of a century later. To their external scientific socialism these Masons added mystic concepts which were thought to be "gnostic" in origin. One of these was the concept of "Gnosticism" itself, called Illumination—which held that heavenly beings directly or indirectly gave humanity its great ideas and would come back to Earth after mankind had achieved sufficient progress. Illumination was a brand of pentecostalism which was persecuted by orthodox Christianity for centuries and had become lodged in Freemasonry through a complex historical process which is impossible to explain without a major digression. It is sufficient to say that the Nazis, being "Illuminated," felt themselves to be divinely inspired and therefore felt justified in rewriting the rules of good and evil to suit their own purposes.

(According to Nazi theory) the heavenly beings, before the present Moon was captured, had lived on the highest ground, in Peru, Mexico, Gondor (Ethiopia), Himalaya, Atlantis and Mu, forming the Uranian Confederation. This was taken quite seriously and British intelligence actually combatted it with the Tolkien fantasy called the "Silmarillion," basis for the famous "Hobbit" books. . . .

Both J. Edgar Hoover and Congressman Otto Passman are high-ranking Masons and both, significantly, reflect this philosophy and its Manichean attitude. The chief danger in Masonic thinking aside from the "divine right of government" is, of course, Manicheanism, the belief that your opponent is opposing God's will and is therefore an agent of Satan. This is the extreme application and Mr. Hoover usually reserves it for "Godless Communism" but it is almost always present to some degree.

Source: "The Nazi Religion: Views on Religious Statism in Germany and America" by J. F. C. Moore, *Libertarian American*, Vol. III, No. 3, August 1969.

Pat

They were using Mace now, and I saw one photographer snapping a picture of a cop while the cop was still Macing him (Heisenberg rides again! From out of the west come the thundering hooves of the great hearse, Joint Phenomenon! Except that I was on acid; if I'd been on weed, then it would really, royally, be a Joint Phenomenon). And I heard later that the photographer got an award for that shot. Right then, he didn't look like he was getting an award. He looked like they had just taken off his skin and touched each raw nerve with a dentist's drill. "Christ," I said to Hagbard, "look at that poor bastard. I hope I come out of this with just another teargassing or two. I don't want any of that Mace." But acid is placid, you know, and a minute later I was on Joyce's juices again and thinking of a drama called "Their Mace and My Gripes." I made the first line fruity, in honor of Padre Pederastia: "What a botch of a pair to plumb this hour's gripes."

"Bism'allah," Hagbard said. "Our karma is made by our deeds, not by our prayers. You're on the set, so you take the action as it comes."

"Oh, cut out that Holy Man craperoo and stop reading

my mind," I protested. "You don't have to go on impressing me." But I was off on another tangent, which went something like this: If this set is Mayor Daley's circus, then Mayor Daley is the ringmaster. If the things below are the things above, as Hermes hermetically hinted, then this set *is* the bigger set. Mr. Microcosm, meet Mr. Macrocosm. "Hi, Mike!" "Hi, Mac." Conclusion: Mayor Daley, in a small way, is what Krishna is, in a large way. QED.

Just then some SDS kids who'd been teargassed across the street came running our way, and Hagbard got busy handing out wet handkerchiefs. They needed them: they were half-blind, like Joyce splitting his Adam into wise hopes. And I wasn't much help, because I was too busy crying myself.

"Hagbard," I gasped in ecstasy. "Mayor Daley is Krishna."

"Worse luck for him," he said curtly, distributing the handkerchiefs. "He doesn't suspect it."

I thought, suddenly:

> Hubert the Hump has coughed and hawked
> And spat on the streets that Lincoln walked

The water turned to blood (Hagbard was a joking jolting Jesus: you expected wine maybe?) and I remembered my mother's story about Dillinger at the Biograph. We all sit there, like him, in the Biograph Theatre, dreaming the drama of our lives, then walk outside to the grandmotherly kindness of the lead kisses that wake us back to our slipping beatitude. Except that he found a way to come back. What was it Charley Mordecai said: "First as tragedy, then as farce?" Marxism-Lennonism: Ed Sanders of the Fugs, the night before, talking about fucking in the streets as if he had read my mind (or had I read his?) and Lennon's "Why Don't We Do It in the Road" was recorded a year in the future. The Marx and our groupies. The bloody handkerchiefs dipped into water, or wine, and the mass rite went on, the mass went Right On, the Mace they rowed. Capone set it up for the Feds, but John was fed up and left the set, so an extra named Frank Sullivan got the bullets. The Autobiograph Theatre, a drama house and a trauma, yes. I maybe should have taken only half a

tab instead of the full 500 mikes, because at that point the
SDS kids, all of them siding with RYM-I at the split next
year, looked like they had altarboy robes on and I thought
Hagbard was distributing communion wafers, not handkerchiefs. He looked at me, suddenly, with that hawk-
faced Egyptian glare, and I observed that he had observed, Hopalong Horus Heisenberg, just where I was at.
You don't have to be a waterman, I thought, to know
which way my mind is blowing.

There was a sound from the crowd, like a subway
opening all its doors with a suck of air, and I saw the police coming, crossing the street to clear the park.

"Here we go again," I said. "All hail Discordia."

"Snafu ueber alles," Hagbard grinned, starting to trot
beside me.

We headed North, figuring that the ones who retreated
eastward would get trapped against the wall and creamed.
"Democracy in action," I said, panting along.

"There thou might'st behold the very image of Authority," he quoted, shifting his water bucket to keep it in balance. I caught the Shakespearean reference and looked
back: my mind had already: each policeman indeed
looked like Shakespeare's dog. I remembered the frantic
semantics at the LBJ anti-birthday party, when Burroughs
insisted Chicago Cops were more like dogs than pigs, in
contradiction to the SDS rhetoric. Terry Southern, taking
his usual maniacal middle course, claimed they were more
akin to the purple-assed mandrill, most surly of the baboon family. But most of them hadn't discovered writing
yet.

"Authority?" I asked, realizing I'd lost something along
the way. We were slowing to a walk, the action was behind us.

"A is not A," Hagbard explained with that tiresome patience of his. "Once you accept A *is* A, you're hooked.
Literally hooked, addicted to the System."

I caught the references to Aristotle, the old man of the
tribe with his unfortunate epistemological paresis, and also
to that feisty little lady I always imagine is really the lost
Anastasia, but I still didn't grok. "What do you mean?" I
asked, grabbing a wet handkerchief as some of the teargas
started to drift to our end of the park.

"Chairman Mao didn't say half of it," Hagbard replied

holding a handkerchief to his own face. His words came through muffled: "It isn't only political power that grows out of the barrel of a gun. So does a whole definition of reality. A set. And the action that has to happen on that particular set and on none other."

"Don't be so bloody patronizing," I objected, looking around a corner in time and realizing this was the night I would be Maced. "That's just Marx: the ideology of the ruling class becomes the ideology of the whole society."

"Not the ideology. The Reality." He lowered his handkerchief. "This was a public park until they changed the definition. Now, the guns have changed the Reality. It *isn't* a public park. There's more than one kind of magic."

"Just like the Enclosure Acts," I said hollowly. "One day the land belonged to the people. The next day it belonged to the landlords."

"And like the Narcotics Acts," he added. "A hundred thousand harmless junkies became criminals overnight, by Act of Congress, in nineteen twenty-seven. Ten years later, in thirty-seven, all the pot-heads in the country became criminals overnight, by Act of Congress. And they really were criminals, when the papers were signed. The guns prove it. Walk away from those guns, waving a joint, and refuse to halt when they tell you. Their Imagination will become your Reality in a second."

And I had my answer to Dad, finally, just as a cop jumped out of the darkness screaming something about freaking motherfucking fag commies and Maced me, as was certain to happen (I knew it as I crumbled in pain) on that set.

ILLUMINATI PROJECT: MEMO #16

8/7

J.M.:

Here's some more info on how Blavatsky, theosophy and the motto under the great pyramid on the U.S. Seal fit into the Illuminati picture (or *don't* fit into the picture. It's getting more confusing the further I dig into it!) This is an article defending Madame Blavatsky, after Truman Capote had repeated the John Birch Society's charge that Sirhan Sirhan was inspired to murder Robert Kennedy by reading Blavatsky's works: "Sirhan Blavatsky Capote" by Ted Zatlyn, *Los Angeles Free Press*, July 26, 1968:

Birchers that attack Madame Blavatsky, though smaller in number and as crazy as ever, find a new home
in an atmosphere of suspicion and violence. Truman
Capote takes them seriously. . . .

Does Mr. Capote know that the Illuminati (according to sacred Birch doctrine) began in the Garden of Eden when Eve made it with the snake and
gave birth to Cain? That all the descendents of
snake-man Cain belong to a super-secret group
known as the Illuminati, dedicated to absolutely
nothing but the meanest low down evil imagined in
the Satanic mind of man?

Anti-Illuminati John Steinbacher writes in his un-
published book, *Novus Ordo Seclorum* (The New
Order of the Ages): "Today in America, many otherwise talented people are flirting with disaster by as-
sociating with those same evil forces . . . Madame
Blavatsky's doctrine was strikingly similar to that of
Weishaupt. . . ."

The author also gives *his* version of the *Bircher's* version
of what the Illuminati are actually trying to accomplish:

Their evil goal is to transcend materiality, and to
bring about one world, denying the sovereignty of
nations and the sanctity of private proverty.

I don't think I can believe, or even understand, this, but at
least it explains how both the Nazis and the Communists
can be pawns of the Illuminati. Or does it?

Pat

"Property is theft," Hagbard said, passing the peace
pipe.

"If the BIA helps those real estate developers take our
land," Uncle John Feather said, "that will be theft. But if
we keep the land, that is certainly not theft."

Night was falling in the Mohawk reservation, but
Hagbard saw Sam Three Arrows nod vigorously in the
gloom of the small cabin. He felt, again, that American
Indians were the hardest people in the world to understand. His tutors had given him a cosmopolitan education,
in every sense of the word, and he usually found no
blocks in relating to people of any culture, but the Indians

did puzzle him at times. After five years of specializing in handling the legal battles of various tribes against the Bureau of Indian Affairs and the land pirates it served, he was still conscious that these people's heads were someplace he couldn't yet reach. Either they were the simplest, or the most sophisticated, society on the planet; maybe, he thought, they were both, and the ultimate simplicity and the ultimate sophistication are identical.

"Property is liberty," Hagbard said. "I am quoting the same man who said property is theft. He also said property is impossible. I speak from the heart. I wish you to understand why I take this case. I wish you to understand in fulness."

Sam Three Arrows drew on the pipe, then raised his dark eyes to Hagbard's. "You mean that justice is not known like a dog who barks in the night? That it is more like the unexpected sound in the woods that must be identified cautiously after hard thinking?"

There it was again: Hagbard had heard the same concreteness of imagery in the speech of the Shoshone at the opposite end of the continent. He wondered, idly, if Ezra Pound's poetry might have been influenced by habits of speech his father acquired from the Indians—Homer Pound had been the first white man born in Idaho. It certainly went beyond the Chinese. And it came, not from books on rhetoric, but from listening to the heart—the Indian metaphor he had himself used a minute ago.

He took his time about answering: he was beginning to acquire the Indian habit of thinking a long while before speaking.

"Property and justice are water," he said finally. "No man can hold them long. I have spent many years in courtrooms, and I have seen property and justice change when a man speaks, change as the caterpillar changes to the butterfly. Do you understand me? I thought I had victory in my hands, and then the judge spoke and it went away. Like water running through the fingers."

Uncle John Feather nodded. "*I* understand. You mean we will lose again. We are accustomed to losing. Since George Washington promised us these lands 'as long as the mountain stands and the grass is green,' and then broke his promise and stole part of them back in ten years—in ten years, my friend!—we have lost, always lost.

We have one acre left of each hundred promised to us then."

"We may not lose," Hagbard said. "I promise you, the BIA will at least know they have been in a fight this time. I learn more tricks, and get nastier, each time I go into a courtroom. I am very tricky and very nasty by now. But I am less sure of myself than I was when I took my first case. I no longer understand what I am fighting. I have a word for it—the Snafu Principle, I call it—but I do not understand what it is."

There was another pause. Hagbard heard the lid on the garbage can in back of the cabin rattling: that was the raccoon that Uncle John Feather called Old Grandfather come to steal his evening dinner. Property was theft, certainly, in Old Grandfather's world, Hagbard thought.

"I am also puzzled," Sam Three Arrows said finally. "I worked, long ago, in New York City, in construction, like many young men of the Mohawk Nation. I found that whites were often like us, and I could not hate them one at a time. But they do not know the earth or love it. They do not speak from the heart, usually. They do not act from the heart. They are more like the actors on the movie screen. They play roles. And their leaders are not like our leaders. They are not chosen for virtue, but for their skill at playing roles. Whites have told me this, in plain words. They do not trust their leaders, and yet they follow them. When we do not trust a leader, he is finished. Then, also, the leaders of the whites have too much power. It is bad for a man to be obeyed too often. But the worst thing is what I have said about the heart. Their leaders have lost it and they have lost mercy. They speak from somewhere else. They act from somewhere else. But from where? Like you, I do not know. It is, I think, a kind of insanity." He looked at Hagbard and added politely. "Some are different."

It was a long speech for him, and it stirred something in Uncle John Feather. "I was in the army," he said. "We went to fight a bad white man, or so the whites told us. We had meetings that were called orientation and education. There were films. It was to show us how this bad white man was doing terrible things in his country. Everybody was angry after the films, and eager to fight. Except me. I was only there because the army paid more than an

Indian can earn anywhere else. So I was not angry, but puzzled. There was nothing that this white leader did that the white leaders in this country do not also do. They told us about a place named Lidice. It was much like Wounded Knee. They told us of families moved thousands of miles to be destroyed. It was much like the Trail of Tears. They told us of how this man ruled his nation, so that none dared disobey him. It was much like the way white men work in corporations in New York City, as Sam has described it to me. I asked another soldier about this, a black white man. He was easier to talk to than the regular white man. I asked him what he thought of the orientation and education. He said it was shit, and he spoke from the heart. I thought about it a long time, and I knew he was right. The orientation and education was shit. When the men from the BIA come here to talk, it is the same. Shit. But let me tell you this: the Mohawk Nation is losing its soul. Soul is not like breath or blood or bone and it can be taken in ways no man understands. My grandfather had more soul than I have, and the young men have less than me. But I have enough soul to talk to Old Grandfather, who is a raccoon now. He thinks as a raccoon and he is worried about the raccoon nation, more than I am worried about the Mohawk Nation. He thinks the raccoon nation will die soon, and all the nations of the free and wild animals. That is a terrible thing and it frightens me. When the nations of the animals die, the earth will also die. That is an old teaching and I cannot doubt it. I see it happening, already. If they steal more of our land to build that dam, more of our soul will die, and more of the souls of the animals will die! The earth will die, and the stars will no longer shine! The Great Mother herself may die!" The old man was crying unashamedly. "And it will be because men do not speak words but speak shit!"

Hagbard had turned pale beneath his olive skin. "You're coming into court," he said slowly, "and you're going to tell the judge that, in exactly those words."

ILLUMINATI PROJECT: MEMO #17

8/8

J.M.:

You may remember that the *East Village Other*'s chart of

the Illuminati Conspiracy (Memo #9) listed "The Holy Vehm" as an Illuminati front. I have finally found out what The Holy Vehm is (or, rather was). My source is Eliphas Levy's *History of Magic,* op. cit., pages 199-200:

> They were a kind of secret police, having the right of life and death. The mystery which surrounded their judgments, the swiftness of their executions, helped to impress the imagination of people still in barbarism. The Holy Vehm assumed gigantic proportions; men shuddered in describing apparitions of masked persons, of summonses nailed to the doors of nobles in the very midst of their watch-guards and their orgies, of brigand chiefs found dead with the terrible cruciform dagger in their breasts and on the scroll attached thereto an extract from the sentence of the Holy Vehm. The Tribunal affected most fantastic forms of procedure: the guilty person, cited to appear at some discredited cross-road, was taken to the assembly by a man clothed in black, who bandaged his eyes and led him forward in silence. This occurred invariably at some unseemly hour of the night, for judgment was never pronounced except at midnight. The criminal was carried into a vast underground vault, where he was questioned by one voice. The hoodwink was removed, the vault was illuminated in all its depth and height, and the Free Judges sat masked and wearing black vestures.
>
> The Code of the Vehmic Court was found in the ancient archives of Westphalia and has been printed in the Reichstheater of Müller, under the following title: "Code and Statutes of the Holy Secret Tribunal of Free Courts and Free Judges of Westphalia, established in the year 772 by the Emperor Charlemagne and revised in 1404 by King Robert, who made those alterations and additions requisite for the administration of justice in the tribunals of the illuminated, after investing them with his own authority."
>
> A note on the first page forbade any profane person to glance at the book under penalty of death. The word "illuminated", here given to the associates of the Secret Tribunal, unfolds their entire mission: they had to track down in the shadows those who

worshipped the darkness; they counterchecked mysteriously those who conspired against society in favour
of mystery; but they were themselves the secret soldiers of light, who cast the light of day on criminal
plottings, and it is this which was signified by a sudden splendour illuminating the Tribunal when it pronounced sentence.

So now we have to add *Charlemagne* to the list of the Illuminated—along with Zoroaster, Joachim of Floris, Jefferson, Washington, Aaron Burr, Hitler, Marx, and Madame Blavatsky. Could this *all* be a hoax?

ILLUMINATI PROJECT: MEMO #18

8/9

J.M.:
My last memo may have been too hasty in using the past
tense in speaking about the Holy Vehm. I find that Darual
thinks they may still exist (*History of Secret Societies,* op.
cit., p. 211):

> These terrible courts were never formally abolished.
> They were reformed by various monarchs, but even
> in the nineteenth century it was said that they still ex-
> isted, though very much underground. The Nazi
> werewolves and resistance organizations fighting the
> Communist occupation of East Germany claimed
> that they were carrying on the tradition of the
> "Chivalrous and Holy Vehm." Perhaps they still are.

Pat

Federal Court for the 17th District of New York State.
Plaintiffs: John Feather, Samuel Arrows, et al. Defendants: Bureau of Indian Affairs, Department of the Interior, and President of the United States. For plaintiffs:
Hagbard Celine. For the defendants: George Kharis, John
Alucard, Thomas Moriarity, James Moran. Presiding: Justice Quasimodo Immhotep.

MR. FEATHER (*concluding*): And it will be because men
do not speak words but speak shit!
MR. KHARIS: Your honor, I move that the last speech be
stricken from the record as irrelevant and immaterial.
We are dealing here with a practical question, the need

of the people of New York for this dam, and Mr. Feather's superstitions are totally beside the point.

MR. CELINE: Your honor, the people of New York have survived a long time without a dam in that particular place. They can survive longer without it. Can anything survive, anything worth having, if our words become, as Mr. Feather says, excrement? Can anything we can reasonably call American Justice survive, if the words of our first President, if the sacred honor of George Washington is destroyed, if his promise that the Mohawk could keep these lands "as long as the mountain stands and the grass is green," if all that becomes nothing but excrement?

MR. KHARIS: Counsel is not arguing. Counsel is making speeches.

MR. CELINE: I am speaking from the heart. *Are you*—or are you speaking excrement that you are ordered to speak by your superiors?

MR. ALUCARD: More speeches.

MR. CELINE: More excrement.

JUSTICE IMMHOTEP: Control yourself, Mr. Celine.

MR. CELINE: I am controlling myself. Otherwise, I would speak as frankly as my client and say that most of the speeches here are plain old shit. Why do I say "excrement" at all, if it isn't, like you people, to disguise a little what we are all doing? It's shit. Plain shit.

JUSTICE IMMHOTEP: Mr. Celine, you are coming very close to contempt of court. I warn you.

MR. CELINE: Your honor, we speak the tongue of Shakespeare, of Milton, of Melville. Must we go on murdering it? Must we tear it away from its last umbilical connection with reality? What is going on in this room, actually? Defendants, the U.S. government and its agents, want to steal some land from my clients. How long do we have to argue that they have no justice, no right, no honor, in their cause? Why can't we say highway robbery is highway robbery, instead of calling it eminent domain? Why can't we say shit is shit, instead of calling it excrement? Why do we never use language to convey meaning? Why must we always use it conceal meaning? Why do we never speak from the heart? Why do we always speak words programmed into us, like robots?

JUSTICE IMMHOTEP: Mr. Celine, I warn you again.

MR. FEATHER: And I warn you. The world will die. The stars will go out. If men and women cannot trust the words spoken, the earth will crack, like a rotten pumpkin.

MR. KHARIS: I call for a recess. Plaintiff and their counsel are both in no emotional state to continue at this time.

MR. CELINE: You even have guns. You have men with guns and clubs, who are called marshals, and they will beat me if I don't shut up. How do you differ from any other gang of bandits, then, except in using language that conceals what you are doing? The only difference is that the bandits are more honest. That's the only difference. The only difference.

JUSTICE IMMHOTEP: Mr. Marshal, restrain the counsel.

MR. CELINE: You're stealing what isn't yours. Why can't you talk turkey for just one moment? Why—

JUSTICE IMMHOTEP: Just hold him, Marshal. Don't use unnecessary force. Mr. Celine, I am tempted to forgive you, considering that you are obviously much involved with your clients, emotionally. However, such mercy on my part would encourage other lawyers to believe they could follow your example. I have no choice. I find you guilty of contempt of court. Sentencing will take place when court reconvenes after a fifteen-minute recess. You may speak at that time, but only on any mitigating grounds that should lighten the degree of your sentence. I will not hear the United States government called bandits again. That is all.

MR. CELINE: You steal land, and you will not hear yourselves called bandits. You order men with guns and clubs to hold us down, and you will not hear yourselves called thugs. You don't act from the heart; where the hell do you act from? What in God's name does motivate you?

JUSTICE IMMHOTEP: Restrain him, Marshal.

MR. CELINE: (Indistinguishable.)

JUSTICE IMMHOTEP: Fifteen-minute recess.

BAILIFF: All rise.

ILLUMINATI PROJECT: MEMO #19

8/9

J.M.:

I wish you would explain to me how your interest in the numbers 5 and 23 fit in with this Illuminati project.

This is all I've been able to unearth so far on the number mystery, and I hope you find it enlightening. It's from a book of mathematical and logical paradoxes: *How to Torture Your Mind,* edited by Ralph L. Woods, Funk and Wagnalls, New York, 1969, page 128.

> 2 and 3 are even and odd;
> 2 and 3 are 5;
> Therefore, 5 is both even and odd.

The damned book, by the way, provides no solutions to the paradoxes. I could sense the fallacy in that one right away, but it took me hours (and a headache) before I could state it in precise words. Hope this helps you. Anyway, for me, it was a relief from the really frightening stuff I've been tracking down lately.

Pat

There were two further memos in the box, on different stationeries and by different typewriters. The first was brief:

April 4
RESEARCH DEPARTMENT:
I am seriously concerned about Pat's absence from the office, and the fact that she doesn't answer the phone when we call her. Would you send somebody to her apartment to talk to the landlord and try to find out what has happened to her?

Joe Malik
Editor

The last memo was the oldest in the lot and already yellowing at the edges. It said:

Dear Mr. "Mallory:"
The information and books, you requested are enclosed, at length. In case you are rushed, here is a quick summary.

1. Billy Graham was in Australia, making public appearances all through last week. There is no way he could have gotten to Chicago.

2. Satanism and witchcraft both still exist in the modern world. The two are often confused by orthodox Christian

writers, but objective observers agree that there is a difference. Satanism is a Christian heresy—the ultimate heresy, one might say—but witchcraft is pre-Christian in origin and has nothing to do with the Christian God *or* the Christian Devil. The witches worship a goddess called Dana or Tana (who goes back to the Stone Age probably).

3. The John Dillinger Died For You Society has its headquarters in Mad Dog, Texas, but was founded in Austin, Texas several years ago. It's some kind of poker-faced joke and is affiliated with the Bavarian Illuminati, another bizarre bunch at the Berkeley campus of the University of California. The Illuminati pretend to be a cabal of conspirators who run the whole world behind the scenes. If you suspect either of these groups of being involved in something sinister, you have probably just fallen for one of their put-ons.

W.H.

"So this thing was already linked to Mad Dog several years ago," Saul said thoughtfully. "And Malik was already assuming an alternative identity, since the letter is obviously addressed to him. And, also as I've begun to suspect as we read this stuff, the Illuminati have their own brand of humor."

"Deduce me one more deduction," Barney said. "Who the hell is this W.H.?"

"People have been asking that for three hundred years," Saul said absently.

"Huh?"

"I'm being whimsical. Shakespeare's sonnets are dedicated to a Mr. W.H., but I don't think we have to worry that this is the same one. This case is as nutty as a squirrel's dinner, but I don't really think it's *that* nutty." He added, "We can be grateful for one thing at least: the Illuminati doesn't really run the world. They're just trying."

Barney frowned, perplexed. "How did you make that one?"

"Simple. Same way I know they're a right-wing organization, not left-wing."

"We're not all geniuses," Barney said. "Take it a step at a time, will you?"

"How many contradictions did you spot in these memos? I counted thirteen. This researcher, Pat, saw it,

too: the evidence is deliberately warped and twisted. All
of it—not just that *East Village Other* chart—is a mixture
of fact and fiction." Saul lit his pipe and settled back in
his chair (in 1921, reading Arthur Conan Doyle, he first
began playing these scenes, in imagination).

"In the first place, either the Illuminati want publicity
or they don't. If they control everything, and want publicity, they'd be on billboards more often than Coca-Cola
and on TV more often than Lucille Ball. On the other
hand, if they control everything, and *don't* want publicity,
none of these magazines and books would have survived—they would have disappeared from libraries, book
stores and publisher's warehouses. This researcher, Pat,
never would have found them.

"In the second place, if you want to recruit people into
a conspiracy, besides idealism and whatever other noble
motives you might exploit in them, you would always exploit hope. You would exaggerate the size and power of
the conspiracy, because most people want to join the winning side. Therefore, all assertions about the actual
strength of the Illuminati should be regarded, *a fortiori,* as
suspect, like the voters' polls released by candidates before
elections.

"Finally, it always pays to frighten the opposition.
Therefore a conspiracy will exhibit the same behavior that
ethologists have observed in animals under attack: it will
puff itself up and try to look bigger. In short, potential or
actual recruits and potential and actual enemies will both
be given the same false impression: that the Illuminati is
twice, or ten times, or a hundred times, its actual size.
This is logical, but my first point was empirical—the
memos do exist—and therefore logic and empiricism confirm each other: the Illuminati are not able to control everything. What then? They've been around a long time
and they are as tireless as the Russian mathematician who
worked out *pi* to the one-thousandth place. The probability, then, is that they control some things and influence a
hell of a lot more. This probability increases as you think
back over the memos. The two chief Arabic branches—
the Hashishim and the Roshinaya—were both wiped out;
the Italian Illuminati were 'crushed' in 1507; Weishaupt's
order was suppressed by the Bavarian government in
1785; and so forth. If they were behind the French Revo-

lution, they influenced rather than controlled, because Napoleon undid everything the Jacobins started. That they had a hand in both Soviet Communism and German Fascism is plausible, considering the many similarities between the two; but if they controlled both, why did the two take opposite sides in the Second World War? And, if they ran both the Federalist party, through Washington, and the Democratic Republicans, through Jefferson, what was the purpose of the Aaron Burr counterrevolution, which they are also supposed to be behind? The picture I get is not a grand Puppet Master moving everybody on invisible strings, but some sort of million-armed octopus—a millepus, let's call it—constantly reaching out tentacles, and often drawing back nothing but a bloody stump, crying, 'Foiled again!'

"But the millepus is very busy and quite resourceful. *If* it controlled the planet, it could choose either operating in the open or retaining secrecy, but since it doesn't have that omnipotence yet, it must choose to be as anonymous as possible. Therefore, many of its tentacles will be probing around in the areas of publication and communications. It wants to know when somebody is investigating it or getting ready to publicize an investigation he has already completed. Finding such a person, it then has two choices: kill him or neutralize him. Killing may be resorted to in certain emergencies, but will be avoided when possible: you never know when a person of that sort has stashed extra copies of his documents in various unexpected places to be released in the event of his death. Neutralization is best, almost always."

Saul paused to relight his pipe, and Muldoon thought, *The most unrealistic aspect of Doyle's stories is Watson's admiration at these moments. I'm just irritated, because he makes me feel like a chump for not seeing it myself.* "Go ahead," he said gruffly, saving his own deductions until Saul was finished.

"The best form of neutralization is recruitment, of course. But any crude and hurried effort at recruitment is known as 'taking your pants down' in the espionage business because it makes you more vulnerable. The safest approach is gradual recruitment, disguised as something else. The best disguise, of course, is the pretense of helping the subject in his investigation. This also opens the second, and preferable, option, which is leading him on a wild

goose chase. Sending him looking for Illuminati in organizations which they have never really infiltrated. Feeding
him balderdash like that stuff about the Illuminati coming
from the planet Vulcan or being descended from Eve and
the Serpent. Best of all, though, is telling him the purpose
of the conspiracy is something other than it actually is,
especially if the story you sell him is in keeping with his
own ideals, since this can then shade over into recruitment.

"Now, the sources this Pat unearthed mostly seem to
come to one of two conclusions: the Illuminati doesn't exist anymore, or the Illuminati is virtually identical with
Russian Communism. The first I reject because Malik and
Pat have both disappeared and two buildings, one here in
New York and one way down in Mad Dog, have been
bombed in a series palpably linked with an investigation
of the Illuminati. You've already accepted that, but the
next step is just as obvious. If the Illuminati tries to distort whatever publicity cannot be avoided, then we should
look at the idea that the Illuminati is communist-oriented
as skeptically as we look at the idea that they don't even
exist.

"So, let's look at the opposite hypothesis. Could the Illuminati be a far-right or fascist group? Well, if Malik's
information was in any way accurate, they seem to have
some kind of special headquarters or central office in Mad
Dog—and that's Ku Klux and God's Lightning territory.
Also, whatever their history before Adam Weishaupt, they
seem to have gone through some reformation and revitali-
zation under his leadership. He was a German and an ex-
Catholic, just like Hitler. One of his Illuminated Lodges
survived long enough to recruit Hitler in 1923, according
to a memo that might be the most accurate one in the lot
for all we know. Considering the proclivities of the German character, Weishaupt could likely be an anti-Semite.
Most historians I've read on Nazi Germany agree to at
least the possibility that there was a 'secret doctrine' which
only the top Nazis shared among themselves and didn't
tell the rest of the party. That doctrine might be pure Illuminism. Take up the many links between Illuminism
and Freemasonry, and the known anti-Catholicism of the
Masonic movement—add in the fact that ex-Catholics are
frequently bitter against the church, and both Weishaupt
and Hitler were ex-Catholics—and we get a hypothetical
anti-Jewish, anti-Catholic, semi-mystical doctrine that

would sell equally well in Germany and in parts of America. Finally, while some left-extremists might want to kill the Kennedys and Reverend King, all three were more likely targets for right-wingers; and the Kennedys would be especially abhorrent to anti-Catholic rightists.

"A last point," Saul said. "Consider the left-wing orientation of *Confrontation*. The editor, Malik, would probably not give much credence to most of the sources quoted in the memos, since the majority are from rightist publications, and most of them allege that the Illuminati is a leftist plot. His most probable reaction would be to dismiss this as another right-wing paranoia, *unless he had other sources besides his own Research Department*. Notice how cagey he is. He doesn't tell his associate editor, Peter Jackson, anything about the Illuminati itself—just that he wants a new investigation of the last decade's assassinations. The bottom memo is so old and yellow it suggests he got his first clue several years ago, but didn't act. Pat asks him why he's hiding all this from the reporter, George Dorn. Finally, he disappears. He was getting information from some place else, and it revealed a plot he could believe in and really fear. That would probably be a Fascist plot, anti-Catholic, anti-Jewish and anti-Negro."

Muldoon grinned. *For once I don't have to play Watson*, he thought. "Brilliant," he said. "You never cease to amaze me, Saul. Would you glance at this, though, and tell me how it fits in?" He handed over a piece of paper. "I found it in a book on Malik's bedside table."

The paper was a brief scrawl in the same handwriting as the occasional jottings on the bottoms of Pat's memos:

Pres. Garfield, killed by Charles Guiteau, a Roman Catholic.

Pres. McKinley, ditto by Leon Czolgosz, a Roman Catholic.

Pres. Theodore Roosevelt, attempted assassination by John Shrank, a Roman Catholic.

Pres. Franklin Roosevelt, attempted assassination by Giuseppe Zangara, a Roman Catholic.

Pres. Harry Truman, attempted assassination by Griselio Torresola and Oscar Collazo, two Roman Catholics.

Pres. Woodrow Wilson, somewhat mysterious death

while tended by a Roman Catholic nurse.

Pres. Warren Harding, another mysterious death (one rumor: it was suicide), also attended by a Catholic nurse.

Pres. John Kennedy, assassination inadequately explained. Head of CIA then was John McCone, a Roman Catholic, who helped write the inconclusive and contradictory Warren Report.

(House of Representatives, March 1, 1964—five Congressmen wounded by Lebron-Miranda-Codero-Rodriguez assassination squad, all Roman Catholics.)

When Saul looked up, Barney said pleasantly, "I found it in a book, like I said. The book was *Rome's Responsibility for the Assassination of Abraham Lincoln* by General Thomas M. Harris. Harris points out that John Wilkes Booth, the Suratt family, and all the other conspirators were Catholics, and argues they are acting under orders from the Jesuits." Barney paused to enjoy Saul's expression and went on, "It occurs to me that, using your principle that most of the memos are full of false leads, we might question the idea that the Illuminati uses the Masons as a front to gather recruits. They would probably need some similar organization, though—one that exists all over the world, has mysterious rites and secrets, inner orders to which a select few are recruited, and a pyramidal authoritarian structure compelling everybody to take commands from above whether they understand them or not. One such organization is the Roman Catholic church."

Saul picked up his pipe from the floor. He didn't seem to remember having dropped it. "My turn to say, 'brilliant,' " he murmured finally. "Are you going to stop going to Mass on Sunday? Do you really believe it?"

Muldoon laughed. "After twenty years," he said, "I finally did it. I got one jump ahead of you. Saul, you were standing face-to-face with the truth, eyeball-to-eyeball, nose-to-nose, mouth-to-mouth—but you were so close that your eyes crossed and you saw it backward. No, it's not the Catholic church. You made a good guess in saying it was anti-Catholic as well as anti-Jewish and anti-Negro. But it's inside the Catholic church and always has been. In fact, the church's efforts to root it out have given Holy Mother Rome a very unfortunate reputation for paranoia and hysteria. Its agents make a special effort to enter the priesthood, in order to obtain holy objects for use in their own bizarre rites. They also try to rise as high in the church as they can, to destroy it from within. Many times they have recruited and corrupted whole parishes, whole orders of clergy, even whole provinces. They probably got to Weishaupt when he was still a Jesuit—they've infiltrated that order several times in history and the Dominicans even more. If caught in criminal acts, they make sure that their cover Catholicism, and not their true faith, is publicized, just like this list of assassins. Their God is called the Light-Bearer and that's probably where the word 'illumination' comes from. And Malik asked about them a long time ago and was told by this W.H., quite correctly, that they still exist. I'm talking about the Satanists, of course."

"Of course," Saul repeated softly, *"of course.* That pentagon that keeps popping up—it's the middle of the pentacle for summoning the Devil. Fascism is only their political facet. Basically, they're a theology—or an anti-theology, I guess. But what in hell—literally in hell—is their ultimate objective, then?"

"Don't ask me," Barney shrugged. "I can follow my brother when he talks about the history of Satanism, but not when he tries to explain its motivations. He uses technical theological terms about 'immanentizing the Eschaton,' but all I can understand is that it has something to do with bringing on the end of the world."

Saul turned ashen. "Barney," he cried, "my God. *Fernando Poo!*"

"But that was settled—"

"That's just it. Their usual technique of the false front. The real threat is coming from somewhere else, and they mean to do it this time."

Muldoon shook his head. "But they must be crazy!"

"Everybody is crazy," Saul said patiently, "if you don't understand his motives." He held up his tie. "Imagine you arrive in a flying saucer from Mars—or from Vulcan, like the Illuminati did according to one of our allegedly reliable sources. You see me get up this morning and for no clear reason wrap this cloth around my neck, in spite of the heat. What explanation can you think of? I'm a fetishist—a nut, in other words. Most human behavior is that sort, not oriented to survival but some symbol-system that people believe in. Long hair, short hair, fish on Friday, no pork, rising when the judge enters the room—all symbols, symbols, symbols. Sure the Illuminati are crazy, from *our* point of view. From *their* point of view, we're crazy. If we can find out what they believe, what their symbols mean to them, we'll understand why they want to kill most of the rest of us, or all of the rest of us. Barney, call your brother. Get him out of bed. I want to find out more about Satanism."

("The devil!" the President shouted on March 27. "Nuclear war over an insignificant place like Fernando Poo? You must be mental. The American people are tired of our army policing the whole world. Let Equatorial Guinea fish its own nuts out of the troubled waters, or whatever that expression is." "Wait," said the Director of the CIA, "let me show you these aerial photographs . . .")

Back at the Watergate, G. Gordon Liddy carefully aims his pistol and shoots out the streetlight: in memory, he is in an old castle at Millbrook, New York, eagerly searching for naked women and not finding any. Beside him Professor Timothy Leary is saying with maddening serenity, "But science is the most ecstatic kick of all. The intelligence of the galaxy is revealed in every atom, every gene, every cell." *We'll get him back,* Liddy thinks savagely, *if we have to assassinate the whole Swiss government. That man is not going to remain free.* Beside him, Bernard Barker shifts nervously as in right-angular time a future president metamorphoses the plumbers into the cesspool cleaners: but now, inside the Watergate, the Illuminati bug is unnoticed by those planting the CREEP bug, although both were subsequently found by the technicians installing the BUGGER bug. "It's the same Intelligence, making endlessly meaningful patterns," Dr. Leary goes on enthusiastically. ("Here, kitty-kitty," Hagbard repeats for the 109th time.)

"The devil?" Father James Augustine Muldoon repeated. "Well, that's a very complicated story. Do you want me to go all the way back to Gnosticism?"

Saul, listening on the extension phone, nodded a vigorous affirmative.

"Go as far back as you have to," Barney said. "This is a complicated matter we're trying to untangle here."

"OK, I'll try to remember you're not in my theology class at Fordham and keep this as brief as I can." The priest's voice faded, then came back—probably he was shifting the phone as he got out of bed and moved to a chair, Saul guessed.

"There were many approaches to Gnosticism," the voice went on in a moment, "all of them centered on *gnosis*—direct experience of God—as distinguished from mere knowledge about God. The search for gnosis, or illumination as it was sometimes called, took many odd forms, some of them probably similar to Oriental yogas and some of them using the very same drugs that modern rebels against the slow path of orthodox religion have rediscovered. Naturally, with such a variety of paths to gnosis, different pilots would land at different ports, each insisting he had found the real New Jerusalem. Mystics are all a bit funny in the head anyway," the priest added cynically, "which is why the church locks them all up in mental hospitals and euphemistically calls these institutions monasteries. But I digress.

"What you're interested in, I guess, is Cainism and Manicheanism. The former regarded Cain as a specially holy figure because he was the first murderer. You have to be a mystic yourself to understand that kind of logic. The notion was that, by bringing murder into the world, Cain created an opportunity for people to renounce murder. But, then, other Cainites went further—paradox always seems to breed more paradox and heresy creates more heresy—and ended up glorifying murder, along with all the other sins. The credo was that you should commit every sin possible, just to give yourself a chance to win a really difficult redemption after repenting. Also, it gave God a chance to be especially generous when He forgave you. Related ideas popped up in Tantric Buddhism about the same time, and it's a great historical mystery which group of lunatics, East or West, was influencing the other. Does any of this help you so far?"

"A bit," Barney said.

"About this gnosis," Saul asked, "is it the orthodox theological position that the illuminations or visions were actually coming from the Devil and not from God?"

"Yes. That's where Manicheanism enters the picture," Father Muldoon said. "The Manicheans made exactly the same charge against the orthodox church. According to their way of looking at it, the God of orthodox Christianity and orthodox Judaism, *was* the Devil. The god they contacted through their own peculiar rites was the real god. This, of course, is still the teaching of Satanists to-day."

"And," Saul asked, beginning to intuit what the answer would be, "what has all this to do with atomic energy?"

"With atomic energy? Nothing at all . . . at least, nothing that I can see. . . ."

"Why is Satan called the light-bringer?" Saul plunged on, convinced he was on the right track.

"The Manicheans reject the physical universe," the priest said slowly. "They say that the true god, their god, would never lower himself to mess around with matter. The God who created the world—our God, Jehovah—they call *panurgia,* which has the connotations of a kind of blind, stupid blundering force rather than a truly intelligent being. The realm which their god inhabits is pure spirit of pure light. Hence, he is called the light-bringer, and this universe is always called the realm of darkness. But they didn't know about atomic energy in those days—did they?" The last sentence had started as a statement and ended as a question.

"That's what *I'm* wondering," Saul said. "Atomic power releases a lot of light, doesn't it? And it sure would immanentize the Eschaton if enough atomic power was unleashed at once, wouldn't it?"

"Fernando Poo!" the priest exclaimed. "Is this connected with Fernando Poo?"

"I'm beginning to think so," Saul said. "I'm also beginning to think we've stayed in one place a long time, using a phone that is almost certainly tapped. We better get moving. Thanks, Father."

"You're quite welcome, although I'm sure I don't know what you're getting at," the priest said. "If you think Satanists control the United States government a few priests would agree with you, especially the Berrigan brothers, but I don't see how this can be a police matter. Does the New York Police Department now maintain a bureau of holy inquisitions?"

"Don't mind him," Barney said softly. "He's very cynical about dogma, like most clergymen these days."

"I heard that," the priest said. "I may be cynical but I really don't think Satanism is a joking matter. And your friend's theory is very plausible, in its way. After all, the Satanist's motive in infiltrating the church, in the old days, was to disgrace the institution thought to represent God on earth. Now that the United States government makes the same claim, well. That may be a joke or a paradox on my part, but it's the way their minds work, too. I am a professional cynic—a theologian must be, these days, if he isn't going to seem a total fool to young people with their skeptical minds—but I'm orthodox, or downright reactionary, about the Inquisitions. I've read all the rationalist historians, of course, and there was certainly an element of hysteria in the church in those days, but, still, Satanism is not any less frightening than cancer or plague. It is totally inimical to human life and, in fact, to all life. The church had good reasons to be afraid of it. Just as people who are old enough to remember have good reasons to be panicky at any hint of a revival of Hitlerism."

Saul thought of the cryptic, evasive phrases in Eliphas Levy: "the monstrous gnosis of Manes . . . the cultus of material fire. . . ." And, nearly ten years ago, the hippies gathered at the Pentagon, hanging flowers on the M.P.'s rifles, chanting "Out, demon, out!" . . . Hiroshima . . . the White Light of the Void. . . .

"Wait," Saul said. "Is there more to it than just *ideas* about killing? Isn't killing a mystical experience to the Satanists?"

"Of course," the priest replied. "That's the whole point—they want gnosis, personal experience, not dogma, which is somebody else's word. Rationalists are always attacking dogma for causing fanaticism, but the worst fanatics start from gnosis. Modern psychologists are just beginning to understand some of this. You know how people in explosive group-therapy sessions talk about sudden bursts of energy occurring in the whole group at once? One can get the same effect with dancing and drumbeating; that's what is called a 'primitive' religion. Use drugs, nowadays, and you're a hippie. Do it with sex, and you're a witch, or one of the Knights Templar. Mass participation in an animal sacrifice has the same effect. Human sacrifice has been used in many religions, including the Aztec cult everybody has heard about, as well as in Satanism. Modern psychologists say that the force released is Freud's libidinal energy. Mystics call it prajna or the Astral Light. Whatever it is, human sacrifice seems to release more of it than sex or drugs or dancing or drumbeating or any less violent method and mass human sacrifice unleashes a ton of it. Now do you understand why I fear Satanism and half apologize for the Inquisition?"

"Yes," Saul said absently, "and I'm beginning to share your fear. . . ." A song he hated was pounding inside his skull: *Wenn das Judenblut vom Messer spritz.* . . .

He realized that he was holding the phone and seeing scenes forty years ago in another country. He jerked himself back to attention as Muldoon thanked his brother again and hung up. Saul raised his eyes and the two detectives exchanged glances of mutual dread.

After a long pause, Muldoon said, "We can't trust anybody with this. We can hardly even trust each other."

Before Saul could answer the phone rang. It was Danny Pricefixer at headquarters. "Bad news. There was only one girl in research at *Confrontation* named Pat. Patricia Walsh to be exact, and—"

"I know," Saul said wearily, "she's disappeared, too."

"What are you going to do now? The FBI is still raising hell and demanding to know where you two are and the Commissioner is having the shits, the fits, and the blind staggers."

"Tell them," Saul said succinctly "that we've disappeared." He hung up carefully and began stuffing the memos back into the box.

"What now?" Muldoon asked.

"We go underground. And we stick to this until we crack it or it kills us."

("How long is this motherfucker?" George asked, gesturing at the Danube six stories below. He and Stella were in their room at the Donau Hotel.

"You won't believe me," Stella replied, smiling. "It's exactly one thousand seven hundred and seventy-six miles in length. One-seven-seven-six, George."

"The same as the date Weishaupt revived the Illuminati?"

"Exactly." Stella grinned. "We keep telling you. Synchronicity is as universal as gravity. When you start looking you find it everywhere.")

"Here's the money," Banana-Nose Maldonado said generously, opening a briefcase full of crisp new bills. (It is now November 23, 1963: they were meeting on a bench near Cleopatra's needle in Central Park: the younger man, however, is nervous.) "I want to tell you that . . . my superior . . . is very pleased. This will definitely decrease Bobby's power in the Justice Department and stop a lot of annoying investigations."

The younger man, Ben Volpe, gulps. "Look, Mr. Maldonado, there's something I've got to tell you. I know how the . . . Brotherhood . . . is when somebody fucks up and hides it."

"You didn't fuck up," Banana-Nose says, bewildered. "In fact, you lucked out amazingly. That schmuck Oswald is going to fry for it. He came along at just the right time. It was a real Fortuna . . . Jesus, Mary and Joseph!" Banana-Nose sits up straight as the thought hits him. "You mean . . . you mean . . . Did Oswald really do it? Did he shoot *before* you?"

"No, no," Volpe is miserable. "Let me explain it as clearly as I can. I'm there on top of the Dallas County Records Building like we planned, see? The motorcade turns onto Elm and heads for the underpass. I use my magnifying sight, swinging the whole gun around to look through it, just to make one last check that I have all the Feds spotted. When I face the School Book Depository, I catch this rifle. That was Oswald, I guess. Then I check out the grassy knoll and, goddam, there's another cat with a rifle. I just went cold. I couldn't figure it out. While I'm in this state, like a zombie, a dog barks and just then the guy in the grassy knoll calm and cool as if he was at a shooting range lays three of them right into the car. That's it," Volpe ends miserably. "I can't take the money. The . . . Brotherhood . . . would have my ass if they ever found out the truth."

Maldonado sat silently, rubbing his famous nose as he did when making a hard decision. "You're a good boy, Bennie. I give you ten percent of the money, just for being honest. We need more honest young boys like you in the Brotherhood."

Volpe swallowed again, and said, "There's one more thing I oughta tell you. I went down to the grassy knoll, after the cops run from there to the School Book Depository. I thought I might find the guy who did the shooting still hanging around and tell you what he looked like. He was long gone, though. But here's what so spooky. I ran into another galoot, who was sneaking down from the triple underpass. Long, skinny guy with buck teeth, kind of reminded me of a python or some kind of snake. He just looks at me and my umbrella and guesses what's in it.

His mouth falls open. 'Jesus Christ and his black bastard brother Harry,' he says, 'how the *fuck* many people does it take to kill a President these days?' "

("And they're teaching them about perversions as well," Smiling Jim was building toward his climax. "Homosexuality and lesbianism are being taught in our schools and we're paying for it out of our tax money. Now is that communism or isn't it?")

"Welcome to the Playboy Club," the beautiful blonde said, "I'm your bunny, Virgin."

Saul took his seat in the dark wondering if he had heard correctly. Virgin was an odd name for a bunny; perhaps she had actually said Virginia. Yes, Virginia, there is a Santa Claus.

"How do you wish your steak, sir?" the bunny was asking. A stake through the heart, for a vampire.

"Medium well," Saul said, wondering why his mind was wandering in such odd directions. ("Odd erections," somebody said in the nearby dark—or was it a distorted echo of his own voice?)

"Medium well," the bunny repeated, seemingly speaking to the wall. A medium wall, Saul thought.

Immediately the wall opened and Saul was looking into a combination kitchen and butcher shop. A steer was standing not five feet from him, but before he could recover from this shock a male figure, stripped to the waist and wearing the hood of a medieval executioner, caught his attention. With one stroke of a huge hammer, this figure knocked the steer unconscious and it fell to the floor with a crash. Immediately the executioner produced an axe and chopped its head off; blood gushed in a crimson pool from its neck.

The wall closed, and Saul had the terrifying feeling that the whole scene had been a hallucination—that he was losing his mind.

"All our lunches are educational today," the bunny said in his ear. "We believe every customer should understand fully what's on the end of his fork and how it got there, before he takes a bite."

"Good God," Saul said, getting to his feet. This wasn't a Playboy Club, it was some den of lunatics and sadists. He stumbled toward the door.

"No way out," a man at another table said softly as he passed.

"Saul, Saul," the maître d' murmured politely, "why dost thou persecute me? *Hab' rochmunas.*"

"It's a drug," Saul said thickly, "you've given me a drug." Of course, that was it—something like mescaline or LSD—and they were guiding his hallucinations by providing proper stimuli. Perhaps they were even faking some of the hallucinations. But how had he fallen into their hands? The last thing he remembered, he was in Joe Malik's apartment with Barney Muldoon. . . . No, there was a voice saying, *"Now,* Sister Victoria," as they came out the door onto Riverside Drive. . . .

"No man should marry a woman more than thirty years younger than himself," the maître d' said mournfully. How did they know about that? Had they investigated his whole life? How long had they held him?

"I'm getting out of here," he shouted, pushing the maître d' aside and bolting for the door.

Hands grasped for him and missed (they weren't really trying, he realized: he was being allowed to reach the door). When he plunged through the doorway, he realized why: he was not on the street but in another room. This was the next ordeal.

A rectangle of light appeared on the wall; somewhere in the darkness there was a projector. A card, light an old silent-movie caption, appeared in the rectangle. It said:

ALL JEW GIRLS LIKE TO BALL WITH BUCK NIGGERS

"Sons of bitches," Saul shouted back at them. They were still working on his feelings about Rebecca. Well, that would get them nowhere: he had ample reason to trust her devotion to him, especially her sexual devotion.

The card moved out of the rectangle, and a picture appeared in its place. It was Rebecca's, in her nightgown, kneeling. Before her stood a naked and enormous black man, six feet six at least, with an equally impressive penis which she held sensuously in her mouth. Her eyes were closed in bliss, like a baby nursing.

"Motherfuckers," Saul screamed. "It's a fake. That's not Rebecca—it's an actress with makeup. You forgot the mole on her hip." They could drug his senses but not his mind.

There was a nasty laugh in the darkness. "Try this one, Saul," a voice said coldly.

A new picture slid into view: Adolph Hitler, in full Nazi uniform, and a naked Rebecca backing up to him, taking his penis in her rectum. Her face showed both pain and pleasure—and the mole on her hip was visible. Another fake—Rebecca was born years after Hitler died. But they hadn't produced the slide in the thirty seconds after his shout, and that meant they knew her body, intimately. . . . And they also knew how skeptical and quick his mind was, and were prepared to administer a series of jolts until something got past his ability to doubt.

"No comment?" the voice asked mockingly.

"I don't believe a man who died thirty years ago would be buggering *any* woman today," Saul said drily. "Your tricks are kind of corny."

"Sometimes, with the vulgar, we must communicate vulgarly," the voice replied—and it was almost gentle and pitying this time.

A new picture appeared—and this time, without doubt, it *was* Rebecca. But it was Rebecca three years ago, when he first met her. She sat at a table in a cheap East Village pad, wearing the emaciated and self-pitying look he remembered from those days; and she was preparing to inject a needle in her arm. It was the real thing, but the terror was in its implications: *they* had been watching him that long ago. Perhaps—it was hard to date the picture precisely, although he remembered her apartment in those days—they even knew he would fall in love with her before he knew it himself. No; more likely, a friend of hers in those days had taken the picture and they had somehow found it when they became interested in him. Their resources must be fantastic.

A new card came on the screen:

ONCE A JUNKIE ALWAYS A JUNKIE

A new picture quickly followed: Rebecca, as she looked today, sitting in his kitchen—with the new café curtains they had just hung last week—once again injecting a needle into her arm.

"You're the vulgar ones, O mighty Illuminati," Saul said caustically. "I would have noticed the tracks on her arm, if she was shooting up again."

The answer was nonverbal: the picture of Rebecca and the giant black man came back on the screen, and was immediately followed by a close-up of her face, eyes closed, mouth open receiving the penis. It was in perfect focus, the work of an artist with the camera, and he could see no sign of any makeup that would help another woman to pass as Rebecca. He held to his memory that the mole on her hip was missing, but, perversely, his mind tasted at last the other possibility—makeup can change a face, and it can also hide a mole. . . . If they wanted him to use his skepticism, so that they could gradually destroy that, and, in the process, undermine his total psyche. . . .

Another sign came on the screen:

THAT WE CAN CALL THESE DELICATE CREATURES OURS BUT NOT THEIR APPETITES

Saul remembered, all too well, Rebecca's passion in bed. "Shakespeare," he called hoarsely. "Advertising your erudition at a time like this is worse than vulgarity. It's petit-bourgeois pretentiousness."

The answer was brutal: a whole series of slides, maybe fifteen or twenty in all, cascaded across the screen in such rapid succession that he couldn't examine them carefully, except that the central character was Rebecca, always Rebecca, Rebecca with the black giant in other sexual positions, Rebecca with another woman, Rebecca with Spiro Agnew, Rebecca with a little seven-year-old boy, Rebecca, Rebecca, in a rising crescendo of perversion and abnormality, Rebecca with a Saint Bernard dog—and a peppermint-colored sine-wave, part of the drug still working on him, cutting across the scene. . . .

"The true sadist has style," Saul gasped fighting for control of his voice. "You people are about as evil and frightening as a bad B-movie."

There was a whirring mechanical sound and a movie began in place of the slides. It was Rebecca and the Saint Bernard, with several close-ups, and her expressions were the ones he knew. Could any actress portray another woman's individual style of sexual response? Yes—if necessary, these people would use hypnosis to get the effect letter-perfect.

The movie stopped abruptly and the projector had another message for him, held on the screen for minutes:

ONLY THE MADMAN IS ABSOLUTELY SURE

When he realized that there would be no further progress until he spoke, Saul said coldly, "Very entertaining.
Where do I go to crumble into a bundle of neuroses?"

There was no answer. No sound. Nothing happened. He
half-saw a latticework of red pentagons, but that was the
drug—and it helped identify which drug, for geometric
patterns were characteristic of the mescaline experience.
As he considered that, the peppermint sine-waves appeared
before the pentagons and the screen gave him a new message:

HOW MUCH IS THE DRUG?
HOW MUCH IS OUR TRICKERY?
HOW MUCH IS REALITY?

Suddenly, Saul was in Copenhagen, on a cruise boat,
passing the mermaid of the harbor. She turned and looked
at him. "This case is fishy," she said—and as she opened
her mouth a school of guppies swam out. "I'm a mouth-
breeder," she explained.

Saul had a reproduction of that famous statue in his
home (which must be the source of the hallucination), yet
he was strangely disturbed. Her punning words seemed to
conceal a deeper meaning than mere casual references to
the *Confrontation* bombing . . . something that went back
. . . back through his whole life . . . and explained why
he had purchased the statue in the first place.

I'm about to have one of those famous drug insights that
hippies always talk about, he thought. But the mermaid
broke apart into pentagons of red, orange, yellow. . . .

And a unicorn winked at him. "Man," it said, "am I
ever horny!"

Those sketches I made the other day, Saul thought . . .
but the screen asked him:

IS THE THOUGHT OF A UNICORN A REAL THOUGHT?

. . . and he suddenly understood for the first time what
the words "a real thought" meant; what Hegel meant by
defining the Absolute Idea as pure thought thinking about
pure thought; what Bishop Berkeley meant by denying the
reality of the physical world in seeming contradiction of
all human experience and common sense; what every detective was secretly attempting to detect, although it was

always right out in the open; why he became a detective in the first place; why the universe itself became; why *everything;*

and then he forgot it;

caught a fleeting glimpse of it again—it had something to do with the eye at the top of the pyramid;

and lost it again in visions of unicorns, stallions, zebras, bars, bars, bars.

Now his whole visual field was hallucinatory . . . octagons, triangles, pyramids, organic shapes of embryos and growing ferns. The drug was taking stronger hold on him. Criminals he had sent to jail appeared—sullen, hating faces—and the screen said

GOODMAN IS A BAD MAN

He laughed to keep from crying. They had touched his deepest doubt about his job—his career, his life's work—precisely at the time the drug also was leading him there, with those damnable accusing faces. It was as if they could read his mind and see his hallucinations. No; it was just one lucky coincidence, because among all their tricks one was statistically likely to occur in tandem with an appropriate drug experience.

WHILE THERE IS A SOUL IN PRISON
I AM NOT FREE

Saul laughed again, more wildly, almost hysterically; and knew, even more clearly than before, the tears hiding behind the laughter. Prisons reform nobody; my life is wasted; I offer society a delusion of security but not a real service. Worse yet, I have known it for years, and lied to myself. The sense of total failure and utter bitterness that washed over Saul at that moment was, he knew, not produced but only magnified by the drug. It had been with him a long, long time but always pushed aside, brushed away from his attention by concentrating on something else; the drug merely allowed him (forced him) to look at the emotion honestly and totally for a few wrenching moments.

A doorway suddenly lit up toward his right and a neon light came on above it, saying, "Absolution and Redemption."

"OK," he said icily, "I'll play the next move." He opened the door.

The room was tiny but furnished like the world's most expensive brothel. Above the fourposter bed was an illustration of Alice and a mushroom labeled "Eat Me." And on the bed, stripped of her Playboy costume, pinkly and beautifully naked with legs spread in anticipation, was the blonde bunny. "Good evening," she said speaking rapidly and fixing his eyes with her own stare, "I'm your Virgin Bunny. Every man wants a Virgin Bunny, to eat on Easter to celebrate the miracle of the Resurrection. Do you understand the miracle of the Resurrection, sir? Do you know that nothing is true and everything is permissible and that a man who dares to break the robot conditioning of society and commit adultery dies in the moment of orgasm with his whore and wakes resurrected to a new life? Did they teach you that in *shule*? Or did they just fill you with a lot of monogamous Yiddish horseshit?" Most hypnotists spoke slowly, but she was obtaining the same effect by talking rapidly. "You thought you were going to eat a dead animal, which is disgusting even if this crazy society accepts it as normal, but instead you're going to eat a desirable woman (and fuck her afterward), which is normal even if this crazy society thinks of it as disgusting. You are one of the Illuminated, Saul, but you never knew it. Tonight you are going to learn. You are going to find your real self as you were before your mother and father conceived you. And I'm not talking about reincarnation. I'm talking about something much more marvelous."

Saul found his voice. "Your offer is appreciated but declined," he said. "Frankly, I find your tawdry mysticism even more adolescent than your sentimental vegetarianism and coarse lasciviousness. The trouble with the Illuminati is that you have no sense of true drama and not even a patina of subtlety."

Her eyes widened as he spoke, but not with surprise at his resistance—either she was really alarmed, and sorry for him, or she was a great actress. "Too bad," she said sadly. "You've refused Heaven, so you must travel the harder path through the halls of Hell."

Saul heard a movement behind him, but before he could turn a sharp sensation pricked his neck: a needle, another drug. Just as he was guessing they had given him a stronger psychedelic to escalate the effect, he felt consciousness slipping away. It was a narcotic or a poison.

The wagon started with a jerk: we were off to see the wizard, the wonderful wizard of arse. What was it Hagbard had said to me, the first time we met, about straight lines, courtrooms, and shit? I couldn't remember, my mind drifted, Joseph K. opening the law books and finding pornographic illustrations (Kafka knew where it was at), deSade keeping a precise mathematical tally in the brothel, how many times he flogged the whores, how many times they flogged him, the Nazis counting every gold filling in the corpses at Auschwitz, Shakespeare scholars debating about that line in Macbeth (was it benches or banks of time?), the prisoner may approach the bench, you can bank on it, buddy, bank on it . . . PIGS EAT SHIT PIGS EAT SHIT . . . and Pound wrote "the buggering bank," he rejected Freud, but even so he got a whiff of the real secret . . . how one homo ominously loopses another. . . .

"My God," the Englishman said. "When do we get out of the teargas area?"

"We're out of it," I told him wearily. "That's regular Chicago air now. Courtesy of Commonwealth Edison and U.S. Steel over in Gary."

The McCarthy woman was weeping quietly, although the Mace had worn off by now. The rest of us rode silently, a little caravan of dried snot and tears, the parmesan cheese odor of stale vomit, some lingering acrid Mace fumes, the urine of somebody who had peed himself, and that high sulphur dioxide and slaughterhouse aroma of Chicago's South Side. The quality of mercy is very strained; it drippeth like the pus from chancre. Abandon hope all ye who enter here. Chairman Mao appeared and lectured us: "Ho is just a poetaster. Now, if you want to hear some real socialist verse, consider *my* latest composition:

> There was a young lady from Queens
> Who gobbled a plateful of beans
>   The beans fermented
>   And she was tormented
> By embarrassing sounds in her jeans!

Indicates the anal orientation of capitalist society," he explained, dwindling into a pool of blood on the floor next to the kid with the broken arm.

* * *

(In 1923, Adolph Hitler stood beneath a pyramidal altar and repeated the words of a goat-headed man: *"Der Zweck heiligte die Mittel."* James Joyce, in Paris, scrawled in crayon words that his secretary, Samuel Beckett, would later type: "Pre-Austeric Man in Pursuit of Pan-Hysteric Woman." In Brooklyn, New York, Howard Phillips Lovecraft, returning from a party at which Hart Crane had been perfectly beastly—thereby confirming Mr. Lovecraft's prejudice against homosexuals—finds a letter in his mailbox and reads with some amusement: "Some of the secrets revealed in your recent stories would better be kept out of the light of print. Believe me, I speak as a friend, but there are those who would prefer such half-forgotten lore to remain in its present obscurity, and they are formidable enemies for any man. Remember what happened to Ambrose Bierce. . . ." And, in Boston, Robert Putney Drake screams, "Lies, lies, lies. It's all lies. Nobody tells the truth. Nobody says what he thinks. . . ." His voice trails off.

"Go on," Dr. Besetzung says, "you were doing fine. Don't stop."

"What the use?" Drake replies, drained of anger, turning on the couch to look at the psychiatrist. "To you, this is just abreaction or acting-out or something clinical. You can't believe I'm right."

"Perhaps I can. Perhaps I agree more than you realize." The doctor looks up from his pad and meets Drake's eye. "Are you sure you're not just *assuming* I'll react like everybody else you've tried to tell this to?"

"If you agreed with me," Drake says carefully, "if you understood what I'm really saying, you'd either be the head of a bank, out there in the jungle with my father, grabbing your own share of the loot, or you'd be a bomb-throwing revolutionary, like those Sacco and Vanzetti fellows. Those are the only choices that make sense."

"The only choices? One must go to one extreme or the other?"

Drake looks back at the ceiling and talks abstractly. "You had to get an M.D. long ago, before you specialized. Do you know any case where germs gave up and went away because the man they were destroying had a noble character or sweet sentiments? Did the tuberculosis baccilli leave John Keat's lungs because he had a few hundred great poems still unwritten inside him? You must have read some history, even if you were never at the front lines like me: do you recall any battle that refutes Napoleon's aphorism about God always being on the side of the biggest cannons and the best tacticians? This bolshie in Russia, Lenin, he has ordered the schools to teach chess to everybody. You know why? He says that chess teaches the lesson that revolutionaries must learn: that if you don't mobilize your forces properly, you lose. No matter how high your morality, no matter how lofty your goal: fight without mercy, use every ounce of intelligence, or you lose. My father understands that. The people who run the world have always understood it. A general who doesn't understand it gets broken back to second lieutenant or worse. I saw a whole platoon wiped out, exterminated like an anthill under a boot. Not because they were immoral or naughty or didn't believe in Jesus. Because at that place, on that day, the Germans had superior fire power. That's the law, the one true law, of the universe, and everything that contradicts it—everything they teach in schools and churches—is a lie." He says the word listlessly now. "Just a lie."

"If you really believe that," the doctor asks, "why do you still have the nightmares and the insomnia?"

Drake's blue eyes stare at the ceiling. "I don't know," he says finally. "That's why I'm here.")

"Moon, Simon," the Desk Sergeant called.

I stepped forward, seeing myself through his eyes: beard, army surplus clothes, stains all over (my own mucus, somebody else's vomit). The archetypcal filthy, dirty, disgusting, hippie-commie revolutionary.

"Well," he said, "another bright red rose."

"I usually look neater," I told him calmly. "You get a bit messed over when you're arrested in this town."

"The only way you get arrested in this town," he said, frowning, "is if you break the laws."

"The only way you get arrested in Russia is you break the laws," I replied cheerfully. "Or by mistake," I added.

That didn't set well at all. "Wise guy," he said gently. "We like wise guys here." He consulted my charge-slip. "Nice record for one night, Moon. Rioting, mob action, assaulting an officer, resisting arrest, disturbing the peace. Nice."

"I wasn't disturbing the peace," I said. "I was disturbing

the war." I stole that one-liner from Ammon Hennacy, a Catholic Anarchist that Mom was always quoting. "The rest of the charges are all bullshit, too."

"Say, I know *you*," he said suddenly. "You're Tim Moon's son. Well, well, well. A second-generation anarchist. I guess we'll be locking you up as often as we locked him up."

"I guess so," I said. "At least until the Revolution. Afterward, we won't be locking you up, though. We're going to establish nice camps in places like Wisconsin, and send you there *free* to learn a useful trade. We believe that all policemen and politicians can be rehabilitated. But if you don't want to go to the camp and learn a productive trade, you don't have to. You can live on Welfare."

"Well, well, well," he said. "Just like your old man. I suppose if I looked the other way, while some of the boys took you in back and worked you over a bit, you'd come out still making wisecracks?"

"I'm afraid so," I smiled. "Irish national character, you know. We see the funny side of everything."

"Well," he said thoughtfully (he was awfully fond of that word), "I hope you can see the funny side of what comes next. You're going to be arraigned before Judge Bushman. You'll find yourself wishing you had fallen into a buzzsaw instead. Give my regards to your father. Tell him Jim O'Malley says hello."

"He's dead," I said.

He looked down at his charge-slips. "Sorry to hear it," he mumbled. "Nanetti, Fred," he bawled, and the kid with the broken arm came forward.

A patrolman led me to the fingerprint room. This guy was a computer: "Right hand." I gave him my right hand. "Left hand." I gave him my left hand. "Follow the officer." I followed the officer, and they took my picture. We went down some halls to the night court, and in a lonely section the patrolman suddenly hit me in the lower back with his club, the exact spot (he knew his business) to give me liver problems for a month. I grunted but refused to say anything that would set him off and get me another clout, so he spoke. "Yellow-bellied faggot," he said.

Just like Biloxi, Mississippi: one cop is nice, another is just impersonal, a third is a mean bastard—and it doesn't really matter. They're all part of the same machine, and what comes out the end of the gears and levers is the same product, whatever their attitude is. I'm sure Buchenwald was the same: some of the guards tried to be as humane as possible, some of them just did their job, some of them went out of their way to make it worse for the prisoners. It doesn't matter: the machine produces the effect it was designed for.

Judge Bushman (we slipped him AUM two years later, but that's another story, coming up on another trip) gave me his famous King Kong scowl. "Here are the rules," he said. "This is an arraignment. You can enter a plea or stand mute. If you enter a plea, you retain the right to change it at your trial. When I set bond, you can be released by paying ten percent to the bailiff. Cash only, no checks. If you don't have the cash, you go to jail overnight. You people have the city tied up in knots and the bail bondsmen are too busy to cover every courtroom, so by sheer bad luck you landed in a courtroom they're not covering." He turned to the bailiff. "Charge sheet," he said. He read the record of my criminal career as concocted by the arresting officer. "Five offenses in one night. You're bad medicine, aren't you, Moon? Trial set for September fifteenth. Bail will be ten thousand dollars. Do you have one thousand dollars?"

"No," I told him wondering how many times he'd made that speech tonight.

"Just a moment," said Hagbard, materializing out of the hallway. "I can make bail for this man."

MR. KHARIS: Does Mr. Celine seriously suggest that the United States Government is in need of a guardian?

MR. CELINE: I am merely offering a way out for your client. Any private individual with a record of such incessant murder and robbery would be glad to cop an insanity plea. Do you insist that your client was in full possession of its reason at Wounded Knee? At Hiroshima? At Dresden?

JUSTICE IMMHOTEP: You become facetious, Mr. Celine.

MR. CELINE: I have never been more serious.

"What is your relationship to this young man?" Bushman asked angrily. He had been about to come when the cop dragged me off to jail, and he was strangling in some kind of gruesome S-M equivalent of coitus interruptus.

"He's my wife," Hagbard said calmly.

"What?"

"Common-law wife," Hagbard went on. "Homosexual marriage is not recognized in Illinois. But homosexuality per se isn't a crime in this state, either, so don't try to make waves, your honor. Let me pay and take him home."

It was too much. "Daddy," I said, camping like our friend the Padre. "You're so masterful."

Judge Bushman looked like he wanted to lay Hagbard out with a gavel upside of his head, but he controlled himself. "Count the money," he told the bailiff. "Make sure he pays every penny. And then," he told us, "I want the two of you out of this courtroom as quickly as possible. I'll see *you* September fifteenth," he added, to me.

MR. KHARIS: And we believe we have demonstrated the necessity of this dam. We believe we have shown that the doctrine of eminent domain is on sure constitutional grounds, and has been held to apply in numerous similar cases. We believe we have shown that the resettlement plan offered by the government will be no hardship for the plaintiffs. . . .

"Fuckin' faggots," the cop said as we went out the door.

"All hail Discordia," I told him cheerfully. "Let's get out of this neighborhood," I added to Hagbard.

"My car is right here," he said, pointing to a goddam Mercedes.

"For an anarchist, you sure live a lot like a capitalist," I commented as we got into that beautiful machine crystallized out of stolen labor and surplus value.

"I'm not a masochist," Hagbard replied. "The world makes me uncomfortable enough. I see no reason to make myself more uncomfortable. And I'm damned if I'll drive a broken-down jalopy that spends half its time in a garage being repaired merely because that would make me seem more 'dedicated' to you left-wing simpletons. Besides," he added practically, "the police never stop a Mercedes and search it. How many times a week do you get stopped and harassed, with your beard and your psychedelic Slaveswagon, you damned moralist?"

"Often enough," I admitted, "that I'm afraid to transport dope in it."

"This car is full of dope," he said blithely. "I'm making

a big delivery to a dealer up in Evanston, on the North-western campus, tomorrow."

"You're in the dope business, too?"

"I'm in every illegal business. Every time a government declares something *verboten*, two groups move in to service the black market created: the Mafia and the LDD. That stands for Lawless Delicacy Dealers."

"I thought it stood for Little Deluded Dupes."

He laughed. "Score one for Moon. Seriously, I'm the worst enemy governments have, and the best protection for the average person. The Mafia has no ethics, you know. If it wasn't for my group and our years and years of experience, everything on the black market, from dope to Canadian furs, would be shoddy and unreliable. We always give the customer his or her money's worth. Half the dope *you* sell probably has passed through my agents on its way to you. The better half."

"What was that homosexual business? Just buggin' old Bushman?"

"Entropy. Breaking the straight line into a curve ball."

"Hagbard," I said, "what the hell is your game?"

"Proving that government is a hallucination in the minds of governors," he said crisply. We turned onto Lake Shore Drive and sped north.

"Thou, Jubela, did he tell you the Word?" asked the goat-headed man.

The gigantic black said, "I beat him and tortured him, but he would not reveal the Word."

"Thou, Jubelo, did he tell you the Word?"

The fishlike creature said, "I tormented and vexed his inner spirit, Master, but he would not reveal the Word."

"And thou, Jubelum, did he tell you the Word?"

The hunchbacked dwarf said, "I cut off his testicles and he was mute. I cut off his penis and he was mute. He did not tell me the Word."

"A fanatic," the goat-head said. "It is better that he is dead."

Saul Goodman tried to move. He couldn't twitch a single muscle: That last drug had been a narcotic, and a powerful one. Or was it a poison? He tried to assure himself that the reason he was paralyzed and laying in a coffin was because they were trying to break down his mind. But he wondered if the dead might tell themselves similar fables, as they struggled to escape from the body before it rotted.

As he wondered, the goat-head leaned over and closed the top of the coffin. Saul was alone in darkness.

"Leave first, Jubela."

"Yes, Master."

"Leave next, Jubelo."

"Yes, Master."

"Leave last, Jubelum."

"Yes, Master."

Silence. It was lonely and dark in the coffin, and Saul couldn't move. Let me not go mad, he thought.

Howard spotted the *Lief Erikson* ahead and sang: "Oh, groovy, groovy, groovy scene/Once again I'll meet Celine." *Maldonado's sleek Bentley edged up the drive to the home of "America's best-known financier-philanthropist," Robert Putney Drake.* (Louis marched toward the Red Widow, maintaining his dignity. An old man in a strange robe pushed to the front of the crowd, trembling with exhaltation. The blade rose: the mob sucked in its breath. The old man tried to look into Louis's eyes, but the king could not focus them. The blade fell: the crowd exhaled. As the head rolled into the basket, the old man raised his eyes in ecstasy and cried out, "Jacques De Molay, thou art avenged!") Professor Glynn lectured his class on medieval history (Dean Deane was issuing the Strawberry Statement on the same campus at the same time) and said, "The real crime of the Templars, however, was probably their association with the Hashishim." George Dorn, hardly listening, wondered if he should join Mark Rudd and the others who wanted to close down Columbia entirely.

"And modern novels are the same," Smiling Jim went on. "Sex, sex, sex—and not normal sex even. Every type of perverted, degenerate, unnatural, filthy, deviated, and sick kind of sex. This is how they're gonna bury us, as Mr. Khrushchev said, without even firing a shot."

Sunlight awakened Saul Goodman.

Sunlight and a headache. A hangover from the combination of drugs.

He was in a bed and his clothes were gone. There was no mistaking the garment he wore: a hospital gown. And the room—as he squinted against the sun—had the dull modern-penitentiary look of a typical American hospital.

He hadn't heard the door open, but a weathered-looking

middle-aged man in a doctor's smock drifted into the room. He was carrying a clipboard; pens stuck their necks out of his smock pocket; he smiled benignly. His horn-rimmed heavily black glasses and crewcut marked him as the optimistic, upward-mobile man of his generation, without either the depression/World War II memories that gave anxiety to Saul's contemporaries or nuclear nightmares that gave rage and alienation to youth. He would obviously think of himself as a liberal and vote conservatively at least half the time.

A hopeless schmuck.

Except that he was probably none of those things, but another of their agents, doing a very convincing performance.

"Well?" he said brightly. "Feeling better, Mr. Muldoon?"

Muldoon, Saul thought. Here we go—another ride into their *kitsch* idea of the Heart of Darkness.

"My name is Goodman," he said thinly. "I'm about as Irish as Moishe Dayan."

"Oh, still playing that little game, are we?" the man spoke kindly. "And are you still a detective?"

"Go to hell," Saul said, no longer in mood to fight back with wit and irony. He would dig into his hostility and make his last stand from a foxhole of bitterness and sullen brevity.

The man pulled up a chair and sat down. "Actually," he said, "these remaining symptoms don't bother us much. You were in a much worse state when you were first brought here six months ago. I doubt that you remember that. Electroshock mercifully removes a great deal of the near past, which is helpful in cases like yours. Do you know that you were physically assaulting people on the street, and tried to attack the nurses and orderlies your first month here? Your paranoia was very acute at that point, Mr. Muldoon."

"Up yours, bubi," Saul said. He closed his eyes and turned the other way.

"Such moderate hostility these days," the man went on, bright as a bird in the morning grass. "A few months ago you would have tried to strangle me. Let me show you something." There was a sound of paper.

Curiosity defeated resistance: Saul turned and looked. The man held out a driver's license, from the State of New

Jersey, for "Barney Muldoon." the picture was Saul's. Saul grinned maliciously, showing his disbelief.

"You refuse to recognize yourself?" the man asked quietly.

"Where is Barney Muldoon?" Saul shot back. "Do you have him in another room, trying to convince him he's Saul Goodman?"

"Where is . . . ?" the "doctor" repeated, seeming genuinely baffled. "Oh, yes, you admit you know the name but claim he was only a friend. Just like a rapist we had in here a while ago. He said all the rapes were committed by his roommate, Charlie. Well, let's try another tack. All those people you beat up on the street—and that Playboy Club bunny you tried to strangle—do you still believe they were agents of this, um, Prussian Illuminati?"

"This is an improvement," Saul said. "A very intriguing combination of reality and fantasy, much better than your group's previous efforts. Let me hear the rest of it."

"You think that's sarcasm," the man said calmly. "Actually, behind it, your recovery is proceeding nicely. You really want to remember, even as you struggle to keep up this Goodman myth. Very well: you are a sixty-year-old police officer from Trenton, New Jersey. You never were promoted to detective and that is the great grievance of your life. You have a wife named Molly, and three sons— Roger, Kerry, and Gregory. Their ages are twenty-eight, twenty-five, and twenty-three. A few years ago, you started a game with your wife; she thought it was harmless at first and learned to her sorrow that it wasn't. The game was, that you pretended to be a detective and, late at night, you would tell her about the important cases you were working on. Gradually, you built up to the most important case of all—the solution to all the assassinations in America during the past decade. They were all the work of a group called the Illuminati, who were surviving top-level Nazis that had never been captured. More and more, you talked about their leader—Martin Borman, of course—and insisted you were getting a line on his whereabouts. By the time your wife realized that the game had become reality to you, it was too late. You already suspected your neighbors of being Illuminati agents, and your hatred for Nazism led you to believe you were Jewish and had taken an Irish name to avoid American anti-Semitism. This particular delusion, I must say, caused you acute guilt, which it took us a long time to understand. It was, we finally realized, a projection of a guilt you have long felt for being a policeman at all. But perhaps at this point, I might aid your struggle for self-recognition (and abort your equal and opposite struggle for self-escape) by reading you part of a report on your case by one of our younger psychiatrists. Are you game to hear it?"

"Go ahead," Saul said. "I still find this entertaining."

The man looked through the papers in his clipboard and smiled disarmingly. "Oh, I see here that it's the Bavarian Illuminati, not the Prussian Illuminati, pardon my mistake." He flipped a few more pages. "Here we are," he said.

"The root of the subject's problems," he began to read, "can be found in the trauma of the primal scene, which was reconstructed under narco-analysis. At the age of three, he came upon his parents in the act of fellatio, which resulted in his being locked in his room for 'spying.' This left him with a permanent horror of being locked up and a pity for prisoners everywhere. Unfortunately, this factor in his personality, which he might have sublimated harmlessly by becoming a social worker, was complicated by unresolved Oedipal hostilities and a reaction formation in favor of 'spying,' which led him to become a policeman. The criminal became for him the father-symbol, who was locked up in revenge for locking him up; at the same time, the criminal was an ego-projection and he received masochistic gratification by identifying with the prisoner. The deep-buried homosexual desire for the father's penis (present in all policemen) was next cathected by denial of the father, *via* denial of paternal ancestory, and he began to abolish all Irish Catholic traces from ego-memory, substituting those of Jewish culture, since the Jew, as persecuted minority, reinforced his basic masochism. Finally, like all paranoids, the subject fancies himself to be of superior intelligence (actually, on his test for the Trenton Police Force, he rated only one hundred ten on the Stanford-Binet IQ index) and his resistance to therapy will take the form of 'outwitting' his doctors by finding the 'clues' which reveal that they, too, are agents of the Illuminati and that his assumed identity as 'Saul Goodman' is, in fact, his actual identity. For therapeutic purposes, I would recommend . . ." The "doctor" broke off. "After that," he said briefly, "it is of no interest to you. Well," he added tolerantly, "do you want to 'detect' the errors in this?"

"I've never been in Trenton in my life," Saul said wearily. "I don't know what anything in Trenton looks like. But you'll just tell me that I've erased those memories. Let's move to a deeper level of combat, *Herr Doktor.* I am quite convinced that my mother and father never performed fellatio in their lives. They were too old-fashioned." This was the heart of the labyrinth, and their real threat: while he was sure that they could not break down his belief in his own identity, they were also insidiously undermining that identity by suggesting it was pathological. Many of the lines in the Muldoon case history could refer to any policeman and might, conceivably, refer to him; as usual, behind a weak open attack they were mounting a more deadly covert attack.

"Do you recognize these?" the doctor asked, producing a sketchbook open to a page with some drawings of unicorn.

"It's my sketchbook," Saul said. "I don't know how you got it but it doesn't prove a damned thing, except that I sketch in my spare time."

"No?" The doctor turned the book around; a bookplate on the cover identified the owner as Barney Muldoon, 1472 Pleasant Avenue, Trenton, N.J.

"Amateur work," Saul said. "Anybody can paste a bookplate onto a book."

"And the unicorn means nothing to you?" Saul sensed the trap and said nothing, waiting. "You are not aware of the long psychoanalytical literature on the unicorn as symbol of the father's penis? Tell me, then, why did you decide to sketch unicorns?"

"More amateurism," Saul said. "If I sketched mountains, they would be symbols of the father's penis, too."

"Very well. You might have made a good detective if your—illness—hadn't prevented your promotion. You do have a quick, skeptical mind. Let me try another approach—and I wouldn't be using such tactics if I weren't convinced you were on the road to recovery; a true psychotic would be driven into catatonia by such a blunt assault on his delusions. But, tell me, your wife mentioned that just before the acute stage of your—problem—you spent a lot of money, more than you could afford on a patrolman's salary, on a reproduction of the mermaid of Copenhagen. Why was that?"

"Damn it," Saul exclaimed, "it wasn't a lot of money."
But he recognized the displaced anger and saw that the
other man recognized it too. He was avoiding the question
of the mermaid . . . and her relation to the unicorn. *There
must be a relationship between fact number one and fact
number two.* . . . "The mermaid," he said, getting there
before the enemy could, "is a mother symbol, right? She
has no human bottom, because the male child dare not
think about that area of the mother. Is that correct jar-
gon?"

"More or less. You avoid, of course, the peculiar rele-
vance in your own case: that the sex act in which you
caught your mother was not a normal one but a very perverted and infantile act, which, of course, is the only sex
act a mermaid can perform—as all collectors of mermaid
statues or mermaid paintings unconsciously know."

"It's not perverted and infantile," Saul protested. "Most
people do it. . . ." Then he saw the trap.

"But not *your* mother and father? They were different
from most people?"

And then it clicked: the spell was broken. Every detail
from Saul's notebook, every physical characteristic Peter
Jackson had described, was there. "You're not a doctor,"
he shouted. "I don't know what your game is but I sure as
hell know who you are. You're Joseph Malik!"

George's stateroom was paneled in teak, the walls hung
with small but exquisite paintings by Rivers, Shahn, De
Kooning, and Tanguy. A glass cabinet built into one wall
held several rows of books. The floor was carpeted in wine
red with a blue stylized octopus in the center, its waving
tentacles radiating out like a sunburst. The light fixture
hanging from the ceiling was a lucite model of that formidable jellyfish, the Portuguese man-of-war.

The bed was full size, with a rosewood headboard
carved with Venetian seashell motifs. Its legs didn't touch
the floor; the whole thing was supported on a huge, rounded beam that allowed the bed to seesaw when the ship
rolled, the sleeper remaining level. Beside the bed was a
small desk. Going to it, George opened a drawer and
found several different sizes of writing paper and half a
dozen felt-tipped pens in various colors. He took out a
legal-size pad and a green pen, climbed on the bed, curled
up at the head and began writing.

April 24

Objectivity is presumably the opposite of schizophrenia. Which means that it is nothing but acceptance of everybody else's notion of reality. But nobody's perception of reality is the same as everybody's
notion of it, which means that the most objective person is the real schizophrenic.

It is hard to get beyond the accepted beliefs of
one's own age. The first man to think a new thought
advances it very tentatively. New ideas have to be
around a while before anyone will promote them
hard. In their first form, they are like tiny, impercep-
tible mutations that may eventually lead to new species. That's why cultural cross-fertilization is so important. It increases the gene-pool of the imagination.
The Arabs, say, have one part of the puzzle. The
Franks another. So, when the Knights Templar meet
the Hashishim, something new is born.

The human race has always lived more or less happily in the kingdom of the blind. But there is an elephant among us. A one-eyed elephant.

George put the pen down and read the green words with
a frown. His thoughts still seemed to be coming from outside his own mind. What was that business about the
Knights Templar? He had never felt the slightest interest in
that period since his freshman year in college, when old
Morrison Glynn had given him a *D* for that paper on the
Crusades. It was supposed to be a simple research paper
displaying one's grasp of proper footnote style, but George
had chosen to denounce the Crusades as an early outbreak
of Western racist imperialism. He'd even gone to the trouble of finding the text of a letter from Sinan, third leader
of the Hashishim, in which he exonerates Richard Coeur
de Lion of any complicity in the murder of Conrad of
Montferret, King of Jerusalem. George felt the episode
demonstrated the essential goodwill of the Arabs. How was
he to know that Morrison Glynn was a staunch conservative Catholic? Glynn claimed, among other dyspeptic criticisms, that the letter from the castle called Messiac was
well known as a forgery. Why were the Hashishim coming
back to mind again? Did it have to do with the weird
dream he'd had of the temple in the Mad Dog jail?

The sub's engine was vibrating pleasantly through the floor, the beam, the bed. The trip so far had reminded George of his first flight in a 747—a surge of power, followed by motion so smooth it was impossible to tell how fast or how far they were going.

There was a knock at the stateroom door, and at George's invitation Hagbard's receptionist came in. She was wearing a tight-fitting golden-yellow slack ensemble. She stared compellingly at George, her pupils huge obsidian pools, and smiled faintly.

"Will you eat me if I can't guess the riddle?" George said. "You remind me of a sphinx."

Her lips, the color of ripe grapes, parted in a grin. "I modeled for it. But no riddle, just an ordinary question. Hagbard wants to know if you need anything. Anything but me. I've got work to do now."

George shrugged. "You beat me to the question. I'd like to get together with Hagbard and find out more about him and the submarine and where we're going."

"We are going to Atlantis. He must have told you that." She shifted her weight from one foot to the other, rolling her hips. She had marvelously long legs. "Atlantis is, roughly speaking, about half way between Cuba and the west coast of Africa, at the bottom of the ocean."

"Yeah, well—That's where it's supposed to be, right?"

"Right. Hagbard's going to want you in the captain's control room later. Meanwhile, smoke some of this, if you want. Helps to pass the time." She held out a gold cigarette case. George took it from her, his fingers brushing the velvety black skin of her hand. A pang of desire for her swept through him. He fumbled with the catch of the case and opened it. There were slender white tubes inside, each one stamped with a gold *K*. He took one out and held it to his nose. A pleasant, earthy smell.

"We've got a plantation and a factory in Brazil," she said.

"Hagbard must be a wealthy man."

"Oh, yeah. He's worth billions and billions of tons of flax. Well, look, George, if you need anything, just press the ivory button on your desk. Someone will come along. We'll be calling you later." She turned with a languid wave and walked down the fluorescent-lit corridor. George's gaze clung to her unbelievable ass till she climbed a narrow flight of carpeted stairs and was out of sight.

What was that woman's name? He lay down on the bed, took out a joint, and lit it. It was marvelous. He was up in seconds, not the usual gradual balloon ascent, but a rocket trip, not unlike the effect of amyl nitrate. He might have known this Hagbard Celine would have something special in the way of grass. He studied the sparkles glinting through the Portuguese man-of-war and wiggled his eyeballs rapidly to make the lights dance. All things that are, are lights. The thought came that Hagbard might be evil. Hagbard was like some robber baron out of the nineteenth century. Also like some robber baron out of the eleventh century. The Normans took Sicily in the ninth century. Which gave you mixtures of Viking and Sicilian, but did they ever look like Anthony Quinn? Or his son Greg La Strade? What son? What the sun done cannot be undone but is well dun. The quintessence of evil. Nemesis of all evil. God bless us, every one. Even One. Odd, the big red one. Eye think it was his I. The eye of Apollo. His luminous I. Aum Shiva.

—Aye, trust me not. Trust not a man who's rich in flax—his morals may be sadly lax. Her name is Stella. Stella Maris. Black star of the sea.

The joint was down to the last half inch. He put it down and crushed it out. With grass flowing like tobacco around here, it was a luxury he could afford. He wasn't going to light another one. That wasn't a high, that was a trip! A Saturn rocket, right out of the world. And back, just as fast.

—George, I want you in the captain's control room.

Clearly, this hallucinating of voices and images meant he wasn't all the way back. Reentry was not completed. He now saw a vision of the layout of that part of the submarine between his stateroom and the captain's control room. He stood up, stretched, shook his head, his hair swirling around his shoulders. He walked to the door, slid it back, and walked on down the hall.

A little later, he stepped through a door onto a balcony which was a reproduction of the prow of a Viking ship. Above, below, in front, to the sides, was green-blue ocean. They seemed to be in a glass globe projecting into the ocean. A long-necked red-and-green dragon with golden eyes and a spiky crest reared above George and Hagbard.

"My approach is fanciful, rather than functional," Hagbard said. "If I weren't so intelligent, it would get me into a lot of trouble." He patted the dragon figurehead with a black-furred hand. Some Viking, George thought. A Neanderthal Viking, perhaps.

"That was a good trick," George said, feeling shrewd but still high. "How you got me up on the bridge with that telepathy thing."

"I called you on the intercom," Hagbard said, with a look of absurd innocence.

"You think I can't tell a voice in my head from a voice in my ears?"

Hagbard roared with laughter, so loud that it made George feel a little uncertain. "Not when you've had your first taste of Kallisti Gold, man."

"Who am I to call a man a liar when he's just turned me on with the best shit I ever had?" said George with a shrug. "I suspect you of making use of telepathy. Most people who have that power would not only not try to hide it, they'd go on television."

"Instead, I put the ocean on television." said Hagbard. He gestured at the globe surrounding their Viking prow. "What you see is simply color television with a few adaptations and modifications. We are inside the screen. The cameras are all over the surface of the sub. The cameras don't use ordinary light, of course. If they did, you wouldn't be able to see anything. The submarine illuminates the sea around us with an infrared laser-radar to which our TV cameras are sensitive. The radiations are of a type that is more readily conducted by the hydrogen in water than by any other element. The result is that we can see the ocean bottom almost as clearly as if it were dry land and we were in a plane flying above it."

"That'll make it easy to see Atlantis when we get to it," George said. "By the way, why did you say we're going to Atlantis, again? I didn't believe it when you told me, and now I'm too stoned to remember."

"The Illuminati are planning to loot one of the greatest works of art in the history of man—the Temple of Tethys. It happens to be a solid-gold temple, and their intention is to melt it down and sell the gold to finance a series of assassinations in the U.S. I intend to get there before them."

The reference to assassinations reminded George that he'd gone down to Mad Dog, Texas, on Joe Malik's hunch that he'd find a clue there to an assassination conspiracy. If Joe knew that the clue was leading 20,000 leagues under

the sea and eons back through time, would he believe it?
George doubted it. Malik was one of those hard-nosed
"scientific" leftists. Though he had been acting and talking
a little strangely lately.

"Who did you say was looting this temple?" he asked
Hagbard.

"The Illuminati. The real force behind all communist
and fascist movements. Whether you're aware of it or not,
they're also already in control of the United States government."

"I thought everybody in your crowd was a right-
winger—"

"And I told you spacial metaphors are inadequate in discussing politics today," Hagbard interrupted.

"Well, you sound like a gang of right-wingers. Up until
the last minute, all I've heard from you and your people
was that the Illuminati were commies, or were behind the
commies. Now you say they're behind fascism and behind
the current government in Washington, too."

Hagbard laughed. "We came on like right-wing
paranoids, at first, to see how you'd react. It was a test."

"And?"

"You passed. You didn't believe us—that was obvious—but you kept your eyes and ears open and were
willing to listen. If you were a right-winger, we would have
done our pro-communist rap. The idea is to find out if a
new man or woman will listen, really listen, or just shut
their minds at the first really shocking idea."

"I'm listening, but not uncritically. For instance, if the
Illuminati control America already, what's the purpose of
the assassinations?"

"Their grip on Washington is still pretty precarious.
They've been able to socialize the economy. But if they
showed their hand now and went totalitarian all the way,
there would be a revolution. Middle-roaders would rise up
with right-wingers, and left-libertarians, and the Illuminati
aren't powerful enough to withstand that kind of massive
revolution. But they can rule by fraud, and by fraud eventually acquire access to the tools they need to finish the job
of killing off the Constitution."

"What sort of tools?"

"More stringent security measures. Universal electronic
surveillance. No-knock laws. Stop and frisk laws. Government inspection of first-class mail. Automatic fingerprint-

ing, photographing, blood tests, and urinalysis of any person arrested before he is charged with a crime. A law making it unlawful to resist even unlawful arrest. Laws establishing detention camps for potential subversives. Gun control laws. Restrictions on travel. The assassinations, you see, establish the need for such laws in the public mind. Instead of realizing that there is a conspiracy, conducted by a handful of men, the people reason—or are manipulated into reasoning—that the entire populace must have its freedom restricted in order to protect the leaders. The people agree that they themselves can't be trusted. Targets for assassination will be mavericks of left or right who are either not part of the Illuminati conspiracy or have been marked as unreliable. The Kennedy brothers and Martin Luther King, for example, were capable of mobilizing a somewhat libertarian left-right-black-white populist movement. But the assassinations that have occurred so far are nothing compared to what will take place. The next wave will be carried out by the Mafia, who will be paid in Illuminati gold."

"Not Moscow gold," said George with a smile.

"The puppets in the Kremlin have no idea that they and the puppets in the White House are working for the same people. The Illuminati control all sorts of organizations and national governments without any of them being aware that others are also controlled. Each group thinks it is competing with the others, while actually each is playing its part in the Illuminati plan. Even the Morituri—the six-person affinity groups which splintered from the SDS Weathermen, because the Weathermen seemed too cautious—are under the control of the Illuminati. They think they're working to bring down the government, but actually they are strengthening its hand. The Black Panthers are also infiltrated. Everything is infiltrated. At present rate, within the next few years the Illuminati will have the American people under tighter surveillance than Hitler had the Germans. And the beauty of it is, the majority of the Americans will have been so frightened by Illuminati-backed terrorist incidents that they will beg to be controlled as a masochist begs for the whip."

George shrugged. Hagbard sounded like a typical paranoid, but there was this submarine and the strange events of the past few days. "So the Illuminati are conspiring to tyrannize the world, is that it? Do you trace them back to the First International?"

"No. They're what happened when the Enlightenment of the eighteenth century collided with German mysticism. The correct name for the organization is Ancient Illuminated Seers of Bavaria. According to their own traditions they were founded or revived in seventeen seventy-six on May first by a man named Adam Weishaupt. Weishaupt was an unfrocked Jesuit and a Mason. He taught that religions and national governments had to be overthrown and the world ruled by an elite of scientifically-minded materialistic atheists, to be held in trust for the masses of mankind who would eventually rule themselves when enlightenment became universal. But this was only Weishaupt's 'Outer Doctrine.' There was also an 'Inner Doctrine,' which was that power is an end in itself, and that Weishaupt and his closest followers would make use of the new knowledge being developed by scientists and engineers to seize control of the world. Back in seventeen seventy-six, things were run largely by the Church and the feudal nobility, with the capitalists slowly getting a bigger and bigger piece of the pie. Weishaupt declared that these groups were obsolete, and it was time for an elite with a monopoly on scientific and technological knowledge to seize power. Instead of eventually producing a democratic society, as the 'Outer Doctrine' promised, the Ancient Illuminated Seers of Bavaria would saddle mankind with a dictatorship that would last forever."

"Well, it would be logical enough that someone around that time would think of that," said George. "And who more likely than a Mason who was an unfrocked Jesuit?"

"You recognize that what I tell you is relatively plausible," said Hagbard. "That's a good sign."

"A sign that it's plausible." laughed George.

"No, a sign that you're the kind of person I'm always looking for. Well, the Illuminati, after staying above ground long enough to recruit a hard-core membership from Masons and freethinkers and to establish international contacts, allowed it to seem that the Bavarian government had suppressed them. Subsequently, the Illuminati launched their first experimental revolution, in France. Here they suckered the middle class, whose true interests lay in laissez faire free enterprise, to follow the Weishaupt slogan of 'Liberty, Equality, Fraternity.' The catch, of course, is that where equality and fraternity rule, there is no liberty. After the career of Napoleon, whose rise and fall was purely the result of Illuminati manipulations, they started planting the seeds of European socialism, leading to the revolutions of eighteen forty-eight, to Marxism, finally to the seizure of Russia, one-sixth of the earth's land mass. Of course, they had to engineer a world war to make the Russian Revolution possible, but by nineteen seventeen they had become quite good at that. World War Two was an even more clever job and resulted in more gains for them."

"Another thing this explains," George said, "is why orthodox Marxism-Leninism, in spite of all its ideals, always turns out to be not worth a shit. Why it's always betrayed the people wherever it established itself. And it explains why there's such an inevitable quality about America's drift toward totalitarianism."

"Right," said Hagbard. "America is the target now. They've got most of Europe and Asia. Once they get America, they can come out into the open. The world will then be much as Orwell predicted in *Nineteen Eighty-four*. They bumped him off after it was published, you know. The book hit a little too close to home. He was obviously on to them—the references to Inner and Outer parties with different teachings, O'Brien's speech about power being an end in itself—and they got him. Orwell, you see, ran across them in Spain, where they were functioning quite openly at one point during the Civil War. But artists also arrive at truth through their imaginations, if they let themselves wander freely. They're more likely to arrive at the truth than more scientific-minded people."

"You've just tied two hundred years of world history up in a theory that would make me feel I should have myself committed if I accepted it," said George. "But I'm drawn to it, I admit. Partly intuitively—I feel you are a person who is essentially sane and not paranoid. Partly because the orthodox version of history that I was taught in school never made sense to me, and I know how people can twist history to suit their beliefs, and therefore I assume that the history I've learned is twisted. Partly because of the very wildness of the idea. If I learned one thing in the last few years, it's that the crazier an idea is the more likely it is to be true. Still and all, given all those reasons for believing you, I would like some further sign."

Hagbard nodded. "All right. A sign. So be it. First, a question for you. Assuming your boss, Joe Malik, was on to something—assuming that the place he sent you did have something to do with assassinations and might lead to the Illuminati: what would be likely to happen to Joe Malik?"

"I know what you're suggesting. I don't like to think about it."

"Don't think." Hagbard suddenly pulled a telephone from under the railing of the ship. "We can tap into the Bell System through the Atlantic cable from here. Dial the New York area code and dial any person in New York, any person who could give you up-to-date information on Joe Malik and on *Confrontation* magazine. Don't tell me who you're dialing. Otherwise, you might suspect I had someone on the ship impersonate the person you want to speak to."

Holding the phone so Hagbard couldn't see, George dialed a number. After a wait of about thirty seconds, after numerous clicks and other strange sounds, George could hear a phone ringing. After a moment, a voice said. "Hello."

"This is George Dorn," said George. "Who is this?"

"Well, who the hell did you think it was? You dialed my number."

"Oh, Christ," said George. "Look, I'm in a place where I don't trust the phones. I have to be sure I'm really talking to you. So I want you to identify yourself without my telling you who you're supposed to be. Do you understand?"

"Of course I understand. You don't have to use that grade school language. This is Peter Jackson, George, as I presume you intended that it should be. Where the hell are you? Are you still in Mad Dog?"

"I'm at the bottom of the Atlantic Ocean."

"Knowing your bad habits, I'm not surprised. Have you heard about what happened to us? Is that why you're calling?"

"No. What happened?" George gripped the telephone tighter.

"The office was blown up by a bomb early this morning. And Joe has disappeared."

"Was Joe killed?"

"Not as far as we know. There weren't any bodies in the wreckage. How about you—are you okay?"

"I'm getting into an unbelievable story, Peter. It's so unbelievable that I'm not going to try to tell you about it. Not till I get back. If you're still running a magazine there then."

"As of now there's still a magazine, and I'm running it from my apartment," said Peter. "I only hope they don't decide to blow me up."

"Who?"

"Whoever. You're still on assignment. And if this has anything to do with what you've been doing down in Mad Dog, Texas, you're in trouble. Reporters are not supposed to go around getting their boss's magazines bombed."

"You sound pretty cheerful, considering Joe might be dead."

"Joe is indestructible. By the way, George, who's paying for this call?"

"A wealthy friend, I think. He's got a corner on flax or something like that. More on him later. I'm going to sign off now, Pete. Thanks for talking."

"Sure. Take care, baby."

George handed the phone to Hagbard. "Do you know what's happened to Joe? Do you know who bombed *Confrontation?* You knew about this before I called. Your people are pretty handy with explosives."

Hagbard shook his head. "All I know is, the pot is coming to a boil. Your editor, Joe Malik, was onto the Illuminati. That's why he sent you to Mad Dog. As soon as you show your face down there, you get busted and Malik's office is bombed. What do you think?"

"I think that what you've been telling me is the truth, or a version of it. I don't know whether to trust you completely. But I've got my sign. If the Bavarian Illuminati don't exist, *something* does. So, then, where do we go from here?"

Hagbard smiled. "Spoken like a true *homo neophilus,* George. Welcome to the tribe. We want to recruit you, because you are so gullible. That is, gullible in the right way. You're skeptical about conventional wisdom, but attracted to unorthodox ideas. An unfailing mark of *homo neophilus.* The human race is not divided into the irrational and the rational, as some idealists think. All humans are irrational, but there are two different kinds of irrationally— those who love old ideas and hate and fear new ones, and those who despise old ideas and joyfully embrace new ones. *Homo neophobus* and *homo neophilus. Neophobus* is the original human stock, the stock that hardly changed at all for the first four million years of human history. Neophilus is the creative mutation that has been popping up at regular intervals during the past million years, giving the race little forward pushes, the kind you give a wheel to make it spin faster and faster. Neophilus makes a lot of mistakes, but he or she moves. They live life the way it should be lived, ninety-nine percent mistakes and one percent viable mutations. Everyone in my organization is *neophilus*, George. That's why we're so far ahead of the rest of the human race. Concentrated neophilus influences, without any neophobe dilution. We make a million mistakes, but we move so fast that none of them catch up with us. Before you get any deeper, George, I'd like you to become one of us."

"Which means what?"

"Become a Legionnaire in the Legion of Dynamic Discord."

George laughed. "Now that sounds like a gas. But it's hard to believe that an organization with an absurd name like that could build anything as serious as this submarine, or work for such a serious end as foiling the Ancient Illuminated Seers of Bavaria."

Hagbard shook his head. "What's serious about a yellow submarine? It's right out of a rock song. And everybody knows people who worry about the Bavarian Illuminati are crackpots. Will you join the Legion—in whatever spirit you choose?"

"Certainly," said George promptly.

Hagbard clapped him on the back. "Ah, you're our type, all right. Good. Back through the door you came, then turn right and through the golden door."

"Is there someone lifting a lamp beside it?"

"There are no honest men on this voyage. Get along with you now." Hagbard's full lips curled in a leer. "You're in for a treat."

("Every perversion," Smiling Jim screamed. "Men having sex with men. Women having sex with women. Obscene desecrations of religious articles for deviant purposes. Even men and women having sex with animals. Why, friends, the only thing they haven't gotten around to yet is people copulating with fruits and vegetables, and I guess that'll be next. Some degenerate getting his kicks with an apple!" The audience laughed at the wit.)

"You've got to run very fast to catch up with the sun. That's the way it is, when you're lost out here," the old woman said, stressing the last five words in a kind of childish singsong. . . . The woods were incredibly thick and dark, but Barney Muldoon stumbled after her. . . . "It's getting darker and darker," she said darkly, "but's always dark, *when you're lost out here*". . . . "Why do we have to catch the Sun?" Barney asked, perplexed. "In search of more light," she cackled gleefully. "You always need more light, *when you're lost out here*". . . .

Behind the golden door stood the lovely black receptionist. She had changed into a short red leather skirt that left all of her long legs in view. Her hands rested lightly on her white plastic belt.

"Hi, Stella," said George. "Is that your name? Is it really Stella Maris?"

"Sure."

"No honest men on this voyage is right. Hagbard *was* talking to me telepathically. He told me your name."

"I told you my name when you boarded the sub. You must have forgotten. You've been through a lot. And sad to say you'll be going through a lot more. I must ask you to remove your clothing. Just shed it on the floor, please."

George unhesitatingly did as he was told. Total or partial nudity was required in lots of initiation rituals; but a twinge of anxiety ran through him. He was trusting these people simply because they hadn't done anything to him *yet*. But there was really no telling what kind of freaks they might be, what kind of ritual torture or murder they might involve him in. Such fears were part of initiation rituals, too.

Stella was grinning at him, eyebrows raised, as he dropped his shorts. He understood the meaning of the grin, and he felt the blood rush hot as a blush to his penis, which grew thicker and heavier in an instant. Being aware that he was standing nude with the start of an erection in front of this beautiful and desirable woman, who was enjoying the spectacle, made him swell and harden still more.

"That's a good-looking tool you've got there. Nice and thick and pink and purple." Stella sauntered over to him, reached out and touched her fingers to the underside of his cock, just where it met his scrotum. He felt his balls draw up. Then her middle finger ran down the central cord, flicking the underside of the head. George's penis rose to full staff in salute to her manual dexterity.

"The sexually responsive male," said Stella. "Good, good, good. Now you're ready for the next chamber. Right through that green door, if you please."

Naked, erect, regretfully leaving Stella behind, George walked through the door. These people were too healthy and good-humored to be untrustworthy, he thought. He liked them and you ought to trust your feelings.

But as the green door slammed shut behind him, his anxiety came back even stronger than before.

In the center of the room was a pyramid of seventeen steps, alternating red and white marble. The room was large, with five walls that tapered together in a gothic arch thirty feet above the pentagonal floor. Unlike the pyramid in the Mad Dog jail, this one had no huge eye goggling down at him. Instead there was an enormous golden apple, a sphere of gold the height of a man with a foot-long stem and a single leaf the size of an elephant's ear. Cut into the side of the apple was the word KALLISTI in Greek letters. The walls of the room were draped with enormous gold curtains that looked like they'd been stolen from a Cinerama theater, and the floor was covered with lush gold carpet into which George's bare feet sank deeply.

This is different, George told himself to quiet his fear. These people are different. There's a connection with the others, but they're different.

The lights went out. The golden apple was glowing in the dark like a harvest moon. KALLISTI was etched in sharp black lines.

A voice that sounded like Hagbard boomed at him from all sides of the room: "There is no goddess but Goddess, and she is your goddess."

This is actually an Elks Club ceremony, George thought. But there were strange, un-BPOE fumes drifting into his nostrils. An unmistakable odor. High-priced incense these people use. An expensive religion, or lodge, or whatever it is. But you can afford the best when you're a flax tycoon. Flax, huh? Hard to see how a man could make such big money in the flax biz. Did you corner the market, or what? Now, mutual funds, that was more down to earth than flax. I do believe I'm feeling the effects. They shouldn't drug a man without his consent.

He found he was holding his penis, which had shrunk considerably. He gave it a reassuring pull.

Said the voice, "There is no movement but the Discordian movement, and it is the Discordian movement."

That would appear to be self-evident. George rolled his eyes and watched the giant, golden-glowing apple wheel and spin above him.

"This is a most sacred and a most serious hour for Discordians. It is the hour when the great, palpitating heart of Discordia throbs and swells, when She What Began It All prepares to ingest into her heaving, chaotic bosom another Legionnaire of the Legion of Dynamic Discord. O minerval are ye willing to make a commitment to Discordia?"

Embarrassed at being addressed directly, George let go of his wang. "Yes," he said, in a voice that sounded muffled to him.

"Are ye a human being, and not a cabbage or something?"

George giggled. "Yes."

"That's too bad," the voice boomed. "Do ye wish to better yerself?"

"Yes."

"How stupid. Are ye willing to become philosophically illuminated?"

Why that word, George wondered briefly. Why *illuminated?* But he said, "I suppose so."

"Very funny. Will ye dedicate yerself to the holy Discordian movement?"

George shrugged, "As long as it suits me."

There was a draft against his belly. Stella Maris, naked and gleaming, stepped out from behind the pyramid. The soft glow from the golden apple illuminated the rich browns and blacks of her body. George felt the blood charging back into his penis. This part was going to be *OK*. Stella walked toward him with a slow, stately stride, gold bracelets sparkling and tinkling on her wrists. George felt hunger, thirst, and a pressure as if a balloon were slowly being inflated in his bowels. His cock rose, heartbeat by heartbeat. The muscles in his buttocks and thighs tightened, relaxed, and tightened again.

Stella approached with gliding steps and danced around him in a circle, one hand reaching out to brush his bare waist. He stepped forward and held out his hands to her. She danced away on tiptoes, spinning, arms over her head, heavy conical breasts with black nipples tilted upward. For once George understood why some men like big boobs.

His eyes moved to the globes of her buttocks, the long muscular shadows in her thighs and calves. He stumbled toward her. She stopped suddenly, legs slightly apart forming an inverse with her patch of very abundant hair at the Royal Arch, her hips swaying in a gentle circular motion. His tool pulled him to her as if it were iron and she were magnetized; he looked down and saw that a little pearl of fluid, gleaming gold in the light from the apple, had appeared in the eye. Polyphemus wanted very much to get into the cave.

George walked up to her until the head of the serpent was buried in the bushy, prickly garden at the bottom of her belly. He put his hands out and pressed them against the two cones, feeling her ribcage rise and fall with heavy breathing. Her eyes were half closed and her lips slightly open. Her nostrils flared wide.

She licked her lips and he felt her fingers lightly circling his cock, lightly brushing it with a friction strong enough to gently electrify it. She stepped back a bit and pushed her finger into the moisture on his tip. George put his hand into the tangle of her pubic hair, feeling the lips hot and swollen, feeling her juices slathering his fingers. His middle finger slid into her cunt, and he pushed it in past the tight opening all the way up to his knuckle. She gasped, and her whole body writhed around his finger in a spiral motion.

"Wow, God!" George whispered.

"Goddess!" Stella answered fiercely.

George nodded. "Goddess," he said hoarsely, meaning Stella as much as the legendary Discordia.

She smiled and drew away from him. "Try to imagine that this is not me, Stella Maris, the youngest daughter of Discordia. She is merely the vessel of Goddess. Her priestess. Think of Goddess. Think of her entering me and acting through me. I *am* her now!" All the while she was stroking Polyphemus gently but insistently. It was already ferocious as a stallion, but it seemed to be getting more inflamed, if that were possible.

"I'm going to go off in your hand in a second," George moaned. He gripped her slender wrist to stop her. "I've *got to fuck you,* whoever you are, woman or goddess. *Please.*"

She stepped back from him, her tan palms turned toward him, her arms held away from her sides in a receiving, accepting gesture. But she said, "Climb the steps now. Climb up to the apple." Her feet twinkling on the thick carpet, she ran backward away from him and disappeared behind the pyramid.

He climbed the seventeen steps, old one-eye still swollen and aching. The top of the pyramid was broad and flat, and he stood facing the apple. He put a hand out and touched it, expecting cold metal, surprised when the softly glowing texture felt warm as a human body to his touch. About half a foot below the level of his waist he saw a dark, elliptical opening in the side of the apple, and a sinister suspicion formed in his mind.

"You got it, George" said the booming voice that presided over his initiation. "Now you're supposed to plant your seeds in the apple. Go to it, George. Give yourself to Goddess."

Shit man, George thought. What a silly idea! They get a guy turned on like this and then they expect him to fuck a goddamn golden idol. He had a good mind to turn his back on the apple, sit down on the top step of the pyramid and jack-off to show them what he thought of them.

"George, would we let you down? It's nice there in the apple. Come on, stick it in. Hurry up."

I am so gullible, thought George. But a hole is a hole. It's all friction. He stepped up to the apple and gingerly placed the tip of his cock in the elliptical opening, half expecting to be sucked in by some mechanical force, half fearing it would be chopped off by a miniature guillotine. But there was nothing. His cock didn't even touch the edges of the hole. He took another small step, and put it halfway in. Still nothing. Then something warm and wet and hairy squirmed up against the tip of his cock. And, whatever it was, he felt it give as he reflexively pushed forward. He pushed some more and it pushed back, and he slid into it. A cunt by all the high hidden Gods, a cunt!—and by the feel it was almost surely Stella's.

George exhaled a deep sigh, planted his hands on the smooth surface of the apple to support himself and began thrusting. The pumping from inside the apple was as fierce. The metal was warm against his thighs and belly. Suddenly the pelvis inside slammed up against the hole, and a hollow scream resounded from the inside of the apple. The echo effect made it seem to hang in the air, containing all the agony, spasm, itch, twitch, moon madness, horror, and ecstasy of life from the ocean's birth to now.

George's prick was stretched like the skin of a balloon about to burst. His lips drew back from his teeth. The delicious electricity of orgasm was building in his groin, in the deepest roots of his penis, in his quick. He was coming. He cried out as he fired his seed into the unseen cunt, into the apple, into Goddess, into eternity.

There was a crash above. George's eyes opened. A nude male body at the end of a rope came hurtling at him from the vaulted ceiling. It jerked to a stop with a horrible crack, its feet quivering above the stem of the apple. Even as the leaps of ejaculation still racked George's body, the penis over his head lifted and spurted thick white gobbets of come, like tiny doves, arcing out over George's uplifted, horrified head to fall somewhere on the side of the pyramid. George stared at the face, canted to one side, the neck broken, a hangman's knot behind the ear. It was his own face.

George went ape. He pulled his penis out of the apple and nearly fell backward down the stairs. He ran down the seventeen steps and looked back. The dead figure was still hanging, through a trap in the ceiling, directly above the apple. The penis had subsided. The body slowly rotated. Enormous laughter boomed out in the room, sounding very much like Hagbard Celine.

"Our sympathies," said the voice. "You are now a legionnaire in the Legion of Dynamic Discord."

The hanging figure vanished soundlessly. There was no trapdoor in the ceiling. A colossal orchestra somewhere began to play *Pomp and Circumstance*. Stella Maris came round from the back of the pyramid again, this time clothed from head to foot in a simple white robe. Her eyes shone. She was carrying a silver tray with a steaming hot towel on it. She put the tray on the floor, knelt, and wrapped George's relaxing dick in the towel. It felt delicious.

"You were beautiful," she whispered.

"Yeah, but—wow!" George looked up at the pyramid. The golden apple gleamed cheerfully.

"Get up off the floor," he said. "You're embarrassing me."

She stood up smiling at him, the broad grin of a woman whose lover has thoroughly satisfied her.

"I'm glad you liked it," said George, his wildly disparate

emotions gradually coalescing as anger. "What was the idea of that last little gag? To turn me off permanently on sex?"

Stella laughed. "George, admit it. Nothing could turn you off sex, right? So don't be such a bad sport."

"Bad *sport*? That sick trick is your idea of sport? What a goddam rotten dirty motherfucking thing to do to a man!"

"Motherfucking? No, that's for when we ordain deacons."

George shook his head angrily. She absolutely refused to be shamed. He was speechless.

"If you have any complaints, sweet man, take them to Episkopos Hagbard Celine of the *Lief Erikson* Cabal," said Stella. She turned and started walking back toward the pyramid. "He's waiting for you back the way you came. And there's a change of clothes in the next room."

"Wait a minute!" George called after her. "What the blazes does *Kallisti* mean?"

She was gone.

In the anteroom of the initiation chamber he found a green tunic and tight black trousers draped over a costumer. He didn't want to put them on. It was probably some sort of uniform of this idiotic cult, and he wanted no part of it. But there weren't any other clothes. There was also a beautiful pair of black boots. Everything fit perfectly and comfortably. There was a full-length mirror on the wall and he looked at himself and grudgingly admitted that the outfit was a gas. A tiny golden apple glinted on the left side of his chest. The only thing was that his hair needed washing. It was getting stringy.

Through two more doors and he was facing Hagbard.

"You didn't like our little ceremony?" said Hagbard with exaggerated sympathy. "That's too bad. I was so proud of it, especially the parts I lifted from William Burroughs and the Marquis de Sade."

"It's *sick*," said George. "And putting the woman inside the apple so I couldn't have any kind of personal sex with her, so I had to *use* her as a receptacle, as, as an *object*. You made it pornographic. And sadistic pornography, at that."

"Dig, George," said Hagbard. "Thou art that. If there were no death, there would be no sex. If there were no sex, there would be no death. And without sex, there would be no evolution toward intelligence, no human race. Therefore death is necessary. Death is the price of orgasm. Only one being on all this planet is sexless, intelligent and immortal. While you were pumping your seeds into the symbol of life, I showed you orgasm and death in one image and brought it home to you. And you'll never forget it. It was a trip, George. Wasn't it a trip?"

George nodded reluctantly. "It was a trip."

"And you know—in your bones—a little more about life than you did before, right, George?"

"Yes."

"Well, then, thank you for joining the Legion of Dynamic Discord."

"You're welcome."

Hagbard beckoned George to the edge of the boat-shaped balcony. He pointed down. Far below in the blue-green medium through which they seemed to be flying George could see rolling lands, hills, winding riverbeds—and then, broken buildings. George gasped. Pyramids rose up below, as high as the hills.

"This is one of the great port cities," Hagbard said. "Galleys from the Americas plied their trade to and from this harbor for a thousand years."

"How long ago?"

"Ten thousand years," said Hagbard. "This was one of the last cities to go. Of course, their civilization had declined quite a bit by then. Meanwhile, we've got a problem. The Illuminati are here already."

A large, undulating, blue-gray shape appeared ahead of them, swam toward them, whirled and matched their speed so it seemed to drift alongside. George felt another momentary leap of fright. Was this another of Hagbard's tricks?

"What is that fish? How does it keep up with us?" George asked.

"It's a porpoise, not a fish, a mammal. And they can swim a lot faster than submarines can sail underwater. We can keep up with them, though. They form a film around their bodies that enables them to slide through the water without setting up any turbulence. I learned from them how to do it, and I applied it to this sub. We can cross the Atlantic under water in less than a day."

A voice spoke from the control panel. "Better go transparent. You'll be within range of their detectors when you've gone another ten miles."

"Right," said Hagbard. "We will maintain present course until further notice, so you'll know where we are."

"I'll know," said the voice.

Hagbard slashed his hand through the air disgustedly. "You're so fucking *superior*."

"Who are you talking to?" said George.

"Howard."

The voice said, "I've never seen machines like this before. They look something like crabs. They've just about got the temple all dug up."

"When the Illuminati do something on their own, they go first class," said Hagbard.

"Who the hell is Howard?" said George.

"It's me. Out here. Hello, Mr. Human," said the voice. "I'm Howard."

Unbelieving, yet knowing quite well what was happening, George slowly turned his head. The dolphin appeared to be looking at him.

"How does he talk to us?" said Hagbard.

"He's swimming alongside the prow of the submarine, which is where we pick up his voice. My computer translates from Delphine to English A mike here in the control room sends our voices to the computer which translates into Delphine and broadcasts the correct sounds through the water to him."

"Lady-oh, oh de-you-day, a new human being has come my way," Howard sang. "He has swum into my ken. I hope he's one of the friendly men."

"They sing a lot," said Hagbard. "Also recite poetry and make it up on the spot. A large part of their culture is poetry. Poetics and athletics—and, of course, the two are very closely related. What they do mostly is swim, hunt, and communicate with each other."

"But we do all with artful complexity and rare finesse," said Howard, looping the loop outside.

"Lead us to the enemy, Howard," said Hagbard.

Howard swam out in front of them, and as he did so, he sang:

Right on, right on, a-stream against the foe
The sallying schools of the Southern seas make their
    course to go.
Attack, attack, with noses sound as rock

No shark or squid can shake us loose or survive our
    dour shock.

"Epics," said Hagbard. "They're mad for epics. They
have their whole story for the past forty thousand years in
epic form. No books, no writing—how could they handle
pens with their fins, you know? All memorization. Which
is why they favor poetry. And their poems are marvelous,
but you must spend years studying their language before
you know that. Our computer turns their works into doggerel. It's the best it can do. When I have the time, I'll add
some circuits that can really translate poetry from one language to another. When the Porpoise Corpus is translated
into human languages, it will advance our culture by centuries or more. It will be as if we'd discovered the works of
a whole race of Shakespeares that had been writing for
forty millennia."

"On the other hand," said Howard, "your civilizations
may be demoralized by culture shock."

"Not likely," said Hagbard grumpily. "We've a few
things to teach you, you know."

"And our psychotherapists can help you over the anguish of digesting our knowledge," said Howard.

"They have psychotherapists?" said George.

"They invented psychoanalysis thousands of years ago
as a means of passing the time on long migrations. They
have highly complex brains and symbol-systems. But their
minds are unlike ours in very important ways. They are all
in one piece, so to speak. They lack the structural differen-
tiation of ego, superego, and id. There is no repression.
They are fully aware, and accepting, of their most primitive wishes. And conscious will, rather than parent-incul-
cated discipline, guides their actions. There is no neurosis,
no psychosis among them. Psychoanalysis for them is an
imaginative poetic exercise in autobiography, rather than a
healing art. There are no difficulties of the mind that require healing."

"Not quite true," said Howard. "There was a school of
thought about twenty thousand years ago that envied humans. They were called the Original Sinners, because they
were like the first parents of your human race who, according to some of your legends, envied the gods and suffered for it. They taught that humans were superior because they could do many more things than dolphins. But

they despaired, and most ended up by committing suicide. They were the only neurotics in the long history of porpoises. Our philosophers mostly hold that we live in beauty all the days of our lives, as no human does. Our culture is simply what you might call a commentary on our natural surroundings, whereas human culture is at war with nature. If any race is afflicted, it is yours. You can do much, and what you can do, you must do. And, speaking of war, the enemy lies ahead."

In the distance George could make out what appeared to be a mighty city rising on hills surrounding a deep depression which must have been a harbor when Atlantis was on the surface. The buildings marched on and on as far as the eye could see. They were mostly low, but here and there a square tower reared up. The sub was heading for the center of the ancient waterfront. George stared at the buildings; he was able to see them better now. They were angular, very modern in appearance, whereas the other city they'd flown—sailed—over had a mixed Greek-Egyptian-Mayan quality to its architecture. Here there were no pyramids. But the tops of many of the structures were broken off, and many others were heaps of rubble. Still, it was remarkable that a city which had sunk so many thousands of feet to the bottom of the ocean in the course of what must have been an enormous earthquake should be this well preserved. The buildings must be incredibly durable. If New York went through a catastrophe like that there'd be nothing left of its glass-and-alloy skyscrapers.

There was one pyramid. It was much smaller than the towers around it. It gleamed a dull yellow. Despite its lack of height, it seemed to dominate the harbor skyline, like a squat, powerful chieftain in the center of a circle of tall, slender warriors. There was movement around its base.

"This is the city of Peos in the region of Poseida," said Hagbard, "and it was great in Atlantis for a thousand years after the hour of the Dragon Star. It reminds me of Byzantium, which was a great city for a thousand years after the fall of Rome. And that pyramid is the Temple of Tethys, goddess of the Ocean Sea. It was seafaring that made Peos great. I have a soft spot in my heart for those people."

Crawling around the base of the temple were strange sea creatures that looked like giant spiders. Lights flashed from their heads and glinted on the sides of the temple. As the submarine swept closer, George could see that the spiders were machines, each with a body the size of a tank. They appeared to be excavating deep trenches around the base of the pyramid.

"Wonder where they had those built," muttered Hagbard. "Hard to keep innovations like that a secret."

As he spoke, the spiders stopped whatever work they were doing around the pyramid. There was no motion among them at all for a moment. Then one of them rose up from the sea bottom, followed by another, and another. They formed quickly into a V shape and started toward the submarine like a pair of arms outstretched to seize it. They picked up speed as they came.

"They've detected us," Hagbard growled. "They weren't supposed to, but they have. It never pays to underestimate the Illuminati. All right, George. Button up your asshole. We're in for a fight."

At that moment but exactly two hours earlier on the clock, Rebecca Goodman awoke from a dream about Saul and a Playboy bunny and something sinister. The phone was ringing (was there a pyramid in the dream?—she tried to remember—something like that) and she reached groggily past the mermaid statue and held the receiver to her ear. "Yes?" she said cautiously.

"Put your hand on your pussy and listen," said August Personage. "I'd like to lift your dress and—" Rebecca hung up.

She suddenly remembered the hit when the needle went in, and all those wasted years. Saul had saved her from that, and now Saul was gone and strange voices on the phone talked of sex the way addicts talked of junk. "In the beginning of all things was Mummu, the spirit of pure Chaos. In the beginning was the Word, and it was written by a baboon." Rebecca Goodman, twenty-five years old, started to cry. If he's dead, she thought, these years have been wasted, too. Learning to love. Learning that sex was more than another kind of junk. Learning that tenderness was more than a word in the dictionary: that it was just what D. H. Lawrence said, not an embellishment on sex but the center of the act. Learning what that poor guy on the phone could never guess, as most people in this crazy country never guessed it. And then losing it, losing it to an aimless bullet fired from a blind gun somewhere.

August Personage, about to leave the phone booth at the

Automat on Fortieth Street and the Avenue of the Americas, catches a flash of plastic on the floor. Bending, he picks up a pornographic tarot card, which he quickly shoves into a pocket to be examined at leisure later.

It was the Five of Pentacles.

And, when the throne room was empty and the believers had departed in wonder and redoubled faith, Hassan knelt and separated the two halves of the vessel which held the head of Ibn Azif. "Very convincing screams," he commented, slipping the trapdoor beneath the plate; and Ibn Azif climbed out, grinning at his own performance. His neck was thick, bull-like, undamaged, and quite solid.

THE FIFTH TRIP, OR GEBURAH
Swift-Kick, Inc

And, behold, thusly was the Law formulated:
IMPOSITION OF ORDER = ESCALATION OF CHAOS!
—Lord Omar Khayaam Ravenhurst,
"The Gospel According to Fred," *The Honest Book of Truth*

The lights flashed; the computer buzzed. Hagbard attached the electrodes.

On January 30, 1939, a silly little man in Berlin gave a silly little speech; among other things, he said: "And another thing I wish to say on this day which perhaps is memorable not only for us Germans: in my life I have many times been a prophet and most of the times I have been laughed at. During the period of my struggle for power, it was in the first case the Jews that laughed at my prophecies that some day I would take over the leadership of the State and thereby of the whole folk and that I would among other things solve also the Jewish problem. I believe that in the meantime the hyenalike laughter of the Jews of Germany has been smothered in their throats. Today I want to be a prophet once more: if the international-finance Jews inside and outside Europe should succeed once more in plunging nations into another world war the consequence will be the annihilation of the Jewish race in Europe." And so on. He was always saying things like that. By 1939 quite a few heads here and there realized that the silly little man was also a murderous little monster, but only a very small number even of these noticed that for the first time in his anti-Semitic diatribes he had used the word *Vernichtung*—annihilation—and even they couldn't believe he meant what that implied. In fact, outside of a small circle of friends, nobody guessed what the little man, Adolf Hitler, had planned.

Outside that small—very small—circle of friends, others came in intimate contact with *der Führer* and never guessed what was in his mind. Hermann Rauschning, the Governor of Danzig, for instance, was a devout Nazi until he began to get some hints of where Hitler's fancies were tending; after fleeing to France, Rauschning wrote a book warning against his former leader. It was called *The Voice of Destruction* and was very eloquent, but the most interesting passages in it were not understood by Rauschning or by most of his readers. "Whoever sees in National Socialism nothing but a political movement doesn't know much about it," Hitler told Rauschning, and this is in the book, but Rauschning and his readers continued to see National Socialism as a particularly vile and dangerous *political movement* and nothing more. "Creation is not yet completed," Hitler said again; and Rauschning again recorded, without understanding. "The planet will undergo an upheaval which you uninitiated people can't understand," *der Führer* warned on another occasion; and, still another time, he remarked that Nazism was, not only more than a political movement, but "more than a new religion"; and Rauschning wrote it all and understood none of it. He even recorded the testimony of Hitler's physician that the silly and murderous little man often awoke screaming from nightmares that were truly extraordinary in their intensity and would shout, "It's HIM, it's HIM, HE's come for me!" Good old Hermann Rauschning, a German of the old school and not equipped to participate in the New Germany of National Socialism, took all this as evidence of mental unbalance in Hitler. . . .

All of them coming back, all of them. Hitler and Streicher and Goebbels and the powers behind them what look like something you can't even imagine, guvnor. . . .

You think they was human, the patient went on as the psychiatrist listened in astonishment, *but wait till you see them the second time. And they're coming—By the end of the month, they're coming. . . .*

Karl Haushofer was never tried at Nuremberg; ask most people to name the men chiefly responsible for the *Vernichtung* (annihilation) decision, and his name will not be mentioned; even most histories of Nazi Germany relegate him to footnotes. But strange stories are told about his many visits to Tibet, Japan, and other parts of the Orient; his gift for prophecy and clairvoyance; the legend that he belonged to a bizarre sect of dissident and most peculiar Buddhists, who had entrusted him with a mission in the Western world so serious that he vowed to commit suicide if he did not succeed. If the last yarn is true, Haushofer must have failed in his mission, for in March 1946 he killed his wife Martha and then performed the Japanese suicide-rite of *sepukku* upon himself. His son, Albrecht, had already been executed for his role in the "officer's plot" to assassinate Hitler. (Of his father, Albrecht had written in a poem: "My father broke the seal/He did not feel the breath of the Evil One/He set It free to roam the world!")

It was Karl Haushofer, clairvoyant, mystic, medium, Orientalist, and fanatic believer in the lost continent of Thule, who introduced Hitler to the Illuminated Lodge in Munich, in 1923. Shortly thereafter, Hitler made his first bid to seize power.

No rational interpretation of the events of August 1968 in Chicago, satisfactory to all participants and observers, has yet been produced. This suggests the need for value-free models, inspired by the structural analysis in von Neumann and Morgenstern's *Theory of Games and Economic Behavior,* which will allow us to express what actually occurred functionally, without tainting our analysis with bias or moral judgments. The model we will employ is that of two teams, an uphill motorcar race and a downhill bicycle race, accidentally intersecting on the same hill. The Picasso statue in the Civic Center will be regarded as "start" for the downhill motorcar race and "finish" for the uphill bicycle race. Pontius Pilate, disguised as Sirhan Sirhan, fires the opening shot, thereby disqualifying Robert F. Kennedy, for whom Marilyn Monroe committed suicide, as recorded in the most trustworthy tabloids and scandal sheets.

THIS IS THE VOICE OF YOUR FRIENDLY NEIGHBORHOOD SPIDER MAN SPEAKING. YOU MUST REALIZE THAT YOU ARE NOT JOSEPH WENDELL MALIK.

Hell's Angels on motorcycles do not fit the structure of the race at all, so they endlessly orbit around the heroic statue of General Logan in Grant Park ("finish" for the uphill crucifixion racers) and can be considered as isolated from the "action," which is, of course, America.

When Jesus falls the first time, this can be considered as a puncture and Simon operates an air pump on his tires, but the threat to throw LSD in the water supply constitutes a "foul" and this team thereby is driven back three squares by Mace, clubs, and the machine guns of the Capone mob unleashed from another time track in the same multiverse. Willard Gibbs, far more than Einstein, created the modern cosmos, and his concept of contingent or statistical reality, when cross-fertilized with the Second Law of Thermodynamics by Shannon and Wiener, led to the definition of information as the negative reciprocal of probability, making the clubbings of Jesus by Chicago cops just another of those things that happens in this kind of quantum jump.

A centurion named Semper Cuni Linctus passes Simon in Grant Park looking for the uphill bike race. "When we crucify a man," he mutters, "he should confounded well *stay* crucified." The three Marys clutch handkerchiefs to their faces as the teargas and Zyklon B pours upward on the hill, to the spot where the crosses and the statue of General Logan stand. . . . "Nor dashed a thousand kim," croons Saint Toad looking through the door at Fission Chips. . . . Arthur Flegenheimer and Robert Putney Drake ascend the chimney. . . . "You don't have to believe in Santa Claus," H. P. Lovecraft explains. . . . "Ambrose," the Dutchman says to him imploringly.

"But it can't be," Joe Malik says, half weeping. "It can't be that crazy. Buildings wouldn't stand. Planes wouldn't fly. Dams would collapse. Engineering colleges would be lunatic asylums."

"They aren't already?" Simon asks. "Have you read the latest data on the ecological catastrophe? You have to face it, Joe. God is a crazy woman."

"There are no straight lines in curved space," Stella adds.

"But my mind is dying," Joe protests, shuddering.

Simon holds up an ear of corn and tells him urgently, "Osiris is a black god!"

(Sir Charles James Napier, bearded, long-haired and sixty-odd years old, General of Her Majesty's Armies in India, met a most engaging scoundrel in January 1843 and immediately wrote to his cronies in England about this remarkable person, whom he described as brave, clever, fabulously wealthy, and totally unscrupulous. Since this curious fellow was also regarded as God by his followers, who numbered over three million, he charged twenty rupees for permission to kiss his hand, asked—and got—the sexual favors of the wives or daughters of any True Believers who took his fancy, and proved his divinity by brazenly and openly committing sins which any mortal would shrivel with shame to have acknowledged. He also proved, at the Battle of Miani, where he aided the British against the rebellious Baluchi tribesmen, that he could fight like ten tigers. All in all, General Napier concluded, a most unusual human being—Hasan ali Shah Mahallat, forty-sixth Imam, or living God, of the Ishmaelian sect of Islam, direct descendant of Hassan i Sabbah, and first Aga Khan.)

Dear Joe:

I'm back in Czechago again, fabulous demesne of Crookbacked Richard, pigbaschard of the world, etc., where the pollution comes up like thunder out of Gary across the lake, etc., and the Padre and I are still working on the heads of the local Heads, etc., so I've finally got time to write you that long letter I promised.

The Law of Fives is all the farther that Weishaupt ever got, and Hagbard and John aren't much interested in any further speculations along those lines. The 23/17 phenomenon is entirely my discovery, except that William S. Burroughs has noted the 23 without coming to any conclusions about it.

I'm writing this on a bench in Grant Park, near the place I got Maced three years ago. Nice symbolism.

A woman just came along from the Mothers March Against Polio. I gave her a quarter. What a drag, just when I was trying to get my thoughts in order. When you come out here, I'll be able to tell you more; this will obviously have to be somewhat sketchy.

Burroughs, anyway, encountered the 23 in Tangiers, when a ferryboat captain named Clark remarked that he'd been sailing 23 years without an accident. That day, his ship sunk, with all hands and feet aboard. Burroughs was thinking about it in the evening when the radio newscast told him that an Eastern Airlines plane, New York to Miami, had crashed. The pilot was another Captain Clark and the plane was Flight 23.

"If you want to know the extent of their control," Simon told Joe (speaking this time, not writing a letter; they were driving to San Francisco after leaving Dillinger), "take a dollar bill out of your wallet and look at it. Go

ahead—do it now. I want to make a point." Joe took out
his wallet and looked for a single. (A year later, in the city
Simon called Czechago in honor of the synchronous invasions in August 1968, the KCUF convention is taking its
first luncheon break after Smiling Jim's sock-it-to-'em
opening speech. Simon brushes against an usher, shouts,
"Hey, you damned faggot, keep your hands off my ass,"
and in the ensuing tumult Joe has no trouble slipping the
AUM in the punch.)

"Do I have to get a library card just to look at one
book?" Carmel asks the librarian in the Main Branch of
the Las Vegas Library, after Maldonado had failed to produce any lead to a communist agent.

*"One of the most puzzling acts of Washington's Pres-
idency," Professor Percival Petsdeloup tells an American
history class at Columbia, back in '68, "was his refusal to
aid Tom Paine when Paine was condemned to death in
Paris."* . . . *Why puzzling? George Dorn thinks in the
back of the class, Washington was an Establishment fink.*
. . . "First of all, look at that face on the front," Simon
says. "It isn't Washington at all, it's Weishaupt. Compare
it with any of the early, authentic pictures of Washington
and you'll see what I mean. And look at that cryptic half-
smile on his face." *(The same smile Weishaupt wore when
he finished the letter explaining to Paine why he couldn't
help him; sealed it with the Great Seal of the United States
whose meaning only he knew; and settling back in his
chair, murmured to himself, "Jacques De Molay, thou art
again avenged!")*

"What do you mean, I'm creating a disturbance? It was
that faggot there, with his big mitts on my ass."

*("Well, I don't know which particular book, honey.
Something that tells how the communists work. You know,
how a patriotic citizen can spot a commie spy ring if
there's one in his neighborhood. That kind of thing," Carmel explained.)*

A swarm of men in blue shirts and white plastic helmets
rushes down the steps at Forty-third Street and UN Plaza,
past the inscription reading, "They shall beat their swords
into plowshares and their spears into pruning hooks, neither shall they study war any more." Waving heavy
wooden crosses and shouting angry battle cries, the helmeted men surge into the crowd like a wave hitting a sand

castle. George sees them coming, and his heart skips a beat.

"And when you turn the bill over, the first thing you see is the Illuminati pyramid. You'll notice it says seventeen seventy-six on it, but our government was founded in seventeen eighty-eight. Supposedly, the seventeen seventy-six is there because that's when the Declaration of Independence was signed. The real reason is that seventeen seventy-six is the year Weishaupt revived the Illuminati. And why do you suppose the pyramid has seventy-two segments in thirteen layers?" Simon asks in nineteen sixty-nine. . . . "Misunderstanding, my eye! When a guy gropes my butt that way I understand exactly what he wants," Simon shouts in nineteen seventy. . . . *George nudges Peter Jackson. "God's Lightning," he says. The plastic hats gleam in the sunlight, more of them jostling down the stairs, a banner, red letters on a white background unfurling above:* "AMERICA: LOVE IT OR WE'LL STOMP YOU. . . . *"Christ on rollerskates," Peter says, "now watch the cops do a vanishing act."* . . . Dillinger settles down cross-legged in a five-sided chamber under the UN meditation room. He curls into the lotus posture with an ease that would appear unusual in an American in his late sixties were there anyone to witness it.

"Seventy-two is the cabalistic number for the Holy Unspeakable Name of God, used in all black magic, and thirteen is the number in a coven," Simon explains. "That's why." The Volkswagen purrs toward San Francisco.

Carmel comes down the steps of the Las Vegas Public Library, a copy of J. Edgar Hoover's *Masters of Deceit* under his arm, an anticipatory smirk on his face, *and Simon is finally ejected from the Sheraton-Chicago shouting, "Faggots! I think you're all a bunch of faggots!"*

"And here's one of their jokes," Simon adds. "Over the eagle's head, do you dig that Star of David? They put that one in—one single six-pointed Jewish star, made up of all the five-pointed stars—just so some right-wing cranks could find it and proclaim it as proof that the Elders of Zion control the Treasury and the Federal Reserve."

Overlooking the crowd in UN Plaza, Zev Hirsch, New York State Commander of God's Lightning, watches his thick-shouldered troops, swinging their wooden crosses like tomahawks, drive back the lily-livered peaceniks. There is an obstacle. A blue line of policemen has formed between the men of God's Lightning and their prey. Over the cops' shoulders, the peaceniks are screeching dirty words at their plastic-hatted enemies. Zev's eyes scan the crowd. He catches the eye of a red-faced cop with gold braid on his cap. Zev gives the Police Captain a questioning look. The Captain winks. A minute later the Captain makes a small gesture with his left hand. Immediately, the line of police vanishes, as if melted in the bright spring sun that beats down on the plaza. The battalion of God's Lightning falls upon their anguished, outraged, and astonished victims. Zev Hirsch laughs. This is a lot more fun than the old days in the Jewish Defense League. All the servants are drunk. And the rain continues.

At an outdoor café in Jerusalem two white-haired old men wearing black are drinking coffee together. They try to mask their emotions from the people around them, but their eyes are wild with excitement. They are staring at an inside page of a Yiddish newspaper, reading two ads in Yiddish, a large, quarter-page announcement of the greatest rock festival of all time to be held near Ingolstadt, Bavaria—bands of all nations, people of all nations, to be known as Woodstock Europa. On the same page is the paper's personals column, and the watery eyes of the two old men are re-reading for the fifth time the statement, in Yiddish, "In thanks to St. Jude for favors granted.—A. W."

One old man points at the page with a trembling finger. "It is coming," he says in German.

The other one nods, a beatific smile on his withered face. "Jawohl. It is coming very soon. Der Tag. Soon we must to Bavaria go. Ewige Blumenkraft!"

Carlo put the gun on the table between us. "This is it, George," he said. "Are you a revolutionary, or are you just on an ego trip playing at being a revolutionary? Can you take the gun?"

I wiped my eyes. The Passaic was flowing below me, a steady stream of garbage from the Paterson falls down to Newark and the Atlantic Ocean. Like the garbage that was my contemptible, cowardly soul. . . . The God's Lightning troopers fan out, clubbing each person wearing an I WON'T DIE FOR FERNANDO POO button. Blood dances in the air, fragile red bubbles, before the tomblike slab of the UN building. . . . *Dillinger's breathing slows down. He stares at the ruby eye atop the 13-step pyramid hidden in the UN building, and he thinks of pentagons.*

"I'm a God's Lightning," Carlo said. "This is no joke, baby, I'm going to do the whole bit." His intense eyes burned into mine as the switchblade came out of his pocket. "Motherfuckin' commie," he screamed suddenly, leaping up so quickly that the chair fell over behind him. "You're not getting off with a beating this time. I'm gonna cut your balls off and take them home as a souvenir." He slashed forward with the knife, deflecting his swing at the last minute. "Made you jump, you long-haired faggotty freak. I wonder if you have any balls to cut off. Well, I'll find out." He inched forward, the knife weaving snakelike patterns in the air.

"Look," I said desperately, "I know you're only play-acting."

"You don't know *nothing,* baby. Maybe I'm FBI or CIA. Maybe this is just an excuse to get you to go for the gun so I can kill you and claim self-defense. Life isn't all demonstrations and play-acting, George. There comes a time when it gets serious." He lunged again with the knife, and I stumbled clumsily backward. "Are you going to take the gun or am I going to cut your balls off and tell the Group you're no fucking good and we couldn't use you?"

He was totally mad and I was totally sane. Is that a more flattering way of telling it, instead of the truth, that he was brave and I was yellow?

"Listen," I said, "I know you won't really stab me and you know I won't really shoot you—"

"Shit on *you know* and *I know,*" Carlo hit me in the chest with his free hand, hard. "I'm a God's Lightning, really a God's Lightning. I'm gonna do the whole scene. This is a test, but the test is for real." He hit me again, jarring my balance, then slapped my face, twice, rapidly, back and forth like a windshield wiper. "I always said you long-haired commie freaks don't have no guts. You can't even fight back. You can't even feel angry, can you? You just feel sorry for yourself, right?"

It was too damned true. A nerve twinged deep down inside at the unfairness of it, of his ability to see into me more than I usually dared see into myself; and at last I grabbed the gun from the table, screaming, "You sadistic *Stalinist* son-of-a-bitch!"

"And look at the eagle," Simon says. "Look real close. That ain't really no olive branch in his left claw, baby.

That's our old friend Maria Juana. You never really looked at a dollar bill before, did you?

"And the real symbolism of the pyramid is alchemical, of course. The traditional code represents the three kinds of sex by a cube, a pyramid, and a sphere. The cube is that travesty we call 'normal' sex, in which the two nervous systems never actually merge at the orgasm, like the two parallel sides of the cube. The pyramid is the two coming together and joining, the magical-telepathic orgasm. The sphere is the Tantric ritual, endlessly prolonged, with no orgasm at all. The alchemists used that code for over two thousand years. The Rosicrucians among the founding fathers used the pyramid as a symbol of their kind of sex magic. Aleister Crowley used that symbol the same way, more recently. The eye on the pyramid is the two minds meeting. Neurological interlock. The opening of the Eye of Shiva. Ewige Schlangekraft—the eternal serpent power. The joining of the Rose and Cross, vagina and penis, into Rose-Cross. The astral leap. Mind escaping from physiology."

The AUM was supposed to work almost instantly, according to what the scientists at ELF had told Hagbard, so Joe approached the first man who had sampled the punch and started a conversation. "Nice talk Smiling Jim gave," he said earnestly. (*I rammed the gun into Carlo's gut and saw him go white about the lips. "No, don't worry," I said, smiling. "I'm not using it on you. But when I come back there'll be a dead pig on the streets somewhere in Morningside Heights." He started to speak, and I jabbed downward with the gun, grinning as he gasped for air. "Comrade," I added.*) "Yeah, Smiling Jim was born with a silver tongue," the other man said.

"A silver tongue," Joe agreed solemnly, then added, holding out his hand, "by the way, I'm Jim Mallison from the New York delegation."

"Knew by your accent," the other said shrewdly. "I'm Clem Cotex from down Little Rock." They shook. "Pleasure to meet you."

"Too bad about that kid that got thrown out," Joe said, lowering his voice. "It looked to me like that usher really was—you know—*touching* him."

Cotex looked surprised for a moment, but then shook his head in doubt. "Can't tell nowadays, especially in big cities. Do you really think an *Andy Frain* usher could be a—fairy?"

"Like you said, nowadays in big cities . . ." Joe shrugged. "I'm just saying that it looked like it to me. Of course, maybe the usher isn't one. Maybe he's just a cheap thief who was trying to pick the kid's pocket. A lot of that goes on these days, too." Cotex involuntarily reached back to check his own wallet, and Joe went on blandly. "But I wouldn't rule out the other, not by a long shot. What sort of man would want to be an usher at a KCUF meeting, if you stop and think about it? You must have observed how many homosexuals there are in our organization."

"What?" Cotex's eyes bulged.

"You haven't noticed it?" Joe smiled loftily. "There are very few of us who are really Christians. Most of the membership are just a *little bit lavender,* know what I mean? I think it's one of our biggest problems, and we ought to bring it out into the open and discuss it frankly. Clear the air, right? For instance, take the way Smiling Jim always puts his arm around your shoulder when he talks to you—"

Cotex interrupted, "Hey, mister, you're pretty darn bright. Just now hit me like a flash—some of the *men* here, when Smiling Jim showed those beaver shots to prove how bad some magazines are getting, they really shuddered. They didn't just disapprove—it really honest-to-Pete revolted them. What kind of *man* actually finds a naked lady disgusting?"

Go, baby, go, Joe thought. The AUM is working. He quickly derailed the conversation. "Another thing that bothers me. Why don't we ever challenge the spherical earth theory?"

"Huh?"

"Look," Joe said. "If all the scientists and eggheads and commies and liberals are pushing it in our schools all the time, there must be something a little fishy about it. Did you ever stop to think that there's no way—just no way at all—to reconcile a spherical earth with the story of the Flood, or Joshua's miracle, or Jesus standing on the pinnacle of the Temple and seeing all the kingdoms of the earth? And I ask you, man to man, in all your travels have you ever *seen* the curvature anywhere? Every place *I've* been is flat. Are we going to trust the Bible and the evidence of our own senses, or are we going to listen to a bunch of agnostics and atheists in laboratory smocks?"

"But the earth's shadow on the moon during an eclipse . . ."

Joe took a dime out of his pocket and held it up. "This casts a circular shadow, but it's flat, not spherical."

Cotex stared into space for a long moment, while Joe waited with suppressed excitement. "You know something?" Cotex said finally, "all the Bible miracles and our own travels and the shadow on the moon would make sense if the earth was shaped like a *carrot* and all the continents were on the flat end—"

Praise be to Simon's god, Bugs Bunny, Joe thought elatedly. It's happening—he's not only gullible—he's creative.

I followed the cop—the pig, I corrected myself—out of the cafeteria. I was so keyed up that it was a Trip. The blue of his uniform, the neon signs, even the green of the lampposts, all were coming in superbright. That was adrenalin. My mouth was dry—dehydration. All the classic flight-fight symptoms. The activation syndrome, Skinner calls it. I let the cop—the pig—get half a block ahead and reached in my pocket for the revolver.

"Come on, George!" Malik shouted. George didn't want to move. His heart was thumping, his arms and legs trembling so hard he knew they'd be useless to him in a fight. But he just didn't want to move. He'd had enough of running from these motherfuckers.

But he couldn't help himself. As the men in blue shirts and white helmets came on, the crowd surged away from them, and George had to move back with the crowd or be knocked down and trampled.

"Come *on*, George." It was Pete Jackson at his side now, with a good, hard grip on his arm, tugging him.

"Goddam it, why do we have to run away from them?" George said, stumbling backward.

Peter was smiling faintly. "Don't you read your Mao, George? Enemy attacks, we retreat. Let the Morituri fanatics stand and get creamed."

I couldn't do it. My hand held the gun, but I couldn't take it out and hold it in front of me any more than I could take out my penis and wave it around. I was sure, even though the street was empty except for me and the pig, that a dozen people would jump out of doorways yell-

ing, "Look, he took it out of his pants."

Just like right now, when Hagbard said, "Button up your asshole. We're in for a fight," I stood frozen like I stood frozen on the embankment above the Passaic.

"Are you on an ego trip playing at being a revolutionary?" Carlo asked.

And Mavis: "All the militant radicals in your crowd ever do is take out the Molotov cocktail diagram that they carefully clipped from *The New York Review of Books,* hang it on the bathroom door, and jack-off in connection with it."

Howard sang:

> The foe is attacking, their ships coming near,
> Now is the time to fight without fear!
> Now is the time to look death in the eye
> Before we submit, we'll fight till we die!

This time I got the gun out of my pocket—standing there, looking down at the Passaic—and raised it to my forehead. If I didn't have the courage for homicide, Jesus knows I have despair enough for a hundred suicides. And I only have to do it once. Just once, and then oblivion. I cock the firing pin. (More play-acting, George? Or will you really do it?) I'll do it, damn you, damn all of you. I pull the trigger and fall, with the explosion, into blackness.

(AUM was a product of the scientists at ELF—the Erisian Liberation Front—and shared by them with the JAMs. An extract of hemp, boosted with RNA, the "learning" molecule, it also had small traces of the famous "Frisco Speedball"—heroin, cocaine, and LSD. The effect seemed to be that the heroin stilled anxiety, the RNA stimulated creativity, the hemp and acid opened the mind to joy, and the cocaine was there to fit the Law of Fives. The delicate balance created no hallucinations, no sense of "high"—just a sudden spurt in what Hagbard Celine liked to call "constructive gullibility.")

It was one of those sudden shifts of movement that occur in a mob scene. Instead of pushing George and Peter back, the crowd between them and the white helmets were parting. A slender man fell heavily against George, anguish in his eyes. There was a terrible thump, and the man fell to the ground.

George saw the dark brown wooden cross before he saw

*the man who wielded it. There was blood and hair at the
end of the crossarm. The God's Lightning man was dark,
broad and muscular, with a blue shadow on his cheeks. He
looked Italian or Spanish—he looked, in fact, a lot like
Carlo. His eyes were wide and his mouth was open and he
was breathing heavily. The expression was neither rage nor
sadistic joy—just the unthinking panting alertness of a
man doing a difficult and fatiguing job. He bent over the
fallen slender man and raised the cross.*

*"All right!" snapped Peter Jackson. He pushed George
aside. There was a silly-looking yellow plastic water pistol
in his hand. He squirted the oblivious God's Lightning
man in the back of the neck. The man screamed, arched
backward, the cross flying end over end into the air. He
fell on his back and lay screaming and writhing.*

*"Come on now, motherfucker!" Pete snarled as he
dragged George into the crowd, broken-field running toward Forty-second Street.*

"An hour and a half to go," Hagbard says, finally beginning to show suppressed tension. George checks his
watch—it's exactly 10:30 P.M., Ingolstadt time. The Plastic Canoe is wailing KRISHNA KRISHNA HARE HARE.

(*Under the noon sun, two days earlier, Carmel speeds in
his jeep away from Las Vegas.*)

"Who am I going to meet at the Norton Cabal?" Joe
asks. "Judge Crater? Amelia Earhart? Nothing would surprise me now."

"A few real together people," Simon replies. "But no
one like that. But you'll have to die, really die, man, before
you're illuminated." He smiles gently. "Aside from death
and resurrection, you won't find anything you'd call 'supernatural' with this bunch. Not even a whiff of old Chicago-
style Satanism."

"God," Joe says, "was that only a week ago?"

"Yep," Simon grins, gunning his VW around a Chevrolet with Oregon license plates, "It's still nineteen sixty-nine,
even if you seem to have lived several years since we met
at the anarchist caucus." His eyes are amused as he half
turns to glance at Joe.

"I suppose that means you know what's been happening
in my dreams. I'm getting the flashforwards already."

"Always happens after a good dirty Black Mass with pot
mixed in the incense," Simon says. "What sort of thing
you getting? Is it happening when you're awake yet?"

"No, only in my dreams." Joe pauses, thinking. "I only know it's the real article because the dreams are so vivid. One set has to do with some kind of pro-censorship rally at the Sheraton-Chicago hotel, I think about a year from now. There's another set that seems farther in the future—five or six years—where I'm impersonating a doctor for some reason. And a third group of images comes to me, now and then, that seems to be the set of a Franken-stein movie, except that the extras are all hippies and there seems to be a rock festival going on."

"Does it bother you?"

"A little. I'm used to waking up in the morning with the future ahead of me, not behind me *and* ahead of me *both*."

"You'll get used to it. You're just beginning to contact what old Weishaupt called *'die Morgensheutegesternwelt'* —the tomorrow-today-yesterday world. It gave Goethe the idea for *Faust,* just like Weishaupt's *'Ewige Blumen-kraft'* slogan inspired Goethe's *'Ewige Weibliche.'* I'll tell you what," Simon suggested, "You might try wearing three wristwatches, like Bucky Fuller does—one showing the time where you're at, one showing the time where you're going, and one showing the time at some arbitrary place like Greenwich Mean Time or your home town. It'll help you get used to relativity. Meanwhile, never whistle while you're pissing. And you might repeat to yourself, when you get disoriented, Fuller's sentence, 'I seem to be a verb.' "

They drove in silence for a while, and Joe pondered on being a verb. Hell, he thought, I have enough trouble un-derstanding what Fuller means when he says *God* is a verb. Simon let him mull it over, and began humming again: "Rameses the Second is dead, my love/He's walking the fields where the BLESSED liiiiive. . . ." Joe realized he was starting to doze . . . *and all the faces at the luncheon table looked at him in astonishment. "No, seriously," he said. "Anthropologists are too timid to say it out in the open, in public, but corner one of them in private and ask him."*

Every detail was clear: it was the same room in the Sheraton-Chicago Hotel, and the faces were the same. (I've been here before and said this before.)

"The rain dances of the Indians work. The rain always comes. So why isn't it possible that their gods are real and ours isn't? Have you ever prayed to Jesus for something

and really gotten it?" There is a long silence and finally an old tight-faced woman smiles youthfully and declares, "Young man, I'm going to try it. How do I meet an Indian in Chicago?"

Like tomahawks the crosses of God's Lightning rose and fell on the slender man's defenseless skull. They'd found their injured comrade lying on the street twisting and moaning beside his erstwhile victim. A couple of them hauled the wounded God's Lightning man away, while the rest took their revenge on the unconscious peace demonstrator.

("You, Luke," says Yeshua ben Yosef, "don't write that down.")

Space-time, then, may be slanted or kiltered when you're lost out here: Fernando Poo looks through his glass at a new island, not guessing that it will be named after himself, not imagining that someday Simon Moon will write "In Fourteen Hundred and Seventy Two, Fernando Poo discovered Fernando Poo," and Hagbard says, "Truth is a tiger," while Timothy Leary does a Crown Point Pavanne out of San Luis Obispo Jail and four billion years earlier one squink says to another, "I've solved the ecology problem on this new planet." The other squink, partner to the first (they own Swift Kick Inc., the shoddiest contractors in the Milky Way) says "How?" The first squink laughs coarsely. "Every organism produced will be programmed with a Death Trip. It'll give them a rather gloomy outlook, I admit, especially the more conscious ones, but it will sure minimize costs for us." Swift Kick Inc. cut the edges every other way they could think, and Earth emerged as the Horrible Example invoked in all classes on planetary design throughout the galaxy.

When Burroughs told me that, I flipped, because I was 23 that year and lived on Clark Street. Besides, I immediately saw the application to the Law of Fives: $2 + 3 = 5$ and Clark has 5 letters.

I was mulling this over when I happened to notice the shipwreck in Pound's Canto 23. That's the only shipwreck mentioned in the whole 800-page poem, in spite of all the nautical voyages described. Canto 23 also contains the line, "with the sun in a golden cup," which Yeats says inspired his own lines, "the golden apples of the sun, the silver apples of the moon."

Golden apples, of course, brought me back to Eris, and I realized I was onto something hot.

Then I tried adding the Illuminati Five to 23, and I got 28. The average menstrual period of Woman. The lunar cycle. Back to the silver apples of the moon— and I'm Moon. Of course, Pound and Yeats both have five letters in their names.

If this be schizophrenia, I said with a P. Henry twist (one better than an O. Henry twist), make the most of it!

I looked deeper.

Through a bullhorn, a police captain began to shout, CLEAR THE PLAZA CLEAR THE PLAZA.

The first reports of the annihilation camps were passed on to the OSS by a Swiss businessman evaluated as being one of the most trustworthy informants on affairs in Nazi Europe. The State Department decided that the stories were not confirmed. That was early in 1943. By autumn of that year, more urgent reports from the same source transmitted still through the OSS forced a major policy conference. It was again decided that the reports were not true. As winter began, the English government asked for another conference to discuss similar reports from their own intelligence networks and from the government of Rumania. The delegates met in Bermuda for a warm, sunny weekend, and decided that the reports were not true; they returned to their work refreshed and tanned. The death trains continued to roll. Early in 1944, Henry Morgenthau, Jr., Secretary of the Treasury, was reached by dissenters in the State Department, examined the evidence, and forced a meeting with President Franklin Delano Roosevelt. Shaken by the assertions in Morgenthau's documents, Roosevelt pledged that he would act at once. He never did. It was said later that the State Department convinced him, once again, of their own analysis: the reports simply were not true. When Mr. Hitler said *Vernichtung* he had not really meant *Vernichtung*. An author, Ben Hecht, then placed an ad in the *New York Times*, presenting the evidence to the public; a group of prominent rabbis attacked him for alarming Jews unnecessarily and undermining confidence in America's Chief Executive during wartime. Finally, late that year, American and Russian troops began liberating the camps, and General Eisenhower insisted that news photographers take detailed movies which were released to the whole world. In the interval between the first suppressed report by the Swiss businessman and the liberation of the first camp, six million people had died.

"That's what we call a Bavarian Fire Drill," Simon explained to Joe. (It was another time; he was driving another Volkswagen. In fact, it was the night of April 23 and they were going to meet Tobias Knight at the UN building.) "It was one official named Winifred who'd been transferred from the Justice Department to a key State Department desk where every bit of evidence passed for evaluation. But the same principles apply everywhere. For instance—we're half an hour early for the meeting anyhow—I'll give you an illustration right now." They were approaching the corner of Forty-third Street and Third Avenue and Simon had observed that the streetlight was changing to red. As he stopped the car, he opened the door and said to Joe, "Follow me."

Puzzled, Joe got out as Simon ran to the car behind them, beat on the hood with his hand and shouted "Bavarian Fire Drill! Out!" He made vigorous but ambiguous motions with his hands and ran to the car next back. Joe saw the first subject look dubiously at his companion and then open the door and get out, obediently trailing behind Simon's urgent and somber figure.

"Bavarian Fire Drill! Out!" Simon was already shouting at the third car back.

As Joe trotted along, occasionally adding his own voice to persuade the more dubious drivers, every car gradually emptied and people formed a neat line heading back toward Lexington Avenue. Simon then ducked between two cars and began jogging toward the front of the line at Third Avenue again, shouting to everybody, "Complete circle! Stay in line!" Obediently, everyone followed in a great circle back to their own cars, reentering from the side opposite to that from which they had left. Simon and Joe climbed back into the VW, the light changed, and they sped ahead.

"You see?" Simon asked. "Use words they've been conditioned to since childhood—'fire drill,' 'stay in line,' like that—and never look back to see if they're obeying. They'll follow. Well, that's the way the Illuminati guaranteed that the Final Solution wouldn't be interrupted. Winifred, one guy who had been around long enough to have an impressive title, and his scrawl 'Evaluation: dubious' on the bottom of each memo . . . and six million died. Hilarious, isn't it?"

And Joe remembered from the little book by Hagbard Celine, *Never Whistle While You're Pissing* (privately printed, and distributed only to members of the JAMs and the Legion of Dynamic Discord): "The individual act of obedience is the cornerstone not only of the strength of authoritarian society but also of its weakness."

(On November 23, 1970, the body of Stanislaus Oedipuski, forty-six, of West Irving Park Road, was found floating in the Chicago river. Death, according to the police laboratory, did not result from drowning but from beating about the head and shoulders with a square-ended object. The first inquiries by homicide detectives revealed that Oedipuski had been a member of God's Lightning and the theory was formed that a conflict between the dead man and his former colleagues might have resulted in his being snuffed with their wooden crosses. Further investigation revealed that Oedipuski had been a construction worker and until very recently well liked on his job, behaving in a normal, down-to-earth manner, bitching about the government, cursing the lazy bums on Welfare, hating niggers, shouting obscene remarks at good-looking dolls who passed construction sites and—when the odds were safely above the 8-to-1 level—joining other middle-aged workers in attacking and beating young men with long hair, peace buttons, or other un-American stigmata. Then, about a month before, all that had changed. He began bitching about the bosses as well as the government—almost sounding like a communist at times; when somebody else cussed the crumb-bums on Welfare, Stan remarked thoughtfully, "Well, you know, our union keeps them from getting jobs, fellows, so what else can they do but go on Welfare? Steal?" He even said once, when some of the guys were good-humoredly giving the finger and making other gallant noises and signals toward a passing eighteen-year-old girl, "Hey, you know, that might really be embarrassing and scaring her . . . !" Worse yet, his own hair begun to grow surprisingly long in the back, and his wife told friends that he didn't look at TV much anymore but instead sat in a chair most evenings reading *books*. The police found that was indeed true, and his small library—gathered in less than a month—was remarkable indeed, featuring works on astronomy, sociology, Oriental mysticism, Darwin's *Origin of the Species*, detective novels by Raymond Chandler, *Alice in Wonderland,* and a college-level text on number theory with the section on primes heavily marked with notes in the margin; the gallant, and now pathetic, tracks of a mind that was beginning to grow after four decades of stagnation, and then had been abruptly stomped. Most mysterious of all was the card found in the dead man's pocket, which although waterlogged, could still be read. One side said

**THERE IS NO ENEMY
ANYWHERE**

and the other side, even more mysteriously, was inscribed:

–ΠΔ♀ ✳ΘΔ☉

The police might have tried to decipher this, but then they discovered that Oedipuski had resigned from God's Lightning—giving his fellow members a lecture on tolerance in the process—the night before his death. That closed the case, definitely. Homicide did not investigate murders clearly connected with God's Lightning, since the Red Squad had its own personal accommodation with that burgeoning organization. "Poor motherfucker," a detective said, looking at Oedipuski's photographs; and closed the file forever. Nobody ever reopened it, or traced the change in the dead man back to his attendance at the meeting, one month before, of KCUF at the Sheraton-Chicago, where the punch was spiked with AUM.)

> In the act of conception, of course, the father contributes 23 chromosomes and the mother contributes another 23. In the *I Ching*, hexagram 23 has connotations of "sinking" or "breaking apart," shades of the unfortunate Captain Clarks. . . .
> Another woman just came by, collecting for the Mothers March against Muscular Dystrophy. I gave her a quarter. Where was I? Oh, yes: James Joyce had five letters in both his front name and his hind name, so he was worth looking into. *A Portrait of the Artist* has five chapters, all well and good, but *Ulysses*

has 18 chapters, a stumper, until I remembered that
5 + 18 = 23. How about *Finnegans Wake?* Alas, that
has 17 chapters, and I was bogged down for a while.

Trying another angle, I wondered if Frank Sullivan, the poor cluck who got shot instead of John at
the Biograph Theatre that night, could have lingered
until after midnight, dying on July 23 instead of July
22 as usually stated. I looked it up in Toland's book,
The Dillinger Days. Poor Frank, sad to say, died before midnight, but Toland included an interesting detail, which I told you that night at the Seminary bar:
23 people died of heat prostration that day in Chicago. He added something else: 17 people had died of
heat prostration the day before. Why did he mention
that? I'm sure he doesn't know—but there it was
again, 23 and 17. Maybe something important is
going to happen in the year 2317? I couldn't check
that, of course (you can't navigate precisely in the
Morgensheutegesternwelt), so I went back to 1723,
and struck golden apples. That was the year Adam
Smith and Adam Weishaupt were both born (and
Smith published *The Wealth of Nations* the same
year Weishaupt revived the Illuminati: 1776.)

Well, 2 + 3 = 5, fitting the Law of Fives, but
1 + 7 = 8, fitting nothing. Where did that leave me?
Eight, I reflected, is the number of letters in Kallisti,
back to the golden apple again, and 8 is also 2^3, hot
damn. Naturally, it came as no surprise when the 8 defendants in the Chicago Conspiracy Trial, which grew
out of our little Convention Week Carnival, were tried
on the 23rd floor of the Federal Building, amid a flurry
of synchronicity—a Hoffman among the defendants, a
Hoffman as judge; the Illuminati pyramid, or Great
Seal of the U.S. right inside the door of the building.
and a Seale getting worse abuse than the other defendants; five-letter names and proliferating—Abbie,
Davis, Foran, Seale, Jerry Rubin (twice), and the
clincher, Clark (Ramsey, not Captain) who was tor-
pedoed and sunk by the judge before he could testify.

I got interested in Dutch Shultz because he died on
October 23. A cluster of synchronicity, that man: he
ordered the shooting of Vincent "Mad Dog" Coll
(remember Mad Dog, Texas); Coll was shot on 23rd
Street, when he was 23 years old; and Charlie Work-

man, who allegedly shot Schultz, served 23 years in prison for it (although rumor has it that Mendy Weiss—two five-letter names, again—did the real shooting.) Does 17 come in? You bet. Shultz was first sentenced to prison at the age of 17.

Around this time I bought Robert Heinlein's *The Puppet Masters,* thinking the plot might parallel some Illuminati operations. Imagine how I felt when Chapter Two began, "23 hours and 17 minutes ago, a flying saucer landed in Iowa . . ."

And, in New York, Peter Jackson is trying to get the next issue of *Confrontation* out on time—although the office is still a shambles, the editor and star researcher have disappeared, the best reporter has gone ape and claims to be at the bottom of the Atlantic with a wax tycoon, and the police are hounding Peter to find out why the first two detectives assigned to the case can't be located. Sitting in his apartment (now the magazine's office) in his shirt and shorts, Peter dials his phone with one hand, adding another crushed cigarette to the pile in the ashtray with the other. Throwing a manuscript onto a basket marked "Ready for Printer," he crosses off "lead article—The Youngest Student Ever Admitted to Columbia Tells Why He Dropped Out by L. L. Durrutti" from a list on the pad before him. His pencil moves down to the bottom, "Book Review," as he listens to the phone ring. Finally, he hears the click of a lifted receiver and a rich, flutey voice says, "Epicene Wildeblood here."

"Got your book review ready, Eppy?"

"Have it tomorrow, dear boy. Can't be any faster, *honestly!*"

"Tomorrow will do," Peter says writing *call again*—A.M. next to "Book Review."

"It's a dreadfully long monster of a book," Wildeblood says pettishly, "and I certainly won't have time to read it, but I'm giving it a thorough *skimming.* The authors are utterly incompetent—no sense of style or structure at all. It starts out as a detective story, switches to science-fiction, then goes off into the supernatural, and is full of the most detailed information of dozens of *ghastly* boring subjects. And the time sequence is all out of order in a very pretentious imitation of Faulkner and Joyce. Worst yet, it has the most raunchy sex scenes, thrown in just to make it sell,

I'm sure, and the authors—whom I've *never* heard of—have the supreme bad taste to introduce real political figures into this mishmash and pretend to be exposing a real conspiracy. You can be *sure* I won't waste time reading such rubbish, but I'll have a perfectly devastating review ready for you by tomorrow noon."

"Well, we don't expect you to read every book you review," Peter says mollifyingly, "just so long as you can be entertaining about them."

"The Foot Fetishist Liberation Front will be participating in the rally at the UN building," Joe Malik said, as George and Peter and he were affixing their black armbands.

"Christ," Jackson said disgustedly.

"We can't afford to take that attitude," Joe said severely. "The only hope for the Left at this time is coalition politics. We can't exclude anybody who wants to join us."

"I've got nothing against faggots personally," Peter begins ("Gays," Joe says patiently). "I've got nothing against Gays personally," Peter goes on, "but they are a bringdown at rallies. They just give God's Lightning more evidence to say we're all a bunch of fruits. But, OK, realism is realism, there are a lot of them, and they swell our ranks, and all that, but, Jesus, Joe. These *toe freaks* are a splinter within a splinter. They're microscopic."

"Don't call them toe freaks," Joe says. "They don't like that."

A woman from the Mothers March Against Psoriasis just came by with another collection box. I gave her a quarter, too. The marching mothers are going to strip Moon of his bread if this keeps up.

Where was I? I meant to add, in relation to the Dutch Shultz shooting that Marty Krompier, who ran the policy racket in Harlem, was also shot on October 23, 1935. The police asked him if there was a connection with phlegmatic Flegenheimer's demise and he said, "It's got to be one of them coincidences." I wonder how he emphasized that—"one of them *coincidences*" or "one of *them* coincidences"? How much did he know?

That brings me to the 40 enigma. As pointed out, 1 + 7 = 8, the number of letters in Kallisti. 8 x 5 = 40.

More interestingly, without invoking the mystic 5, we still arrive at 40 by adding 17 + 23. What, then, is the significance of 40? I've run through various associations—Jesus had his 40 days in the desert, Ali Baba had his 40 thieves, Buddhists have their 40 meditations, the solar system is almost exactly 40 astronomical units in radius (Pluto yo-yos a bit)—but I have no definite theory yet. . . .

The color television set in the Three Lions Pub in the Tudor Hotel at Forty-second Street and Second Avenue shows the white-helmeted men carrying wooden crosses fall back as the blue-helmeted men carrying billy clubs move forward. The CBS camera pans over the plaza. There are five bodies on the ground scattered like flotsam tossed on a beach by a receding wave. Four of them are moving, making slow efforts to get up. The fifth is not moving at all.

George said, "I think that's the guy we saw getting clubbed. My God, I hope he isn't dead."

Joe Malik said, "If he is dead, it may get people to demand that something be done about God's Lightning."

Peter Jackson laughed mirthlessly. "You still think some honky peacenik getting killed is going to make people indignant. Don't you understand, nobody in this country *cares* what happens to a peace freak. You're in the same boat with the niggers now, you silly sons-of-bitches."

Carlos looked up in astonishment as I burst into the room, still wet from the Passaic, and threw the gun at his feet, screaming, "You silly sons-of-bitches, you can't even make bombs without blowing yourselves up, and when you buy a gun the motherfucker is defective and misfires. You can't expel me—I quit!" You silly sons-of-bitches. . . .

"You silly sons-of-bitches!" Simon shouted. Joe woke as the VW swerved amid a flurry of Hell's Angels bike roaring by. He was back in "real" time again—but the word had quotes around it, in his mind, now, and it always would.

"Wow," he said, "I was in Chicago again, and then at that rock festival . . . and then I was in somebody else's lifeline. . . ."

"Goddam Harley-Davidsons," Simon mutters as the last Angel thunders by. "When fifty or sixty of them swarm by like that, it's as bad as trying to drive on the sidewalk in

Times Square at high noon without hitting a pedestrian."

"Later-for-that," Joe said, conscious of his growing ease in using Simon's own language. "This tomorrow-today-yesterday time is beginning to get under my skin. It's happening more and more often. . . ."

Simon sighed, "You want words to put around it. You can't accept it until it has labels dangling off it, like a new suit. OK. And your favorite word-game is science. Fine, right on! Tomorrow we'll drop by the Main Library and you can look up the English science journal *Nature* for Summer nineteen sixty-six. There's an article in there by the University College physicist F. R. Stannard about what he calls the Faustian Universe. He tells how the behavior of K-mesons can't be explained assuming a one-way time-track, but fits into a neat pattern if you assume our universe overlaps another where time runs in the opposite direction. He calls it the Faustian universe, but I'll bet he has no idea that Goethe wrote *Faust* after experiencing that universe directly, just as you're doing lately. Incidentally, Stannard points out that everything in physics is symmetrical, except our present concept of one-way time. Once you admit two-way time traffic, you've got a completely symmetrical universe. Fits the Occamite's demand for simplicity. Stannard'll give you lots of *words*, man. Meanwhile, just settle for what Abdul Alhazred wrote in the *Necronomicon:* 'Past, present, future: all are one in Yog-Sothoth.' Or what Weishaupt wrote in his *Konigen, Kirchen und Dummheit:* 'There is but one Eye and it is all eyes; one Mind and it is all minds; one time and it is Now.' Grok?" Joe nods dubiously, faintly hearing the music:

RAMA   RAMA   RAMA   HAAAAARE
Two big rhinoceroses, three big rhinoceroses . . .

Dillinger made contact with the mind of Richard Belz, forty-three-year-old professor of physics at Queens College, as Belz was being loaded into an ambulance to be taken to Bellevue Hospital where X rays would reveal severe skull fractures. Shit, Dillinger thought, why does somebody have to be half dead before I can reach him? Then he concentrated on his message: Two universes flowing in opposite directions. Two together form a third entity which is synergetically more than the sum of its two parts. Thus two always leads to three. Two and Three. Duality and trinity. Every unity is a duality and a trinity. A pentagon. Sheer energy, no matter involved. From the pentagon depend five more pentagons, like the petals of a flower. A white rose. Five petals and a center: six. Two times three. The flower interlocks with another flower just like it, forming a polyhedron made of pentagons. Each such polyhedron could have common surfaces with other polyhedrons, forming infinite latticeworks based on the pentagonal unit. They would be immortal. Self-sustaining. Not computers. Beyond computers. Gods. All space for their habitation. Infinitely complex.

The howl of a siren reached the unconscious ears of Professor Belz. Consciousness is present in the living body, even in one that is apparently unconscious. Unconsciousness is not the absence of consciousness, but its temporary immobility. It is not a state resembling death. It is not like death at all. Once the necessary complexity of brain-cell interconnections is reached, substantial energy relationships are set up. These can exist independently of the material base that brought them into being.

All of this, of course, is merely visual structural metaphor for interactions on the energy level that cannot be visualized. The siren howled.

In the Three Lions pub, George said to Peter, "What was in that water pistol?"

"Sulphuric acid."

"Acid is just the first stage," said Simon. "Like matter is the first stage of life and consciousness. Acid launches you. But once you're out there, if the mission is successful, you jettison the first stage and you're traveling free of gravity. Which means free of matter. Acid dissolves the barriers which prevent the maximum possible complexity of energy relationships from building up in the brain. At Norton Cabal, we'll show you how to pilot the second stage."

(*Waving their crosses over their heads and howling incoherently, the men of God's Lightning formed wavering ranks and marched around the territory they had conquered. Zev Hirsch and Frank Ochuk carried the banner that read* "LOVE IT OR WE'LL STOMP YOU.")

Howard sang:

> The tribes of the porpoise are fearless and strong
> Our land is the ocean, our banner's a song
> Our weapon is speed and our noses like rock
> No foe can withstand our terrible shock.

A cloud of porpoise bodies swam out from somewhere behind Hagbard's submarine. Through the pale blue-green medium which Hagbard's TV cameras made out of water, they seemed to fly toward the distant spiderlike ships of the Illuminati.

"What's happening?" said George. "Where's Howard?"

"Howard is leading them," said Hagbard. He flipped a toggle on the railing of the balcony on which they stood in the center of a globe that looked like a bubble of air at the bottom of the Atlantic Ocean. "War room, get missiles ready. We may have to back up the porpoise attack."

"*Da, tovarish Celine,*" came a voice.

The porpoises were too far away to be seen now. George discovered that he was not afraid. The whole thing was too much like watching a science-fiction movie. There was too much illusion involved in this submarine of Hagbard's. If he were able to realize, in his glands and nerves, that he was in a vulnerable metal ship thousands of feet below the surface of the Atlantic, under such enormous pressure that the slightest stress could crack the hull and send water bursting in that would crush them to death, then he might be afraid. If he were really able to accept the fact that those little distant globes with waving legs appended to them were undersea craft manned by people who intended to destroy the vessel he was in, then he could be afraid. Actually, if he could not see as much as he was seeing, but only feel and sense things and be told what was happening, as in the average airplane flight, then he would be afraid. As it was, the 20,000-year-old city of Peos looked like a tabletop model. And though he might intellectually accept Hagbard's statement that they were over the lost continent of Atlantis, in his bones he didn't believe in Atlantis. As a result, he didn't believe in any of the rest of this, either.

Suddenly Howard was outside their bubble. Or some other porpoise. That was another thing that made this hard to accept. Talking porpoises.

"Ready for destruction of enemy ships," said Howard.

Hagbard shook his head. "I wish we could communicate with them. I wish I could give them a chance to surrender. But they wouldn't listen. And they have communications systems on their ships that I can't get through to." He turned to George. "They use a type of insulated telepathy to communicate. The very thing that tipped off Sheriff Jim

Cartwright that you were in a hotel room in Mad Dog smoking Weishaupt's Wonder Weed."

"You don't want them too close when they go." said Howard.

"Are your people out of the way?" said Hagbard.

(Five big rhinoceroses, six big rhinoceroses. . . .)

"Of course. Quit this hesitating. This is no time to be a humanitarian."

"The sea is crueler than the land," said Hagbard, "sometimes."

"The sea is cleaner than the land," said Howard. "There's no hate. Just death when and as needed. These people have been your enemies for twenty thousand years."

"I'm not that old," said Hagbard, "and I have very few enemies."

"If you wait any longer you'll endanger the submarine and my people."

George looked out at the red and white striped globes which were moving toward them through the blue-green water. They were much larger now and closer. Whatever was propelling them wasn't visible. Hagbard reached out a brown finger, let it rest on a white button on the railing in front of him, then pressed it decisively.

There was a bright flash of light, dimmed slightly by the medium through which it traveled, on the surface of each of the globes. It was like watching fireworks through tinted glasses. Next, the globes crumbled as if they were ping-pong balls being struck by invisible sledge hammers.

"That's all there is to it," said Hagbard quietly.

The air around George seemed to vibrate, and the floor under him shook. Suddenly he was terrified. Feeling the shock wave from the simultaneous explosions out there in the water made it real. A relatively thin metal shell was all that protected him from total annihilation. And nobody would ever hear from him or know what happened to him.

Large, glittering objects drifted down through the water from one of the nearby Illuminati spider ships. They vanished among the streets of the city that George now knew was real. The buildings in the area near the explosion of the Illuminati ships looked more ruined than they had before. The ocean bottom was churned up in brown clouds. Down into the brown clouds drifted the crushed spider ships. George looked for the Temple of Tethys. It stood, intact, in the distance.

"Did you see those statues fall out of the lead ship?" said Hagbard. "I'm claiming them." He hit the switch on the railing. "Prepare for salvage operation."

They dropped down among buildings deeply buried in sediment, and at the bottom of their television globe George saw two huge claws reach out, seemingly from nowhere—actually he guessed, from the underside of the submarine—and pick up four gleaming gold statues that lay half-buried in the mud.

Suddenly a bell rang and a red flash lit up the interior of the bubble. "We're under attack again," said Hagbard. Oh, no, George thought. Not when I'm starting to believe that all this is real. I won't be able to stand it. Here goes Dorn doing his world-famous coward act again. . . . Hagbard pointed. A white globe hovered like an underwater moon above a distant range of mountains. On its pale surface a red emblem was painted, a glaring eye inside a triangle.

"Give me missile visibility," said Hagbard, flicking a switch. Between the white globe and the *Lief Erickson* four orange lights appeared in the water rushing toward them.

"It just doesn't pay to underestimate them—ever," said Hagbard. "First it turns out they can detect me when they shouldn't have equipment good enough to do that, now I find that not only do they have small craft in the vicinity, they've got the *Zwack* herself coming after me. And the *Zwack* is firing underwater missiles at me, though I'm supposed to be indetectable. I think we might be in trouble, George."

George wanted to close his eyes, but he also didn't want to show fear in front of Hagbard. He wondered what death at the bottom of the Atlantic would feel like. Probably something like being under a pile driver. The water would hit them, engulf them, and it wouldn't be like any ordinary water—it would be like liquid steel, every drop striking with the force of a ten-ton truck, prying cell apart from cell and crushing each cell individually, reducing the body to a protoplasmic dishrag. He remembered reading about the disappearance of an atomic submarine called the *Thresher* back in the '60s, and he recalled that the *New*

York Times had speculated that death by drowning in water under extreme pressure would be exceedingly painful, though brief. Every nerve individually being crushed. The spinal cord crushed everywhere along its length. The brain squeezed to death, bursting, rupturing, bleeding into the steel-hard water. The human form would doubtless be unrecognizable in minutes. George thought of every bug he had ever stepped on, and bugs made him think of the spider ships. That's what we did to *them*. And I define them as enemies only on Hagbard's say so. Carlo was right. I can't kill.

Hagbard hesitated, didn't he? Yes, but he did it. Any man who can cause a death like that to be visited upon other men is a monster. No, not a monster, only too human. But not my kind of human. Shit, George, he's your kind of human, all right. You're just a coward. Cowardice doth make consciences for us all.

Hagbard called out, "Howard, where the hell are you?"

The torpedo shape appeared on the right side of the bubble. "Over here, Hagbard. We've got more mines ready. We can go after those missiles with mines like we did the spider ships. Think that would work?"

"It's dangerous," said Hagbard, "because the missiles might explode on contact with the metal and electronic equipment in the mines."

"We're willing to try," said Howard, and without another word he swam away.

"Wait a minute," Hagbard said. "I don't like this. There's too much danger to the porpoises." He turned to George and shook his head. "I'm not risking a goddamned thing, and they stand to be blown to bits. It's not right. I'm not that important."

"You are risking something," said George, trying to control the quaver in his voice. "Those missiles will destroy us if the dolphins don't stop them."

At that moment, there were four blinding flashes where the orange lights had been. George gripped the railing, sensing that the shock wave of these explosions would be worse than that caused by the destruction of the spider ships. It came. George had been readying himself for it, but unable to tell when it would come, and it still took him by surprise. Everything shook violently. Then the bottom dropped out of his stomach, as if the submarine had suddenly leaped up. George grabbed the railing with both arms, clinging to it as the only solid thing near him. "O God, we're gonna be killed!" he cried.

"They got the missiles," Hagbard said. "That gives us a fighting chance. Laser crew, attempt to puncture the *Zwack*. Fire at will.

Howard reappeared outside the bubble. "How did your people do?" Hagbard asked him.

"All four of them were killed," said Howard. "The missiles exploded when they approached them, just as you predicted."

George, who was standing up straight now, thankful that Hagbard had simply ignored his episode of terror, said, "They were killed saving our lives. I'm sorry it happened, Howard."

"Laser-beam firing, Hagbard," a voice announced. There was a pause. "I think we hit them."

"You needn't be sorry," said Howard. "We neither look forward to death in fear nor back upon it in sorrow. Especially when someone has died doing something worthwhile. Death is the end of one illusion and the beginning of another."

"What other illusion?" asked George. "When you're dead, you're dead, right?"

"Energy can neither be created nor destroyed," said Hagbard. "Death itself is an illusion."

These people were talking like some of the Zen students and acid mystics George had known. If I could feel that way, he thought, I wouldn't be such a goddamned coward. Howard and Hagbard must be enlightened. I've got to become enlightened. I can't stand living this way any more. Whatever it took, acid alone wasn't the answer. George had tried acid already, and he knew that, while the experience might be wholly remarkable, for him it left little residue in terms of changed attitudes or behavior. Of course, if you *thought* your attitudes and behavior should change, you mimicked other acidheads.

"I'll try to find out what's happening to the *Zwack*," said Howard, and swam away.

"The porpoises do not fear death, they do not avoid suffering, they are not assailed by conflicts between intellect and feeling and they are not worried about being ignorant of things. In other words, they have not decided that they

know the difference between good and evil, and in consequence they do not consider themselves sinners. Understand?"

"Very few humans consider themselves sinners
nowadays," said George. "But everyone is afraid of
death."

"All human beings consider themselves sinners. It's just
about the deepest, oldest, and most universal human hangup there is. In fact, it's almost impossible to speak of it in
terms that don't confirm it. To say that human beings have
a universal hangup, as I just did, is to restate the belief
that all men are sinners in different languages. In that
sense, the Book of Genesis—which was written by early
Semitic opponents of the Illuminati—is quite right. To arrive at a cultural turning point where you decide that all
human conduct can be classified in one of two categories,
good and evil, is what creates all sin—plus anxiety, hatred,
guilt, depression, all the peculiarly human emotions. And,
of course, such a classification is the very antithesis of
creativity. To the creative mind there is no right or wrong.
Every action is an experiment, and every experiment yields
its fruit in knowledge. To the moralist, every action can be
judged as right or wrong—and, mind you, *in advance*—
without knowing what its consequences are going to be—
depending upon the mental disposition of the actor. Thus
the men who burned Giordano Bruno at the stake *knew*
they were doing good, even though the consequence of
their actions was to deprive the world of a great scientist."

"If you can never be sure whether what you are doing is
good or bad," said George, "aren't you liable to be pretty
Hamlet-like?" He was feeling much better now, much less
afraid, even though the enemy was still presumably out
there trying to kill him. Maybe he was getting *darshan*
from Hagbard.

"What's so bad about being Hamlet-like?" said Hagbard.
"Anyway, the answer is no, because you only become hesi-
tant when you believe there is such a thing as good and
evil, and that your action may be one or the other, and
you're not sure which. That was the whole point about
Hamlet, if you remember the play. It was his *conscience*
that made him indecisive."

"So he should have murdered a whole lot of people in
the first act?"

Hagbard laughed. "Not necessarily. He might have decisively killed his uncle at the earliest opportunity, thus saving the lives of everyone else. Or he might have said, 'Hey, am I really obligated to avenge my father's death?' and done nothing. He was due to succeed to the throne anyway. If he had just bided his time everyone would have been a lot better off, there would have been no deaths, and the Norwegians would not have conquered the Danes, as they did in the last scene of the last act. Though being Norwegian myself I would hardly begrudge Fortinbras his triumph."

At that moment Howard appeared again outside their bubble. "The *Zwack* is retreating. Your laser beam punctured the outer shell, causing a leak in the fuel-storage cells and putting excessive stress on the pressure-resisting system. They were forced to climb to higher levels, which put them so far away from you that they're now heading south toward the tip of Africa."

Hagbard expelled a great sigh of relief. "That means they're heading for their home base. They'll enter a tunnel in the Persian Gulf which will bring them into the great underground Sea of Valusia, which is deepest beneath the Himalayas. That was the first base they established. They were preparing it even before the fall of High Atlantis. It's devilishly well defended. One day we'll penetrate it though."

The thing that puzzled Joe most after his illuminization was John Dillinger's penis. The rumors about the Smithsonian Institute, he knew, were true: even though any casual phone-caller would get a flat denial from Institute officials, certain high-placed government people could provide a dispensation and the relic would be shown, in the legendary alcohol bottle, all legendary 23 inches of it. But if John was alive, it wasn't his, and, if it wasn't his, whose was it?

"Frank Sullivan's," Simon said, when Joe finally asked him.

"And who the hell was Frank Sullivan to have a tool like that?"

But Simon only answered, "I don't know. Just some guy who looked like John."

Atlantis also bothered Joe, after he saw it the first time Hagbard took him for a ride in the *Lief Erikson*. It was all too pat, too plausible, too good to be true, especially the ruins of cities like Peos, with their architecture that obviously combined Egyptian and Mayan elements.

"Science has been flying on instruments, like a pilot in a fog, ever since nineteen hundred," he said casually to Hagbard on the return trip to New York. (This was in '72, according to his later recollections. Fall of '72—almost two years exactly after the test of AUM in Chicago.)

"You've been reading Bucky Fuller," was Hagbard's cool reply. "Or was it Korzybski?"

"Never mind who I've been reading," Joe said directly. "The thought in my head is that I never saw Atlantis, any more than I ever saw Marilyn Monroe. I saw moving pictures which you told me were television reception of cameras outside your sub. And I saw moving pictures of what Hollywood assured me was a real woman, even though she looked more like a design by Petty or Vargas. In the Marilyn Monroe case, it is reasonable to believe what I am told: I don't believe a robot that good has been built yet. But Atlantis . . . I know special-effects men who could build a city like that on a tabletop, and have dinosaurs walking through it. And your cameras trained on it."

"You suspect me of trickery?" Hagbard asked raising his eyebrows.

"Trickery is your metier," Joe said bluntly. "You are the Beethoven, the Rockefeller, the Michelangelo of deception. The Shakespeare of the gypsy switch, the two-headed nickel, and the rabbit in the hat. What little liver pills are to Carter, lies are to you. You dwell in a world of trapdoors, sliding panels, and Hindu ropetricks. Do I suspect you? Since I met you, I suspect *everybody.*"

"I'm glad to hear it," Hagbard grinned. "You are well on your way to paranoia. Take this card and keep it in your wallet. When you begin to understand it, you'll be ready for your next promotion. Just remember: *it's not true unless it makes you laugh.* That is the one and sole and infallible test of all ideas that will ever be presented to you." And he handed Joe a card saying

THERE IS NO FRIEND

ANYWHERE

Burroughs, incidentally, although he discovered the 23 synchronicity principle, is unaware of the correlation with 17. This makes it even more interesting that his date for the invasion of earth by the Nova Mob (in *Nova Express)* is September 17, 1899. When I asked him how he picked that date, he said it just came to him out of the air.

Damn. I was just interrupted by another woman, collecting for the Mothers March Against Hernia. I only gave her a dime.

W, the 23rd letter, keeps popping up in all this. Note: Weishaupt, Washington, William S. Burroughs, Charlie Workman, Mendy Weiss, Len Weinglass in the Conspiracy Trial, and others who will quickly come to mind. Even more interesting, the first physicist to apply the concept of synchronicity to physics, after Jung published the theory, was Wolfgang Pauli.

Another suggestive letter-number transformation: Adam Weishaupt (A.W.) is 1-23, and George Washington (G.W.) is 7-23. Spot the hidden 17 in there? But, perhaps, I grow too imaginative, even whimsical. . . .

There was a click. George turned. All the time he'd been in the control center with Hagbard, he had never looked back at the door through which he had come. He was surprised to see that it looked like an opening in thin air—or thin water. On either side of the doorway was blue-green water and a dark horizon which was actually the ocean bottom. Then, in the center, the doorway itself and a golden light silhouetting the figure of a beautiful woman.

Mavis strode onto the balcony, pulling the door shut behind her. She was wearing forest-green tights with white patent leather boots and a wide white belt. Her small but well-shaped breasts jiggled naturally under her blouse. George found himself thinking back to the scene on the beach. That was only this morning, and what time was it anyway? What time where? Back in Florida it was probably two or three in the afternoon. Which would make it one P.M. in Mad Dog, Texas. And probably about six out here in the Atlantic. Did time zones extend beneath the water? He supposed they did. On the other hand, if you were at the North Pole, you could skip around the Pole and be in a different time zone every few seconds. And cross the International Date Line every five minutes if you wanted to. Which would not, he reminded himself, make it possible to travel in time. But if he could go back to this morning and replay Mavis's demand for sex, this time he would respond! He now wanted her desperately.

Well and good, but why did she say he was *not* a schmuck, why did she imply admiration for him because he would not fuck her? If he had fucked her because she asked him and he felt he should but without wanting to, he would have been a pure and simple schmuck. But he could have pronged her simply because she would have been nice to fuck, regardless of whether she would have admired him or despised him. But that was their game—Mavis's and Hagbard's game of saying I do what I want to do, and I don't give a damn what you think. George cared a great deal about what other people thought, so not fucking Mavis at the time was at least honest, even if he was beginning to see some merit in the Discordian (he supposed it was Discordian) attitude of super self-sufficiency.

Mavis smiled at him. "Well, George, had your baptism of fire?"

George shrugged. "Well, there was the Mad Dog jail. And I've been in a few other bad scenes." For instance, there was the time I held a pistol to my head and pulled the trigger.

She'd sucked his cock, he'd watched her in manic manustupration, but he was desperate to get inside her, all the way, up the womb, riding her ovarian trolley to the wonderful land of fuck, as Henry Miller said. What the hell was so special about Mavis's cunt? Especially after that induction ceremony scene. Hell, Stella Maris seemed like a less neurotic woman and was certainly a classic lay. After Stella Maris, who needed Mavis?

A sudden question struck him. How did he know he'd laid Stella? It could have been Mavis inside that golden apple. It could have been some woman he'd never met. He was pretty sure it was a woman, unless it was a goat or a cow or a sheep. Best not put that kind of joke past Hagbard either. But even if it was a woman, why visualize Stella or Mavis or somebody like them? It was probably some diseased old Etruscan whore that Hagbard kept around for religious purposes. Some Sibyl. Some wop witch. Maybe it was Hagbard's rotten old Sicilian mother with no teeth, a black shawl, and three kinds of VD. No, it was Hagbard's father who was Sicilian. His mother was Norwegian.

"What color were they?" he said suddenly to Hagbard.

"Who?"

"The Atlanteans."

"Oh." Hagbard nodded. "They were covered with fur over most of their bodies, like any normal ape. At least, the High Atlanteans were. A mutation occurred around the time of the Hour of the Evil Eye—the catastrophe that destroyed High Atlantis. Later Atlanteans, like modern humans, were hairless. Those of the oldest Atlantean ancestry tend to be rather furry." George couldn't help looking down at Hagbard's hand as it rested on the railing. It was covered with thick black hair.

"All right," said Hagbard, "it's time to head back to our North American base. Howard? You out there?"

The long, streamlined shape performed a somersault on their right. "What's happening, Hagbard?"

"Have some of your people keep an eye on things here. We've got work to do on land. And—Howard, as long as I live I will be in debt to your people for the four who died to save me."

"Haven't you and the *Lief Erickson* saved us from several kinds of deaths planned for us by the shore people?" said Howard. "We'll keep watch over Atlantis for you. And the seas in general, and that which Atlantis has spawned. Hail and farewell, Hagbard and other friends—

> "The sea is wide and the sea is deep
> But warm as blood through it there rolls
> A tide of friendship that will keep
> Us close in Ocean's blackest holes."

He was gone. "Lift off," Hagbard called. George felt the surge of the sub's colossal engines, and they were sailing high above the hills and valleys of Atlantis. With the special lighting of Hagbard's television screen system, it seemed much like flying in a jet plane over one of the continents above the ocean's surface.

"Too bad we don't have time to get deeper into Atlantis," said Hagbard. "There are many mighty cities to see. Though of course none of them can approach the cities that existed before the Hour of the Evil Eye."

"How many of these Atlantean civilizations were there?" asked George.

"Basically, two. One leading up to the Hour, and one afterward. Before the Hour, there was a civilization of about a million human beings on this continent. Technically, they were further advanced than the human race is today. They had atomic power, space travel, genetic technology and much else. This civilization was struck a death blow in the Hour of the Evil Eye. Two-thirds of them were killed —almost half the human population of the planet at that time. After the Hour, something made it impossible for them to make a comeback. The cities that came through the first catastrophe relatively undamaged were destroyed in later disasters. The inhabitants of Atlantis were reduced to savagery in a generation. Part of the continent sank under the sea, which was the beginning of the process that ended when all of Atlantis was under water, as it is today."

"Was this the earthquakes and tidal waves that you always read about?" George asked.

"No," said Hagbard with a curious closed expression. "It was manmade. High Atlantis was destroyed in a kind of war. Probably a civil war, since there was no other power on the planet that could have matched them."

"Anyway, if there'd been a victor, they'd still be around now," said George.

"They are," said Mavis. "The victors are still around. Only they're not what you might visualize. Not a conquering nation. And we are the descendants of the defeated."

"Now," said Hagbard, "I'm going to show you something I promised when we first met. It has to do with the catastrophe I've been talking about. Look there."

The submarine had risen high above the continent, and it was possible to see landscapes stretching for hundreds of miles. Looking in the direction in which Hagbard pointed, George saw a vast expanse of black, glazed plain. Out of its center jutted something white and pointed, like a canine tooth.

"It is said of them that they even controlled the comets in their courses." said Hagbard. He pointed again.

The submarine sailed closer to the jutting white object. It was a four-sided white pyramid.

"Don't say it," said Mavis, giving him a warning look, and George remembered the tattoo he had seen between her breasts. He looked down again. They were above the pyramid now and George could see the side that had been hidden from him as they approached. He saw what he had half-feared, half-expected to see: a blood-red design in the shape of a baleful eye.

"The Pyramid of the Eye," Hagbard said. "It stood in the center of the capital of High Atlantis. It was built in the last days of that civilization by the founders of the world's first religion. It doesn't look very big from up here, but it's five times the size of the Great Pyramid of Cheops, which was modeled after it. It's made of an imperishable ceramic substance which repels even ocean sediment. As if the builders knew that to last it would have to survive tens of thousands of years of ocean burial. And maybe—depending on who they were—they did know that. Or maybe they just built well in those days. Peos, as you saw, was a pretty durable city, and that was built after High Atlantis fell, by the second civilization I spoke of. That second civilization reached a level somewhat more advanced than that of the Greeks and Romans, but it was nothing like its predecessor. And some malevolent force seemed bent on destroying it, too, and it was destroyed, about ten thousand years ago. Of that civilization we have the evidence of ruins. But of High Atlantis we have only records and legends dug up from the later civilization—and, of course, poetry from the Porpoise Corpus. This is the only artifact, this pyramid. But its existence and durability prove that as long ago as ten Egypts, a race of men existed whose technology was far advanced beyond what we know today. So advanced that it took twenty thousand years for that civilization's successor culture to disappear completely. The men who destroyed High Atlantis did their best to make it disappear. But they couldn't quite manage it. The Pyramid of the Eye, for instance, is indestructible. Though it's probable that they didn't want to destroy it."

Mavis nodded sombrely. "That is their most sacred shrine."

"In other words," said George, "you're telling me that the people who destroyed Atlantis still exist. Do they have the powers they had then?"

"Substantially, yes," said Hagbard.

"Is this the Illuminati you told me about?"

"Illuminati, or Ancient Illuminated Seers of Bavaria is one of the names they have used, yes."

"So they didn't start in seventeen seventy-six—they go a long way back before that, right?"

"Right," said Mavis.

"Then why did you lie to me about their history? And why the hell haven't they taken over the world by now, if they're all that powerful? When our ancestors were savages, they could have dominated them completely."

Hagbard replied, "I lied to you because the human mind can only accept a little of the truth at a time. Also, initiation into Discordianism has stages. The answer to the other question is complicated. But I'll try to give it to you simply. There are five reasons. First, there are organizations like the Discordians which are almost as powerful and which know almost as much as the Illuminati and which are able to thwart them. Second, the Illuminati are too small a group to enjoy the creative cross-fertilization necessary to progress of any kind, and they have been unable to advance much beyond the technological level they reached thirty thousand years ago. Like Chinese Mandarins. Third, the Illuminati are hamstrung in their actions by the superstitious beliefs that set them apart from the other Atlanteans. As I told you, they're the world's first religion. Fourth, the Illuminati are too sophisticated, ruthless and decadent to want to take over the world—it amuses them to *play* with world. Fifth, the Illuminati *do* rule the world and everything that happens, happens by their sufferance."

"Those reasons contradict each other," said George.

"That's the nature of logical thought. All propositions are true in some sense, false in some sense and meaningless in some sense." Hagbard didn't smile.

The submarine had described a great arc as they talked and now the Pyramid of the Eye was far behind them. The eye itself, since it faced eastward, was no longer visible. Below, George could see the ruins of several small cities at the edges of tall cliffs that fell away into darker depths—cliffs that doubtless had been the seacoast of Atlantis at one time.

Hagbard said, "I've got a job for you, George. You're going to like it, and you're going to want to do it, but it is going to make you shit a brick. We'll talk about it when we get to Chesapeake Base. Now, though, let's go down into the hold and have a look at our acquisitions." He flicked a switch. "FUCKUP, get your finger out of your ass and drive this thing for a while."

"I'll see the statues later," said Mavis. "I've got other things to do just now."

George followed Hagbard down carpeted staircases and halls paneled in glowing, polished oak. At last they came to a large hall which was apparently paved with marble flagstones. A group of men and women wearing horizontally striped nautical shirts similar to Hagbard's were clustered around four tall statues in the center of the room. When Hagbard entered the room they stopped talking and stepped away to give him a clear look at the sculptures. The floor was covered with puddles of water and the statues themselves were dripping.

"No wiping them dry," Hagbard said. "Every molecule is precious just as it is, and the less disturbed the better." He stepped closer to the nearest one and looked at it for a long moment. "What do you say about a thing like this? It's beyond exquisite. Can you imagine what their art was like *before* the disaster? And to think the Unbroken Circle destroyed every trace of it, except for that crude, stupid pyramid."

"Which is the greatest piece of ceramic technology in the history of the human race," said one of the women. George looked around for Stella Maris, but she wasn't there.

"Where's Stella?" he asked Hagbard.

"Upstairs minding the store. She'll see them later."

The sculptures were unlike the work of any culture George knew, which was to be expected, after all. They were at once realistic, fanciful and abstractly intellectual. They bore resemblance to Egyptian and Mayan, Classical Greek, Chinese and Gothic, combined with a surprisingly modern-looking note. There were some qualities in the statues that were totally unique, though, qualities doubtless lost by the civilizations to which Atlantis was ancestral, but that might have been found in known world art, had there been other civilizations to preserve and emphasize them. This, George realized, was the Ur-Art; and looking at the statues was like hearing a sentence in the first language spoken by men.

An elderly sailor pointed at the statue farthest from where they were standing. "Look at that beatific smile. A woman thought of that statue, I'll bet. That's every woman's dream—to be totally self-sufficient."

"Some of the time, Joshua," said the Oriental woman who had spoken before, "but not all of the time. Now what I prefer is that." She pointed to another statue.

Hagbard laughed. "You think that's just nice, healthy oragenitalism, Tsu-Hsi. But the child in the woman's arms is the Son Without a Father, the Self-Begotten, and the couple at the base represent the Unbroken Circle of Gruad. Usually it's a serpent with its tail in its mouth, but in some of the earlier representations the couple in oral intercourse symbolizes sterile lust. The Unloved Mother has her foot on the man's head to indicate that she conquers lust. The whole sculpture is the product of the foulest cult to come out of Atlantis. They originated human sacrifice. First they practiced castration, but then they escalated to killing men instead of just cutting off their balls. Later, when women were subjugated, the sacrifice became a virgin female, supposedly to give her to the Unloved Ones while she was still pure."

"That halo around the child's head looks like the peace symbol," said George.

"Peace symbol, my ass," said Hagbard. "That's the oldest symbol of evil there is. Of course, in the cult of the Unbroken Circle it was a symbol of good, but that's the same difference."

"They can't have been so vicious if they produced that statue," said the Oriental woman stubbornly.

"Could you deduce the Spanish Inquisition from a painting of the manger at Bethlehem?" said Hagbard. "Don't be naive, Miss Mao." He turned to George, "The value of any one of these statues is beyond calculation. But not many people know that. I'm sending you to one who does—Robert Putney Drake. One of the finest art connoisseurs in the world, and the head of the American branch of the world crime syndicate. You're going to see him with a gift from me—these four statues. The Illuminati were planning to buy his support with gold from the Temple of Tethys. I'm going to get to him first."

"If they only needed four statues, why were they trying to raise the whole temple?" George asked.

"I think they wanted to remove the temple to Agharti, their stronghold under the Himalayas, for safekeeping. I haven't been any closer to the Temple of Tethys than we were today, but I suspect it's a treasure-house of evidence of High Atlantis. As such, it would be something the Illuminati would want to remove. Until now there was no reason to, because no one had access to the seabottom other than the Illuminati. Now I can get around down here just as well, better in fact, than they can, and pretty soon others will be following. Several nations and many groups of private persons are exploring the undersea world. It's time for the Illuminati to finish taking away whatever tells of High Atlantis."

"Will they destroy that city we saw? And what about the Pyramid of the Eye?"

Hagbard shook his head. "They'd be willing to let later Atlantean ruins to be found. That wouldn't say anything about their existence. As for the Pyramid of the Eye, I suspect they have a real problem with that. They can't destroy it, and even if they could they wouldn't want to. But it's a dead giveaway to the existence of a supercivilization in the past."

"Well," said George, not at all wanting to meet the head of the American crime syndicate, "what we ought to do is go back and raise the Temple of Tethys ourselves, before the Illuminati grab it."

"Good grief," said Miss Mao. "This happens to be the most critical moment in the history of this civilization. We don't have time to fiddle-fuck around with archeology."

"He's just a legionnaire," said Hagbard. "Though after this mission he'll know the Fairest and become a deacon. He'll understand more then. George, I want you to act as a go-between for the Discordian movement and the Syndicate. You're going to bring these four statues to Robert Putney Drake and tell him there are more where they came from. Ask Drake to stop working for the Illuminati, to take the heat off our people, wherever he's after them, and to drop the assassination project the Illuminati have been working on with him. And as an earnest of good faith, he's to snuff twenty-four Illuminati agents for us in the next twenty-four hours. Their names will be contained in a sealed envelope which you'll give him."

FIVES. SEX. HERE IS WISDOM. The mumble of the breast is the mutter of man.

State's Attorney Milo A. Flanagan stood on the roof of the high rise condominium on Lake Shore Drive in which he lived, scanning blue-gray Lake Michigan with powerful binoculars. It was April 24, and Project Tethys should be completed. At any moment Flanagan expected to sight what would look like another Great Lakes freighter heading for the Chicago River locks. Only this one would be carrying a dismantled Atlantean temple crated in its hold. The ship would be recognizable by a red triangle painted on the funnel.

After being inspected by Flanagan (whose name in the Order was Brother Johann Beghard) and after his report had been sent on to Vigilance Lodge, the North American command center, the crated temple would be moved downriver to Saint Louis, where, by prior agreement with the President of the United States, it would be trucked overland to Fort Knox under the guard of the U.S. Army. The President didn't know with whom he was dealing. The CIA had informed him that the source of the artifacts was the Livonian Nationalist Movement, now behind the Iron Curtain, and that the crates would contain Livonian art treasures. Certain high officers in the CIA did know the real nature of the organization which the U.S. was helping, because they were members of it. Of course, the Syndicate (without even a cover story) was keeping three-quarters of its gold in with the government store at Fort Knox these days. "Where could you find a safer place?" Robert Putney Drake once asked.

But the freighter was behind schedule. The wind battered at Flanagan, whipping his wavy white hair and the well-tailored jacket sleeves and trouser legs. The goddamned Chicago wind. Flanagan had been fighting it all his life. It had made him the man he was.

Police Sergeant Otto Waterhouse emerged from the doorway to the roof. Waterhouse was a member of Flanagan's personal staff, which meant he was on the Police Department payroll, the Syndicate payroll, and another payroll that regularly deposited a fixed sum in the account of Herr Otto Wasserhaus in a Bavarian bank. Waterhouse was a six-and-a-half-foot-tall black man who had made a career for himself in the Chicago Police Department by being more willing and eager to harass, torture, maim, and kill members of his race than the average Mississippi sheriff. Flanagan had early spotted Waterhouse's ice-cold, self-hating love affair with death, and had attached him to his staff.

"A message from CFR communications center in New York," said Waterhouse. "The word has come through from Ingolstadt that Project Tethys was aborted."

Flanagan lowered his binoculars and turned to look at Waterhouse. The State's Attorney's florid face with its bushy pepper-and-salt eyebrows was shrewd and distinguished, the sort of face people vote for, especially in Chicago. It was a face that had once belonged to a kid who had run with the Hamburgers in Chicago's South Side Irish ghetto and bashed out the brains of black men with cobblestones for the fun of it. It was a face that had come from that primitive beginning to knowing about ten-thousand-year-old sunken temples, spider ships, and international conspiracies. It was stamped indelibly with the lines of Milo A. Flanagan's ancestors, the ancestors of the Gauls, Britons, Scots, Picts, Welsh, and Irish. Around the time the Temple of Tethys was sinking into the sea, they had been driven forth on orders from Agharti from that thick ancient forest that is now the desert country of Outer Mongolia. But Flanagan was only a Fourth-degree Illuminatus and not fully instructed in the history. Though he did not display much emotion there were blue-white flames of murderous madness burning deep in his eyes. Waterhouse was one of the few people in Chicago who could meet Flanagan's baleful stare head-on.

"How did it happen?" Flanagan asked.

"They were attacked by porpoises and an invisible submarine. The spider craft were all blown to bits. The *Zwack* came in and counterattacked, was damaged by a laser beam and forced to disengage."

"How did they find out we had spider ships at the temple site?"

"Maybe the porpoises told them."

Flanagan looked at Waterhouse coldly and thoughtfully. "Maybe it leaked at this end, Otto. There are JAMs active in this town, more here than anywhere in the country right now. Dillinger has been spotted twice in the last week. By Gruad, how I'd like to be the one to *really* get him, once and for all! What would Hoover's ghost say then, huh, Otto?" Flanagan grinned, one of his rare genuine smiles, exposing prominent canine teeth. "We know there's a JAM cult center somewhere on the North Side. Someone's been stealing hosts from my brother's church for the past ten years—even at times when I've had as many as thirty men staked out there. And my brother says that there have been more cases of demonic possession in his parish in the last five years than in all of Chicago in all its previous history. One of our sensitives has reported emanations of the Old Woman in this area at least once a month during the past year. It's long past time we found them. They could be reading our minds, Otto. That could be the leak. Why haven't we got a fix on them?"

Waterhouse, who only a few years ago had known nothing more unconventional than how to turn a homicide into "killed while resisting arrest," looked back calmly at Flanagan and said, "We need ten sensitives of the fifth grade to form the pentacle, and we've only got seven."

Flanagan shook his head. "There are seventeen fifth graders in Europe, eight in Africa, and twenty-three scattered around the rest of the world. You'd think they could spare us three for a week. That's all it would take."

Waterhouse said, "Maybe you've got enemies in the higher circle. Maybe somebody wants to see us get it."

"Why the hell do you say things like that, Waterhouse?"

"Just to fuck you up, man."

Eight floors below, in an apartment which was regularly used for black masses, a North Clark street hippie named Skip Lynch opened his eyes and looked at Simon Moon and Padre Pederastia. "Time's getting very short," he said. "We've got to finish off Flanagan soon."

"It can't be too soon for me," said Padre Pederastia. "If Daddy hadn't favored him so outrageously he'd be the priest today and I'd be State's Attorney."

Simon nodded. "But then we'd be snuffing you instead of Milo. Anyway, I believe George Dorn will be taking care of the problem for us right now."

Squinks? It all began with the squinks—and that sentence is more true than you will realize until long after this mission is over, Mr. Muldoon.

It was the night of February 2, 1776, and it was dark and windy in Ingolstadt; in fact, Adam Weishaupt's study looked like a set for a Frankenstein movie, with its windows rattling and candles flickering, and old Adam himself casting terrifying shadows as he paced back and forth with his peculiar lurching gait. At least the shadows were terrifying to *him,* because he was flying high on the new hemp extract that Kolmer had brought back from his last visit to Baghdad. To calm himself, he was repeating his English vocabulary-building drill, working on the new words for that week. "Tomahawk . . . Succotash . . . Squink. *Squink?*" He laughed out loud. The word was "skunk," but he had short-circuited from there to "squid" and emerged with "squink." A new word: a new concept. But what would a squink look like? Midway between a squid and a skunk, no doubt: it would have eight arms and smell to *hoch Himmel.* A horrible thought: it reminded him, uncomfortably, of the shoggoths in that damnable *Necron-omicon* that Kolmer was always trying to get him to read when he was stoned, saying that was the only way to understand it.

He lurched over to the Black Magic and Pornography section of his bookshelves—which he kept, sardonically, next to his Bible commentaries—and took down the long-forbidden volume of the visions of the mad poet Abdul Alhazred. He turned to the first drawing of a shoggoth. Strange, he thought, how a creature so foul could also, from certain angles and especially when you were high, look vaguely like a crazily grinning rabbit. *"Du haxen Hase,"* he chortled to himself. . . .

Then his mind made the leap: five sides on the borders on the shoggoth sketches . . . five sides, always, on all the shoggoth sketches . . . and "squid" and "skunk" both had five letters in them. . . .

He held up his hands, looked at the five fingers on each, and began to laugh. It was all clear suddenly: the Sign of the Horns made by holding up the first two fingers in a V and folding the other three down: the two, the three and their union in the five. Father, Son and Holy Devil . . . the Duality of good and evil, the Trinity of the Godhead . . . the bicycle and the tricycle. . . . He laughed louder and louder, looking—despite his long, thin face—like the Chinese statues of the Laughing Buddha.

While the gas chambers were operating, other features of life in the camps were also contributing to the Final Solution. At Auschwitz, for instance, many perished from beatings and other forms of ill treatment, but the general neglect of elementary sanitary and health precautions had the most memorable results. First there was spotted fever, then paratyphoid fever and abdominal typhus erysipelas. Tuberculosis, of course, was rampant, and—particularly amusing to certain of the officers—incurable diarrhea brought death to many inmates, degrading as it killed. No attempt was made, either, to prevent the ubiquitous camp rats from attacking those too ill to move or defend themselves. Never before witnessed by twentieth-century doctors, noma also appeared and was recognized only from the descriptions in old textbooks: it is the complication of malnutrition which eats holes in the cheeks until you can see right through to the teeth. *"Vernichtung,"* a survivor said later, "is the most terrible word in any language."

Even so, the Aztecs grew more frantic toward the end, increasing the number of sacrifices, doubling and tripling the days of the year that called for spilled blood. But nothing saved them: just as Eisenhower's army advanced across Europe to end the ovens of Auschwitz, Cortez and his ships moved toward the great pyramid, the statue of Tlaloc, the confrontation.

Seven hours after Simon spoke of George Dorn to Padre Pederastia, a private jet painted gold landed at Kennedy International Airport. Four heavy crates were moved by crane from the belly of the plane into a truck which bore on its side the sign "GOLD & APPEL TRANSFERS." A young man with shoulder-length blond hair, wearing a fashionable cutaway and knee breeches of red velvet with bottle-green silk stockings, stepped down from the plane and climbed into the cab of the truck. Holding an alligator briefcase in his lap, he sat silently beside the driver.

Tobias Knight, the driver, kept his thoughts to himself and asked no questions.

George Dorn was frightened. It was a feeling he was getting used to, so accustomed in fact that it no longer seemed to stop him from doing insane things. Besides, Hagbard had given him a talisman against harm, assuring him that it was 100 percent infallible. George slipped it out of his pocket and glanced at it again, curiously and with a wan hope. It was gold-tinted card with the strange glyphs:

It was probably another of Hagbard's jokes, George decided. It might even be Etruscan for "Kick this boob in the ass." Hagbard's refusal to translate it suggested some such Celinean irony, and yet he had seemed very sober—almost religious—about the symbols.

One thing was sure: George was still frightened, but the fear was no longer paralyzing. If I was this casual about fear a few years ago, he thought, there'd be one less cop in New York. And I wouldn't be here either, probably. No, that's not right, either. I would have told Carlo to go fuck himself. I wouldn't have let the fear of being called a cop-out stop me. George had been scared when he went to Mad Dog, when Harry Coin tried to fuck him up the ass, when Harry Coin was killed, when he escaped from the Mad Dog jail, when he saw his own death just as he was coming, and when the Illuminati spider ships had attacked the *Lief Erickson*. Being scared was beginning to seem a normal condition to him.

So now he was going to meet the men who ran organized crime in the U.S. He knew practically nothing about the Syndicate and the Mafia, and what little he did know he tended to disbelieve on the grounds that it was probably myth. Hagbard had sketched in a little additional information for him while he was preparing for this flight. But the one thing that George was absolutely certain about was that he was going unprotected among men who killed human beings as easily as a housewife kills silverfish. And he was supposed to negotiate with them. The Syndicate had been working with the Illuminati until now. Now they were supposed to switch over to the Discordians, on George's say-so. With, of course, the help of four priceless statues. Except, what were Robert Putney Drake and Federico Maldonado going to say when they heard these statues had been dredged up from the bottom of the ocean floor out of the ruins of Atlantis? They would probably express their skepticism with pistols and send George back to the place he claimed the statues came from.

"Why me?" George had asked Hagbard earlier that day.

"Why me?" Hagbard repeated with a smile. "The question asked by the soldier as the enemy bullets whistle around him, by the harmless homeowner as the homicidal maniac steps through the kitchen door hunting knife in hand, by the woman who has given birth to a dead baby, by the prophet who has just had a revelation of the word of God, by the artist who knows his latest painting is a work of genius. Why you? Because you're there, schmuck. Because something has to happen to you. OK?"

"But what if I fuck it up? I don't know anything about your organization or the Syndicate. If times are as crucial as you say, it's silly to send somebody like me on this mission. I have no experience meeting people like this."

Hagbard shook his head impatiently. "You underrate yourself. Just because you're young and afraid you think you can't talk to people. That's stupid. And it's not typical of your generation, so you should be all the more ashamed of yourself. Furthermore, you are experienced with even. worse people than Drake and Maldonado. You spent part of a night in a cell with the man who killed John F. Kennedy."

"What?" George felt the blood rush out of his face and he thought he might faint.

"Oh, sure," said Hagbard casually. "Joe Malik was on the right track when he sent you to Mad Dog, you know."

After all that, Hagbard told George he was perfectly free to turn down the mission if he didn't want to go. And George said he would go for the same reason he had agreed to accompany Hagbard on his golden submarine. Because he knew that he would have been a fool to pass up the experience.

A two-hour drive brought the truck to the outskirts of Blue Point, Long Island, to the gates of an estate. Two heavy-set men in green coveralls searched George and the driver, pointed the bell-shaped nozzle of an instrument at the truck and studied some dials, and then waved them through. They drove up a winding, narrow asphalt road through woods just beginning to show the light green budding of early spring. Shadowy figures prowled among the trees. Suddenly the road burst out of the woods and into a meadow. From here there was a long gentle rising slope to the top of a hill that was crowned by houses. From the edge of the woods George could see four large, comfortable-looking cottages, each three stories high, a little smaller than Newport, a little larger than Atlantic City. They were made of brick painted in seaside pastel colors and formed a semicircle on the crest of the hill. The grass of the meadow was cut very short, and halfway up the hill it became a beautifully manicured lawn The woods screened the houses from the road, the meadow made it impossible for anyone emerging from woods to approach the houses without being seen, and the houses themselves constituted the elements of a fortress.

The Gold & Appel truck followed the driveway, which led between two of the houses, rolling over slots in the driveway where a section might be hydraulically raised to form a wall. The driver stopped at a gesture from one of two men in khakis who approached. George could now see the Syndicate fortress consisted of eight separate houses forming an octagon around a lawn. Each house had its own fenced-in yard, and George noticed with surprise that there was play equipment for children in front of several cottages. In the center of the compound was a tall white pole from which flew an American flag.

George and the driver stepped down from the cab of the truck. George identified himself and was ushered to the far side of the compound. The hill was much steeper on this side, George saw. It sloped down to a narrow boulder-strewn beach drenched by huge Atlantic waves. A nice view, George thought. And eminently secure. The only way Drake's enemies could get at him would be to shell his home from a destroyer.

A slender, blond man—at least sixty and maybe a well-preserved seventy—came down the steps of the house George was approaching. He had a concave nose that end-ed in a sharp point, a strong, cleft chin, ice-blue eyes. He shook hands vigorously.

"Hi. I'm Drake. The others are inside. Let's go. Oh—is it OK with you if we go ahead and unload your truck?" He gave George a sharp, birdlike look. George realized with a sinking feeling that Drake was saying that they would take the statues regardless of whether any deal went through. Why, then, should they inconvenience themselves by changing sides in this underground war? But he nodded in acquiescence.

"You're young, aren't you?" said Drake as they went into the house. "But that's the way it is nowadays. Boys do men's work." The house was handsome inside, but not as one might expect, incredible. The carpets were thick, the woodwork heavy, dark and polished, the furnishings prob-ably genuine antiques. George didn't see how Atlantean statues would fit into the decor. There was a painting at the top of the stairs to the second floor of a woman who looked slightly like Queen Elizabeth II. She wore a white gown with diamonds at her neck and wrists. Two small, fragile-looking blond boys in navy blue suits with white satin ties stood with her, staring solemnly out of the paint-ing.

"My wife and sons," said Drake with a smile.

They entered a large study full of mahogany, oak pan-eling, leatherbound books and red and green leather furni-ture. Theodore Roosevelt would have loved it, George thought. Over the desk hung a painting of a bearded man in Elizabethan costume. He was holding a bowling ball in his hand and looking superciliously at a messenger type who pointing out to sea. There were sailing ships in the distant background.

"An ancestor," said Drake simply. He pressed a button in a panel on the desk. A door opened and two men came in, the first a tall young Chinese with a boney face and unruly black hair, the second a short, thin man who bore a faint resemblance to Pope Paul VI.

"Don Federico Maldonado, a man of the greatest respect," said Drake. "And Richard Jung, my chief counselor." George shook hands with both of them. He couldn't understand why Maldonado was known as "Banana-Nose"; his proboscus was on the large side, but bore little resemblance to a banana. It was more like an eggplant. The name must be a sample of low Sicilian humor. The two men took seats on a red leather couch. George and Drake sank into armchairs facing them.

"And how are my favorite musicians doing?" Jung said genially.

Was this some kind of password? George was sure of one thing: his survival depended on sticking absolutely to truth and sincerity with these people, so he said, very sincerely, "I don't know. Who are your favorite musicians?"

Jung smiled back, saying nothing, until George, his heart racing inside his chest like a hamster determined to run clear off the treadmill, reached into his briefcase and took out a parchment scroll.

"This," he said, "is the fundamental agreement proposed by the people I represent." He handed it to Drake. Maldonado, he noticed, was staring fixedly, expressionlessly, at him in the most unnerving way. The man's eyes looked as if they were made of glass. His face was a waxen mask. He was, George decided, a wax dummy of Pope Paul VI which had been stolen from Madame Tussaud's, dressed in a business suit, and brought to life to serve as the head of the Mafia. George had always thought there was something witchy about Sicilians.

"Do we sign this in blood?" said Drake, removing the cloth-of-gold ribbon from the parchment and unrolling it.

George laughed nervously. "Pen and ink will do fine."

Saul's angry, triumphant eyes stare into mine, and I look away guiltily. *Let me explain,* I say desperately. *I really am trying to help you. Your mind is a bomb.*

"What Weishaupt discovered that night of February second, seventeen seventy-six," Hagbard Celine explained to Joe Malik in 1973, on a clear autumn day in Miami, about the same time that Captain Tequilla y Mota was reading Luttwak on the coup d'etat and making his first moves toward recruiting the officer's cabal that later seized Fernando Poo, "was basically a simple mathematical relationship. It's so simple, in fact, that most administrators and bureaucrats never notice it. Just as the householder doesn't notice the humble termite, until it's too late. . . . Here, take this paper and figure for yourself. How many permutations are there in a system of four elements?"

Joe, recalling his high school math, wrote 4 x 3 x 2 x 1, and read aloud his answer "Twenty-four."

"And if you're one of the elements, the number of coalitions—or to be sinister, conspiracies—that you may have to confront would be twenty-three. Despite Simon Moon's obsessions, the twenty-three has no particularly mystic significance," Hagbard added quickly. "Just consider it pragmatically—it's a number of possible relationships which the brain can remember and handle. But now suppose the system has five elements . . . ?"

Joe wrote 5 x 4 x 3 x 2 x 1 and read aloud, "One hundred and twenty." "You see? One always encounters jumps of that size when dealing with permutations and combinations. But, as I say, administrators as a rule aren't aware of this. Korzybski pointed out, back in the early thirties, that nobody should ever *directly* supervise more than four subordinates, because the twenty-four possible coalitions ordinary office politics can create are enough to tax any brain. When it jumps up to one hundred and twenty, the administrator is lost. That, in essence, is the sociological aspect of the mysterious Law of Fives. The Illuminati always has five leaders in each nation, and five international Illuminati Primi supervising all of them, but each runs his own show more or less independent of the other four, united only by their common commitment to the Goal of Gruad." Hagbard paused to relight his long, black Italian cigar.

"Now," he said, "put yourself in the position of the head of any counterespionage organization. Imagine, for instance, that you're poor old McCone of the CIA at the time of the first of the New Wave of Illuminati assassinations, ten years ago, in sixty-three. Oswald was, of course, a double agent, as everybody always knew. The Russians wouldn't have let him out of Russia without getting a commitment from him to do 'small jobs,' as they're called in the business, although he'd be a 'sleeper.' That is, he'd go about his ordinary business most of the time, and only be called on occasionally when he was in the right place at the right time for a particular 'small job.' Now, of course, Washington knows this; they know that no expatriate comes back from Moscow without some such agreement. And Moscow knows the other side: that the State Department wouldn't take him back unless he accepted a similar status with the CIA. Then, November twenty-second, Dealy Plaza—blam! the shit hits the fan. Moscow and Washington both want to know, the sooner the quicker, who was he working for when he did it, or was it his own idea? Two more possibilities loom at once: could a loner with confused politics like him have been recruited by the Cubans or the Chinese? And, then, the kicker: could he be innocent? Could another group—to avoid the obvious, let's call them Force X—have stage-managed the whole thing? So, you've got MVD and CIA and FBI and who-all falling over each other sniffing around Dallas and New Orleans for clues. And Force X gets to seem more and more implausible to all of them, because it is intrinsically incredible. It is incredible because it has no skeleton, no shape, no flesh, nothing they can grab hold of. The reason is, of course, that Force X is the Illuminati, working through five leaders with five times four times three times two times one, or one hundred and twenty different basic vectors. A conspiracy with one hundred and twenty vectors doesn't look like a conspiracy: it looks like chaos. The human mind can't grasp it, and hence declares it nonexistent. You see, the Illuminati is always careful to keep a random element in the one hundred and twenty vectors. They didn't *really* need to recruit both the leaders of the ecology movement *and* the executives of the worst pollution-producing corporations. They did it to create ambiguity. *Anybody* who tries to describe their operations sounds like a paranoid. What clinched it," Hagbard concluded, "was a real stroke of luck for the Weishaupt gang: there were two other elements involved, which nobody had planned or foreseen. One was the Syndicate."

"It always starts with nonsense," Simon is telling Joe in another time-track, between Los Angeles and San Francisco, in 1969. "Weishaupt discovered the Law of Fives while he was stoned and looking at one of those shoggoth pictures you saw in Arkham. He imagined the shoggoth was a rabbit and said, '*du hexen Hase*,' which has been preserved as an in-joke by Illuminati agents in Hollywood. It runs through the Bugs Bunny cartoons: 'You wascal wabbit!' But out of that schizzy mixture of hallucination and logomania, Weishaupt saw both the mystic meaning of the Five and its pragmatic application as a principal of international espionage, using permutations and combinations that I'll explain when we have a pencil and paper. That same mixture of revelation and put-on is always the language of the supra-conscious, whenever you contact it, whether through magic, religion, psychedelics, yoga, or a spontaneous brain nova. Maybe the put-on or nonsense part comes by contamination from the unconscious, I don't know. But it's always there. That's why serious people never discover anything of real importance."

"You mean the Mafia?" Joe asks.

"What? I didn't say anything about the Mafia. Are you in another time-track again?"

"No, not the Mafia alone," Hagbard says. "The Syndicate is much bigger than the Maf." The room returns to focus: it is a restaurant. A seafood restaurant. On Biscayne Avenue, facing the bay. In Miami. In 1973. The walls are decorated with undersea motifs, including a huge octopus. Hagbard, undoubtedly, had chosen this meeting place just because he liked the decor. Crazy bastard thinks he's Captain Nemo. Still: we've got to deal with him. As John says, the JAMs can't do it alone. Hagbard, grinning, seemed to be noting Joe's return to present time. "You're reaching the critical stage," he said changing the subject. "You now only have two mental states: high on drugs and high without drugs. That's very good. But as I was saying, the Syndicate is more than just the Maf. The only Syndicate, up until October twenty-third, nineteen thirty-five, was nothing more than the Mafia, of course. But then they killed the Dutchman, and a young psychology student, who also happened to be a psychopath with a power drive like Genghis Khan, was assigned to do a paper on how the Dutchman's last words illustrate the similarity between somatic damage and schizophrenia. The Dutchman had a bullet in his gut while the police interviewed him, and they recorded everything he said, but on the surface it was all gibberish. This psychology student wrote the paper that his professor expected, and got an *A* for the course—but he also wrote another interpretation of the Dutchman's words, for his own purposes. He put copies in several bank vaults—he came from one of the oldest banking families in New England, and he was even then under family pressure to give up psychology and go into banking. His name was

(Robert Putney Drake visited Zurich in 1935. He personally talked to Carl Jung about the archetypes of the collective unconscious, the *I Ching*, and the principle of synchronicity. He talked to people who had known James Joyce before that drunken Irish genius had moved to Paris, and learned much about Joyce's drunken claims to be a prophet. He read the published portions of *Finnegans Wake* and went back for further conversations with Jung. Then he met Hermann Hesse, Paul Klee and the other members of the Eastern Brotherhood and joined them in a mescaline ritual. A letter from his father arrived about then, asking when he was going to give up wasting his time and return to Harvard Business School. He wrote that he would return for the fall semester, but not to study business administration. A great psychologist was almost born then, and Harvard might have had its Timothy Leary scandal thirty years earlier.

Except for Drake's power drive.)

I. THE FAUST PARSON, SINGULAR. Napalm sundaes for How Chow Mein, misfortune's cookie.

Josephine Malik lies trembling on the bed, trying to be brave, trying to hide her fear. Where, now, is the mask of masculinity?

This delusion that you are a man trapped in a woman's body can only be cured one way. I might be kicked out of the American Psychoanalystical Association if they knew about my methods. In fact, already had a spot of bother with them when one of my patients cured his Oedipus complex by actually fucking his mother, convincing himself extensionally as the semanticists would say that she really was an old lady and not the woman he remembered from infancy. Nevertheless, the whole world is going bananas as you must have observed, my poor girl, and we have to use heroic measures to save whatever sanity remains in any patient we encounter. (*The psychiatrist is now naked. He joins her on the bed.*) Now, my little frightened dove, I will convince you that you really are a true-born, honest-to-God woman. . . .

Josephine feels his finger in her cunt and screams. Not

at the touch: at the reality of it. She hadn't believed until then that the change was real.

> *Weishaupt bridge is falling down*
> *Falling down*
> *Falling down*

And modern novels are the same: in the YMCA on Atlantic Avenue in Brooklyn, looking out the window at the radio tower atop Brooklyn Technical High School, a man named Chaney (no relative of the movie family) spreads his pornographic tarot cards across the bed. One of them, he notes, is missing. Quickly, he arranges them in suits, and hunts for the lost card: it is the Five of Pentacles. He curses softly: that was one of his favorite orgy tableux.

Rebecca. The Saint Bernard.

"It's probably all jumbled in your head," I went on, furious that our plan was falling apart, that I needed his trust now but had no way to earn it. "We've been disintoxicating and dehypnotizing you, but you almost certainly can't tell where the Illuminati left off and we rescued you and started reversing the treatment. You're due to explode into psychosis within twenty-four hours and we're using the only techniques that can defuse that process."

"Why am I hearing everything twice?" Saul asked, balancing between wary skepticism and a sense that Malik was not playing games any more but urgently trying to help him.

"The stuff they gave you was an MDA derivative—very high on mescaline and methedrine both. It has an echo effect for seventy-two hours minimum. You're hearing what I'm going to say before I say it and then again when I do say it. That'll pass in a few minutes, but it'll be back, every half hour or so, for the next day yet. The end of the chain is psychosis, unless we can stop it." "Unless we can stop it."

"It's easing up now," Saul said carefully, "Less of an echo that time. I still don't know whether to trust you. Why were you trying to turn me into Barney Muldoon?"

"Because the psychic explosion is on Saul Goodman's time-track, not on Barney Muldoon's."

Ten big rhinoceroses, eleven big rhinoceroses ...

"You Wascal Wabbit," Simon whispers through the Judas Window. Immediately the door opens and a grinning young man with the Frisco-style Jesus Christ hair-and-beard says, "Welcome to the Joshua Norton Cabal." Joe sees to his relief that it was a normal but untypically clean hippie hangout, and there are none of the sinister accoutrements of the Lake Shore Drive coven. At the same time, he hears the strange man in the bed asking, "Why were you trying to turn me into Barney Muldoon?" *My God, now it's happening when I'm awake as well as when I'm asleep.* Simu-multi-taneously, he hears the alarm and cries, "The Illuminati must be attacking!"

"Attacking this building?" Saul asks confusedly.

"Building? You're on a submarine, man. The *Lief Erickson,* on its way to Atlantis!"

Twenty big rhinoceroses, twenty-one big rhinoceroses ...

"Number Seventeen," read Professor Curve, " 'Law and anarchists will give the American people a speedy Cadillac.' "

All the Helen Hokinson types are out today. Another one just hit me for the Mothers March Against Dandruff. I gave her a nickel.

1923 was a very interesting year for the occult, by the way. Not only did Hitler join the Illuminati and attempt the Munich putsch, but, glancing through the books of Charles Fort, I found quite a few suggestive events. On March 17th—which not only fits our 17-23 correlation but is also the anniversary of the defeat of the Kronstadt rebellion, the day the Lord Nelson statue was bombed in Dublin in 1966 and, of course, good Saint Patrick's holy day—a naked man was seen mysteriously running about the estate of Lord Caernarvon in England. He appeared several times in the following days, but was never caught. Meanwhile, Lord Caernarvon himself died in Egypt—some said he was a victim of the curse of Tut-Ankh-Amen, whose tomb he had burglarized. (An archaeologist is a ghoul with credentials.) Fort also records two cases that May of a synchronistic phenomenon he has traced through the centuries: a volcanic eruption coinciding with the discovery of a new star. In September, there was a Mumiai scare in India—Mumiais are invisible demons that grab people in broad daylight. Throughout the year, there were reports of exploding coal in England; some tried to explain this by saying the embittered miners (it was a time of labor troubles) were putting dynamite in the coal, but the police couldn't prove this. The coal went on exploding. In the summer, French pilots began having strange mishaps, whenever they flew over Germany, and it was suggested that the Germans were testing an invisible ray machine. Considering the last three phenomena together—invisible demons in India, exploding coal in England, invisible rays over Germany—I guess somebody was testing something. . . .

You can call me Doc Iggy. My full name, at present, is Dr. Ignotum P. Ignotius. The P. stands for Per. If you're a Latinist, you'll realize that translates as "the unknown explained by the still more unknown." I think it's a quite appropriate name for my function tonight, since Simon brought you here to be illuminized. My slave name, before I was turned on myself, is totally immaterial. As far as I'm concerned, your slave name is equally pointless, and I'll call you by the password of the Norton Cabal, which Simon used at the door. Until tomorrow morning, when the drug starts wearing off, you are U. Wascal Wabbit. That's U., the initial, not why-oh-you, by the way.

We accept Bugs Bunny as an exemplar of Mummu here, too, but otherwise we have little in common with the SSS. That's the Satanist, Surrealists and Sadists—the crew who began your illuminization in Chicago. All we share with them actually is use of the Tristero anarchist postal system, to evade the government's postal inspectors, and a financial agreement whereby we accept their DMM script—Divine Marquis Memorial script—and they accept our hempscript and the flaxscript of the Legion of Dynamic Discord. Anything to avoid Federal Reserve notes, you know.

It'll be a while yet before the acid starts working, so I'll just chat like this, about things that are more or less trivial—or quadrivial, or maybe pentivial—until I can see that you're ready for more serious matters. Simon's in the chapel, with a woman named Stella who you'll really dig, getting things ready for the ceremony.

You might wonder why we're called the Norton Cabal. The name was chosen by my predecessor, Malaclypse the Younger, before he left us to join the more esoteric group known as ELF—the Erisian Liberation Front. They're the Occidental branch of the Hung Mung Tong Cong and all their efforts go into a long-range anti-Illuminati project known only as Operation Mindfuck. But that's another, very complicated, story. One of Malaclypse's last writings, before he went into the Silence, was a short paragraph saying, "Everybody understands Mickey Mouse. Few understand Hermann Hesse. Hardly anyone understands Albert Einstein. And nobody understands Emperor Norton." I guess Malaclypse was already into the Mindfuck mystique when he wrote that.

(Who was Emperor Norton? Joe asks, wondering if the drug is beginning to work already or Dr. Ignotius just has a tendency to speak more slowly than most people.)

Joshua Norton, Emperor of the United States and Protector of Mexico. San Francisco is proud of him. He lived in the last century and got to be emperor by proclaiming himself as such. *For some mysterious reason,* the newspapers decided to humor him and printed his proclamations. When he started issuing his own money, the local banks *went along with the joke* and accepted it on par with U.S. currency. When the Vigilantes got into a lynching mood one night and decided to go down to Chinatown and kill some Chinese, Emperor Norton stopped them *just by standing in the street with his eyes closed reciting the Lord's Prayer.* Are you beginning to understand Emperor Norton a little, Mr. Wabbit?

(A little, Joe said, a little . . .)

Well, chew on this for a while, friend: there were two very sane and rational anarchists who lived about the same time as Emperor Norton across the country in Massachusetts: William Green and Lysander Spooner. They also realized the value of having competing currencies instead of one uniform State currency, and they tried logical arguments, empirical demonstrations and legal suits to get this idea accepted. They accomplished nothing. The government broke its own laws to find ways to suppress Green's Mutual Bank and Spooner's People's Bank. That's because they were obviously sane, and their currency did pose a real threat to the monopoly of the Illuminati. But Emperor Norton was so crazy that people *humored* him and his currency was allowed to circulate. Think about it. You might begin to understand why Bugs Bunny is our symbol and why our currency has the ridiculous name hempscript. Hagbard Celine and his Discordians, even more absurdly, call their money flaxscript. That commemorates the Zen

Master who was asked, "What is the Buddha?" and replied, "Five pounds of flax." Do you begin to see the full dimensions of our struggle with the Illuminati?

At least, for now, you can probably grasp this much: their fundamental fallacy is the Aneristic Delusion. They *really* believe in law 'n' order. As a matter of fact, since everybody in this crazy, millennia-old battle has his own theory about what the Illuminati are really aiming at, I might as well tell you mine. I think they're all scientists and they want to set up a scientific world government. The Jacobins were probably following precise Illuminati instructions when they sacked the churches in Paris and proclaimed the dawn of the Age of Reason. You know the story about the old man who was in the crowd when Louis XVI went to the guillotine and who shouted as the king's head fell, "Jacques De Molay, thou art avenged"? All the symbols that De Molay introduced into Masonry are scientific implements—the T-square, the architect's triangle, even that pyramid that has caused so much bizarre speculation. If you count the eye as part of the design, the pyramid has 73 divisions, you know, not 72. What's 73 mean? Simple: multiply it by five, in accordance with Weishaupt's *funfwissenschaft*, the science of fives, and you get 365, the days of the year. The damn thing is some kind of astronomical computer, like Stonehenge. The Egyptian pyramids are facing to the East, where the sun rises. The great pyramid of the Mayans has exactly 365 divisions, and is also facing to the East. What they're doing is worshipping the "order" they have found in Nature, never realizing that they projected the order there with their own instruments.

That's why they hate ordinary mankind—because we're so disorderly. They've been trying for six or seven thousand years to reestablish Atlantis-style high civilization— law 'n' order—the Body Politic, as they like to call it. A giant robot is what their Body Politic really amounts to, you know. A place for everything and everything in its place. A place for everybody and everybody in his place. Look at the Pentagon—look at the whole army, for Goddess's sake! That's what they want the planet to be like. Efficient, mechanical, orderly—very orderly—and inhuman. That's the essence of the Aneristic Delusion: to imagine you have found Order and then to start manipulating the quirky, eccentric chaotic things that really exist into some kind of platoons or phalanxes that correspond to your concept of the Order they're supposed to manifest. Of course, the quirkiest, most chaotic things that exist are other people—and that's why they're so obsessed with trying to control us.

Why are you staring like that? Am I changing colors or growing bigger or something? Good: the acid is starting to work. Now we can really get to the nitty-gritty. First of all, most of what I've been telling you is bullshit. The Illuminati have no millennia-old history; neither do the JAMs. They invented their great heritage and tradition—Jacques De Molay and Charlemagne and all of it—out of whole cloth in 1776, picking up all sorts of out-of-context history to make it seem plausible. We've done the same. You might wonder why we copy them, and even deceive our own recruits about this. Well, part of illumination—and we've got to be illuminized ourselves to fight them—is in learning to doubt everything. That's why Hagbard has that painting in his stateroom saying "Think for yourself, schmuck," and why Hassan i Sabbah said *"Nothing* is true." You've got to learn to doubt us, too, and everything we tell you. There are no honest men on this voyage. In fact, maybe *this part* is the only lie I've told you all evening, and the Illuminati history before 1776 really is true and not an invention. Or maybe we're just a front for the Illuminati . . . to recruit you indirectly. . . .

Feeling paranoid? Good: illumination is on the other side of absolute terror. And the only terror that is truly absolute is the horror of realizing that you can't believe anything you've ever been told. You have to realize fully that you *are* "a stranger and afraid in a world you never made," like Houseman says.

Twenty-two big rhinoceroses, twenty-three big rhinoceroses . . .

The Illuminati basically were structure-freaks. Hence, their hangup on symbols of geometric law and architectural permanence, especially the pyramid and the pentagon. (God's Lightning, like all authoritarian Judeo-Christian heresies, had its own share of this typically Occidental straight-line mystique, which was why even the Jews among them, like Zev Hirsch, accepted the symbol first suggested by Atlanta Hope: that most Euclidean of all religious emblems: the Cross.) The Discordians made their own sardonic commentary on the legal and scientific basis

of law 'n' order by using a 17-step pyramid—17 being a
number with virtually no interesting geometric, arithmetic
or mystic properties, outside of Java, where it was the basis of a particularly wierd musical scale—and topping it
with the Apple of Discord, symbol of the un-rational, un-
geometrical, and thoroughly disorderly spontaneity of the
vegetable world of creative evolution. The Erisian Liberation Front (ELF) had no symbol, and when asked for
one by new recruits, replied loftily that their symbol could
not be pictured, since it was a circle whose circumference
was everywhere and its center nowhere. They were the
most far-out group of all, and only the most advanced Discordians could begin to understand their gibberish.

The JAMs, however, had a symbol that anyone could
understand, and, just as Harry Pierpont showed it to John
Dillinger midway through a nutmeg high in Michigan City
prison, Dr. Ignotius showed it to Joe midway through his
first acid trip.

"This," he said dramatically, "is the Sacred Chao."

"That's a symbol of technocracy," Joe said, giggling.

"Well," Dr. Ignotius smiled, "at least you're original.
Nine out of ten new members mistake it for the Chinese
yin-yang or the astrological symbol of Cancer. It's similar
to both of them—and also to the symbols of the Northern
Pacific Railroad and the Sex Information and Education
Council of the United States, all of which is eventually
going to lead to some interesting documents being produced at John Birch headquarters, I'm sure, proving that
sex educators run the railroads or that astrologers control
the sex educators or something of that sort. No, this is different. It is the Sacred Chao, symbol of Mummu, God of
Chaos.

"On the right, O nobly born, you will see the image of
your 'female' and intuitive nature, called *yin* by the
Chinese. The yin contains an apple which is the golden ap-

ple of Eris, the forbidden apple of Eve, and the apple which used to disappear from the stage of the Flatbush Burlesque House in Brooklyn when Linda Larue did the split on top of it at the climax of her striptease. It represents the erotic, libidinal, anarchistic, and subjective values worshiped by Hagbard Celine and our friends in the Legion of Dynamic Discord.

"Now, O nobly born, as you prepare for Total Awakening, turn your eyes to the left, yang side of the Sacred Chao. This is the image of your 'male,' rationalistic ego. It contains the pentagon of the Illuminati, the Satanists, and the U.S. Army. It represents the anal, authoritarian, structural, law 'n' order values which the Illuminati have imposed, through their puppet governments, on most of the peoples of the world.

"This is what you must understand, O newborn Buddha: neither side is complete, or true, or real. Each is an abstraction, a fallacy. Nature is a seamless web in which both sides are in perpetual war (which is another name for perpetual peace). The equation always balances. Increase one side, and the other side increases by itself. Every homosexual is a latent heterosexual, every authoritarian cop is the shell over an anarchistic libido. There is no *Vernichtung*, no Final Solution, no pot of gold at the end of the rainbow, and you are not Saul Goodman, when you're lost out here."

Listen: the chaos you experience under LSD is not an illusion. The orderly world you *imagine you experience,* under the artificial and poisonous diet which the Illuminati have forced on all civilized nations, is the real illusion. I am not saying what you are hearing. The only good fnord is a dead fnord. Never whistle while you're pissing. An obscure but highly significant contribution to sociology and epistemology occurs in Malignowski's study "Retroactive Reality," printed in *Wieczny Kwiat Wtadza,* the journal of the Polish Orthopsychiatric Psociety, for Autumn 1959.

"All affirmations are true in some sense, false in some sense, meaningless in some sense, true and false in some sense, true and meaningless in some sense, false and meaningless in some sense, and true and false and meaningless in some sense. Do you follow me?"

(*In some sense,* Joe mutters. . . .)

The author, Dr. Malignowski, was assisted by three graduate students named Korzybski-1, Korzybski-2, and

Korzybski-3 (Siamese triplets born to a mathematician and, hence, indexed rather than named). Malignowski and his students interviewed 1,700 married couples, questioning husband and wife separately in each case, and asked 100 key questions about their first meeting, first sexual experience, marriage ceremony, honeymoon, economic standing during the first year of marriage, and similar subjects which should have left permanent impressions on the memory. Not one couple in the 1,700 gave exactly the same answers to 100 questions, and the highest single score was made by a couple who gave the same answers to 43 of the questions.

"This study demonstrated graphically what many psychologists have long suspected: the life-history which most of us carry around in our skulls is more our own creation (at least seven percent more) than it is an accurate recording of realities. As Malignowski concludes, 'Reality is retroactive, retrospective and illusory.'

"Under these circumstances, things not personally experienced but recounted by others are even more likely to be distorted, and after a tale passes through five tellers it is virtually one hundred percent pure myth: another example of the Law of Fives.

"Only Marxists," Dr. Iggy concluded, opening the door to usher Joe into the chapel room, "still believe in an objective history. Marxists and a few disciples of Ayn Rand."

Jung took the parchment from Drake and stared at it. "It's not to be signed in blood? And what the hell is this yin-yang symbol with the pentagon and the apple? You're a fucking fake." His lips curled tightly in against his teeth.

"What do you mean?" said George through a throat that was rapidly closing up.

"I mean you're not from the goddam Illuminati," said Jung. "Who the hell are you?"

"Didn't you know that before I came here—that I'm not from the Illuminati?" said George. "I'm not trying to fake anybody out. Honest, really, I thought you knew the people who sent me. I never *said* I was from the Illuminati."

Maldonado nodded, a slight smile bringing his face to life. "I know who he is. The people of the Old *Strega*. The Sybil of Sybils. All hail Discordia, kid. Right?"

"Hail Eris," said George with a slight feeling of relief.

Drake frowned. "Well, we seem to be at cross purposes. We were contacted by mail, then by telephone, then by messenger, by parties who made it quite clear that they knew all about our business with the Illuminati. Now, to the best of my knowledge—perhaps Don Federico knows better—there is only one organization in the world that knows anything about the AISB, and that is the AISB itself." George could tell he was lying.

Maldonado raised a warning hand. "Wait. Up, everybody. To the bathroom."

Drake sighed. "Oh, Don Federico! You and your tired notions of security. If my house isn't safe, we're all dead men as of this moment. And if the AISB is as good as it's said to be, an old trick like running water will be no obstacle to them. Let's conduct this discussion like civilized men, for God's sake, and *not* huddled around my shower stall."

"There are times when dignity is suicide," said Maldonado. He shrugged. "But, I yield. I'll settle the question with you in hell if you're wrong."

"I'm still in the dark," said Richard Jung. "I don't know who this guy is or where he's from."

"Look, Chinaman," said Maldonado. "You know who the Ancient Illuminated Seers of Bavaria are, right? Well, every organization has opposition, right? So do the Illuminati. Opposition that's like them, religious, magical, spooky stuff. Not simply interested in becoming rich, as is our gentlemanly aim in life. Playing supernatural games. *Capeesh?*"

Jung looked skeptical. "You could be describing the Communist party, the CIA, or the Vatican."

"Superficial," said Maldonado scornfully. "And upstarts, compared with the AISB. Because the Bavarian Illuminati aren't Bavarians, you understand. That's just a recent name and manifestation for their order. Both the Illuminati and their opposition, which this guy represents, go back a long ways before Moscow, Washington or Rome. A little imagination is called for to understand this, Chinaman."

"If the Illuminati are yang," George said helpfully, "we're yin. The only solution is a Yin Revolution. Dig?"

"I am a graduate of Harvard Law School," said Jung loftily, "and I do *not* dig it. What are you, a bunch of hippies?"

"We never made a deal with your bunch before," said Maldonado. "They never had enough to offer us."

Robert Putney Drake said, "Yes, but wouldn't you *like* to, though, Don Federico? Haven't you had a bellyfull of the others? I know I have. I know where you're from now, George. And you people have been making giant strides in recent decades. I'm not surprised that you're able to tempt us. It's worth our lives—and we are supposedly the most secure men in the United States—to betray the Illuminati. But I understand you offer us statues from Atlantis. By now they should be uncrated. And that there are more where these came from? Is that right, George?"

Hagbard had said nothing about that, but George was too worried about his own survival to quibble. "Yes," he said. "There are more."

Drake said, "Whether we want to risk our lives by working with your people will depend on what we find when we examine the *objets d'art* you are offering. Don Federico, being a highly qualified expert in antiquities, particularly in those antiquities which have been carefully kept outside of the ken of conventional archaeological knowledge, will pronounce on the value of what you've brought. As a Sicilian thoroughly versed in his heritage, Don Federico is familiar with things Atlantean. The Sicilians are about the only extant people who do know about Atlantis. It is not generally realized that the Sicilians have the oldest continuous civilization on the face of the planet. With all due respects to the Chinese." Drake nodded formally to Jung.

"I consider myself an American," said Jung. "Though my family knows a thing or two about Tibet that might surprise you."

"I'm sure," said Drake. "Well, you shall advise, as you are able. But the Sicilian heritage goes back thousands of years before Rome, as does their knowledge of Atlantis. There were a few things washed up on the shores of North Africa, a few things found by divers. It was enough to establish a tradition. If there were a museum of Atlantean arts, Don Federico is one of the few people in the world qualified to be a curator."

"In other words," said Maldonado with a ghastly smile, "those statues better be authentic, kid. Because I will know if they are not."

"They are," said George. "I saw them picked up off the ocean bottom myself."

"That's impossible," said Jung.

"Let's look," said Drake.

He stood up and placed the palm of his hand flat against an oak panel which immediately slid to one side, revealing a winding metal staircase. Drake leading the way, the four of them descended what seemed to George five stories to a door with a combination lock. Drake opened the door and they passed through a series of other chambers, ending up in a large underground garage. The Gold & Appel truck was there and beside it the four statues, freed of their crates. There was no one in the room.

"Where did everybody go?" said Jung.

"They're Sicilians," said Drake. "They saw these and were afraid. They did the job of uncrating them and left." His face and Maldonado's wore a look of awe. Jung's craggy features bore an irritated, puzzled frown.

"I'm beginning to feel that I've been left out of a lot," he said.

"Later," said Maldonado. He took a small jeweler's glass out of his pocket and approached the nearest statue. "This is where they got the idea for the great god Pan," he said. "But you can see the idea was more complicated twenty thousand years ago than two thousand." Fixing the jeweler's glass in his eye, he began a careful inspection of a glittering hoof.

At the end of an hour, Maldonado, with the help of a ladder, had gone over each of the four statues from bottom to top with fanatical care and had questioned George about the manner of their seizure as well as what little he knew of their history. He put his jeweler's glass away, turned to Drake and nodded.

"You got the four most valuable pieces of art in the world."

Drake nodded. "I surmised as much. Worth more than all the gold in all the Spanish treasure ships there ever were."

"If I have not been dosed with a hallucinogenic drug," said Richard Jung, "I gather you are all saying these statues come from Atlantis. I'll take your word for it that they're solid gold, and that means there's a lot of gold there."

"The value of the matter is not worth one one ten-thousandth the value of the form," said Drake.

"That I don't see," said Jung. "What is the value of Atlantean art if no reputable authority anywhere in the world believes in Atlantis?"

Maldonado smiled. "There are a few people in the world who know that Atlantis existed, and who know there is such a thing as Atlantean art. And believe me, Richard, those few got enough money to make it worth anyone's while who has a piece from the bottom of the sea. Any one of these statues could buy a middle-sized country."

Drake clapped his hands with an air of authority. "I'm satisfied if Don Federico is satisfied. For these and for four more like them—or the equivalent if four such statues simply don't exist—my hand is joined with the hand of the Discordian movement. Let us go back upstairs and sign the papers—in pen and ink. And then, George, we would like you to be our guest at dinner."

George didn't know if he had the authority to promise four more statues, and he was certain that total openness was the only safe approach with these men. As they were climbing the stairs, he said to Drake, who was above him, "I wasn't authorized by the man who sent me to promise anything more. And I don't believe he has any more at the moment, unless he has a collection of his own. I know these four statues are the only ones he captured on this trip."

Drake let out a small fart, an incredible thing, it seemed to George, for the leader of all organized crime in the United States to do. "Excuse me," he said. "The exertion of these stairs is too much for me. Would love to put in an elevator, but that wouldn't be as secure. One of these days my heart will give out, going up and down those stairs." The fart smelled moderately bad, and George was glad when he had climbed out of its neighborhood. He was surprised that a man of Drake's importance would acknowledge that he farted. Perhaps that kind of straightforwardness was a factor in Drake's success. George doubted that Maldonado would admit to a fart. The Don was too devious. He was not your earthy sort of Latin—he was paper-thin and paper-pale, like a Tuscan aristocrat of attenuated bloodline.

They reentered Drake's office, and Drake and Maldonado each signed the parchment scroll. After the phrase, "for valuable considerations received," Drake inserted the words, "and considerations of equal value yet to come."

He smiled at George. "Since you can't guarantee the additional objects, I'll expect to hear from your boss within twenty-four hours after you leave here. This whole deal is contingent upon the additional payment from you."

ORGASM. HER BUBBIES FRITCHID BY THE GYNING DEEP-SEADOODLER. All in a lewdercrass chaste for a moulteeng fawkin. In fact, hearing Drake say that he was to be leaving the Syndicate fortress made George feel a bit better. He signed in behalf of the Discordians and Jung signed as a witness.

Drake said, "You understand, there is no way the organizations which Don Federico and I represent can be bound by anything we sign. What we agree to here is to use our influence with our many esteemed colleagues and to hope that they will grant us the favor of cooperation in the mutual enterprise."

Maldonado said, "I couldn't have said it better myself. We, of course, personally pledge our lives and our honor to further your purposes."

Robert Putney Drake took a cigar out of a silver humidor. Slapping George on the back, he shoved the cigar into his mouth. "You know, you're the first hippie I've ever done business with. I suppose you'd like to have some marijuana. I don't keep any around the house, and as you probably know we don't deal much in the stuff. Too bulky to transport, considering the amount you can make on it. Aside from that, I think you'll like the food and drink here. We'll have a big dinner and some entertainment."

The dinner was steak Diane, and it was served to the four men at a long table in a dining room hung with large, old paintings. They were waited on by a series of beautiful young women, and George wondered where the gang leaders kept their wives and mistresses. In some sort of *purdah*, perhaps. There was something Arabic about this whole setup.

During the main course a blonde in a long white gown which left one breast bare played the harp in a corner of the room and sang. There was conversation with the coffee; four young women sat down briefly with the men and regaled them with witticisms and funny stories.

With the brandy came Tarantella Serpentine. She was an amazingly tall woman, at least six feet two, with long blond hair that was piled high on her head and fell below her shoulders. She was wearing tinkling gold bracelets around her wrists and ankles, and there were diaphonous veils wrapped around her slender body, and nothing else. George could see pink nipples and dark crotch hair. When she strode through the door Banana-Nose Maldonado wiped his mouth with his napkin and began applauding gleefully. Robert Putney Drake smiled proudly and Richard Jung swallowed hard.

George just stared. "The star of our little rural retreat," said Drake by way of introduction. "May I present—Miss Tarantella Serpentine." Maldonado's applause continued, and George wondered if he should join in. Music, Oriental but with a touch of rock, flooded the room. The sound reproduction equipment was excellent, nigh perfect. Tarantella Serpentine began to dance. It was a strange, hybrid sort of dance, a synthesis of belly-dancing, go-go, and modern ballet. George licked his lips and he felt his face get warm and his penis begin to throb and swell as he watched. Tarantella Serpentine's dance was even more sensuous than the dance Stella Maris had done when he was being initiated into the Discordian movement.

After she had done three dances, Tarantella bowed and left. "You must be tired, George," said Drake, resting his hand on George's shoulder.

Suddenly, George realized he had been going on almost no sleep except for the times he'd dozed off in the car on the way from Mad Dog to the Gulf. He had been under incredible physical, and even more important, emotional pressure.

He agreed that he was tired, and, praying that he would not be murdered in his sleep, he let Drake lead him to a bedroom.

The bed was an enormous fourposter with a cloth-of-gold canopy. Naked, George slid between cool, crisp sheets, and clutching the top sheet around his neck, lay flat on his back, shut his eyes tight and sighed. That morning he had been on a beach in the Gulf of Mexico watching naked Mavis masturbate. He had fucked an apple. He had been to Atlantis. And now he was lying on a downy-soft mattress in the home of the chief of all organized crime in America. If he closed his eyes he might find himself back in the Mad Dog jail. He shook his head. There was nothing to fear.

He heard the bedroom door open. There was nothing to fear. To prove it, he kept his eyes closed. He heard a board squeak. Squeaky boards in this place? Sure—to warn the sleeper that there was someone sneaking up on him. He opened his eyes.

Tarantella Serpentine was standing over the bed. "Bobby-baby sent me," she said.

George closed his eyes again. "Sweetheart," he said, "you are beautiful. You really are. You're beautiful. Make yourself comfortable."

She reached down and turned on a bedside lamp. She was wearing a gold metallic bikini top with a short matching skirt. Her breasts were delightfully small, George thought. Although, on a five-foot-two girl they'd be ample. But Tarentella was built like a *Vogue* model. George liked her looks. He had always been partial to tall, slender boyish women.

"I'm not intruding on you, am I?" she asked. "You sure you wouldn't rather sleep?"

"Well it's not so much what I'd *rather* do," said George. "I doubt that I can do anything other than sleep. I have had a very trying day." Masturbated once, he thought, had one blow job, and fucked one apple. Forgive us our debts as we forgive our debtors. Plus been scared out of my wits 90 percent of the time.

Tarantella said, "My name is known in rarified circles for what I can achieve with men whose days are *all* trying. Presidents, kings, Syndicate heads—naturally—rock stars, oil billionnaires, people like that. My thing is, I can make men come. Over and over and over and *over* again. Ten times, sometimes even twenty times, no matter how old or how tired. I get paid a lot. Tonight, Bobby-baby is paying for my services, and I'm to service you. Which I like very much, because most of my clientele is on the middle-aged side, and you're nice and young and have a firm body." She gently pulled the sheet loose from George's grip—he had forgotten he was still holding it up around his neck—and caressed his bare shoulder.

"How old are you, George—twenty-two?"

"Twenty-three," said George. "But I don't want to disappoint you. I'm willing and I'm interested. In fact, I'm curious about what you do. But I'm pretty tired."

"Honey, you *can't* disappoint me. The more limp you are, the more I like it. The more of a challenge you are to me. Let me show you my specialty."

Tarantella doffed her bra, skirt, and panties quickly but

deliberately enough to let George enjoy watching her. Smiling at him, she stood before him, her legs spread wide apart. Her fingernails tickled her nipples, and George watched them swell up. Then, her left hand playing with her left breast, her right hand snaked down to her groin and began massaging the golden-brown hairs of her mons. Her middle finger disappeared between her legs. After a few moments a scarlet flush spread over her face, neck, and chest, her body arched backward, and she gave a single, agonized cry. Her skin, from head to toe, was glowing with a fine coating of sweat.

After a momentary pause she smiled and looked at him. Her right hand caressed his cheek and he felt the wetness on his face and smelled the Lobster Newburg aroma of a young cunt. Her fingers drifted to the sheets, and with a sudden movement she stripped them away from George's body. She grinned down at his stiff cock and in a moment was on top of him, holding his prick, inserting it into herself. Two minutes of smooth pistonlike movements on her part brought him to an unexpectedly pleasant orgasm.

"Baby," he said. "You could wake the dead."

He enjoyed his second orgasm about a half hour later, and his third a half hour after that. The second time Tarantella lay on her back and George lay on top of her, and the third time she was on her stomach and he was straddling her from the rear. There was something about the mood Tarantella created that was crucial to what she called her "specialty." Though she had boasted about her ability to make a man come repeatedly, when it came right down to doing things she made him feel that it didn't really matter what happened with him. She was fun-loving, playful, carefree. He did not feel obligated in any sense to stiffen, to come. Tarantella might view men as a challenge, but she made it clear that George was not to see her as a challenge.

After a short nap, he woke to find her sucking his rapidly hardening penis. It took much longer this time for him to come, but he enjoyed every second of mounting pleasure. After that they lay side by side and talked for a while. Then Tarantella went to the bedside table and took a tube of petroleum jelly out of a drawer. She began applying it to his penis, which grew erect during the process. Then she rolled over and presented him with her rosy asshole. It was the first time George had had a woman that way, and he came rather quickly after insertion from the novelty and excitement of it all.

They slept for a while and he awoke to find her masturbating him. Her fingers were very clever and seemed quickly to find their way to all the most sensitive parts of his penis—with special attention to that area just behind the crown of the head. He opened his eyes wide when he came and saw, after a few seconds, a small, pale, pearl-like drop of semen appear on the end of his dick. A wonder there was any at all.

It was getting to be a trip. His ego went away somewhere, and he was all body, letting it all happen. *It* was fucking Tarantella, and *it* was coming—and, judging by the sounds she was making and the wetness in which his penis was sloshing, she was coming, too.

There followed two more blow jobs. Then Tarantella pulled something that looked like an electric razor out of the bed-table drawer. She plugged it into the wall and began to stroke his penis with its vibrating head, pausing every so often to lick and lubricate the areas she was working on.

George closed his eyes and rolled his hips from side to side as he felt yet another orgasm coming on. From a great distance he heard Tarantella Serpentine say, "My greatness lies in the life I can generate in limp pricks."

George's pelvis began to pump up and down. It was really going to be that superorgasm Hemingway described. It began to happen. It was pure electricity. No juice—all energy pouring out like lightning through the magic wand at the center of his being. He wouldn't be surprised to discover that his balls and cock were disintegrating into whirling electrons. He screamed, and behind his tight-clenched eyes, he saw, very clearly, the smiling face of Mavis.

He awoke in the dark, and his instinctive groping motion told him that Tarantella was gone.

Instead, Mavis, in a white doctor's smock, stood at the foot of the bed, watching him with large bright eyes. The darkened Drake bedroom had turned into a hospital ward, and was suddenly brightly lit.

"How did you get here?" he blurted. "I mean—how did I get here?"

"Saul," she said kindly, "it's almost all over. You've come through it."

And suddenly he realized that he felt, not twenty-three, but sixty-three years old.

"You've won," he admitted, "I'm no longer sure who I am."

"You've won," Mavis contradicted. "You've gone through ego loss and now you're beginning to discover who you really are, poor old Saul."

He examined his hands: old man's. Wrinkled. Goodman's hands.

"There are two forms of ego loss," Mavis went on, "and the Illuminati are masters of both. One is schizophrenia, the other is illumination. They set you on the first track, and we switched you to the other. You had a time bomb in your head, but we defused it."

Malik's apartment. The Playboy Club. The submarine. And all the other past lives and lost years. "By God," Saul Goodman cried, "I've got it. I *am* Saul Goodman, but I am all the other people, too."

"And all time is this time," Mavis added softly.

Saul sat upright, tears gleaming in his eyes. "I've killed men. I've sent them to the electric chair. Seventeen times. Seventeen suicides. The savages who cut off fingers or toes or ears for their gods are more sensible. We cut off whole egos, thinking they are not ourselves but separate. God God God," and he burst in sobs.

Mavis rushed forward and held him, cradling his head to her breast. "Let it out," she said. "Let it all out. It's not true unless it makes you laugh, but you don't understand until it makes you weep."

QUEENS. Psychoanalysts in living cells, moving in military ordure, and a shitty outlook on life and sex, dancing coins in harry's krishna. It all coheres, even if you approach it bass ackwards. It coheres.

"Gruad the grayface!" Saul screamed, weeping, beating his fist against the pillow as Mavis held his head, stroked his hair. "Gruad the damned! And I have been his servant, his puppet, sacrificing myselves on his electric altars as burnt offerings."

"Yes, yes," Mavis cooed in his ear. "We must learn to give up our sacrifices, not our joys. They have taught us to give up everything except our sacrifices, and those are what we must give up. We must sacrifice our sacrifices."

"The Grayface, the lifehater!" Saul shrieked. "The bastard motherfucker! Osiris, Quetzalcoatl, I know him

under all his aliases. Grayface, Grayface, Grayface! I
know his wars and his prisons, the young boys he shafts up
the ass, the George Dorns he tries to turn into killers like
himself. And I have served him all my life. I have sacrificed men on his bloody pyramid!"

"Let it out," Mavis repeated, holding the old man's
trembling body "Let it all out, baby. . . ."

NOTHUNG. Woden you gnaw it, when you herd those
flying sheeps with wagner's loopy howls? Hassan walked
this loony valley, he had to wake up by himself. August
23, 1966: before he ever heard of the SSS, the Discordians, the JAMs or the Illuminati: stoned and beatific, Simon Moon is browsing in a Consumer Discount store on
North Clark street, digging the colors, not really intending
to buy anything. He stops in a frieze, mesmerized by a sign
above the timeclock:

NO EMPLOYEE MAY, UNDER ANY CIRCUMSTANCES, PUNCH
THE TIME CARD FOR ANY OTHER EMPLOYEE.
ANY DEVIATION WILL RESULT IN TERMINATION.
THE MGT.

"God's pajamas," Simon mutters, incredulous.

"Pajamas? Aisle seven," a clerk says helpfully.

"Yes. Thanks," Simon speaks very distinctly, edging
away, hiding his high. God's *pajamas and spats,* he thinks
in a half-illuminated trance, either I'm more stoned than I
think or that sign is absolutely the whole clue to how the
show runs.

RAGS. Hail Ghoulumbia, her monadmen are fled and all
she's left now is a bloody period. "The funny part," Saul
said, smiling while a few tears still flowed, "is that I'm not
ashamed of this. Two days ago I would have rather died
than be seen weeping—especially by a woman."

"Yes," Mavis said, *"especially by a woman."*

"That's it—isn't it?" Saul gasped. "That's their whole
gimmick. I couldn't see you without seeing a *woman.* I
couldn't see that editor, Jackson, without seeing a *Negro.* I
couldn't see anybody without seeing the attached label and
classification."

"That's how they keep us apart," Mavis said gently.
"And that's how they train us to keep our masks on. Love
was the hardest bond for them to smash, so they had to
create patriarchy, male supremacy, and all that crap—and

the 'masculine protest' and 'penis envy' in women came in as a result—so even lovers couldn't look at one another without seeing a separate category."

"O my God, my God," Saul moaned, beginning to weep heavily again. " 'A rag, a bone, a hank of hair.' O my God. *And you were with them!"* he cried suddenly, raising his head. "You're a former Illuminatus—that's why you're so important to Hagbard's plan. And that's why you have that tattoo!"

"I was one of the Five who run the U.S.," Mavis nodded. "One of the Insiders, as Robert Welch calls them. I've been replaced now by Atlanta Hope, the leader of God's Lightning."

"I've got it, I've got it!" Saul said, laughing. "I looked every way but the right way before. *He's* inside the Pentagon. That's why they build it in that shape, so *he* couldn't escape. The Aztecs, the Nazis . . . and now us . . ."

"Yes," Mavis said grimly. "That's why thirty thousand Americans disappear every year, without trace, and their cases end up in the unsolved files. *He* has to be fed."

" 'A man, though naked, may be in rags.' " Saul quoted. "Ambrose Bierce knew about it."

"And Arthur Machen," Mavis added. "And Lovecraft. But they had to write in code. Even so, Lovecraft went too far, mentioning the *Necronomicon* by name. That's why he died so suddenly when he was only forty-seven. And his literary executor, August Derleth, was persuaded to insert a note in every edition of Lovecraft's works, claiming that the *Necronomicon* doesn't exist and was just part of Lovecraft's fantasy."

"And the *Lloigor?"* Saul asked. "And the *dols?"*

"Real," Mavis said. "All real. That's what causes bad acid trips and schizophrenia. Psychic contact with *them* when the ego wall breaks. That's where the Illuminati were sending you when we raided their fake Playboy Club and short-circuited the process."

"Du hexen Hase," Saul quoted. And he began to tremble.

UNHEIMLICH. Urvater whose art's uneven, horrid be thine aim. Harpoons in him, corpus whalem: take ye and hate.

Fernando Poo was given prominent attention in the world press only once before the notorious Fernando Poo

Incident. It occurred in the early 1970s (while Captain Tequilla y Mota was first studying the art of the Coup d'Etat and laying his first plans,) and was occasioned by the outrageous claims of the anthropologist J. N. Marsh, of Miskatonic University, that artifacts he had found on Fernando Poo proved the existence of the lost continent of Atlantis. Although Professor Marsh had an impeccable reputation for scholarly caution and scientific rigor before this, his last published book, *Atlantis and Its Gods,* was greeted with mockery and derision by his professional colleagues, especially after his theories were picked up and sensationalized by the press. Many of the old man's friends, in fact, blame this campaign of ridicule for his disappearance a few months later, which they suspect was the suicide of a broken-hearted and sincere searcher after truth.

Not only were Marsh's theories now beyond all scientific credibility, but his methods—such as quoting Allegro's *The Sacred Mushroom and the Cross* or Graves' *The White Goddess* as if they were as reputable as Boas, Mead, or Frazer—seemed to indicate senility. This impression was increased by the eccentric dedication "To Ezra Pound, Jacques De Molay and Emperor Norton I." The real scientific scandal was not the theory of Atlantis (that was a bee that had haunted many a scholarly bonnet) but Marsh's claim that the gods of Atlantis actually existed; not as supernatural beings, of course, but as a superior class of life, now extinct, which had preexisted mankind and duped the earliest civilization into worshiping them as divine and offering terrible sacrifices at their altars. That there was absolutely no archaeological or paleontological evidence that such beings ever existed, was the mildest of the scholarly criticisms aimed at this hypothesis.

Professor Marsh's rapid decline, in the few months between the book's unanimous rejection by the learned world and his sudden disappearance, caused great pain to colleagues at Miskatonic. Many recognized that he had acquired some of his notions from Dr. Henry Armitage, generally regarded as having gone somewhat bananas after too many years devoted to puzzling out the obscene metaphysics of the *Necronomicon.* When the librarian Miss Horus mentioned at a faculty tea shortly after the disappearance that Marsh had spent much of the past month with that volume, one Catholic professor urged, only half-jokingly, that Miskatonic should rid itself of scandals once and for all by presenting "that damned book" (he emphasized the word very deliberately) to Harvard.

Missing Persons Department of the Arkham police assigned the Marsh case to a young detective who had previously distinguished himself by tracing several missing infants to one of the particularly vile Satanist cults that have festered in that town since the witch-hunting days of 1692. His first act was to examine the manuscript on which the old man had been working since the completion of *"Atlantis and Its Gods."* It seemed to be a shortish essay, intended for an anthropological magazine, and was quite conservative in tone and concept, as if the professor regretted the boldness of his previous speculations. Only one footnote, expressing guarded and qualified endorsement of Urquhart's theory about Wales being settled by survivors from Mu, showed the bizarre preoccupations of the Atlantis book. However, the final sheet was not related to this article at all and seemed to be notes for a piece which the Professor evidently intended to submit, brazenly and in total contempt of academic opinion, to a pulp publication devoted to flying saucers and occultism. The detective puzzled over these notes for a long time:

> *The usual hoax: fiction presented as fact. This hoax described here opposite to this: fact presented as fiction.*
>
> *Huysmans' La-Bas started it, turns the Satanist into hero.*
>
> *Machen in Paris 1880s, met with Huysman's circle.*
>
> *"Dols" and "Aklo letters" in Machen's subsequent "fiction."*
>
> *Same years: Bierce and Chambers both mention Lake of Hali and Carcosa. Allegedly, coincidence.*
>
> *Crowley recruiting his occult circle after 1900.*
>
> *Bierce disappears in 1913.*
>
> *Lovecraft introduces Hali, dols, Aklo, Cthulhu after 1923.*
>
> *Lovecraft dies unexpectedly, 1937.*
>
> *Seabrook discusses Crowley, Machen, etc. in his "Witchcraft," 1940.*
>
> *Seabrook's "suicide," 1942.*
>
> *Emphasize: Bierce describes Oedipus Complex in "Death of Halpin Frazer," BEFORE Freud, and*

relativity in "Inhabitant of Carcosa," BEFORE Einstein. Lovecraft's ambiguous descriptions of Azathoth as "blind idiot-god," "Demon-Sultan" and "nuclear chaos" circa 1930: fifteen years before Hiroshima.

Direct drug references in Chambers' "King in Yellow," Machen's "White Powder," Lovecraft's "Beyond the Wall of Sleep" and "Mountains of Madness."

The appetites of the Lloigor or Old Ones in Bierce's "Damned Thing." Machen's "Black Stone," Lovecraft (constantly.)

Atlantis known as Thule both in German and Panama Indian lore, and of course, "coincidence" again the accepted explanation. Opening sentence for article: "The more frequently one uses the word 'coincidence' to explain bizarre happenings, the more obvious it becomes that one is not seeking, but evading, the real explanation." Or, shorter: "The belief in coincidence is the prevalent superstition of the Age of Science."

The detective then spent an afternoon at Miskatonic library, browsing through the writings of Ambrose Bierce, J-K Huysmans, Arthur Machen, Robert W. Chambers, and H. P. Lovecraft. He found that all repeated certain key words; dealt with lost continents or lost cities; described superhuman beings trying to misuse or victimize mankind in some unspecified manner; suggested that there was a cult, or group of cults, among mankind who served these beings; and described certain books (usually not giving their titles: Lovecraft was an exception) that reveal the secrets of these beings. With a little further research, he found that the occult and Satanist circles in Paris in the 1880s had influenced the fiction of both Huysmans and Machen, as well as the career of the egregious Aleistair Crowley, and that Seabrook (who knew Crowley) hinted at more than he stated outright in his book on Witchcraft, published two years before his suicide. He then wrote a little table:

Huysmans—hysteria, complaints about occult attacks, final seclusion in a monastery.
Chambers—abandons such subjects, turns to light romantic fiction.

Bierce—disappears mysteriously.
Lovecraft—dead at an early age.
Crowley—hounded into silence and obscurity.
Machen—becomes a devout Catholic. (Huysmans' escape?)
Seabrook—alleged suicide.

The detective then went back and reread, not skimming this time, the stories by these writers in which drugs were specifically mentioned, according to Marsh's notes. He now had a hypothesis: the old man had been lured into a drug cult, as had these writers, and had been terrified by his own hallucinations, finally ending his own life to escape the phantoms his own narcotic-fogged brain had created. It was a good enough theory to start with, and the detective conscientiously set about interviewing every friend on campus of old Marsh, leading into the subject of grass and LSD very slowly and indirectly. He made no headway and was beginning to lose his conviction when good fortune struck, in the form of a remark by another anthropology professor about Marsh's preoccupation in recent years with *amanita muscaria,* the hallucinogenic mushroom used in ancient Near Eastern religions.

"A very interesting fungus, *amanita,*" this professor told the detective. "Some sensationalists without scholarly caution have claimed it was every magic potion in ancient lore: the soma of the Hindus, the sacrament used in the Dionysian and Eleusinian mysteries in Greece, even the Holy Communion of the earliest Christians and Gnostics. One chap in England even claims amanita, and not hashish, was the drug used by the Assassins in the Middle Ages, and there's a psychiatrist in New York, Puharich, who claims it actually does induce telepathy. Most of that is rubbish, of course, but amanita certainly is the strongest mind-altering drug in the world. If the kids ever latch onto it, LSD will seem like a tempest in a teapot by comparison."

The detective now concentrated on finding somebody—anybody—who had actually seen old Marsh when he was stoned out of his gourd. The testimony finally came from a young black student named Pearson, who was majoring in anthropology and minoring in music. "Excited and euphoric? Yeah," he said thoughtfully. "I saw old Joshua

that way once. It was in the library of all places—that's
where my girl works—and the old man jumped up from a
table grinning about a yard wide and said out loud, but
talking to himself, you know, 'I saw them—I saw the
fnords!' Then he ran out like Jesse Owens going to get his
ashes hauled. I was curious and went over to peek at what
he'd been reading. It was the *New York Times* editorial
page, and not a picture on it, so he certainly didn't see the
fnords, whatever the hell they are, *there*. You think he was
maybe bombed a little?"

"Maybe, maybe not," the detective said noncomittally,
obeying the police rule of never accusing anyone of anything in hearing of a witness unless ready to make an arrest. But he was already quite sure that Professor Marsh
would never reappear to be subject to arrest or any other
harassment by those who had not entered his special world
of lost civilizations, vanished cities, lloigors, dols, and
fnords. To this day, the file on the Joshua N. Marsh case
in the Arkham police department bears the closing line:
"Probable cause of death: suicide during drug psychosis."
Nobody ever traced the change in Professor Marsh back to
a KCUF meeting in Chicago and a strangely spiked punch;
but the young detective, Daniel Pricefixer, always retained
a nagging doubt and a shapeless disquiet about this particular investigation, and even after he moved to New York
and went to work for Barney Muldoon, he was still addicted to reading books on pre-history and thinking strange
thoughts.

SIMON MAGUS. You will come to know gods.

After the disappearance of Saul Goodman and Barney
Muldoon, the FBI went over the Malik apartment with a
fine-tooth comb. Everything was photographed, finger-
printed, analyzed, catalogued, and where possible shipped
back to the crime laboratory in Washington. Among the
items was a short note on the back of a Playboy Club
lunch receipt, not in Malik's handwriting, which meant
nothing to anybody and was included only for the sake of
the completeness so loved by the Bureau.

The note said: "Machen's *dols* = Lovecraft's *dholes?*"

VECTORS. You will come to no gods.

On April 25, most of New York was talking about the
incredible event that had occurred shortly before dawn at
the Long Island mansion of the nation's best-known
philanthropist, Robert Putney Drake. Danny Pricefixer of

the Bomb Squad, however, was almost oblivious of this bizarre occurrence, as he drove through heavy traffic from one part of Manhattan to another interviewing every witness who might have spoken to Joseph Malik in the week before the *Confrontation* explosion. The results were uniformly disappointing: aside from the fact that Malik had grown increasingly secretive in recent years, none of the interviews seemed to provide any useful information. A killer smog had again settled on the city, for the seventh straight day, and Danny, a nonsmoker, was very aware of the wheeze in his chest, which did nothing to improve his mood.

Finally, at three in the afternoon, he left the office of **ORGASM** at 110 West Fortieth Street (an associate editor there was an old friend of Malik's and frequently lunched with him, but had nothing substantial to offer in leads) and remembered that the main branch of the New York Public Library was only half a block away. The hunch had been in the back of his mind, he realized, ever since he glanced at Malik's weird Illuminati memos. *What the hell,* he thought, *it'll only be a few more wasted minutes in a wasted day.*

For once, the congestion at the window in the main reference room was not quite as bad as a Canal Street traffic jam. *Atlantis and Its Gods* by Professor J. N. Marsh was delivered to him in seventeen minutes, and he began leafing through it looking for the passage he vaguely remembered. At last, on page 123, he found it:

Hans Stefan Santesson points out the basic similarity of Mayan and Egyptian investiture rituals, as previously indicated in Colonel Churchward's insightful but wrongheaded books on the lost continent of Mu. As we have demonstrated, Churchward's obsession with the Pacific, based on his having received his first clues about our lost ancestors in an Asiatic temple, led him to attribute to the fictitious Mu much of the real history of the actual Atlantis. But this passage from Santesson's *Understanding Mu* (Paperback Library, New York, 1970, page 117) needs little correction:

Next he was taken to the Throne of Regeneration of the Soul, and the Ceremony of Investiture or Illumination took place. Then he experienced further ordeals before attaining to the Chamber of the Orient, to the Throne of Ra, to become truly a Master. He could see for himself in the distance the uncreated light from which was pointed out the whole happiness of the future . . . In other words, as Churchward puts it, both in Egypt and in Maya the initiate had to "sustain" (i.e., survive) "the fiery ordeal" to be approved as an adept. The adept had to become justified. The justified must then become illuminate. . . . The destruction of Mu was commemorated by the possibly symbolic House of Fire of the Quiche Mayas and by the relatively later Chamber of Central Fire of the Mysteries which we are told were celebrated in the Great Pyramid.

Substituting Atlantis for Mu, Churchward and Santesson are basically correct. The god, of course, could choose the shape in which He would appear in the final ordeal, and, since these gods, or *lloigor* in the Atlantean language, possessed telepathy, they would read the initiate's mind and manifest in the form most terrifying to the specific individual, although the *shoggoth* form and the classic Angry Giant form such as appears in Aztec statues of Tlaloc were most common. To employ an amusing conceit, if these beings had survived to our time, as some occultists claim, they would appear to the average American as, say, King Kong or, perhaps, Dracula or the Wolf-Man.

The sacrifices demanded by these creatures evidently contributed significantly to the fall of Atlantis, and we can conjecture that the mass burnings practised by the Celts at Beltain and even the Aztec religion, which turned their altars into abbatoirs, were minor in comparison, being merely the result of persistent tradition after the real menace of the *lloigor* had vanished. We, of course, cannot fully understand the purpose of these bloody rituals, since we cannot fathom the nature, or even the sort of matter or energy, that comprised the *lloigor*. That the chief of these beings, is known in the *Pnakotic Manuscripts* and the Eltdown Shards as Iok-Sotot, "Eater of

Souls," suggests that it was some energy or psychic vibration of the dying victim that the *lloigor* needed; the physical body was, as in the case of the corpse-eating cult of Leng, consumed by the priests themselves, or merely thrown away, as among the Thuggee of India.

Thoughtfully and quietly, Danny Pricefixer returned the book to the clerk at the checkout window. Thoughtfully and quietly, he walked out on Fifth Avenue and stood between the two guardian lions. Who was it, he wondered, who had asked, "Since nobody wants war, why do wars keep happening?" He looked at the killer smog around him and asked himself another riddle, "Since nobody wants air pollution, why does air pollution keep increasing?"

Professor Marsh's words came back to him: *"if these beings had survived to our time, as some occultists claim. . . ."*

Walking toward his car, he passed a newsstand and saw that the disaster at the Drake Mansion was still the biggest headline even in the afternoon editions. It was irrelevant to his problem, however, so he ignored it.

Sherri Brandi continued the chant in her mind, maintaining the rhythm of her mouth movements . . . *fifty-three big rhinoceroses, fifty-four big rhinoceroses, fifty-five*—Carmel's nails dug into her shoulders suddenly and the salty gush splashed hot on her tongue. Thank the Lord, she thought, the bastard finally made it. Her jaw was tired and she had a crick in her neck and her knees hurt, but at least the son-of-a-bitch would be in a good mood now and wouldn't beat her up for having so little to report about Charley and his bugs.

She stood up, stretching her leg and neck muscles to remove the cramps, and looked down to see if any of Carmel's come had dribbled on her dress. Most men wanted her naked during a blow job, but not creepy Carmel; he insisted she wear her best gown, always. He liked soiling her, she realized: but, hell, he wasn't as bad as some pimps and we've all got to get our kicks some way.

Carmel sprawled back in the easy chair, his eyes still closed. Sherri fetched the towel she had been warming over the radiator and completed the transaction, drying him and gently kissing his ugly wand before tucking it back inside his fly and zippering him up. He *does* look like a goddam frog, she thought bitterly, or a nasty-tempered chipmunk.

"Terrif," he said finally. "The johns really get their money's worth from you, kid. Now tell me about Charley and his bugs."

Sherri, still feeling cramped, pulled over a footstool and perched on its edge. "Well," she said, "you know I gotta be careful. If he knows I'm pumping him, he might drop me and take up with some other girl. . . ."

"So you were too damned cautious and you didn't get anything out of him?" Carmel interrupted accusingly.

"Oh, he's over the loop," she answered, still vague. "I mean, really crazy now. That must be . . . uh, important . . . if you have to deal with him. . . ." She came back into focus. "How I know is, he thinks he's going to other planets in his dreams. Some planet called Atlantis. Do you know which one that is?"

Carmel frowned. This was getting stickier: first, find a commie: then, find how to get the info out of Charley despite the FBI and CIA and all the other government people; and now, how to deal with a maniac. . . . He looked up and saw that she was out of focus again, staring into space. *Dopey broad,* he thought, and then watched as she slid slowly off the stool onto a neat sleeping position on the floor.

"What the hell?" he said out loud.

When he kneeled next to her and listened for her heart, his own face paled. *Jesus, Jesus, Jesus,* he thought standing up, now I got to *get rid of a fucking corpus delectus. The damned bitch went and died.*

"I can see the fnords!" Barney Muldoon cried, looking up from the *Miami Herald* with a happy grin.

Joe Malik smiled contentedly. It had been a hectic day—especially since Hagbard had been tied up with the battle of Atlantis and the initiation of George Dorn—but now, at last, he had the feeling their side was winning. Two minds set on a death trip by the Illuminati had been successfully saved. Now if everything worked out right between George and Robert Putney Drake . . .

The intercom buzzed and Joe answered, calling across the room without rising, "Malik."

"How's Muldoon?" Hagbard's voice asked.

"Coming all the way. He sees the fnords in a Miami paper."

"Excellent," Hagbard said distractedly. "Mavis reports that Saul is all the way through, too, and just saw the fnords in the *New York Times*. Bring Muldoon up to my room. We've located that other problem—the sickness vibrations that FUCKUP has been scanning since March. It's somewhere around Las Vegas and it's at a critical stage. We think there's been one death already."

"But we've got to get to Ingolstadt before Walpurgis night. . . ." Joe said thoughtfully.

"Revise and rewrite," Hagbard said. "*Some* of us will go to Ingolstadt. Some of us will have to go to Las Vegas. It's the old Illuminati one-two punch—two attacks from different directions. Get your asses in gear, boys. They're immanentizing the Eschaton."

WEISHAUPT. Fnords? Prffft!

Another interruption. This time it was the Mothers March Against Muzak. Since that seems the most worthwhile cause I've been approached for all day, I gave the lady $1. I think that if Muzak can be stamped out, a lot of our other ailments will disappear too, since they're probably stress symptoms, caused by noise pollution.

Anyway, it's getting late and I might as well conclude this. One month before our KCUF experiment—that is, on September 23, 1970—Timothy Leary passed five federal agents at O'Hare Airport here in Chicago. He had vowed to shoot rather than go back to jail, and there was a gun in his pocket. None of them recognized him . . . And, oh, yes, there was a policeman named Timothy O'Leary in the hospital room where Dutch Schultz died on October 23, 1935.

I've been saving the best for last. Aldous Huxley, the first major literary figure illuminated by Leary, died the same day as John F. Kennedy. The last essay he wrote revolved around Shakespeare's phrase, "Time must have a stop"—which he had previously used for the title of a novel about life after death. "Life is an illusion." he wrote, "but an illusion which we must take seriously."

Two years later, Laura, Huxley's widow, met the medium, Keith Milton Rinehart. As she tells the story in her book, *This Timeless Moment*, when she asked if Rinehart could contact Aldous, he replied that Aldous wanted to transmit "classical evidence of survival," a message, that is, which could not be explained "merely" as telepathy, as something Rinehart picked out of *her* mind. It had to be something that could only come from Aldous's mind.

Later that evening, Rinehart produced it: instructions to go to a room in her house, a room he hadn't seen and find a particular book, which neither he nor she was familiar with. She was to look on a certain page and a certain line. The book was one Aldous had read but she had never even glanced at; it was an anthology of literary criticism. The line indicated—I have memorized it—was: "Aldous Huxley does not surprise us in this admirable communication in which paradox and erudition in the poetic sense and the sense of humor are interlaced in such an efficacious form." Need I add that the page was 17 and the line was, of course, line 23?

(I suppose you've read Seutonius and know that the late J. Caesar was rendered exactly 23 stab wounds by Brutus and Co.)

Brace yourself, Joe. Worse attacks on your Reason are coming along. Soon, you'll see the fnords.

Hail Eris,

P.S. Your question about the vibes and telepathy is easily answered. The energy is always moving in us, through us, and out of us. That's why the vibes have to be right before you can read someone without static. Every emotion is a motion.

ILLUMINATUS!
PART II

The Golden Apple

To Arlen and Yvonne

There is no god but man.

Man has the right to live by his own law—to live in the way that he wills to do: to work as he will: to play as he will: to rest as he will: to die when and how he will.

Man has the right to eat what he will: to drink what he will: to dwell where he will: to move as he will on the face of the earth.

Man has the right to think what he will: to speak what he will: to write what he will: to draw, paint, carve, etch, mold, build as he will: to dress as he will.

Man has the right to love as he will.

Man has the right to kill those who thwart these rights.

—*The Equinox: A Journal of Scientific Illuminism,* 1922 (edited by Aleister Crowley)

BOOK THREE

UNORDNUNG

Believe not one word that is written in *The Honest Book of Truth* by Lord Omar nor any that be in *Principia Discordia* by Malaclypse the Younger; for all that is there contained are the most pernicious and deceptive truths.

— "Epistle to the Episkopi," *The Dishonest Book of Lies,* by Mordecai Malignatus, K.N.S.

THE SIXTH TRIP, OR TIPARETH
(THE MAN WHO MURDERED GOD)

> To choose order over disorder, or disorder over order, is
> to accept a trip composed of both the creative and the
> destructive. But to choose the creative over the destructive
> is an all-creative trip composed of both order and disorder.
> —"The Curse of Grayface and the Introduction
> of Negativism," *Principia Discordia,* by
> Malaclypse the Younger, K.S.C.

April 25 began, for John Dillinger, with a quick skimming of the *New York Times;* he noticed more fnords
than usual. "The fit's about to hit the shan," he thought
grimly, turning on the eight o'clock news—only to
catch the story about the Drake Mansion, another bad
sign. In Las Vegas, in rooms where the light never
changed, none of the gamblers noticed that it was now
morning; but Carmel, returning from the desert, where
he had buried Sherri Brandi, drove out of his way to
look over Dr. Charles Mocenigo's home, hoping to see
or hear something helpful; he heard only a revolver
shot, and quickly sped away. Looking back, he saw
flames leaping toward the sky. And, over the mid-At-
lantic, R. Buckminster Fuller glanced at his three
watches, noting that it was two in the morning on the
plane, midnight at his destination (Nairobi) and 6 A.M.
back home in Carbondale, Illinois. (In Nairobi itself,
Nkrumah Fubar, maker of voodoo dolls that caused
headaches to the President of the United States,
prepared for bed, looking forward to Mr. Fuller's lecture at the university next morning. Mr. Fubar, in his
sophisticated-primitive way, like Simon Moon in his

primitive-sophisticated way, saw no conflict between magic and mathematics.)

In Washington, D.C., the clocks were striking five when Ben Volpe's stolen Volkswagen pulled up in front of the home of Senator Edward Coke Bacon, the nation's most distinguished liberal and leading hope of all those young people who hadn't yet joined Morituri groups. "In quick and out quick," Ben Volpe said tersely to his companions, "a *cowboy*." Senator Bacon turned in his bed (Albert "the Teacher" Stern fires directly at the Dutchman) and mumbled, "Newark." Beside him, his wife half woke and heard a noise in the garden (*Mama mama mama*, the Dutchman mumbles): "Mama," she hears her son's voice saying, as she sinks back toward a dream. The rain of bullets jolts her awake into a sea of blood and in one flash she sees her husband dying beside her, her son twenty years ago weeping for a dead turtle, the face of Mendy Weiss, and Ben Volpe and two others backing out of the room.

But, in 1936, when Robert Putney Drake returned from Europe to accept a vice presidency in his father's bank in Boston, the police already knew that Albert the Teacher really hadn't shot the Dutchman. There were even a few, such as Elliot Ness, who knew the orders had come from Mr. Lucky Luciano and Mr. Alphonse "Scarface" Capone (residing in Atlanta Penitentiary) and had been transmitted through Federico Maldonado. Nobody, outside the Syndicate itself, however, could name Jimmy the Shrew, Charley the Bug and Mendy Weiss as the actual killers—nobody except Robert Putney Drake.

On April 1, 1936, Federico Maldonado's phone rang and, when he answered it, a cultivated Boston voice said conversationally, "Mother is the best bet. Don't let Satan draw you too fast." This was followed by an immediate click as the caller hung up.

Maldonado thought about it all day and finally mentioned it to a very close friend that evening. "Some nut calls me up today and gives me part of what the Dutch-man told the cops before he died. Funny thing about it—he gives one of the parts that would really sink us all, if anybody in the police or the Feds could under-stand it."

"That's the way some nuts are," pronounced the other Mafioso don, an elegant elderly gentleman re-sembling one of Frederick II's falcons. "They're tuned in like gypsies. Telepathy, you know? But they get it all scrambled because they're nuts."

"Yeah, I guess that's it," Maldonado agreed. He had a crazy uncle who would sometimes blurt out a Broth-erhood secret that he couldn't possibly know, in the middle of ramblings about priests making it with altar boys and Mussolini hiding on the fire escape and non-sense like that. "They tune in—like the Eye, eh?" And he laughed.

But the next morning, the phone rang again, and the same voice said with elaborate New England intona-tion, "Those dirty rats have tuned in. French Canadian bean soup." Maldonado broke into a cold sweat; it was that moment, in fact, when he decided his son, the priest, would say a mass for the Dutchman every Sun-day.

He thought about it all day. Boston—the accent was Boston. They had witches up there once. French Cana-dian bean soup. Christ, Harvard is just outside Boston and Hoover is recruiting Feds from the Harvard Law School. Were there lawyers who were witches, too? Cowboy the son of a bitch, I told them, and they found him in the men's crapper. That damned Dutch-man. A bullet in his gut and he lives long enough to blab everything about the *Segreto*. The goddam *tedeschi* . . .

Robert Putney Drake dined on lobster Newburg that evening with a young lady from one of the lesser-known branches of the House of Morgan. Afterward, he took her to see *Tobacco Road* and, in the cab back to his hotel, they talked seriously about the sufferings of the poor and the power of Henry Hull's performance as Jeeter. Then he took her up to his room and fucked her from hell to breakfast. At ten in the morning, after she had left, he came out of the shower, stark naked, thirty-three years old, rich, handsome, feeling like a healthy and happy predatory mammal. He looked down at his penis, thought of snakes in mescaline visions back in Zurich and donned a bathrobe which cost enough to feed one of the starving families in the nearby slums for about six months. He lit a fat Cuban cigar and sat down by the phone, a male mammal, predatory, happy. He began to dial, listening to the clicks, the dot and the dot and the dot-dot, remembering the perfume his mother had worn leaning over his crib one night thirty-two years ago, the smell of her breasts, and the time he experimentally tried homosexuality in Boston Common with the pale faggot kneeling before him in the toilet stall and the smell of urine and Lysol disinfectant, the scrawl on the door saying ELEANOR ROOSEVELT SUCKS and his instant fantasy that it wasn't a faggot genuflecting in church before his hot hard prick but the President's wife . . . "Yes?" said the taut, angry voice of Banana Nose Maldonado.

"When I reached the can, the boy came at me," Drake drawled, his mild erection becoming warm and rubbery. "What happened to the other sixteen?" He hung up quickly. ("The analysis is brilliant," Professor Tochus at Harvard had said of his paper on the last words of Dutch Schultz. "I particularly like the way you've combined both Freud and Adler in finding sexuality and power drives expressed in the same image at certain places. That is quite original." Drake laughed and said: "The Marquis de Sade anticipated me by a century and a half, I fear. Power—and possession—*are* sexual, to some males.")

Drake's brilliance had also been noted by Jung's circle in Zurich. Once—when Drake was off taking mescaline with Paul Klee and friends on what they called their Journey to the East—Drake had been a topic of long and puzzled conversation in Jung's study. "We haven't seen his like since Joyce was here," one woman psychiatrist commented. "He is brilliant, yes," Jung said sadly, "but evil. So evil that I despair of comprehending him. I even wonder what old Freud would think. This man doesn't want to murder his father and possess his mother; he wants to murder God and possess the cosmos."

Maldonado got two phone calls the third morning. The first was from Louis Lepke, and was crudely vehement: "What's up, Banana Nose?" The insult of using the forbidden nickname in personal conversation was deliberate and almost unforgivable, but Maldonado forgave it.

"You spotted my boys following you, eh?" he asked genially.

"I spotted your *soldiers*," Lepke emphasized the word, "and that means you wanted me to spot them. What's up? You know if I get hit, you get hit."

"You won't get hit, *caro mio*," Don Federico replied, still cordial. "I had a crazy idea about something I thought might be coming from inside and you're the only one who would know enough to do it, I thought. I was wrong. I can tell by your voice. And if I was right, you wouldn't have called me. A million apologies. Nobody will be following you anymore. Except maybe Tom Dewey's investigators, eh?" he laughed.

"Okay," Lepke said slowly, "Call them off, and I'll forget it. But don't try to scare me again. I do crazy things when I'm scared."

"Never again," Maldonado promised.

He sat frowning at the phone, after Lepke hung up. *Now I owe him,* he thought. *I'll have to arrange to bump off somebody who's annoying him, to show the proper and most courteous apology.*

But, Virgin Mother, if it isn't the Butcher, who is it? A real witch?

The phone rang again. Crossing himself and calling on the Virgin silently, Maldonado lifted the receiver.

"Let him harness himself to you and then bother you," Robert Putney Drake quoted pleasantly, "fun is fun." He did not hang up.

"Listen," Don Federico said, "who is this?"

"Dutch died three times," Drake said in a sepulchral tone. "When Mendy Weiss shot him, when Vince Coll's ghost shot *him* and when that dumb junkie, the Teacher, shot him. But Dillinger never even died once."

"Mister, you got a deal," Maldonado said. "I'm sold. *I'll meet you anywhere.* In *broad daylight.* In Central Park. *Any place* you'll feel safe."

"No, you will not meet me just now," Drake said coolly. "You are going to discuss this with Mr. Lepke and Mr. Capone, first. You will also discuss it with—" he read, off a card in his hand, fifteen names. "Then, after you have all had time to consider it, you will be hearing from me." Drake farted, as he always did in the nervous moments when an important deal was being arranged, and hung up quickly.

Now, he said to himself, *insurance.*

A photostat of his second analysis of the last words of Dutch Schultz—the private one, not the public version which he had turned in to the Department of Psychology at Harvard—was on the hotel desk before him. He folded it smartly and pinned on top of it a note saying, "There are five copies in the vaults of five different banks." He then inserted it in an envelope, addressed it to Luciano and strolled out to drop it down the hotel mail chute.

Returning to his room he dialed Louis Lepke, born Louis Buchalter, of the organization later to be named Murder Inc. by the sensational press. When Lepke answered, Drake recited solemnly, still quoting the Dutchman, "I get a month. They did it. Come on, Illuminati."

"Who the hell is this?" Lepke's voice cried as Drake gently cradled the phone. A few moments later, he completed checking out of the hotel and flew home on the noon flight, to spend five grueling twenty-hour days reorganizing and streamlining his father's bank. On the fifth night he relaxed and took a young lady of the Lodge family to dance to Ted Weems's orchestra and

listen to their new young vocalist, Perry Como. Afterwards, he fucked her thirteen to the dozen and seven
ways to a Sunday. The next morning, he took out a
small book, in which he had systematically listed all the
richest families in America, and placed her first name
and a check after *Lodge,* as he had done with *Morgan*
the week before. A Rockefeller would be next.

He was on the noon flight to New York and spent
the day negotiating with Morgan Trust officials. That
night he saw a breadline on Fortieth Street and became
profoundly agitated. Back in his hotel, he made one of
his rare, almost furtive diary entries:

> Revolution could occur at any time. If Huey Long
> hadn't been shot last year, we might have it al-
> ready. If Capone had let the Dutchman hit
> Dewey, the Justice Department would be strong
> enough now, due to the reaction, to ensure that
> the State would be secure. If Roosevelt can't
> maneuver us into the war when it starts, all will be
> lost. And the war may be three or four years away
> yet. If we could bring Dillinger back, the reaction
> might strengthen Hoover and Justice, but John
> seems to be with the other side. My plan may be
> the last chance, and the Illuminati haven't con-
> tacted me yet, although they must have tuned in.
> Oh, Weishaupt, what a spawn of muddleheads
> are trying to carry on your work.

He tore the page out nervously, farted and crumbled
it in the ashtray, where he burned it slowly. Then, still
agitated, he dialed Mr. Charles Luciano on the phone
and said softly, "I am a pretty good pretzler, Winifred.
Department of Justice. I even got it from the department."

"Don't hang up," Luciano said softly. "We've been
waiting to hear from you. Are you still there?"

"Yes," Drake said carefully, with tight lips and a
tighter sphincter.

"Okay," Mr. Lucky said. "You know about the Illuminati. You know what the Dutchman was trying to say to the police. You even seem to know about the *Liberteri* and Johnnie Dillinger. How much do you want?"

"Everything," Drake replied. "And you are all going to offer it to me. But not yet. Not tonight." And he hung up.

(The wheel of time, as the Mayans knew, spins three ways; and just as the earth revolves on its own axis, simultaneously orbits about the sun and at the "same" time trails after the sun as that star traverses the galaxy's edge, the wheel of time, which is a wheel of *ifs,* is come round again, as Drake's phone clicks off, to Gruad the Grayface calculating the path of a comet and telling his followers: "See? Even the heavenly bodies are subject to law, and even the lloigor, so must not men and women also be subject to law?" And in a smaller cycle, Semper Cuni Linctus, centurion stationed in a godforsaken outpost of the Empire, listens in boredom as a subaltern tells him excitedly: "That guy we crucified last Friday—people all over town are swearing they've seen him walking around. One guy even claims to have put a hand through his side!" Semper Cuni Linctus smiles cynically. "Tell that to the gladiators," he says. And Albert Stern turns on the gas, takes one last fix, and full of morphine and euphoria, dies slowly, confident that he will always be remembered as the man who shot Dutch Schultz, not knowing that Abe Reles will reveal the truth five years later.)

Camp-town racetrack five miles long . . .

During Joe's second trip on the *Leif Erikson,* they went all the way to Africa, and Hagbard had an important conference with five gorillas. At least, he said afterwards that it was important; Joe couldn't judge, since the conversation was in Swahili. "They speak some English," Hagbard explained back on the sub, "but I prefer Swahili, since they're more eloquent in it and can express more nuances."

"Are you the first man to teach an ape to speak," Joe asked, "in addition to your other accomplishments?"

"Oh, not at all," Hagbard said modestly. "It's an old Discordian secret. The first person to communicate with a gorilla was an Erisian missionary named Malaclypse the Elder, who was born in Athens and got exiled for opposing the imposition of male supremacy when the Athenians created patriarchy and locked up their women. He then wandered all over the ancient world, learning all sorts of secrets and leaving behind a priceless collection of mind-blowing legends—he's the Phoenix Madman mentioned in the Confucian scriptures, and he passed himself off as Krishna to recite that gorgeous Bible of revolutionary ethics, the Bhagavad Gita, to Arjuna in India, among other feats. I believe you met him in Chicago while he was pretending to be the Christian Devil."

"But how have you Discordians concealed the fact that gorillas talk?"

"We're rather close-mouthed, you might say, and when we do speak it's usually to put somebody on or blow their minds—"

"I've noticed that," Joe said.

"And the gorillas themselves are too shrewd to talk to anybody but another anarchist. They're all anarchists themselves, you know, and they have a very healthy wariness about people in general and government people in particular. As one of them told me once, 'If it got out that we can talk, the conservatives would exterminate most of us and make the rest pay *rent* to live on our own land; and the liberals would try to train us to be engine-lathe operators. Who the fuck wants to operate an engine lathe?' They prefer their own pastoral and Eristic ways, and I, for one, would never interfere with them. We do communicate, though, just as we communicate with the dolphins. Both species are intelligent enough to realize that it's in their interest, as part of earth's biosphere, to help the handful of human anarchists to try to stop, or at least

slow down, the bloodletting and slaughter of our Aneristic rulers and Aneristic mobs."

"Sometimes I still get confused about your theological terms—or are they psychological? The Aneristic
forces, especially the Illuminati, are structure freaks:
they want to impose their concept of order on everybody else. But I still get confused about the differences
between the Erisian, the Eristic and the Discordian.
Not to mention the JAMs."

"The Eristic is the opposite of the Aneristic,"
Hagbard explained patiently, "and, therefore, identical
with it. Remember the Hodge-Podge. Writers like De
Sade, Max Stirner and Nietzsche are Eristic; so are the
gorillas. They represent total supremacy of the individual, total negation of the group. It isn't necessarily the
war-of-all-against-all, as Aneristic philosophers imagine, but it can, under stress, degenerate into that. More
often, it's quite pacifistic, like our hairy friends in the
trees back there. The Erisian position is modified; it
recognizes that Aneristic forces are part of the world
drama, too, and can never be totally abolished. We
merely stress the Eristic as a balance, because human
society has been tilted grotesquely toward the Aneristic
side all through the Piscean age. We Discordians are
the activists in the Erisian movement; we do things.
The pure Erisians work in more mysterious ways, in
accordance with the Taoist principle of *wu-wei*—doing
nothing effectively. The JAMs are left-wingers, who
might have become Aneristic except for special circumstances that led them in a libertarian direction. But
they've fucked it all up with typical left-wing hatred
trips. They haven't mastered the *Gita*: the art of fighting with a loving heart."

"Strange," Joe said. "Dr. Iggy, in the San Francisco
JAM cabal, explained it to me differently."

"What would you expect?" Hagbard replied. "No
two who *know,* know the same in their knowing. By
the way, why haven't you told me that you're sure
those gorillas back there were just men I dressed up in
gorilla suits?"

"I'm becoming more gullible," Joe said.

"Too bad," Hagbard told him sadly. "They really *were* men in gorilla suits. I was testing how easily you could be bamboozled, and you flunked."

"Now, wait a minute. They smelled like gorillas. That was no fake. You're putting me on *now*."

"That's right," Hagbard agreed. "I wanted to see if you'd trust your own senses or the word of a Natural-Born Leader and Guru like me. You trusted your own senses, and you pass. My put-ons are not just jokes, friend. The hardest thing for a man with dominance genes and piratical heredity like me is to avoid becoming a goddam authority figure. I need all the feedback and information I can get—from men, women, children, gorillas, dolphins, computers, any conscious entity—but nobody contradicts an Authority, you know. *Communication is possible only between equals:* that's the first theorem of social cybernetics—and the whole basis of anarchism—and I have to keep knocking down people's dependence on me or I'll become a fucking Big Daddy and won't get accurate communication anymore. If the pig-headed Illuminati and their Aneristic imitators in all the governments, corporations, universities and armies of the world understood that simple principle, they'd occasionally find out what's actually going on and stop screwing up every project they start. I am Freeman Hagbard Celine and I am not anybody's bloody leader. As soon as you fully understand that I'm your equal, and that my shit stinks just like yours, and that I need a lay every few days or I get grouchy and make dumb decisions, and that there is One more trustworthy than all the Buddhas and sages but you have to find him for yourself, then you'll begin to understand what the Legion of Dynamic Discord is all about."

"One more trustworthy than all the Buddhas and sages . . . ?" Joe repeated, finding himself most confused when he had been closest to total comprehension a second earlier.

"To receive light you must be receptive," Hagbard

said curtly. "Work that one out for yourself. Meanwhile, take this back to New York and chew on it a bit." And he presented Joe with a book entitled *Never Whistle While You're Pissing: A Guide to Self-Liberation,* by Hagbard Celine, H.M., S.H.

Joe read the book carefully in the following weeks—while Pat Walsh, in *Confrontation*'s research department, checked out every assertion about the Illuminati that Joe had picked up from Hagbard, Simon, Dillinger and Dr. Ignotius—but, although some of the book was brilliant, much was obscure, and he found no clue to the One more trustworthy than all Buddhas. Then, one night high on Alamout Black hashish, he started working on it with expanded and intensified consciousness. Malaclypse the Elder? No, he was wise, and somewhat benevolent in a fey sort of style, but certainly not trustworthy. Simon? For all his youth and nuttiness, he had moments of incredible perception, but he was almost certainly less enlightened than Hagbard. Dillinger? Dr. Ignotius? The mysterious Malaclypse the Younger, who had disappeared, leaving behind only the inscrutable *Principia Discordia?*

Christ, Joe thought, what a male chauvinist I am! Why didn't I think of Stella? The old joke came back to him . . . "Did you see God?" "Yes, and she's black." *Of course.* Hadn't Stella presided over his initiation, in Dr. Iggy's chapel? Hadn't Hagbard said she would preside over George Dorn's initiation, when George was ready? *Of course.*

Joe always remembered that moment of ecstasy and certainty: it taught him a lot about the use and misuse of drugs and why the Illuminati went wrong. For the unconscious, which always tries to turn every good lay into a mother figure, had contaminated the insight which his supraconscious had almost given him. It was many months later, just before the Fernando Poo crisis, that he finally discovered beyond all doubt the One who was more trustworthy than all Buddhas and all sages.

Do-da, do-da, do-da-do-da-DAY . . .

(And Semper Cuni Linctus, the very night that he reamed his subaltern for taking native superstitions seriously, passed an olive garden and saw the Seventeen . . . and with them was the Eighteenth, the one they had crucified the Friday before. *Magna Mater,* he swore, creeping closer, *am I losing my mind?* The Eighteenth, whatshisname, the preacher, had set up a wheel and was distributing cards to them. Now, he turned the wheel and called out the number at which it stopped. The centurion watched, in growing amazement, as the process was repeated several times, and the cards were marked each time the wheel stopped. Finally, the big one, Simon, shouted "Bingo!" The scion of the noble Linctus family turned and fled . . . Behind him, the luminous figure said, "Do this in commemoration of me."

"I thought we were supposed to do the bread and wine bit in commemoration of you?" Simon objected.

"Do both," the ghostly one said. "The bread and wine is too symbolic and arcane for some folks. This one is what will bring in the mob. You see, fellows, if you want to bring the Movement to the people, you have to start from where the people are at. You, Luke, don't write that down. This is part of the *secret* teachings.")

Slurp, slurp . . . *Camp-town ladies sing this song . . .*

(But how do you account for a man like Drake? one of Carl Jung's guests asked at the Sunday afternoon *Kaffeeklatsch* where the strange young American had inspired so much speculation. Jung sucked on his pipe thoughtfully—wondering, actually, how he could ever cure his associates of treating him like a guru—and answered finally, "A fine mind strikes on an idea like the arrow hitting bull's-eye. The Americans have not yet produced such a mind, because they are too assertive, too outgoing. They land on an idea, even an important idea, like one of their fullbacks making a tackle. Hence, they always crumple or cripple it. Drake has such a mind. He has learned everything about power—more than Adler knows, for all his obsession

on the subject—but he has not learned the important thing. That is, of course, how to *avoid* power. What he needs, and will probably never achieve, is religious humility. Impossible in his country, where even the introverts are extroverted most of the time.")

It was a famous novelist, who was later to win the Nobel Prize, who actually gave Drake his first lead on what the Mafia always called *il Segreto*. They had been talking about Joyce and his unfortunate daughter, and the novelist mentioned Joyce's attempts to convince himself that she wasn't really schizophrenic. "He told Jung, 'After all, I do the same sorts of things with language myself.' Do you know what Jung, that old Chinese sage disguised as a psychiatrist, answered? 'You are diving, but she is sinking.' Incisive, of course; and yet, all of us who write anything that goes below the surface of naturalism can understand Joyce's skepticism. We never know for sure whether we're diving or just sinking."

That reminded Drake of his thesis, and he went and got the last words of Mr. Arthur Flegenheimer, a.k.a. Dutch Schultz, from his bureau. He handed the sheets to the novelist and asked, "Would you say the author of this was diving or sinking?"

The novelist read slowly, with increasing absorption, and finally looked up to regard Drake with extremely curious eyes. "Is it a translation from the French?" he asked.

"No," Drake said. "The author was an American."

"So it's not poor Artaud. I thought it might be. He's been around the bend, as the English say, since he went to Mexico. I understand he's currently working on some quite remarkable astrological charts involving Chancellor Hitler." The novelist lapsed into silence, and then asked, "What do you regard as the most interesting line in this?"

" 'A boy has never wept nor dashed a thousand kim,' " Drake quoted, since that was the line that bothered him most.

"Oh, that boy imagery is all personal, just repressed

homosexuality, quite ordinary," the novelist said impatiently. " 'I was in the can and the boy came at me.' I think the author hurt the boy in some way. All the references are tinged with more than normal homosexual guilt."

My God, Drake thought, *Vince Coll. He was young enough to seem like a boy to Schultz. The Dutchman thought Coll's ghost was shooting at him in that john in Newark.*

"I would imagine the author killed himself, or is in a mental hospital by now," the novelist went on thoughtfully.

"He's dead," Drake said grudgingly. "But I won't give you any more clues. It's fascinating to see how well you're doing on your own."

"This is the interesting line," the novelist said. "Or three lines rather. 'I would hear it, the Circuit Court would hear it, and the Supreme Court might hear it. If that ain't the payoff. Please crack down on the Chinaman's friends and Hitler's commander.' You swear this author was American?"

"Well, he came of German ancestry," Drake said, thinking of Jung's theory of genetic memory. "But Chancellor Hitler would hate to admit it. His people were not Aryan."

"He was Jewish?" the novelist exclaimed.

"What's so surprising about that?"

"Only that scarcely two or three people in the whole world, outside the inner circle of the Nazi Party, would understand what was meant by the Chinaman and Hitler's commander. This author must have delved very deeply into occult literature—things like Eliphas Levi, or Ludvig Prinn, or some of the most closely guarded Rosicrucian secrets, and then made a perfectly amazing guess in the right direction."

"What in the world are you talking about?"

The novelist looked at Drake for a long time, then said, "I hate to even discuss it. Some things are too vile. Some books, as your Mr. Poe said, should not allow themselves to be read. Even I have coded things in my most famous work, which is admired for all the wrong reasons. In my search for the mystical, I have learned things I would rather forget, and the real goal of Herr Hitler is one of those things. But you must tell me: who was this remarkable author?"

("He just called me," Luciano told Maldonado, "and I got this much at least: he's not a shakedown artist. He's aiming big, and he's big already himself. I'm getting my lawyer out of bed, to run down all the best Boston families, and find one with a son who shows signs of having the old larceny in his heart. I bet it's a banking family. I can hear money in a voice, and he has it.")

Drake was persistent, and finally the novelist said, "As you know, I refuse to live in Germany because of what is happening there. Nevertheless, it is my home, and I do hear things. If I try to explain, you must get your mind out of the arena of ordinary politics. When I say Hitler does have a Master, that doesn't mean he is a front man in the pedestrian political sense." The novelist paused. "How can I present the picture so you will understand it? You are not German . . . How can you understand a people of whom it has been said, truthfully, that they have one foot in their own land and one foot in Thule? Have you even heard of Thule? That's the German name for the fabulous kingdom the Greeks called Atlantis. Whether this kingdom ever existed is immaterial; the belief in it has existed since the dawn of history and beliefs motivate actions. In fact, you cannot understand a man's actions unless you understand his beliefs."

The novelist paused again, and then began talking about the Golden Dawn Society in England in the 1890s. "Strange things were written by the members. Algernon Blackwood, for instance, wrote of intelligent beings who preexisted mankind on earth. Can you take such a concept seriously? Can you think about Blackwood's warnings, of his guarded phrases, such as, 'Of such great powers or beings there may conceivably be a survival, of which poetry and legend alone caught a

flying memory and called them gods, monsters, myth-
ical beings of all sorts and kinds'? Or, Arthur Machen,
who wrote of the 'miracles of Mons' during the Great
War, describing the angels, as they were called, and
published this two days before the soldiers at the scene
sent back reports of the incident. Machen was in the
Golden Dawn, and he left it to rejoin the Catholic
Church, warning, 'There are sacraments of Evil as well
as of Good.' William Butler Yeats was a member, too,
and you must certainly know his remarkable lines,
'What rough beast/ Its hour come round at last/
Slouches toward Bethlehem to be born?' And the
Golden Dawn was just the outer portal of the Myster-
ies. The things that Crowley learned after leaving the
Golden Dawn and joining the Ordo Templi Orientis
. . . Hitler suppressed both the Dawn and the Ordo
Templi Orientis, you know. He belonged to the Vril
Society himself, where the really extraterrestrial secrets
are kept . . ."

"You seem to be having a hard time getting to the
point," Drake said.

"Some things need to be approached in hints, even
in allegories. You have taken mescaline with Klee and
his friends, and spent the night seeing the Great
Visions. Do I need to remind you that reality is not a
one-level affair?"

"Very well," Drake said. "Behind the Golden Dawn
and the OTO and the Vril Society is a hidden group of
real Initiates. There was a German branch of the
Golden Dawn, and Hitler was a member. You want me
to understand that to treat these sacraments of Evil
and these beings from Atlantis as no more than fictions
would be to oversimplify; is that right?"

"The Golden Dawn was founded by a German
woman, carrying on a tradition that was already a hundred years old in Bavaria. As for these powers or
beings from Thule, they do not exist in the sense that
bricks and beefsteak exist, either. The physicist, by
manipulating these fantastic electrons—which, I remind you, have to be imagined as moving from one

place to another without passing through any intervening space like a fairy or a ghost—produces real phenomena, visible to the senses. Say, then, that by manipulating these beings or powers from Thule, certain men are able to produce effects that can also be seen and experienced."

"What was the Golden Dawn?" Drake asked, absorbed. "How did it begin?"

"It's very old, more than medieval. The modern organization began in 1776, with a man who quit the Jesuits because he thought he was an atheist, until his researches into Eastern history had surprising results . . ."

(It's him! Hitler screamed, *He has come for me!* And then, as Herman Rauschning recorded, "he lapsed into gibberish." *The boss himself,* Dutch Schultz moaned, *Oh, mama, I can't go through with it. Please. Come on, open the soap duckets. The chimney sweeps. Take to the sword. Shut up. You got a big mouth.)*

We've got two real possibilities, Lepke's lawyer reported. *But one of them is Boston Irish and what you described was the old original Boston accent. The second one is probably your man, then. His name is Robert Putney Drake.*

Standing before the house on Benefit Street, Drake could see, across the town, the peak of Sentinel Hill and the old deserted church that had harbored the Starry Wisdom Sect in the 1870s. He turned back to the door and raised the old Georgian knocker *(remembering: Lillibridge the reporter and Blake the painter had both died investigating that sect)*, then rapped smartly three times.

Howard Phillips Lovecraft, pale, gaunt, cadaverous, opened the door. "Mr. Drake?" he asked genially.

"It was good of you to see me," Drake said.

"Nonsense," Lovecraft replied, ushering him into the Colonial hallway. "Any admirer of my poor tales is always welcome here. They are so few that I could have them all here on a single day without straining my aunt's dinner budget."

He may be one of the most important men alive, Drake thought, *and he doesn't really suspect.*

("He left Boston by train this morning," the soldier reported to Maldonado and Lepke. "He was going to Providence, Rhode Island.")

"Of course, I have no hesitation in discussing it," Lovecraft said after he and Drake were settled in the old book-lined study and Mrs. Gamhill had served them tea. "Whatever your friend in Zurich may feel, I am and always have been a strict materialist."

"But you have been in touch with *these* people?"

"Oh, certainly, and an absurd lot they are, all of them. It began after I published a story called 'Dagon' in, let me see, 1919. I had been reading the Bible and the description of the Philistine sea god, Dagon, reminded me of sea serpent legends and of the reconstructions of dinosaurs by paleontologists. And the notion came to me: suppose Dagon were real, not a god, but simply a long-lived being vaguely related to the great saurians. Simply a story, to entertain those who enjoy the weird and Gothic in literature. You can't imagine my astonishment when various occult groups began contacting me, asking which group I belonged to and which side I was on. They were all terribly put out when I made perfectly clear that I didn't believe any such rubbish."

"But," Drake asked perplexed, "why did you pick up more and more of these hidden occult teachings and incorporate them in your later stories?"

"I am an artist," Lovecraft said, "a mediocre artist, I fear—and don't contradict me. I value honesty above all the other virtues. I would like to believe in the supernatural, in a world of social justice and in my own possession of genius. But reason commands that I accept the facts: the world is made of blind matter, the wicked and brutal always have and always will trample on the weak and innocent, and I have a very microscopic capacity to create a small range of esthetic effects, all macabre and limited in their appeal to a very special audience. Nevertheless, I would that things were otherwise. Hence, although a conservative, I support certain social legislation that might improve the conditions of the poor, and, although a poor writer, I try to elevate the status of my own wretched prose. Vampires and ghosts and werewolves are worn out; they provoke chuckles rather than terror. Thus, when I began to learn of the old lore, after 'Dagon' was published, I began to use it in my stories. You can't imagine the hours I have spent with those old volumes at Miskatonic, wading through tons of trash—Alhazred and Levi and Von Juntzt were all mental cases, you know—to sift out the notions that were unfamiliar enough to cause a genuine shock, and a real shudder, in my readers."

"And you've never received threats from any of these occult groups for mentioning Iok Sotot or Cthulhu outright in your stories?"

"Only when I mentioned Hali," Lovecraft said with a wry smile. "Some thoughtful soul reminded me of what happened to Bierce after *he* wrote a bit frankly on that subject. But that was a friendly warning, not a threat. Mr. Drake, you are a banker and a businessman. Certainly, you don't take any of this seriously?"

"Let me reply with a question of my own," Drake said carefully. "Why, in all the esoteric lore which you have chosen to make exoteric through your stories, have you never mentioned the Law of Fives?"

"In fact," Lovecraft said, "I did hint at it, rather broadly, in 'At the Mountains of Madness.' Have you not read that? It's my longest, and, I think, my best effort to date." But he seemed abruptly paler.

"In 'The Case of Charles Dexter Ward,'" Drake pursued, "you quote a formula from Eliphas Levi's *History of Magic*. But you don't quote it in full. Why was that?"

Lovecraft sipped his tea, obviously framing his answer carefully. Finally he said, "One doesn't have to believe in Santa Claus to recognize that people will exchange presents at Christmas time. One doesn't have to believe in Yog Sothoth, the Eater of Souls, to realize how people will act who do hold that belief. It is not my intent, in any of my writings, to provide information that will lead even one unbalanced reader to try experiments that will result in the loss of human life."

Drake arose. "I came here to learn," he said, "but it appears that my only possible function is to teach. Let me remind you of the words of Lao-tse: 'Those who speak do not know; those who know do not speak.' Most occult groups are in the first class, and their speculations are as absurd as you think. But those in the second class are not to be so lightly dismissed. They have left you alone because your stories appear only in magazines that appeal to a small minority. These magazines, however, have lately been printing stories about rockets and nuclear chain reactions and other matters that are on the edge of technological achievement. When these fantasies start coming true, which will probably occur within a decade, there will be much wider interest in such magazines, and your stories will be included in that renaissance. Then you will receive some very unwelcome attention."

Lovecraft remained seated. "I think I know of whom you are speaking; I can also read newspapers and make deductions. Even if they are mad enough to attempt it, they do not have the means. They would have to take over not one government but many. That project would keep them busy enough, I should think, to distract them from worrying about a few lines here and there in stories that are published as fiction. I can conceive of the next war leading to breakthroughs in rocketry and nuclear energy, but I doubt that even that will lead many people to take my stories seriously, or to see the connections between certain rituals, which I have never described explicitly, and acts which will be construed as the normal excesses of despotism."

"Good day, sir," Drake said formally. "I must be off to New York, and your welfare is really not a major concern in my life."

"Good day," Lovecraft said, rising with Colonial

courtesy. "Since you have been so good as to give me a warning, I will return the favor. I do not think your interest in these people is based on a wish to oppose them, but to serve them. I beg you to remember their attitude toward servants."

Back out on the street, Drake experienced a momentary dejection. *For nearly twenty years he's been writing about them and they haven't contacted him. I've been rocking the boat on two continents, and they haven't contacted me. What does it take to make them show their hand? And if I don't have an understanding with them, anything I work out with Maldonado and Capone is written on the wind. I just can't afford to deal with the Mafia before I deal with them. What should I do—put an ad in the* New York Times: *"Will the All-Seeing Eye please look in my direction? R. P. Drake, Boston"?*

And a Pontiac (stolen an hour before in Kingsport) pulled away from the curb, several houses back, and started following Drake as he left Benefit Street and walked back toward the downtown area. He wasn't looking back, so he didn't see what happened to it, but he noticed an old man coming toward him stop in his tracks and turn white.

"Jesus on a pogo stick," the old man said weakly.

Drake looked over his shoulder and saw nothing but an empty street. "What is it?" he asked.

"Never mind," the old man replied. "You'd *never* believe me, mister." And he cut across the sidewalk toward a saloon.

("What do you mean, you lost four soldiers?" Maldonado screamed into the phone.

"Just what I'm saying," Eddie Vitelli, of the Providence gambling, heroin and prostitution Vitellis, said. "We found your Drake at a hotel. Four of the best soldiers we've got followed him. They called in once to say he was at a house on Benefit Street. I told them to pick him up as soon as he comes out. And that's it, period, it's all she wrote. They're all gone, like something picked them off the face of the earth. I've got everybody looking for the car they were in, and that's gone, too.")

Drake canceled his trip to New York and went back to Boston, plunging into bank business and mulling over his next move. Two days later, the janitor came to his desk, hat in hand, and asked, "Could I speak to you, Mr. Drake?"

"Yes, Getty, what is it?" Drake replied testily. His tone was deliberate; the man was probably about to ask for a raise, and it was best to put him on the defensive immediately.

"It's this, sir," the janitor said, laying a card on Drake's desk. Drake looked down impatiently and saw a rainbow of colors—the card was printed on some unknown plastic and created a prismatic effect recalling his mescaline trips in Zurich. Through the rainbow, shimmering and radiant, he saw the outlines of a thirteen-step pyramid, with a red eye at the top. He stared up at the janitor and saw a face without subservience or uncertainty.

"The Grand Master of the Eastern United States is ready to talk to you," the janitor said softly.

"Holy Cleopatra!" Drake cried, and tellers turned to stare at him.

"Kleopatra?" Simon Moon asked, twenty-three years later. "Tell him about Kleopatra."

It was a sunny afternoon in October and the drapes in the living room of the apartment on the seventeenth floor of 2323 Lake Shore Drive were pulled back to reveal a corner window view of Chicago's Loop skyscrapers and the whitecap-dotted blue surface of Lake Michigan. Joe sprawled in a chair facing the lake. Simon and Padre Pederastia were on a couch under an enormous painting titled "Kleopatra." She looked a good deal like Stella Maris and was holding an asp to her bosom. The eye-and-pyramid symbol appeared several times in the hieroglyphs on the tomb wall behind her. Sitting in an armchair opposite the painting was a slender man with sharp, dark features, shoulder-length chestnut hair, a forked brown beard and green eyes.

"Kleopatra," said the man, "was an instant study. Would have made her Polymother of the great globe itself, if she'd lived. She damned near brought down the Roman Empire, and she did shorten its life by centuries. She forced Octavius to bring so much Aneristic power to bear that the Empire went prematurely into the state of bureaucracy."

"What do I call you?" said Joe. "Lucifer? Satan?"

"Call me Malaclypse the Elder," said the fork-bearded man with a smile that seemed to beam through endless shifting veils of warm self-regard.

"I don't get it," said Joe. "The first time I saw you, we were all terrified out of our minds. Though when you finally showed up looking like Billy Graham, I didn't know whether to laugh or go catto. But I know I was scared."

Padre Pederastia laughed. "You were so terrified, my son, that you were trying to climb right inside our little redhead's big red bird's nest. You were so frightened that that hefty cock of yours"—he licked his lips—"was squirting juice all over the carpet. Oh, you were terrified, all right. Oh, my, yes."

"Well, I wasn't so scared just at that moment you mention," said Joe with a smile. "But a little later, when our friend here was about to appear. You were terrified yourself, Padre Pederastia. You kept hollering, 'Come not in that form! Come not in that form!' Now we're all sitting around the living room behaving like old chums—and this—this *being* here is reminiscing about the good old days with Kleopatra."

"They were terrible days," said Malaclypse. "Very cruel days, very sad days. Constant wars, tortures, mass murders, crucifixions. Bad times."

"I believe you. And what's worse, I can understand what it means if I believe you, and I can live knowing that you exist. And even sit down in this living room and smoke a cigarette with you."

Two lit cigarettes appeared between Malaclypse's

fingers. He passed one to Joe. Joe drew on it; it tasted sweet, with just a hint of marijuana.

"That's a corny trick," said Joe.

"Just so you don't lose your old associations to me too quickly," said Malaclypse. "Too quick to understand, too soon to misunderstand."

Padre Pederastia said, "The night of that Black Mass, I simply had worked myself up to the point where I totally believed. That's what magic is, after all. The people who were here that night relate to left-hand magic, to the Satan myth, to the Faust legend. It's a quick way to get them involved. It worked with you at the time, but we've brought you along fast, because we want more help from you. So now you don't need the trappings."

"You don't have to be a Satanist to love Malaclypse," said Malaclypse.

"In fact, its better if you're not," said Simon. "Satanists are creeps. They skin dogs alive and shit like that."

"Because most Satanists are Christians," said Joe. "Which is a very masochistic religion."

"Now, just a minute—" said Padre Pederastia with some asperity.

"He's right, Pederastia," said Malaclypse. "Nobody knows that better than you—or me, for that matter."

"Did you ever meet Jesus?" Joe asked, awed in spite of his skepticism.

Malaclypse smiled. "I *was* Jesus."

Padre Pederastia flapped his hands and bounced up and down in his chair. "You're telling too much!"

"For me, trust is total or nonexistent," said Malaclypse. "I perceive that I can trust Joe. I wasn't the original Jesus, Joe, the one they crucified. But—this happened a few centuries after I experienced transcendental illumination at Melos—I was passing through Judea in the persona of a Greek merchant when they crucified Jesus. I met some of his followers the day he died, and I talked with them. If you think Christianity is a bloody religion as it is, this is nothing to what it would have been if Jesus hadn't seemed to come back. If the seventeen original apostles—five of them have been purged from the records—had been left on their own, they would have passed from horror and terror at Jesus's death to vindictive fury. It would have been as if Islam had come seven centuries earlier. Instead of slowly taking over the Roman Empire and preserving much of the Greco-Roman world intact, it would have swept and mobilized the East, destroyed most of Western civilization and replaced it with a theocracy more oppressive than Pharaonic Egypt. I stopped that with a few magic tricks. Appearing in the persona of the resurrected Jesus, I taught there was no need for hatred and vengeance after my death. I even tried to get them to realize that life is a game by teaching them Bingo. To this day, nobody understands and critics call it part of the *commercialism* of the Church. The sacred Tarot wheel, the moving Mandala! So despite my influence, Christianity focused obsessively on the crucifixion of Jesus—which is really irrelevant to what he taught while he was alive—and remained a kind of death worship. When Paul went to Athens and made the link-up with the Illuminati, who were using Plato's Academy as a front, the ideology of Plato combined with the mythology of Christ to deliver the knockout blow to pagan humanism and lay the foundations for the modern world of superstates. After that, I changed my appearance again and took the name of Simon Magus and had some success spreading ideas contradictory to Christianity."

"You can change your appearance at will, then," said Joe.

"Oh, sure thing. I'm just as quick with a thought projection as anybody." He pushed his pinkie thoughtfully into his left nostril and worked it around. Joe stiffened; he didn't care to watch people picking their noses in public. He looked resolutely over Malaclypse's left shoulder. "Now that you know as much as you do about us, Joe, it's time you started working with us. Chicago, as you know, is the Illuminati nerve center in this hemisphere, so we'll use this town to test AUM, a new drug with astonishing properties, if ELF's technicians are correct. It's supposed to turn neophobes into neophiles."

Simon slapped his forehead and shouted "Wow, man!" and started laughing. Pederastia gasped and whistled.

"You look blank, Joe," said Malaclypse. "Has no one explained to you that the human race is divided into two distinct genotypes—neophobes, who reject new ideas and accept only what they have known all their lives, and neophiles, who love new things, change, invention, innovation? For the first four million years of man's history, all humans were neophobes, which is why civilization did not develop. Animals are all neophobes. Only mutation can change them. Instinct is simply the natural behavior of a neophobe. The neophile mutation appeared about a hundred thousand years ago, and speeded up thirty thousand years ago. However, there has never been more than a handful of neophiles anywhere on the planet. The Illuminati themselves sprang from one of the oldest neophile-neophobe conflicts on record."

"I take it the Illuminati were trying to hold back progress," said Joe. "Is that their general aim?"

"You're still thinking like a liberal," said Simon. "Nobody gives a fuck for progress."

"Right," said Malaclypse. "They were the innovators in that instance. All the Illuminati were—and are—neophiles. Even today, they see their work as directed toward progress. They want to become like gods. It's possible for humans, given the right methods, to translate themselves into sentient latticeworks of pure energy that will be more or less permanent. The process is called transcendental illumination, to distinguish it from the acquisition of insight into the true nature of man and the universe, which is ordinary illumination. I've gone through transcendental illumination and am a being composed altogether of energy, as you may have guessed. However, prior to becoming energy fields men often fall victim to hubris. Their actions cause pain to others and make them insensitive, uncreative and irrational. Mass human sacrifice is the most reliable method of achieving transcendental illumination. Human sacrifice can, of course, be masked as other things, such as war, famine and plague. The vision of the Four Horsemen vouchsafed to Saint John is actually a vision of mass transcendental illumination."

"How did you achieve it?" Joe asked.

"I was present at the massacre of the male inhabitants of the city of Melos by the Athenians in 416 B.C. Have you read Thucydides?"

"A long time ago,"

"Well, Thucydides had it wrong. He presented it as an out-and-out atrocity, but there were extenuating circumstances. The Melians had been stabbing Athenian soldiers in the back, poisoning them, filling them full of arrows from ambush. Some of them were working for the Spartans and some were on the side of Athens, but the Athenians didn't know which ones they could trust. They didn't want to do any unnecessary killing, but they did want to get back to Athens alive. So they rounded up all the Melian men one day and hacked them to pieces in the town square. The women and children were sold into slavery."

"What did you do?" said Joe. "Were you there with the Athenians?"

"Yes, but I didn't do any killing. I was a chaplain. Of the Erisian denomination, of course. But I was prepared to perform services to Hermes, Dionysus, Heracles, Aphrodite, Athena, Hera and some of the other Olympians. I almost went mad with horror—I didn't understand that Pangenitor is Panphage. I was praying to Eris to deliver me or deliver the Melians or do something, and she answered me."

"Hail, she what done it all," said Simon.

"I almost believe you," said Joe. "But every once in

a while the suspicion creeps in that you're simply doing a two-thousand-year-old man routine and the butt of the joke is me."

Malaclypse stood up with a little smile. "Come here, Joe."

"What for?"

"Just come here." Malaclypse held his hands away from his sides, palms turned toward Joe appealingly. Joe walked over and stood before him.

"Put your hand into my side," said Malaclypse.

"Oh, come on," said Joe. Pederastia snickered. Malaclypse just looked at him with a gentle, encouraging smile, so he reached out to touch Malaclypse's shirt. His hands still felt nothing. He closed his eyes to verify that. There was no sensation whatever. Thin air. Eyes still shut, he moved his hand forward. He opened his eyes, and when he saw his arm sunk into Malaclypse's body up to the elbow, he almost barfed his cookies.

He drew back. "It can't be a movie. I'd be almost willing to say a moving holograph, but the illusion is too perfect. You're looking right at me. To my eyes you are unquestionably there."

"Try a few karate chops," said Malaclypse. Joe obliged, swinging his hand like a scythe through Malaclypse's waist, chest and head. For a finale, Joe brought his hand straight down through the top of the being's head.

"I suspend judgment," said Joe. "Maybe you are what you say you are. But it's pretty hard to take. Can you feel anything?"

"I can create temporary sensory organs for myself whenever I want to. I can enjoy just about anything a human enjoys or experiences. But my primary mode of perception is a very advanced form of what you would call intuition. Intuition is a kind of sensitivity in the mind to events and processes; what I have is a highly developed intuitional receptor which is completely controllable."

Joe went back and sat down, shaking his head. "You

certainly are in an enviable position."

"Like I said, it's the real reason for human sacrifice," said Malaclypse. He, too, sat down, and Joe now noticed that the soft upholstery of his chair didn't sink beneath his weight. He seemed to rest on the surface of the cushions. "Any sudden or violent death releases a burst of consciousness energy, which can be controlled and channeled as any explosive energy can be. The Illuminati would all like to become as gods. That has been their ambition for longer than I care to say."

"Which means they have to perpetrate mass murder," said Joe, thinking of nuclear weapons, gas chambers, chemical-biological warfare.

Malaclypse nodded. "Now, I don't disapprove of that on moral grounds, since morals are purely illusory. I do have a personal distaste for that sort of thing. Although, when you've lived as long as I have, you have lost so many friends and lovers that it is impossible not to take the deaths of humans as a matter of course. So it goes. And, since I achieved my own immortality and nonmateriality as the result of a mass murder, it would be hypocritical of me to condemn the Illuminati. For that matter, I don't condemn hypocrisy, though it is also personally distasteful to me. But I do say that the method of the Illuminati is stupid and wasteful, since everybody is already everything. So, why fuck around with things? It is absurd to try to be something else when there is nothing else."

"That kind of statement is simply beyond my comprehension," said Joe. "I don't know, maybe it's my engineering training. But even after my own partial illumination in San Francisco with Dr. Iggy, this kind of talk doesn't make any more sense than Christian Science to me."

"Soon you'll understand more," said Malaclypse. "About the history of man, about some of the esoteric knowledge that has been lying around for tens of thousands of years. Eventually you'll know all that's worth knowing about absolutely everything."

(Tobias Knight, the FBI agent monitoring the bugging equipment in Dr. Mocenigo's home, heard the pistol shot the same time Carmel did. "What the hell?" he said out loud, sitting up straight. He had heard the door open and footsteps walking about and had been waiting for a conversation . . . and then, without warning, he had heard the shot. Now a voice spoke, "Sorry, Dr. Mocenigo. You were a great patriot, and this is a dog's death. But I will share it with you." Then there were more footsteps and *something else* . . . Knight recognized the sound: it was liquid being poured. The steps and the pouring liquid continued, and Knight abruptly tore himself out of his state of shock and pressed the intercom. "Knight?" asked a voice which he recognized as Esperando Despond, the Special Agent in Charge for Las Vegas. "Mocenigo's house," Knight said crisply. "Get a whole crew out there double-quick. Something is happening, one killing at least." He released the intercom and listened, paralyzed, to the footsteps and the liquid sounds, which were now mixed with subdued humming. A man doing an unpleasant job, but trying to keep his cool. Knight recognized the tune, finally: "Camp-town Races." The humming and walking and slurping continued. "Do-da-Do-da . . ." Then the voice spoke again: "This is General Lawrence Stewart Talbot, speaking to the CIA, the FBI and whoever else has this house bugged. I discovered at two this morning that several people in our Anthrax Leprosy Pi project have accidentally been subjected to live cultures. All of them are living at the installation, and can easily be isolated while the antidote works. I have already given orders to that effect. Dr. Mocenigo himself unknowingly received the worst dose, and was in advanced morbidity, a few minutes from death, when I arrived. His whole house, obviously, will have to be burned down, and I am also, due to my proximity while examining him, too far gone to be saved. I will therefore shoot myself after setting fire to the house. There is one remaining problem. I found evidence that a woman had been in Dr.

Mocenigo's bed earlier—that's what comes of allowing important people to live off base—and she must be found and given the antidote and each of her contacts must be traced. Needless to say, this must be done quietly, or there will be a nationwide panic. Tell the President to see that my wife gets the medal for this. Tell my wife that with my last breath I still insist she was wrong about that girl in Red Lion, Pennsylvania. In closing, I firmly believe that this is the greatest country in the history of the world, and can still be saved if Congress will lock up those damned college kids for once and for all. God bless America!" There was a scratching sound—my God! Knight thought, the match—and the sound of flames, in the midst of which General Talbot tried to add a postscript but couldn't get the words out because he was screaming. Finally, the second shot came, and the screaming stopped. Knight raised his head, jaw clenched, repressed tears in his steely eyes. "That was a great American," he said aloud.)

Over cigars and brandy, after George had been sent off to bed to be distracted by Tarantella, Richard Jung asked pointedly, "Just how sure are you that this Discordian bunch is a match for the Illuminati? It's kind of late in the game to change sides."

Drake started to speak, then turned to Maldonado. "Tell him about Italy in the 19th century," he said.

"The Illuminati are just men and women," Maldonado replied obligingly. "More women than men, in fact. It was Eve Weishaupt who started the whole show; Adam just acted as her front because people are used to taking orders from men. This Atlantis stuff is mostly bullshit. Everybody who knows about Atlantis at all traces his family, or his clan, or his club, back there. Some of the old dons in the Maf even try to trace *la Cosa Nostra* back there. All bullshit. Just like all the WASPs tracing themselves back to the *Mayflower*. For everyone who can prove it, like Mr. Drake, there's a hundred who are just bluffing.

"You see," Maldonado went on more intensely,

chewing his cigar ferociously, "originally the Illuminati was just a—how do you call it—a kind of 18th-century women's liberation front. Behind Adam Weishaupt was Eve; behind Godwin, who started all this socialism and anarchism with his *Political Justice* book, was his mistress Mary Wollstonecraft, who started the woman revolution with a book called, uh . . ."

"Vindication of the Rights of Women," Drake contributed.

"And they got Tom Paine to write on women's lib, too, and to defend their French Revolution and try to import it here. But that all fell through and they didn't get a real controlling interest in the U.S. until they hoodwinked Woody Wilson into creating the Federal Reserve in 1914. And that's the way it usually goes. In Italy they had a front called the Haute Vente, that was so damn secret Mazzini was a member all his life and never knew the control came from Bavaria. My grandpa told me all about those days. We had a three-way dogfight. The Monarchists on one side, the Haute Vente and the Liberteri, the anarchists, on the other, and the Maf in the middle trying to roll with the punches and figure out which way the bread was buttered, you know? Then the Liberteri got wise to the Haute Vente and split from it, and it was a four-way fight. You look it up in the history books, they tell it like it was except they don't mention who ran the Haute Vente. And then the good old Law of Fives came into it, and we had the Fascisti and it was a five-way dogfight. Who won? Not the Illuminati. It wasn't until 1937, manipulating the English government to discourage Mussolini's peace plans and using Hitler to get Benito into the Berlin-Tokyo axis, that the Illuminati had some kind of control in Italy. And even then it was indirect. When we made our deal with the CIA—it was called the OSS back in those days—Luciano got out of the joint and we turned over Italy and delivered Mussolini dead."

"And the point of all this?" Jung asked coldly.

"The point is," Maldonado said, "the Maf has been

against the Illuminati more of the time than we've been with them, and we're still doing business and we're stronger than ever. Believe me, their bark is much worse than their bite. Because they know some magic, they scare everybody. We've had magicians and belladonnas—witches, to you—in Sicily since before Paris got hot pants for Helen, and believe me a bullet kills them as dead as it kills anybody else."

"The Illuminati *do* have a bite," Drake interjected, "but it is my judgment that they are going out with the Age of Pisces. The Discordians, I think, represent an Aquarian swing."

"Oh, I don't go for that mystic stuff," Jung said. "Next thing you'll be quoting *I Ching* at me, like my old man."

"You're an anal type, like most accountants," Drake replied coolly. "And a Capricorn as well. Down-to-earth and conservative. I won't attempt to persuade you about this aspect of the matter. Just take my word, I didn't get where I am by ignoring significant facts just because they won't fit on a profit-and-loss statement. On the profit-and-loss level, however, I have had reasons to believe that the Discordians can currently outbid the Illuminati. These reasons date back many months before the appearance of those marvelous statues today."

Later, in bed, Drake turned the matter around in his head and looked at it from several sides. Lovecraft's words came back to him: "I beg you to remember their attitude toward their servants." That was it, basically. He was an old man, and he was tired of being their servant, or satrap, or satellite. When he was thirty-three, he was ready to take them over, as Cecil Rhodes had once done. Somehow, he had been maneuvered into taking over just one section of their empire. If he could think, truthfully, that he owned the United States more thoroughly than any President in four decades, the fact remained that he did not own himself. Not until he signed his Declaration of Independence tonight by joining the Discordians. The other Jung, the *alter Zauber* in Zurich, had tried to tell him something about power once, but he had dismissed it as sentimental slop. Now he tried to remember it . . . and, suddenly, all the old days came back, Klee and his numinous paintings, the Journey to the East, old Crowley saying, "Of course, mixing the left-hand and right-hand paths is dangerous. If you fear such risks, go back to Hesse and Jung and those old ladies. Their way is safe and mine isn't. All that can be said for me is that I have real power and they have dreams." But the Illuminati had crushed Crowley, just as they smashed Willie Seabrook, when those men revealed too much. *"I beg you to remember their attitude toward their servants."* Damn it, what was it Jung had said about power?

And he turned the card over, and on the back was an address on Beacon Hill with the words "8:30 tonight." He looked up at the janitor, who backed away deferentially, saying, "Thank you, Mr. Drake, sir," without a touch of irony in his face or voice. And it hadn't surprised him at all that, for deliberate contrast, the Grand Master he met that night, one of the five Illuminati Primi for the U.S., was an official of the Justice Department. (And what had Jung said about power?) "A few of them will have to fall. Lepke, I would recommend. Perhaps Luciano also." No mystical trappings: just a businesslike meeting. "Our interest is the same as yours: increasing the power of the Justice Department. An equal increment in the power of the other branches of government will proceed nicely when we get the war into gear." Drake remembered his excitement: it was all as he had foreseen. The end of the Republic, the dawn of the Empire.

"After Germany, Russia?" Drake asked once.

"Very good; you are indeed farseeing," the Grand Master replied. "Mr. Hitler, of course, is only a medium. Virtually no ego at all, on his own. You have no idea how dull and prosaic such types are, except when under proper Inspiration. Naturally, his supplied ego will collapse, he will become psychotic, and we will have no control over him at all, then. We are prepared to help him fall. Our real interest now is here. Let me show you something. We do not work in general outlines; our plans are always specific, to the last detail." He handed Drake a sheaf of papers. "The war will probably end in '44 or '45. We will have Russia built up as the next threat within two years. Read this carefully."

Drake read what was to become the National Security Act of 1947. "This abolishes the Constitution," he said almost in ecstasy.

"Quite. And believe me, Mr. Drake, by '46 or '47, we will have Congress and the public ready to accept it. The American Empire is closer than you imagine."

"But the isolationists and pacifists—Senator Taft and that crowd—"

"They will wither away. When communism replaces fascism as the number one enemy, your small-town conservative will be ready for global adventures on a scale that would make the heads of poor Mr. Roosevelt's liberals spin. Trust me. We have every detail pinpointed. Let me show you where the new government will be located."

Drake stared at the plan and shook his head. "Some people will recognize what a pentagon means," he said dubiously.

"They will be dismissed as superstitious cranks. Believe me, this building will be constructed within a few years. It will become the policeman of the world. Nobody will dare question its actions or judgments without being denounced as a traitor. Within thirty years, Mr. Drake, *within thirty years,* anyone who attempts to restore power to the Congress will be cursed and vilified, not by liberals but by conservatives."

"Holy God," Drake said.

The Grand Master rose and walked to an old-fashioned globe nearly as large as King Kong's head. "Pick a spot, Mr. Drake. Any spot. I guarantee you we will have American troops there within thirty years. The Empire that you dreamed of while reading Tacitus."

Robert Putney Drake felt humbled for an instant,

even though he recognized the gimmick: using one single example of telepathy, plucking Tacitus out of his head, to climax the presentation of the incredible dream. At last he understood firsthand the awe that the Illuminati created in both its servitors and its enemies.

"There will be opposition," the Grand Master went on. "In the 1960s and early 1970s especially. That's where your notion for a unified crime syndicate fits into our plan. To crush the opposition, we will need a Justice Department equivalent in many ways to Hitler's Gestapo. If your scheme works—if the Mafia can be drawn into a syndicate that is not entirely under Sicilian control, and the various other groups can be brought under the same umbrella—we will have a nationwide outlaw cartel. The public itself will then call for the kind of Justice Department that we need. By the mid-1960s, wiretapping of all sorts must be so common that the concept of privacy will be archaic." And, tossing sleeplessly, Drake thought how smoothly it had all worked out; why then was he rebelling against it? Why did it give him no pleasure? And what *was* it Jung had said about power?

Richard Jung, wearing Carl Jung's old sweater and smoking his pipe, said, "And next the solar system." The room was crowded with white rabbits, Playboy bunnies, Bugs Bunny, the Wolf Man, Ku Kluxers, Mafiosos, Lepke with accusing eyes, a dormouse, a mad hatter, the King of Hearts, the Prince of Wands, and Jung was shouting over the din. "Billions to reach the moon. Trillions to get to Mars. All pouring into our corporations. Better than the gladiatorial games." Linda Lovelace elbowed him aside. "Call me Ishmaelian," she said suggestively; but Jung handed Drake the skeleton of a Biafran baby. "For Petruchio's feast," he explained, producing a piece of ticker tape. "We now own," he began to read, "seventy-two percent of earth's resources, and fifty-one percent of all the armed troops in the world are under our direction. Here," he said, passing the body of an infant that had died in Appalachia, "see that this one gets an apple in its mouth."

A bunny passed Drake a 1923 Thompson machine gun, the model that had been called an automatic rifle because the Army had no funds to buy submachine guns that year. "What's this for?" Drake asked, confused. "We have to defend ourselves," the bunny said. "The mob is at the gates. The hungry mob. An astronaut named Spartacus is leading them." Drake handed the gun to Maldonado and crept upstairs to his private heliport. He passed through the lavatory to the laboratory (where Dr. Frankenstein was attaching electrodes to Linda Lovelace's jaws) and entered the golf course again, where the door opened to the airplane cabin.

He was escaping in his 747 jet, and below he could see Black Panthers, college kids, starving coal miners, Indians, Viet Cong, Brazilians, an enormous army pillaging his estate. "They must have seen the fnords," he said to the pilot. But the pilot was his mother and the sight of her threw him into a rage. "Leaving me alone!" he screamed. "Always leaving me alone to go to your damned parties with father. I never had a mother, just one nigger maid after another acting as mothers. Were the parties that fucking important?"

"Oh," she said reddening, "how can you use that word in front of your own mother?"

"To hell with that. All I remember is your perfume hanging in the air, and some strange black face coming when I called for you."

"You're such a baby," she said sadly. "All your life, you've always been a big baby." It was true: he was wearing diapers. A vice president of Morgan Guarantee Trust stared at him incredulously. "I say, Drake, do you really think that is appropriate garb for an important business meeting?" Beside him Linda Lovelace bent in ecstasy to kiss the secret ardor of Ishmael. "A whale of a good time," the vice president said, suddenly giggling inanely.

"Oh, fuck you all," Drake screamed. "I've got more money than any of you."

"The money is gone," Carl Jung said, wearing

Freud's beard. "What totem will you use now to ward off insecurity and the things that go bump in the night?" He sneered. "What childish codes! M.A.F.I.A.—*Morte Alla Francia Italia Anela*. French Canadian bean soup—the Five Consecrated Bavarian Seers. *Annuit Coeptis Novus Ordo Seclorum*—Anti-Christ Now Our Savior. A boy has never wept nor dashed a thousand kim—Asmodeus Belial Hastur Nyarlathotep Wotan Niggurath Dholes Azathoth Tindalos Kadith. Child's play! *Glasspielen!*"

"Well, if you're so damned smart, who are the inner Five right now?" Drake asked testily.

"Groucho, Chico, Harpo, Zeppo and Gummo," Jung said, riding off on a tricycle. "The Illuminati is your mother's breast, sucker," added Albert Hoffman, peddling after Jung on a bicycle.

Drake awoke as the Eye closed. It was all clear in an instant, without the labor he had spent working over the Dutchman's words. Maldonado stood by the bedside, his face Karloff's, and said, "We deserve to be dead." Yes: that was what it was like when you discovered you were a robot, not a man, like Karloff in the last scene of *Bride of Frankenstein*.

Drake awoke again and this time he was really awake. It was clear, crystal clear, and he had no regrets. Far away over Long Island Sound came the first distant rumble of thunder, and he knew this was no storm that any scientist less heretical than Jung or Wilhelm Reich would ever understand. "Our job," Huxley wrote before death, "is waking up."

Drake put on his robe quickly and stepped out into the dark Elizabethan hallway. Five hundred thousand dollars this house and grounds had cost, including the cottages, and it was only one of his eight estates. Money. What did it mean when Nyarlathotep appeared and "the wild beasts followed him and licked his hands" as that damned stupid-smart Lovecraft wrote? What did it matter when "the blind idiot God Chaos blew earth's dust away"?

Drake pushed open the dark paneled doorway of

George's room. Good: Tarantella was gone. The thunder rumbled again, and Drake's own shadow looming over the bed reminded him once more of a Karloff movie.

He bent over the bed and shook George's shoulder gently. "Mavis," the boy said. Drake wondered who the hell Mavis was; somebody terrific, obviously, if George could be dreaming about her after a session with the Illuminati-trained Tarantella. Or was Mavis another ex-Illuminatus? There were a lot of them with the Discordians lately, Drake had surmised. He shook George's shoulder again, more vigorously.

"Oh, no, I can't come again," George said. Drake gave another shake, and two weary and frightened eyes opened to look at him.

"What?"

"Up," Drake grunted, grabbing George under the arms and pulling him to a sitting position. "Out of bed," he added, panting, rolling the boy to the edge.

Drake was looking through waves upward at George. *Damn it, the thing has already found my mind.* "You've got to get out," he repeated. "You're in danger here."

October 23, 1935: Charley Workman, Mendy Weiss and Jimmy the Shrew charge through the door of the Palace Chop House and, according to orders, cowboy the joint . . . Lead pellets like rain; and rain like lead pellets hitting George's window, "Christ, what is it?" he asked. Drake stood him up stark naked and handed him his drawers, repeating "Hurry!" *Charley the Bug looked over the three bodies: Abadaba Berman, Lulu Rosenkrantz and somebody he didn't recognize. None of them was the Dutchman. "My God, we fucked up,"* he said, *"Dutch ain't here."* But a commotion has started in the alleys of the dream: Albert Stern, taking his last fix of the night, suddenly recalls his fantasy of killing somebody as important as John Dillinger. *"The can," Mendy Weiss says excitedly; he had a hard-on, like he always did on this kind of job.* "Man is a giant," Drake says, "forced to live in a pigmy's hut." "What does that mean?" George asks. "It means we're all fools," Drake says excitedly, smelling the old whore Death, "especially those of us who try to act like giants by bullying the others in the hut instead of knocking the goddam walls down. Carl Jung told me that, only in more elegant language." George's dangling penis kept catching his eye: homosexuality (an occasional thing with Drake), heterosexuality (his normal state) and the new lust for the old whore Death were all tugging at him. *The Dutchman dropped his penis, urine squirting his shoes, and went for his gun as he heard the shots in the barroom. He turned quickly, unable to stop pissing, and Albert Stern came through the door, shooting before Dutch could take aim. Falling forward, he saw that it was really Vince Coll, a ghost. "Oh, mama mama mama," he said, lying in his urine.*

"Which way do we go?" George asked, buttoning his shirt.

"You go," Drake said. "Down the stairs and out the back, to the garage. Here's the key to my Silver Wraith Rolls Royce. It won't be any use to me anymore."

"Why aren't you coming?" George protested.

"We deserve to be dead," Drake said, "all of us in this house."

"Hey, that's crazy. I don't care what you've done, a guilt trip is always crazy."

"I've been on a crazier trip, as you'd call it, all my life," Drake said calmly. "The power trip. Now, move!"

"George, don't make no bull moves," the Dutchman said. "He's talking," Sergeant Luke Conlon whispered at the foot of the hospital bed; the police stenographer, F. J. Lang, began taking notes. "What have you done with him?" the Dutchman went on. "Oh, mama, mama, mama. Oh, stop it. Oh, oh, oh, sure. Sure, mama." Drake sat down in the window seat and, too nervous for a cigar, lit one of his infrequent cigarettes. One hundred and fifty-seven, he thought, remembering the last entry in his little notebook. One hundred and fifty-seven rich women, one wife, and seventeen boys.

And never once did I really make contact, never once did I smash the walls . . . The wind and the rain were now deafening outside . . . Fourteen billion dollars, thirteen billion illegal and tax-free; more than Getty or Hunt, even if I could never publicize the fact. And that Arab boy in Tangier who picked my pocket after he blew me, my mother's perfume, hours and hours in Zurich puzzling over the Dutchman's words.

Outside Flegenheimer's livery stable in the Bronx, Phil Silverberg is teasing young Arthur Flegenheimer in 1913, holding the burglar's tools out of reach, asking mockingly, "Do you really think you're big enough to knock over a house on your own?" In the Newark hospital, the Dutchman cries angrily, "Now listen, Phil, fun is fun." The seventeen Illuminati representatives vanished in the dark; the one with the goat's head suddenly returned. "What happened to the other sixteen?" Dutch asked the hospital walls. The blood from his arm signed the parchment. "Oh, he done it. Please," he asked vaguely. Sergeant Conlon looks bemusedly at the stenographer, Lang. *The lightning seemed dark, and the darkness seemed light. It's taking hold of my mind completely, Drake thought, sitting by the window.*

I will hold onto my sanity, Drake swore silently. What was that rock song about Jesus I was remembering?

"Only five inches between me and happiness," was it? No, that's from *Deep Throat*. The whiteness of the whale.

The waves covered his vision again: wrong song, obviously. I have to reach him, to unify the forces. No, dammit, that's not *my* thought. That's his thought. He's coming up, up out of the waves. I must rise. I must rise. To unify the forces.

Dillinger said, "You're right, Dutch. Fuck the Illuminati. Fuck the Maf. The Justified Ancients of Mummu would be glad to have you." The Dutchman looked right into Sergeant Conlon's eyes and asked, "John, please, oh, did you buy the whole tale? You promised a million, sure. Get out, I wished I knew.

Please make it quick. Fast and furious. Please. Fast and furious. Please help me get out."

I should have gotten out in '42, when I first learned about the camps, Drake thought. I never realized until then that they really meant to do it. And next Hiroshima. Why did I stay after Hiroshima? It was so obvious, it was just the way Lovecraft wrote, the idiot God Chaos blew earth's dust away, and back in '35 I knew the secret: if a cheap hoodlum like Dutch Schultz had a great poet buried in him, what might be released if any man looked the old whore Death in the eye? Say that I betrayed my country and my planet, but worse, add that I betrayed Robert Putney Drake, the giant of psychology I murdered when I used the secret for power and not for healing.

I see the plumbers, the cesspool cleaners, the colorless all-color of atheism. I am the Fate's lieutenant: I act under ardors. White, White void. Ahab's eye. Five inches from happiness, the Law of Fives, always. Ahab schlurped down, down.

"This Bavarian stuff is all bullshit," Dillinger said. "They're mostly Englishmen, since Rhodes took command in 1888. And they've already infiltrated Justice, State and Labor, as well as the Treasury. That's who you're playing ball with. And let me tell you what they plan to do with your people, the Jews, in this war they're cooking up."

"Listen," the Dutchman interrupted. "Capone would have a bullet in me if he knew I was even talking to you, John."

"Are you afraid of Capone? He arranged to have the Feds put a bullet in me at the Biograph and I'm still sassy and lively as ever."

"I'm not afraid of Capone or Lepke or Maldonado or . . ." The Dutchman's eyes brought back the hospital room. "I'm a pretty good pretzler," he told Sergeant Conlon anxiously. "Winifred, Department of Justice. I even got it from the department." The pain shot through him, sharp as ecstasy. "Sir, please stop it!" He had to explain about DeMolay and Weishaupt. "Listen," he urged, "the last Knight. I don't want to holler." It was so hard, with the pulsings of the pain. "I don't know, sir. Honestly, I don't. I went to the toilet. I was in the can and the boy came at me. If we wanted to break the Ring. No, please. I get a month. Come on, Illuminati, cut me off." It was so hard to explain. "I had nothing with him and he was a cowboy in one of the seven days. *Ewige!* Fight . . . No business, no hang-outs, no friends. Nothing. Just what you pick up and what you need." The pain wasn't just the bullet; they were working on his mind, trying to stop him from saying too much. He saw the goat head. "Let him harness himself to you and then bother you," he cried. "They are Englishmen and they are a type and I don't know who is best, they or us." So much to say, and so little time. He thought of Francie, his wife. "Oh, sir, get the doll a rofting." The Illuminati formula to summon the lloigor: he could at least reveal that. "A boy has never wept nor dashed a thousand kim. Did you hear me?" They had to understand how high it went, all over the world. "I would hear it, the Circuit Court would hear it, and the Supreme Court would hear it. If that ain't the payoff. Please crack down on the China-man's friends and Hitler's Commander." Eris, the Great Mother, was the only alternative to the Illumi-nati's power; he had to tell them that much. "Mother is the best bet and don't let Satan draw you too fast."

"He's blabbing too much," the one who wore the goat head, Winifred, from Washington, said. "Increase the pain."

"The dirty rats have tuned in," Dutch shouted.

"Control yourself," Sergeant Conlon said soothingly.

"But I am dying," Dutch explained. Couldn't they understand anything?

Drake met Winifred at a cocktail party in Washington, in '47, just after the National Security Act was passed by the Senate. "Well?" Winifred asked, "do you have any further doubts?"

"None at all," Drake said. "All my open money is now invested in defense industries."

"Keep it there," Winifred smiled, "and you'll get richer than you ever dreamed. Our present projection is that we can get Congress to approve *one trillion dollars* in war preparations before 1967."

Drake thought fast and asked softly, "You're going to add another villain beside Russia?"

"Watch China," Winifred said calmly.

For once, curiosity surpassed cupidity in Drake; he asked, "Are you really keeping *him* in the Pentagon?"

"Would you like to meet him, face to face?" Winifred asked with a faint hint of a sneer in his voice.

"No thank you," Drake said coolly. "I've been reading Herman Rauschning. I remember Hitler's words about the Superman: 'He is alive, among us. I have met him. He is intrepid and terrible. I was afraid of him.' That's enough for my curiosity."

"Hitler," Winifred replied, not hiding the sneer now. "Saw him in his more human form. He's . . . progressed . . . since then."

Tonight, Drake thought, as the thunder rose to a maddening crescendo, I will see him, or one of them. Surely, I could have picked a more agreeable form of suicide? The question was pointless; Jung had been right all along, with his Law of Opposites. Even Freud knew it: every sadist becomes a masochist at last.

On an impulse, Drake arose and fetched a pad and pen from the bedside Tudor table. He began to scribble by the light of the increasing electrical storm outside:

> What am I afraid of? Haven't I been building up to this rendezvous ever since I threw the bottle at mother when I was 1½ years old?
>
> And it is kin to me. We both live on blood, do we not, even if I have prettied it over by taking the blood money instead of the blood itself?
>
> Dimensions keep shifting, whenever it gets a fix on me. Prinn was right in his *De Vermis Mysteriis*, they don't really participate in the same space-time as us. That's what Alhazred meant when he wrote, "Their hand is at your throat but

you see them not. They walk serene and unsuspected, not in the spaces we know, but between them."

"Pull me out," the Dutchman moaned. "I am half crazy. They won't let me get up. They dyed my shoes. Give me something. I am so sick."

I can see Kadath and the two magnetic poles. I must unify the forces by eating the entity.

Which me is the real me? Is it so easy to flow into my soul because there is so little soul left? Is that what Jung was trying to tell me about power?

I see Newark Hospital and the Dutchman. I see the white light and then the black that does not pulsate or move. I see George trying to drive the Rolls in this damnable rain. I see the whiteness of whiteness is black.

"Anybody," the Dutchman pleaded, "kindly take my shoes off. No, there's a handcuff on them. The Baron says these things."

I see Weishaupt and the Iron Boot. No wonder only five ever withstand the ordeal to become the top of the pyramid. Baron Rothschild won't let Rhodes get away with that. What is time or space, anyway? What is soul, that we claim to judge it? Which is real—the boy Arthur Flegenheimer, seeking for his mother, the gangster Dutch Schultz, dealing in murder and corruption with the cool of a Medici or a Morgan, or the mad poet being born in the Newark hospital bed as the others die?

And Elizabeth was a bitch. They sang "The Golden Vanity" about Raleigh, but none could speak a word against me. Yet he received the preference. The Globe Theatre, new drama by Will Shakespeare, down the street they torture Sackerson the bear for sport.

Christ, they opened the San Andreas Fault to

hide the most important records about Norton. Sidewalks opening like mouths, John Barrymore falling out of bed, Will Shakespeare in his mind, my mind, Sir Francis's mind. Roderick Usher. Starry Wisdom, they called it.

"The sidewalk was in trouble," the Dutchman tried to explain, "and the bears were in trouble and I broke it up. Please put me in that room. Please keep him in control."

I can hear it! The very sounds recorded by Poe and Lovecraft: Tekeli-li, tekeli-li! It must be close.

I didn't mean to throw the bottle, mother. I just wanted your attention. I just wanted attention.

"Okay,' the Dutchman sighed. "Okay, I am all through. Can't do another thing. Look out, mama, look out for her. You can't beat Him. Police. Mama. Helen. Mother. Please take me out."

I can see it and it can see me. In the dark. There are things worse than death, vivisections of the spirit. I should run. Why do I sit here? The bicycle and the tricycle. 23 skiddoo. Inside the pentagon, the cold of interstellar space. They came from the stars and brought their images with them. Mother. I'm sorry.

"Come on, open the soap duckets," the Dutchman said hopelessly. "The chimney sweeps. Take to the sword."

It is like a chimney without end. Up and up forever, in deeper and deeper darkness. And the red all-seeing eye.

"Please help me up. French Canadian bean soup. I want to pay. Let them leave me alone."

I want to join it. I want to become it. I have no more will of my own. I take thee, old whore Death, as my lawful wedded wife. I am mad. I am half mad. Mother. The bottle. Linda, schlurped, sucked down.

Unity.

A nine-year-old girl named Patty Cohen lived three miles down the coast from the Drake estate, and she went mad in those early morning hours of April 25. At first, her parents thought she had gotten hold of some of the LSD which was known to be infiltrating the local grammar school and, being fairly hip, they fed her niacin and horse doctor's doses of vitamin C as she ran about the house alternately laughing and making faces at them, howling about "he's laying in his own piss" and "he's still alive inside it" and "Roderick Usher." By morning they knew it was more than acid, and months of sadness began as they took her to clinics and private psychiatrists and more clinics and more private psychiatrists. Finally, just before Chanukah in December, they took her to an elegant shrink on Park Avenue, and she had a virtual epileptic fit in the waiting room, staring at a statue on the end table and screaming, "Don't let him eat me! Don't let him eat me!" Her recovery began from that day, and the sight of that miniature representation of the giant Tlaloc in Mexico City.

But three hours after Drake's death, George Dorn lay on his bed in the Hotel Tudor, holding a phone to his ear, listening to it ring. A young woman's voice on the other end suddenly said hello.

"I'd like to speak to Inspector Goodman," said George.

There was a momentary pause, then the voice said, "Who's calling, please?"

"My name is George Dorn, but it probably wouldn't mean anything to the Inspector. But would you ask him to come to the phone please and tell him I have a message for him about the case of Joseph Malik."

There was a constricted silence, as if the woman on the other end of the phone wanted to scream and had stopped breathing. Finally she said, "My husband is working just now, but I'll be glad to give him any message you have."

"That's funny," said George. "I've been told Inspector Goodman's duty hours are noon to 9 P.M."

"I don't think it's any of your business where he is," the woman suddenly blurted. George felt a little shock. Rebecca Goodman was frightened and she didn't know where her husband was: something in the tone of her last three words revealed her mental state to George. I must be getting more sensitive to people, he thought.

"Do you ever hear from him?" he said gently. He was feeling sorry for Mrs. Inspector Saul Goodman, who was, come to think of it, the wife of a pig. If, just a few years ago, George had read in the paper that this woman's husband had been shot down at random by some unknown revolutionary-type assailants, he would probably have whispered, "Right on." One of George's own friends of that period might have killed Inspector Goodman. There was even a moment when George himself might have done it. Once, one of the kids in George's group had called up the young widow of a policeman killed one December by young blacks and called her a bitch and the wife of a pig and told her that her husband was guilty of crimes against the people and that those who had shot him would go down in history as heroes. George had approved of this verbal action as a means of hardening oneself against bourgeois sentimentality. The papers had been full of stories about how this policeman's three little kids would have no Christmas this year; such tripe made George urgently want to throw up.

But now this woman's anguish was coursing through the wire and he was feeling it, just because her husband was not known to be dead, just missing. And probably not dead at all; otherwise why would Hagbard have said that George should get in touch with him?

"I—I don't know what you mean," she said. She was starting to break, George thought. In another minute she'd be blurting out all her fears to him. Well, for Christ's sake, *he* didn't know where Goodman was.

"Look," he said sharply, pushing back against the flow of emotion coming through to him, "if you hear from Inspector Goodman, tell him if he wants to know more about the Bavarian Illuminati he should call George Dorn at the Hotel Tudor. That's D-O-R-N, Hotel *Tudor*. Have you got that?"

"The Illuminati! Look, uh, Mr. Dorn, whatever you want to tell, you can tell me. I'll pass it on to him."

"I can't do that, Mrs. Goodman. Thank you, now. Good-bye."

"Wait! Don't hang up."

"I can't help you, Mrs. Goodman. I don't know where he is, either." George dropped the phone into its cradle with a sigh. His hands were cold and moist. Well, he'd have to tell Hagbard he couldn't reach Inspector Goodman. But he had learned something—that Saul Goodman, who was supposed to be investigating Joe Malik's disappearance, had himself disappeared, and the words "Bavarian Illuminati" meant something to his wife. George crossed the small room and turned on the TV. The noon news would be on. He went back to his bed, lay down and lit a cigarette. He was still exhausted, from his sexual bout of the night before with Tarantella Serpentine.

The announcer said, "The Attorney General has announced that he will speak at six this evening on the early morning epidemic of gangland-style assassinations at widely separated locations all over the country. The death toll from killings of this type has reached twenty-seven, though local officials refuse to say whether all—or any—of these deaths are connected. Among those shot are Senator Edward Coke Bacon; two high-ranking Los Angeles police officers; the mayor of a town called Mad Dog, Texas; a New York fight promoter; a Boston pharmacist; a Detroit ceramicist; a Chicago Communist; three New Mexico hippie leaders; a New Orleans restaurateur; a barber in Yorba Linda, California; and a sausage manufacturer in Sheboygan, Wisconsin. There were bomb explosions at fifteen locations, killing thirteen more people. Six persons around the country have disappeared, and four of these were seen being forced into cars at different times last night and this morning. The Attorney General today called this 'a reign of terror perpetrated by organized crime,' pointing out that though the motives for the widely scattered slayings is obscure they bear the earmarks of gangster killings. However, new FBI director George Wallace, who has ordered FBI agents around the country into action, issued a written statement declaring—quote—'Once again the Attorney General has treed the wrong coon, proving that law enforcement should be left to the experienced professionals. We have reason to think that these murders are the work of Negro Communists directed from Peking.'—end of quote. Meanwhile, the office of the Vice President has issued an apology to the Italian-American Anti-Defamation League for his reference to 'Mafioso rubouts' and the League has withdrawn its picket line from the White House. Remember, the Attorney General will address the nation at 6 P.M. tonight." The announcer suddenly changed his facial expression from neutral newscaster to pugnacious patriot. "Certain dissident elements keep complaining that people don't get a chance to participate in decisions made by their government. Yet, at a time like this, when the whole nation has an opportunity to hear the Attorney General, the ratings are not always as good as they should be. So let's do everything we can to build up those ratings tonight, and let the whole world know that this is still a democracy."

"Fuck!" George shouted at the screen. He didn't recall TV newscasters being that obnoxious. Must be a fairly recent development, something that had happened after he left for Mad Dog—maybe a late outgrowth of the Fernando Poo crisis. It was in this very hotel, George remembered, just after the bloody Fernando Poo demonstrations at the UN that Joe Malik had first broached the subject of Mad Dog. Now Joe had disappeared, not unlike those people who, as George knew, the Syndicate had snuffed in earnest of their good intentions, having accepted Hagbard's gift of objets d'art. Not unlike Inspector Saul Goodman who perhaps had gone down the same rabbit hole as Joe.

There was a knock at the door. George went to it, turning off the TV set in passing. It was Stella Maris.

"Well, glad to see you, baby. Strip off that dress and come over to the bed, so we can reaffirm my initiation rites."

Stella put her hands on his shoulders. "Never mind that now, George. We've got things to worry about. Robert Putney Drake and Banana Nose Maldonado are dead. Come on. We've got to get back to Hagbard right away."

Traveling first by helicopter, then by executive jet and finally by motorboat to Hagbard's Chesapeake Bay submarine base, George was exhausted and dazed in terror's aftermath. He rallied when he saw Hagbard again.

"You motherfucker! You sent me to get goddam killed!"

"And that has given you the courage to tell me off," said Hagbard with an indulgent smile. "Fear is a funny thing, isn't it, George? If we weren't afraid of dying of diseases, we'd never develop the science of microbiology. That science in turn creates the possibility of germ warfare. And each superpower is so afraid that the others may wage germ warfare against it, each develops its own plagues to wipe out the human race."

"Your mind is wandering, you stupid old fart," said Stella. "George isn't kidding about nearly being killed."

"The fear of death is the beginning of slavery," Hagbard said simply.

Even though it was early, George found himself on the verge of collapse, ready to sleep for twenty-four hours or more. The submarine's engines vibrated under his feet as he trudged to his cabin, but he wasn't even curious about where they were going. He lay down on his bed, and picked a book off the headpost bookshelf, part of his getting-ready-for-sleep ritual. *Sexuality, Magic and Perversion* said the binder. Well, that sounded juicy and promising. Author named Francis King, whoever that is. Citadel Press, 1972. Only a few years ago.

Well, then. George opened at random:

> Within a few years Frater Paragranus had become Chief of the Swiss section of the OTO, had entered into friendly relationships with the disciples of Aleister Crowley—notably Karl Germer—and had established a magazine. Subsequently Frater Paragranus inherited the chieftainship of Krumm-Heller's Ancient Rosicrucian Fraternity and the Patriarchate of the Gnostic Catholic Church—this latter dignity he derived from Chevillon, murdered by the Gestapo in 1944, who was himself the successor of Johnny Bricaud. Frater Paragranus is also the head of one of the several groups who claim to be the true heirs and successors of the Illuminati of Weishaupt as revived (circa 1895) by Leopold Engel.

George blinked. *Several* Illuminati? He had to ask Hagbard about this. But he was already beginning to visualize into hypnogogic revery and sleep was coming.

In less than a half-hour, Joe had distributed ninety-two paper cups of tomato juice containing AUM, the drug that promised to turn neophobes into neophiles. He stood in Pioneer Court, just north of the Michigan Avenue Bridge, at a table from which hung a poster reading FREE TOMATO JUICE. Each person who took a cupful was invited to fill out a short questionnaire and leave it in a box on Joe's table. However, Joe explained, the questionnaire was optional, and anyone who wanted to drink the tomato juice and run was welcome to do so.

AUM would work just as well either way, but the questionnaire would give ELF an opportunity to trace its effect on some of the subjects.

A tall black policeman was suddenly standing in front of the table. "You got a permit for this?"

"You bet," said Joe with a quick smile. "I'm with the General Services Corporation, and we're running a test on a new brand of tomato juice. Care to try some, officer?"

"No thanks," said the cop unsmilingly. "We had a bunch of yippies threatening to put LSD in the city's water supply two years ago. Let's just see your credentials." There was something cold, hard and homicidal in this cop's eyes, Joe thought. Something beyond the ordinary. This would be a unique guy, and the stuff would affect him uniquely. Joe looked down at the nameplate on the policeman's jacket, which read WATERHOUSE. The line behind Patrolman Waterhouse was getting longer.

Joe found the paper Malaclypse had given him. He handed it to Waterhouse, who glanced at it and said, "This isn't enough. You apparently didn't tell them you were going to set up your stand in Pioneer Court. You're blocking pedestrian traffic here. This is a busy area. You'll have to move."

Joe looked out at the street where crowds walked back and forth, at the bridge across the green, greasy Chicago river and at the buildings surrounding Pioneer Court. The brick-paved area was an ample public square, and there was clearly room for everyone. Joe smiled at Waterhouse. He was in Chicago and knew what to do. He took a ten-dollar bill out of his pocket, folded it twice lengthwise and wrapped it around a cup of the tomato juice, which he deftly filled from the plastic jug on his table. Waterhouse drained the tomato juice without comment, and when he tossed the cup into the wastebasket the ten-dollar bill was gone.

A bunch of baldheaded, cackling small-town businessman types was lined up in front of the table. Each one wore an acetate-covered badge bearing a red

Crusaders' cross, the letters KCUF and the words, "Dominus Vobiscum! My name is ———— ." Joe smilingly handed them cups of tomato juice, noting that the lapels of several bore an additional decoration, a square white plastic cross with the letters CL printed across it. Any of these men, Joe knew, would love to put him in jail for the rest of his life because he was the publisher of a radical magazine that occasionally got very explicit about sex and several times had published what Joe considered very beautiful erotica. The Knights of Christianity United for the Faith were rumored to be behind the firebombing of two theaters in the Midwest and the lynching of a news dealer in Alabama. And, of course, they had close ties with Atlanta Hope's God's Lightning Party.

AUM would be strong medicine for this bunch, Joe thought. He wondered if it would get them off their censorship kick or just make them more formidable. In either case, they would be bound to bust loose from Illuminati control for a time. If only there were a way he and Simon could get into their convention and administer AUM to more of them . . .

Behind the KCUF contingent there was a small man who looked like a rooster with a gray comb. When Joe read the questionnaire later, he found out that he had administered AUM to Judge Caligula Bushman, a shining ornament of the Chicago judiciary.

There followed a succession of faces Joe did not find memorable. They all had that complex, stupid, shrewd, angry, defeated, cynical, gullible look characteristic of Chicago, New York and other big cities. Then he found himself confronting a tall redhead whose features seemed to combine the best of Elizabeth Taylor and Marilyn Monroe. "Any vodka in that?" she asked him.

"No, ma'am, just straight tomato juice," said Joe.

"Too bad," she said as she tossed it down." "I could use one."

Caligula Bushman, known as the toughest judge on the Chicago bench, was trying six people who were charged with attacking a draft board, destroying all its furniture, ruining its files and dumping a wheelbarrow full of cow manure on the floor. Suddenly Bushman interrupted the trial about halfway through the prosecution's presentation of its case with the announcement that he was going to hold a sanity hearing. To the bewilderment of all, he then asked State's Attorney Milo A. Flanagan a series of rather odd questions:

"What would you think of a man who not only kept an arsenal in his home, but was collecting at enormous financial sacrifice a second arsenal to protect the first one? What would you say if this man so frightened his neighbors that they in turn were collecting weapons to protect themselves from him? What if this man spent ten times as much money on his expensive weapons as he did on the education of his children? What if one of his children criticized his hobby and he called that child a traitor and a bum and disowned it? And he took another child who had obeyed him faithfully and armed that child and sent it out into the world to attack neighbors? What would you say about a man who introduces poisons into the water he drinks and the air he breathes? What if this man not only is feuding with the people on his block but involves himself in the quarrels of others in distant parts of the city and even in the suburbs? Such a man would clearly be a paranoid schizophrenic, Mr. Flanagan, with homicidal tendencies. This is the man who should be on trial, though under our modern, enlightened system of jurisprudence we would attempt to cure and rehabilitate him rather than merely punish.

"Speaking as a judge," he continued, "I dismiss this case on several grounds. The State is clinically insane as a corporate entity and is absolutely unfit to arrest, try and incarcerate those who disagree with its policies. But I doubt that this judgment, though obvious to any man of common sense, quite fits into the rules of our American jurisprudential game. I also rule, therefore, that the right to destroy government property is protected by the First Amendment to the U.S. Constitution and therefore the crime with which these people are charged is not a crime under the Constitution. Government property belongs to all of the people, and the right of any of the people to express displeasure with their government by destroying government property is precious and shall not be infringed." This doctrine had come to Judge Bushman suddenly while he was speaking without his robe. It startled him, but he had noticed that his mind was working better and faster this afternoon.

He went on, "The State does not exist as a person or thing exists, but is a legal fiction. A fiction is a form of communication. Anything said to be owned by a form of communication must also thereby be itself a form of communication. Government is a map and government paper is a map of the map. The medium, in this case, is definitely the message, as any semanticist would agree. Furthermore, any physical act directed against a communication is itself a communication, a map of the map of the map. Thus, destruction of government property is protected by the First Amendment. I will issue a more ample written opinion on this point, but I feel now that the defendants need suffer in durance no longer. Case dismissed."

Many spectators trooped out of the courtroom sullenly, while those who loved the defendants surrounded them with tears, laughter and hugs. Judge Bushman, who stepped down from the bench but remained in the courtroom, was the benign center of a cluster of reporters. (He was thinking that his opinion would be a map of the map of the map of the map, or a fourth-order map. How many potential further orders of symbolism were there? He barely heard the praises showered on him. Of course, he knew his decision would be overturned; but the judge business already bored him. It would be interesting to get into mathematics, really deep.)

Harold Canvera had not bothered to fill out a questionnaire and therefore was not under observation and was not protected. He returned to his home, and his job as an accountant, and his avocation, which was recording telephone spiels against the Illuminati, the Communists, the Socialists, the Liberals, the Middle-of-the-Roaders and all insufficiently conservative Republicans. (Mr. Canvera also mailed out similar pamphlets whenever anybody was intrigued enough by his phone messages to send him twenty-five cents for additional information. He performed these worthy educational services for a group calling itself White Heroes Opposing Red Extremism, which was a splinter off Taxpayers Warring Against Tyranny, which was a splinter off God's Lightning.) In the following weeks, however, strange new ideas began to appear in Canvera's taped phone messages.

"*Lower* taxes aren't enough," he said, for instance. "When you hear some so-called conservative Bircher or some follower of William Buckley Jr. call for lower taxes, *beware*. There's a man who's *squishy soft* on Illuminism. All taxes are robbery. Instead of attacking Joan Baez, a real American should support her for refusing to pay any more money into the Illuminati treasury in Washington."

The next week was even more interesting: "White Heroes Opposing Red Extremism has often told you that there's no real difference between the Democrats and Republicans. Both are pawns of the Illuminati scheme to destroy private property and make everybody a slave of the State, so the International Bankers *of a certain minority group* can run everything. Now it's time for all thinking patriots to take an even more skeptical look than ever before at the so-called anti-Illuminati John Birch Society. Why are they always putting up those stickers saying, 'Support Your Local Police'? Ever wonder about that? What's the most important thing to a police state? Isn't it police? And if we got rid of the police, how could we ever have a police state? Think about it, fellow Americans, and Remember the Alamo!"

A few of these new strange ideas had come from

various right-wing anarchist periodicals (all secretly subsidized by Hagbard Celine) that Canvera had mysteriously received three months earlier and hadn't glanced at until swallowing the AUM. The periodicals had been mailed by Simon Moon, as a joke, in an envelope with the return address Illuminati International, 34 East 68th Street, New York City—the headquarters of the Council on Foreign Relations, long regarded by the Birchers as an Illuminati hotbed. "Remember the Alamo," Canvera had picked up from *Bowie Knife,* a publication of the Davy Crockett Society, a paramilitary right-wing fascist group which had splintered off God's Lightning when their leader, a Texas oil millionaire of gigantic paranoias, became convinced that many apparent Mexicans were actually Red Chinese agents in slight disguise. Later, the dogma became retroactive and he claimed that the Chinese had always been Communists, *all* Mexicans had always been Chinese, and the attack on the Alamo was the first Communist assault against American capitalism.

The third week was quite remarkable. Evidently, AUM, like LSD, changed some personality traits but left others fairly intact; in any event, in Canvera's irregular evolution from right-wing authoritarianism to right-wing libertarianism, he had somehow managed to arrive at a thesis never before enunciated except by Donatien Alphonse François de Sade. What this rare man did was to give a three-minute spiel in favor of the right of any person, of either sex, to use any other person, of either sex, *with or without* their consent, for sexual gratification of any sort needed or at least *desired.* The only option he granted the recipients of these intimate invasions was the reciprocal right to use the initiator for their own needs or desires. Now, most of the people who regularly called Canvera's phone service were not offended by any of this; they were Lincoln Avenue hippies and dialed him only when stoned, for what they called "a really weird and far-out head trip," and they were bored that he was no longer as funky as in his old Negro-baiting, Jew-hating and Illuminati-castigating days. However, there were a few members of White Heroes Opposing Red Extremism who called occasionally to check that their contributions were still financing the dissemination of true Americanism, and these people were severely puzzled and finally disturbed. Some of them even wrote to WHORE headquarters in Mad Dog, Texas, to complain that there was something a little bit peculiar in the Americanism lately. However, the president of WHORE, Dr. Horace Naismith, who also ran the John Dillinger Died for You Society, Veterans of the Sexual Revolution, and the Colossus of Yorba Linda Foundation, was in it only for the money, sad to say, and had no time for such petty complaints. He was too busy implementing his newest fund-raising scheme, the Male Chauvinist Organization (MACHO), which he hoped would milk *mucho* denaros from Russ Meyers, illegal abortionists, pimps, industrialists who regularly paid female workers thirty percent of the salaries of men doing the same jobs, and all others threatened by the Women's Liberation Movement.

The fourth week was, to be frank about it, definitely bizarre. Canvera discoursed at length on the lost civilization that once existed in the Gobi Desert and denounced those, such as Brion Gysin, who believed it had destroyed itself in atomic war. Rather, he asserted, it had been obliterated when the Illuminati arrived from the planet Vulcan in flying saucers. "Remember the Alamo" was now replaced by "Remember Carcosa," Canvera having discerned that both Ambrose Bierce and H. P. Lovecraft were describing this tragic Gobian society in their fiction. The hippies were again delighted—this was the funky kind of trip that had originally made Canvera a mock folk hero among them—and they especially appreciated his call for the U.S. to abandon the next moon shot and launch a punitive expedition to Vulcan both to wipe out Illuminism at its source and to avenge poor Carcosa. The

WHORE regulars, however, were again upset; all that concern with Carcosa struck them as creeping one-worldism.

The fifth week, Canvera took a new turn, denouncing the masses for their stupidity and proclaiming that the boobs probably deserved being governed by the Illuminati since most of them were too dumb to find their own behinds in a dark room even using both hands. He had been browsing through a volume of H. L. Mencken (sent to him over a year earlier by El Haj Stackerlee Mohammed, né Pearson, after one of his put-prayers-back-in-the-public-schools tirades); but he had also been pondering an invitation to *join* the Illuminati. This document, which came in an envelope with no return address, informed him that he was too smart to stay with the losers all his life and ought to climb on the winning side before it was too late. It added that membership dues were $3125, which should be put in a cigar box and buried in his back yard, after which it promised "one of our underground agents will contact you." At first, Canvera had considered this a hoax—he received many put-ons in the mail, together with pornography, Rosicrucian pamphlets, illustrated with the eye-and-pyramid design, and pretended fan letters signed by such names as *Eldridge Cleaver, Fidel Castro, Anton Szandor Levay* or *Judge Crater,* all of course cooked up by his Lincoln Avenue audience. Later, however, it struck him that 3125 was *five to the fifth power* and that convinced him a True Illuminatus was indeed communicating with him. He took the $3125 out of his savings account, buried it as instructed, made a pro-Illuminati recording as a gesture of good faith and waited. The next day he was shot, several times, in the head and shoulders, dying of natural causes as a result.

(In present time again, Rebecca Goodman enters the Hotel Tudor lobby in answer to the second mysterious phone call of the day, while Hagbard decides George Dorn needs to be illuminized further before Ingolstadt, and Esperando Despond clears his throat

and says, "I want to explain the mathematics of plague to you men . . .")

Actually, poor old Canvera's death had nothing to do with the Illuminati or with his former compatriots in WHORE. The man had been practicing the libertine philosophy of his post-AUM phone editorials and had tampered with Cassandra Acconci, the beloved daughter of Ronald Acconci, Chicago Regional Commander of God's Lightning and a long-time contributor to KCUF. Acconci arranged, via State's Attorney Milo A. Flanagan, for the local Maf to do a hit on Canvera. But there are no endings, any more than there are any beginnings; it next developed that Canvera's seed lived on in wedlock with Cassandra's ovum and was in danger of becoming a human being within her previously trim abdomen.

Saul Goodman had no idea that the room he was in had last been rented to George Dorn; he was conscious only of his impatience, not knowing that Rebecca was at that moment on an elevator approaching his floor . . . And a mile north, Peter Jackson, still trying to put together the July issue of *Confrontation* virtually singlehanded, dives into the slush pile (which is the magazine industry's elegant name for unsolicited manuscripts) and comes up with more fallout from the Moon-Malik AUM project of 1970. "Orthodox Science: The New Religion," he reads. *Well, let's sample it, what the hell.* Opening at random he finds:

Einstein's concept of spherical space, furthermore, suffers from the same defect as the concept of a smoothly or perfectly spherical earth: it rests upon the use of the irrational number, π. This number has no operational definition; there is no place on any engineer's scale to which one can point and say "This is exactly π," although these scales are misleadingly marked with such a spot. π, in fact, can never be found in the real world, and there are historical and archeological reasons to believe it was created by a Greek mathematician under the influence of the mind-warping hallucinogenic mushroom *Amanita muscaria*. It is pure surrealism. You cannot write π as a real number; you can only approximate it, as 3.1417 . . . etc. Chemistry knows no such units: three atoms of an element may combine with four atoms of another element, but you will never find π atoms combining with anything. Quantum physics reveals that an electron may jump three units or four units, but it will not jump π units. Nor is π necessary to geometry, as is sometimes claimed; R. Buckminster Fuller has created an entire geometric system, at least as reliable as that of the ancient Greek dope fiends, in which π does not appear at all. Space, then, may be slanted or kiltered in various ways, but it cannot be smoothly spherical . . .

"What the ring-tailed rambling hell?" Peter Jackson said aloud. He flipped to the end:

In conclusion, I want to thank a strange and uncommon man, James Mallison, who provided the spark which set me thinking about these matters. In fact, it was due to my meeting with Mr. Mallison that I sold my hardware business, returned to college and majored in cartography and topology. Although he was a religious fanatic (as I was at the time of our meeting) and would, therefore, not appreciate many of my discoveries, it is due to this man's perverse, peculiar and yet brilliant prodding that I embarked on the search which has lead to this new theory of a Pentahedroidal Universe.

W. Clement Cotex, Ph.D

"Far fucking *out*," Peter muttered. James Mallison was a pen name Joe Malik sometimes used, and here was another James Mallison inspiring this guy to become a Ph.D. and invent a new cosmological theory. What was the word Joe used for such coincidences? Synch-something . . .

("1472," Esperando Despond concludes his gloomy mathematical calculations. "That's the number of plague cases we might have right now, at noon, if the girl had only two contacts after leaving Dr. Mocenigo. Now, if she had three contacts . . ." The assembled FBI agents are gradually turning a pale greenish color from the neck up. Carmel, the only actual contact, is busy two blocks away stuffing money into a briefcase.)

"That's him!" Mrs. Edward Coke Bacon cried excitedly, addressing Basil Banghart, another FBI agent, in an office in Washington. She is pointing at a photo of Albert "the Teacher" Stern. "Ma'am," Banghart says kindly, "that can't be him. I don't even know why his picture's still in the file. That's a no-account junkie who once got on our most-wanted list because he confessed to a murder he didn't even commit." In Cincinnati, an FBI artist is completing a portrait under the direction of the widow of a slain TV repairman: the face of the killer, gradually emerging, combines various features of Vincent "Mad Dog" Coll, George Dorn and the lead vocalist of the American Medical Association, which group was at that moment boarding a plane at Kennedy International Airport for the Ingolstadt gig. Rebecca Goodman, rising in the Hotel Tudor elevator, has a flash memory of a nightmare of the night before: Saul being shot by the same vocalist, dressed as a monk, in red-and-white robes, while a Playboy bunny danced in front of some kind of giant pyramid. In Princeton, New Jersey, a nuclear physicist named Nils Nosferatu—one of the few survivors of the early morning shootings—babbles to the detective and police stenographer at his bedside, "Tlaloc sucks. You can't trust them. The midget is the one to watch. We'll be moved, all right, when the tear gas hits. Fun is fun. Omega. George's brother met the dolphins first, and that was the psychic hook that brought George in. She's at the door. She's buried in the desert. Any devia-

tion will result in termination. Unify the forces. You hold the hose. I'll get Mark."

"I've got to start telling you the truth, George," Hagbard began hesitantly, *as the Midget, Carmel and Dr. Horace Naismith collided in front of the door of the Sands Hotel ("Watch the fuck where you're going," Carmel growled),* and she was at the door, her heart was pounding, an intuition was forming in her mind, and she knocked *(and Peter Jackson began dialing Epicene Wildeblood),* and she was sure of it, and she was afraid of being sure because she might be wrong, *and the Midget said to Dr. Naismith "Rude bastard, wasn't he?"* and the door opened, *and the door of Milo O. Flanagan's office opened to admit Cassandra Acconci,* and her heart stopped, *and Dr. Nosferatu screamed, "The door. She's in the door. The door in the desert. He eats Carmels,"* and it was him and she was in his arms and she was weeping and laughing and asking, "Where have you *been,* baby?" And Saul closed the door behind her and drew her further into the room. "I'm not a cop anymore," he said, "I'm on the other side."

"What?" Rebecca noticed there was a new thing in his eyes, a thing for which she had no word.

"You can stop worrying that you'll get back on horse," he went on gaily. "And if you've ever been afraid of your sexual fantasies, don't be. We've all got them. Saint Bernards!"

But even that wasn't as weird as the new thing in his eyes.

"Baby," she said, *"baby.* What the hell is this?"

"I wanted sex with my father, when I was two years old. When did you have that thing about the Saint Bernard?"

"When I was eleven or twelve, I think. Just before my first period. My God, you must have been a lot further away than I ever imagined." She was beginning to recognize the new thing. It wasn't intelligence; he had always had that. With awe, she realized it was what the ancients called wisdom.

"I've always had a thing about black women, just like your thing about black men," he went on. "I think everybody in this country has a touch of it. The blacks have it about *us,* too. I was in one head, a brilliant black guy, musician, scientist, poet, a million talents, and white women were like the Holy Grail to him. And your fantasy about Spiro Agnew—I had one just like that about Ilse Koch, a Nazi bitch from before your time. It was the same thing in both cases, revenge. Not real sex, hate-sex. Oh, we're all so crazy-in-the-head."

Rebecca backed up and sat down on the bed. "It's too much, too fast, I'm scared. I can see you don't have any contempt for me, but, Lord, can I *live* knowing that somebody else knows every single repressed desire I have?"

"Yes," Saul said calmly. "And you're mistaken about Time. I can't know every secret, darling. I've only had a smattering of them. A handful. There are a dozen people right now who've been through my head the same way, and I can look any one of them in the eye. The things I know about *them!*" He laughed.

"It's still too fast," Rebecca said. "You disappear, and then you come back knowing things about me that I only half know myself, and you're not a cop anymore . . . What do you mean, you've joined 'the other side'? The Mafia? The Morituri groups?"

"No," Saul answered happily. "Much further out than that. Darling, I've been driven mad by the world's best brainwashers and put back together again by a computer that does psychotherapy, predicts the future and steers a submarine all at once. On the way, I learned things about humanity and the universe that it would take a year to tell you. And I don't have much time right now, because I've got to fly to Las Vegas. In two or three days, if everything works out, I'll be able to show you, not just tell you—"

"Are you reading my mind right now?" Rebecca asked, still awed and nervous.

Saul laughed again. "It isn't that simple. It takes years of training, and even then it's like an old radio full of static. If I 'tune in' right now, I'll get a flash of whatever's in your head, but it will be so jumbled with other things that relate to my resonance in one way or another that I won't know for sure which part is you."

"Do it," Rebecca said. "I'll be more comfortable with you if I see a sample of whatever-it-is that you've become."

Saul sat down on the bed beside her and took her hand. "Okay," he said thoughtfully, "I'll do it aloud, and don't be afraid. I'm the same man, darling, there's just more of me now." He inhaled deeply. "Here goes . . . Five million bucks. Never find her where I buried her. 1472. George, don't make no bull moves. Unify the forces. One helping hand deserves another. New York Jew doctors. Remember Carcosa! In quick and out quick, a cowboy. They're all coming back. Lie down on the floor and keep calm. It's a League of Nations, a young people's League of Nations. One was for fighting, the other for fun . . . *Good Lord,*" he broke off and closed his eyes. "I've got a whole street and I can see them. They're still singing. 'We rose up in arms and none failed to come, we're the Vets of the Sex Revolooooootion!' *What the hell?*" He turned to her and explained, "It's like a split-screen movie, but split a thousand ways, and with a thousand soundtracks. I only pick up a few random bits. When one jumps out like that last one, it's important; I'll bet that street is in Las Vegas and I'll be walking on it myself in a few hours. Anyway," he added, "none of that seemed to come from you. Did it?"

"No," she said, "and I'm glad. This takes some re-orientation. When you said you're going to show me in a few days, did you mean show me how to do it?"

"You *are* doing it. Everybody is. All the time."

"But?"

"But most of the time it's just background noise. I can teach you to become more aware of it. Learning to focus—to pick out one person and one time—that takes years, decades."

Rebecca finally smiled. "You sure did go a long way in a day and a half."

"If it were a year and a half," Saul said simply, "or a century and a half—I'd still be trying to find my way back to you all through it."

She kissed him. "Yes, it's still you," she said, "just *more* of you. Tell me: if we both studied it for years and years could we get to the point where we were reading each other's minds constantly, tuned in on each other completely?"

"Yes," Saul said, "there are couples like that."

"Mm. That's even more intimate than sex."

"No. It *is* sex."

An intimation came to Rebecca, like a voice whispering far down at the end of a dark hall, and she knew that some part of her already knew, and had always known, what Saul was about to explain. "Your new friends who taught all this," she said quietly. "They're way ahead of Freud, aren't they?"

"Way ahead. For instance, what am I thinking now?"

"You're feeling horny," Rebecca grinned. "But that's not my background noise, or telepathy, that picked that up. It's your breathing and the kind of light in your eyes and all sorts of other small cues that a woman learns to recognize. The way you moved a little closer after I kissed you. Things like that."

Saul took her hand again. "*How* horny am I?" he asked.

"*Very* horny. In fact, you've already decided that you've got time enough and *that's* more important than talking . . ."

Saul touched her cheek gently. "Did you read that from kinesic cues, or was it the background noise or telepathy?"

"I guess the background noise helped me to read the cues . . ."

Saul glanced at his watch. "I have to meet Barney Muldoon in the lobby in exactly fifty minutes. How would you like to hear a scientific lecture while you're being laid? That's a perversion we've never tried before." His hand moved down from her cheek to her neck and then began unbuttoning her blouse.

("There's a Morituri bomb factory in your building," Cassandra Acconci said flatly. "On the seventeenth floor. The name on the buzzer is the same as yours."

"My brother!" Milo O. Flanagan bellowed. "Right under my nose! That freaking faggot!")

"Oh, Saul. Oh, Saul, Saul," Rebecca closed her eyes as the mouth tightened on her nipple . . . *and Dr. Horace Naismith crossed the lobby of the Sands, affixing the VSR badge to his lapel, and passed the Midget again* . . . "Well," the Attorney General told the President, "one solution, of course, is to *nuke* Las Vegas. But that wouldn't solve the problem of the possible carriers who could have hopped a plane already and might be anywhere in the country now, or anywhere in the world." While the President washes down three Librium, a Tofranil and an Elavil, the Vice President asks thoughtfully, "Suppose we just distribute the antidote to party workers and ride this thing out?" He is feeling more than usually misanthropic, having had an appalling evening in New York due to his impulsiveness in answering a personal ad which had touched his heart . . .

("Thank you Cassandra," Milo A. Flanagan said fervently. "I'm eternally grateful to you."

"One helping hand deserves another," Cassandra replied; she remembered how Milo and Smiling Jim Trepomena had helped her get the abortion the time she was knocked up by that Canvera character. Her father had wanted to send her to New York for a legal D & C, but Milo had pointed out that it would look kind of funny to some people for the daughter of a high KCUF spokesman to have an *official* abortion. "Besides," Smiling Jim had added, "you don't want to fool around with them New York Jew doctors. They might do dirty things to you. Just trust me, child; we've got the coun-

try's best-qualified criminal abortionists in Cincinnati."
Actually, though, the real reason Cassandra was blowing the whistle on Padre Pederastia's bomb emporium
was to annoy Simon Moon, whom she had been trying
to get into her bed ever since she met him at the
Friendly Stranger Coffee House six months before. Simon hadn't been interested, due to his obsession with
black women, who represented the Holy Grail to him.)

"Wildeblood here," the cultured drawl came over
the wire.

"Have you finished your review yet?" Peter Jackson
asked, crushing another cigarette butt in his ashtray
and worrying about lung cancer.

"Yes, and you'll love it. I really tear these two
smart-asses apart." Wildeblood was enthusiastic. "Listen to this: 'a pair of nursery Nietzsches dreaming of a
psychedelic Superman.' And this: 'a plot that is only a
put-on, characters who are cardboard, and a pretense
of scholarship that amounts to sheer bluff.' But *this* is
the crusher; listen: 'a constant use of obscene language
for shock effect until the reader begins to feel as depressed as an unwilling spectator at a quarrel between
a fishwife and a lobster-pot pirate.' Don't you think
that will get quoted at all the best cocktail parties this
season?"

"I suppose so. The book's a real stinker, eh?"

"Heavens, I wouldn't know for sure. I told you yesterday, it's absurdly *long*. Three volumes, in fact. Boring as hell. I only had time to skim it. But listen to this,
dear boy: 'If *The Lord of the Rings* is a fairy tale for
adults, sophisticated readers will quickly recognize this
monumental miscarriage as a fairy tale for paranoids.'
That refers to the ridiculous conspiracy theory that the
plot, if there is one, seems to revolve around. Nicely
worded, wouldn't you say?"

"Yeah, sure," Peter said, crossing off *book review*
on his pad. "Send it over. I'll pay the messenger."

Epicene Wildeblood, hanging up, crossed off *Confrontation* on his own pad, found *Time* next on the list,
and picked up another book to be immortalized by his

devastating witticisms. He was feeling more than usually misanthropic, having had a disastrous evening the
night before. Somebody had answered his personal ad
about his "interest in Greek Culture" and he had
thrilled at the thought of a new asshole to conquer; the
asshole, unfortunately, had turned out to be the Vice
President of the United States, who was interested only
in declaiming about the glorious achievements of the
military junta that had ruled in Athens. When Eppy,
despairing of sex, had tried to steer the conversation to
Plato at least, the VP asked, "Are you sure he was a
Greek? That sounds like a wop name to me."

(Tobias Knight and two other FBI agents elbow
past the Midget searching for whores who might have
been with Dr. Mocenigo the night before, while outside
the VSR's first contingent, the Hugh M. Hefner
Brigade, led by Dr. Horace Naismith himself, marches
by singing: "We're Vet'rans of the *Sexule* Revolution/
Our rifles were issued, we had our own guns/ One was
for fighting, the other for fun/ We rose up in arms and
none failed to come/ We're Vets of the Sex Revo-
loooooooooootion!")

You see, darling, it all revolves around sex, but not
in the sense that Freud thought. Freud never understood sex. Hardly anybody understands sex, in fact,
except a few poets here and there. Any scientist who
starts to get an inkling keeps his mouth shut because
he knows he'd be drummed out of the profession if he
said what he knew. Here, I'll help you unhook that.
What we're feeling now is supposed to be tension, and
what we'll feel after orgasm is supposed to be relaxation.
Oh, they're so pretty. Yes, I know I always say that. But
they are pretty. Pretty, pretty, pretty. Mmmm. Mmmm.
Oh, yes, yes. Just hold it like that a moment. Yes. Tension? Lord, yes that's what I mean. How can this be
tension? What's it got in common with worry or anxiety or anything else that we call tension? It's a strain,
but not a tension. It's a drive to break out, and a tension is a drive to hold in. Those are the two polarities.
Oh, stop for a minute. Let me do this. You like that?

Oh, darling, yes, darling, I like it, too. It makes me happy to make you happy. You see, we're trying to break through our skins into each other. We're trying to break the walls, walls, walls. Yes, Yes. Break the walls. Tension is trying to hold up the walls, to keep the outside from getting in. It's the opposite. Oh, Rebecca. Let me kiss them again. They're so pretty. Pretty pretty titties. Mmm. Mmm. Pretty. And so big and round. Oh, you've got two hard-ons and I've only got one. And this, this, ah, you like it, don't you, that's three hard-ons. You want me to take my finger away and kiss it? Oh, darling, pretty belly, pretty. Mmm. Mmm. Darling, Mmm. MMMMM. Mmm. Lord, Lord. You never came so fast before, oh, I love you. Are you happy? I'm so happy. That's right, just for a minute. Oh, God, I love watching you do that. I love to see it go into your mouth. Lord, God, Rebecca, I love it. Yes, now I'll put him in. Little Saul, there, coming up inside you, there. Does little Rebecca like him? I know, I know. They love each other, don't they? The way we love each other. She's so warm, she welcomes him so nicely. You're inside me, too. That's what I'm trying to say. My field. You're inside my field, just like I'm inside yours. It's the fields, not the physical act. That's what people are afraid of. That's why they're tense during sex. They're afraid of letting the fields merge. It's a unifying of the forces. God, I can't keep talking. Well, if we slow way down, yes, this is nicer, isn't it? That's why it's so fast for most people. They rush, complete the physical act, before the fields are charged. They never experience the fields. They think it's poetry, fiction, when somebody who's had it describes it. One scientist knew. He died in prison. I'll tell you about him later. It's the big taboo, the one all the others grow out of. It isn't sex itself they're trying to stop. That's too strong, they can't stop it. It's this. Darling, yes. This. The unifying. It happens at death, but they try to steal it even then. They've taken it out of sex. That's why the fantasies. And the promiscuity. The search. Blacks, homosexuality, our parents, people we know we hate, Saint Bernards. Everything. It's not neuroses or perversion. It's a search. A desperate search. Everybody wants sex with an enemy. Hate mobilizes the field, too, you see. And hate. Is safer. Safer than love. Love too dangerous. Lord, Lord, I love you. I love you. Let me more. Get the weight on my elbows, hold your ass with my hands. Yes. Poetry isn't poetry. I mean it doesn't lie. It's true when I say I worship you. Can't say it outside bed. Can only say love then, usually. Worship too scary. Some people can't even say love in bed. Searching, partner to partner. Never able to say love. Never able to feel it. Under control. They can't let us learn, or the game is up. Their name? They got a million names. Monopolize it. Keep it to themselves. They had to stamp it out in the rest of us, to control. To control us. Drove it underground, into background noise. Mustn't break through. That's how. How it happened. Darling. First they repressed telepathy, then sex. That's why schizos. Darling. Why schizos break into crazy sex things first. Why homosexuals dig the occult. Break one taboo, come close to the next. Finally break the wall entirely. Get through. Like we get through, together. They can't have that. Got to keep us apart. Schisms. Always splitting and schisms. White against black, men against women, all the way down the line. Keep us apart. Don't let us merge. Make sex a dirty joke. A few more minutes. A few more. My tongue in your ear. Oh, God. Soon. So fast. A miracle. Whole society set up to prevent this. To destroy love. Oh, I do love you. Worship you. Adore you. Rebecca. Beautiful, beautiful. Rebecca. They don't want us to. Unify. The. Forces. Rebecca. Rebecca. Rebecca.

THE SEVENTH TRIP, OR NETZACH
(THE SNAFU PRINCIPLE)

The most thoroughly and relentlessly Damned, banned, excluded, condemned, forbidden, ostracized, ignored, suppressed, repressed, robbed, brutalized and defamed of all Damned Things is the individual human being. The social engineers, statisticians, psychologists, sociologists, market researchers, landlords, bureaucrats, captains of industry, bankers, governors, commissars, kings and presidents are perpetually forcing this Damned Thing into carefully prepared blueprints and perpetually irritated that the Damned Thing will not fit into the slot assigned to it. The theologians call it a sinner and try to reform it. The governor calls it a criminal and tries to punish it. The psychotherapist calls it a neurotic and tries to cure it. Still, the Damned Thing will not fit into their slots.

—*Never Whistle While You're Pissing,*
by Hagbard Celine, H.M., S.H.

The Midget, whose name was Markoff Chaney, was no relative of the famous Chaneys of Hollywood, but people *did* keep making jokes about that. It was bad enough to be, by the standards of the gigantic and stupid majority, a freak; how much worse to be so named as to remind these big oversized clods of the cinema's two most famous portrayers of monstro-freaks; by the time the Midget was fifteen, he had built up a detestation for ordinary mankind that dwarfed (he hated that word) the relative misanthropies of Paul of Tarsus, Clement of Alexandria, Swift of Dublin and even Robert Putney Drake. Revenge, for sure, he would have. He would have revenge.

It was in college (Antioch, Yellow Springs, 1962)

that Markoff Chaney discovered another hidden joke in his name, and the circumstances were—considering that he was to become the worst headache the Illuminati ever encountered—appropriately synchronistic. It was in a math class, and, since this was Antioch, the two students directly behind the Midget were ignoring the professor and discussing their own intellectual interests; since this was Antioch, they were a good six years ahead of intellectual fads elsewhere. They were discussing ethology.

"So we keep the same instincts as our primate ancestors," one student (he was from Chicago, his name was Moon, and he was crazy even for Antioch) was saying. "But we superimpose culture and law on top of this. So we get split in two, dig? You might say," Moon's voice betrayed pride in the aphorism he was about to unleash, "mankind is a statutory ape."

". . . and," the professor, old Fred "Fidgets" Digits, said at just that moment, "when such a related series appears in a random process, we have what is known as a Markoff Chain. I hope Mr. Chaney won't be tormented by jokes about this for the rest of the term, even if the related series of his appearances in class do seem part of a notably random process." The class roared; another ton of bile was entered in the Midget's shit ledger, the list of people who were going to eat turd before he died.

In fact, his cuts were numerous, both in math and in other classes. There were times when he could not bear to be with the giants, but hid in his room, *Playboy* gatefold open, masturbating and dreaming of millions and millions of nubile young women built like Playmates. Today, however, *Playboy* would avail him not; he needed something raunchier. Ignoring his next class, Physical Anthropology (always good for a few humiliating moments), he hurried across David Street, passing Atlanta Hope without noticing her, and slammed into his room, chain-bolting the door behind him.

Damn old Fidgets Digits, and damn the science of mathematics itself, the line, the square, the average, the whole measurable world that pronounced him a bizarre random factor. Once and for all, beyond fantasy, in the depth of his soul he declared war on the statutory ape, on law and order, on predictability, on negative entropy. He would be a random factor in every equation; from this day forward, unto death, it would be civil war: the Midget versus the Digits.

He took out the pornographic Tarot deck, which he used when he wanted a really far-out fantasy for his orgasm, and shuffled it thoroughly. Let's have a Markoff Chain masturbation to start with, he thought with an evil grin.

And, thus, without ever contacting the Legion of Dynamic Discord, the Erisian Liberation Front or even the Justified Ancients of Mummu, Markoff Chaney began his own crusade against the Illuminati, not even knowing that they existed.

His first overt act—his Fort Sumter, as it were—began in Dayton the following Saturday. He was in Norton's Emporium, a glorified 5 & 10¢ store, when he saw the sign:

NO SALESPERSON MAY LEAVE THE FLOOR WITHOUT
THE AUTHORIZATION OF A SUPERIOR.
THE MGT.

What!, he thought, are the poor girls supposed to pee in their panties if they can't find a superior? Years of school came back to him ("Please, may I leave the room, sir?") and rituals which had appeared nonsensical suddenly made sense in a sinister way. Mathematics, of course. They were trying to reduce us all to predictable units, robots. Hah! not for nothing had he spent a semester in Professor "Sheets" Kelly's intensive course on textual analysis of modern poetry. The following Wednesday, the Midget was back at Norton's and hiding in a coffee urn when the staff left and locked up. A few moments later, the sign was down and a subtly different one was in its place:

NO SALESPERSON MAY LEAVE THE FLOOR OR GO TO THE
DOOR WITHOUT THE AUTHORIZATION OF A SUPERIOR.
THE MGT.

He came back several times in the next few weeks,
and the sign remained. It was as he suspected: in a
rigid hierarchy, nobody questions orders that seem to
come from above, and those at the very top are so isolated from the actual work situation that they never see
what is going on below. It was the chains of communication, not the means of production, that determined a
social process; Marx had been wrong, lacking cybernetics to enlighten him. Marx was like the engineers of
his time, who thought of electricity in terms of work
done, before Marconi thought of it in terms of information transmitted. Nothing signed "THE MGT."
would ever be challenged; the Midget could always
pass himself off as the Management.

At the same time, he noticed that the workers were
more irritable; the shoppers picked this up and became
grouchier themselves; sales, he guessed correctly, were
falling off. Poetry was the answer: poetry in reverse.
His interpolated phrase, with its awkward internal
rhyme and its pointlessness, bothered everybody, but in
a subliminal, preconscious fashion. Let the market researchers and statisticians try to figure this one out
with their computers and averages.

His father had been a stockholder in Blue Sky Inc.,
generally regarded as the worst turkey on the Big
Board (it produced devices to be used in making land-
ings on low-gravity planets); profits had soared when
John Fitzgerald Kennedy had announced that the U.S.
would put a man on the moon before 1970; the Midget
now had a guaranteed annuity amounting to thirty-six
hundred dollars per year, three hundred dollars per
month. It was enough for his purposes. Revenge, in
good measure, he would have. He would have revenge.

Living in Spartan fashion, dining often on a tin of
sardines and a pint of milk from a machine, traveling
always by Greyhound bus, the Midget criss-crossed the

country constantly, placing his improved surrealist signs whenever the opportunity presented itself. A slowly mounting wave of anarchy followed in his wake. The Illuminati never got a fix on him: he had little ego to discover, burning all his energies into Drive, like a dictator or a great painter—but, unlike a dictator or a great painter, he had no desire for recognition. For years, the Illuminati attributed his efforts to the Discordians, the JAMs or the esoteric ELF. Watts went up, and Detroit; Birmingham, Buffalo, Newark, a flaming picnic blanket spread across urban America as the Midget's signs burned in the stores that had flaunted them; one hundred thousand marched to the Pentagon and some of them tried to expel the Demon (the Illuminati foiled that at the last minute, forbidding them to form a circle); a Democratic convention was held behind barbed wire; in 1970 a Senate committee announced that there had been three thousand bombings in the year, or an average of ten per day; by 1973 Morituri groups were forming in every college, every suburb; the SLA came and came back again; Atlanta Hope was soon unable to control God's Lightning, which was going in for its own variety of terrorism years before Illuminati planning had intended.

"There's a random factor somewhere," technicians said at Illuminati International; "There's a random factor somewhere," Hagbard Celine said, reading the data that came out of FUCKUP; "There's a random factor somewhere," the Dealy Lama, leader of ELF, said dreamily in his underground hideout beneath Dealy Plaza.

Drivers on treacherous mountain roads swore in confusion at signs that said:

SLIPPERY WHEN WET
MAINTAIN 50 M.P.H.
FALLING ROCK ZONE
DO NOT LITTER

Men paid high initiation fees to revel in the elegance

of all-WASP clubs whose waiters were carefully trained to be almost as snobbish as the members, then felt vaguely let down by signs warning them:

WATCH YOUR HAT AND COAT
NOT RESPONSIBLE FOR LOST PROPERTY.
THE MGT.

The Midget became an electronic wizard in his spare time. All over the country, pedestrians stood undecided on curbs as electric signs said WALK while the light was red and then switched to DON'T WALK when the light went green. He branched out and expanded his activities; office workers received memos early in the morning (after he had spent a night with a Xerox machine) and puzzled over:

1. All vacation requests must be submitted in triplicate to the Personnel Department at least three weeks before the planned vacation dates.

2. All employees who change their vacation plans must notify Personnel Department by completing Form 1472, Vacation Plan Change, and submitting it three weeks before the change in plans.

3. All vacation plans must be approved by the Department Supervisor and may be changed if they conflict with the vacation plans of employees of higher rank and/or longer tenure.

4. Department Supervisors may announce such cancellations at any time, provided the employee is given 48 hours notice, or two working days, whichever is longer, as the case may be. (Employees crossing the International Date Line, see Form 2317.)

5. Employees may not discuss vacation plans with other employees or trade preferred dates.

6. These few simple rules should prevent a great deal of needless friction and frustration if all

employees cooperate, and we will all have a
happy summer.

THE MGT.

On April 26 of the year when the Illuminati tried to
immanentize the Eschaton, the Midget experienced
aches, pains, nausea, spots before his eyes, numbness
in his legs and dizziness. He went to the hotel doctor,
and a short while after describing his symptoms he was
rushed in a closed car to a building that had a Hopi Indian Kachina Doll Shop in front and the Las Vegas
CIA office in the back. He was fairly delirious by then,
but he heard somebody say, "Ha, we're ahead of the
FBI *and* the Cesspool Cleaners on this one." Then he
got an injection and began to feel better, until a
friendly silver-haired man sat down by his cot and
asked who "the girl" was.

"What girl?" the Midget asked irritably.

"Look, son, we know you've been with a girl. She
gave you this."

"Was it the clap?" the Midget asked, dumbfounded.
Except for his pornographic Tarot cards, he was still a
virgin (the giant women were all so damned patronizing, but his own female equivalents bored him; the
giantesses were the Holy Grail to him, but he had
never had the courage to approach one). "I never
knew the clap could be this bad," he added, blushing.
His greatest fear was that somebody would discover his
virginity.

"No, it wasn't the clap," said the kindly man (who
didn't deceive the Midget one bit; if this guy couldn't
pump him, he knew, they would send in the mean,
tough one; the nice cop and the nasty cop; oldest con
in the business). "This girl had a certain, uh, rare disease, and we're with the U.S. Public Health Service."
The gentle man produced forged credentials to "prove"
this last allegation. Horseshit, the Midget thought.
"Now," the sweet old codger went on, "we've got to
track her down, and see that she gets the antidote, or a

lot of people will get this disease. You understand?"

The Midget understood. This guy was Army Intelligence or CIA and they wanted to crack this before the FBI and get the credit. The disease was started by the government, obviously. Some fuckup in one of their biological war laboratories, and they had to cover it up before the whole country got wise. He hesitated; none of his projects had ever been consciously intended to lead to death, just to make things a little unpredictable and spooky for the giants.

"The U.S. Public Health Service will be eternally grateful to you." the grandfatherly man said, eyes crinkling with sly affection. "It isn't often that a *little* man gets a chance to do such a *big* job for his country."

That did it. "Well," the Midget said, "she was blonde, in her mid-twenties I guess, and she told me her name was Sarah. She had a scar on her neck—I suppose somebody tried to cut her throat once. She was, let's see, about five-five and maybe 110-115 pounds. And she was superb at giving head," he concluded, thinking that was a very plausible Las Vegas whore he had just created. His mind was racing rapidly; they wouldn't want people running around loose knowing about this. The antidote had been to keep him alive while they pumped him. He needed insurance. "Oh, and here's a real lead for you," he said "I just remembered. First, I want to explain something about, uh, people who are below average in stature. We're very sexy. You see, our sex gland or whatever it's called works extra, because our growth gland doesn't work. So we never get enough." He was making this up off the top of his head and enjoying it. He hoped it would spread; he had a beautiful vision of bored rich women seeking midgets as they now seek blacks. "So you see," he went on, "I kept her a long time, having encores and encores and encores. Finally, she told me she'd have to raise her price, because she had another customer waiting. I couldn't afford it so I let her go." Now the clincher. "But she mentioned his name. She said, 'Joe Blotz will be pissed if I disappoint him,' only the name wasn't Joe Blotz."

"Well, what was it?"

"That's the problem," the Midget said sadly. "I can't remember. But if you leave me alone awhile," he added brightly, "maybe it'll come back to me." He was already planning his escape.

And, twenty-five hours earlier, George Dorn, quoting Pilate, asked, "What is Truth?" (Barney Muldoon just then, was lounging in the lobby of the Hotel Tudor, waiting for Saul to finish what he had called "a very important, very private conversation" with Rebecca; Nkrumah Fubar was experimentally placing a voodoo doll of the president of American Express inside a tetrahedron—their computer was still annoying him about a bill he'd paid over two months ago, on the very daynight that Soapy Mocenigo dreamed of Anthrax Leprosy Pi; R. Buckminster Fuller, unaware of this new development in his geodesic revolution, was lecturing the Royal Institute of Architects in London and explaining why there were no nouns in the real world; August Personage was breathing into a telephone in New York; Pearson Mohammed Kent was exuberantly balling a female who was not only *white* but *from Texas;* the Midget himself was saying "Rude bastard, isn't he?" to Dr. Naismith; and our other characters were variously pursuing their own hobbies, predilections, obsessions and holy missions). *But Hagbard, with uncharacteristic gravity, said,* "Truth is the opposite of lies. The opposite of most of what you've heard all your life. The opposite of most of what you've heard from me."

They were in Hagbard's funky stateroom and George, after his experience at the demolished Drake mansion, found the octopi and other sea monsters on the wall murals distinctly unappetizing. Hagbard, as usual, was wearing a turtleneck and casual slacks; this time the turtleneck was lavender—an odd, faggoty item for him. George remembered, suddenly, that

Hagbard had once told him, anent homosexuality, "I've tried it, of course," but added something about liking women better. (Goodness, was that only two mornings ago?) George wondered what it would be like to "try it" and if he would ever have the nerve. "What particular lies," he asked cautiously, "are you about to confess?"

Hagbard lit a pipe and passed it over. "Alamout Black hash," he said croakingly, holding the smoke down. "Hassan i Sabbah's own private formula. Does wonders when heavy metaphysics is coming at you."

George inhaled and felt an immediate *hit* like cocaine or some other forebrain stimulant. "Christ, what's this shit cut with?" he gasped, as somebody somewhere seemed to turn colored lights on in the gold-and-nautical-green room and on that outasight lavender sweater.

"Oh," Hagbard said casually, "a hint of belladonna and stramonium. That was old Hassan's secret, you know. All that crap in most books about how he had turned his followers on with hash, and they'd never had it before so they thought it was magic, is unhistorical. Hashish was known in the Mideast since the neolithic age; archeologists have dug it up in tombs. Seems our ancestors buried their priests with a load of hash to help them negotiate with their gods when they got to Big Rock Candy Mountain or wherever they thought they were going. Hassan's originality was blending hashish with just the right chemical cousins to produce a new synergetic effect."

"What's *synergetic?*" George asked slowly, feeling seasick for the first time aboard the *Leif Erikson.*

"Nonadditive. When you put two and two together and get five instead of four. Buckminster Fuller uses synergetic gimmicks all the time in his geodesic domes. That's why they're stronger than they look." Hagbard took another toke and passed the pipe again.

What the hell? George thought. Sometimes increasing the dose got you past the nausea. He toked, deeply. Hadn't they started out to discuss Truth, though?

George giggled. "Just as I suspected. Instead of using your goddam *prajna* or whatever it is to spy on the Illuminati, you're just another dirty old man. You use it to play Peeping Tom in other people's heads."

"Heads?" Hagbard protested, laughing. "I never scan the *heads*. Who the hell wants to watch people eliminating their wastes?"

"I thought you were going to be Socrates," George howled between lunatic peals of tin giggles, "and I was prepared to be Plato, or at least Glaucon or one of the minor characters. But you're as stoned as I am. You can't tell me anything important. All you can do is make bad puns."

"The pun," Hagbard replied with dignity (ruined somewhat by an unexpected chortle), "is mightier than the sword. As James Joyce once said."

"Don't get pedantic."

"Can I get semantic?"

"Yes. You can get semantic. Or antic. But not pedantic."

"Where were we?"

"Truth."

"Yes. Well, Truth is like marijuana, my boy. A drug on the market."

"I'm getting a hard-on."

"You too? That's the way the balling bounces. At least, with Alamout Black. Nausea, then microamnesia, then the laughing jag, then sex. Be patient. The clear light comes next. Then we can discuss Truth. As if we haven't been discussing it all along."

"You're a hell of a guru, Hagbard. Sometimes you sound even dumber than me."

"If the Elder Malaclypse were here, he'd tell you a few about some other gurus. And geniuses. Do you think Jesus never whacked off? Shakespeare never got on a crying jag at the Mermaid Tavern? Buddha never picked his nose? Gandhi never had the crabs?"

"I've still got a hard-on. Can't we postpone the philosophy while I go look for Stella—I mean, Mavis?"

"That's Truth."

"What is Truth?"

"Up in the cortex it makes a difference to you whether it's Stella or Mavis. Down in the glands, no difference. My grandmother would do as well."

"That's not Truth. That's just cheap half-assed Freudian cynicism."

"Oh, yes. You saw the mandala with Mavis."

"And you were inside my head somehow. Dirty voyeur."

"Know thyself."

"This will never take its place beside the Platonic Dialogues, not in a million years. We're both stoned out of our gourds."

"I love you, George."

"I guess I love you, too. You're so damned overwhelming. Everybody loves you. Are we gonna fuck?"

(Mavis had said, "Wipe the come off your trousers." Fantasizing Sophia Loren while he masturbated. Or fantasizing that he masturbated while actually . . .)

"No. You don't need it. You're starting to remember what really happened in Mad Dog jail."

"Oh, no." Coin's enormous, snaky cock . . . the pain . . . the pleasure . . .

"I'm afraid so."

"Damn it, now I'll never know. Did you put that in my head, or did it really happen? Did I fantasize the interruption then or did I fantasize the rape just now?"

"Know thyself."

"Did you say that twice or did I just hear it twice?"

"What do you think?"

"I don't know. I don't know, right now. I just don't know. Is this some devious homosexual seduction?"

"Maybe. Maybe it's a murder plot. Maybe I'm leading up to cutting your throat."

"I wouldn't mind. I've always had a big self-destructive urge. Like all cowards. Cowardice is a defense against suicide."

Hagbard laughed. "I never knew a young man who had so much pussy and risked death so often. And there you sit, still worrying about being whatever it was they called you when you first started letting your hair grow long in your early teens."

"Sissy. That was the word in good old Nutley, New Jersey. It meant both faggot and coward. So I've never cut my hair since then, to prove *they* couldn't intimidate *me*."

"Yeah. I'm tracking a black guy now, a musician, who's balling a white lady, a fair flower from Texas. Partly, because she really turns him on. But partly because she could have a brother who might come after him with a gun. He's proving *they* can't intimidate *him*."

"That's the Truth? We spend all our time proving we can't be intimidated? But all the time we are intimidated on another level?" The colors were coming back strong again; it was that kind of trip. Every time you thought you were the pilot, it would go off in an unexpected direction to remind you that you were just a passenger.

"That's part of the Truth, George. Another part is that every time you think you're intimidated you're really rebelling on another level. Oh, what idiots the Illuminati really are, George. I once collected statistics on industrial accidents in a sample city—Birmingham, England, actually. Fed all the relevant facts into FUCKUP and got just what I expected. Sabotage. Unconscious sabotage. Every case was a blind insurrection. Every man and woman is in rebellion, but only a few have the guts to admit it. The others jam the system by accident, har har har, or by stupidity, har har har again. Let me tell you about the Indians, George."

"What Indians?"

"Did you ever wonder why nothing works right? Why the whole world seems completely fucked up all the time?"

"Yeah. Doesn't everybody?"

"I suppose so. Pardon me, I've got to get more stoned. In a little while, I go into FUCKUP and we put our heads together—literally, I attach electrodes to my temples—and I'll try to track down the problem in Las

Vegas. I don't spend *all* my time on random voyeurism," Hagbard pronounced with dignity. He refilled the pipe, asking pettishly, "Where was I?"

"The Indians in Birmingham. How did they get there?"

"There weren't any fucking Indians in Birmingham. You're getting me confused." Hagbard toked deeply.

"You're getting yourself confused. You're bombed out of your skull."

"Look who's talking." Hagbard toked again. "The Indians. The Indians weren't in Birmingham. Birmingham was where I did the study that convinced me most industrial accidents are unconscious sabotage. So are most misfiled documents among white-collar workers, I'd wager. The Indians are another story. I was a lawyer once, when I first came to your country and before I went in for piracy. I usually don't admit that, George. I usually tell people I played the piano in a whorehouse or something else not quite so disreputable as the truth. If you want to know why nothing makes sense in government forms, remember there are two hundred thousand lawyers working for the bureaucracy these days.

"The Indians were a band of Shoshones. I was defending them against the Great Land Thief, or as it pretentiously titles itself, the Government, in Washington. We were having a conference. You know what an Indian conference is like? Nobody talks for hours sometimes. A good yoga. When somebody does finally speak, you can be sure it comes from the heart. That old movie stereotype, 'White man speak with forked tongue,' has a lot of truth in it. The more you talk, the more your imagination colors things. I'm one of the most long-winded people alive and one of the worst liars." Hagbard toked again and finally held the pipe out inquiringly; George shook his head. "But the story I wanted to tell was about an archeologist. He was hunting for relics of the Devonian culture, the Indians who lived in North America just before the ecological catastrophe of 10,000 B.C. He found what he thought was a burial mound and asked to dig into it. Grok this, George. The Indians looked at him. They looked at me. They looked at each other. Then the oldest man spoke and, very gravely, gave permission. The archeologist hefted his pick and shovel and went at it like John Henry trying to beat that steam drill. In two minutes he disappeared. Right into a cesspool. Then the Indians laughed.

"*Grok,* George. I knew them as well as any white man ever knows Indians. They had learned to trust me, and I, them. And yet I sat there, while they played their little joke, and I didn't get a hint of what was about to happen. Even though I had begun to discover my telepathic talents and even focus them a little. Think about it, George. Think about all the pokerfaced blacks you've seen. Think about every time a black has done something so fantastically, outrageously stupid that you had a flash of racism—which, being a radical, you were ashamed of, right?—and wondered if maybe they *are* inferior. And think of ninety-nine percent of the women in the Caucasian world, outside Norway, who do the Dumb Dora or Marilyn Monroe act all the time. Think a minute, George. Think."

There was a silence that seemed to stretch into some long hall of near-Buddhist emptiness—George recognized a glimpse, *at last!,* into the Void all his acidhead friends had tried to describe—and then he remembered this was not the trip Hagbard was pushing him toward. But the silence lingered as a quietness of spirit, a calm in the tornado of those last few days, and George found himself ruminating with total dispassion, without hope or dread or smugness or guilt; if not totally without ego, or in full *darshana,* at least without the inflamed and voracious ego that usually either leaped forward or shrunk back from naked fact. He contemplated his memories and was unmoved, objective, at peace. He thought of blacks and women and of their subtle revenges against their Masters, acts of sabotage that could not be recognized clearly as such because they took the form of acts of obedience; he thought of the Shoshone Indians and their crude joke, so similar to the jokes of oppressed peoples everywhere; he saw, suddenly, the meaning of Mardi Gras and the Feast of Fools and the Saturnalia and the Christmas Office Party and all the other limited, permissible, structured occasions on which Freud's Return of the Repressed was allowed; he remembered all the times he had gotten his own back against a professor, a high school principal, a bureaucrat, or, further back, his own parents, by waiting for the occasion when, by doing exactly what he was told, he could produce some form of minor catastrophe. He saw a world of robots, marching rigidly in the paths laid down for them from above, and each robot partly alive, partly human, waiting its chance to drop its own monkey wrench into the machinery. He saw, finally, why everything in the world seemed to work wrong and the Situation Normal was All Fucked Up. "Hagbard," he said slowly. "I think I get it. Genesis is exactly backwards. Our troubles started from obedience, not disobedience. And humanity is not yet created."

Hagbard, more hawk-faced than ever, said carefully, "You are approaching Truth. Walk cautiously now, George. Truth is not, as Shakespeare would have it, a dog that can be whipped out to kennel. Truth is a tiger. Walk cautiously, George." He turned in his chair, slid open a drawer in his Danish Modern quasi-Martian desk and took out a revolver. George watched, as cool and alone as a man atop Everest, as Hagbard opened the chamber and showed six bullets inside. Then, with a snap, the gun was closed and placed on the desk blotter. Hagbard did not glance at it again. He watched George; George watched the pistol. It was the scene with Carlo all over again, but Hagbard's challenge was unspoken, gnomic; his level glance did not even admit that a contest had begun. The gun glittered maliciously; it whispered of all the violence and stealth in the world, treacheries undreamed of by Medici or Machiavelli, traps set for victims who were innocent and blameless; it seemed to fill the room with an aura of its presence, and yes, it even had the more subtle menace of a knife, weapon of the sneak, or of a whip in the hands of a man whose smile is too sensual, too intimate, too knowing; into the middle of George's tranquility it had come, inescapable and unexpected as a rattlesnake in the path on the afternoon of the sweetest spring day in the world's most manicured and artificial garden. George heard the adrenalin begin to course into his bloodstream; saw the "activation syndrome" moisten his palms, accelerate his heart, loosen his sphincter a micrometer; and still, high and cool on his mountain, felt nothing.

"The robot," he said, glancing finally at Hagbard, "is easily upset."

"Don't put your hand in that fire," Hagbard warned, unimpressed. "You'll get burned." He watched; he waited; George could not tear his glance from those eyes and in them, then, he saw the merriment of Howard, the dolphin, the contempt of his grade school principal ("A high IQ, Dorn, does not justify arrogance and insubordination"), the despairing love of his mother, who could never understand him, the emptiness of Nemo, his tomcat of childhood days, the threat of Billy Holtz, the school bully, and the total otherness of an insect or a serpent. More: he saw the child Hagbard, proud like himself of intellectual superiority and frightened like himself of the malice of stupider but brawnier boys, and the very old Hagbard, years hence, wrinkled as a reptile but still showing an endless searching intelligence. The ice melted; the mountain, with a roar of protest and defiance, crumbled; and George was borne down, down in the river racing toward the rapids where the gorilla howled and the mouse trotted quickly, where the saurian head raised above the Triassic foliage, where the sea slept and the spirals of DNA curled backward toward the flash that was this radiance now, this raging eternally against the quite impossible dying of the light, this storm and this centering.

"Hagbard . . ." he said at last.

"I know. I can see it. Just don't fall back into that other thing. It's the Error of the Illuminati."

George smiled weakly, still not quite back into the world of words. " 'Eat and ye shall be as gods'?" he said.

"I call it the no-ego ego trip. It's the biggest ego trip of all, of course. Anybody can learn it. A child of two months, a dog, a cat. But when an adult rediscovers it, after the habit of obedience and submission has crushed it out of him for years or decades, what happens can be a total disaster. That's why the Zen Roshis say, 'One who achieves supreme illumination is like an arrow flying straight to hell.' Keep in mind what I said about caution, George. You can release at any moment. It's great up there, and you need a mantra to keep you away from it until you learn how to use it. Here's your mantra, and if you knew the peril you are in you'd brutally burn it into your backside with a branding iron to make sure you'd never forget it: I Am The Robot. Repeat it."

"I Am The Robot."

Hagbard made a face like a baboon and George laughed again, at last. "When you get time," Hagbard said, "look into my little book, *Never Whistle While You're Pissing*—there are copies all over the ship. That's *my* ego tip. And keep it in mind: you are the robot and you'll never be anything else. Of course, you're also the programmer, and even the meta-programmer; but that's another lesson, for another day. For now, just remember the mammal, the robot."

"I know," George said. "I've read T. S. Eliot, and now I understand him. 'Humility is endless.' "

"And humanity *is* created. The . . . other . . . is not human."

George said then, "So I've arrived. And it's just another starting place. The beginning of another trip. A harder trip."

"That's another meaning in Heracleitus. 'The end is the beginning.' " Hagbard rose and shook himself like a dog. "Wow," he said. "I better get to work with

FUCKUP. You can stay here or go to your own room, but I suggest that you don't rush off and talk about your experience to somebody else. You can talk it to death that way."

George remained in Hagbard's room and reflected on what had happened. He had no urge to scribble in his diary, the usual defense against silence and aloneness since his early teens. Instead, he savored the stillness of the room and of his inner core. He remembered Saint Francis of Assisi called his body "Brother Ass," and Timothy Leary used to say when exhausted, "The robot needs sleep." Those had been their mantras, their defenses against the experience of the mountaintop and the terrible arrogance it triggered. He remembered, too, the old classic underground press ad: "Keep me high and I'll ball you forever." He felt sorry for the woman who had written that: pitiful modern version of the maddened Saint Simon on his pillar in the desert. And Hagbard was right: any dog or cat could do it, could make the jump to the mountaintop and wait without passion until the robot, Brother Ass, survived the ordeal or perished in it. That was what primitive rites of initiation were all about—driving the youth through sheer terror to the point of letting go, the mountaintop point, and then bringing him back down again. George suddenly understood how his generation, in rediscovering the sacred drugs, had failed to rediscover their proper use . . . had failed, or had been prevented. The Illuminati, it was clear, didn't want any competition in the godmanship business.

You could talk it to death in your own head as well as in conversation, he realized, but he went back over it again trying to dissect it without mutilating it. The homosexuality bit had been a false front (with its own reality, of course, like all false fronts). Behind that was the conditioned terror against the Robot: the fear, symbolized in Frankenstein and dozens of other archetypes, that if it were let loose, unrestrained, the Robot would run amok, murder, rape, go mad . . . And then Hagbard had waited until the Alamout Black brought him to freedom, showed him the peak, the place where the cortex at last could idle, as a car motor or a dog or cat idles, the last refuge where the catatonic hides. When George was safely in that harbor, Hagbard produced the gun—in a more primitive, or more sophisticated, society, it would have been the emblem of a powerful demon—and George saw that he could, indeed, idle there and not blindly follow the panic signals from the Robot's adrenalin factory. And, because he was a human and not a dog, the experience had been ecstasy to him, and temptation, so Hagbard, with a few words and a glance from those eyes, pushed him off the peak into . . . what?

Reconciliation was the word. Reconciliation with the robot, with the Robot, with himself. The peak was not a victory; it was the war, the eternal war against the Robot, carried to a higher and more dangerous level. The end of the war was his surrender, the only possible end to that war, since the Robot was three billion years old and couldn't be killed.

There were two great errors in the world, he perceived: the error of the submissive hordes, who fought all their lives to control the Robot and please their masters (and who always sabotaged every effort without knowing it, and were in turn sabotaged by the Robot's Revenge: neuroses, psychoses and all the tiresome list of psychosomatic ailments); and the error of those who recaptured the animal art of letting the Robot run itself, and who then tried to maintain this split from their own flesh indefinitely, until they were lost forever in that eternally widening chasm. One sought to batter the Robot to submission, the other to slowly starve it; both were wrong.

And yet, on another plane of his still-zonked mind, George knew that even this was a half truth; that he was, indeed, just beginning his journey, not arriving at his destination. He rose and walked to the bookshelves and, as he expected, found a stack of Hagbard's little pamphlets on the bottom: *Never Whistle While You're Pissing*, by Hagbard Celine, H.M., S.H. He wondered what the H.M. and S.H. stood for, then flipped open to the first page, where he found only the large question:

WHO
IS THE ONE
MORE TRUSTWORTHY
THAN
ALL THE BUDDHAS
AND SAGES
? ?

George laughed out loud. The Robot, of course. Me. George Dorn. All three billion years' worth of evolution in every gene and chromosome of me. And that, of course, was what the Illuminati (and all the petty would-be Illuminati who made up power structures everywhere) never wanted a man or woman to realize.

George turned to the second page and began reading:

> If you whistle while you're pissing, you have two minds where one is quite sufficient. If you have two minds, you are at war with yourself. If you are at war with yourself, it is easy for an external force to defeat you. This is why Mong-tse wrote, "A man must destroy himself before others can destroy him."

That was all, except for an abstract drawing on page three that seemed to suggest an enemy figure moving out toward the viewer. About to turn to page four, George got a shock: from another angle, the drawing was two figures engaged in attacking each other. I and It. The Mind and the Robot. His memory leaped back twenty-two years and he saw his mother lean over the crib and remove his hand from his penis. Christ, no wonder I grab it when I'm frightened: the Robot's Revenge, the Return of the Repressed.

George started to turn the page again, and saw another trick in Hagbard's abstraction: from a third angle, it might be a couple making love. In a flash, he saw his mother's face above his crib again, in better focus, and recognized the concern in her eyes. The cruel hand of repression was moved by love: she was trying to save him from Sin.

And Carlo, dead three years now, together with the rest of that Morituri group—what had inspired Carlo when he and the four others (all of them less than eighteen, George remembered) blasted their way into a God's Lightning rally and killed three cops and four Secret Service agents in their attempts to gun down the Secretary of State? Love, nothing but mad love . . .

The door opened and George tore his eyes from the text. Mavis, back again in her sweater and slacks outfit, walked in. For a proclaimed right-wing anarchist, she sure dresses a lot like a New Leftist, George thought; but then Hagbard wrote like a cross between Reichian Leftist and an egomaniacal Zen Master—there was obviously more to the Discordian philosophy than he could grasp yet, even though he was now convinced it was the system he himself had been groping toward for many years.

"Mmm," she said, "I like that smell. Alamout Black?"

"Yeah," George said, having trouble meeting her eyes. "Hagbard's been illuminating me."

"I can tell. Is that why you suddenly feel uncomfortable with me?"

George met her eyes, then looked away again; there was tenderness there but it was, as he had expected, sisterly at best. He muttered, "It's just that I realize our sex" (why couldn't he say fucking or, at least, balling?) "was less important to you than to me."

Mavis took Hagbard's chair and smiled at him affectionately. "You're lying, George. You mean it was *more* important to me than to you." She began to refill the pipe; *Christ God,* George thought, *did Hagbard send her in to take me to the next stage, whatever it is?*

"Well, I guess I mean both," he said cautiously. "You were more emotionally involved than I was *then,* but *now* I'm more emotionally involved. And I know that what I want, I can't have. Ever."

"Ever is a long time. Let's just say you can't have it now."

" 'Humility is endless,' " George repeated.

"Don't start feeling sorry for yourself. You've discovered that love is more than a word in poetry, and you want it right away. You just had two other things that used to be just words to you—*sunyata* and *satori.* Isn't that enough for one day?"

"I'm not complaining. I know that 'humility is endless' also means surprise is endless. Hagbard promised me a happy truth and that's it."

Mavis finally got the pipe lit and, after toking deeply, passed it over. "You can have Hagbard," she said.

George, sipping very lightly since he was still fairly high, mumbled "Hm?"

"Hagbard will love you as well as ball you. Of course, it's not the same. He loves everybody. I'm not at that stage yet. I can only love my equals." She grinned wickedly. "Of course, I can still get horny about you. But now that you know there's more than that, you want the whole package deal, right? So try Hagbard."

George laughed, feeling suddenly lighthearted. "Okay! I will."

"Bullshit," Mavis said bluntly. "You're putting us both on. You've liberated some of the energies and right away, like everybody else at this stage, you want to prove that there are no blocks anywhere anymore. That laugh was not convincing, George. If you have a block, face it. Don't pretend it isn't there."

Humility is endless, George thought. "You're right," he said, unabashed.

"That's better. At least you didn't fall into feeling guilty about the block. That's an infinite regress. The next stage is to feel guilty about feeling guilty . . . and pretty soon you're back in the trap again, trying to be the governor of the nation of Dorn."

"The Robot," George said.

Mavis toked and said, "Mm?"

"I call it the Robot."

"You picked that up from Leary back in the mid-'60s. I keep forgetting you were a child prodigy. I can just see you, with your eyeglasses and your shoulders all hunched, poring over one of Tim's books when you were eight or nine. You must have been quite a child. They've sure mauled you over since then, haven't they?"

"It happens to most prodigies. And nonprodigies, too, for that matter."

"Yeah. Eight years' grade school, four high school, four college, then postgraduate studies. Nothing left but the Robot at the end. The ever-rebellious nation of Me with poor old I sitting on the throne trying to govern it."

"There's no governor anywhere," George quoted.

"You *are* coming along nicely."

"That's Chuang Chou, the Taoist philosopher. But I never understood him before."

"So that's where Hagbard stole it! He has little cards that say, 'There is no enemy anywhere.' And ones that say, 'There is no friend anywhere.' He said once he could tell in two minutes which card was right for a particular person. To jolt them awake."

"But words alone can't do it. I've known most of the words for years . . ."

"Words can help. In the right situation. If they're the wrong words. I mean, the right words. No, I *do* mean the wrong words."

They laughed, and George said, "Are we just goofing, or are you taking up the liberation of the nation of Dorn where Hagbard left off?"

"Just goofing. Hagbard did tell me that you had passed one of the gateless gates and that I might drop in, *after* you had a while alone."

"A gateless gate. That's another one I've known for years, without understanding it. The gateless gate and the governorless nation. The chief cause of socialism is capitalism. What the hell does that bloody apple have to do with all this?"

"The apple is the world. Who did Goddess say owns it?"

" 'The prettiest one.' "

"Who is the prettiest one?"

"You are."

"Don't make a pass right now. Think."

George giggled. "I've been through too much already. I think I'm getting sleepy. I have two answers, one communist and one fascist. Both are wrong, of course. The correct answer has to fit in with your anarcho-capitalism."

"Not necessarily. Anarcho-capitalism is just *our* trip. We don't mean to impose it on everybody. We have an alliance with an anarcho-communist group called the JAMs. John Dillinger's their leader."

"Come off it. Dillinger died in 1935 or something."

"John Dillinger is alive and well today, in California, Fernando Poo and Texas," Mavis smiled. "As a matter of fact, he shot John F. Kennedy."

"Give me another toke. If I have to listen to this, I might as well be in a state where I won't try to understand it."

Mavis passed the pipe. "The prettiest one has quite a few levels to it, like all good jokes. I'll give you the Freudian one, as beginners. You know the prettiest one, George. You gave it to the apple just yesterday.

"Every man's penis is the prettiest thing in the world to him. From the day he's born until the day he dies. It never loses its endless fascination. And, I kid you not, baby, the same is true of every woman and her pussy. It's the closest thing to a real, blind, helpless love and religious adoration that most people ever achieve. But they'd rather die than admit it. Homosexuality, the urge to kill, petty spites and treacheries, fantasies of sadism, masochism, transvestism, any weird thing you can name, they'll confess all that in a group therapy session. But that deep submerged constant narcissism, that perpetual mental masturbation, is the earliest and most powerful block. They'll never admit it."

"From what I've read of psychiatric literature, I thought most people had rather squeamish and negative feelings about their genitals."

"That, to quote Freud himself, is a reaction formation. The primordial emotional tone, from the day the infant discovers the incredible pleasure centers there, is perpetual astonishment, awe and delight. No matter how much society tries to crush it and repress it. For instance, everybody has some pet name for their genitals. What's yours?"

"Polyphemus," he confessed.

"What?"

"Because it has one eye, you know? Also, Polyphemus rhymes with penis, I guess. I mean, I can't remember exactly what my mental process was when I invented that in my early teens."

"Polyphemus was a giant, too. Almost a god. You see what I mean about the primary emotional tone? It's the origin of all religion. Adoration of your own genitals and of your lover's genitals. *There's* Pan Pangenitor and the Great Mother."

"So," George said owlishly, still not sure whether this was profundity or nonsense, "the earth belongs to our genitalia?"

"To their offspring, and their offspring's offspring, and so on, forever. The world is a verb, not a noun."

"The prettiest one is three billion years old."

"You've got it, baby. We're all tenants here, including the ones who think they're owners. Property is impossible."

"Okay, okay, I think I've got most of it. Property is theft because the Illuminati land titles are arbitrary and unjust. And so are their banking charters and railroad franchises and all the other monopoly games of capitalism—"

"Of state capitalism. Not of true laissez-faire."

"Wait. Property is impossible because the world is a verb, a burning house as Buddha said. All things are fire. My old pal Heracleitus. So property is theft and property is impossible. How do we get to property is liberty?"

"Without private property there can be no private decisions."

"So we're back where we started from?"

"No, we're one flight higher up on the spiral staircase. Look at it that way. Dialectically, as your Marxist friends say."

"But we *are* back at private property. After proving it's an impossible fiction."

"The Statist form of private property is an impossible fiction. Just like the Statist form of communal property is an impossible fiction. Think outside the State framework, George. Think of property in freedom."

George shook his head. "It beats the hell out of my ass. All I can see is people ripping each other off. The war of all against all, as what's-his-name said."

"Hobbes."

"Hobbes, snobs, jobs. Whoever. Or whatever. Isn't he right?"

"Stop the motor on this submarine."

"What?"

"Force me to love you."

"Wait, I don't . . ."

"Turn the sky green or red, instead of blue."

"I still don't get it."

Mavis took a pen off the desk and held it between two fingers. "What happens when I let go of this?"

"It falls."

"Where do you sit if there are no chairs?"

"On the floor?" *If I wasn't so stoned, I would have had it by then. Sometimes drugs are more a hindrance than a help.* "On the ground?" I added.

"On your ass, that's for sure." Mavis said. "The point is, if the chairs all go away, you still sit. Or you build new chairs." She was stoned, too; otherwise she'd be explaining it better, I realized. "But you can't stop the motor without learning something about marine engineering first. You don't know what switch to pull. Or switches. And you can't change the sky. And the pen will fall without a gravity-governing demon rushing into the room to make it fall."

"Shit and pink petunias," I said disgustedly. "Is this some form of Thomism? Are you trying to sell me the Natural Law argument? I can't buy that at all."

"Okay, George. Here's the next jolt. Keep your asshole tight." She spoke to the wall, to a hidden microphone, I guessed. "Send *him* in now."

The Robot is easily upset; my sphincter was already tightening as soon as she warned me there was a jolt coming and she didn't really need to add that bit about my asshole. Carlo and his gun. Hagbard and his gun. Drake's mansion. I took a deep breath and waited to see what the Robot would do.

A panel in the wall opened and Harry Coin was pushed into the room. I had time to think that I should have guessed, in this game where both sides were playing with illusion constantly, Coin's death could have been faked, artificial intestines dangling and all, and of course Mavis and her raiders could have taken him out of Mad Dog jail even before they took me out of course, and I remembered the pain when he slapped my face and when his cock entered me, and the Robot was already moving, and I hardly had time to aim of course, and then his head was banging against the wall, blood spurting from his nose, and I had time to clip him again on the jaw as he went down of course, and then I came all the way back and stopped myself as I was about to kick him in the face as he lay there unconscious. Zen in the art of face-punching. I had knocked a man out with two blows; I who hated Hemingway and Machismo so much that I'd never taken a boxing lesson in my life. I was breathing hard, but it was good and clean, the feeling of after-an-orgasm; the adrenalin was flowing, but a fight reflex instead of a flight reflex had been triggered, and now it over, and I was calm. A glint in the air: Hagbard's pistol was in Mavis's hand, then flying toward me. As I caught it, she said, "Finish the bastard."

But the rage had ended when I held back the kick on seeing him already unconscious.

"No," I said. "It *is* finished."

"Not until you kill him. You're no good to us until you're ready to kill, George."

I ignored her and rapped on the wall. "Haul the bastard out," I said clearly. The panel opened, and two Slavic-looking seamen, grinning, grabbed Coin's arms and dragged him out. The panel closed again, quietly.

"I don't kill on command," I said, turning back to Mavis. "I'm not a German shepherd or a draftee. *My* case with him is settled, and if you want him dead, do the dirty work yourself."

But Mavis was smiling placidly. "Is that a Natural Law?" she asked.

And twenty-three hours later Tobias Knight listened to the voice in his earphones: "That's the problem. I can't remember. But if you leave me alone for a while maybe it'll come back to me." Smoothing his mustache nervously, Knight set the button for automatic record, removed the earphones and buzzed Esperando Despond's office.

"Despond," the intercom said.

"The CIA has one. A man who was with the girl after Mocenigo. Send somebody down for the tape—it's got a pretty good description of the girl."

"Wilco," Despond said tersely. "Anything else?"

"He thinks he might remember the name of her next customer. She mentioned it to him. We might get that, too."

"Let's hope so," Despond said and clicked off. He sat back in his chair and addressed the three agents in his office. "The guy we've got—what's his name? Naismith—is probably the next customer. We'll check the two descriptions of the girl against each other and get a much more accurate picture than the CIA has, since they're working from only one description."

But fifteen minutes later, he was staring in puzzlement at the chart which had been chalked on the blackboard:

DESCRIPTIONS OF SUSPECT

	First Witness	*Second Witness*
Height	5'2"	5'5"
Weight	90-100 lbs	110-115 lbs
Hair	Black	Blond
Race	Negro	Caucasian
Name or alias	Bonnie	Sarah
Scars, etc.	None	Scar on throat
Age	Late teens	Mid-twenties
Sex	Female	Female

A tall, bearish agent named Roy Ubu said thoughtfully, "I've never seen two eyewitness descriptions match exactly, but *this* . . ."

A small, waspish agent named Buzz Vespa snapped, "One of them is lying for some reason. But which one?"

"Neither of them has any reason to lie," Despond said. "Gentlemen, we've got to face the facts. Dr. Mocenigo was unworthy of the trust that the U.S. government placed in him. He was a degenerate sex maniac. He had *two* women last night, one of them a Nigra."

"What do you mean that little sawed-off bastard is gone?" Peter Kurten of the CIA was shouting at that very moment. "The only way out of his room was right through that door, there, and we've all had it under constant surveillance. The door was only opened once when DeSalvo took out the coffee urn to have it refilled at the sandwich shop next door. Oh . . . my . . . *God* . . . the . . . *coffee* . . . *urn* . . ." As he slumped back in his chair, mouth hanging open, an agent with a device that looked like a mine sweeper stepped forward.

"Daily sweep for FBI bugs, sir," he said uncomfortably. "I'm afraid the machine is registering one under your desk. If you'll let me just reach in and . . . uh . . . that gets it . . ."

And Tobias Knight, listening, heard no more. It would be a few hours, at least, until their man in the CIA was able to plant a new bug.

And Saul Goodman stepped hard on the brakes of his rented Ford Brontosaurus as a tiny and determined figure, dashing out of the Papa Mescalito Sandwich Shop, ran right in front of the fender. Saul heard a sickening thud and Barney Muldoon's voice beside him saying, "Oh Christ, no . . ."

I was at the end of my ropes. The Syndicate I could see, but why the Feds? I was flabbygastered. I said to that dumb cunt Bonnie Quint, "Are you a thousand percent sure?"

"Carmel," she says. "I know the Syndicate. They're not that smooth. These guys were just what they claimed. Feds."

Oh, Christ Jesus. Christ Jesus with egg in his beard. I couldn't help myself, I just hauled off and bopped her in the kisser, the dumb cunt. "What'd you tell them?" I screamed. "What'd you tell them?"

She started to snivel. "I didn't tell them nothing," she says.

So I had to bop her again. Christ, I hate hitting women, they always blubber so much. "I'll use the belt," I howled. "So help me, God, I'll use the belt. Don't tell me you didn't tell them nothing. Everybody tells them something. Even a clam would sing like Sinatra when they're finished with him. So what'd you tell them?" I bopped her again, Christ, this was terrible.

"I just told them I wasn't with this Mocenigo. Which I wasn't."

"So who did you tell them you were with?"

"I made up a prescription. A midget. A guy I saw on the street. I wouldn't give the name of a real john, I know that could come back against you. And me."

I didn't know what to do, so I bopped her again. "Go away," I says. "Be missing. Let me think."

She goes out, still blubbering, and I go over to the window and look at the desert to calm my head. My rose fever was starting to act up; it was that time of year. Why did people have to bring roses to the desert? I tried to contemplate hard on the problem and forget my health. There was only one explanation: that damned Mocenigo figured out that Sherri was pumping him and told the Feds. The Syndicate wasn't in it yet. They were all still running around the East like chickens with their legs cut off, trying to figure who rubbed Maldonado, and why it happened at the house of a straight like this banker Drake. So they hadn't got the time yet to find out that five million of Banana Nose's money had disappeared into my own safe as soon as I heard he was dead. The Feds weren't in on that at all, and the connection was circumsubstantial.

And then it hit me so hard that I almost fell over. Besides my own girls, who wouldn't talk, there were a dozen or two cab drivers and bartenders and whatnots who knew that Sherri worked for me. The Feds would get it out of somebody sooner or later, and probably sooner. It was like a light bulb going on over my head in a comic strip: TREASON. AIDING AND ABEDDING THE ENEMY. I remembered from when I was a kid those two Jewish scientists who the Feds got for that. The hot squat. They fried them, Christ Jesus, I thought I'd vomit. Why does the fucking government have to be that way about somebody just trying to make a buck? Even the Syndicate would only shoot you or give you a lead enema, but the cocksucking government has to go and put you in an electrical chair. Christ Jesus, I was hot as a chimney.

I took a candy out of my pocket and started chewing it, trying to think what to do. If I ran, the Syndicate would guess I was the one who emptied the till when Maldonado was rubbed, and they'd get me. If I *didn't* run, the Feds would be at the door with a high treason warrant. It was a double whammy. I might try to highjack a plane to Panama, but I didn't know nearly enough about Mocenigo's bugs to make a deal with the Commie government down there. They'd just send me right back. It was hopeless, like trying to fill a three-card inside straight. The only thing to do was find a hole and bury myself.

And then it was just like a light bulb in my head

again, and I thought: Lehman Cave.

"What does the computer say now?" the President asked the Attorney General.

"What does the computer say now?" the Attorney General barked into the open phone before him.

"If the girl had two contacts before she died, at this moment the possible carriers number," the phone paused, "428,000. If the girl had three contacts, 7,-656,000."

"Get the Special Agent in Charge," the President snapped. He was the calmest man at the table—ever since Fernando Poo, he had been supplementing his Librium, Tofranil and Elovil with Demerol, the amazing little pills that had kept Hermann Goering so chipper and cheerful during the Nuremberg Trials while all the other Nazis crumbled into catatonic, paranoid or other dysfunctional conditions.

"Despond," a second open phone said.

"This is your President," the President said. "Give it to us straight. Have you treed the coon?"

"Uh, sir, no, sir. We have to find the procurer, sir. The girl can't possibly be alive, but we haven't found her. It is now mathematically certain that somebody hid her body. The obvious theory, sir, is that her procurer, being in an illegal business, hid the body rather than report it. We have two descriptions of the girl, sir, and, uh, although they don't tally *completely* they should lead us to her procurer. Of course, he should die soon, sir, and then we'll find him. That's the Rubicon of the case, sir. Meanwhile, I'm happy to report, sir, that we're lucking out amazingly. Only two definite cases off the base so far and both of them injected with the antidote. It is possible, just possible, that the procurer went into hiding after disposing of the body. In that case, he hasn't contacted another human being and is not spreading it. Sir."

"Despond," the President said, "I want *results*. Keep us informed. Your country depends on you."

"Yes, sir."

"Tree that coon, Despond."

"We will, sir."

Esperando Despond turned from the phone as an agent from the computer section entered the room. "Got something?" he snapped nervously.

"The first girl, the Nigra, sir. She was one of the pros we questioned yesterday. Her name is Bonnie Quint."

"You look worried. Is there a hitch?" Despond asked shrewdly.

"Just another of the puzzles. She didn't admit being with Mocenigo the night before, but that kind of lying we expected. Here's what's weird: her description of the guy she says she *was* with." The computer man shook his head dubiously. "It doesn't fit Naismith, the guy who said he was with *her*. It fits the little mug, the dwarf, that the CIA grabbed. Only *he* said she was the second girl."

Despond mopped his brow. "What the heck has been going on in this town?" he asked the ceiling. "Some kind of *sex* orgy?"

In fact, several kinds of sex orgies had been going on in Las Vegas ever since the Veterans of the Sexual Revolution had arrived two days earlier. The Hugh M. Hefner Brigade had taken two stories of the Sands, hired a herd of professional women, and hadn't yet come out to join the Alfred Kinsey Brigade, the Norman Mailer Guerrillas and the others in marching up and down the Strip, squirting young girls in the crotch with water pistols, passing bottles of hooch back and forth and generally blocking traffic and annoying pedestrians. Dr. Naismith himself, after a few token appearances, had avoided most of the merriment and retired to a private suite to work on his latest fund-raising letter for the Colossus of Yorba Linda Foundation. Actually, the VSR, like White Heroes Opposing Red Extremism, was one of Naismith's lesser projects and brought in only peanuts. Most of the real veterans of the sexual revolution had succumbed to syphilis, marriage, children, alimony or some such ailment, and few white heroes were prepared to oppose red extremism in the bizarre manner suggested by Naismith's pamphlets; in both of those cases, he had recognized two nut markets that nobody else was exploiting and had quickly moved in. Even the John Dillinger Died For You Society, of which he was inordinately proud since it was probably the most implausible religion in the long history of humanity's infatuation with metaphysics, didn't earn much less per annum than these fancies. The real bread was in the Colossus of Yorba Linda Foundation, which had been successfully raising money for several years to erect a heroic monument, in solid gold and *ten feet taller than the statue of Liberty,* honoring the martyred former president Richard Milhous Nixon. This monument, paid for entirely by the twenty million Americans who still loved and revered Nixon despite the damnable lies of the Congress, the Justice Department, the press, the TV, the law courts, *et al.,* would stand outside Yorba Linda, Tricky Dicky's boyhood home, and scowl menacingly toward Asia, warning those gooks not to try to get the jump on Uncle Sammie. Beside the gigantic idol's right foot, Checkers looked adoringly upward; beneath the left foot was a crushed allegorical figure representing Cesar Chavez. The Great Man held a bunch of lettuce in his right hand and a tape recording in the left. It was all most tasteful, and so appealed to Fundamentalist Americans that hundreds of thousands of dollars had already been collected by the Colossus fund, and Naismith planned to hop to Nepal with the loot at the first sign that contributors or postal inspectors were beginning to wonder when the statue would actually start rising on the plot he had purchased, amid much publicity, after the first few thousand arrived.

Naismith was a small, slight man and, like many Texans, affected a cowboy hat (although he had never herded cattle) and a bandito mustache (although his thefts were all based on fraud rather than force). He was also, for his nation at this time in history, an uncommonly honest man, and, unlike most corporations of the epoch, none of his enterprises had poisoned or mutilated the customers whose money he took. His one vice was cynicism based on lack of imagination: he reckoned most of his countrymen as total mental basket cases and fondly believed that he was exploiting their folly when he told them that a vast Illuminati conspiracy controlled the money supply and interest rates or that a bandit of the 1930s was, in a sense, a redeemer of the atrophying human spirit. That there was an element of truth in these bizarre notions never crossed his mind. In short, even though born in Texas, Naismith was as alienated from the pulse, the poetry and the profundity of American emotion as a New York intellectual.

But his cynicism served him well when, after reporting certain strange symptoms to the hotel doctor, he found himself rushed to a supposed U.S. Public Health Service station which was manned by individuals he quickly recognized as *laws*. This is an old Texas word, probably an abbreviation of *lawmen* (Texans don't know much about abbreviating) and is as charged with suspicion and wariness, although not quite so much rage, as the New Left's word *pig*. Bonnie Parker had used it, eloquently, in her last ballad:

> Someday they'll go down together
> They'll bury them side by side
> For some it means grief
> For the laws a relief
> But it's death for Bonnie and Clyde.

That about summed it up: the *laws* were not necessarily fascist Gestapo racist pigs (words largely unknown in Texas), but they were people who would find it a relief if bothersome and rebellious individualism disappeared, however bloody the disappearance might be. If you were ornery enough, the laws would bushwhack you—shoot you dead from ambush, without a chance to surrender, as they did to Miss Parker and Mr. Barrow—but even if you were merely a mildly larcenous hoaxter like Dr. Naismith, they would be much cheered to put you someplace where you couldn't throw any more entropy into the functioning of the Machine they served. And so, recognizing laws, Dr. Naismith narrowed his eyes, thought deeply, and when they began their questioning, lied as only an unregenerate old-school Texas confidence man can lie.

"You got it from somebody who had body contact with you. So either you were in a very crowded elevator or you got it from a prostitute. Which was it?"

Naismith thought of the collision on the sidewalk with the Midget and the weasel-faced character with the big suitcase, but he also thought that the questioner leaned heavily on the second possibility. They were looking for a woman; and, if you tell the laws what they want to hear, they don't keep coming back and asking more personal questions. "I was with a prostitute," he said, trying to sound embarrassed.

"Can you describe her?"

He thought back over the pros he had seen with other VSR delegates, and one stood out. Being a kindly man, he didn't want to implicate an innocent whore in this messy business (whatever it was), so he combined her with another woman, the first that he ever successfully penetrated in his long-ago youth in the 1950s.

Unfortunately for Dr. Naismith's kindly intentions, the laws never expect an eyewitness description to match the person described in *all* respects, so when his information was coded into an IBM machine, three cards came out. Each one had more similarities to his fiction than differences from it, and they came from a card file of several hundred prostitutes whose descriptions had been gathered and coded in the past twenty-four hours. Running the three cards through a different sorting in the machine, limited to outstanding bodily characteristics most commonly remembered correctly, the technicians emerged, after all, with Bonnie Quint. Forty-five minutes later she was in Esperando Despond's office, nervously twirling her mink stole, picking at the hem of her mini-skirt, evading questions nimbly and remembering intensely Carmel's voice saying, "I'll use the belt. So help me, God. I'll use the belt." She was also smarting from the injection.

"You *don't* work free-lance," Despond told her, nastily, for the fifth time. "In this town, the Maf would put a knife up your ass and break off the handle if you tried that. You've got a pimp. Now, do we throw the book at you or do we get his name?"

"Don't be too hard on her," Tobias Knight said. "She's only a poor, confused kid. Not twenty yet, are you?" he asked her kindly. "Give her a chance to think. She'll do the right thing. Why should she protect a lousy pimp who exploits her all the time?" He gave her a reassuring glance.

"Poor confused kid, my ass!" Despond exploded. "This is a matter of life and death and no Nigra whore is going to sit here lying her head off and get away with it." He did a good imitation of a man literally trembling with repressed fury. "I'd like to kick her head in," he screamed.

Knight, still playing the friendly cop, looked shocked. "That's not very professional," he said sadly. "You're overtired, and you're frightening the child."

Three hours later—after Despond had nearly done a complete psycho schtick and virtually threatened to behead poor Bonnie with his letter opener, and Knight had become so fatherly and protective that both he and she were beginning to feel that she was actually his very own six-year-old daughter being set upon by Goths and Vandals—a sobbing but accurate description of Carmel emerged, including his address.

Twelve minutes later, Roy Ubu, calling via car radio, reported that Carmel was not in his house and had been seen driving toward the Southwest in a jeep with a large suitcase beside him.

In the next eighteen hours, eleven men in jeeps were stopped on various roads southwest of Las Vegas, but none of them was Carmel, although most of them were around the height and weight and general physical description given by Bonnie Quint, and two of them even had large suitcases. In the twenty-four hours after that, nearly a thousand men of all sizes and shapes were stopped on roads, north, south, east and west, in cars not remotely like jeeps and some driving toward, not away from, Las Vegas. None of them was Carmel either.

Among all the men wandering around the Desert Door base and the city of Las Vegas with credentials from the U.S. Public Health Service, one who really was employed by USPHS, had a long lean body, a mournful countenance, a general resemblance to the late great Boris Karloff, and the name Fred Filiarisus. By special authority of the White House, Dr. Filiarisus was able to gain access to everything known by the scientists at Desert Door, including the course of the disease in those originally infected, among whom two had died before the antidote took effect and three had shown a total lack of symptoms even though exposed along with the others. He also had access to both FBI and CIA information as it came in, without having to bug either office. It was he, therefore, who finally put together the correct picture, on April 30, and reported directly to the White House at eleven that morning.

"Some people are naturally immune to Anthrax Leprosy Pi, Mr. President," Filiarisus said. "Unfortunately, they serve as carriers. We found three like that at the base, and it is mathematically, scientifically certain that a fourth is still at large.

"Everybody was lying to the FBI and CIA, sir. They were all afraid of punishment for various activities forbidden by our laws. No variation or permutation on their stories will hang together reasonably. Each witness lied about something, and usually about several things. The truth is other than it appeared. In short, the government, being an agency of punishment, acted as a distorting factor from the beginning, and I had to use information-theory equations to determine the degree of distortion present. I would say that what I finally discovered may have universal application: no governing body can ever obtain an accurate account of reality from those over whom it holds power. From the perspective of communication analysis, government is not an instrument of law and order, but of law and disorder. I'm sorry to have to say this so bluntly, but it needs to be kept in mind when similar situations arise in the future."

"He sounds like an *eff*ing anarchist," the Vice President muttered.

"The true picture, with a ninety-seven percent probability, is this," Filiarisus continued. "Dr. Mocenigo had only one contact, and she died. The FBI hypothesis is correct: her body was then hidden, probably in the desert, by an associate wishing to avoid involvement with law enforcement agencies. If prostitution were legal, we might never have had this nightmare."

"I told you he was an *eff*ing anarchist," the Vice President growled. "And a sex maniac, too!"

"The associate who hid the body," Filiarisus went on, "is our fourth carrier, personally immune but lethal to others. It was this person who infected Mr. Chaney and Dr. Naismith. This person was probably not a prostitute. These men lied, among other reasons, because they knew what the government agents wanted them to say. When power is wielded over people, they *say* as well as *do* what they think is expected of them—another reason government always finds it difficult to learn the truth about anything.

"The only hypothesis that mathematical logic will accept, when all the known data was fed into a computer, is that the fourth carrier is the procurer who disappeared, Mr. Carmel. Experiencing no symptoms himself, he is unaware that he carries the world's most dangerous disease. For reasons of his own, which we cannot guess, he has been hiding since he disposed of the woman's body. Probably, he feared that the corpse might be found and a case of manslaughter or homicide could be made against him. Or he might have a motive completely unrelated to her death. Only twice has he contacted other human beings. I would suggest that his contact with Miss Quint was typical of their professional relationship; he either hit her or had sex relations with her. His contact with Dr. Naismith and Mr. Chaney was some sort of accident—perhaps the crowded elevator that has been suggested by Mr. Despond. Otherwise, he had been, as it were, underground.

"This is why we only found three cases instead of the thousands or millions we feared.

"However, the problem still remains. Carmel is immune, will never know he has the disease unless he is told it, and will eventually surface somewhere. When he does, we will learn of it through the outbreak of Anthrax Leprosy Pi cases in the vicinity. At that point, the whole nightmare begins again, sir.

"Our best hope, and the computer backs me on this, is public disclosure. The panic we tried to avoid will have to be faced. Every medium of communication in the nation must be given the full facts, and Carmel's description must be circulated everywhere. This is our last chance. The man is a walking biological Doomsday Machine and he must be found.

"Psychologists and social psychologists have fed all the relevant facts about this case, and about previous panics and plagues, into the computer also. The conclusion, with ninety-three percent certainty, is that the panic will be nationwide and martial law will have to be declared everywhere. Liberals in Congress should be placed under house arrest as the first step, and the Supreme Court must be stripped of its powers totally. The Army and the National Guard will have to be sent into every city with authority to override any policies of local officials. Democracy, in short, must cease until the emergency is ended."

"He's not an anarchist," the Secretary of the Interior said. "He's a goddam fascist."

"He's a realist," said the President, clear-minded, crisp, quick on the uptake and stoned clear round the corner of schizophrenia by his usual three tranquilizers, a stronger dose of amphetamines than usual, and loads of those happy little Demerol tablets. "We start implementing his suggestions right now."

And so those few tattered remnants of the Bill of Rights which had survived into the fourth decade of the Cold War were laid to rest—temporarily, it was thought by those present. Dr. Filiarisus, whose name in the Ancient Illuminated Seers of Bavaria was Gracchus Gruad, had completed on the day known as May Eve or *Walpurgisnacht* the project begun when the first dream of Anthrax Leprosy Pi was planted in Dr. Mocenigo's mind on the day known as Candelmas. These dates were known by much older names in the Illuminati, of course, and the burial of the Bill of Rights was expected, by them, to be permanent.

(Two hours before Dr. Filiarisus spoke to the President, four of the world's five Illuminati Primi met in an old graveyard in Ingolstadt; the fifth could not be present. They agreed that all was going as scheduled, but one danger remained: nobody in the order, however developed his or her ESP, had been able to trace Carmel. Leaning on a tombstone—where Adam Weishaupt had once performed rites so unique that the psychic vibration had bounced off every sensitive mind in Europe, leading to such decidedly peculiar literary productions as Lewis's *The Monk*, Maturin's *Melmoth*, Walpole's *Castle of Otranto*, Mrs. Shelley's *Frankenstein*, and DeSade's *One Hundred Twenty Days of Sodom*—the eldest of the four said, "It can still fail, if one of the mehums finds the pimp before he infects a city or two." Mehums was an abbreviation for all descendants of those not part of the original Unbroken Circle; it meant *mere humans*.

"Why can none of our ultra-sensitives find him?" a second asked. "Does he have no ego or soul at all?"

"He has a vibration but it's not distinctly human. Whenever we seem to have a fix on it, we're usually picking up a bank vault or the safe of some paranoid millionaire," the eldest replied.

"We have that problem with an increasing number of Americans," the third commented morosely. "In that nation, we have done our work too well. The conditioning to those pieces of paper is so strong that no other psychic impulse remains to be read."

The fourth spoke. "Now is no time for trepidation, my brothers. The plan is virtually realized, and this man's lack of ordinary mehum qualities will prove an advantage when we do fix on him. No ego, no resistance. We will be able to move him at our whim. The stars are right, He Who Is Not To Be Named is impatient, and now we must be intrepid!" She spoke with fervor.

The others nodded. *"Heute die Welt, Morgens das Sonnensystem!"* the eldest cried out fiercely.

"Heute die Welt," all repeated, *"Morgens das Sonnensystem!")*

But two days earlier, as the *Leif Erikson* left the Atlantic and entered the underground Ocean of Valusia beneath Europe, George Dorn was listening to a different kind of chorus. It was, Mavis had explained to him in advance, the weekly Agape Ludens, or Love Feast Game, of the Discordians, and the dining hall was newly bedecked with pornographic and psychedelic posters, Christian and Buddhist and Amerindian mystic designs, balloons and lollypops dangling from the ceiling on Day-Glo-dabbed strings, numinous paintings of Discordian saints (including Norton I, Sigismundo Malatesta, Guillaume of Aquitaine, Chuang Chou, Judge Roy Bean, various historical figures even more obscure, and numerous gorillas and dolphins), bouquets of roses and forsythia and gladiolas and orchids, clusters of acorns and gourds, and the inevitable proliferation of golden apples, pentagons and octopi.

The main course was the best Alaskan king crab Newburg that George had ever tasted, only lightly dusted with a mild hint of Panamanian Red grass. Dozens of trays of dried fruits and cheeses were passed back and forth among the tables, together with canapes of an exquisite caviar George had never encountered before ("Only Hagbard knows where those sturgeon spawn," Mavis explained) and the beverage was a blend of the Japanese seventeen-herb Mu tea with

Menomenee Indian peyote tea. While everyone gorged, laughed and got gently but definitely zonked, Hagbard—who was evidently satisfied that he and FUCKUP had located "the problem in Las Vegas"—merrily conducted the religious portion of the Agape Ludens.

"Rub-a-dub-dub," he chanted, "O hail Eris!"

"Rub-a-dub-dub," the crew merrily chorused, "O Hail Eris!"

"*Sya-dasti,*" Hagbard chanted. "All that I tell you is true."

"*Sya-dasti,*" the crew repeated, "O hail Eris!" George looked around; there were three, or five, races present (depending upon which school of physical anthropology you credited) and maybe half a hundred nationalities, but the feeling of brotherhood and sisterhood transcended any sense of contrast, creating instead a blend, as in musical progression.

"*Sya-davak-tavya,*" Hagbard chanted now. "All that I tell you is false."

"*Sya-davak-tavya,*" George joined in, "O hail Eris!"

"*Sya-dasti-sya-nasti,*" Hagbard intoned. "All that I tell you is meaningless."

"*Sya-dasti-sya-nasti,*" all agreed, some jeeringly, "O hail Eris!"

If they had services like this in the Baptist church back in Nutley, George thought, I never would have told my mother religion is all a con and had that terrible quarrel when I was nine.

"*Sya-dasti-sya-nasti-sya-davak-tav-yaska,*" Hagbard sang out. "All that I tell you is true and false and meaningless."

"*Sya-dasti-sya-nasti-sya-davak-tav-yaska,*" the massed voices replied, "O hail Eris!"

"Rub-a-dub-dub," Hagbard repeated quietly. "Does anyone have a new incantation?"

"All hail crab Newburg," a Russian-accented voice shouted.

That was an immediate hit. "All hail crab Newburg," everyone howled.

"All hail these bloody fucking beautiful roses," an

Oxfordian voice contributed.

"All hail these bloody fucking beautiful roses," all agreed.

Miss Mao arose. "The Pope is the chief cause of Protestantism," she recited softly.

That was another roaring success; everybody chorused, and one Harlem voice added, "Right *on!*"

"Capitalism is the chief cause of socialism," Miss Mao chanted, more confident. That went over well, too, and she then tried, "The State is the chief cause of anarchism," which was another smashing success.

"Prisons are built with the stones of law, brothels with the bricks of religion," Miss Mao went on.

"PRISONS ARE BUILT WITH THE STONES OF LAW, BROTHELS WITH THE BRICKS OF RELIGION," the hall boomed.

"I stole that last one from William Blake," Miss Mao said quietly and sat down.

"Any others?" Hagbard asked. There was none, so he went on after a moment, "Very well, then, I will preach my weekly sermon."

"Balls!" cried a Texas voice.

"Bullshit!" added a Brazilian female.

Hagbard frowned. "That wasn't much of a demonstration," he commented sadly. "Are the rest of you so passive that you're just going to sit here on your dead asses and let me bore the piss out of you?"

The Texan, the Brazilian lady and a few others got up. "We are going to have an orgy," the Brazilian said briefly, and they left.

"Well, sink me, I'm glad there's some life left on this old tub," Hagbard grinned. "As for the rest of you—who can tell me, without uttering a word, the fallacy of the Illuminati?"

A young girl—she was no more than fifteen, George guessed, and the youngest member of the crew; he had heard she was a runaway from a fabulously rich Italian family in Rome—slowly raised her hand and clenched her fist.

Hagbard turned on her furiously. "How many times

must I tell you people: no faking! You got that out of some cheap book on Zen that neither the author nor you understood a damned word of. I hate to be dictatorial, but phony mysticism is the one thing Discordianism can't survive. You're on shitwork, in the kitchen. for a week, you wise-ass brat."

The girl remained immobile, in the same position, fist raised, and only slowly did George read the slight smile that curled her mouth. Then he started to smile himself.

Hagbard lowered his eyes for a second and gave a Sicilian shrug. *"O oi che siete in piccioletta barca,"* he said softly, and bowed. "I'm still in charge of nautical and technical matters," he announced, "but Miss Portinari now succeeds me as *episkopos* of the *Leif Erikson* cabal. Anyone with lingering spiritual or psychological problems, take them to her." He lunged across the room, hugged the girl, laughed with her happily for a moment and placed his golden apple ring on her finger. "Now I don't have to meditate every day," he shouted joyously, "and I'll have more time for some thinking."

In the next two days, as the *Leif Erikson* slowly crossed the Sea of Valusia and approached the Danube, George discovered that Hagbard had, indeed, put all his mystical trappings behind him. He spoke only of technical matters concerning the submarine, or other mundane subjects, and was sublimely unconcerned with the role-playing, role-changing and other mind-blowing tactics that had previously made up his persona. What emerged—the new Hagbard, or the old Hagbard of days before his adoption of guru-hood—was a tough, pragmatic, middle-aged engineer, with wide intelligence and interests, an overwhelming kindness and generosity, and many small symptoms of nervousness, anxiety and overwork. But mostly he seemed happy, and George realized that the euphoria derived from his having dropped an enormous burden.

Miss Portinari, meanwhile, had lost the self-effacing quality that made her so eminently forgettable before, and, from the moment Hagbard passed her the ring, she was as remote and gnomic as an Etruscan sybil. George, in fact, found that he was a little afraid of her—an annoying sensation, since he thought he had transcended fear when he found that the Robot was, left to itself, neither cowardly nor homicidal.

George tried to discuss his feelings with Hagbard once, when they happened to be seated together at dinner on April 28. "I don't know where my head is at anymore," he said tentatively.

"Well, in the immortal words of Marx, putta your hat on your neck, then," Hagbard grinned.

"No, seriously," George murmured as Hagbard hacked at a steak. "I don't feel really awakened or enlightened or whatever. I feel like K. in *The Castle*: I've seen it once, but I don't know how to get back there."

"Why do you *want* to get back?" Hagbard asked. "I'm damned glad to be out of it all. It's harder work than coal mining." He munched placidly, obviously bored by the direction of the conversation.

"That's not true," George protested. "Part of you is still there, and always will be. You've just given up being a guide for others."

"I'm *trying* to give up," Hagbard said pointedly. "Some people seem to be trying to reenlist me. Sorry. I'm not a German shepherd or a draftee. *Non serviam,* George."

George fiddled with his own steak for a minute, then tried another approach. "What was that Italian phrase you used, just before you gave your ring to Miss Portinari?"

"I couldn't think of anything else to say," Hagbard explained, embarrassed. "So, as usual with me, I got arty and pretentious. Dante addresses his readers, in the First Canto of the *Paradiso*, '*O voi che siete in piccioletta barca*'—roughly, Oh, you who are sailing in a very small boat astern of me. He meant that the readers, not having had the Vision, couldn't really understand his words. I turned it around, '*O oi che siete in piccioletta barca,*' admitting I was behind her in understanding. I should get the Ezra Pound Award for hiding emotion in tangled erudition. That's why I'm glad to give up the guru gig. I never was much better than second-rate at it."

"Well, I'm still way astern of *you* . . ." George began.

"Look," Hagbard growled. "I'm a tired engineer at the end of a long day. Can't we talk about something less taxing to my depleted brain? What do you think of the economic system I outline in the second part of *Never Whistle While You're Pissing?* I've decided to start calling it techno-anarchism; do you think that's more clear at first sight than anarcho-capitalism?"

And George found himself, frustrated, engaged in a long discussion of non-interest-bearing currencies, land stewardship replacing land ownership, the inability of monopoly capitalism to adjust to abundance, and other matters which would have interested him a week ago but now were very unimportant compared to the question which Zen masters phrased as "getting the goose out of the bottle without breaking the glass"—or specifically, getting George Dorn out of "George Dorn" without destroying GEORGE DORN.

That night, Mavis came again to his bed, and George said again, "No. Not until you love me the way I love you."

"You're turning into a stiff-necked prig," Mavis said. "Don't try to walk before you can crawl."

"Listen," George cried. "Suppose our society crippled every infant's legs systematically, instead of our minds? The ones who tried to get up and walk would be called neurotics, right? And the awkwardness of their first efforts would be published in the all psychiatric journals as proof of the regressive and schizzy nature of their unsocial and unnatural impulse toward walking, right? And those of you who know the secret would be superior and aloof and tell us to wait, be patient, you'll let us in on it in your own good time, right? Crap. I'm going to do it on my own."

"I'm not holding anything back," Mavis said gently.

"There's no field until *both* poles are charged."

"And I'm the dead pole? Go to hell and bake bagels."

After Mavis left, Stella arrived, wearing cute Chinese pajamas. "Horny?" she asked bluntly.

"Christ Almighty, yes!"

In ninety seconds they were naked and he was nibbling at her ear while his hand rubbed her pubic mat; but a saboteur was at work at his brain. "I love you," he thought, and it was not untrue because he loved all women now, knowing partially what sex was really all about, but he couldn't bring himself to say it because it was not totally true, either, since he loved Mavis more, much more. "I'm awfully fond of you," he almost said, but the absurdity of it stopped him. Her hand cupped his cock and found it limp; her eyes opened and looked into his enquiringly. He kissed her lips quickly and moved his hand lower, inserting a finger until he found the clitoris. But even when her breathing got deeper, he did not respond as usual, and her hand began massaging his cock more desperately. He slid down, kissing nipples and bellybutton on the way, and began licking her clitoris. As soon as she came, he cupped her buttocks, lifted her pelvis, got his tongue into her vagina and forced another quick orgasm, immediately lowering her slightly again and beginning a very gentle and slow return in spiral fashion back to the clitoris. But still he was flaccid.

"Stop," Stella breathed. "Let me do you, baby."

George moved upward on the bed and hugged her. "I love you," he said, and suddenly it did not sound like a lie.

Stella giggled and kissed his mouth briefly. "It takes a lot to get those words out of you, doesn't it?" she said bemusedly.

"Honesty is the worst policy," George said grimly. "I was a child prodigy, you know? A freak. It was rugged. I had to have some defense, and somehow I picked honesty. I was always with older boys so I never won a fight. The only way I could feel superior, or escape total inferiority, was to be the most honest bastard on the planet earth."

"So you can't say 'I love you' unless you mean it?" Stella laughed. "You're probably the only man in America with *that* problem. If you could only be a woman for a while, baby! You can't imagine what liars most men are."

"Oh, I've said it at times. When it was at least half true. But it always sounded like play-acting to me, and I felt it sounded that way to the woman, too. This time it just came out, perfectly natural, no effort."

"That *is* something," Stella grinned. "And I can't let it go unrewarded." Her black body slid downward and he enjoyed the esthetic effect as his eyes followed her—black on white, like the *yin-yang* or the Sacred Chao—what was the psychoses of the white race that made this beauty seem ugly to most of them? Then her lips closed over his penis and he found that the words had loosened the knot: he was erect in a second. He closed his eyes to savor the sensation, then opened them to look down at her Afro hairdo, her serious dark face, his cock slipping back and forth between her lips. "I love you," he repeated, with even more conviction. "Oh, Christ, Oh, Eris, oh baby baby, I love you!" He closed his eyes again, and let the Robot move his pelvis in response to her. "Oh, stop," he said, "stop," drawing her upward and turning her over, "together," he said, mounting her, "together," as her eyes closed when he entered her and then opened again for a moment meeting his in total tenderness, "I love you, Stella, I love," and he knew it was so far along that the weight wouldn't bother her, collapsing, using his arms to hug her, not supporting himself, belly to belly and breast to breast, her arms hugging him also and her voice saying, "I love you, too, oh, I love you," and moving with it, saying "angel" and "darling" and then saying nothing, the explosion and the light again permeating his whole body not just the penis, a passing through the mandala to the other side and a long sleep.

The next morning, he and Stella fucked some more, wildly and joyously; they said "I love you" so many times that it became a new mantra to him, and they were still whispering at breakfast. The problem of Mavis and the problem of reaching total enlightenment had both vanished from his mind. Enjoying bacon and eggs that seemed tastier than he had ever eaten before, exchanging pointless and very private jokes with Stella, George Dorn was at peace.

(But nine hours earlier, at that "same" time, the Kachinas gathered in the center of the oldest city in North America, Orabi, and began a dance which an excited visiting anthropologist had never seen before. As he questioned various old men and old women among the People of Peace—which is what *ho-pi* means—he found that the dance was dedicated to She-Woman-Forever-Not-Change. He knew enough not to try to convert that title into his own grammar, since it represented an important aspect of the Hopi philosophy of Time, which is much like the Simon Moon and Adam Weishaupt philosophies of Time and nothing like what physics students learn, at least until they reach graduate level studies. Only four times, he was told, had this dance ever been necessary: four times when the many worlds were all in danger, and this was the time of the fifth and greatest danger. The anthropologist, who happened to be a Hindu named Indole Ringh, quickly jotted in his notebook: "Cf. four yugas in *Upanishads,* Wagadu legend in Sudan, and Marsh's queer notions about Atlantis. This could be big." The dance went on, the drums pounded monotonously, and Carmel, far away, broke into a sudden perspiration . . .)

And, in Los Angeles, John Dillinger calmly loaded his revolver, dropped it in his briefcase and set a Panama hat on his neatly combed silver-gray hair. He was humming a song from his youth: "Those wedding bells are breaking up that old gang of mine . . ." I hope that pimp is where Hagbard says, he thought; I've only got eighteen hours before they declare martial law

. . . "Good-bye forever," he hummed on, "old fellows and pals . . ."

I saw the fnords the same day I first heard about the plastic martini. Let me be very clear and precise about this, since many of the people on this trip are deliberately and perversely obscure: I would not, *could not,* have seen the fnords if Hagbard Celine hadn't hypnotized me the night before, on the flying saucer.

I had been reading Pat Walsh's memos, at home, and listening to a new record from the Museum of Natural History. I was adding a few new samples to my collection of Washington-Weishaupt pictures on the wall, when the saucer appeared hovering outside my window. Needless to say, it didn't particularly surprise me; I had saved a little of the AUM, after Chicago, contrary to the instructions from ELF, and had dosed myself. After meeting the Dealy Lama, not to mention Malaclypse the Elder, and seeing that nut Celine actually talk to gorillas, I assumed my mind was a point of receptivity where the AUM would trigger something truly original. The UFO, in fact, was a bit of a letdown; so many people had seen them already, and I was ready for something nobody had ever seen or imagined.

It was even more a disappointment when they psyched me, or slurped me aboard, and I found, instead of Martians or Insect Trust delegates from the Crab Galaxy, just Hagbard, Stella Maris and a few other people from the *Leif Erikson.*

"Hail Eris," said Hagbard.

"All hail Discordia," I replied, giving the three-after-two pattern, and completing the pentad. "Is this something important, or did you just want to show me your latest invention?"

The inside of the saucer was, to be trite, eerie. Everything was non-Euclidean and semitransparent; I kept feeling that I might fall through the floor and hurtle to the ground to smash myself on the sidewalk. Then we started moving and it got worse.

"Don't let the architecture disturb you," Hagbard

said. "My own adaptation of some of Bucky Fuller's synergetic geometry. It's smaller, and more solid, than it looks. You won't fall out, believe me."

"Is this contraption behind all the flying saucer reports since 1947?" I asked curiously.

"Not quite," Hagbard laughed. "That's basically a hoax. The plan was created in the United States government, one of the few ideas they've had without direct Illuminati inspiration since about the middle of Roosevelt's first term. A reserve measure, in case something happens to Russia and China."

"Hi, baby," I said softly to Stella, remembering San Francisco. "Would you tell me, minus the Celine rhetoric and paradox, what the hell he's talking about?"

"The State is based on threat," Stella said simply. "If people aren't afraid of something, they'll realize they don't need that big government hand picking their pockets all the time. So, in case Russia and China collapse from internal dissension, or get into a private war and blow each other to hell, or suffer some unexpected natural calamity like a series of earthquakes, the saucer myth has been planted. If there are no earthly enemies to frighten the American people with, the saucer myth will immediately change. There will be 'evidence' that they come from Mars and are planning to invade and enslave us. Dig?"

"So," Hagbard added, "I built this little gizmo, and I can travel anywhere I want without interference. Any sighting of this craft, whether by a radar operator with twenty years' experience or a little old lady in Perth Amboy, is regarded by the government as a case of autosuggestion—since they know they didn't plant it themselves. I can hover over cities, like New York, or military installations that are Top Secret, or any place I damned well please. Nice?"

"Very nice," I said. "But why did you bring me up here?"

"It's time for you to see the fnords," he replied. Then I woke up in bed and it was the next morning. I made breakfast in a pretty nasty mood, wondering if

I'd seen the fnords, whatever the hell they were, in the hours he had blacked out, or if I would see them as soon as I went out in the street. I had some pretty gruesome ideas about them, I must admit. Creatures with three eyes and tentacles, survivors from Atlantis, who walked among us, invisible due to some form of mind shield, and did hideous work for the Illuminati. It was unnerving to contemplate, and I finally gave in to my fears and peeked out the window, thinking it might be better to see them from a distance first.

Nothing. Just ordinary sleepy people, heading for their buses and subways.

That calmed me a little, so I set out the toast and coffee and fetched in the *New York Times* from the hallway. I turned the radio to WBAI and caught some good Vivaldi, sat down, grabbed a piece of toast and started skimming the first page.

Then I saw the fnords.

The feature story involved another of the endless squabbles between Russia and the U.S. in the UN General Assembly, and after each direct quote from the Russian delegate I read a quite distinct "Fnord!" The second lead was about a debate in Congress on getting the troops out of Costa Rica; every argument presented by Senator Bacon was followed by another "Fnord!" At the bottom of the page was a *Times* depth-type study of the growing pollution problem and the increasing use of gas masks among New Yorkers; the most distressing chemical facts were interpolated with more "Fnords."

Suddenly I saw Hagbard's eyes burning into me and heard his voice: "Your heart will remain calm. Your adrenalin gland will remain calm. Calm, all-over calm. You will not panic. You will look at the fnord and see it. You will not evade it or black it out. You will stay calm and face it." And further back, way back: my first-grade teacher writing FNORD on the blackboard, while a wheel with a spiral design turned and turned on his desk, turned and turned, and his voice droned on, IF YOU DON'T SEE THE FNORD IT CAN'T EAT YOU, DON'T

SEE THE FNORD, DON'T SEE THE FNORD . . .

I looked back at the paper and still saw the fnords.

This was one step beyond Pavlov, I realized. The first conditioned reflex was to experience the panic reaction (the activation syndrome, it's technically called) whenever encountering the word "fnord." The second conditioned reflex was to black out what happened, including the word itself, and just to feel a general low-grade emergency without knowing why. And the third step, of course, was to attribute this anxiety to the news stories, which were bad enough in themselves anyway.

Of course, the essence of control is fear. The fnords produced a whole population walking around in chronic low-grade emergency, tormented by ulcers, dizzy spells, nightmares, heart palpitations and all the other symptoms of too much adrenalin. All my left-wing arrogance and contempt for my countrymen melted, and I felt genuine pity. No wonder the poor bastards believe anything they're told, walk through pollution and overcrowding without complaining, watch their sons hauled off to endless wars and butchered, never protest, never fight back, never show much happiness or eroticism or curiosity or normal human emotion, live with perpetual tunnel vision, walk past a slum without seeing either the human misery it contains or the potential threat it poses to their security . . . Then I got a hunch, and turned quickly to the advertisements. It was as I expected: no fnords. That was part of the gimmick, too: only in consumption, endless consumption, could they escape the amorphous threat of the invisible fnords.

I kept thinking about it on my way to the office. If I pointed out a fnord to somebody who hadn't been deconditioned, as Hagbard deconditioned me, what would he or she say? They'd probably read the word before or after it. "No *this* word," I'd say. And they would again read an adjacent word. But would their panic level rise as the threat came closer to consciousness? I preferred not to try the experiment; it might have ended with a psychotic fugue in the subject. The conditioning, after all, went back to grade school. No wonder we all hate those teachers so much: we have a dim, masked memory of what they've done to us in converting us into good and faithful servants for the Illuminati.

When I arrived at my desk, Peter Jackson handed me a press release. "What do you make of this?" he asked with a puzzled frown, and I looked at the mimeographed first page. The old eye-and-pyramid design leaped out at me. "DeMolay Frères invites you to the premiere debut of the world's first plastic nude martini . . . ," the press release declared. On second glance the eye in the triangle turned into the elliptical rim of a martini glass, while the pupil in the eye was actually the olive floating in the cocktail.

"What the hell is a plastic nude martini?" said Peter Jackson. "And why would they invite us to a press party for one?"

"You can bet that it's nonbiodegradable," said Joe.

"Which will make it very unfashionable with honky ecology freaks," said Peter sarcastically.

Joe squinted at the design again. It could be a coincidence. But coincidence was just another word for synchronicity. "I think I'll go," he said. "And what's that?" he added as his eye fell upon a half-unfolded poster on his desk.

"Oh, that came with the latest American Medical Association album," said Peter. "I don't want it, and I thought you might. It's time you took those pictures of the Rolling Stones off your wall. This is the age of constantly accelerating change, and a man who displays old pictures of the Stones is liable to be labeled a reactionary."

Four owl-eyed faces stared at him. They were dressed in one-piece white suits, and three of them were joining extended hands to form a triangle, while the fourth, Wolfgang Saure, generally acknowledged to be the leader of the group, stood with his arms folded in the center. The picture was taken from above so that the most prominent elements were the four heads, while the outstretched arms clearly made the sides of the triangle, and the bodies seemed unimportant, dwindling away to nothing. The background was jet black. The three young men and the woman, with their smooth-shaven bony faces, their blond crew-cuts and their icy blue eyes seemed extremely sinister to Joe. If the Nazis had won the war and Heinrich Himmler had followed Hitler as ruler of the German Empire, kids like this would be running the world. And they almost were, in a different sense, because they had succeeded the Beatles and Stones as kings of music, which made them emperors among youth. Although long hair remained the general fashion, the kids had accepted the American Medical Association's antiseptic-clean appearance as a needed reaction against a style that had become too commonplace.

As Wolfgang himself had said, "If you need an outward sign to know your own, you don't really belong."

"They give me the creeps," said Joe.

"What did you think when the Beatles first came out?" said Peter.

Joe shrugged. "They gave me the creeps. They looked ugly and sexless and like teenage werewolves with all that hair. And they seemed to be able to mesmerize twelve-year-old girls."

Peter nodded. "The bulk of the AMA's fans are even younger. So you might as well start conditioning yourself to them now. They're going to be around for a long time."

"Peter, let's you and me have lunch," Joe said. "Then I'm going to get some work done, and then I'm going to leave here at four to go to this plastic martini party. First of all, though, hold the chair for me while I take down the Stones and put up the American Medical Association."

The DeMolay Frères group wasn't kidding, he found. There were martinis, olives and all (or cocktail onions for those who preferred them) in transparent plastic bags that were shaped like nude women. Pretty terrible taste the manufacturer had, thought Joe. Briefly, Joe wondered if it would be a good idea to infiltrate this company so as to get dosages of AUM in all the plastic nude martinis. But then he remembered the emblem and thought maybe this company was already infiltrated. But by which side?

There was a beautiful Oriental girl in the room. She had black hair that reached all the way down to the small of her back, and when she raised her arms to adjust a head ornament, Joe was surprised to see thick black hair in her armpits. Orientals did not normally have much body hair, he thought. Could she be some relation to the hairy Ainu of northern Japan? It intrigued him, turned him on as he'd never thought armpit hair would, and he went over to her to talk. The first thing he noticed was that the headband she wore had a golden apple with the letter K printed on it right in the center of her forehead. She is one of Us, he thought. His hunch about coming to this party was right.

"These martini bags sure have a silly shape," said Joe.

"Why? Don't you care for nude women?"

"Well, this has about as much to do with nude women as any other piece of plastic," said Joe. "No, my point is that it's in such execrable taste. But, then, all of American industry is nothing but a giant obscene circus to me. What's your name?"

The black eyes fixed his intently. "Mao Tsu-hsi."

"Any relation?"

"No. My name means 'cat' in Chinese. His doesn't. His name is *Mao* but mine is *Mao*." Joe was enchanted by her enunciation of the two different tones.

"Well, Miss Cat, You are the most attractive woman I've met in ages."

She responded with a silent flirtation of her own and they were soon in a wonderfully interesting conversation—which he could never remember afterwards. Nor did he notice the pinch of powder she dropped into his drink. He began feeling strangely groggy. Tsu-hsi took his arm and led him to the checkroom. They got their coats, left the building and hailed a cab. In the back seat they kissed for a long time. She opened her coat and he pulled the zipper that went all the way down the front of her dress. He felt her breasts and stroked her belly, then dropped his head into her bush. She was wearing no underwear. She draped her legs over his, using her coat to screen what was going on from the cab driver, and helped him expose his erect penis. With a few quick, agile movements she had swept her skirt out of the way, raised her little seat into the air and slid her well-lubricated cunt down over his cock and was fucking him sidesaddle. It could have been difficult and awkward, but she was so light and well coordinated that she managed to bring herself to orgasm easily and voluptuously. She drew in her breath sharply through her teeth and a shudder ran through her body. She rested her head momentarily on his shoulder, then raised herself slightly and helped Joe to a pleasant climax with a rotary motion of her ass.

The experience, Joe realized, would have been more exquisite a few months, or a few years, earlier. Now, with his growing sensitivity, he was conscious of what had been missing: the actual energetic contact. The effect of the JAMs and the Discordians on him, he reflected, had been paradoxical by ordinary standards. He was no more puritanical than before they started tinkering with his nervous system (he was less), but at the same time casual sex was less appealing to him. He remembered Atlanta Hope's diatribes against "sexism" in her book *Telemachus Sneezed*—the Bible of the God's Lightning Movement—and he suddenly saw some weird kind of sense in her rantings. "The Sexual Revolution in America was as much of a fraud as the Political Revolutions in China and Russia," Atlanta had written with her usual exuberant capitalization; she was, in a way, quite right. People today were still wrapped in a cellophane of false ego, and even if they fucked and had orgasms together the cellophane was still there and no real contact had been made.

And yet if Mao was what he suspected she would know this even better than he did. Was this quick, cool spasm some kind of test or some lesson or demonstration? If so, how was he supposed to respond?

And then he remembered that she had not given an address to the driver. The cab had been waiting only for them to take them to a predetermined place, for reasons unknown.

I've seen the fnords, he thought; *now I'm going to see more.*

The cab stopped on a narrow, heavily shadowed street that seemed to be all empty stores, factory buildings, loading docks and warehouses.

With Miss Mao leading, they entered an old dilapidated-looking loft building with the aid of a key she had in her handbag, climbed some clanging cast-iron stairs, walked hand in hand down a long dark corridor and came at last through a series of anterooms, each better appointed than the last, to a splendid boardroom. Joe shook his head, amazed at what he saw, but there was something—he suspected a drug—that was keeping him docile and passive.

Around a table sat men and women costumed from various eras of human history. Joe recognized Indian, Chinese, Japanese, Mongol and Polynesian dress, also classical Greek and Roman, medieval and Renaissance. There were other outfits more difficult to recognize at first glance. A flying Dutch board meeting, Joe thought to himself. They were talking about the Illuminati, the Discordians, the JAMs and the Erisians.

A man wearing a steel breastplate and helmet with gold inlay and a neatly trimmed mustache and goatee said, "It is now possible to predict with ninety-eight percent probability of accuracy that the Illuminati are setting up Fernando Poo for an international crisis. The question is, do we raid the island and get the records now, making sure they're not endangered, or do we wait and take advantage of the trouble as a cover for our raid?"

A man in a dragon-embroidered red silk robe said,

"There will be no way to take advantage of the trouble, in my opinion. It will seem like chaos on the surface, but underneath the Illuminati will have everything very much under control. Now is the time to move."

A woman in a translucent silk blouse whose little vest did not hide her dark, rounded breasts, said, "You realize this could be a lovely scoop for your magazine, Mr. Malik. You could send a reporter there to look into conditions on Fernando Poo. Equatorial Guinea has all the usual problems of a developing African nation. Will tribal rivalries flare up between the Bubi and the Fang, preventing the further development of national cooperation? Will the poverty of the mainland province lead to attempts to expropriate the wealth of Fernando Poo? And what of the army? What, for example, of a certain Captain Jesus Tequila y Mota? An interview with the captain might prove to be a journalistic coup three years from now."

"Yes," said a big woman in colorfully dyed furs who played incessantly with the carved leg bone of some large animal. "We don't expect C. L. Sulzberger to grasp the importance of Fernando Poo until the crisis is upon the world. So, if advance warning is desirable—as we think it is—why not through *Confrontation?*"

"Is that why you asked me here?" said Joe. "To tell me something is going to happen in Fernando Poo? Where the hell is Fernando Poo, anyway?"

"Look it up in an atlas when you get back to work. It's one of several volcanic islands off the coast of Africa," said a dark-skinned, slit-eyed man wearing a buffalo hide decorated with feathers. "Of course, you understand that you could only hint at the real forces at work there," he added. "For instance, we wouldn't want you to mention that Fernando Poo is one of the last outcroppings of the continent of Atlantis, you know."

Mao Tsu-hsi was standing beside Joe with a glass containing a pinkish liquid. "Here, drink this," she said. "It will sharpen your perceptions."

A man in gold-braid-encrusted field marshal's uniform said, "Mr. Malik is the next business in order on our agenda. We are to educate him, to some extent. Let's do it, to that extent."

The lights in the room went out. There was a rustling at one end, and suddenly Joe was looking at a brightly lit movie screen.

WHEN ATLANTIS RULED THE EARTH

The title appears in letters that look like blocks of stone piled on top of one another to form a kind of step pyramid. It is followed by shots of the earth as it looked thirty thousand years ago, during the great ice ages, showing woolly mammoths, saber-toothed tigers and Cro-Magnon hunters, while a narrator explains that at the same time the greatest civilization ever known by man is flourishing on the continent of Atlantis. The Atlanteans do not know anything about good or evil, the narrator explains. However, they all live to be five hundred years old and have no fear of death. The bodies of all Atlanteans are covered with fur, as with apes.

After seeing various domestic scenes in Zukong Gimorlad-Siragosa, the largest and most central city on the continent (but not the capital, because the Atlanteans do not have a government), we move to a laboratory where the young (one hundred years old) scientist GRUAD is displaying a biological experiment to an associate, GAO TWONE. The experiment is a giant water-dwelling serpent-man. Gao Twone is impressed, but Gruad declares that he is bored; he wishes to change himself in some unexpected way. Gruad is already strange—unlike other Atlanteans, he is not covered with fur, but has only short blond hair on top of his head and a close-cropped beard. In comparison to other Atlanteans he seems hideously naked. He wears a high-collared pale green robe and gauntlets. He tells Gao Twone that he is tired of accumulating knowledge for the sake of knowledge. "It's just another guise for the pursuit of pleasure, to which too many of our fellow Atlanteans devote their lives. Of course, there's nothing wrong with pleasure—it moves the energies—but I feel that there is something higher and more heroic. I have no name for it yet, but I know it exists."

Gao Twone is somewhat shocked. "You, as a scientist, can talk of *knowing* something exists when you have no evidence?"

Gruad is dejected by this and admits, "My lens needs polishing." But after a moment he bounces back. "And yet, even though I have my moments of doubt, I think my lens really is clear. Of course, I must find the evidence. But even now, before I start, I feel that I know what I will find. We could be greater and finer than we are. I look at what I am and sometimes I despise myself. I'm just a clever animal. An ape who has learned to play with tools. I want to be much more. I say we can be what the lloigor are, and even more. We can conquer time and seize eternity, even as they have. I mean to achieve that or destroy myself in the attempt."

The scene shifts to a banquet hall where INGEL RILD, a venerable Atlantean scientist, has called together prominent Atlanteans to celebrate a space research achievement, the production of a solar flare. Ingel Rild and his associates have developed a missile which, when it strikes the sun, can cause an explosion. He tells the marijuana-smoking gathering, "We can control to the second the timing of the flare and to the millimeter the distance it will spring out from the sun. A flare of sufficient magnitude could burn our planet to a crisp. A smaller flare could bombard the earth with radiations such that the area closest to the sun would be destroyed, while the rest of our world would suffer drastic changes. Most serious of all, perhaps, would be the biological changes these excessive radiations would bring about. Life forms would be damaged and perhaps become extinct. New life forms would arise. All of nature would undergo a tremendous upheaval. This has happened naturally once or twice. It happened seventy

million years ago when the dinosaurs were suddenly
wiped out and replaced by mammals. We still have
much to learn about the mechanism that produces
spontaneous solar flares. However, to be able to cause
them artificially is a step toward predicting and possibly controlling them. When that stage is reached, our
planet and our race will be protected from the kind of
catastrophe that destroyed the dinosaurs."

After the applause, a woman named KAJECI asks
whether it might not be disrespectful to tamper with
"our father, the sun." Ingel Rild replies that man is a
part of nature and what he does is natural and can't be
construed as tampering. Now Gruad interrupts angrily,
pointing out that he, an unattractive mutation, is the
product of tampering with nature. He tells Ingel Rild
that the Atlanteans do not truly understand nature and
the order that controls it. He declares that man is subject to laws. All things in nature are, but man is different because he can disobey the natural laws that govern him. Gruad goes on, "With humanity we can
speak, as we speak of our own machines, in terms of
performance expected and performance delivered. If a
machine does not do what it is designed for, we try to
correct it. We want it to do what it *ought* to do, what it
should do. I think we have the right and the duty to demand the same of people—that they perform as they
ought to and *should* perform." An aged and merry-
eyed scientist named LHUV KERAPHT interrupts, "But
people are not machines, Gruad."

"Exactly," Gruad answers. "I have already considered that. Therefore, I have created new words, words
even stronger than *should* and *ought*. When a person
performs as he or she should and ought, I call that
Good; and anything less than this I call *Evil*." This
outlandish notion is greeted with general laughter.
Gruad tries to speak persuasively, conscious of his
lonely position as a pioneer, trying desperately to communicate with the closed minds all around him. After
further argument, though, he becomes threatening, declaring, "The people of Atlantis do not live according

to the law. In their pride, they strike the sun itself, and boast of it, as you have, Ingel Rild, this day. I say that if Atlanteans do not live according to the law, a disaster will befall them. A disaster that will shake the entire earth. You have been warned! Heed my words!" Gruad strides majestically out of the banquet hall, seizing his cloak at the door and sweeping it about him as he leaves. Kajeci follows him and tells him that she thinks she partly understands what he has been trying to say. The laws he speaks of are like the wishes of parents, and, "The great bodies of the universe are our parents. Isn't that so?" Gruad's naked hand strokes Kajeci's furred cheek, and they go off into the darkness together.

Within six months Gruad has formed an organization called the Party of Science. Their banner is an eye inside a triangle which in turn is surrounded by a serpent with its tail in its mouth. The Party of Science demands that Atlantis publish the natural laws Gruad has discovered and make them binding on all with systems of reward and punishment to enforce them. The word "punishment" is another addition to the Atlantean vocabulary coined by Gruad. One of Gruad's opponents explains to friends of his that it means torture, and everyone's fur bristles. Ingel Rild announces to a gathering of his supporters that Gruad has proven to his own satisfaction—and the demonstration runs to seventy-two scrolls of logical symbols—that sex is part of what he calls Evil. Only sex for the good of the community is to be permitted under Gruad's system, to keep the race alive.

A scientist called TON LIT exclaims, "You mean we must be thinking about conception during the act? That's impossible. Men's penises would droop, and women's vaginas wouldn't get moist. It's like—well, it's like making the shrill mouth-music while you are urinating. It would take great training, if it can be done at all." Ingel Rild proposes the formation of a Party of Freedom to oppose Gruad. Discussing Gruad's personality, Ingel Rild says he checked the genealogical records and found that several of the most agitated-energy people in all Atlantean history were among his ancestors. Gruad is a mutation, and so are many of his followers. The energy of normal Atlanteans flows slowly. Gruad's people are impatient and frustrated, and this is what makes them want to inflict suffering on their fellow humans.

Joe sat up with a jolt. If he understood that part of the movie, Gruad—evidently the first Illuminatus—was also the first *homo neophilus*. And the Party of Freedom, which seemed to be the origin of the Discordian and JAM movements, was pure *homo neophobus*. How the hell could that be squared with the generally reactionary attitude of current Illuminati policies, and the innovativeness of the Discordians and JAMs? But the film was moving on—

In a disreputable-looking tavernlike place where men and women smoke dope in pipes that they pass from one to another, while people grope in couples and groups in dark corners, SYLVAN MARTISET proposes a Party of Nothingness that rejects the positions of both the Party of Science and the Party of Freedom.

After this we see street fighting, atrocities, the infliction of punishment on harmless people by men wearing Gruad's eye-and-triangle badge. The Party of Freedom proclaims its own symbol, a golden apple. The fighting spreads, the numbers of the dead mount and Ingel Rild weeps. He and his associates decide on a desperate expedient—unleashing the lloigor Yog Sothoth. They will offer this unnatural soul-eating energy being from another universe its freedom in return for its help in destroying Gruad's movement. Yog Sothoth is imprisoned in the great Pentagon of Atlantis on a desolate moor in the southern part of the continent. The Atlantean electric plane bearing Ingel Rild, Ton Lit and another scientist drifts, trailing feathery sparks, to a landing in a flat field overgrown with gray weeds. Within the Pentagon, an enormous black stone structure, the ground is scorched and the air shimmers like a heat mirage. Flickers of static electricity run through the shimmering from time to time, and an unpleasant noise, like flies around a corpse, pervades the whole moor. The faces of the three Atlantean sages register disgust, sickness and terror. They climb the nearest tower and talk to the guard. Suddenly Yog Sothoth takes control of Ton Lit, speaking in an oily, rich, deep and reverberating voice, and asks them what they seek of him. Ton Lit lets out a terrible shriek and claps his hands over his ears. Froth slips from the side of his mouth, his fur bristles and his penis stands erect. His eyes are delirious and suffering, like those of a dying gorilla. The guard uses an electronic instrument that looks like a magician's wand topped with a five-pointed star to subdue Yog Sothoth. Ton Lit bays like a hound and leaps for Ingel Rild's throat. The electronic ray drives him back and he stands panting, tongue hanging loose, as the Pentagon first and then the ground begin to soften into asymptotic curves. Yog Sothoth chants, "Ia-nggh-ha-nggh-ha-nggh-fthagn!   Ia-nggh-ha-nggh-ha-nggh-hgual! The blood is the life . . . The blood is the life . . ." All faces, bodies and perspectives are skewed and there is a greenish tinge on everything. Suddenly the guard strikes the nearest wall of the Pentagon directly with his electronic wand and Ton Lit shrieks, human intelligence coming back into his eyes together with great shame and revulsion. The three sages flee the Pentagon under a sky slowly turning back to its normal shape and color. The laughter of Yog Sothoth follows them. They decide that they cannot release the lloigor.

Meanwhile Gruad has called his closest followers, known as the Unbroken Circle of Gruad, to announce that Kajeci has conceived. Then he shows them a group of manlike creatures with green, scaly skin, wearing long black cloaks and black skullcaps with scarlet plumes. These he calls his Ophidians. Since Atlanteans have a kind of instinctive check on themselves that prevents them from killing except in blind fury,

Gruad has developed these synthetic humanoids from the serpent, which he has found to be the most intelligent of all reptiles. They will have no hesitation about destroying men and will act only on Gruad's command. Some of his followers protest, and Gruad explains that this is not really killing. He says, "Atlanteans who will not accept the teachings of the Party of Science are swinish beings. They are a sort of robot who has no inner spiritual substance to control it. Our bodies, however, are deceived into feeling as if they are our own kind, and we cannot raise our hands against them. Now, however, the light of science has given us hands to raise." At this meeting Gruad also addresses his men for the first time as the "illuminated ones."

At the next meeting of the Party of Freedom the Ophidians attack, using iron bars to club people to death and slashing throats with their fangs. Then the Party of Freedom holds a funeral for a dozen of its dead at which Ingel Rild gives an oration describing the ways in which the struggle between Gruad's followers and the other Atlanteans is changing the character of all human beings:

"Hitherto, Atlanteans have enjoyed knowledge but not worried over the fact that there is much that we do not know. We are conservative and indifferent to new ideas, we have no inner conflicts and we feel like doing the things that seem wise to us. We think that the things we feel like doing will usually work out for the best. We consider pain and pleasure a single phenomenon, which we call sensation, and we respond to unavoidable pain by relaxing or becoming ecstatic. We do not fear death. We can read each other's minds because we are in touch with all the energies of our bodies. The followers of Gruad have lost that ability, and they are thankful that they have. The Scientists dote on new things and new ideas. This love of the new thing is a matter of genetic manipulation. Gruad is even encouraging people in their twenties to have children, though it is our custom never to have children before we reach a hundred. The generations of Gruad's followers come thick and fast, and they are not like us. They agonize over their ignorance. They are full of uncertainty and inner conflict between what they should do and what they feel like doing. The children, who are brought up on Gruad's teachings, are even more disturbed and conflict-filled than their parents. One doctor tells me that the attitudes and the way of life Gruad is encouraging in his people is enough to shorten their life spans considerably. And they are afraid of pain. They are afraid of death. And even as their lives grow shorter, they desperately seek for some means of achieving immortality."

Gruad tells a meeting of his Unbroken Circle that the time has come to intensify the struggle. If they can't rule the Atlanteans, they will destroy Atlantis. "Atlantis will be destroyed by light," says Gruad. "By the light of the sun." Gruad introduces the worship of the sun to his followers. He reveals the existence of gods and goddesses. "They are all energy, conscious energy," says Gruad. "This conscious and powerfully directed and focused pure energy I call spirit. All motion is spirit. All light is spirit. All spirit is light."

Under Gruad's direction, the Party of Science builds a great pyramid, thousands of feet high. It is in two halves; the upper half, made of an indestructible ceramic substance and inscribed with a terrible staring eye, floats five hundred feet above the base, held in place by antigravity generators.

A band of men and women led by LILITH VELKOR, chief spokeswoman for the Party of Nothingness, gathers at the base of the great pyramid and laughs at it. They carry Nothingarian signs:

DON'T CLEAN OUR LENSES, GRUAD—
GET THE CRACK OUT OF YOUR OWN

EVERY TIME I HEAR THE WORD "PROGRESS" MY
FUR BRISTLES

THE SUN SUCKS

FREEDOM DEFINED IS FREEDOM DENIED

THE MESSAGE ON THIS
SIGN IS A FLAT LIE

Lilith Velkor addresses the Nothingarians, satirizing all Gruad's beliefs, claiming that the most powerful god is a crazy woman and she is the goddess of chaos. To the accompaniment of laughter she declares, "Gruad says the sun is the eye of the sun god. That's more of his notion that males are superior and reason and order are superior. Actually, the sun is a giant golden apple which is the plaything of the goddess of chaos. And it's the property of anyone she thinks is fair enough to deserve it." Suddenly a band of Ophidians attacks followers of Lilith Velkor and kills several of them. Lilith Velkor leads her people in an unprecedented attack on the Ophidians. They storm up the side of the great pyramid and throw the Ophidians down to the street, killing them. Amazingly, they succeed in wiping out all the Ophidians. Gruad declares that Lilith Velkor must die. When the opportunity presents itself, his men seize her and take her to a dungeon. There an enormous wheel has been constructed with four spokes in the shape

Lilith Velkor is crucified with ropes, upside down, on this device. Several members of the Party of Science lounge about, watching her die. Gruad enters, goes to the wheel and looks at the dying woman, who says, "This is as good a day to die as any." Gruad remonstrates with her, saying that death is a great evil and she should fear it. She laughs and says, "All my life I have despised tradition and now I despise innovation also. Surely, I must be a most wicked example for the world!" She dies laughing. Gruad's rage is unbearable. He vows that he will wait no longer; Atlantis is too wicked to save and he will destroy it.

On a windswept plain in the northern regions of Atlantis a huge teardrop-shaped rocket with graceful fins is poised on the launching pad. Gruad is in the control room making last-minute adjustments while Kajeci and Wo Topod argue with him. Gruad says, "The human race will survive. It will survive the better purged of these Atlanteans, who are nothing but swine, nothing but robots, nothing but creatures who do not understand good and evil. Let them perish." His finger strikes a red button and the rocket hurtles on its way to the sun. It will take several days to reach there, and meanwhile Gruad has gathered the Unbroken Circle on an airship which takes them away from Atlantis and into the huge mountains to the east in a region that will one day be called Tibet. Gruad calculates that by the time the missile strikes the sun, they will have been landed and underground for two hours. The sun rides blinding yellow over the plains of Atlantis. It is a beautiful day in Zukong Gimorlad-Siragosa, the sun shining down on its slender, graceful towers with spiderweb bridges spiraling among them, its parks, its temples, its museums, its fine public buildings and magnificent private palaces. Its handsome, richly furred people gracefully stride amidst the beauties of the first and finest civilization man has ever produced. Families, lovers, friends and enemies, all unsuspecting what is about to happen, enjoy their private moments. A quintet plays the melodious zinthron, balatet, mordan, swaz and fendrar. Over all, however, the great eye on the side of Gruad's pyramid glares horrid and red.

Suddenly the sun's body rages. Coiled flames, balls of gas, roll out. The sun looks like a giant fiery arachnid or octopus. One great flame comes rolling toward the earth, burning red gas which turns yellow, then green, then blue, then white.

There is nothing left of Zukong Gimorlad-Siragosa, except the pyramid with its upper segment now resting on the base, the antigravity generators having been destroyed. The baleful eye looks out over an absolutely flat, burnt-black plain. The ground shakes, great cracks open. The blackened area is a great circle, hundreds of miles in diameter, beyond which is a dark brown and still desolate wasteland. Thousands of cracks appear in the brittle surface of the continent, the strength of whose rocks has been destroyed by the incredible heat of the solar flare. A tide of mud starts crawling over the empty plain. It leaves only the top of the pyramid, with the great eye, showing. Water sweeps over the mud, at first sinking in and standing in pools, then rising higher so that only the tip of the pyramid sticks out of a great lake. Under the water enormous parallel fissures open in the ground on either side of the blackened central circle. The midsection of the continent, including the pyramid, begins to sink. The pyramid falls into the depths of the ocean with cliffs rising on either side of it to the parts of Atlantis that still remain above the ocean. They will remain for many thousands of years more, and they will be the Atlantis remembered in the legends of men. But the true Atlantis—high Atlantis—is gone.

Gruad stares into his crimson-glowing viewplate, watching the destruction of Atlantis. The light changes color, from red to gray, and the face of Gruad turns gray. It is a terrible face. It has aged a hundred years in the last few minutes. Gruad may claim to be in the right, but deep down he knows that what he has done isn't nice. And yet deep down there is satisfaction, too, for Gruad, long tortured by unreasonable guilt, now has something he can really feel guilty about. He turns to the Unbroken Circle and proposes, since it appears that the earth will survive the cataclysm (he was not really sure that it would), that they plan for the future. Most of them, however, are still in shock. Wo Topod, inconsolable, stabs himself to death, the first recorded time that a member of the human race has deliberately killed himself. Gruad calls upon his followers to destroy all remains of the Atlantean civilization and then,

later, to build a perfect civilization when even the ruins
of Atlantis have been forgotten.

The great beasts that inhabited Europe, Asia and
North America die off as a result of mutations and diseases caused by the solar flare. All relics of the Atlantean civilization are destroyed. The people who were
Gruad's erstwhile countrymen are either killed or
driven forth to wander the earth. Besides Gruad's
Himalayan colony there is one other remnant of the
High Atlantean era: the Pyramid of the Eye, whose
ceramic substance resisted solar flare, earthquake, tidal
wave and submersion in the depths of the ocean.
Gruad explains that it is right that the eye should remain. It is the eye of God, the One, the scientific-tech-
nical eye of ordered knowledge that looks down on the
universe and by perceiving it causes it to be. If an
event is not witnessed, it does not happen; therefore,
for the universe to happen there must be a Witness.

Among the primitive hunters and gatherers a mutation has appeared that seems to be spreading rapidly.
More and more people are being born without fur and
with hair in the same pattern as Gruad's. The Hour of
God's Eye has caused mutations in every species.

From the Himalayas the rocket ships of the Unbroken Circle, painted red and white, swoop out in
squadrons. They sweep across Europe and land on the
brown islands where Atlantis used to be. There they
land and raid a city of refugees from the Atlantean
disaster. They kill many of the leaders and intellectuals
and herd the rest aboard the ships, fly to the Americas
and deposit the helpless people on a vast plain. Far below their route of passage lies the Pyramid of the Eye
at the bottom of the Atlantic. The base of the pyramid
is covered with silt and the break where the upper part
of the pyramid had floated on antigravity projectors is
also covered. Still the pyramid itself towers over the
mud around it, taller by three times than the Great
Pyramid of Egypt, the building of which lies twenty-
seven thousand years in the future. A vast shadow descends upon the pyramid. There is a suggestion in the

darkness of the ocean bottom of giant tentacles, of sucker disks wide as the rims of volcanos, of an eye as big as the sun looking at the eye on the pyramid. Something touches the pyramid, and enormous as it is, it moves slightly. Then the presence is gone.

The pentagonal trap in which the people of Atlantis had heroically and brilliantly caught the dread ancient being Yog Sothoth has been, amazingly, undamaged by the catastrophe. Being on the southern plain, which was relatively uninhabited, the Pentagon of Yog Sothoth becomes the center of a migration of people who survived the disaster. Emergency cities are set up, those dying of radiation sickness are treated. A second Atlantis begins to take root. And then, from the Himalayas, the ships of the Unbroken Circle come swooping down on one of their raids. Lines of Atlantean men and women are marched to the walls of the Pentagon and there mowed down by laser fire. Then explosive charges are placed amid the heaps of bodies and the masked, uniformed men of the Unbroken Circle withdraw. There is a series of explosions; horrid yellow smoke goes coiling up. The gray stone walls crumble. There is a moment of stillness, balance, tension. Then the piled-up boulders of one side of the wall fly apart as if thrust by the hand of a giant. An enormous claw print appears in the soft soil around the ruins of the Pentagon. The masked men of the Unbroken Circle race frantically for their ships and take off. The ships dart into the sky, stop suddenly, waver and plummet like stones to explosive crashes on the earth. The surviving refugees scream and scatter. Like a scythe going through wheat, death sweeps among them in great arcs as they run in massed mobs. Mouths open in soundless screams, they fall. Only a handful escapes. Over the scene a colossal reddish figure of indeterminate shape and number of limbs stands triumphant.

In the Himalayas, Gruad and the Unbroken Circle watch the destruction of the Pentagon and the massacre of the Atlanteans. The Unbroken Circle cheers, but Gruad strangely weeps. "You think I hate walls?"

he says. "I love walls. I love any kind of wall. Anything that separates. Walls protect good people. Walls lock away the evil. There must always be walls and the love of walls, and in the destruction of the great Pentagon that held Yog Sothoth I read the destruction of all that I stand for. Therefore I am stricken with regret."

At this the face of EVOE, a young priest, takes on a reddish glow and a demoniac look. There is more than a hint of possession. "It is good to hear you say that," he says to Gruad. "No man yet has befriended me, though many have tried to use me. I have prepared a special place for your soul, oh first of the men of the future." Gruad attempts to speak to Yog Sothoth, but the possession has apparently passed, and the other members of the Unbroken Circle praise a new beverage that Evoe has prepared, made of the fermented juice of grapes. At dinner, later that day, Gruad tries the new beverage and praises it, saying, "This juice of grapes relaxes me and does not cause the disturbing visions and sounds that makes the herb the Atlanteans used to smoke so unpleasant for a man of conscience." Evoe gives him more to drink from a fresh jar, and Gruad takes it. Before drinking he says, "Any culture that arises in the next twenty thousand years or so is going to have the rot of Atlantis in it. Therefore I decree a noncultural time of eight hundred generations. After that we may allow man free reign on his propensity for building civilizations. The culture he builds will be under our guidance, with our ideas implicit in its every aspect, with our control at every stage. Eight hundred generations from now the new human culture will be planted. It will follow the natural law. It will have the knowledge of good and evil, the light that comes from the sun, the sun that blasphemers say is only an apple. It is no apple, I tell you, though it is a fruit, even as this beverage of Evoe's that I now quaff is from a fruit. From the grape comes this drink and from the sun comes the knowledge of good and evil, the separation of light and darkness over the whole earth. Not an apple, but the fruit of knowledge!" Gruad drinks. He puts down his glass, clutches his throat and staggers back. His other hand goes to his heart. He topples over and lies on his back, his eyes staring upward.

Naturally, everyone accuses Evoe of poisoning Gruad. But Evoe calmly answers that it was Lilith Velkor who did it. He was doing research on the energies of the dead and had learned how to take them into him. But sometimes the energies of the dead could take control of him, so that he would be just a medium through which they act. He cries, "When you write this tragedy into the archives, you must say, not that Evoe the man did it, but Evoe-Lilith, possessed by the evil spirit of a woman. The woman did tempt me, I tell you! I was helpless." The Unbroken Circle is persuaded, and agree that since Lilith Velkor and the crazy goddess she worshipped were responsible for Gruad's death, henceforward women must be subordinate to men so such evils will not be repeated. They decide to build a tomb for Gruad and to inscribe upon it, "The First Illuminated One: Never Trust A Woman." They decide that since the lloigor is loose they will offer sacrifices to it, and the sacrifices will be pure young women who have never lain with a man. Evoe seems to be taking control of the group and Gao Twone protests this. To prove his dedication to the true and the good, Evoe declares, he has had his penis amputated as a sacrifice to the All-Seeing Eye. He pulls open his robe. All look at his truncated crotch and immediately retch. Evoe goes on, "Furthermore, it is decreed by the Eye and Natural Law that all male children who would be close to goodness and truth must imitate my sacrifice, at least to the extent of losing the foreskin or being cut enough to bleed." Kajeci comes in at this point, and they plan a great funeral, agreeing that they will not burn Gruad as was the Atlantean custom, signifying that one is dead forever, but will preserve his body, symbolizing the hope that he is not really dead but will rise again.

There follow several thousand years of warfare between the remnants of the Atlanteans and the inhabitants of Agharti, the stronghold of the Scientists, who now call themselves variously the Knowledgeable or the Enlightened Ones. The last remnants of the Atlantean culture are destroyed. Great cities were built, then destroyed by nuclear explosions. All the inhabitants of the city of Peos are killed in one night by the eater of souls. Chunks of the continent break off and sink into the sea. There are earthquakes and tidal waves. Finally, only outcroppings like the cone-shaped island of Fernando Poo rise alone from the sea where Atlantis had been.

About 13,000 B.C. a new culture is planted on a hillside near the headwaters of the Euphrates and it starts to spread. A tribe of Cro-Magnons, magnificently tall, strong, large-headed people, is marched at gunpoint down from the snows of Europe to the fertile lands of the Middle East. They are taken to the site chosen for the first agricultural settlement and shown how to plant crops. For several years they do so while the Unbroken Circle's men guard them with flame throwers. Their generations pass rapidly, and once the new way of life has taken hold the Illuminated Ones leave them alone. The tribe divides into kings, priests, scribes, warriors, and farmers. A city surrounded by farms rises up. The kings and priests are soft, weak and fat. The peasants are stunted and dulled by malnutrition. The warriors are big and strong, but brutal and unintelligent. The scribes are intelligent, but thin and bloodless. Now the city makes war on neighboring tribes of barbarians. Being well organized and technologically superior, the people of the city win. They enslave the barbarians and plant other cities nearby. Then a great tribe of barbarians comes down from the north and conquers the civilized people and burns their city. This is not the end of the new civilization, though. It only revitalizes it. Soon the conquerors have learned to play the roles of kings, priests and warriors, and now there is a kind of nation consisting of several cities with a large body of armed men who must be kept occupied. Marching robotlike in great square formations, they set out over the plain to find new peoples to conquer. The sun shines down on the civilization created by the Illuminati. And below the sea the eye on the pyramid glares balefully upward.

THE END

Lights flashed on suddenly. The screen rolled up into its receptacle with a snap. Blinded, Joe rubbed his eyes. He had a ferocious headache. He also had a ferocious need to urinate at once, before his bladder exploded. He'd had an awful lot of drinks at the plastic martini party, then made love to that Chinese girl in the cab, then sat down to watch this movie without once taking time out to go to the bathroom. The pain in his groin was excruciating. He imagined it felt something like what Evoe, that fellow in the movie, had experienced after he castrated himself.

"Where the hell is the john?" said Joe loudly. There was no one in the room. While he was absorbed in the movie, they, doubtless having seen it before, had crept away softly, leaving him alone to watch the death of Atlantis.

"Christ's sake," he muttered. "Gotta take a leak. If I don't find the bathroom right away I'll pee in my pants." Then he noticed a wastepaper can under the table. It was walnut with a metal lining. He bent over and picked it up, sending new tremors of anguish through a body on the verge of bursting. He decided to use it as a receptacle, set it down again, unzipped his fly, took out his dick and let go into the can. What if they all came trooping back into the room now, he thought. Well, he would be embarrassed, but what the hell. It was their fault for springing this movie on him without giving him a chance to make himself comfortable. Joe looked somberly down into the foam.

"Piss on Atlantis," he muttered. Who the hell were those people he'd seen tonight? Simon and Padre and Big John had never told him about a group like this. Nor had they ever said anything about Atlantis. But there was the clear implication, if this movie was to be believed, that the Ancient Illuminated Seers of Bavaria might better be called the Ancient Illuminated Seers of Atlantis. And that the word "Ancient" meant a lot older than 1776.

It was clearly time to leave this place. He could try searching the offices, but he doubted whether he'd find anything, and, anyway, he was much too tired and hung over—not only from the alcohol he'd drunk, but also from the strange drug the Oriental girl had given him before the movie. Still, it had been a very nice drug. It had been Joe's habit since 1969, when he wasn't too busy and didn't have to get up early in the morning, to get stoned and watch late movies on television. He found this so enjoyable a pastime that he'd lost two girlfriends to it; they'd both wanted to go to bed when he was just settling down in front of the tube, laughing himself silly at the incredibly clever witticisms, marveling at the profundity of the philosophical aphorisms tossed off by the characters (such as Johnny's line in *Bitter Rice:* "I work all week and then on Sundays I watch other people ride the merry-go-round"—what a world of pathos had been expressed in that simple summation of a man's life) or appreciating, as one wordsmith does another, the complex subtlety of the commercials and the secret links between them and the movies into which they were inserted (like the slogan: "You can take the Salem out of the country but you can't take the country out of Salem," in the middle of *The Wolf Man).* All of this capacity for appreciating movies had been raised to a new high with the drug Mao Tsu-hsi had given him, and added to this it was a full-color movie on a large screen uninterrupted by commercials or, come to think of it, by fnords—and commercials no matter how trickily interwoven with the plot of the movie did tend to *seem* like interruptions, even to one who was stoned enough to know better. It had been a great movie. The best movie of his life. He would never forget it.

Joe tried the knob of the boardroom door and it

opened at once. He stopped, considering whether he should take out his pocket knife and carve "Malik was here" or some obscenity into the beautiful wood of the table. That would, he felt in an obscure way, let them know that he knew where they were at. But it would be a shame to spoil the wood, and besides, he was dreadfully tired. He walked through darkened outer corridors, staggered down the stairs and let himself out into the street. Looking toward the East River, he thought he could see light in the sky over Queens. Was the sun coming up? Had he been there that long?

A cab cruised by with its light on. Joe hailed it. Sinking into the back seat as he gave the driver his home address, he noticed that the man's name on his hack license was Albert Feather.

> Well, here's that ladder now,
> Come on, let's climb.
> The first rung is yours,
> The rest are mine.

Funny, thought Lieutenant Otto Waterhouse of the State's Attorney's Police. Every time things get hairy, that damn song starts going through my head. I must be an obsessive-compulsive neurotic. He'd first heard the song, "To Be a Man" by Len Chandler, at the home of a chick he was balling back in '65. It expressed pretty well for him his condition as a member of the tribe. The tribe, that was how he thought of black people; he'd heard a Jew refer to the Jews that way, and he liked it better than that soul brother shit. Deep down, he hated other blacks and he hated being black. You had to climb, that was the thing. You had to climb, each man alone.

When Otto Waterhouse was eight years old, a gang of black kids on the South Side had beaten him, knifed him and thrown him into Lake Michigan to drown. Otto didn't know how to swim, but somehow he'd pulled himself along the concrete pilings, clinging to rusty steel where there was nothing to cling to, his blood seeping out into the water, and he'd stayed there, hidden, till the gang went away. Then he pulled himself along to a ladder, climbed up and dragged himself onto the concrete pier. He lay there, almost dead, wondering if the gang would come back and finish him.

Someone did come along. A cop. The cop nudged Otto's body with his toe, rolled it over and looked down. Otto looked up at the Irish face, round, pig-nosed and blue-eyed.

"Oh, shit," said the cop, and walked on.

Somehow Otto lived till morning, when a woman came along and found him and called an ambulance. Years later, it seemed logical enough to him to join the police force. He knew the members of the gang that nearly killed him. He didn't bother with them until after he got on the force. Then he found cause to kill each of the gang members—several of whom had by then become respectable citizens—one by one. Most of them didn't know who he was or why he was killing them. The number he killed made his reputation in the Chicago Police Department. He was a nigger cop who could be trusted to deal with niggers.

Otto never did know who the cop was who'd left him to die—he remembered the face, more or less, but they all looked alike to him.

He had another oddly vivid memory, of a fall day in 1970 when he'd been walking through Pioneer Court and had hassled a dude who was giving out free samples of—of all things—tomato juice. Otto took a ten from the dude and drank some tomato juice. The guy had a crew haircut and wore horn-rimmed glasses. He didn't seem to mind having to pay a bribe, and he looked at Otto with an odd gleam in his eye as the tomato juice went down. For a moment, Otto thought the tomato juice might be poisoned. There were cop haters everywhere; many people seemed to have sworn to kill the "pigs" as they called them. But dozens of people had already drunk the juice and gone away happy. Otto shrugged and walked off.

Thinking back over the strange changes that had

come over him, Otto always traced them back to that moment. There had been something in the juice.

It wasn't till Stella Maris told him about AUM that he realized how he'd been had. And by then it was too late. He was a three-way loser, working for the Syndicate, the Illuminati and Discordian Movement. The only way out was down—down into the chaos with Stella pointing the way.

"Just tell me one thing, baby," he said to her one afternoon as they lay naked together in his apartment in Hyde Park. "Why did they pick you to contact me?"

"Because you hate niggers," said Stella calmly, running her finger down his dick. "You hate niggers worse than any white man does. That's why the way to freedom for you lies through me."

"And what about you?" he said angrily, pulling away from her and sitting up in bed. "I suppose you can't tell the difference between black and white. Black meat and white meat, it's all the same to you, ain't it, you goddamned *whore!*"

"You'd like to think so," said Stella. "You'd like to think only a nigger whore would lay you, a whore who'd lay anybody regardless of race. But you know you are wrong. You know that Otto Waterhouse, the black man who is better than all black men because he hates all black men, is a lie. It's you who can't tell the difference between black and white and thinks the black man should be where the white man is and hates the black man because he isn't white. No, I see color. But I see everything else about a person, too, baby. And I know that nobody is where they should be and everybody should be where they are."

"Oh, fuck your goddam philosophy," said Waterhouse. "Come here."

But he learned. He thought he'd learned everything Stella and Hagbard and the rest of them had to teach him. And that was a lot, piled on top of all that Illuminati garbage. But now they'd thrown him a total curve.

He was to kill.

The message came, as all the messages did, from Stella.

"Hagbard said to do this?"

"Yes."

"And I suppose, if I go along with this, I'll be told why later on, or I'll figure it out for myself? Goddam, Stella, this is asking a lot, you know."

"I know. Hagbard told me you have to do this for two reasons. First, for the honor of the Discordians, so that they will have respect."

"He *sounds* like a wop for once. But he's right. I understand that."

"Second. He said because Otto Waterhouse must kill a white man."

"What?" Otto started to tremble in the phone booth. He picked nervously, without reading it, at a sticker that said, THIS PHONE BOOTH RESERVED FOR CLARK KENT.

"Otto Waterhouse must kill a white man. He said you'd know what that meant."

Otto's hand was still shaking when he hung up. "Oh, *damn,"* he said. He was almost crying.

So now on April 28 he stood at a green metal door marked "1723." It was the service entrance to a condominium apartment at 2323 Lake Shore Drive. Behind him stood a dozen State's Attorney's police. All of them, like himself, were wearing body armor and baby-blue helmets with transparent plastic visors. Two were carrying submachine guns.

"All right," said Waterhouse, glancing at his watch. It had amused Flanagan to set the time for the raid at 5:23 A.M. It was 5:22:30. "Remember—shoot everything that moves." He kept his back to the men so they would not see the damned tears that insisted on welling up in his eyes.

"Right on, lieutenant," said Sergeant O'Banion satirically. Sergeant O'Banion hated blacks, but worse than that he hated filthy, lice-ridden, long-haired, homosexual, Communist-inspired Morituri bomb manufacturers. He believed that there was a whole disgusting nest of them, sleeping together, dirty naked bodies entwined, like a can full of worms, just on the other side of that green metal door. He could see them. He licked his lips. He was going to clean them out. He hefted the machine gun.

"Okay," said Waterhouse. It was 5:23. Shielding himself with one gloved hand, he pointed his .45 at the lock on the door. The instructions given orally by Flanagan at the briefing were that they would not show a warrant or even knock before entering. The apartment was said to be full of enough dynamite to wipe out the entire block of luxury high-rise apartment houses. Presumably the kids, if they knew they were caught, would set them off. That way they could take a bunch of pigs with them, preserve their reputation for suicidal bravery, protect themselves from giving away any information, use the explosives and avoid having to live with the shaming knowledge that they'd been dumb enough to get caught.

O'Banion was imagining finding a white girl in the arms of a black boy and finishing them off with one burst from his machine gun. His cock swelled in his pants.

Waterhouse fired.

In the next instant he threw his weight against the door and smashed it open. He was in a hallway next to the kitchen. He walked into the apartment. His shoes rang on a bare tile floor. Tears ran down his cheeks.

"My God, my God, why have you forsaken me?" he sobbed.

"Who's that?" a voice called. Waterhouse, whose eyes had adjusted to the darkness, looked across the empty living room into the foyer, where Milo A. Flanagan stood silhouetted in the light from the exterior hall.

Waterhouse raised the heavy automatic in his hand to arm's length, sighted carefully, took a deep breath and held it and squeezed the trigger. The pistol blasted and kicked his hand and the black figure went toppling backwards into the startled arms of the men behind him.

A bat which had been sitting on a windowsill flew out the open window toward the lake. Only Waterhouse saw it.

O'Banion came clumping into the room. He took a bent-kneed stance and fired a burst of six rounds in the direction of the front door.

"Hold it!" Waterhouse snapped. "Hold your fire. Something's wrong." Something would really be wrong if the guys at the front door came through again, shooting. "Turn on the lights, O'Banion," Waterhouse said.

"There's somebody in here shooting."

"We're standing here talking, O'Banion. No one is shooting at us. Find a light switch."

"They're gonna set off the bombs!" O'Banion's voice was shrill with fear.

"With the lights on, O'Banion, we'll see them doing it. Maybe we'll even be able to stop them."

O'Banion ran to the wall and began slapping it with the palm of one hand while he kept his machine gun cradled in the free arm. One of the other men who had followed O'Banion through the service entrance found the light switch.

The apartment was bare. There was no furniture. There were no rugs on the floor, no curtains on the windows. Whoever had been living here had vanished.

The front door opened a crack. Before they could start shooting Waterhouse yelled, "It's all right. It's Waterhouse in here. There's nobody here." He wasn't crying anymore. It was done. He had killed his first white man.

The door swung all the way open. "Nobody *there?*" said the helmeted policeman. "Who the hell shot Flanagan?"

"Flanagan?" said Waterhouse.

"Flanagan's dead. They got him."

"There isn't anybody here," said O'Banion, who had been looking through side rooms. "What the hell went wrong? Flanagan set this up personally."

Now that the light was on, Waterhouse could see that someone had drawn a pentagram in chalk on the floor. In the center of the pentagram was a gray envelope. Otto picked it up. There was a circular green seal on the back with the word ERIS embossed on it. Otto opened it and read:

> Good going, Otto. Now proceed at once to Ingolstadt, Bavaria. The bastards are trying to immanentize the Eschaton.
>
> S-M

Folding the note and shoving it into his pocket as he holstered his pistol with his other hand, Otto Waterhouse strode across the living room. He barely glanced down at the body of Milo A. Flanagan, the bullet hole in the center of his forehead like a third eye. Hagbard had been right. Despite all the advance terror and sorrow, once he'd done it, he didn't feel a thing. I have met the enemy and he is mine, he thought.

Otto pushed past the men crowded around Flanagan's body. Everyone assumed he was going somewhere to make some sort of report. No one had figured out who shot Flanagan.

By the time O'Banion had puzzled it out, Otto was already in his car. Six hours later, when they had set up blockades at the airports and railway terminals, Otto was in Minneapolis International Airport buying a ticket to Montreal. He had to fly back to Chicago, but he sat out the brief stopover at O'Hare International Airport aboard the plane, while his brother officers searched the terminals for him. Twelve hours later, carrying a passport supplied by Montreal Discordians, Otto Waterhouse was on his way to Ingolstadt.

"Ingolstadt," said FUCKUP. Hagbard had programmed the machine to converse in reasonably good English this week. "The largest rock festival in the history of mankind, the largest temporary gathering of human beings ever assembled, will take place near Ingolstadt on the shore of Lake Totenkopf. Two million young people from all over the world are expected. The American Medical Association will play."

"Did you know or suspect before this that the American Medical Association, Wolfgang, Werner, Wilhelm and Winifred Saure, are four of the Illuminati Primi?" asked Hagbard.

"They were on a list, but fourteenth in order of probability," said FUCKUP. "Perhaps some of the other groups I suspected are Illuminati Veri."

"Can you now state the nature of the crisis that we will face this week?"

There was a pause. "There were three crises for this month. Plus several subcrises designed to bring the three major crises to a peak. The first was Fernando Poo. The world nearly went to war over the Fernando Poo coup, but the Illuminati had a countercoup in reserve and that resolved the problem satisfactorily. Heads of state are human and this feint has helped to make them jumpier and more irrational. They are in no shape to react wisely to the next two jolts. Unless you wish me to continue discussing the character structures of the present heads of state—which are important elements in the crises through which the world is passing—I will proceed to the next crisis. This is Las Vegas. I still do not know exactly what is going on there, but the sickness vibrations are still coming through strongly. There is, I have deduced from recently acquired information, a bacteriological warfare research center located in the desert somewhere near Las Vegas. One of my more mystical probes came up with the sentence, 'The ace in the hole is poisoned candy.' But that's one of those things that we probably won't understand until we find out what's going on in Las Vegas by more conventional means."

"I've already dispatched Muldoon and Goodman there," said Hagbard. "All right, FUCKUP, obviously the third crisis is Ingolstadt. What's going to happen at that rock festival?"

"They intend to use the Illuminati science of strategic biomysticism. Lake Totenkopf is one of Europe's famed 'bottomless lakes,' which means it has an outlet into the underground Sea of Valusia. At the end of World War II Hitler had an entire S.S. division in reserve in Bavaria. He was planning to withdraw to Obersalzburg and, with this fanatically loyal division, make a glorious last stand in the Bavarian Alps. Instead the Illuminati convinced him that he still had a chance to win the war, if he followed their instructions. Hitler, Himmler and Bormann fed cyanide to all the troops, killing several thousand of them. Then their bodies, dressed in full field equipment, were placed by divers on a huge underground plateau near where the Sea of Valusia surfaces as Lake Totenkopf. Their boots were weighted at the bottom so that they would stand at attention. The airplanes, tanks and artillery assigned to the division were also weighted and sunk along with the troops. Many of them, by the way, knew that there was cyanide in their last supper, but they ate it anyway. If the Fuehrer thought it best to kill them, that was good enough for them."

"I can't imagine there would be much left of them after over thirty years," said Hagbard.

"You are wrong as usual, Hagbard," said FUCKUP. "The S.S. men were placed under a biomystical protective field. The entire division is as good as it was the day it was placed there. Of course, the Illuminati had tricked Hitler and Himmler. The real purpose of the mass sacrifice was to provide enough explosively released consciousness energy to make it possible to translate Bormann to the immortal energy plane. Bormann, one of the Illuminati Primi of his day, was to be rewarded for his part in organizing World War II. The fifty million violent deaths of that war helped many Illuminati to achieve transcendental illumination and were most pleasing to their elder brothers and allies, the lloigor."

"And what will happen at Ingolstadt during the festival?"

"The American Medical Association's fifth number

at Woodstock Europa will send out biomystical waves that will activate the Nazi legions in the lake, and send them marching up the shore. They will be, in their resurrection, endowed with supernormal strength and energy, making them almost impossible to kill. And they will achieve even greater powers as a result of the burst of consciousness energy that will be released when they massacre the millions of young people on the shore. Then, led by the Saures, they will turn against Eastern Europe. The Russians, already made extremely nervous by the Fernando Poo incident, will think an army is attacking them from the West. Their old fear that Germany will once again, with the help of the capitalist powers, rise up and attack Russia and slaughter Russians for the third time in this century will become a reality. They will find that conventional weapons will not stop the resurrected Nazis. They will believe they are up against some new kind of American superweapon, that the Americans have decided to launch a sneak attack. The Russians will then start bringing superweapons of their own into play. Then the Illuminati will play their ace in the hole in Las Vegas, whatever that is." The voice of the computer, coming from Hagbard's Polynesian teakwood desk, was suddenly silent.

"What happens after that?" said Hagbard, leaning forward tensely. George saw perspiration on his forehead.

"It doesn't matter what happens after that," said FUCKUP. "If the situation develops as I project, the Eschaton will have been immanentized. For the Illuminati, that will mean the fulfillment of the project that has been their goal since the days of Gruad. A total victory. They will all simultaneously achieve transcendental illumination. For the human race, on the other hand, that will be extinction. The end."

BOOK FOUR

BEAMTENHERRSCHAFT

Well, Hoover performed. He would have fought.
That was the point. He would have defied a few
people. He would have scared them to death. He
has a file on everybody.
—Richard Milhous Nixon

THE EIGHTH TRIP, OR HOD
(TELEMACHUS SNEEZED)

There came unto the High Chapperal one who had studied in the schools of the Purple Sage and of the Hung Mung Tong and of the Illuminati and of the many other schools; and this one had found no peace yet.

Yea: of the Discordians and the teachers of Mummu and of the Nazarene and of the Buddha he had studied; and he had found no peace yet.

And he spake to the High Chapperal and said: Give me a sign, that I may believe.

And the High Chapperal said unto him: Leave my presence, and seek ye the horizon and the sign shall come unto you, and ye shall seek no more.

And the man turned and sought of the horizon; but the High Chapperal crept up behind him and raised his foot and did deliver a most puissant kick in the man's arse, which smarted much and humiliated the seeker grievously.

He who has eyes, let him read and understand.

—"The Book of Grandmotherly Kindness,"
The Dishonest Book of Lies, by Mordecai Malignatus, K.N.S.

The Starry Wisdom Church was not 00005's idea of a proper ecclesiastical shop by any means. The architecture was a shade too Gothic, the designs on the stained-glass windows a bit unpleasantly suggestive for a holy atmosphere ("My God, they must be bloody wogs," he thought), and when he opened the door, the altar was lacking a proper crucifix. In fact, where the crucifix should have been he found instead a design that was more than suggestive. It was, in his opinion, downright tasteless.

Not High Church at all, Chips decided.

He advanced cautiously, although the building appeared deserted. The pews seemed designed for bloody reptiles, he observed—a church, of course, should be uncomfortable, that was good for the soul, but this was, well, gross. They probably advertise in the kink newspapers, he reflected with distaste. The first stained-glass window was worse from inside than outside; he didn't know who Saint Toad was, but if that mosaic with his name on it gave any idea of Saint Toad's appearance and predelictions, then, by God, no self-respecting Christian congregation would ever think of sanctifying him. The next feller, a shoggoth, was even less appetizing; at least they had the common decency not to canonize *him*.

A rat scurried out from between two pews and ran across the center aisle, right before Chip's feet.

Fair got on one's nerves, this place did.

Chips approached the pulpit and glanced up at the Bible. That was, at least, one civilized touch. Curious as to what text might have been preached last in this den of wogs, he scrambled up into the pulpit and scanned the open pages. To his consternation, it wasn't the Bible at all. A lot of bragging and bombast about some Yog Sothoth, probably a wog god, who was both the Gate and the Guardian of the Gate. Absolute rubbish. Chips hefted the enormous volume and turned it so he could read the spine. *Necronomicon,* eh? If his University Latin could be trusted, that was something like "the book of the names of the dead." Morbid, like the whole building.

He approached the altar, refusing to look at the abominable design above it. Rust—now what could one say of brutes who let their altar get rusty? He scraped with his thumbnail. The altar was marble, *and marble doesn't rust.* A decidedly unpleasant suspicion crossed his mind, and he tasted what his nail had lifted. Blood. Fairly fresh blood.

Not High Church at all.

Chips approached the vestry, and walked into a web.

"Damn," he muttered, hacking at it with his flash-light—and something fell on his shoulder. He brushed it off quickly and turned the light to the floor. It started to run up his trouser leg and he brushed it off again, beginning to breathe heavily, and stepped on it hard. There was a satisfactory snapping sound and he stomped again to be sure. When he removed his shoe and turned the light down again, it was dead.

A damned huge ugly brute of a spider. Black gods, Saint Toads, rats, mysterious and heathenish capital-ized Gates, that nasty-looking shoggoth character, and now spiders. A buggering tarantula it looked like, in fact. Next, Count Dracula, he thought grimly, testing the vestry door. It slid open smoothly and he stepped back out of visible range, waiting a moment.

They were either not home or cool enough to allow him the next move.

He stepped through the door and flashed his light around.

"Oh, God, no," he said. "No. God, *no*."

"Good-bye, Mr. Chips," said Saint Toad.

Did you ever take the underground from Charing Cross to one of the suburbs? You know, that long ride without stops when you're totally in the dark and ev-erything seems to be rushing by outside in the opposite direction? Relativity, the laboratory-smock people call it. In fact, it was even more like going up a chimney than going forward in a tunnel, but it was like both at the same time, if you follow me. Relativity. A bitter-looking old man went by, dressed in turn-of-the-cen-tury Yankee clothing, muttering something about "Carcosa." An antique Pontiac car followed him, with four Italians in it looking confused—it was slow enough for me to spot the year, definitely 1936, and even to read the license plates, Rhode Island AW-1472. Then a black man, not a Negro or a wog, but a really truly black man, without a face and I'd hate to tell you what he had where the face should have been. All the while, there was this bleating or squealing that seemed to say "Tekeli-li! Tekeli-li!" Another man, English-looking but in early 19th-century clothing; he looked my way, surprised, and said, "I only walked around the horses!" I could sympathize: I only opened a bleeding door. A giant beetle, who looked at me more intelligently than any bug I ever saw before—he seemed to be going in a different direction, if there was direction in this place. A white-haired old man with startling blue eyes, who shouted "Roderick Usher!" as he flew by. Then a whole parade of pentagons and other mathematical shapes that seemed to be talking to each other in some language of the past or the future or wherever they called home. And by now it wasn't so much like a tunnel or even a chimney but a kind of roller coaster with dips and loops but not the sort you find in a place like Brighton—I think I saw this kind of curve once, on a blackboard, when a class in non-Euclidean geometry had used the room before my own class in Eng Lit Pope to Swinb. and Neo-Raph. Then I passed a shoggoth or it passed me, and let me say that their pictures simply do not do them justice: I am ready to go anywhere and confront any peril on H.M. Service but I pray to the Lord Harry I never have to get that close to one of those chaps again. Next came a jerk, or cusp is probably the word: I recognized something: Ingolstadt, the middle of the university. Then we were off again, but not for long, another cusp: Stonehenge. A bunch of hooded people, right out of a Yank movie about the KKK, were busy with some gruesome mummery right in the center of the stones, yelling ferociously about some ruddy goat with a thousand young, and the stars were all wrong overhead. Well, you pick up your education where you can—now I know, even if I can't tell any bloody academic how I know, that Stonehenge is much older than we think. Whizz, bang, we're off again, and now ships are floating by—everything from old Yankee clippers to modern luxury liners, all of them signaling the old S.O.S. semaphore desperately—and a bunch of airplanes following in their wake. I realized that part must be the Bermuda Triangle, and about then it dawned that the turn-of-the-century Yank with the bitter face might be Ambrose Bierce. I still hadn't the foggiest who all those other chaps were. Then along came a girl, a dog, a lion, a tin man and a scarecrow. A real puzzler, that: was I visiting real places or just places in people's minds? Or was there a difference? When the mock turtle, the walrus, the carpenter and another little girl came along, my faith in the difference began to crumble. Or did some of those writer blokes know how to tap into this alternate world or fifth dimension or whatever it was? The shoggoth came by again (or was it his twin brother?) and shouted, or I should say, gibbered, "Yog Sothoth Neblod Zin," and I could tell that was something perfectly filthy by the tone of his voice. I mean, after all, I can take a queer proposition without biffing the offender on the nose—one must be cosmopolitan, you know—but I would vastly prefer to have such offers coming out of human mouths, or at the very least out of mouths rather than orifices that shouldn't properly be talking at all. But you would have to see a shoggoth yourself, God forbid, to appreciate what I mean. The next stop was quite a refrigerator, miles and miles of it, and that's where the creature who kept up that howling of "Tekeli-li! Tekeli-li!" hung his hat. Or its hat. I shan't attempt to do him, or it, justice. That *Necronomicon* said about Yog Sothoth that "Kadath in the cold waste hath known him," and now I realized that "known" was used there in the Biblical sense. I just hope he, or it, stays in the cold waste. You wouldn't want to meet him, or it, on the Strand at midday, believe me. His habits were even worse than his ancestry, and why he couldn't scrape off some of the seaweed and barnacles is beyond me; he was rather like Saint Toad in his notions of sartorial splendor and table etiquette, if you take my meaning. But I was off again, the curvature was getting sharper and the cusps more frequent. There was no mistaking the Heads where I arrived next: Easter Island. I had a moment to reflect on how those Heads resembled Tlaloc and the lloigor of Fernando Poo and then this

kink's version of a Cook's Tour moved on, and there I
was at the last stop.

"Damn, blast and thunder!" I said, looking at Manolete turning his veronica and Concepcion lying there
with her poor throat cut. "Now that absolutely does
tear it."

I decided not to toddle over to the Starry Wisdom
Church this time around. There *is* a limit, after all.

Instead, I went out into Tequila y Mota Street and
approached the church but kept my distance, trying to
figure where BUGGER kept the Time Machine.

While I was reflecting on that, I heard the first pistol
shot.

Then a volley.

The next thing I knew the whole population of Fernando Poo—Cubans descended from the prisoners
shipped there when it was a penal colony in the 19th
century, Spaniards from colonial days, blacks, wogs,
and whatnot—were on Tequila y Mota street using up
all the munitions they owned. It was the countercoup,
of course—the Captain Puta crowd who unseated
Tequila y Mota and prevented the nuclear war—but I
didn't know that at the time, so I dashed into the
nearest doorway and tried to duck the flying bullets,
which were coming, mind you, as thick as the darling
buds in May. It was hairy. And one Spanish bloke—
gay as a tree full of parrots from his trot and his car-
riage, goes by waving an old cutlass out of a book and
shouting, "Better to die on our feet than to live on our
knees!"—headed straightway into a group of Regular
Army who had finally turned out to try to stop this
business. He waded right into them, cutting heads like
a pirate, until they shot him as full of holes as Auntie's
drawers. That's your Spaniards: even the queers have
balls.

Well, this wasn't my show, so I backed up, opened
the door and stepped into the building. I just had a moment to recognize *which* building I had picked, when
Saint Toad gave me his bilious eye and said, "You
again!"

The trip was less interesting this time (I had seen it before, after all) and I had time to think a bit and realize that old frog-face wasn't using a Time Machine or any mechanical device at all. Then I was in front of a pyramid—they missed that stop last time—and I waited to arrive back in the Hotel Durrutti. To my surprise, when there was a final jerk in the dimensions or whatever they were, I found myself someplace else.

00005, in fact, was in an enormous marbled room deliberately designed to impress the bejesus out of any and all visitors. Pillars reached up to cyclopean heights, supporting a ceiling too high and murky to be visible, and every wall, of which there seemed to be five, was the same impenetrable ivory-grained marble. The eyes instinctively sought the gigantic throne, in the shape of an apple with a seat carved out of it, and made of a flawless gold which gleamed the more brightly in the dim lighting; and the old man who sat on the throne, his white beard reaching almost to the lap of his much whiter robe, commanded attention when he spoke: "If I may be trite," he said in a resonant voice, "you are welcome, my son."

This still wasn't High Church, but it was a definite improvement over the digs where Saint Toad and his loathsome objets d'art festered. Still, 00005's British common sense was disturbed. "I say," he ventured, "you're not some sort of mystic, are you? I must tell you that I don't intend to convert to anything heathen."

"Conversion, as you understand it," the aged figure told him placidly, "consists of pounding one's own words into a man's ears until they start coming out of his mouth. Nothing is of less interest to me. You need have no fear on that ground."

"I see." 00005 pondered. "This wouldn't be Shangri-La or some such place, would it?"

"This is Dallas, Texas, my son." The old man's eyes bore a slight twinkle although his demeanor otherwise remained grave. "We are below the sewers of Dealy Plaza, and I am the Dealy Lama."

00005 shook his head. "I don't mind having my leg pulled," he began.

"I am the Dealy Lama," the old man repeated, "and this is the headquarters of the Erisian Liberation Front."

"A joke's a joke," Chips said, "but how did you manage that frog-faced creature back in the Starry Wisdom Church?"

"Tsathoggua? He is not managed by us. We saved you from him, in fact. Twice."

"Tsathoggua?" Chips repeated. "I thought the swine's name was Saint Toad."

"To be sure, that is one of his names. When he first appeared, in Hyperborea, he was known as Tsathoggua, and that is how he is recorded in the Pnakotic Manuscripts, the *Necronomicon* and other classics. The Atlantean high priests, Klarkash Ton and Lhuv Kerapht, wrote the best descriptions of him, but their works have not survived, except in our own archives."

"You *do* put on a good front," 00005 said sincerely. "I suppose, fairly soon, you'll get around to telling me that I have been brought here due to some karma or other?" He was actually wishing there were some place to sit down. No doubt, it added to the Lama's dignity to sit while Chips had to stand, but it had been a hard night already and his feet hurt.

"Yes, I have many revelations for you," the old man said.

"I was afraid of that. Isn't there some place where I can bring my arse to anchor, as my uncle Sid would say, before I listen to your wisdom? I'm sure it's going to be a long time in the telling."

The old man ignored this. "This is the turning point in history," he said. "All the forces of Evil, dispersed and often in conflict before, have been brought together under one sign, the eye in the pyramid. All the forces of Good have been gathered, also, under the sign of the apple."

"I see," 00005 nodded. "And you want to enlist me on the side of Good?"

"Not at all," the old man cried, bouncing up and down in his seat with laughter. "I want to invite you to stay here with us while the damned fools fight it out aboveground."

00005 frowned. "That isn't a sporting attitude," he said disapprovingly; but then he grinned. "Oh, I almost fell for it, didn't I? You *are* pulling my leg!"

"I am telling you the truth," the old man said vehemently. "How do you suppose I have lived to this advanced age? By running off to join in every idiotic barroom brawl, world war, or Armageddon that comes along? Let me remind you of the street where we picked you up; it is entirely typical of the proceedings during the Kali Yuga. Those imbeciles are using live ammunition, son. Do you want me to tell you the secret of longevity, lad—*my* secret? I have lived so outrageously long because," he spoke with deliberate emphasis, "I don't give a fuck for Good and Evil."

"I should be ashamed to say so, if I were you," Chips replied coolly. "If the whole world felt like you, we'd all be a sorry kettle of fish."

"Very well," the old man started to raise an arm. "I'll send you back to Saint Toad."

"Wait!" Chips stirred uneasily. "Couldn't you send me to confront Evil in one of its, ah, more human forms?"

"Aha," the old man sneered. "You want the lesser Evil, is it? Those false choices are passing away, even as we speak. If you want to confront Evil, you will have to confront it on its own terms, not in the form that suits your own mediocre concepts of a Last Judgment. Stay here with me, lad. Evil is much more nasty than you imagine."

"Never," Chips said firmly. " 'Ours not to reason why, Ours but to do or die!' Any Englishman would tell you the same."

"No doubt," the old man snickered. "Your countrymen are as fat-headed as these Texans above us. Glorifying that idiotic Light Brigade the way these bumpkins brag about their defeat at the Alamo! As if stepping in front of a steamroller were the most admirable thing a man could do with his time. Let me tell you a story, son."

"You may if you wish," 00005 said stiffly. "But no cynical parable will change my sense of Right and Duty."

"Actually, you're glad of the interlude; you're not all that eager to face the powers of Tsathoggua again. Let that pass." The old man shifted to a more comfortable position and, still oblivious of Chips' tired shifting from leg to leg, began:

This is the story of Our Lady of Discord, Eris, daughter of Chaos, mother of Fortuna. You have read some of it in Bullfinch, no doubt, but his is the exoteric version. I am about to give you the Inside Story.

Is the thought of a unicorn a real thought? In a sense, that is the basic question of philosophy—

I thought you were going to tell me a story, not launch into some dreary German metaphysics. I had enough of that at the University.

Quite so. The thought of a unicorn is a real thought, then, to be brief. So is the thought of the Redeemer on the Cross, the Cow who Jumped Over the Moon, the lost continent of Mu, the Gross National Product, the Square Root of Minus One, and anything else capable of mobilizing emotional energy. And so, in a sense, Eris and the other Olympians were, and are, real. At the same time, in another sense, there is only one True God and your redeemer in His only begotten son; and the lloigor, like Tsathoggua, are real enough to reach out and draw you into their world, which is on the other side of Nightmare. But I promised to keep the philosophy to a minimum.

You recall the story of the Golden Apple, in the exoteric and expurgated version at least? The true version is the same, up to a point. Zeus, a terrible old bore by the way, did throw a bash on Olympus, and he did slight Our Lady by not inviting Her. She did make an apple, but it was Acapulco Gold, not metallic gold. She wrote Korhhisti, on it, *to the prettiest one,* and rolled it into the banquet hall. Everybody—not just the goddesses; that's a male chauvinist myth—started fighting over who had the right to smoke it. Paris was never called in to pass judgment; that's all some poet's fancy. The Trojan War was just another imperialistic rumble and had no connection with these events at all.

What really happened was that everybody was squabbling over the apple and working up a sweat and pushing one another around and pretty soon their vibrations—Gods have very high vibration, exactly at the speed of light, in fact—heated up the apple enough to unleash some heavy fumes. In a word, the Olympians all got stoned.

And they saw a Vision, or a series of Visions.

In the first Vision, they saw Yahweh, a neighboring god with a world of his own which overlapped theirs in some places. He was clearing the set to change its valence and start a new show. His method struck them as rather barbarous. He was, in fact, drowning everybody—except one family that he allowed to escape in an Ark.

"This is Chaos," said Hermes. "That Yahweh is a *mean* mother', even for a god."

And they looked at the Vision more closely, and because they could see into the future and were all (like every intelligent entity) rabid Laurel and Hardy fans and because they were zonked on the weed, they saw that Yahweh bore the face of Oliver Hardy. All around him, below the mountain on which he lived (his world was flat), the waters rose and rose. They saw drowning men, drowning women, innocent babes sinking beneath the waves. They were ready to vomit. And then Another came and stood beside Yahweh, looking at the panorama of horrors below, and he was Yahweh's Adversary, and, stoned as they were, he looked like Stanley Laurel to them. And then Yahweh spoke, in the eternal words of Oliver Hardy: "Now look what *you* made me do," he said.

And that was the first Vision.

They looked again, and they saw Lee Harvey Os-

wald perched in the window of the Texas School Book
Depository; and he, again, wore the face of Stanley
Laurel. And, because this world had been created by a
great god named Earl Warren, Oswald fired the only
shots that day, and John Fitzgerald Kennedy was, as
the Salvation Army charmingly expresses it, "promoted
to glory."

"This is Confusion," said Athena with her owl-eyes
flashing, for she was more familiar with the world
created by the god Mark Lane.

Then they saw a hallway, and Oswald-Laurel was
led out between two policemen. Suddenly Jack Ruby,
with the face of Oliver Hardy, stepped forward and
fired a pistol right into that frail little body. And then
Ruby spoke the eternal words, to the corpse at his feet:
"Now look what *you* made me do," he said.

And that was the second Vision.

Next, they saw a city of 550,000 men, women and
children, and in an instant the city vanished; shadows
remained where the men were gone, a firestorm raged,
burning pimps and infants and an old statue of a happy Buddha and mice and dogs and old men and lovers;
and a mushroom cloud arose above it all. This was in
a world created by the cruelest of all gods, *Realpolitik*.

"This is Discord," said Apollo, disturbed, laying
down his lute.

Harry Truman, a servant of Realpolitik, wearing the
face of Oliver Hardy, looked upon his work and saw
that it was good. But beside him, Albert Einstein, a
servant of that most elusive and gnomic of gods, Truth,
burst into tears, the familiar tears of Stanley Laurel
facing the consequences of his own karma. For a brief
instant, Truman was troubled, but then he remembered
the eternal words: "Now look what *you* made me do,"
he said.

And that was the third Vision.

Now they saw trains, many trains, all of them running on time, and the trains criss-crossed Europe and
ran 24 hours a day, and they all came to a few destina-

tions that were alike. There, the human cargo was stamped, catalogued, processed, executed with gas, tabulated, recorded, stamped again, cremated and disposed.

"This is Bureaucracy," said Dionysus, and he smashed his wine jug in anger; beside him, his lynx glared balefully.

And then they saw the man who had ordered this, Adolf Hitler, wearing still the mask of Oliver Hardy, and he turned to a certain rich man, Baron Rothschild, wearing the mask of Stanley Laurel, and they knew this was the world created by the god Hegel and the angel Thesis was meeting the demon Antithesis. Then Hitler spoke the eternal words: "Now look what *you* made me do," he said.

And that was the fourth Vision.

They did then look further and, lo, high as they were they saw the founding of a great republic and proclamations hailing new gods named Due Process and Equal Rights for All. And they saw many in high places in the republic form a separate cult and worship Mammon and Power. And the Republic became an Empire, and soon Due Process and Equal Rights for All were not worshipped, and even Mammon and Power were given only lip-service, for the true god of all was now the impotent What Can I Do and his dull brother What We Did Yesterday and his ugly and vicious sister Get Them Before They Get Us.

"This is Aftermath," said Hera, and her bosom shook with tears for the fate of the children of that nation.

And they saw many bombings, many riots, many rooftop snipers, many Molotov cocktails. And they saw the capital city in ruins, and the leader, wearing the face of Stanley Laurel, taken prisoner amid the rubble of his palace. And they saw the chief of the revolutionaries look about at the rubble and the streets full of corpses, and they heard him sigh, and then he addressed the leader, and he spoke the eternal words: "Now look what *you* made me do," he said.

And that was the fifth Vision.

And now the Olympians were coming down and they looked at each other in uncertainty and dismay. Zeus himself spoke first.

"Man," he said, "that was Heavy Grass."

"Far fuckin out," Hermes agreed solemnly.

"Tree fuckin mendous," added Dionysus, petting his lynx.

"We were really fuckin *into* it," Hera summed up, for all.

And they turned their eyes again on the Golden Apple and read the word Our Lady Eris had written upon it, that most multiordinal of all words, Korhhisti. And they knew that each god and goddess, and each man and woman, was in the privacy of the heart, the prettiest one, the fairest; the most innocent, the Best. And they repented themselves of not having invited Our Lady Eris to their party, and they summoned her forth and asked her, "Why did you never tell us before that all categories are false and all Good and Evil a delusion of limited perspective?"

And Eris said, "As men and women are actors on a stage of our devising, so are we actors on the stage devised by the Five Fates. You had to believe in Good and Evil and pass judgments on your creatures, the men and women below. It was a curse the Fates put upon you! But now you have come to the Great Doubt and you are free."

The Olympians thereupon lost interest in the god-game and soon were forgotten by humanity. For She had shown them a great Light, and a great Light destroys shadows; and we are all, gods and mortals, nothing else but gliding shadows. Do you believe that?

"No," said Fission Chips.

"Very well," the Dealy Lama said somberly. "Begone, back to the world of maya!"

And Fission Chips whirled head over heels into a vortex of bleatings and squealings, as time and space were given another sharp tug and, nearly a month later, head *over heels, the Midget is up and tottering*

across Route 91 as the rented Ford Brontosaurus
shrieks to a stop and Saul and Barney are out the
doors (every cop instinct telling them that a man who
runs from an accident is hiding something) but John
Dillinger, driving toward Vegas from the north, continues to hum "Good-bye forever, old sweethearts and
gals, God . . . bless . . . you . . ." *and the same tug*
in space-time grips Adam Weishaupt two centuries ear-
lier, causing him to abandon his planned soft sell and
blurt out to an astonished Johann Wolfgang von
Goethe, "Spielen Sie Strip Schnipp-Schnapp?" and
Chips, hearing Weishaupt's words, is back in the
graveyard at Ingolstadt as four dark figures move away
in dusk.

"*Strip Schnipp-Schnapp?*" Goethe asks, putting hand
on chin in a pose that was later to become famous,
"*Das ist dein hoch Zauberwerk?*"

"*Ja, ja,*" Weishaupt says nervously, "*Der Zweck*
heiligte die Mittel."

Ingolstadt always reminds me of the set of a bleeding Frankenstein movie, and, after Saint Toad and that
shoggoth chap and the old Lama with his wog metaphysics, it was no help at all to have an invisible voice
ask me to join him in a bawdy card game. I've faced
some weird scenes in H.M. Service but this Fernando
Poo caper was turning out to be outright unwholesome,
in fact *unheimlich* as these krauts would say. And, in
the distance, I began to hear wog music, but with a
Yank beat to it, and suddenly I knew the worst: that
blasted Lama or Saint Toad or somebody had lifted
nearly a month out of my life. I had walked into Saint
Toad's after midnight on March 31 (call it April 1,
then) and this would be April 30 or May 1. *Walpur-*
gisnacht. When all the kraut ghosts are out. And I was
probably considered dead back in London. And if I
called in and tried to explain what had happened, old
W. would be downright *psychiatric* about the matter,
oh, he'd be sure I was well around the bend. It was a
rum go either way.

Then I remembered that the old Lama in Dallas had

said he was sending me to the final battle between Good and Evil. This was probably it, right here, right now, this night in Ingolstadt. A bit breathtaking to think of that. I wondered when the Angels of the Lord would appear: bloody soon, I hoped. It would be nice to have them around when Old Nick unleashed the shoggoth and Saint Toad and that lot.

So I toddled out into the streets of Ingolstadt and started sniffing around for the old sulphur and brimstone.

And half a mile below and twelve hours earlier, George Dorn and Stella Maris were smoking some Alamout Black hash with Harry Coin.

"You haven't got a bad punch for an intellectual," Coin said with warm regard.

"You're pretty good at rape yourself," George replied, "for the world's most incompetent assassin."

Coin started to draw back his lips in an angry snarl, but the hash was too strong. "Hagbard told you, Ace?" he asked bashfully.

"He told me most of it," George said. "I know that everybody on this ship once worked for the Illuminati directly or for one of their governments. I know that Hagbard has been an outlaw for more than two decades—"

"Twenty-three years exactly," Stella said archly.

"That figures," George nodded. "Twenty-three years, then, and never killed anybody until that incident with the spider ships four days ago."

"Oh, he *killed* us," Harry said dreamily, drawing on the pipe. "What he does is worse than capital punishment, while it's going on. I can't say I'm the same man I was before. But it's pretty bad until you come through."

"I know," George grinned. "I've had a few samples myself."

"Hagbard's system," Stella said, "is very simple. He just gives you a good look at your own face in a mirror. He lets you see the puppet strings. It's still up to you to break them. He's never forced anyone to do anything that goes against their heart. Of course," she frowned in concentration, "he does sort of maneuver you into places where you have to find out in a hurry just what your heart *is* saying to you. Did he ever tell you about the Indians?"

"The Shoshone?" George asked. "The cesspool gag?"

"Let's play a game," Coin interrupted, sinking lower in his chair as the hash hit him harder. "One of us in this room is a Martian, and we've got to guess from the conversation which one it is."

"Okay," Stella said easily. "Not the Shoshone," she told George, "the Mohawk."

"You're not the Martian," Coin giggled. "You stick to the subject, and that's a human trait."

George, trying to decide if the octopus on the wall was somehow connected with the Martian riddle, said, "I want to hear about Hagbard and the Mohawk. Maybe that will help us identify the Martian. You think up good games," he added kindly, "for a guy who was sent on seven assassination missions and fucked up every one of them."

"I'm dumb but I'm lucky," Coin said. "There was always somebody else there blasting away at the same time. Politicians are *awfully* unpopular these days, Ace."

This was a myth, Hagbard had confided to George. Until Harry Coin had completed his course in the Celine System, it was better if he believed himself the world's most unsuccessful assassin rather than face the truth: that he had goofed only on his first job (Dallas, November 22, 1963) and really had killed five men since then. Of course, even if Hagbard wasn't a holy man any longer, he was still tricky: maybe Harry had, indeed, missed every time. Perhaps Hagbard was keeping the image of Harry as mass murderer in George's mind to see if George could relate to the man's present instead of being hung up on his "past."

At least I've learned this much, George thought. The word "past" is always in quotes for me, now.

"The Mohawk," Stella said, leaning back lazily (George's male organ or penis or dick or whatever the hell is the natural word, if there is a natural word, well, my cock, then, my delicious ever-hungry cock rose a centimeter as her blouse tightened on her breasts, Lord God, we'd been humping like wart hogs in rutting season for hours and hours and hours and I was still horny and still in love with her and I probably always would be, but then again maybe I'm the Martian). Well, in fact, the old pussy hunter didn't rise more than a millimeter, not a centimeter, and he was as slow as an old man getting out of bed in January. I had just about fucked until my brains came out my ears, even before Harry brought in the hash and wanted to talk. Looking for the Martian. Looking for the governor of Dorn. Looking for the Illuminati. Krishna chasing his tail around the curved space of the Einsteinian universe until he disappears up his own ass, leaving behind a behind: the back of the void: the Dorn theory of circutheosodomognosis. "Owned some land," she continued. That beautiful black face, like ebon melody: yes, no painter could show but Bach could hint the delight of those purple-tinted lips in that black face, saying, "And the government wanted to steal the land. To build a dam." The inside of her cunt had that purple hue to it, also, and there was a tawny beige in her palm, like a Caucasian's skin, there were so many delights in her body, and in mine, too, treasures that couldn't be spent in a million years of the most tender and violent fucking. "Hagbard was the engineer hired to build the dam, but when he found out that the Indians would be dispossessed and relocated on less fertile ground, he refused the job." Eris, Eros spelled sideways. "He broke his contract, so the government sued him," she said. "That's how he got to be a close friend with the Mohawk."

Which was all pure crapperoo. Obviously, Hagbard had gone to court as a lawyer for the Indians, but that one touch of shame in him had kept him from admitting to Stella that he had once been a lawyer, so he made up that bit about being the engineer on the dam to explain how he got involved in the case.

"He helped them move when they were dispossessed." I could see bronze men and women moving in twilight, a hill in the background. "This was a long time ago, back in the '50s, I think. (Hagbard was a hell of a lot older than he looked.) One Indian was carrying a raccoon he said was his grandfather. He was a very old man himself. He said Grandfather could remember General Washington and how he changed after he became President. (He would be there tonight, that being who had once been George Washington and Adam Weishaupt: he of whom Hitler had said, "He is already among us. He is intrepid and terrible. I am afraid of him.") Hagbard says he kept thinking of Patrick Henry, the one man who saw what had happened at the Constitutional Convention. It was Henry who had looked at the Constitution and said right away, 'I smell a rat. It squints toward monarchy.' The Old Indian, whose name was Uncle John Feather, said that Grandfather, when he was a man, could speak to all animals. He said the Mohawk Nation was more than the living, it was the soul and the soil joined together. When the land was taken, some of the soul died. He said that was why he couldn't speak to all animals but only to those who had once been part of his family." The soul is in the blood, moving the blood. It is in the night especially. Nutley is a typical Catholic-dominated New Jersey town, and the Dorns are Baptists, so I was hemmed in two ways, but even as a boy I used to walk along the Passaic looking for Indian arrowheads, and the soul would move when I found one. Who was the anthropologist who thought the Ojibway believed all rocks were alive? A chief had straightened him out: "Open your eyes," he said, "and you'll see *which* rocks are alive." We haven't had our Frobenius yet. American anthropology is like virgins writing about sex.

"I know *who* the *Martian* is," Coin crooned in a singsong. "But I'm not telling. Not yet." That man who was either the most successful or the most unsuccessful

assassin of the 20th century and who had raped me (which was supposed to destroy my manhood forever according to some idiots) was smashed out of his skull and he looked so happy that I was happy *for* him.

"Hagbard," Stella went on, "stood there like a tree. He was paralyzed. Finally, old Uncle John Feather asked what was the matter."

Stella leaned forward, her face more richly black against the golden octopus on the wall. "Hagbard had foreseen the ecological catastrophe. He had seen the rise of the Welfare State, Warrior Liberalism (as he calls it) and the spread of Marxism out of Russia across the world. He saw why it all had to happen, with or without the Illuminati helping it along. He understood the Snafu Principle."

He had worked all that night, after explaining to Uncle John Feather that he was troubled in his heart at the tragedy of the Mohawk (not mentioning the more enormous tragedy coming at the planet, the tragedy which the old man understood already in his own terms); hard work, carrying pitiful cheap furniture from cabins onto trucks, tying whole households' possessions with tough ropes; he was sweating and winded when they finished shortly before dawn. The next day, he had burned his naturalization papers and put the ashes in an envelope addressed to the President of the United States, with a brief note: "Everything relevant is ruled irrelevant. Everything material is ruled immaterial. An ex-citizen." The ashes of his Army Reserve discharge went to the Secretary of Defense with a briefer note: *"Non serviam.* An ex-slave." That year's income tax form went to the Secretary of the Treasury, after he wiped his ass on it; the note said: "Try robbing a poor box. *Der Einziege."* His fury still mounting, he grabbed his copy of *Das Kapital* off the bookshelf, smiling bitterly at the memory of his sarcastic marginal notes, scrawled "Without private property there is no private life" on the flyleaf, and mailed it to Josef Stalin in the Kremlin. Then he buzzed his secretary, gave her three months pay in lieu of notice of dismissal and walked out of his law office forever. He had declared war on all governments of the world.

His afternoon was spent giving away his savings, which at that time amounted to seventy thousand dollars. Some he gave to drunks on the street, some to little boys or little girls in parks; when the Stock Exchange closed, he was on Wall Street, handing out fat bundles of bills to the wealthiest-looking men he could spot, telling them, "Enjoy it. Before you die, it won't be worth shit." That night he slept on a bench in Grand Central Terminal; in the morning, flat broke, he signed on as A.B.S. aboard a merchant ship to Norway.

That summer he tramped across Europe working as tourist guide, cook, tutor, any odd job that fell his way, but mostly talking and listening. About politics. He heard that the Marshall Plan was a sneaky way of robbing Europe under the pretense of helping it; that Stalin would have more trouble with Tito than he had had with Trotsky; that the Viet Minh would surrender soon and the French would retake Indo-China; that nobody in Germany was a Nazi anymore; that everybody in Germany was still a Nazi; that Dewey would unseat Truman easily.

During his last walking tour of Europe, in the 1930s, he had heard that Hitler only wanted Czechoslovakia and would do anything to avoid war with England; that Stalin's troubles with Trotsky would never end; that all Europe would go socialist after the next war; that America would certainly enter the war when it came; that America would certainly stay out of the war when it came.

One idea had remained fairly constant, however, and he heard it everywhere. That idea was that more government, tougher government, more honest government was the answer to all human problems.

Hagbard began making notes for the treatise that later became *Never Whistle While You're Pissing*. He began with a section that he later moved to the middle of the book:

It is now theoretically possible to link the human nervous system into a radio network so that, micro-miniaturized receivers being implanted in people's brains, the messages coming out of these radios would be indistinguishable to the subjects from the voice of their own thoughts. One central transmitter, located in the nation's capital, could broadcast all day long what the authorities wanted the people to believe. The average man on the receiving end of these broadcasts would not even know he was a robot; he would think it was his own voice he was listening to. The average woman could be treated similarly.

It is ironic that people will find such a concept both shocking and frightening. Like Orwell's *1984,* this is not a fantasy of the future but a parable of the present. Every citizen in every authoritarian society already has such a "radio" built into his or her brain. This radio is the little voice that asks, each time a desire is formed, "Is it safe? Will my wife (my husband/my boss/my church/my community) approve? Will people ridicule and mock me? Will the police come and arrest me?" This little voice the Freudians call "The Superego," with Freud himself vividly characterized as "the ego's harsh master." With a more functional approach, Perls, Hefferline and Goodman, in *Gestalt Therapy,* describe this process as "a set of conditioned verbal habits."

This set, which is fairly uniform throughout any authoritarian society, determines the actions which will, and will not, occur there. Let us consider humanity a biogram (the basic DNA blueprint of the human organism and its potentials) united with a logogram (this set of "conditioned verbal habits"). The biogram has not changed in several hundred thousand years; the logogram is different in each society. When the logogram reinforces the biogram, we have a libertarian society, such as still can be found among some American

Indian tribes. Like Confucianism before it became authoritarian and rigidified, American Indian ethics is based on speaking from the heart and acting from the heart—that is, from the biogram.

No authoritarian society can tolerate this. All authority is based on conditioning men and women to act from the logogram, since the logogram is a set created by those in authority.

Every authoritarian logogram divides society, as it divides the individual, into alienated halves. Those at the bottom suffer what I shall call the *burden of nescience*. The natural sensory activity of the biogram—what the person sees, hears, smells, tastes, feels, and, above all, what the organism as a whole, or as a potential whole, *wants* —is always *irrelevant and immaterial*. The authoritarian logogram, not the field of sensed experience, determines what is relevant and material. This is as true of a highly paid advertising copywriter as it is of an engine lathe operator. The person acts, not on personal experience and the evaluations of the nervous system, but on the orders from above. Thus, personal experience and personal judgment being nonoperational, these functions become also less "real." They exist, if at all, only in that fantasy land which Freud called the Unconscious. Since nobody has found a way to prove that the Freudian Unconscious really exists, it can be doubted that personal experience and personal judgment exist; it is an act of faith to assume they do. The organism has become, as Marx said, "a tool, a machine, a robot."

Those at the top of the authoritarian pyramid, however, suffer an equal and opposite *burden of omniscience*. All that is forbidden to the servile class—the web of perception, evaluation and participation in the sensed universe—is demanded of the members of the master class. They must attempt to do the seeing, hearing, smelling, tasting, feeling and decision-making for the whole society.

But a man with a gun is told onl$_{1}$
people assume will not provoke hin
trigger. Since all authority and go$_{1}$
based on force, the master class, wiu$_{10}$ $_{--}$
of omniscience, faces the servile class, with its
burden of nescience, precisely as a highwayman
faces his victim. *Communication is possible only
between equals.* The master class never abstracts
enough information from the servile class to know
what is actually going on in the world where the
actual productivity of society occurs. Furthermore, the logogram of any authoritarian society
remains fairly inflexible as time passes, but everything else in the universe constantly changes. The
result can only be progressive disorientation
among the rulers. The end is debacle.

The schizophrenia of authoritarianism exists
both in the individual and in the whole society.

I call this the Snafu Principle.

That autumn, Hagbard settled in Rome. He worked
as a tourist guide, amusing himself by combining authentic Roman history with Cecil B. DeMille (none of
the tourists ever caught him out); he also spent long
hours scrutinizing the published reports of Interpol.
His *Wanderjahr* was ending; he was preparing for action. Never subject to guilt or masochism, he had one
reason only for his dispersal of his savings: to prove to
himself that what he intended could be done starting
from zero. When winter arrived, his studies were complete: Interpol's crime statistics had very kindly provided him with a list of those commodities which,
either because of tariffs intended to stifle competition
or because of "morals" laws, could become the foundation of a successful career in smuggling.

One year later, in the Hotel Claridge on Forty-
fourth Street in New York, Hagbard was placed under
arrest by two U.S. narcotics agents named Calley and
Eichmann. "Don't take it too hard," Calley said.
"We're only following orders."

"It's okay," Hagbard said, "don't feel guilty. But what are you going to do with my cats?"

Calley knelt on the floor and examined the kittens thoughtfully, scratching one under the chin, rubbing the ear of the other. "What's their names?" he asked.

"The male is called Vagina," Hagbard said. "The female I call Penis."

"The male is called *what?*" Eichmann asked, blinking.

"The male is Vagina, and the female is Penis," Hagbard said innocently, "but there's a metaphysic behind it. First, you have to ask yourself, which appeared earlier on this planet, life or death? Have you ever thought about that?"

"This guy is nuts," Calley told Eichmann.

"You've got to realize," Hagbard went on, "that life is a coming apart and death is a coming together. Does that help?"

("I never know whether Hagbard is talking profundity or asininity," George said dreamily, toking away.)

"Reincarnation works *backward in time,*" Hagbard went on, as the narcs opened drawers and peered under chairs. "You always get reborn into an earlier historical period. Mussolini is a witch in the 14th century now, and catching hell from the Inquisitors for his bum karma in this age. People who 'remember' the past are all deluded. The only ones who really remember past incarnations remember the *future,* and they become science-fiction writers."

(A little old lady from Chicago walked into George's room with a collection can marked Mothers March Against Phimosis. He gave her a dime and she thanked him and left. After the door closed, George wondered if she had been a hallucination or just a woman who had fallen through a space-time warp and landed on the *Leif Erikson.)*

"What the hell are these?" Eichmann asked. He had been searching Hagbard's closet and found some red, white and blue bumper stickers. The top half of each letter was blue with white stars, and the bottom half was red-and-white stripes; they looked patriotic as all get-out. The slogan formed this way was

LEGALIZE ABORTION
PREGNANCY IS A JEWISH PLOT!

Hagbard had been circulating these in neighborhoods like the Yorkville section of Manhattan, the western suburbs of Chicago, and other places where old-fashioned Father Coughlin-Joe McCarthy style Irish Catholic fascism was still strong. This was a trial run on the logogram-biogram double-bind tactic out of which the Dealy Lama later developed Operation Mindfuck.

"Patriotic stickers," Hagbard explained.

"Well, they *look* patriotic . . ." Eichmann conceded dubiously.

("Did a little woman from Chicago just walk through this room?" George asked.

"No," Harry Coin said, toking again. "I didn't see any woman from Chicago. But *I* know *who* the Martian *is*.")

"What the hell are these?" Calley asked. He had found some business-size cards saying RED in green letters and GREEN in red letters.

("When you're out of it all the way, on the mountain," George asked, "that's neither the biogram nor the logogram, right? What the hell is it, then?")

"An antigram," Hagbard explained, still helpful.

"The cards are an antigram?" Eichmann repeated, bewildered.

"I may have to place you under arrest and take you downtown," Hagbard warned. "You've both been very naughty boys. Breaking and entering. Pointing a gun at me—that's technically assault with a deadly weapon. Seizing my narcotics—that's theft. All sorts of invasion of privacy. Very, very naughty."

"*You* can't arrest *us*," Eichmann whined. "*We're* supposed to arrest *you*."

"Which is red and which is green?" Hagbard asked.

"Look again," They looked and RED was now really red and GREEN was really green. (Actually, the tints changed according to the angle at which Hagbard held the card, but he wasn't giving away his secrets to them.) "I can also change up and down," he added. "Worse yet, I clog zippers. Neither one of you can open your fly right now, for instance. My real gimmick, though, is reversing revolvers. Try to shoot me and the bullets will come out the back and you'll never use your good right hand again. Try it and see if I'm bluffing."

"Can't you go a little easy on us, officer?" Eichmann took out his wallet. "A cop's salary ain't the greatest in the world, eh?" He nudged Hagbard insinuatingly.

"Are you trying to bribe me?" Hagbard asked sternly.

"Why not?" Harry Coin whined. "You got nothing to gain by killing me. Take the money and put me off the sub at the first island you pass."

"Well," Hagbard said thoughtfully, counting the money.

"I can get more," Harry added. "I can send it to you."

"I'm sure." Hagbard put the money in his clam-shell ashtray and struck a match. There was a brief, merry blaze, and Hagbard asked calmly, "Do you have any other inducements to offer?"

"I'll tell you anything you want to know about the Illuminati!" Harry shrieked, really frightened now, realizing that he was in the hands of a madman to whom money meant nothing.

"I know more about the Illuminati than you do," Hagbard replied, looking bored. "Give me a philosophic reason, Harry. Is there any purpose in allowing a specimen like you to go on preying on the weak and innocent?"

"Honest, I'll go straight. I'll join your side. I'll work for you, kill anybody you want."

"That's a possibility," Hagbard conceded. "It's a

slim one, though. The world is full of killers and potential killers. Thanks to the Illuminati and their governments, there's hardly an adult male alive who hasn't
had some military training. What makes you think I
couldn't go out on the streets of any large city and find
ten better-qualified killers than you inside an afternoon?"

"Okay, okay," Harry said, breathing hard. "I don't
have no college education, but I'm not a fool either.
Your men dragged me from Mad Dog Jail to this submarine. You want *something*, Ace. Otherwise, I'd be
dead already."

"Yes, I want something." Hagbard leaned back in
his chair. "Now you're getting warm, Harry. I want
something but I won't tell you what it is. You've got to
produce it and show it to me without any clues or
hints. And if you can't do that, I really will have you
killed. I shit you not, fellow. This is my version of a
trial for your past crimes. I'm the judge and the jury
and you've got to win an acquittal without knowing the
rules. How do you like that game?"

"It ain't fair."

"It's more of a chance than you gave any of the men
you shot, isn't it?"

Harry Coin licked his lips. "I think you're bluffing,"
he ventured finally. "You're some chicken-shit liberal
who doesn't believe in capital punishment. You're
looking for an excuse to *not* kill me."

"Look into my eyes, Harry. Do you see any mercy
in them?"

Coin began to perspire and finally looked down into
his lap. "Okay," he said hollowly. "How much time do
I have?"

Hagbard opened his drawer and took out his
revolver. He cracked it open, showing the bullets,
and quickly snapped it closed again. He slipped the
safety catch—a procedure he later found unnecessary
with George Dorn, who knew nothing about guns—
and aimed at Harry's belly. "Three days and three minutes are both too long," he said casually. "If you're

ever going to get it, you're going to get it now."

"Mama," Coin heard himself exclaim.

"You're going to shit your pants in a moment," Hagbard said coldly. "Better not. I find bad smells offensive, and I might shoot you just for that. And mama isn't here, so don't call her again."

Coin saw himself lunging across the room, the gun roaring in mid-leap, but at least trying to get his hands on this bastard's throat before dying.

"Pointless," Hagbard grinned icily. "You'd never get out of the chair." His finger tightened slightly, and Coin's gut churned; he knew enough about guns to know how easy it was to have an accident, and he thought of the gun going off even before the bastard Celine intended it to, maybe even as he was on the edge of guessing the goddam riddle, the pointlessness of it was the final horror, and he looked again into those eyes without guilt or pity or any weakness he could exploit; then, for the first time in his life, Harry Coin knew peace, as he relaxed into death.

"Good enough," Hagbard said from far away, snapping the safety back in place. "You've got more on the ball than either of us realized."

Harry slowly came back and looked at that face and those eyes. "God," he said.

"I'm going to give you the gun in a minute," Hagbard went on. "Then it's *my* turn to sweat. Of course, if you kill me you'll never get off this sub alive, but maybe you'll think that's worthwhile, just for revenge. On the other hand, maybe you'll be curious about that instant of peace—and you'll wonder if there's an easier way to get back there and if I can teach it to you. Maybe. One more thing, before I toss you the gun. Everybody who joins me does it by free choice. When you said you'd come over to my side just because you were afraid of dying, you had no value to me at all. Here's the gun, Harry. Now, I want you to check it. There are no gimmicks, no missing firing pin or anything like that. No other tricks, either—nobody watching you through a peephole and ready to gun you down the minute you aim at me, or anything like that. I'm totally at your mercy. What are you going to do?"

Harry examined the gun carefully, and looked back at Hagbard. He had never studied kinesics and orgonomy as Hagbard had, but he could read enough of the human face and body to know what was going on in the other man. Hagbard had that same peace he himself had experienced for a moment.

"You win, you bastard," Harry said, tossing the gun back. "I want to know how you do it."

"Part of you already knows," Hagbard smiled gently, putting the gun back in the drawer. "You just did it, didn't you?"

"What would he have done if I did block?" Harry asked Stella in present time.

"Something. I don't know. A sudden act of some sort that scared you more than the gun. He plays it by ear. The Celine System is never twice the same."

"Then I was right, he *wouldn't* have killed me. It was all bluff."

"Yes and no." Stella looked past Harry and George, into the distance. "He wasn't acting with you, he was manifesting. The mercilessness was quite real. There was no sentimentality involved in saving you. He did it because it's part of his Demonstration."

"His Demonstration?" George asked, thinking of geometry problems and the neat Q.E.D. at the bottom, back in Nutley years and years ago.

"I've known Hagbard longer than she has," Eichmann said. "In fact, Calley and I were among the first people he enlisted. I've watched him over the years, and I still don't understand him. But I understand the Demonstration."

"You know," George said absently, "when you two first came in, I thought you were a hallucination."

"You never saw us at dinner, because we work in the kitchen," Calley explained. "We eat after everybody else."

"Only a small part of the crew are former criminals," Stella told George, who was looking confused. "Rehabilitating a Harry Coin—pardon me, Harry—doesn't really excite Hagbard much. Rehabilitating policemen and politicians, and teaching them useful trades, is work that really turns Hagbard on."

"But not for sentimental reasons," Eichmann emphasized. "It's part of his Demonstration."

"It's his Memorial to the Mohawk Nation, too," Stella said. "That trial set him off. He tried a direct frontal assault that time, attempting to cut through the logogram with a scalpel. It didn't work, of course; it never does. Then he decided: 'Very well, I'll put them where words can't help, and see what they do then.' That's his Demonstration."

Hagbard, actually—well, not *actually;* this is just what he told me—had started with two handicaps, intending to prove that they weren't handicaps. The first was that he would have a bank balance of exactly $00.00 at the beginning, and the second was that he would never kill another human being throughout the Demonstration. That which was to be proved (namely, that government is a hallucination, or a self-fulfilling prophecy) could be shown only if all his equipment, including money and people, came to him through honest trade or voluntary association. Under these rules, he could not shoot even in self-defense, for the biogram of government servants was to be preserved, and only their logograms could be disconnected, deactivated and defused. The Celine System was a consistent, although flexible, assault on the specific conditioned reflex—that which compelled people to look outside themselves, to a god or a government, for direction or strength. The servants of government all carried weapons; Hagbard's insane scheme depended on rendering the weapons harmless. He called this the Tar-Baby Principle ("You Are Attached To What You Attack").

Being a man of certain morbid self-insight, he realized that he himself exemplified the Tar-Baby Principle and that his attacks on government kept him perpetually attached to it. It was his malign and insidious notion that government was even more attached to *him;* that his existence *qua* anarchist *qua* smuggler *qua* outlaw aroused greater energetic streaming in government people than their existence aroused in him: that, in short, he was the Tar Baby on which they could not resist hurling themselves in anger and fear: an electrochemical reaction in which he could bond them to himself just as the Tar Baby captured anyone who swung a fist at it.

More (there was always more, with Hagbard), he had been impressed, on reading Weishaupt's *Uber Strip Schnipp-Schnapp, Weltspielen and Funfwissenschaft,* by the passage on the Order of Assassins, which read:

> Surrounded by Moslem maniacs on one side and Christian maniacs on the other, the wise Lord Hassan preserved his people and his cult by bringing the art of assassination to esthetic perfection. With just a few daggers strategically placed in exactly the right throats, he found Wisdom's alternative to war, and preserved the peoples by killing their leaders. Truly, his was a most exemplary life of grandmotherly kindness.

"Grossmutterlich Gefälligkeit," muttered Hagbard, who had been reading this in the original German, "now where have I heard that before?"

In a second, he remembered: the *Mu-Mon-Kan* or "Gateless Gate" of Rinzai Zen contained a story about a monk who kept asking a Zen Master, "What is the Buddha?" Each time he asked, he got hit upside the head with the Master's staff. Finally discouraged, he left and sought enlightenment with another Master, who asked him why he had left the previous teacher. When the poor gawk explained, the second Master gave him the ontological hotfoot: "Go back to your previous Master at once," he cried, "and apologize for not showing enough appreciation of his grandmotherly kindness!"

Hagbard was not surprised that Weishaupt evidently knew, in 1776 when *Uber Strip Schnipp-Schnapp* was written, about a book which hadn't yet been translated into any European tongue; he was astonished, however, that even the evil Ingolstadt *Zauberer* had understood the rudiments of the Tar-Baby Principle. It never pays to underestimate the Illuminati, he thought then —for the first time. He was to think it many times in the next two and a half decades.

On April 24, when he told Stella to deliver some Kallisti Gold to George's stateroom, Hagbard had already asked FUCKUP the odds that Illuminati ships would arrive in Peos within the time he intended to be there. The answer was better than 100-to-1. He thought about what that meant, then buzzed to have Harry Coin sent in.

Harry swaggered to a chair, trying to look insolent, and said, "So you're the leader of the Discordians, eh?"

"Yes," Hagbard said evenly, "and on this ship, my word is law. *Wipe that silly grin off your face and sit up straight.*" He observed the involuntary stiffening of Harry's body before the man caught himself and remembered to maintain his slouch. Typical: Coin could resist the key conditioning phrases, but only with effort. "Listen," he said softly *"I will tell you only one more time"*—another Bavarian Fire Drill, that—"This is my ship. You will address me as Captain Celine. You will *come to attention* when I talk to you. Otherwise . . ." he let the phrase trail off.

Slowly, Coin shifted to a more respectful kinesic posture—immediately modifying it by grinning more insolently. Well, that was good; the streak of rebellion ran deep. The breathing was not bad for a professional criminal: the only block seemed to be at the bottom of the exhalation. The grin was a defense against tears, of course, as with most chronic American smilers. Hagbard attempted a probe: Harry's father was the kind who pretended to consider the case and to toy with forgiveness before he would administer the thrashing.

"Is that better?" Harry asked, accentuating his respectful posture and grinning more sarcastically.

"A little," Hagbard said, sounding mollified. "But I don't know what I'm going to do with you, Harry. That's a bad bunch you've been mixed up with, very *un-American*." He paused to get a reaction to the word; it came at once.

"Their money is as good as anyone's," Harry said defiantly. His shoes crept backwards, as he spoke, and his neck decreased an inch—the turtle reflex, Hagbard called it; and it was a sure sign of the repressed guilt denied by the man's voice.

"You were born pretty poor, weren't you?" Hagbard asked, in a neutral tone.

"Poor? We was white niggers."

"Well, I guess there's some excuse for you . . ." Hagbard watched: the grin grew wider, the body imperceptibly moved back toward slouching. "But, to turn on *your own country*, Harry. That's bad. That's the lowest thing a human being can do. It's like turning against *your own mother*." The toes curled inward again, tentatively. What did Harry's father say before wielding the belt? Hagbard caught it: "Harry," he repeated it gravely, "you haven't been acting like a *proper white man*. You've been acting like you got *nigger blood*."

The grin stretched to the breaking point and became a grimace, the body stiffened to the most respectful possible posture. "Now, look here, sir," Harry began, "you got no call to talk to me that way—"

"And you're not even *ashamed*," Hagbard ran over him. "You don't show any *remorse*." He shook his head with profound discouragement. "I can't let you wander around loose, committing more crimes and treasons. I'm going to have to feed you to the sharks."

"Listen, Captain Celine, sir, I've got a money belt under this shirt and it's full of more hundred-dollar bills than you ever saw at one time . . ."

"Are you trying to bribe me?" Hagbard asked sternly; the rest of the scene would be easy, he reflected. Part of his mind drifted to the Illuminati ships he would meet at Peos. There was no way to use the Celine System without communicating, and he knew the crew would be "protected" against him by some Illuminati variation on the ear wax of Ulysses' men passing the Sirens. The money would go in the giant clam-shell ashtray, a real shocker for a man like Coin, but what would he do about the Illuminati ships?

When the time came to produce the gun, he slipped the safety off viciously. If I'm going to join the ancient brotherhood of killers, he thought morosely, maybe I should have the stomach to start with a visible target. "Three days and three minutes are both too long," he said, trying to sound casual, "if you're ever going to get it, you're going to get it now." They would be at Peos in less than an hour, he thought, as Coin involuntarily cried "Mama." Like Dutch Schultz, Hagbard reflected; like how many others? It would be interesting to interview doctors and nurses and find out how many people passed out with that primordial cry for the All-Protector on their lips . . . but Harry finally surrendered, abdicated, left the robot running itself according to the biogram. He was no longer sitting in an insolent slouch, a respectful attention, a guilty cramp . . . He was simply sitting. He was ready for death.

"Good enough," Hagbard said. "You've got more on the ball than either of us realized." The man would now transfer his submissive reflexes to Hagbard; and the next stage would be longer and harder, before he learned to stop playing roles entirely and just manifest as he had in the face of extinction.

The gun gambit was variation #2 of the third basic tactic in the Celine System; it had five usual sequels. Hagbard picked the most dangerous one—he usually did, since he didn't much like the gun gambit at all, and could only stomach it if he gave most of the subjects a chance at the other role. This time, however, he knew he had another motive: somewhere, deep inside, a coward in him hoped Harry Coin was crazier than he had estimated and would, in fact, shoot; that way

Hagbard could avoid the decision awaiting him in Peos.

"You win, you bastard," Coin's voice said; Hagbard came back and quickly rushed through a small verbal game involving Hell images picked up from Harry's childhood. When he had Coin sent back to his room, under light security, he slouched in his chair and rubbed his eyes tiredly. He probed for Dorn and found the Dealy Lama was on that channel, broadcasting.

—Leave the kid alone, he beamed. It's my turn now. Go contemplate your navel, you old fraud.

A shower of rose petals was the nonverbal answer. The Lama faded out. George went on rapping to himself on the themes planted by the ELF leader: Odd, the big red one. Eye think it was his I. The eye of Apollo. His luminous I.

—Aye, trust me not, Hagbard beamed. Trust not a man who's rich in flax—his morals may be sadly lax. (Some of my own doubts getting in here, he thought.) Her name is Stella Maris. Black star of the seas. (I won't tell him who she and Mavis really are.) George, I want you in the captain's control room.

George should start with variation #1, the *Liebestod* or orgasm-death trip, Hagbard decided. Make him aware of the extent to which he treats women as objects—and, of course, give him some mystical hogwash later to gloss it over temporarily, so the doubt will be pushed into the unconscious for a while. Yes: George was already on a pornography trip, very similar to Atlanta Hope and Smiling Jim Treponema, except that in his case it was ego-dystonic.

"That was a good trick," George said a few moment's later in the captain's control room, "how you got me up on the bridge with that telepathy thing."

Hagbard, still thinking about the decision in Peos, tried to look innocent when he replied, "I called you on the intercom." He realized that he was whistling and pissing at once, worrying about Peos as well as about George, and brought himself back sharply. "Ab-

surd" was the word in George's mind—absurd innocence. Well, Hagbard thought, I fucked that one up.

"You think I can't tell a voice in my head from a
voice in my ears?" George demanded. Hagbard roared
with laughter, totally in the present again; but after
George had been sent to the chapel for his initiation,
the problem returned. Either the Demonstration failed,
or the Demonstration failed. Double bind. Damned
both ways. It was infuriating, but all the books had
warned him long ago: "As ye give, so shall ye get." He
had used the Celine System on quite a few people over
nearly three decades, and now he was in the middle of
a classic Celine Trap himself. There was no correct answer, except to give up trying.

When the moment came, though, he found that part
of him had not given up trying. "Ready for destruction
of enemy ships," said Howard.

Hagbard shook his head. George was remembering
some crazy incident in which he had tried to commit
suicide while standing by the Passaic River, and
Hagbard kept picking up parts of that bum trip while
trying to clear his own head. "I wish we could communicate with them," he said aloud, realizing that he was
possibly blowing the guru game by revealing his inner
doubts to George. "I wish I could give them a chance
to surrender . . ."

"You don't want them too close when they go," said
Howard.

"Are your people out of the way?" Hagbard asked
in agony.

"Of course," the dolphin replied irritably. "Quit this
hesitating. This is no time to be a humanitarian."

"The sea is crueler than the land," Hagbard protested, but then he added "sometimes."

"The sea is cleaner than the land," Howard replied.
Hagbard tried to focus—the dolphin was obviously
aware of his distress, and soon George would be (no: a
quick probe showed George had retreated from the
scene into the past and was shouting, "You silly sons
of bitches," at somebody named Carlo). "These people

have been your enemies for thirty thousand years."

"I'm not that old," Hagbard said wearily. The Demonstration had failed. He was committed, and others with him were now committed. Hagbard reached out a brown finger, let it rest on a white button on the railing in front of him, then pressed it decisively. "That's all there is to it," he said quietly.

("Be a wise-ass then! When you start flunking half your subjects, perhaps you'll come back to reality." A voice long, long ago . . . at Harvard . . . And once, in the South, he had been moved by a very simple, a ridiculously simple, Fundamentalist hymn:

> Jesus walked this lonesome valley
> He had to walk it all alone
> Nobody else could walk there for Him
> He had to walk it by Himself.

I will walk this lonesome valley, Hagbard thought bitterly, all by myself, all the way to Ingolstadt and the final confrontation. But it's meaningless now, the Demonstration has failed; all I can do is pick up the pieces and salvage what I can. Starting with Dorn right here and right now.)

Hate, like molten lead, drips from the wounded sky . . . they call it air pollution . . . August Personage dials slowly, with the cunt-starved eyes of a medieval saint . . . "God lies!" Weishaupt cried in the middle of his first trip, "God is Hate!" . . . Harry Coin is crumpled in his chair . . . George's head hangs at an angle, like a doll with a broken spring . . . Stella doesn't move . . . They are not dead but stoned . . .

Abe Reles blew the whistle on the entire Murder Inc. organization in 1940 . . . He named Charley Workman as the chief gun in the Dutch Schultz massacre . . . He gave the details proving the roles of Lepke (who was executed) and Luciano (who was imprisoned and, later, exiled) . . . He kept his mouth shut about certain other things, however . . . But Drake was worried. He gave orders to Maldonado, who conveyed them to a capo, who passed them on to some soldiers . . . Reles was guarded by five policemen but nonetheless he went out his hotel window and spread like jam on the ground below . . . There were mutterings in the press . . . The coroner's jury couldn't believe that five cops were on the take from the Syndicate . . . Reles's death was declared to be suicide . . . But in 1943, as the Final Solution moved into high gear, Lepke announced he wanted to talk before his execution . . . Tom Dewey, alive by grace of the Dutchman's death, was governor, and he granted a stay of execution . . . Lepke spent twenty-four hours with Justice Department officials and it was announced later that he refused to reveal anything of significance . . . One of the officials had been brought back from State to work with Justice because of his background on Schultz and the Big Six Syndicate . . . He said little, but Lepke read a lot in his eyes . . . His name, of course, was Winifred . . . Lepke understood: as Bela Lugosi once said, there are worse things than dying . . .

In 1932 the infant son of aviator Charles Lindbergh Jr. was kidnapped . . . Already at that time, a heist of that dimension could not be permitted in the Northeast without the consent of a full-fledged don of the Mafia . . . Even a capo could not authorize it alone . . . The aviator's father, Congressman Charles Lindbergh Sr., had been an outspoken critic of the Federal Reserve monopoly . . . Among other things, he had charged on the floor of Congress, "Under the Federal Reserve Act panics are scientifically created; the present one is the first scientifically created one worked out as we figure a mathematical problem . . ." The go-between in delivering the ransom money was Jafsie Condon, Dutch Schultz's old high school principal . . . "It's got to be one of them coincidences," as Marty Krompier said later . . . ·

John Dillinger arrived in Dallas on the morning of November 22, 1963, and rented an Avis at the airport. He drove out to Dealy Plaza and scouted the terrain. The Triple Underpass where Harry Coin was supposed to stand when doing the job was under observation from a railroadman's shack, he noted; it occurred to him that the man in that shack would not have a long life expectancy. There would be a lot of other eyewitnesses, he realized, and the JAMs couldn't protect them all, not even with the help of the LDD. It was going to be bad all around . . . In fact, the man in the railroad shack, S. M. Holland, told a story that didn't jibe with the Earl Warren version, and later died when his car went off the road under circumstances that aroused speculation among those given to speculating; the coroner's jury called it an accident . . . Dillinger found his spot in the thickly wooded part of the Grassy Knoll and waited until Harry Coin appeared on the Underpass. He made himself relax and looked around to be sure that he was invisible from everywhere but a helicopter (there were no helicopters: the Illuminati's top double agent within the Secret Service had seen to that). A movement in the School Book Depository caught his eye. Something not kosher up there. He swung his binoculars . . . and caught another head, ducking quickly, atop the Dal-Tex building. An Italian, very young . . . That was bad. If one of Maldonado's soldiers was here, either the Illuminati were aware they had a double agent in their midst and had hired two assassins, or else the Syndicate was acting on its own. John panned back to the School Book Depository: whoever that clown was, he had a rifle, too, and he was being cagey: definitely not Secret Service.

This was a piss-cutter.

John's original plan was to plug Harry Coin before Coin could get a bead on the young Hegelian from Boston. Now, he had three men to knock out at once. It couldn't be done. There was no human way of hitting more than two of those targets—all three of them in different areas and at different elevations—before the fuzz were swarming all over him. The third would have time to do the job while that was happening. It was what Hagbard called an existential *koan.*

"Shit, piss and industrial waste," John muttered, quoting another Celinism.

Well, save what you can, as Harry Pierpont always said when a bank job went sour in the middle. Save what you can and haul ass out of that place.

If Kennedy had to die, and obviously it was in the cards or in the *I Ching* at least (which probably explained why Hagbard, after consulting that computer of his, refused to get involved in this caper), then "save what you can" could only be applied, in this case, to mean: screw the Illuminati. He would give them a mystery they would never solve.

The motorcade was already in front of the School Book Depository, and the gazebo up there might start blasting at any minute, if Harry Coin or the Mafiosos weren't quicker. Dillinger hoisted his rifle, quickly sighted on John F. Kennedy's skull, and thought briefly, *Even if it falls through and doesn't remain an enigma to bug the Illuminati, think of those wild headlines when I'm caught: PRESIDENT SHOT BY JOHN DILLINGER, people will think Orson Welles is publishing the papers now,* and then he tightened his finger.

("Murder?" George asked. "It's hard not to think of Good and Evil when a man's games get that hairy."

"During the Kali Yuga," Stella replied, "almost all our games are played with live ammunition. Haven't you noticed?")

The three shots blew brains into Jackie Kennedy's lap and Dillinger, whirling in amazement, saw the man start to run out of the Grassy Knoll down into the street. John set off in pursuit and caught a glimpse of the face as the killer mingled in the crowd below.

"Christ!" John said. *"Him?"*

Stella toked again—she never seemed to think she was sufficiently stoned. "Wait," she said. "There's a passage in *Never Whistle While You're Pissing* that goes into this a bit." She got up, walking quite slowly like all potheads, and rummaged among the books on the wall shelf. "You know the old saying, 'different strokes for different folks'?" she asked over her shoulder. "Hagbard and FUCKUP have classified sixty-four thousand personality types, depending on which strokes, or gambits, they use most often in relating to others." She found the book and carefully walked back to her chair. "For instance," she said slowly. "Right now, you can intersect my life line in a number of ways, from kissing my hand to slitting my throat. Between those extremes, you can, let's say, carry on an intellectual conversation with sexual flirtation underneath it, or an intellectual conversation with sexual flirtation and also with kinesic signals indicating that the flirtation is only a game and you don't really want me to respond, and on an even deeper level you can be sending other signals indicating that actually you do want me to respond after all but you're not ready to admit that to yourself. In authoritarian society, as we know it, people are usually sending either very simple dominance signals—'I'm going to master you, and you better accept it before I get really nasty'—or submissive signals—'You're going to master me, and I'm reconciled to it.' "

"Lord in Heaven," Harry Coin said softly. "That was what my first session with him was all about. I tried dominance signals to bluff him, and it didn't work. So I tried submissive signals, which is the only other gimmick I ever knew, and that didn't work either. So I just gave up."

"Your brain gave up," Stella corrected. "The strategy center, for dealing with human relations in authoritarian society, was exhausted. It had nothing left to try. Then the Robot took over. The biogram. You acted from the heart."

"But what has redundance got to do with this?" George asked.

"Here's the passage," Stella said. She began to read aloud:

People exist on a spectrum from the most redundant to the most flexible. The latter, unless they are thoroughly trained in psychodynamics, are always at a disadvantage to the former in social interactions. The redundant do not change their script; the flexible continually keep changing, trying to find a way of relating constructively. Eventually, the flexible ones find the "proper" gambit, and communication, of a sort, is possible. They are now on the set created by the redundant person, and they act out his or her script.

The steady exponential growth of bureaucracy is not due to Parkinson's Law alone. The State, by making itself ever more redundant, incorporates more people into its set and forces them to follow its script.

"That's heavy," George said, "but I'll be damned if I can see how it applies to Jesus *or* Emperor Norton."

"Exactly!" Harry Coin chortled. "And that ends the game. You've just proven what I suspected all along. *You're* the Martian!"

"Don't raise your voices," Calley said drowsily from the floor. "I can see hundreds of blissful Buddhas floating through the air . . ."

A single blissful Buddha, meanwhile—together with an inverted Satanic cross, a peace symbol, a pentagon and the Eye in the Triangle—were taking up Danny Pricefixer's attention, back in New York. He had finally decided to play his hunch about the *Confrontation* bombing and the five associated disappearances. The decision came after he and the acting head of Homicide received a thorough ass-chewing from the Police Commissioner himself. "Malik is gone. The Walsh woman is gone. This Dorn kid was taken right out of a jail in Texas. Two of my best men, Goodman and Muldoon, are gone. The Feds are nasty and I can tell they know something that makes this case even more important than five possible murders alone would account for. I want you to report some kind of progress before the day is over, or I'll replace you with Post-Toasties Junior G-Men."

When they escaped into the hall, Pricefixer asked the man from Homicide, Van Meter, "What are you going to do?"

"Go back and give my men the same ass-chewing. They'll produce." Van Meter didn't really sound convinced. "What are *you* going to do?" he added lamely.

"I'm going to play a hunch," Danny said, and he walked down to Bunco-Fraud, where he exchanged some words with a detective named Sergeant Joe Friday who always insisted on trying to act like his namesake in the famous television series.

"I want a mystic," Danny said.

"Palmist, crystal-gazer, witch, astrologer . . . any preference?" Friday asked.

"The technique doesn't matter. I want one you've never been able to pin anything on. One you investigated and found a little scary . . . as if she or he really did have something on the ball."

"I know the one you want," Friday said emphatically, hitting the intercom button on his phone. "R & I," he said and waited. "Carella? Send up the package on Mama Sutra."

The package, when it shot out of the interoffice tube, proved to be all that Danny had hoped for. Mama Sutra had no arrests. She had been investigated several times—usually at the demand of rich husbands who thought she had too much influence over their wives, and once at the demand of the board of directors of a public utility who thought the president of the firm consulted too often with her—but none of her activities involved any claims that could be construed to be in violation of the fraud laws. Furthermore, she had dealt with the extremely wealthy for many years and had never played any games remotely like an *okanna borra* or Gypsy Switch on any of them. Her business card, included in the package, modestly offered only "spiritual insight," but she evidently delivered it in horse doctor's doses: one detective, after interviewing her, quit the force and entered a Trappist monastery in Kentucky, a second became questionable and finally useless in the eyes of his superiors because of an incessant series of memos he wrote urging that New York be the first American city to experiment with the English system of unarmed policemen, and a third announced that he had been a closet queen for two decades and began sporting a Gay Liberation button, necessitating his immediate transfer to the Vice Squad.

"This is my woman," Pricefixer said; and an hour later, he sat in her waiting room studying the blissful Buddha and other occult accessories, feeling like a horse's ass. This was really going way out on a limb, he knew, and his only excuse was that Saul Goodman frequently cracked hopeless cases by making equally bizarre jumps. Danny was ready to jump: the disappearance of Professor Marsh, in Arkham, was connected with the *Confrontation* mystery, and both were connected with Fernando Poo and the gods of Atlantis.

The receptionist, an attractive young Chinese woman named Mao something-or-other, put down her phone and said, "You can go right in."

Danny opened the door and walked into a completely austere room, white as the North Pole. The white walls had no paintings, the white rug was solid white without any design in it, and Mama Sutra's desk and the Danish chair facing it were also white. He realized that the total lack of occult paraphernalia, together with the lack of color, was certainly more impressive than heavy curtains, shadows, smoldering candles and a crystal ball.

Mama Sutra looked like Maria Ouspenskaya, the old actress who was always popping up on the late late show to tell Lon Chaney Jr. that he would always walk the "thorny path" of lycanthropy until "all tears empty into the sea."

"What can I do for you?" she asked in a brisk, businesslike manner.

"I'm a detective on the New York Police," Danny

said, showing her his badge. "I'm not here to hassle you or give you any trouble. I need knowledge and advice, and I'll pay for it out of my own pocket."

She smiled gently. "The other officers, who investigated me for fraud in the past, must have created quite a legend at police headquarters. I promise no miracles, and my knowledge is limited. Perhaps I can help you; perhaps not. There will be no fee, in either case. Being in a sensitive profession, I would like to keep on friendly terms with the police."

Danny nodded. "Thanks," he said. "Here's the story . . ."

"Wait." Mama Sutra frowned. "I think I am picking up something already. Yes. *District Attorney Wade. Clark. The ship is sinking. 2422. If I can't live as please, let me die when I choose.* Does any of that mean anything to you?"

"Only the first part," Danny said, perplexed. "I suspect that the matter I'm investigating goes back at least as far as the assassination of John F. Kennedy. The man who handled the original investigation of that killing, in Dallas, was District Attorney Henry Wade. The rest of it doesn't help at all, though. Where did you get it from?"

"There are . . . vibrations . . . and I register them." Mama Sutra smiled again. "That's the best explanation I can offer. It just happens, and I've learned how to use it. Somewhat. I hope someday before I die a psychologist will go far enough out in his investigations to find something that will explain to *me* what I do. The sinking ship is meaningless? How about the date, *June 15, 1904?* That seems to be on the same wave."

Pricefixer shook his head. "No help, as they say in poker."

"Wait," Mama Sutra said. "It means something to me. There was an Irish writer, James Joyce, who studied the theosophy of Blavatski and the mysticism of the Golden Dawn Society. He wrote a novel in which all the action takes place on June 16, 1904. The novel is called *Ulysses,* and is impregnated on every page with coded mystical revelations. And, yes, now I remember, there is a shipwreck mentioned in it. Joyce made all the background details historically accurate, so he included what was actually in the Dublin papers that day—the book takes place in Dublin, you see—and one of the stories concerned the sinking of the ship, *General Slocum,* in New York Harbor the day before, June 15."

"Did you say Golden Dawn?" Pricefixer demanded excitedly.

"Yes. Does that help?"

"It just adds to the confusion, but at least it shows you're on the right track. The case I'm working on seems to be connected with the disappearance of a professor from a university in Massachusetts several years ago, and he left behind some notes that mentioned the Golden Dawn Society and . . . let's see . . . some of its members. Aleister Crowley is one name I remember."

"To Mega Theiron," Mama Sutra said slowly, beginning to pale slightly. "Young man, what you are involved in is very serious. Much more than an ordinary police officer could understand. But you are not an ordinary police officer or you wouldn't have come to me in the first place. Let me tell you flatly, then, that what you have stumbled upon is something that could very easily involve both James Joyce's mysticism and the assassination of President John Kennedy. But to understand it you will have to stretch your mind to the breaking point. Let me suggest that you wait while I have my receptionist make you a rather stiff drink."

"Can't drink on duty, ma'am," Danny said sadly. Mama Sutra took a deep breath. "Very well. You'll have to take it cold and struggle with it as best you can."

"Does it involve the lloigor?" Danny asked hesitantly.

"Yes. You already have a large part of the puzzle if you know that much."

"Ma'am," Danny said, "I think I'll have that drink. Bourbon, if you have it."

2422, he thought while Mama Sutra spoke to the receptionist, that's even crazier than the rest of this. 2 plus 4 plus 2 plus 2. Adds up to 10. The base of the decimal system. What the hell does that mean? Or 24 plus 22 adds up to 46. That's two times 23, the number missing in between 24 and 22. Another enigma. And 2 times 4 times 2 times 2 is, let's see, 32. Law of falling bodies. High school physics class. 32 feet per second per second. And 32 is 23 backwards. Nuts.

Miss Mao entered with a tray. "Your drink, sir," she said softly. Danny took the glass and watched her gracefully walk back toward the door. *Mao* is Chinese for cat, he remembered from his years in Army Intelligence, and she certainly moved like a cat. *Mao:* onomatopoeia they call that. Like kids calling a dog "woof-woof." Come to think of it, that's how we got the word "wolf." Funny, I never thought of that before. Oh, the pentagram outside, and the pentagram in those old Lon Chaney Wolf Man movies. Malik's mystery mutts. Enough of that.

He took a stiff wallop of the bourbon and said, "Go ahead. Start. I'll take some more of the medicine when my mind starts crumbling."

"I'll give it to you raw," Mama Sutra said quietly. "The earth has already been invaded from outer space. It is not some threat in the future, for writers to play with. It happened, a long time ago. Fifty million years ago, to be exact."

Danny took another belt of his drink. "The lloigor," he said.

"That was their generic name for themselves. There were several races of them. Shoggoths and Tcho-Tchos and Dholes and Tikis and Wendigos, for instance. They were not entirely composed of matter as we understand it, and they do not occupy space and time in the concrete way that furniture does. They are not sound waves or radio waves or anything like that either, but think of them that way for a while. It's better than not having any mental picture of them at all. Did you take any physics in high school?"

"Nothing like relativity," Danny said, realizing that he was believing all this.

"Sound and light?" she asked.

"A little."

"Then you probably know two elementary experiments. Project a white light through a prism and a spectrum appears on the screen behind the prism. You've seen that?"

"Yes."

"And the experiment with a glass tube that has a thin layer of colored powder on the bottom, when you send a sound wave through it?"

"Yeah. And the wave leaves little marks at each of its valleys and you can see them in the powder." The track of the invisible wave in a visible medium.

"Very well. Now you can picture, perhaps, how the lloigor, although not made of matter as we understand it, can manifest themselves in matter, leaving traces that show, let us say, a cross section of what they really are."

Danny nodded, totally absorbed.

"From our point of view," Mama Sutra went on, "they are intolerably hideous in these manifestations. There is a reason for that. They were the source of the worst terrors experienced by the first humans. Our DNA code still carries an aversion and terror toward them, and this activates a part of our minds which the psychologist Jung called the Collective Unconscious. That is where all myth and art come from. Everything frightening, loathsome and terrible—in the folklore, in the paintings and statues, in the legends and epics of every people on earth—contains a partial image of a manifestation of the lloigor. 'As a foulness shall ye know Them,' a great Arab poet wrote."

"And they've been at war with us through all history?" Danny asked unhappily.

"Not at all. Are the stockyards at war with the cattle? It's nothing like war at all," Mama Sutra said simply. "It's just that they *own* us."

"I see," Danny said. "Yes, of course. I see." He looked into his empty glass dismally. "Could I have another?" he murmured.

After Miss Mao had brought him another bourbon, he took a huge swallow and slouched forward in his chair. "There's nothing we can do about it?" he asked.

"There is one group that has been trying to liberate humanity," Mama Sutra said. "But lloigor have great powers to warp and distort minds. This group is the most maligned, slandered and hated people on earth. All the evil they seek to prevent has been attributed to them. They operate in secret because otherwise they would be destroyed. Even now, the John Birch Society and various other fanatics—including an evil genius named Hagbard Celine—struggle ceaselessly to combat the group of whom I speak. They have many names, the Great White Brotherhood, the Brethren of the Rosy Cross, the Golden Dawn . . . usually, though they are known as the Illuminati."

"Yes!" Danny cried excitedly. "There was a whole bunch of memos about them at the scene of the crime that started this case."

"And the memos, I would wager, portrayed them in an unfavorable light?"

"Sure did," Danny agreed. "Made them seem the worst bastards in history. Pardon me, ma'am." I'm getting drunk, he thought.

"That is how they are usually portrayed," Mama Sutra said sadly. "Their enemies are many, and they are few . . ."

"Who are their enemies?" Danny leaned forward eagerly.

"The Cult of the Yellow Sign," Mama Sutra replied. "This is a group serving one particular lloigor called Hastur. They live in such terror of this being that they usually call him He Who Is Not To Be Named. Hastur resides in a mysterious place called Hali, which was formerly a lake but is now just desert. Hali was by a great city in the lost civilization of Carcosa. You look as if those names mean something to you?"

"Yes. They were in the notes of the professor who disappeared. The other case that I was convinced was connected with this one."

"They have been mentioned—unwisely, I think—by certain writers, such as Bierce and Chambers and Lovecraft and Bloch and Derleth. Carcosa was located where the Gobi Desert is at present. The major cities were Hali, Mnar and Sarnath. The Cult of the Yellow Sign has managed to conceal all this rather thoroughly, although a few archeologists have published some interesting speculations about the Gobi area. Most of the evidence of a great civilization before Sumer and Egypt has been either hidden or doctored so that it seems to point to Atlantis. Actually, Atlantis never existed, but the Cult of the Yellow Sign carefully keeps the myth alive so nobody will discover what went on, and still goes on, in the Gobian wastelands. You see, the Cult of the Yellow Sign still goes there, on certain occasions, to worship and make certain transactions with Hastur, and with Shub Niggurath, a lloigor who is known in mystical literature as the Black Goat with a Thousand Young, and with Nyarlathotep, who appears either as a solid black man, not a Negro but black as an abyss, or else as a gigantic faceless flute player. But I repeat: you cannot understand the lloigor by these manifestations or cross sections into our space-time continuum. Do you believe in God?"

"Yes," Danny answered, startled by the sudden personal question.

"Take a little more of your drink. I must tell you now that your God is another manifestation of some lloigor. That is how religion began, and how the lloigor and their servants in the Cult of the Yellow Sign continue it. Have you ever had what is called a religious or mystical experience?"

"No," Danny said, embarrassed.

"Good. Then your religion is just a matter of believing what you have been told and not of a personal emotional experience. All such experiences come from the lloigor, to enslave us. Revelations, visions, trances, miracles, all of it is a trap. Ordinary, normal people instinctively avoid such aberrations. Unfortunately, due to their gullibility and a concerted effort to brainwash them, they are willing to follow the witches and wizards and shamans who traffic in these matters. You see, and I urge you to take another drink right now, *every religious leader in human history has been a member of the Cult of the Yellow Sign and all their efforts are devoted to hoaxing, deluding and enslaving the rest of us.*"

Danny finished his glass and asked meekly, "May I have more?"

Mama Sutra buzzed for Miss Mao and said, "You're taking this part very well. People who *have* had religious visions take it very poorly; they don't want to know what foul source those experiences actually came from. The lloigor, of course, can be considered gods—or demons—but it is more profitable, at this point in history, to just consider them another life form cast up by the universe, unfortunately superior to us and even more unfortunately inimical to us. You see, religion is always a matter of sacrifice, and whenever there is a sacrifice there is a victim—and also a person or entity profiting from the sacrifice. There is no religion in the world—not one—that is not a front for the Cult of the Yellow Sign. The Cult itself, like the lloigor, is of prehuman origin. It began among the snake people of Valusia, the peninsula that is now Europe, and then spread eastward to be adopted by the first humans in Carcosa. Always the purpose of the Cult has been to serve the lloigor, at the expense of other human beings. Since the rise of the Illuminati, the Cult has also acted to combat their work and discredit them."

Danny was glad that Miss Mao arrived then with his third stiff bourbon. "And who are the Illuminati and what is their goal?" he asked, belting away a strong swallow.

"Their founder," Mama Sutra said, "was the first man to think rationally about the lloigor. He realized that they were not supernatural, but just another aspect of nature; not all-powerful, but just more powerful than us; and that when they came 'out of the heavens' they came from other worlds like this one. His name has come down to us in certain secret teachings and documents. It was Ma-lik."

"Jesus," Danny said, "that's the name of the guy whose disappearance started all this."

"The name meant 'one who knows' in the Carcosan tongue. Among the Persians and some Arabs today it still exists but means 'one who leads.' His followers, the Illuminati, are those who have seen the light of reason—which is quite distinct from the stupefying and mind-destroying light in which the lloigor sometimes appear to overwhelm and mystify their servants in the Cult of the Yellow Sign. What Ma-lik sought, what the Illuminati still seek, is scientific knowledge that will surpass the powers of the lloigor, end mankind's enslavement and allow us to become self-owners instead of property."

"How large is the Illuminati?"

"Very small. I don't know the exact number." Mama Sutra sighed. "I have never been accepted for membership. Their standards are quite high. One must virtually be a walking encyclopedia to qualify for an initial interview. You must remember that this is the most dedicated, most persecuted, most secret group in the world. Everything they do, if not wiped off the records by the Cult of the Yellow Sign, is always misrepresented and pictured as malign, devious and totally evil. Indeed, any effort to be rational, to think scientifically, to discover or publish a new truth, even by those outside the Illuminati, is always pictured in those colors by the Cult and all the religions which serve as its fronts. All churches, Protestant, Catholic, Jewish, Moslem, Hindu, Buddhist or whatever, have always opposed and persecuted science. The Cult of the Yellow Sign even fills the mass media with this propaganda. Their favorite stories are the one about the scientist who isn't fully human until he has a religious insight and recognizes 'the higher powers'—the lloigor, that is—and the other one about the scientist who seeks truth without fear and causes a disaster. 'He meddled with things man should leave alone' is always the punch line on that one. The same hatred of knowledge and glorification of superstition and ignorance permeates all human societies. How much more of this can you stand?" Mama Sutra asked abruptly.

"I don't honestly know," Danny said wearily. "It seems if I do get to the bottom of this business, it'll bring every power in this country down on my head. The least that'll happen is that I'll get kicked out of my job. More likely, I'll disappear like the man I'm looking for and the first two detectives on this case. But for my own satisfaction, I'd like to know the rest of the truth, before I bid you good day and look for a hole to hide in. You might also tell me how you can survive, knowing as much as you do."

"I have studied much. I have a Shield. I cannot explain the Shield anymore than I can explain my ESP. I only know that it works. As to answering your other questions, first tell me about your investigation. Then I will be able to relate it to the Illuminati and the Cult of the Yellow Sign."

Danny took another drink, closed his eyes for a minute and launched into his story. He began with the Marsh disappearance in Arkham four years earlier, his perusal of the missing professor's notes, his reading in the books mentioned in those notes and his conclusion that a drug cult was involved. Then he told of the *Confrontation* bombing, his skimming of the Illuminati memos, the disappearance of Malik, Miss Walsh, Goodman and Muldoon, and the frantic curiosity of the FBI. "That's it," he concluded. "That's about all I know."

Mama Sutra nodded thoughtfully, "It is as I feared," she said finally. "I think I can shed light on the matter, but you will be well advised to leave the police force and seek the protection of the Illuminati after you have heard. You are already, at this very moment, in great peril." She lapsed into silence again, and then said, "You will not see the picture of what is happening now, until I give you more of the background."

For the next hour, Danny Pricefixer sat transfixed as Mama Sutra told him of the longest war in history, the battle for the freedom of the human mind waged by the Illuminati against the forces of slavery, superstition and sorcery.

It began, she repeated, in ancient Carcosa when the first humans were contacted by the serpent people of Valusia. The latter brought with them certain fruits with strange powers. These fruits would be called hallucinogens or psychedelics today, Mama Sutra said, but what they did to the brain of the eater was not in any sense a hallucination. It opened him to invasion by the lloigor. The chief fruit used in these rites was a botanical cousin of the modern apple, yellowish or golden in color, and the snake people promised, "Eat of this and you shall become all-powerful." In fact, the eaters became enslaved by the lloigor, and especially by Hastur, who took up residence in the Lake of Hali; distorted versions of what happened have come down to us in various African legends about people who had commerce with snakes and lost their souls, in the Homeric tale of the lotus eaters, in Genesis, and in the Arabic lore utilized in the fiction of Robert W. Chambers, Ambrose Bierce and others. Soon, the Cult of the Yellow Sign was formed among the eaters of the golden apples, and its first high priest, Gruad, bargained with Hastur for certain powers in return for which the lloigor were fed on human sacrifices. The people were told that the sacrifices were good for the crops—and this, in fact, was partially true, for the lloigor ate only the energy of the victim, and the body, buried in the fields, gave back its nitrogen to the soil. This was the beginning of religion—and of government. Gruad controlled the Temple, and the Temple soon controlled Hali, and, then, all of Carcosa.

So things went for many thousands of years, until the priests were rich, fat and decadent, while the citizens lived in terror and slavery. The number of sacrifices increased ever, for Hastur grew with each victim whose energy he absorbed and his appetite grew with him. Finally, among the people, there arose one who had been refused admission to the priesthood, Ma-lik, and he taught that humanity could become all-powerful, not through eating the golden apples and sacrificing to the lloigor, but through a process he called rational thought. He was, of course, fed to Hastur as soon as the priests heard of this teaching, but he had followers, and they quickly learned to keep their thoughts private and plan their activities in secret. This was the age of midnight arrests, purge trials and accelerating sacrifices in Carcosa, Mama Sutra said, and eventually the followers of Ma-lik—the few who had escaped extermination—fled to the Thuranian subcontinent, which is now Europe.

There they met little people who had come down from the north after the snake folk had exterminated each other in some form of slow, insidious and stealthy civil war. (Apparently, the snakes never met in a single battle during all this time: the poison in the wine cup, the knife in the back and similar subtle activities had slowly escalated to the deadly level of actual warfare. The serpent people had an aversion to *facing* an enemy as they killed him.) The little people had had their own experiences with the lloigor, long ago, but all they remembered were confused legends about Orcs (whom Mama Sutra identified with the Tcho-Tchos) and a great hero named Phroto who battled a monster called Zaurn (evidently a shoggoth, Mama Sutra said.)

Many millenniums passed, and the little people and the followers of Ma-lik intermarried, producing basically the human race of today. A great law-giver named Kull tried to establish a rational society on Ma-lik's principles, and fought a battle with some of the serpent people who had surprisingly survived in hidden places; most of this got lost in exaggeration and legend. After more thousands of years, a barbarian named Konan or Conan arose, somehow, to the throne of

Aquilonia, mightiest kingdom on the Thuranian sub-continent; Konan brooded much about the continuing horrors in Carcosa, which he sensed as a threat to the rest of the world. Finally, he disappeared, abdicating in favor of his son, Conn, and reputedly sailing *to the west*.

Konan, Mama Sutra said, was the same person who appeared in the Yucatan peninsula at that time and became known as Kukulan. He was evidently seeking, among the Mayan scientists, some knowledge or technology to use against the lloigor. Whatever happened, he left them, and only the legend of Kukulan, "the feathered serpent," remained. When the Aztecs came down from the north, Kukulan became Quetzalcoatl, and human sacrifice was instituted in his name. The lloigor, in some fashion, had turned the work of Konan around and made it serve their own ends.

Carcosa meanwhile perished. What happened is unknown, but some students of ancient lore suspect that Konan actually circumnavigated the globe, collecting knowledge as he went, and descended upon Carcosa with weapons that destroyed both the Cult of the Yellow Sign and all traces of the civilization that served it.

Throughout the rest of history, Mama Sutra went on, the Cult of the Yellow Sign never regained its former powers, but it has come very close in certain times and certain places. The lloigor continued to exist, of course, but could no longer manifest in our kind of space-time continuum unless the Cult performed very complicated technical operations, which were sometimes disguised as religious rituals and sometimes as wars, famines or other calamities.

Over the intervening ages, the Cult waged steady warfare against the one power that threatened them: rationality. When they couldn't manifest a lloigor to blast a mind, they learned to fake it; if real magic wasn't available, stage magic served in its place. "By 'real magic,' of course," Mama Sutra explained, "I mean the technology of the lloigor. As science-fiction writer Arthur C. Clarke has commented, any sufficiently advanced technology is indistinguishable from magic. The lloigor have that κind of technology. That's how they got to earth from their star."

"You mean their planet, don't you?" Danny asked.

"No, they lived originally on a star. I told you they were not made of matter as we understand it. Incidentally, their origin on a star explains why the pentagram or star shape always attracts their attention and is one of the best ways of summoning them. They invented that design. A star doesn't look five-pointed to a human being, but that's what it looks like to *them*."

Finally, in the 18th century, the Age of Reason appeared to be at hand. Tentatively, as an experiment, one branch of the Illuminati surfaced in Bavaria. They were led by an ex-Jesuit named Adam Weishaupt who had inside knowledge of how the Cult of the Yellow Sign operated and performed its hoaxes and "miracles." The real brain behind this movement, however, was Weishaupt's wife, Eve; but they knew that, even in the Age of Reason, humanity was not ready yet for a liberation movement led by a woman, so Adam fronted for her.

The experiment was unsuccessful. The Cult of the Yellow Sign planted fake documents in the home of an Illuminatus named Zwack, whispered some hints to Bavarian government and then watched with glee as the movement was disbanded and hounded out of Germany.

A simultaneous experiment began in America, started by two Illuminati named Jefferson and Franklin. Both preached reason, like Weishaupt, but carefully did not make his mistake of stating explicitly how this contradicted religion and superstition. (This latter matter they discussed only in their private letters.) Since Jefferson and Franklin were national heroes, and since the rationalistic government they helped to create seemed well established, the Cult of the Yellow Sign dared not denounce them openly. One trial balloon was attempted: the Reverend Jebediah Morse, a high Yellow Sign adept, openly accused Jefferson of being an Illuminatus and charged him and his party with most of the crimes that had discredited Weishaupt in Bavaria. The American public was not deceived—but all subsequent Yellow Sign propaganda in America has rested on the original anti-Illuminati claims of Reverend Morse.

Due to Jefferson, one Illuminati symbol was adopted by the new government: the Eye on the Pyramid, representing knowledge of geometry and, hence, of the order of nature. This was to be used in later generations, if necessary, to indicate the truth about the founding of the U.S. government, since it was well understood that the Cult of the Yellow Sign would try to distort the facts as soon as possible. Another Illuminati work, of more immediate importance, was the Bill of Rights (the part of the Constitution still under most vigorous attack by the Yellow Sign fanatics) and certain key expressions in early documents, such as the reference to "Nature and Nature's God" in the Declaration of Independence—as far as Jefferson dared to go in leavening traditional superstition with a natural-science admixture. And, of course, the first half-dozen Presidents were all high-ranking Masons and Rosicrucians who understood at least the fundamentals of Illuminati philosophy.

Mama Sutra sighed briefly, and went on. All this, she said, is only the tip of the iceberg. Government actually plays a minor role in controlling people; far more important are the words and images that make up the semantic environment. The Cult of the Yellow Sign not only suppresses words and images that threaten their power, but infiltrates every branch of communications with their own ideology. Science and reason are forever mocked or portrayed as menacing. Wishful thinking, fantasy, religion, mysticism, occultism and magic are forever preached as the real solutions to all problems. Best-selling books teach people to *pray,* not *work,* for success. Movies win awards by showing a child's ignorant faith justified over the skepticism of adults. There is an astrology column in virtually every newspaper. More and more, the ideology of the Cult of the Yellow Sign is set forth openly, as the ideas of the Illuminati and the Founding Fathers are forgotten or distorted. One only has to think of any antidemocratic, antirational or antihumane idea out of the Dark Ages, Mama Sutra said, and one can immediately think of some popular religious columnist or some movie star who is blatantly expounding it and calling it "Americanism."

The Cult of the Yellow Sign, the old woman continued, is determined to destroy the United States, because it came closer than any other nation to the Illuminati ideals of free minds and free people and because it still retains a few tattered relics of Illuminism in its laws and customs.

This is where Mr. Hagbard Celine enters the picture, Mama Sutra said grimly.

Celine, she went on, was a brilliant but twisted personality, the son of an Italian pimp and a Norwegian prostitute. Raised in the underworld, he early developed a contempt and hatred for ordinary, decent society. The Mafia, recognizing his talents and predilections, took him in and financed his way through Harvard Law School. After graduation, he became an important mouthpiece for Syndicate hoodlums in trouble with the law. On the side, however, he also took some cases for American Indians, since this was a way of frustrating the government. In one particularly bitter battle, he attempted to stop the construction of a much-needed dam in upstate New York; his unbalanced behavior in the courtroom (which helped lose the case) indicated his deep attraction for the occult, since he had obviously been taken in by the superstitions of the Indians he served. Mafia dons conferred with leaders of the Cult of the Yellow Sign, and soon, Hagbard, who had been wandering around Europe aimlessly, was recruited to start a new front for the Cult, to fight the United States both politically and religiously. This front, Mama Sutra said, was called the Legion of Dynamic Discord, and, while it pretended to be against all governments, it was actually devoted only to harming the U.S. He was given a submarine (which he later claimed to have designed himself) and became an important cog in the Mafia heroin-smuggling business. More important, his crew—renegades and misfits from all nations—were indoctrinated in a deliberately nonsensical variety of mysticism.

An important center of Celine's heroin network, Mama Sutra added, was a fake church in Santa Isobel on the island of Fernando Poo.

Obviously, Mama Sutra concluded, Joseph Malik, the editor of *Confrontation,* was investigating the Illuminati, deceived by the lies spread against them by Celine and the Yellow Sign adepts. As for Professor Marsh, his explorations in Fernando Poo may have revealed something about Celine's heroin ring.

"Then you think they're both dead," Danny said somberly. "And, probably, Goodman and Muldoon and Pat Walsh, the researcher, also."

"Not necessarily. Celine, as I have told you, is both brilliant and quite insane. He has perfected his own form of brainwashing and it amuses him to recruit rather than destroy any possible opponent. It is quite possible that all of these people are working for him right now, against the Illuminati and the United States, which they will believe to be the major enemies of humanity." Mama Sutra paused thoughtfully. "However, that is far from sure. Events in the last few days have changed Celine for the worse. He is more insane, and more dangerous, than ever. The assassinations of April 25 all across the nation appear to be his work, engineered through the Mafia. He is striking out blindly against anyone he imagines may be an Illuminatus. Needless to say, most of the victims were not actually in the Illuminati, which is, as I have mentioned, a very small organization. Since he is in this violent and paranoid frame of mind, I fear for the lives of anyone associated with him."

Danny was slumped forward in his chair, drunk, dejected and depressed. "Now that I know," he asked rhetorically, "what can I do about it? My God, what can I do about it?"

I finally got around to reading *Telemachus Sneezed* on the flight to Munich, a touch of appropriate synchronicity, since Atlanta Hope (like the Illuminati's pet paperhanger) had an umbilical connection backward toward Clark Kent's old enemy Lothar and his festive burgher's unsure God. In fact, Atlanta wrote as if she had her own Diet of Worms for breakfast every morning. What made it even more fan-fuckin'-tastic was that she was on the same flight with me, sitting, in fact, a few seats ahead of me and to port, or starboard, or whatever is the correct word for right when you're in the air.

Mary Lou was with me; she was a hard woman to get out of your system once you'd made it with her. John had advanced me only enough money for my own passage, so I'd hustled some Alamout Black on Wells Street to raise the extra fare for her, and then I had to explain that it wasn't just a pleasure trip.

"What's all the mystery?" she had asked. "Are you CIA or a Commie or something for Christ's sake?"

"If I told you," I said, "you wouldn't believe it. Just enjoy the music and the acid and whatever else is coming down, and when it happens you'll see it. You'd never believe it before you see it."

"Simon Motherfucking Moon," she told me gravely, "after the yoga and sex you've taught me these last three days, I'm ready to believe anything."

"Ghosts? The *grand zombi?*"

"Oh, there you go again, putting me on," she protested.

"See?"

So it was more or less left at that and we smoked two joints and hopped a cab out to O'Hare, passing all the signs where they were tearing down lower-middle-class neighborhoods to turn them into upper-middle-class high-rise neighborhoods and each sign said, THIS IS ANOTHER IMPROVEMENT FOR CHICAGO—RICHARD J.

DALEY, MAYOR. Of course, in the lower-class neighborhoods, they weren't tearing anything down, just waiting for the people to go on another rampage and burn it down. The signs there were all done with spray cans and had more variety: OFF THE PIG, BLACK P. STONE RUNS IT, POWER TO THE PEOPLE, FRED LIVES, ALMIGHTY LATIN KINGS RUN IT, and one that would have pleased Hagbard, OFF THE LANDLORDS. Then we got into the traffic on the Eisenhower Expressway (Miss Doris Day standing before Ike's picture in my old schoolroom flashed through memory like the ghost of an old hard-on, the flesh of her mammary) and we put on our gas masks and sat while the cab crawled along fast enough to possibly catch a senile snail with arthritis.

Mary Lou bought Edison Yerby's seventieth or eightieth novel in the airport, which suited me fine since I like to read on airplanes myself. Looking around, I spotted *Telemachus Sneezed* and decided, what the hell, let's see how the other half thinks. So there we were at fifty thousand feet a few yards from the author herself and I was plunged deeply into the *donner-und-blitzen* metaphysics of God's Lightning. Unlike the lamentable Austrian monorchoid, Atlanta wrote like she had balls, and she expressed her philosophy in a frame of fiction rather than autobiography. Pretty soon, I was in her prose up to my ass and sinking rapidly. Fiction always does that to me: I buy it completely and my critical faculties come into action only after I'm finished.

Briefly, then, *Telemachus Sneezed* deals with a time in the near future when we dirty, filthy, freaky, lazy, dope-smoking, frantic-fucking anarchists have brought Law and Order to a nervous collapse in America. The heroine, Taffy Rhinestone, is, like Atlanta was once herself, a member of Women's Liberation and a believer in socialism, anarchism, free abortions and the charisma of Che. Then comes the rude awakening: food riots, industrial stagnation, a reign of lawless looting and plunder, everything George Wallace ever warned us against—but the Supreme Court, who are all anarchists with names ending in -*stein* or -*farb* or -*berger* (there is no *overt* anti-Semitism in the book), keeps repealing laws and taking away the rights of policemen. Finally, in the fifth chapter—the climax of Book One—the heroine, poor toughy Taffy, gets raped *fifteen* times by an oversexed black brute right out of *The Birth of a Nation,* while a group of cops stand by cursing, wringing their hands and frothing at the mouth because the Supreme Court rulings won't allow them to take any action.

In Book Two, which takes place a few years later, things have degenerated even further and factory pollution has been replaced by a thick layer of marijuana smoke hanging over the country. The Supreme Court is gone, butchered by LSD crazed Mau-Maus who mistook them for a meeting of the Washington chapter of the Policemen's Benevolent Association. The President and a shadowy government-in-exile are skulking about Montreal, living a gloomy emigre existence; the Blind Tigers, a rather thinly disguised caricature of the Black Panthers, are terrorizing white women everywhere from Bangor to Walla Walla; the crazy anarchists are forcing abortions on women whether they want them or not; and television shows nothing but Maoist propaganda and Danish stag films. Women, of course, are the worst sufferers in this blightmare, and, despite all her karate lessons, Taffy has been raped so many times, not only by standard vage-pen but orally and anally as well, that she's practically a walking sperm bank. Then comes the big surprise, the monstro-rape to end all rapes, committed by a pure Aryan with hollow cheeks, a long lean body, and a face that never changes expression. "Everything is fire," he tells her, as he pulls his prick out afterwards, "and don't you ever forget it." Then he disappears.

Well, it turns out that Taffy has gone all icky-sticky-gooey over this character, and she determines to find him again and make an honest man of him. Meanwhile, however, a subplot is brewing, involving Taffy's evil brother, Diamond Jim Rhinestone, an unscrupulous dope pusher who is mixing heroin in his grass to make everybody an addict and enslave them to him. Diamond Jim is allied with the sinister Blind Tigers and a secret society, the Enlightened Ones, who cannot achieve world government as long as a patriotic and paranoid streak of nationalism remains in America.

But the forces of evil are being stymied. A secret underground group has been formed, using the cross as their symbol, and their slogan is appearing scrawled on walls everywhere:

> SAVE YOUR FEDERAL RESERVE NOTES, BOYS,
> THE STATE WILL RISE AGAIN!

Unless this group is found and destroyed, Diamond Jim will not be able to addict everyone to horse, the Blind Tigers won't be able to rape the few remaining white women they haven't gotten to yet, and the Enlightened Ones will not succeed in creating one world government and one monotonous soybean diet for the whole planet. But a clue is discovered: the leader of the Underground is a pure Aryan with hollow cheeks, a long lean body, and a face that never changes expression. Furthermore, he is in the habit of discussing Heracleitus for like seven hours on end (this is a neat trick, because only about a hundred sentences of the Dark Philosopher survive—but our hero, it turns out, gives lengthy comments on them).

At this point there is a major digression, while a herd of minor characters get on a Braniff jet for Ingolstadt. It soon develops that the pilot is tripping on acid, the copilot is bombed on Tangier hash and the stewardesses are all speed freaks and dykes, only interested in balling each other. Atlanta then takes you through the lives of each of the passengers and shows that the catastrophe that is about to befall them is richly deserved: all, in one way or another, had helped to create the Dope Grope or Fucks Fix culture by denying the "self-evident truth" of some hermetic saying by Heracleitus. When the plane does a Steve Brodie into the North Atlantic, everybody on board, including the acid-tripping Captain Clark, are getting just what they merit for having denied that reality is really fire.

Meanwhile, Taffy has hired a private detective named Mickey "Cocktails" Molotov to search for her lost Aryan rapist with hollow cheeks. Before I could get into that, however, I was wondering about the synchronistic implications of the previous section, and called over one of the stewardesses.

"Could you tell me the pilot's name?" I asked.

"Namen?" she replied. *"Ja, Gretchen."*

"No, not your name," I said, "the pilot's name. *Namen unser,* um, *Winginmacher?"*

"Winginmacher?" she repeated, dubiously, *"Ein Augenblick."* She went away, while I looked up *Augenblick* in a pocket German-English dictionary, and another stewardess, with the identical uniform, the identical smile and the identical blue eyes, came over, asking, *"Was wollen sie haben?"*

I gave up on *Winginmacher,* obviously a bad guess. *"Gibt mir, bitte,"* I said, *"die Namen unser Fliegenmacher."* I spread my arms, imitating the plane. *"Luft Fliegenmacher,"* I repeated, adding helpfully, "How about *Luft Piloten?"*

"It's *Pilot,* not *Piloten,*" she said with lots of teeth. "His name is Captain Clark. Heathcliffe Clark."

"Danke— Thanks," I said glumly, and returned to *Telemachus Sneezed,* imagining friend Heathcliffe up front there weathering heights of *saure*-soaring and plunging into the ocean because, as Mallory said, it's there. An Englishman piloting a kraut airline, no less, just to remind me that I'm surrounded by the paradoxical paranoidal paranormal parameters of synchronicity. Their wandering ministerial Eye. Lord, I buried myself again in Atlanta Hope's egregious epic.

Cocktails Molotov, the private dick, starts looking for the Great American Rapist, with only one clue: an architectural blueprint that fell out of his pocket while he was tupping Taffy. Cocktails's method of investiga-

tion is classically simple: he beats up everybody he
meets until they confess or reveal something that gives
him a lead. Along the way he meets an effete snob type
who makes a kind of William O. Douglas speech putting down all this brutality. Molotov explains, for seventeen pages, one of the longest monologues I ever
read in a novel, that life is a battle between Good and
Evil and the whole modern world is corrupt because
people see things in shades of red-orange-yellow-
green-blue-indigo-violet instead of in clear black and
white.

Meanwhile, of course, everybody is still mostly involved in fucking, smoking grass and neglecting to in-
vest their capital in growth industries, so America is
slipping backward toward what Atlanta calls "crapu-
lous precapitalist chaos."

At this point, another character enters the book,
Howard Cork, a one-legged madman who commands a
submarine called the *Life Eternal* and is battling *everybody*—the anarchists, the Communists, the Diamond
Jim Rhinestone heroin cabal, the Blind Tigers, the Enlightened Ones, the U.S. government-in-exile, the still-
nameless patriotic Underground and the Chicago
Cubs—since he is convinced they are *all* fronting for a
white whale of superhuman intelligence who is trying
to take over the world on behalf of the cetaceans.
("No normal whale could do this," he says after every
TV newscast reveals further decay and chaos in America, "but a whale of superhuman intelligence . . . !")
This megalomaniac tub of blubber—the whale, not
Howard Cork—is responsible for the release of the famous late-1960s record *Songs of the Blue Whales*,
which has hypnotic powers to lead people into wild
frenzies, dope-taking, rape and loss of faith in Christianity. In fact, the whale is behind most of the cultural
developments of recent decades, influencing minds
through hypnotic telepathy. "First, he introduced W.
C. Fields," Howard Cork rages to the dubious first
mate, "Buck" Star, "then, when America's moral fiber
was sufficiently weakened, Liz and Dick and Andy

Warhol and rock music. Now, the Songs of the Blue Whales!" Star becomes convinced that Captain Cork went uncorked and wigged when he lost his leg during a simple ingrown toenail operation bungled by a hip young chiropodist stoned on mescaline. This suspicion is increased by the moody mariner's insistence on wearing an old cork leg instead of a modern prosthetic model, proclaiming, "I was born all Cork and I'm not going to die only three-fourths Cork!"

Then comes a turnabout scene, and it is revealed that Cork is actually not bananas at all but really a smooth apple. In a meeting with a pure Aryan with hollow cheeks, a long lean body, and a face that never changes expression, it develops that the Captain is an agent of the Underground which is called God's Lightning because of Heracleitus's idea that God first manifested himself as a lightning bolt which created the world. Instead of hunting the big white whale, as the crew thinks, the *Life Eternal* is actually running munitions for the government-in-exile and God's Lightning. When the hollow-cheeked leader leaves, he says to Cork, "Remember: the *way up* is the *way down.*"

Meanwhile, the Gateless Gate swung creakingly open and I started picking up some of the "real" world. That is, I began to recognize myself, again, as the ringmaster. All of this information gets fed into me, entropy and negentropy all synergized up in a wodge of wonderland, and I compute it as well as my memory banks give it unto me to understand these doings.

But, as Harry Coin, I enter Miss Portinari's suite somewhat diffidently. I am conscious of the ghosts of dead pirates, only partly induced by this room's surrealist variety of Hagbard's nautical taste in murals. In fact, Harry, in his own language, had an asshole tight enough to shit bricks. It was easy, now, to accept that long-haired hippie, George, and even his black girlfriend as equals, but it just didn't seem right to be asked to accept a *teenage girl* as a superior. A couple days ago I would have been thinking how to get into her panties. Now I was thinking how to get her into my head. That Hagbard and his dope sure have screwed up my sense of values worse than anything since I left Biloxi.

And, for some reason, I could hear the Reverend Hill pounding the Bible and hollering up a storm back there in Biloxi, long ago, "No remission without blood! No remission without blood, brothers and sisters! Saint Paul says it and don't you forget it! No remission without the blood of our Lord and Saviour Jesus Christ! Amen."

And Hagbard reads FUCKUP's final analysis of the strategy and tactics in the Battle of Atlantis. All the evidence is consistent with Assumption A, and inconsistent with Assumption B, the mathematical part of FUCKUP has decided. Hagbard grinds his teeth in a savage grimace: Assumption A is that the Illuminati spider ships were under remote control, and Assumption B is that there were human beings aboard them.

—Trust not a man who's rich in flax—his morals may be sadly lax.

"Ready for destruction of enemy ships," Howard's voice came back to him.

"Are your people out of the way?"

"Of course. Quit this hesitating. This is no time to be a humanitarian."

(Assumption A is that the Illuminati spider ships were under remote control.)

The sea is crueler than the land. Sometimes.

(None of the evidence is consistent with Assumption B.)

Hagbard reached out a brown finger, let it rest on a white button on the railing in front of him, then pressed it decisively. *That's all there is to it,* he said.

But that wasn't all there was to it. He had decided, coolly and in his wrong mind, that if he was a murderer already the final gambit might as well be one that would salvage part of the Demonstration. He had sent George to Drake (Bob, you're dead now, but did you ever understand, even for a moment, what I tried to tell you? What Jung tried to tell you even earlier?) and then twenty-four real men and women were dead, and now the bloodshed was escalating, and he wasn't sure that any part of the Demonstration could be saved.

"No remission without blood! No remission without blood, brothers and sisters . . . No remission without the blood of our Saviour and Lord Jesus Christ!"

I got into the Illuminati in 1951, when Joe McCarthy was riding high and everybody was looking for conspiracies everywhere. In my own naive way (I was a sophomore at New York University at the time) I was seeking to find myself, and I answered one of those Rosicrucian ads in the back of a girlie magazine. Of course, the Rosicrucians aren't a front in the simple way that the Birchers and other paranoids think; only a couple of plants at AMORC headquarters are Illuminati agents. But they select possible candidates at random, and we get slightly different mailings than those sent to the average new member. If we show the proper spirit, our mailings get more interesting and a personal contact is made. Well, pretty soon I swore the whole oath, including that silly part about never visiting Naples, which is just an expression of an old grudge of Weishaupt's, and I was admitted as Illuminatus Minerval with the name Ringo Erigena. Since I was majoring in law, I was instructed to seek a career in the FBI.

I met Eisenhower only once, at a very large and sumptuous ball. He called another agent and myself aside. "Keep your eye on Mamie," he said. "If she has five martinis, or starts quoting John Wayne, get her upstairs *quick.*"

Kennedy I never even talked to, but Winifred (whose name in the order is Scotus Pythagoras) used to bitch about him a lot. "This New Frontier stuff is dangerous," Winfred would say testily. "The man thinks he's living in a western movie. One big showdown, and the bad guys bite the dust. We'd best not let him last too long."

You can imagine how upset I was when the Dallas caper began to throw light on the whole overall pattern. Of course, I didn't know what to do: Winifred was my only superior in the government who was also a superior in the Illuminati, but I had a lot of hunches and guesses about some others, and I wouldn't want to bet that John Edgar wasn't one of them, for instance. When the feeler came from the CIA I went on what these kids today call a paranoid trip. It could have been coincidence or synchronicity, but it could have been the Order, scanning me, and ensuring that my involvement would get deeper.

("Most people in espionage don't know who they're working for," Winifred told me once, in that voice of silk and satin and stilettos, "especially the ones who only do 'small jobs.' Suppose we find a French Canadian separatist in Montreal who's in a position to provide certain information at certain times. We certainly don't ask him to work for American Intelligence. That's no concern of his, and even inimical to his real interests. So he's approached by another very convincing French Canadian who has 'evidence' to prove he's an agent of the most secret of all Quebec Libre underground movements. Or, if the Russians find a woman in Nairobi who has access to certain offices and happens to be anti-Communist and pro-English: no sense in trying to recruit her for the MVD, right? The contact she meets has a full set of credentials and just the right Oxford tone to convince her he's with M.5 in London. And so it goes," he ended dreamily, "so it goes . . .")

My CIA contact really was CIA; I'm almost absolutely willing to give odds around 60-40 on that. At least, he knew the proper passwords to show that he was acting under presidential orders, whatever that proves.

It was Hoover himself who ordered me to infiltrate God's Lightning. Well, he didn't pick me alone; I was part of a group, and a rousing pep talk he gave us. I can still remember him saying, "Don't let their American flags fool you. Look at those lightning bolts, right out of Nazi Germany, and, remember, the next thing to a godless Commie is a godless Nazi. They're both against Free Enterprise." Of course, as soon as I was admitted to the Arlington chapter of God's Lightning, I found out that Free Enterprise stood second only to Heracleitus in their pantheon. J. Edgar did get some queer hornets in his headgear at times—like his fear that John Dillinger was really still alive some place, laughing at him. That was the dread that turned him against Melvin Purvis, the agent who gunned Dillinger down in Chicago, and he rode Purvis right out of the Bureau. Those of you with long memories will recall that poor Purvis ended up working for a breakfast cereal company, acting as titular head of the Post-Toasties Junior G-Men.

It was in God's Lightning that I read *Telemachus Sneezed,* which I still think is a rip-roaring good yarn. That scene where Taffy Rhinestone sees the new King on television and it's her old rapist friend with the gaunt cheeks and he says, "My name is John Guilt"— man, that's *writing*. His hundred-and-three-page-long speech afterwards, explaining the importance of guilt and showing why all the anti-Heracleiteans and Freudians and relativists are destroying civilization by destroying guilt, certainly is persuasive—especially to somebody like me with three-going-on-four personalities each of which was betraying the others. I still quote his last line, "Without guilt there can be no civilization." Her nonfiction book, *Militarism: The Unknown Ideal for the New Heracleitean* is, I think, a distinct letdown, but the God's Lightning bumper stickers asking "What Is John Guilt?" sure give people the creeps until they learn the answer.

I met Atlanta Hope herself at the time of the New York Draft Riots. That was, you will remember, when God's Lightning, disgusted with reports that the FBI was swamped in two years' backlog in draft resistance and draft evasion cases, decided to organize vigilante groups to hunt down the hippie-yippie-commie-pacifist scum themselves. As soon as they entered the East Village—which harbored, as they suspected, hundreds of thousands of bearded, long-haired and otherwise semivisible fugitives from the Vietnam, Cambodia, Thailand, Laos, Taiwan, Costa Rica, Chile and Tierra del Fuego conflicts—they began to encounter both suspects and resistance. After the third hour, the Mayor ordered the police to cordon the area. The police, of course, were on the side of God's Lightning and did all they could to aid their mayhem against the Great Unwashed while preventing reciprocal mayhem. After the third day, the Governor called out the National Guard. The Guard, who were mostly draft-dodgers at heart themselves, tried to even the score, and even help the Dregs and Drugs a bit. After the third week, the President declared that part of Manhattan a disaster area and sent in the Red Cross to help the survivors.

I was in the thick and din of it (you have no idea how bizarre civil war gets when one side uses trash cans as a large part of their arsenal) and even met Joe Malik, prematurely, under a Silver Wraith Rolls Royce where he had crawled to take notes near the front line and I had crept to nurse wounds received while being pushed through the window of the Peace Eye Bookstore—I have scars I could show you still—and a voice over my shoulder says that I should put in the fact that August Personage was trapped in a phone booth only a few feet away, suffering hideous paranoid delusions that in spite of all this chaos the police would trace his last obscene call and find him still in the booth afraid to come out and face the trash can covers and bullets and other miscellaneous metals in the air—and I even remember that the Rolls had license plate RPD-1, which suggests that a certain person of importance was also in that odd vicinity on some doubtless even odder errand. I met Atlanta herself a day later and a block north, on the scene where Taylor Mead was making his famous Last Stand. Atlanta grabbed my right arm (the wounded one: it made me wince) and howled something like, "Welcome, brother in the True Faith! War is the Health of the State! Conflict is the creator of all things!" Seeing she was on a heavy Heracleitus wavelength, I quoted, with great passion, "Men should fight for the Laws as they would for the walls of the city!" That won her and I was Atlanta's Personal Lieutenant for the rest of the battle.

Atlanta remembered me from the Riots and I was summoned to organize the first tactical strikes against Nader's Raiders. If I do say so myself, I did a commendable job; it earned me a raise from the Bureau, a tight but genuinely pleased smile from my CIA drop, a promotion to Illuminatus Prelator from Winifred—and another audience with Atlanta Hope which led to my initiation into the A∴A∴, the supersecret conspiracy for which she was really working. (The A∴A∴ is so arcane that even now I can't reveal the full name hinted in those initials.) My secret name was Prince of Wands E; I got the Prince of Wands by picking a Tarot card at random, and she gave me the E herself—from which I deduced that there were four other Princes of Wands, together with five Kings of Swords, and so forth, meaning that the A∴A∴ was something special in even esoteric realms, since it was a worldwide conspiracy with no more than three hundred ninety members (five times the number of cards in the Tarot deck). The name fairly suited me—I wouldn't want to be Hanged Man D or Fool A—and I was happy that the Prince is known for his multiple personalities.

If I had been three and a half agents before (my role in God's Lightning a fairly straightforward one, at least from GL's point of view, since I was only asked to smash, not to spy) there was no doubt that I was four agents now, belonging to the FBI, the CIA, the Illuminati and the A∴A∴ and betraying each of them to at least one and sometimes two or three of the others. (Yes, I had been converted to the A∴A∴ during their initiation; if I could describe that most amazing ritual you would not wonder why.) Then came the Vice President's brainstorm about economizing on agents, and I began to get transferred on loan to the CIA frequently, whereupon the Bureau discreetly asked me to report anything interesting that I observed. This, however, I perceive as a further complexification of my four-way psychic stretch and not as the inevitable, irrefragable and synergetic fifth step.

And I was right. For it was only in the last year that I entered the terminal stage, or *Grumment* as the Order calls it, due to those curious events which led me from Robert Putney Drake to Hagbard Celine.

I was sent to the Council on Foreign Relations banquet carrying the credentials of a Pinkerton detective; my supposed role as private dick was to keep an eye on the jewels of the ladies and other valuables. My real job was to place a small bug on the table where Robert Putney Drake would be sitting; I was on loan to IRS that week, and they didn't know that Justice had standing orders never to prosecute him for anything, so they were trying to prove he had concealed income. Naturally, I also had an ear peeled for anything that might be of import for the Illuminati, the A∴A∴ and the CIA, if my Lincoln Memorial contact really was CIA and not Military or Naval Intelligence or somebody else entirely. (You can be sure I often meditated on the possibility that he might be Moscow, Peking or Havana, and Winifred told me once that the Illuminati had reason to believe him part of an advance-guard fifth column sent by invaders from Alpha Centauri—but Grand Masters of the Illuminati are notorious put-on artists, and I didn't buy that yarn any more than I bought the tale that had originally brought me into the Illuminati, the one about them being a conspiracy to establish a world government run by British Israelites.) Conspiracy was its own reward to me, now; I didn't care what I was conspiring *for*. Art for art's sake. Not whether you betray or preserve but how you play the game. I sometimes even identified it with the A∴A∴ notion of the Great Work, for in the twisting labyrinths of my selves I was beginning to find the rough sketch for a soul.

There was a hawk-faced wop at Drake's table, very elegant in a spanking new tuxedo, but the cop in me

made him as illegit. Sometimes you can make a subject
precisely, as bunco-con, safe-blower, armed robber or
whatnot, but I could only place him vaguely somewhere on that side of the game; in fact, I associated
him with images of piracy on the high seas or the kind
of gambits the Borgias played. Somehow the conversation got around to a new book by somebody named
Mortimer Adler who had already written a hundred or
so great books if I understood the drift. One banker
type at the table was terribly keen on this Adler and
especially on his latest great book. "He says that we
and the Communists share the same Great Tradition"
(I could hear the caps by the way he pronounced the
term) "and we must join together against the one force
that really does threaten civilization—anarchism!"

There were several objections, in which Drake didn't
take part (he just sat back, puffing his cigar and looking agreeable to everyone, but I could see boredom under the surface) and the banker tried to explain the
Great Tradition, which was a bit over my head, and,
judging by the expressions around the table, a bit over
everybody else's head, too, when the hawk-faced dago
spoke up suddenly.

"I can put the Great Tradition in one word," he said
calmly. "Privilege."

Old Drake suddenly stopped looking agreeable-but-
bored—he seemed both interested and amused. "One
seldom encounters such a refreshing freedom from euphemism," he said, leaning forward. "But perhaps I am
reading too much into your remark, sir?"

Hawk-face sipped at his champagne and patted his
mouth with a napkin before answering. "I think not,"
he said at last. "Privilege is defined in most dictionaries
as a right or immunity giving special favors or benefits
to those who hold it. Another meaning in Webster is
'not subject to the usual rules or penalties.' The invalu-
able thesaurus gives such synonyms as power, authority, birthright, franchise, patent, grant, favor and, I'm
sad to say, pretension. Surely, we all know what privilege is in *this* club, don't we, gentlemen? Do I have to

remind you of the Latin roots, *privi*, private, and *lege*, law, and point out in detail how we have created our Private Law over here, just as the Politburo have created their own private law in their own sphere of influence?"

"But that's not the Great Tradition," the banker type said (later, I learned that he was actually a college professor; Drake was the only banker at that table). "What Mr. Adler means by the Great Tradition—"

"What Mortimer means by the Great Tradition," hawk-face interrupted rudely, "is a set of myths and fables invented to legitimize or sugar-coat the institution of privilege. Correct me if I'm wrong," he added more politely but with a sardonic grin.

"He means," the true believer said, "the undeniable axioms, the time-tested truths, the shared wisdom of the ages, the . . ."

"The myths and fables," hawk-face contributed gently.

"The sacred, time-tested wisdom of the ages," the other went on, becoming redundant. "The basic bedrock of civil society, of civilization. And we do share that with the Communists. And it is just that common humanistic tradition that the young anarchists, on both sides of the Iron Curtain, are blaspheming, denying and trying to destroy. It has nothing to do with privilege at all."

"Pardon me," the dark man said. "Are you a college professor?"

"Certainly. I'm head of the Political Science Department at Harvard!"

"Oh," the dark man shrugged. "I'm sorry for talking so bluntly before you. I thought I was entirely surrounded by men of business and finance."

The professor was just starting to look as if he spotted the implied insult in that formal apology when Drake interrupted.

"Quite so. No need to shock our paid idealists and turn them into vulgar realists overnight. At the same time, is it absolutely necessary to state what we all know in such a manner as to imply a rather hostile and outside viewpoint? Who are you and what is your trade, sir?"

"Hagbard Celine. Import-export. Gold and Appel Transfers here in New York. A few other small establishments in other ports." As he spoke my image of piracy and Borgia stealth came back strongly. "And we're not children here," he added, "so why should we avoid frank language?"

The professor, taken aback a foot or so by this turn in the conversation, sat perplexed as Drake replied:

"So. Civilization is privilege—or Private Law, as you say so literally. And we all know where Private Law comes from, except the poor professor here—out of the barrel of a gun, in the words of a gentleman whose bluntness you would appreciate. Is it your conclusion, then, that Adler is, for all his naivete, correct, and we have more in common with the Communist rulers than we have setting us at odds?"

"Let me *illuminate* you further," Celine said—and the way he pronounced the verb made me jump. Drake's blue eyes flashed a bit, too, but that didn't surprise me: anybody as rich as IRS thought he was, would *have* to be On the Inside.

"Privilege implies exclusion from privilege, just as advantage implies disadvantage," Celine went on. "In the same mathematically reciprocal way, profit implies loss. If you and I exchange equal goods, that is trade: neither of us profits and neither of us loses. But if we exchange unequal goods, one of us profits and the other loses. Mathematically. Certainly. Now, such mathematically unequal exchanges will always occur because some traders will be shrewder than others. But in total freedom—in anarchy—such unequal exchanges will be sporadic and irregular. A phenomenon of unpredictable periodicity, mathematically speaking. Now look about you, professor—raise your nose from your great books and survey the actual world as it is—and you will not observe such unpredictable functions. You will observe, instead, a mathematically smooth function, a steady profit accruing to one group and an equally steady loss accumulating for all others. Why is this, professor? Because the system is not free or random, any mathematician would tell you *a priori*. Well, then, where is the determining function, the factor that controls the other variables? You have named it yourself, or Mr. Adler has: the Great Tradition. Privilege, I prefer to call it. When A meets B in the marketplace, they do not bargain as equals. A bargains from a position of privilege; hence, he always profits and B always loses. There is no more Free Market here than there is on the other side of the Iron Curtain. The privileges, or Private Laws—the rules of the game, as promulgated by the Politburo and the General Congress of the Communist Party on that side and by the U.S. government and the Federal Reserve Board on this side—are slightly different; that's all. And it is this that is threatened by anarchists, and by the repressed anarchist in each of us," he concluded, strongly emphasizing the last clause, staring at Drake, not at the professor.

The professor had a lot more to say in a hurry then, about the laws of society being the laws of nature and the laws of nature being the laws of God, but I decided it was time to circulate a bit more so I didn't hear the rest of the conversation. The IRS has a complete tape of it, I'm sure, since I had placed the bug long before the meal.

The next time I saw Robert Putney Drake was a turning point. I was being sent to New York again, on a mission for Naval Intelligence this time, and Winifred gave me a message that had to be delivered to Drake personally; the Order wouldn't trust any mechanical communication device. Strangely, my CIA drop also gave me a message for Drake, and it was the same message. That didn't jar me any, since it merely confirmed some of what I had begun to suspect by then.

I went to this office on Wall Street, near the corner of Broad (just about where I'd be toiling at Corporate Law, if my family had had its way) and I told his secretary, "Knigge of Pyramid Productions to see Mr.

Drake." That was the password that week; Knigge had been a Bavarian baron and second-in-command to Weishaupt in the original AISB. I sat and cooled my heels awhile, studying the decor, which was heavily Elizabethan and made me wonder if Drake had some private notion about being a reincarnation of his famous ancestor.

Finally, Drake's door opened and who stood there but Atlanta Hope, looking kind of wild-eyed and distraught. Drake had his arm on her shoulder and he said piously, "May your work hasten the day when America returns to purity." She stumbled past me in a kind of daze and I was ushered into his office. He motioned me to an overstuffed chair and stared at my face until something clicked. "Another Knigge in the woodpile," he laughed suddenly. "The last time I saw you, you were a Pinkerton detective." You had to admire a memory like that; it had been a year since the CFR banquet and I hadn't done anything to attract his attention that night.

"I'm FBI as well as being in the Order," I said, leaving out a few things.

"You're more than that," he said flatly, sitting behind a desk as big as some kids' playgrounds. "But I have enough on my mind this week without prying into how many sides you're playing. What's the message?"

"It comes from the Order and the CIA both," I said, to be clear and relatively above-board. "This it is: *The Taiwan heroin shipments will not arrive on time. The Laotian opium fields are temporarily in the hands of the Pathet Lao. Don't believe the Pentagon releases about our troops having the Laotian situation under control.* No answer required." I started to rise.

"Wait, damn it," Drake said, frowning. "This is more important than you realize." His face went blank and I could tell his mind was racing like an engine with governor off; it was impressive. "What's your rank in the Order?" he asked finally.

"Illuminatus Prelator," I confessed, humbly.

"Not nearly high enough. But you have more practical espionage experience than a great many higher members. You'll have to do." The old barracuda relaxed, having come to a decision. "How much do you know about the Cult of the Black Mother?" he asked.

"The most militant and most secret Black Power group in the country," I said carefully. "They avoid publicity instead of seeking it, because their strategy is based on an eventual coup d'etat, not on revolution. Until a minute ago, I thought no white man in the country even knew of their existence, except those of us in the FBI. The Bureau has never reported on them to other government agencies, because we're ashamed to admit we've never been able to keep an informer inside for long. They all die of natural causes, that's what bugs us."

"Nobody in the Order has ever told you the truth?" Drake demanded.

"No," I said, curious. "I thought what I just told you was the truth."

"Winifred is more closed-mouth than he needs to be," Drake said. "The Cult of the Black Mother is entirely controlled by the Order. They monitor ghetto affairs for us. Right now, they predict a revival of 1960s-style uprisings for late summer in Harlem, on the West Side of Chicago, and in Detroit. They need to up the addiction rate at least eighteen percent, hopefully twenty or twenty-five percent, in all those areas, or the property damage will be even more enormous than we are prepared to absorb.

"They can't do it, if they have to cut their present stock even more than it's already cut. There just has to be more junk in the ghettoes or all hell will break loose by August."

I began to realize that he had used the word "monitor" in its strict cybernetic meaning.

"There's only one alternative," Drake went on. "The black market. There's a very cunning and well-organized group that's been trying to crack the CIA-Syndicate heroin monopoly for quite a while now. The Cult of the Black Mother will have to deal with them directly. I don't want the Order involved at all—that would make it messy, and besides we'll have to crush this group later, when we're able to pierce their cover."

The upshot of it was that I found myself on One Hundred Tenth Street in Harlem, feeling very white and un-bulletproof, entering a restaurant called The Signifying Monkey. Walking through a lot of hostile stares, I went direct to the coffee-colored woman at the cash register and said, "I've got a tombstone disposition."

She gave me a piercing look and muttered, "Upstairs, after the men's room, the door marked Private. Knock five times." She grinned maliciously, "And if you're not kosher, kiss your white ass good-bye, brother."

I went up the stairs, found the door, knocked five times, and one eye in an ebony face looked out at me stonily. "White," he said.

"Man," I replied.

"Native," he came back.

"Born," I finished. A bolt slipped on a chain and the door opened the rest of the way. I never did find out whose idea of a joke that password was—they had lifted it from the Ku Klux Klan, of course. The room I was in was heavy with marijuana smoke, but I could see that it was decently furnished and dominated by an enormous statue of Kali, the Black Mother; I had visions of weird *Gunga Din* rites and shouts of "Kill for the love of Kali!" There were four other men in the room, in addition to the one who let me in, and two reefers were circulating, one deosil and one widdershins.

"Who you from?" a voice asked in the murk.

"AISB," I answered carefully, "And I'm to speak to Hassan i Sabbah X."

"You're speaking to him," said the tallest and blackest character in the bunch, passing me a reefer. I took a quick, deep draw and, Christ, it was good. I'd been half addicted ever since the March on the Pentagon in 1967, where I walked right behind Norman

Mailer part of the way, and later fell in with some hippies who were sitting on the steps smoking it. I say I was half addicted since then, because two of me believe, as a loyal government employee, that the old government publications claiming marijuana is addicting must be true or the government wouldn't have printed them. Fortunately, the other two of me know that it isn't addicting, so I don't go through very bad withdrawal when it's scarce.

I started to outline the situation to Hassan i Sabbah X but the other joint came around, widdershins, and I took a drag on that. "A man could get stoned doing this," I said facetiously.

"*Yeah,*" a satisfied black voice agreed in the gloom.

Well, by the time I explained the problem to Hassan, I was so bombed that I immediately let him recruit me for the next step, on his rationalization that a white man could handle it easier than a black man. Actually, I was curious to contact this group of heroin pirates.

Hassan wrote the address carefully. "Now, here's the passwords," he said. "You say, 'Do what thou wilt shall be the whole of the Law.' Don't say 'Do what you will'—they can't stand anybody fucking around with the words, it has something to do with magic. She replies, 'Love is the law, love under will.' Then you finish it with 'Every man and every woman is a star.' Got it?"

You can bet your ass I got it. I was almost goggle-eyed. It was the passwords of the A∴A∴

"One more thing," Hassan added, "be sure to ask for Miss Mao, *not* Mama Sutra. Mama isn't cleared for this."

(As the Braniff jet took off from Kennedy International, Simon was already deep into *Telemachus Sneezed* again. He didn't notice the preoccupied-looking red-headed young man who took the seat across the aisle; if he had, he would have immediately made the identification, *cop*. He was reading, "Factory smog is a symbol of progress, of the divine fire of industry, of the flaming deity of Heracleitus.")

HARRY KRISHNA HARRY KRISHNA HARRY HARRY

Harry Coin didn't know what the drug was; Miss Portinari had merely said, "It takes you further than pot," and handed him the tablet. It might be that LSD the hippies use, he reflected, or it might be something else entirely that Hagbard and FUCKUP had concocted in the ship's laboratory. Miss Portinari went on chanting:

HARRY RAMA HARRY RAMA HARRY HARRY

Obediently, he continued to stare into the aquamarine pool between them; she wore a yellow robe and sat placidly in the lotus position.

("I've gotta know," he had told her. "I can't go around with two sets of memories and never be sure which are real and which Hagbard just put in my head like a man puts a baby into a woman. Did I kill all those people or didn't I?"

"You must be in the proper frame of mind before you can accept the answer," she had replied remotely.)

HARRY COINSHA HARRY COINSHA HARRY HARRY

Was she changing the chant or was it the drug? He tried to keep calm and continue staring into the pool, as she had ordered, but the porcelain design around it was changing. Instead of two dolphins chasing each other's tails like the astrological sign of Pisces (the age that was ending, according to Hagbard), it was now one long serpentlike creature trying to swallow *its own* tail.

That's me, he thought. A lot of people have told me I'm as thin and long as a snake.

And it's everybody else, too (he realized suddenly). I'm seeing what George told me: the Self pursuing the Self and trying to govern it, the Self trying to swallow the Self.

But as he stared, fascinated, the pool turned red,

blood red, the color of guilt, and he felt it reach out and try to pull him down into it, into red oblivion, a void made flush.

"It's alive," he screamed. "Jesus Motherfucking Christ!"

Miss Portinari casually stirred the pool, remote and calm, and its spiral inward slowly turned back to aquamarine. Harry felt himself blushing, *it was only a hallucination,* and muttered, "Pardon my language, ma'am."

"Don't apologize," she said sharply. "The most important truths always appear first as blasphemies or obscenities. That's why every great innovator is persecuted. And the sacraments look obscene, too, to an outsider. The eucharist is just sublimated cannibalism, to the unawakened. When the Pope kisses the feet of the laity, he looks like an old toe-queen to some people. The rites of Pan look like a suburban orgy. Think about what you said. Since it has five words and fits the Law of Fives, it is especially significant."

This is a weird bunch, but they know important things, Harry reminded himself. He looked deep into the blue spiral and silently repeated to himself, "It's alive, Jesus Motherfucking Christ, it's alive . . ."

Jesus, looking strangely hawk-faced and Hagbardian, rose from the pool. "This is my *bodhi,*" he said, pointing. Harry looked and saw Buddha sitting beneath the bodhi-tree. "Tat TVam Asi," he said, and the falling leaves of the tree turned into millions of TV sets all broadcasting the same Laurel and Hardy movie. "Now look what you made me do," Hardy was saying . . . In a previous incarnation, Harry saw himself as a centurion, Semper Cuni Linctus, driving the nails into the cross. "Look," he said to Jesus, "nothing personal. I'm only following orders." "So am I," Jesus said, "My Father's orders. Aren't we all?"

"Look into the pool," Miss Portinari repeated. "Just look into the pool."

It was like each Chinese box had another Chinese box inside it; but the best of all belonged to Miss Mao

Tsu-hsi. We were reclining in her trim but elegant pad on West Eighty-seventh Street, passing a joint back and forth and comparing multiple identities. We were naked on a bearskin rug, a dream come true, for she was my ideal woman. "I got into the A∴A∴ first, Tobias," she was saying. "They recruited me at a Ba'Hai meeting—they have cruisers out, looking for likely prospects, in every mystical group from Subud to Scientology, you know. Then Naval Intelligence contacted me and I reported to them on what the A∴A∴ was up to. I'm not flexible as you, though, and my loyalties tend to stay fairly constant—chiefly I was reporting to A∴A∴ what I gleaned from Naval Intelligence. I did believe in the A∴A∴ basically. Until I met *Him*."

"That reminds me," I said, jealous of the worshipful way she said *Him* as if talking about a god. "If he's coming soon, shouldn't we get up and put some clothes on?"

"If you want to be bourgeois," she said.

While we were dressing, I remembered something. "By the way," I asked casually, "who are you spying on Mama Sutra for—the A∴A∴, Naval Intelligence, or *Him?*"

"All three of them." She was starting to pull her panties on, and I said suddenly, "Wait." I knelt and kissed her pussy one last time, "For the nicest Chinese box I've opened in this whole case," I said gallantly. That was my Illuminati training; as an FBI man, I was ashamed of such a perverted act.

We finished dressing and she was pouring some wine (a light German vintage from, of all places, Bavaria) when the knock came.

Miss Mao sidled over to the door in her slinky Chinese dress and said softly, "Hail Eris."

"All hail Discordia," came a voice from outside. She slipped the lock and a little fat man walked in. My first reaction was astonishment; he didn't look anything like the superintellectual superhero she had described.

"Hagbard couldn't come," he said briefly. "I'll handle the sale, and initiate *you,*" with a glance at me, "into the Legion of Dynamic Discord, if you're really ready, as Miss Mao says, to battle every government on earth and the Illuminati to boot."

"I'm ready," I said passionately. "I'm tired being a puppet on four sets of strings." (Actually, I know I just wanted a fifth set.)

"Good," he said. "Put her there," and he held out his hand. As we shook, he said, *"Episkopos* Jim Cartwright of the Mad Dog Cabal."

"Tobias Knight," I said, "of the FBI, the CIA, the A∴A∴ and the Illuminati."

He blinked briefly. "I've met double agents and triple agents, but you're the first quadruple agent in my experience. I guess this was inevitable, by the Law of Fives. Welcome to the fifth ring of the world's oldest continuous Five Ring Circus. Prepare for Death and Rebirth."

JESUS   MOTHERFUCKING   CHRIST   IT'S ALIVE . . .

ILLUMINATUS!
PART III

LEVIATHAN

The mutation from terrestrial to interstellar life
must be made, because the womb planet itself is going
to blow up within a few billion years . . . Planet Earth
is a stepping stone on our time-trip through the galaxy.
Life has to get its seed-self off the planet
to survive . . .
There are also some among us who are bored with the
amniotic level of mentation on this planet and look
up in hopes of finding someone entertaining to talk to.
—TIMOTHY LEARY, Ph.D., and
L. WAYNE BRENNER, *Terra II*

THE NINTH TRIP, OR YESOD
(WALPURGISNACHT ROCK)

SINK is played by Discordians and people of much ilk.
PURPOSE: To sink object or an object or a thing . . . in
water or mud or anything you can sink something in.
RULES: Sinking is allowed in any manner. To date, ten-
pound chunks of mud have been used to sink a tobacco can.
It is preferable to have a pit of water or a hole to drop things
into. But rivers—bays—gulfs—I dare say even oceans—can
be used.
TURNS are taken thusly: whosoever gets the junk up and in
the air first.
DUTY: It shall be the duty of all persons playing SINK to help
find more objects to sink, once one object is sunk.
UPON SINKING: The sinker shall yell, "I sank it!" or something equally as thoughtful.
NAMING OF OBJECTS is sometimes desirable. The object is
named by the finder of such object, and whoever sinks it can
say (for instance), "I sank Columbus, Ohio."

> —ALA HERA, E.L., N.S., Rayville Apple Panthers,
> quoted in *Principia Discordia*, by Malaclypse the
> Younger, K.S.C.

For over a week the musicians had been boarding planes
and heading for Ingolstadt. As early as April 23, while Simon and Mary Lou listened to Clark Kent and His Supermen and George Dorn wrote about the sound of one eye
opening, the Fillet of Soul, finding bookings sparse in London, drove into Ingolstadt in a Volvo painted seventeen
Day-Glo colors and flaunting Ken Kesey's old slogan,
"Furthur!" On April 24 a real trickle began, and while Harry Coin looked into Hagbard Celine's eyes and saw no mercy there (Buckminster Fuller, just then, was explaining
"omnidirectional halo" to his seatmate on a TWA Whisper-

jet in mid-Pacific), the Wrathful Visions, the Cockroaches, and the Senate and the People of Rome all drove down Rathausplatz in bizarre vehicles, while the Ultra-Violet Hippopotamus and the Thing on the Doorstep both navigated Friedrich-Ebert-Strasse in even more amazing buses. On April 25, while Carmel looted Maldonado's safe and George Dorn repeated "I Am the Robot," the trickle turned to a stream and in came Science and Health with Key to the Scriptures, the Glue Sniffers, King Kong and His Skull Island Dinosaurs, the Howard Johnson Hamburger, the Riot in Cell Block Ten, the House of Frankenstein, the Signifying Monkey, the Damned Thing, the Orange Moose, the Indigo Banana, and the Pink Elephant. On April 26 the stream became a flood, and while Saul and Barney Muldoon tried to reason with Markoff Chaney and he struggled in their grip, Ingolstadters found themselves inundated by Frodo Baggins and His Ring, the Mouse That Roars, the Crew of the Flying Saucer, the Magnificent Ambersons, the House I Live In, the Sound of One Hand, the Territorial Imperative, the Druids of Stonehenge, the Heads of Easter Island, the Lost Continent of Mu, Bugs Bunny and His Fourteen Carrots, the Gospel According to Marx, the Card-Carrying Members, the Sands of Mars, the Erection, the Association, the Amalgamation, the St. Valentine's Day Massacre, the Climax, the Broad Jumpers, the Pubic Heirs, the Freeks, and the Windows. Mick Jagger and his new group, the Trashers, arrived on April 27, while the FBI was interviewing every whore in Las Vegas, and there quickly followed the Roofs, Moses and Monotheism, Steppenwolf, Civilization and Its Discontents, Poor Richard and His Rosicrucian Secrets, the Wrist Watch, the Nova Express, the Father of Waters, the Human Beings, the Washington Monument, the Thalidomide Babies, the Strangers in a Strange Land, Dr. John the Night Tripper, Joan Baez, the Dead Man's Hand, Joker and the One-Eyed Jacks, Peyote Woman, the Heavenly Blues, the Golems, the Supreme Awakening, the Seven Types of Ambiguity, the Cold War, the Street Fighters, the Bank Burners, the Slaves of Satan, the Domino Theory, and Maxwell and His Demons. On April 28, while Dillinger loaded his gun and the kachinas of Orabi began the drum-beating, the Acapulco Gold-Diggers arrived, followed by the Epic of Gilgamesh, the Second Law of Thermodynamics, Dracula and His Brides, the

Iron Curtain, the Noisy Minority, the International Debt, Three Contributions to the Theory of Sex, the Cloud of Unknowing, the Birth of a Nation, the Zombies, Attila and His Huns, Nihilism. the Catatonics. the Thorndale Jag Offs, the Haymarket Bomb, the Head of a Dead Cat, the Shadow Out of Time, the Sirens of Titan, the Player Piano, the Streets of Laredo, the Space Odyssey, the Blue Moonies, the Crabs, the Dose, the Grassy Knoll, the Latent Image, the Wheel of Karma, the Communion of Saints, the City of God, General Indefinite Wobble, the Left-Handed Monkey Wrench, the Thorn in the Flesh, the Rising Podge, SHA-ZAM, the Miniature Sled, the 23rd Appendix, the Other Cheek, the Occidental Ox, Ms. and the Chairperson, Cohen Cohen Cohen and Kahn, and the Joint Phenomenon.

On April 29, while Danny Pricefixer listened raptly to Mama Sutra, the deluge descended upon Igolstadt: Buses, trucks, station wagons, special trains, and every manner of transport except dog sleds, brought in the Wonders of the Invisible World, Maule's Curse, the Jesus Head Trip, Ahab and His Amputation, the Horseless Headsmen, the Leaves of Grass, the Gettysburg Address, the Rosy-Fingered Dawn, the Wine-Dark Sea, Nirvana, the Net of Jewels, Here Comes Everybody, the Pisan Cantos, the Snows of Yesteryear, the Pink Dimension, the Goose in the Bottle, the Incredible Hulk, the Third Bardo, Aversion Therapy, the Irresistible Force, MC Squared, the Enclosure Acts, Perpetual Emotion, the 99-Year Lease, the Immovable Object, Spaceship Earth, the Radiocarbon Method, the Rebel Yell, the Clenched Fist, the Doomsday Machine, the Rand Scenario, the United States Commitment, the Entwives, the Players of Null-A, the Prelude to Space, Thunder and Roses, Armageddon, the Time Machine, the Mason Word, the Monkey Business, the Works, the Eight of Swords, Gorilla Warfare, the Box Lunch, the Primate Kingdom, the New Aeon, the Enola Gay, the Octet Truss, the Stochastic Process, the Fluxions, the Burning House, the Phantom Captain, the Decline of the West, the Duelists, the Call of the Wild, Consciousness III, the Reorganized Church of the Latter-Day Saints, Standard Oil of Ohio, the Zig-Zag Men, the Rubble Risers, the Children of Ra, TNT, Acceptable Radiation, the Pollution Level, the Great Beast, the Whores of Babylon, the Waste Land, the Ugly Truth, the Final Diagnosis, Solution Unsatisfactory, the Heat Death of the Universe, Mere Noise, I Opening, the Nine Unknown Men, the Horse of Another Color, the Falling Rock Zone, the Ascent of the Serpent, Reddy Willing and Unable, the Civic Monster, Hercules and the Tortoise, the Middle Pillar, the Deleted Expletive, Deep Quote, LuCiFeR, the Dog Star, Nuthin' Sirius, and Preparation H.

(But, on April 23, while Joe Malik and Tobias Knight were setting the bomb in *Confrontation*'s office, the Dealy Lama broadcast a telepathic message to Hagbard Celine saying *It's not too late to turn back* and Joe hesitated a moment, blurting finally, "Can we be sure? Can we be really sure?" Tobias Knight raised weary eyes. "We can't be sure of anything," he said simply. "Celine has popped up at banquets and other social occasions where Drake was present five times now, and each conversation eventually got around to the puppet metaphor and Celine's favorite bit about the unconscious saboteur in everybody. What else can we assume?" He set the timer for 2:30 A.M. and then met Joe's eyes again. "I wish I could have given George a few more hints," Joe said lamely. "You gave him too damned many hints as it is," Knight replied, closing the bomb casing.)

On April 1, while God's lightning paraded about UN Plaza and Captain Tequila y Mota was led before a firing squad, John Dillinger arose from his cramped lotus position and stopped broadcasting the mathematics of magic. He stretched, shook all over like a dog, and proceeded down the tunnel under the UN building to Alligator Control. OTO yoga was always a strain, and he was glad to abandon it and return to more mundane matters.

A guard stopped him at the AC door, and John handed over his plastic eye-and-pyramid card. The guard, a surly-looking woman whose picture John had seen in the newspapers as a leader of the Radical Lesbians, fed the card into a wall slot; it came out again almost at once, and a green light flashed.

"Pass," she said. *"Heute die Welt."*

"Morgens das Sonnensystem," John replied. He entered the beige plastic underworld of Alligator Control, and walked through geodesic corridors until he came to the door marked MONOTONY MONITOR. After he inserted his card in the appropriate slot, another green light blinked and the door opened.

Taffy Rheingold, wearing a mini-skirt and still pert and attractive despite her years and gray hair, looked up from her typing. She sat behind a beige plastic desk that matched the beige plastic of the entire Alligator Control headquarters. A broad smile spread across her face when she recognized him.

"John," she said happily. "What brings you here?"

"Gotta see your boss," he answered, "but before you buzz him, do you know you're in another book?"

"The new Edison Yerby novel?" She shrugged philosophically. "Not quite as bad as what Atlanta Hope did to me in *Telemachus Sneezed*."

"Yeah, I suppose, but how did this guy find out so much? Some of those scenes are *absolutely true*. Is he in the Order?" John demanded.

"A mind leak," Taffy said. "You know how it is with writers. One of the Illuminati Magi scanned Yerby and he thought he had invented all of it. Not a clue. The same kind of leak we had when Condon wrote *The Manchurian Candidate*." She shrugged. "It just happens sometimes."

"I suppose," John said absently. "Well, tell your boss I'm here."

In a minute he was in the inner office, being effusively greeted by the old man in the wheelchair. "John, John, it's so *good* to see you again," said the crooning voice that had hypnotized millions; otherwise, it was hard, in this aged figure, to recognize the once handsome and dynamic Franklin Delano Roosevelt.

"How did you get stuck with a job like this?" Dillinger asked finally, after the amenities had been exchanged.

"You know how it is with the new gang in Agharti," Roosevelt murmured. " 'New blood, new blood'—that's their battle cry. All of us old and faithful servants are being pushed into minor bureaucratic positions."

"I remember your funeral," John said wistfully. "I was envious, thinking of you going to Agharti and working directly with the Five. And now it's come to this . . . Monotony Monitor in Alligator Control. Sometimes I get pissed with the Order."

"Careful," Roosevelt said. "They might be scanning. And a double agent, such as you are, John, is always under special surveillance. Besides, this isn't really so bad, considering how they reacted in Agharti when the Pearl Harbor revelations started coming out in the late forties. I did not handle that matter too elegantly, you know, and they had a right to demote me. And Alligator Control is interesting."

"Maybe," John said dubiously. "I never have understood this project."

"It's very significant work," Roosevelt said seriously. "New York and Chicago are our major experiments in testing the *mehum* tolerance level. In Chicago we concentrate on mere ugliness and brutality, but in New York we're simultaneously carrying on a long-range boredom study. That's where Alligator Control comes in. We've got to keep the alligators in the sewers down to a minimum so the Bureau of Sanitation doesn't reactivate their own Alligator Control Project, which would be an opportunity for adventure and a certain natural *mehum* hunting-band mystique among some of the young males. It's the same reason we took out the trolley cars: Riding them was more fun than buses. Believe me, Monotony Monitoring is a very important part of the New York project."

"I've seen the mental-health figures," John said, nodding. "About seventy percent of the people in the most congested part of Manhattan are already prepsychotic."

"We'll have it up to eighty percent by 1980!" Roosevelt cried, with some of his old steely-eyed determination. But then he fixed a joint in his ivory holder and, clenching it at his famous jaunty angle, added, "And *we're* immune, thanks to Sabbah's Elixir." He quoted cheerfully: " 'Grass does more than Miltown can/ To justify God's ways to man.' But what *does* bring you here, John?"

"A 'small job,' " Dillinger said. "There's a man in my organization named Malik who is getting a little too close to the secret of the whole game. I need some help here in New York to set him off on a snark hunt until after May first. I'd like to know who you've got on your staff closest to him."

"Malik," Roosevelt said thoughtfully. "That would be the Malik of *Confrontation* magazine?" John nodded, and Roosevelt sat back in his wheelchair, smiling. "This is a lead-pipe cinch. We've got an agent in his office."

(But neither of them realized that ten days later a dolphin swimming through the ruins of Atlantis would discover that no Dragon Star had ever fallen. Nor could they have guessed how Hagbard Celine would reevaluate Illuminati history when that revelation was reported to him, and they had no clue of the decision he would then make, which would change everybody's conspiracies shockingly and unexpectedly.)

"Here are the five alternate histories," Gruad said, his wise old eyes crinkling humorously. "Each of you will be responsible for planting the evidence to make one of these histories seem fairly credible. Wo Topod, you get the Carcosa story. Evoe, you get the lost continent of Mu." He handed out two bulky envelopes. "Gao Twone, you get this charming snake story—I want variations of it scattered throughout Africa and the Near East." He handed out another envelope. "Unica, you get the Urantia story, but that one isn't to be released until fairly late in the Game." He picked up the fifth envelope and smiled again. "Kajeci, my love, you get the Atlantis story, with certain changes that make us out to be the most double-dyed bastards in all history. Let me explain the purpose behind that . . ."

And in 1974 the four members of the American Medical Association gazed somberly down at Joe Malik from his office wall. It looked to be a long day, and there was nothing to anticipate as exciting as last night had been. There was a thick manuscript in a manila envelope in the IN box; he noticed that the stamps had been removed. That was doubtless Pat Walsh's work; her kid brother was a stamp collector. Joe smiled, remembering the diary he'd kept when he was a teen-ager. In case his parents found it, he always referred to masturbation as stamp collecting. "Collected five stamps today—a new record." "After five days of no stamps, collected a beauty in several colors. Enormous, but the negotiations were tiring." Doubtless today's kids, if they kept diaries (they probably used casette tape recorders), either talked openly about it or considered it too incidental to mention. Joe shook his head. The Catholic teen-ager he had been in 1946 was no more remote than the crumbling liberal he'd been in 1968. And yet, in spite of all he'd been through, much of the time he felt that all of the knowledge didn't make a difference. People like Pat and Peter still treated him as if he were the same man, and he still did the same job in the same way.

He took the heavy manuscript out and shook the envelope. Damn it, there was no return envelope. Well, working at a magazine like *Confrontation*, whose contributors were mostly radicals and the kind of kooks who were willing to write for no bread, you didn't really expect them to enclose stamped self-addressed envelopes. There was a covering letter. Joe sucked in his breath when he saw the golden apple embossed in the upper left-hand corner.

Hail Eris and Hi, Joe,

Here is a brilliant, original interpretation of international finance called "Vampirism, the Heliocentric Theory and the Gold Standard." It's by Jorge Lobengula, a really far-out young Discordian thinker. JAMs don't go in much for writing, but Discordians, fortunately, do. If you find it worth printing, you may have it at your usual rates. Make the check payable to the Fernando Poo Secessionist Movement and sent it to Jorge at 15 Rue Hassan, Algiers 8.

Incidentally, Jorge will not be involved in the Fernando Poo coup. He is turning toward a synergistic economics, which will gradually lead him to see the folly of Fernando Poo going it alone. And the coup itself, of course, will not be any of our doing. But Jorge will be a key figure in Equatorial Guinea's subsequent economic recovery—assuming the world pulls through that particular mess. If you can't use this paper, burn it. Jorge has plenty of copies.

Five tons of flax,

Mal

P.S. The Fernando Poo rebellion may still be one or two years in the future, so don't jump to the conclusion that the pot is coming to a boil already. Remember what I told you about the goose in the bottle.

M.

(Down the hall in the lady's room, bolting the door for privacy, Pat Walsh takes her transistorized transmitter from her pantyhose and broadcasts to the receiver at the Council on Foreign Relations headquarters half a block east. "I'm still writing lots of Illuminati research papers, and they'll give him plenty of false leads. The big news today is an article on Erisian economics by a Fernando Poo national. It came with a covering letter signed 'Mal,' and from the context, I feel fairly certain it's the original—Malaclypse the Elder himself. If not, at last we've got a lead on that damned elusive Malaclypse the Younger. The envelope was postmarked Mad Dog, Texas . . .")

Joe put down Mal's letter, trying to remember the obscure references to Fernando Poo before the movie last night. Someone had said something was going to happen there. Maybe he should get a stringer on the island, or even send somebody over. A malicious grin crossed his face: It might be interesting to send Peter. First some AUM, then a trip to Fernando Poo. That might fix Peter up.

Joe flipped through the Lobengula manuscript quickly, scanning. There were no fnords. That was a relief. He had become painfully conscious of them since Hagbard had removed the aversion reflex, and each fnord had sent a pang through him that was a ghost of the low-grade emergency in which he had previously lived. He turned back to the first page and began to read in earnest:

VAMPIRISM, THE HELIOCENTRIC THEORY AND THE GOLD STANDARD
by Jorge Lobengula
Do What Thou Wilt Shall Be The Whole Of The Law

Joe stopped. That sentence had been used in the Black Mass in Chicago and further back, he knew, it was the code of the Abbey of Theleme in Rabelais; but there was something else about it that chewed at his consciousness, something that suggested a hidden meaning. This was not just a first axiom of anarchism—there was something else there, something more hermetic. He looked back at Mal's letter: "Remember what I told you about the goose in the bottle."

That was a simple riddle used by Zen Masters in the training of monks, Joe remembered. You take a newborn gosling and slip it through the neck of a bottle. Month after month you keep it in there and feed it, until it is a full-grown goose and can no longer be passed through the bottle's neck. The question is: Without breaking the bottle, how do you get the goose out?

Neither riddle seemed to shed much light on the other.
Do what thou wilt shall be the whole of the law.
How do you get the goose out of the bottle?

"Holy God." Joe laughed. "Do what *thou* wilt shall be the whole of the law."

The goose gets out of the bottle the same way John Dillinger got out of the "escape-proof" Crown Point jail.

"Jesus motherfucking Christ," Joe gasped. *"It's alive!"*

JUST LIKE A TREE THAT'S STANDING BY THE WAAATER

WE SHALL NOT   WE SHALL NOT BE MOVED

The only place where all five Illuminati Primi met was the Great Hall of Gruad in Agharti, the thirty-thousand-year-old Illuminati center on the peaks of the Tibetan Himalayas, with a lower-level water front harbor on the vast underground Sea of Valusia.

"We will report in the usual order," said Brother Gracchus Gruad, pressing a button in the table before him so his words would automatically be recorded on impervium wire for the Illuminati archives. "First of all, Fernando Poo. Jorge Lobengula, having decided that the combined resources of Fernando Poo and Rio Muni can be reallocated so as to increase the per-capita wealth of citizens of both provinces, has accordingly broken with the Fernando Poo separatists and returned to Rio Muni, where he hopes to persuade Fang leaders to go along with his schemes for economic redevelopment. Our plans now center on a Captain Ernesto Tequila y Mota, one of the few Caucasians left on Fernando Poo. He has good contacts among the wealthier Bubi, the ones who favor separatism, and he is inordinately ambitious. I don't think we need contemplate a change in timetable."

"I should hope not," said Brother Marcus Marconi. "It would be such a shame not to immanentize the Eschaton on May first."

"Well, we can't count on May first," said Brother Gracchus Gruad. "But with three distinct plans pointing in that direction, one of them is bound to hit. Let's hear from you, Brother Marcus."

"Charles Mocenigo has now reached Anthrax Leprosy Mu. A few more nightmares at the right moment and he'll be home."

Sister Theda Theodora spoke next. "Atlanta Hope and God's Lighting are becoming more powerful all the time. The President will be scared shitless of her when the time comes, and he'll be ready to be even more totalitarian than her, just to keep her from taking over."

"I don't trust Drake," said Brother Marcus Marconi.

"Of course," said Brother Gracchus Gruad. "But he has builded his house by the sea."

"And he who builds by the sea builds on sand," said Brother Otto Ogatai. "My turn. Our record, *Give, Sympathize, Control*, is an international hit. Our next tour of Europe should be an extraordinary success. Then we can begin, very slowly and tentatively, negotiations for the *Walpurgisnacht* festival. Anyone who tries to develop the idea prematurely, of course, will have to be deflected."

"Or liquidated," said Brother Gracchus Gruad. He looked down the long table at the man who sat by himself at the far end. "Now you. You've been silent all this time. What do you have to say?"

The man laughed. "A few words from the skeleton at the feast, eh?" This was the fifth and most formidable Illuminatus Primus, Brother Henry Hastur, the only one who would have the gall to name himself after a lloigor. "It is written," he said, "that the universe is a practical joke by the general at the expense of the particular. Do not be too quick to laugh or weep, if you believe this saying. All I can say is, there is a serious threat in being to all your plans. I warn you. You have been warned. You may all die. Are you afraid of death? You need not answer—I see that you are. That in itself may be a mistake. I have tried to explain to you about not fearing death, but you will not listen. All your other problems follow from that."

The other four Illuminati Primi listened in cold, disdainful silence and did not reply.

"If all are One," the fifth Illuminatus added significantly, "all violence is masochism."

"If all are One," Brother Otto replied nastily, "all sex is masturbation. Let's have no more *mehum* metaphysics here."

HARE KRISHNA HARE HARE

"George!"

Then George was here, with Celine, in Ingolstadt. This was going to be tricky. George's head was bent over an earthenware stein, doubtless full of the local brew.

"George!" Joe called again. George looked up, and Joe was astonished. He had never seen George like this before. George shook his shoulder-length blond hair to clear it away from his face, and Joe looked deep into his eyes.

They were strange eyes, eyes without fear or pity or guilt, eyes that acknowledged that the natural state of man was one of perpetual surprise, and therefore could not be greatly surprised by any one thing, even the unexpected appearance of Joe Malik. What has Celine done to him in the past seven days? Joe wondered. Has he destroyed his mind or has he—illuminated him?

Actually, it was George's tenth stein of beer that day, and he was very, very drunk.

HARRY ROBOT HARRY HARRY

(Civil liberties were suspended and a state of national emergency declared during a special presidential broadcast on all channels between noon and 12:30 on April 30. Fifteen minutes later the first rioting started in New York, at the Port Authority on Forty-first Street, where a mob attempted to overrun the police and steal buses in which to escape to Canada. It was 6:45 P.M. just then in Ingolstadt, and Count Dracula and His Brides were giving forth a raga-rock version of an old Walt Disney cartoon song . . . And in Los Angeles, where it was 9:45 A.M., a five-person Morituri group, hurriedly convened, decided to use up all its bombs against police stations immediately. "Cripple the motherfucker before it's *heavy*," said their leader, a sixteen-year-old girl with braces on her teeth . . . Her idiom, in standard English, meant: "Paralyze the fascist state before it's entrenched" . . . and Saul, trusting the pole-vaulter in the unconscious, was leading Barney and Markoff Chaney into the mouth of Lehman Cavern . . . Carmel, nearly a kilometer south of them, and several hundred feet closer to the center of the earth, still clutched his briefcase and its five million green gods, but he did not move . . . Near him were the bones of a dozen bats he had eaten . . .)

TO BE A BAT'S A BUM THING

A SILLY AND A DUMB THING

BUT AT LEAST A BAT IS SOMETHING

AND YOU'RE NOT A THING AT ALL

Joe Malik, hit by the raga rock as if by an avalanche of separate notes which were each boulders, felt his body dissolve. Count Dracula wailed it again (YOU'RE NOT A THING AT ALL), and Joe felt mind crumble along with body and could find no center, no still point in the waves of sound and energy; the fucking acid was Hagbard's ally and had turned against him, he was dying; even the words "Hey that cat's on a bummer" came from far away, and his effort to determine if they really meant him collapsed into an effort to remember what the words were, which imploded into an uncertainty about what effort he was trying to make, mental or physical, and why. "Because," he cried out, "because, because—" . . . but "because" meant nothing.

YOU'RE NOTHING BUT A NOTHING

NOTHING BUT A NOTHING

"But I can't take acid now," George had protested. "I'm so damned drunk on this Bavarian beer, it's sure to be a down trip."

"Everybody takes acid," Hagbard said coldly. "Those are Miss Portinari's orders, and she's right. We can only face this thing if our minds are completely open to the Outside."

"Hey, dig," Clark Kent said. "That French cat eating the popsicle."

"Yeah?" said one of the Supermen.

"It's Jean-Paul Sartre. Who'd ever expect to see *him* here?" Kent shook his head. "Hope to hell he stays long enough to hear our gig. Sheee-it, the influence that *man* has had on me! He should hear it come back at him in music."

"That's your trip, baby," a second Superman said. "I don't give a fuck what *any* motherfuckin' honky thinks about our music."

YOU'RE NOTHING BUT A NOTHING

"Mick Jagger hasn't even played 'Sympathy for the Devil' yet and already the trouble has started," an English voice drawled . . . Attila and His Huns were trying to do acute bodily damage to the Senate and the People of Rome . . . Both groups were speeding, and they had gotten into a very intellectual discussion of the meaning of one of Dylan's lyrics . . . A Hun bopped a Roman with a beer stein as another voice mumbled something about Tyl Eulenspiegel's merry pranks.

YOU'RE NOT A THING AT ALL

Joe had always had the policy at *Confrontation* that real screwballs should be sent to him for interviewing, but the little fat man who came in didn't seem particularly crazy. He just had the bland, regular, somewhat smallish features of a typical WASP.

"The name is James Cash Cartwright," the fat man said, holding out his hand, "and the subject is consciousness energy."

"The subject of what?"

"Oh—this here article I have written for you." Cartwright reached into his alligator briefcase and pulled out a thick sheaf of typewritten paper. It was an odd size, possibly eight by ten. He handed the manuscript to Joe.

"What kind of paper is this?" said Joe.

"It's the standard size in England," said Cartwright. "When I was over there in 1963 visiting the tombs of my ancestors, I bought ten reams of it. I took the plane from Dallas on November 22, the day Kennedy was shot. Synchronicity. Also, I sneezed the moment the gunman squeezed. More synchronicity. But about this paper, I've never used anything else for my writing since then. Kind of gives a man a nice feeling to know that all the trees that went into my paper were chopped down over ten years ago, and no trees have died since then to support the proliferation of Jim Cartwright's philosophical foliage."

"That certainly is a wonderful thing," said Joe, thinking how much he loathed ecological moralists. During the height of the ecology fad, back in 1970 and '71, several people actually had had the nerve to write Joe saying that ecologically responsible journals like *Confrontation* had a duty to cease publication in order to save trees. "Just what fruit have your philosophical researches borne, Mr. Cartwright?" he asked.

"Golden apples of the sun, silver apples of the moon," said Cartwright with a smile. Joe saw Lilith Velkor defying Gruad atop the Pyramid of the Eye.

"Well, sir," said Cartwright, "my basic finding is that life energy pervades the entire universe, just as light and gravity do. Therefore, all life is one, just as all light is one. All energies, you see, are broadcast from a central source, yet to be found. If four amino acids—adenine, cytosine, guanine, and thymine—suddenly become life when you throw them together, then all chemicals are potentially alive. You and me and the fish and bugs are that kind of life made from adenine, cytosine, guanine, and thymine: DNA life. What we call dead matter is another kind of life: non-DNA life. Okay so far? If awareness is life and if life is one, then the awareness of the individual is just one of the universe's sensory organs. The universe produces beings like us in order to perceive itself. You might think of it as a giant, self-contained eye."

Joe remained impassive.

Cartwright went on. "Consciousness is therefore also manifested as telepathy, clairvoyance, and telekinesis. Those phenomena are simply non-localized versions of consciousness. I'm very interested in telepathy, and I've had a lot of success with telepathic research. These cases of communication are just further evidence that consciousness is a seamless web throughout the universe."

"Now wait a minute," said Joe. "Automobiles run on mechanical energy, heat energy, and electrical energy, but that doesn't mean that all the automobiles in the world are in contact with each other."

"What burns?" said Cartwright, smiling.

"You mean in a car? Well, the gas ignites explosively in the cylinder—"

"Only organic matter burns," said Cartwright smugly. "And all organic matter is descended from a single cell. All fire is one. And all automobiles do communicate with each other. You can't tell me anything about gas or oil. Or cars. I'm a Texan. Did I tell you that?"

Joe shook his head. "Just what part of Texas are you from?"

"Little place called Mad Dog."

"Had a notion you might be. Tell me, Mr. Cartwright, do you know anything about a conspiratorial organization called the Ancient Illuminated Seers of Bavaria?"

"Well, I know three organizations that have similar names: the Ancient Bavarian Conspiracy, the New Bavarian Conspiracy, and the Conservative Bavarian Seers."

Joe nodded. Cartwright didn't seem to have the facts straight—as Joe knew them. Perhaps the fat man had other pieces of the puzzle, perhaps fewer pieces than Joe had. Still, if they were different, they might be useful.

"Each of these organizations controls one of the major TV networks in the U.S.," said Cartwright. "The initials of each network have been intentionally chosen to refer back to the name of the group that runs it. They also control all the big magazines and newspapers. That's why I came to you. Judging by the stuff you've been getting away with printing lately, not only do the Illuminati not control your magazine, but you seem to have the benefit of some pretty powerful protection."

"So, there are three separate Illuminati groups, and

among them they dominate all the communications media —is that correct?" said Joe.

"That's right," said Cartwright, his face as cheerful as if he were explaining how his wife made ice cream with a hand freezer. "They dominate the motion-picture industry too. They took a hand in the making of hundreds of movies, the best known of which are *Gunga Din* and *Citizen Kane.* Those two movies are especially full of Illuminati references, symbols, code messages, and subliminal propaganda. 'Rosebud,' for instance, is their code name for the oldest Illuminati symbol, the so-called Rosy Cross. You know what that means." He snickered lewdly.

Joe nodded. "So—you know about 'flowery combat.' "

Cartwright shrugged. "Who doesn't? Dr. Horace Naismith, a learned friend of mine, and head of the John Dillinger Died for You Society, has written an analysis of *Gunga Din*, pointing out the real meaning of the thuggee, the evil goddess Kali, the pit full of serpents, the elephant medicine, the blowing of the bugle from the top of the temple, and so forth. *Gunga Din* celebrates the imposition of law and order in an area terrorized by the criminal followers of a goddess who breeds evil and chaos. The thuggee are a caricature of the Discordians, and the English represent the Illuminati's view of themselves. The Illuminati love that movie."

"Sometimes I wonder if we're not all working for them, one way or another," said Joe, trying deliberately to be ambivalent to see which way Cartwright would move.

"Well, sure we are," said Cartwright. "Everything we do that contributes to a lack of harmony in the human race helps them. They are forever shaking up society with experiments involving suffering and death for large numbers of people. For instance, consider the *General Slocum* disaster on June 15, 1904. Note that 19 plus 04 equals 23, by the way."

Him too? Joe groaned mentally. He's got to be either one of us or one of them, and if he's one of them, why is he telling me so much?

"You tell me," Cartwright said, "if all consciousness is not *one,* just how did Joyce happen to pick the very next day for *Ulysses,* so the *General Slocum* disaster would be in the newspaper his characters read? You see, Joyce knew he was a genius, but he never did understand the nature of genius, which is to be in better touch with the universal consciousness than the average man is. Anyway, the Illuminati were trying, with the *General Slocum* disaster, a new, more economical technique for achieving transcendental illumination—one that would require only a few hundred sudden deaths instead of thousands. Not that they care about saving lives, you understand, though the desire might result from the return of the repressed original purpose of the Illuminati, which was benign."

"Really?" said Joe. "What was the benign purpose?"

"The preservation of human knowledge after the natural catastrophe that destroyed the continent of Atlantis and the first human civilization, thirty thousand years ago," said Cartwright.

"Natural catastrophe?"

"Yes. A solar flare that erupted just when Atlantis was turned toward the sun. The original Illuminati were scientists who predicted the solar flare but were scoffed at by their fellows, so they fled by themselves. The benevolence of those early Illuminati was replaced by elitist attitudes in their successors, but the benign purpose keeps coming back in the form of factions which arise among the Illuminati and split off. The factions preserve traditional Illuminati secrecy, but they aim to thwart the destructiveness of the parent body. The Justified Ancients of Mummu were expelled from the Illuminati back in 1888. But the oldest anti-Illuminati conspiracy is the Erisian Liberation Front, which splintered off before the beginnings of the current civilization. Then there's the Discordian Movement—another splinter faction, but they're almost as bad as the Illuminati. They're sort of like a cross between followers of Ayn Rand and Scientologists. They've got this guy named Hagbard Celine, their head honcho. You didn't read about it because the governments of the world were too scared shitless to do anything about it, but five years ago this Celine character infiltrated the nuclear-submarine service of the U.S. Navy for the Illuminati—and stole a sub. He's a supersalesman, Celine is—he could talk old H. L. Hunt right out of half his oil wells. He was a Chief Petty Officer. First he converted about half the crew with the most incredible line of bullshit you've heard since Tim Leary was in his prime. Then he put some kind of drug in the ship's air supply, and while they were under the influence he converted most of the others. The ones that were stubborn he just blew out through the torpedo tubes. Nice guy. Now, mind you, this sub was armed with Polaris missiles. So the next thing Celine does is get himself off to someplace in the ocean where they can't find him and blackmail the fucking governments of the U.S., the U.S.S.R., and Red China to each give him ten million dollars in gold, and after he gets the thirty million he will scuttle his missiles. Otherwise he will dump 'em on a city of one of those three countries."

"Was Celine still working for the Illuminati at that point?"

"Hell, no!" Cartwright snorted. "That's not how they play the game. They like to operate stealthily, behind the throne-room curtains. They work with poison and daggers and things, not H-bombs. No, Celine told the Illuminati to go fuck themselves, and there was nothing they could do but grind their teeth. He's been operating like a pirate ever since. And I'll tell you something else. There's more than one world leader, including the Illuminati leaders, that hasn't been able to sleep at night because of what else Hagbard Celine has on that submarine."

"What's that, Mr. Cartwright?"

"Well, see, the U.S. Government did a very dumb thing. They weren't satisfied to have just nuclear weapons aboard their Polaris submarines for a while. They also thought the subs should be armed with the other kind of weapon—bugs."

Joe felt himself go cold, and the back of his neck prickled. Let others worry about the nuclear devastation all they want. Disease—the extinction of the human race through the spread of some manmade plague for which man would have no remedy—was his particular nightmare. Maybe because at the age of seven he'd very nearly died of polio; though he'd been healthy ever since, the fear of fatal illness had been impossible to shake.

"This Hagbard Celine—these Discordians—have a bacteriological weapon aboard the submarine?"

"Yeah. Something called Anthrax Tau. All Celine has to do is release it in the water and within a week the whole human race would be dead. It spreads faster'n a two-dollar whore on Saturday night. Any living thing can carry it. But one nice thing about it—it's fatal only to man. If Celine ever gets crazy enough to use it—and he's pretty crazy these days, and getting worse all the time—it'll give the planet a fresh start, so to speak. Some other life form could evolve into sentience. Now, if we have a nuclear war, or if we pollute the planet to death, there won't be *any* life left worth talking about. Might be the best thing that ever happened if Hagbard Celine shot that Anthrax Tau down the tube. It would sure prevent worse things from happening."

"If there were no one left alive," said Joe, "from whose point of view would it be the best thing that ever happened?"

"Life's," said Cartwright. "I told you, all life is one. Which gets me back to my manuscript. I'll just leave it with you. I realize it's much longer than what you usually publish, so feel free to excerpt from it as you please, and to pay me at your usual rates for whatever you publish."

That evening Joe stayed till nine at his office. He was, as usual, a day late getting copy to the typesetter on his editorial column and the letters column. These were two parts of the magazine that he felt only he could do right, and he refused to delegate either job to Peter or anyone else on the staff. First he ran the letters through his typewriter, shortening and pointing them up, then adding brief editorial answers where called for. After that he put aside his notes and research for the editorial he'd planned for this August issue, and instead he wrote an impassioned plea that each reader make himself personally responsible for doing something about the menace of bacteriological warfare. Even if what Cartwright had told him was a crock, it reminded him of his long-held conviction that germ warfare was far more likely to put the quietus to the human race than nuclear weapons. It was just too easy to unleash. He envisioned Hagbard in his submarine spewing the microbes of all-destroying plague out into the seas, and he shuddered.

His briefcase weighed down by Cartwright's manuscript, which he'd decided to take home with him, he stood in the lobby of his office building, gazing gloomily at the tanks full of tropical fish in the window of the pet store. One tank had, as an ornament, a china model of a sunken pirate ship. It made Joe think again of Hagbard Celine. Did he trust Hagbard or didn't he? Was it possible to really believe in a Hagbard with the Captain Nemo psychosis, brooding over tubes and jars full of bacteria cultures, one hairy finger hovering tentatively over a button that would send a torpedo full of Anthrax Tau germs out into the inky waters of the Atlantic? Within a week all humans would die, Cartwright had said. And it was hard to think that Cartwright was lying, since he knew so much about so many other things.

When Joe got home he put on his favorite Museum of National History record, *The Language and Music of the Wolves*, and lit up a joint. He liked listening to the wolves when he was high, and trying to understand their language. Then he took Cartwright's manuscript out of his briefcase and looked at the title page. It didn't say a word about consciousness energy, indeed, it referred to a subject Joe found much more interesting:

HOW THE ANCIENT BAVARIAN CONSPIRACY
   PLOTTED AND CARRIED OUT

THE ASSASSINATIONS OF MALCOLM X, JOHN F. KENNEDY, MARTIN LUTHER KING, JR., GEORGE LINCOLN ROCKWELL, ROBERT KENNEDY, RICHARD M. NIXON, GEORGE WALLACE, JANE FONDA, GABRIEL CONRAD, AND HANK BRUMMER

"Well," said Joe, "I'll be fucked."

"It was quite a trip," said Hagbard Celine.

"You're quite a tripper," Miss Portinari replied. "You really did Harry Coin very well. Probably just the way he'll do it, when he gets up the nerve to come see me."

"It was simpler than doing my own trip," Hagbard said wearily. "My guilt is much deeper, because I know more. It was easier to take his guilt trip than to take my own."

"And it's over? Your fur no longer bristles?"

"I know who I am and why I'm here. Adenine, cytosine, guanine, thymine."

"How did you ever forget?"

Hagbard grinned. "It's easy to forget. You know that." She smiled back. "Blessed be, Captain."

"Blessed be," he said.

Returning to his stateroom, he was still subdued. The vision of the self-begotten and the serpent eating its own tail had broken the lines of word, image, and emotional energy that were steering him toward the Dark Night of the Soul again—but resolving his personal problem did not rescue the Demonstration or help him cope with the oncoming disaster. It merely freed him to begin anew. It merely reminded him that the end is the beginning and humility is endless.

It merely, merrily, turned the Wheel another Tarot-towery connection . . .

He realized he was still tripping a little. That was readily fixed: Harry Coin was tripping, and he wasn't Harry Coin right now.

Hagbard, remembering again who he was and why he was there, opened his stateroom door. Joe Malik sat in a chair, under an octopus mural, and regarded him with a level glance.

"Who killed John Kennedy?" Joe asked calmly. "I want a straight answer this time, H.C."

Hagbard relaxed into another chair, smiling gently. "That one finally registered, eh? I told John, all those years ago, to emphasize that you should never trust anyone with the initials H.C., and yet you've gone on trusting me and never noticing."

"I noticed. But it seemed too wild to take seriously."

"John Kennedy was killed by a man named Harold Canvera who lived on Fullerton Avenue in Chicago, near the Seminary Restaurant, where you and Simon first discussed his theories of numerology. Dillinger had moved back to that neighborhood for a while in the late fifties, because he liked to go to the Biograph Theatre for old times' sake, and Canvera was his landlord. A very sane, ordinary, rather dull individual. Then, in Dallas in 1963, John saw him blow the President's head off before Oswald or Harry Coin or the Mafia gun could fire." Hagbard paused to light a cigar. "We investigated Canvera afterward, like scientists investigating the first extraterrestrial life form. You can imagine how thorough we were. He had no politics at all at the time, which puzzled the hell out of us. It turned out that Canvera had put a lot of money into Blue Sky, Inc., a firm that made devices for landing on low-gravity planets. That was back in the very early fifties. Finally, Eisenhower's hostility to the space program drove Blue Sky to the bottom of the board, and Canvera sold out at a terrible loss. Then Kennedy came in and announced that the U.S. was going to put a man on the moon. The stocks he'd sold were suddenly worth millions. Canvera's brain snapped—that was all. Killing Kennedy and getting away with it turned him schizzy finally. He went in for spiritualism for a while, and then later joined White Heroes Opposing Red Extremism, one of the really paranoid anti-Illuminati groups, and ran a telephone message service giving WHORE propaganda."

"And nobody else ever suspected?" Joe asked. "Canvera is still there in Chicago, going about his business, just another face on the street?"

"Not quite. He was shot a few years ago. Due to you."

"Due to *me?*"

"Yes. He was one of the subjects in the first AUM test. He subsequently made the mistake of knocking up the daughter of a local politician. It appears that the AUM made him susceptible to libertine ideas."

WE'RE GONNA ROCK ROCK ROCK TILL BROAD DAYLIGHT

"You sound very convincing, and I almost believe you," Joe said slowly. "Why, all of a sudden? Why no more put-ons and runarounds?"

"We're getting to the chimes at midnight," Hagbard replied simply, with a Latin shrug. "The spell is ending. Soon the coach turns back to a pumpkin, Cinderella goes back to the kitchen, everybody takes their masks off, and the carnival is over. I mean it," he added, his face full of sincerity. "Ask me anything and you get the truth."

"Why are you keeping George and me apart? Why do I have to skulk around the sub like a wanted fugitive and eat with Calley and Eichmann? Why don't you want George and me to compare notes?"

Hagbard sighed. "The real explanation for that would take a day. You'd have to understand the whole Celine System first. In the baby talk of conventional psychology, I'm taking away George's father figures. You're one: his first and only boss, an older man he trusts and respects. I became another very quickly, and that's one of the thousand and one reasons I turned the guru-hood over to Miss Portinari. He had to confront Drake, the bad father, and lose you and me, the good fathers, before he could really learn to ball a woman. The next step, if you're curious, is to take the woman away from him. Temporarily," Hagbard added quickly. "Don't be so jumpy. You've been through a large part of the Celine System, and it hasn't killed you. You're stronger because of it, aren't you?"

Joe nodded, accepting this, but shot the next question immediately. "Do you know who bombed *Confrontation?*"

"Yes, Joe. And I know *why* you did it."

YOU'RE NOT A THING AT ALL

"Okay, then, here's the payoff, and your answer better be good. Why are you helping the Illuminati to immanentize the Eschaton, Hagbard?"

"It steam-engines when it comes steam-engine time, as a very wise man once said."

"Jesus," Joe said wearily. "I thought I had crossed that *pons asinorum*. When I figured out how you get the goose out of the bottle in the Zen riddle—you do nothing and wait for the goose to peck its way out, just like a chick pecks its way out of an egg—I realized 'Do what thou wilt' becomes 'the whole of the law' by a mathematical process. The equation balances when you realize who the 'thou' is, as distinguished from the ordinary 'you.' The whole fucking works, the universe—all of it alive in the same way we're alive, and mechanical in the same way we're mechanical. The Robot. The one more trustworthy than all the Buddhas and sages. Oh, Christ, yes, I thought I understood it all. But this, this . . . this stone fatalism—*what the hell are we going to Ingolstadt for, if we can't do anything?*"

"The coin has two sides. It's the only coin that comes up at this time, but it still has two sides." Hagbard leaned forward intensely. "It's mechanical *and* alive. Let me give you a sexual metaphor, since you usually hang out with New York intellectuals. You look at a woman across a room and you know you're going to bed with her before the night is over. That's mechanical: Something has happened when your eyes met. But the orgasm is organic; what it will be like, neither of you can predict. And I know, just as the Illuminati know, that immanentization is going to happen on May first because of a mechanical process Adam Weishaupt started on another May first two centuries ago, and because of other processes other people started before then and since then. But neither I nor the Illuminati know what form immanentization will take. It doesn't have to be hell on earth. It can be heaven on earth. And that's why we're going to Ingolstadt."

THREE O'CLOCK   TWO O'CLOCK   ONE O'CLOCK
ROCK

I became a cop because of Billie Freshette. Well, I don't want to jive you—that wasn't the whole reason. But she sure as hell was one bodacious big part of the reason, and that's the curious thing about what finally happened, and how Milo Flanagan assigned me to infiltrate the Lincoln

Park anarchist group, getting me in right up to my black ass in all that international intrigue and yoga-style balling with Simon Moon. But maybe I should start over from the beginning again, from Billie Freshette. I was a little kid and she was an old woman—it was in the early 1950s, you see (Hassan i Sabbah X was operating in the open then, going around the South Side preaching that the greatest of the White Magicians had just died recently in England and now the age of the Black Magicians was beginning; everybody thought he was one stone-crazy stud), and my father was a cook in a restaurant on Halsted. He pointed her out to me on the street once (it must have been just a while before she went back to the reservation in Wisconsin to die). "See that old woman, child? She was John Dillinger's girl friend."

Well, I looked, and I saw she was really heavy and together and that whatever the law had done to her never broke her, but I also saw that sorrow hung around her like a dark halo. Daddy went on and told me a lot more about her, and about Dillinger, but it was the sorrow that got printed all over every cell in my little baby brain. It took years for me to figure it out, but what it really meant, as an omen or conjure, was that she was basically just like the women of the black gang leaders on the South Side, even if she was an Indian. There's just one way for a black in Chicago, and that's to join a gang—Solidarity Forever, as Simon would say—but I dug that there was only one gang that was really safe, the biggest gang of all, Mister Charlie's boys, the motherfucking establishment.

I guess every black cop has that in the back of his head, before he finds out that we never really can join that gang, not as full members anyway. I found out quicker, being not just black but female. So I was in the gang, the baddest and heaviest gang, but I was always looking for something better, the impossible, the boss gimmick that would get me off the Man's black-and-white chessboard entirely into some place where I was myself and not just a pawn being moved around at Charlie's whim.

Otto Waterhouse never had that feeling, at least not until near the end of the game. I never did get inside his head enough to know what was going on there (he was a real cop and got into my head almost as soon as we met, and I could always feel him watching me, waiting for the time when I would round on Charlie and go over to the other side), so the best I can do in making him is to say that he was no Tom in the ordinary sense: He didn't screw blacks for the Man, he screwed blacks for himself; it was strictly his own trip.

Otto was my drop after I got assigned to underground work. We met in a place that I could always have an excuse to visit, a rundown law firm called Washington, Weishaupt, Budweiser and Kief, on 23 North Clark. Later, for some reason I was never told, they changed the name to Ruly, Kempt, Sheveled and Couth, and then to Weery, Stale, Flatt and Profitable, and to keep up the front they actually did hire a couple of lawyers and did some real law work for a corporation called Blue Sky, Inc.

On April 29, still harboring a cargo of doubt about Hagbard, Joe Malik decided to try the simplest method of Tarot divination. Concentrating all his energy on the question, he cut the deck and picked out one card that would reveal Hagbard Celine's true nature, if the divination worked. With a sinking heart, he saw that he had come up with the Hierophant. Running the mnemonics Simon had taught him, Joe quickly identified this figure with the number five, the Hebrew letter *Vau* (meaning "nail"), and the traditional interpretation of a false show: a hypocrisy or a trick. Five was the number of *Grummet*, the destructive and chaotic end of a cycle. *Vau* was the letter associated with quarrels, and the meaning "nail" was often related to the implement of Christ's death. The card was telling him that Hagbard was a hypocritical trickster aiming at destruction, a murderer of the Dreamer-Redeemer aspect of humanity. Or, taking a more mystical reading, as was usually advisable with the Tarot, Hagbard only seemed to be these things, and was actually an agent of Resurrection and Rebirth—as Christ had to die before he could become the Father, as (in Vedanta) the false "self" must be obliterated to join the great Self. Joe swore. The card was only reflecting his own uncertainty. He rummaged in the bookshelf Hagbard had provided for his stateroom and found three books on the Tarot. The first, a popular manual, was absolutely useless: It identified the Hierophant with the letter of religion in contrast to the spirit, with conformity, and with all the plastic middle-class values Hagbard conspicuously lacked. The second (by a true adept of the Tarot) just led him back to his own confused reading of the card, remarking that the Hierophant is "mysterious, even sinister. He seems to be enjoying a very secret joke at somebody's expense." The third work raised more doubts: It was *Liber 555*, by somebody named Mordecai Malignatus, which vaguely reminded Joe that the old *East Village Other* chart of the Illuminati conspiracy showed a "Mordecai the Foul" in charge of the Sphere of Chaos—and "Mordecai Malignatus" was a fair Latinization of "Mordecai the Foul." Mordecai, Joe remembered, was, according to that half-accurate and half-deceptive chart, in dual control (along with Richard Nixon, then living) of the Elders of Zion, the House of Rothschild, the Politburo, the Federal Reserve System, the U.S. Communist Party, and Students for a Democratic Society. Joe flipped the pages to see what the semimythical Mord had to say about the Hierophant. The chapter was brief; it was in "The Book of Republicans and Sinners," and said:

5	*Vau* (nail)	THE HIEROPHANT	They nailed Love to a Cross Symbolic of their Might But Love was undefeated It simply didn't fight.

Five stoned men were in a courtyard when an elephant entered.

The first man was stoned on sleep, and he saw not the elephant but dreamed instead of things unreal to those awake.

The second man was stoned on nicotine, caffeine, DDT, carbohydrate excess, protein deficiency, and the other chemicals in the diet which the Illuminati have enforced upon the half-awake to keep them from fully waking. "Hey," he said, "there's a big, smelly beast in our courtyard."

The third stoned man was on grass, and he said, "No, dads, that's the Ghostly Old Party in its true nature, the Dark Nix on the Soul," and he giggled in a silly way.

The fourth stoned man was tripping on peyote, and

he said, "You see not the mystery, for the elephant is a poem written in tons instead of words," and his eyes danced.

The fifth stoned man was on acid, and he said nothing, merely worshipping the elephant in silence as the Father of Buddha.

And then the Hierophant entered and drove a nail of mystery into all their hearts, saying, "You are all elephants!"

Nobody understood him.

(At eight o'clock in Ingolstadt an unscheduled group called the Cargo Cult managed to get the mike and began blasting out their own outer-space arrangement of an old children's song:

SHE'LL BE COMING 'ROUND THE MOUNTAIN WHEN SHE
    COMES
SHE'LL BE COMING 'ROUND THE MOUNTAIN WHEN SHE
    COMES

And, in Washington, where it was still only two in the afternoon, the White House was in flames, while the National Guard machine-gunned an armed mob crossing the Mall in front of the Washington Monument, a single finger pointing upward in an eloquent and vulgar gesture which only the Illuminati knew meant "Fuck you!" . . . In Los Angeles, where it was eleven in the morning, the bombs started to go off in police stations . . . And in Lehman Cavern, Markoff Chaney disgustedly pointed out a graffito to Saul and Barney: HELP STAMP OUT SIZEISM: TAKE A MIDGET TO LUNCH. "You see?" he demanded. "That's supposed to be funny. It's not funny at all. Not one damned bit.")

SHE'LL BE DRIVING SIX WHITE HORSES
SHE'LL BE DRIVING SIX WHITE HORSES
SHE'LL BE DRIVING SIX WHITE HORSES WHEN SHE COMES

On April 29 Hagbard invited George to join him on the bridge of the *Leif Erikson*. They had been sailing through a smooth-walled tubular passage that was completely filled with water and was both underground and below sea level. It had been built by the Atlanteans and not only had survived the catastrophe but had been maintained in good condition for the next thirty thousand years by the Illuminati. There was even a salt lock, located, roughly, under Lyon,

France, which served to keep the salt water of the Atlantic out of the further reaches of the passage and the underground freshwater Sea of Valusia. The underground waterways were connected with many lakes in Switzerland, Bavaria, and eastern Europe, Hagbard explained, and if salt water were found in all of those lakes the existence of the weird subsurface world of the Illuminati would be suspected. As the submarine approached a huge circular hatchway barring the passage, Hagbard turned off the devices that rendered the craft indetectable. Immediately the enormous round metal door swung toward them.

"Won't the Illuminati know we've activated this machinery?" said George.

"No. This works automatically," said Hagbard. "It's never occurred to them that anyone else might use this passageway."

"But they know *you* could. And you guessed wrong about their spider-ships being able to detect you."

Hagbard whirled on George, a hairy arm lifted to punch him in the chest. "Shut up about the fucking spider-ships! I don't want to hear any more about the spider-ships! Portinari's running the show now. And she says it's safe. Okay?"

"Commander, you're out of your fucking mind," George said firmly.

Hagbard laughed, his shoulders slumping slightly in relaxation. "All right. You can get off the sub any time you want to. We'll just open the hatch and let you swim out."

"You're out of your fucking mind, but I'm stuck with you," said George, clapping Hagbard on the shoulder.

"You're either on the sub or off the sub," said Hagbard. "Watch this."

The *Leif Erikson* had sailed through the round metal gateway, which closed behind it. Here the ceiling of the underwater passage was about fifty feet higher than it had been in the section they just left, and the tunnel was only partially filling with water. The air seemed to be coming from vents in the ceiling. There was another metal hatchway in the distance down the tunnel.

"This lock is pretty big," George said. "The Illuminati must have sailed some enormous submarines through here."

"And animals," said Hagbard.

The hatchway ahead of them opened, and fresh water

came pouring in. The water level in the lock rose until it reached the ceiling, and the *Leif Erikson*'s engines turned over and began to propel it forward once more.

Now George is writing in his diary again:

April 29

And what the hell does it mean to say that life shouldn't change too rapidly? How fast is evolution? Do you measure it in terms of lifetime? A year is more than a lifetime to many kinds of animals, while seventy years is an hour in the lifetime of a sequoia. And the universe is only ten billion years old. How fast do ten billion years go? To a god they might go very fast indeed. They might all happen at once. Suppose the lifetime of your typical basic god was a hundred quintillion years. The whole lifetime of this universe would be to him no more than the amount of time it takes us to watch a movie.

So, from the point of view of a god or of the universe, things evolve very quickly. It's like one of those Walt Disney films where you watch a plant growing before your eyes and the whole cycle from bud to fruit takes about two minutes. To a god, life is a single organism proliferating in all directions all over the earth, and now on the moon and Mars, and the whole process from the first of the protobionts to George Dorn and fellow humans takes no longer than

Hagbard's voice over the intercom jolted him out of his reverie. "Come on back up, George. There's more to see."

This time Mavis was on the bridge with Hagbard. As George entered, Hagbard withdrew his hand from her left breast in an unhurried movement. George wanted to kill Hagbard, but he was thankful that he hadn't seen Mavis touching Hagbard in any sexual way. That would have been past bearing. He might have tested his new-found courage by taking a poke at Hagbard, and Goddess only knows what karate or yoga or magic would be the response. Besides, Mavis and Hagbard must be balling all the time. Who else but Hagbard would a woman like Mavis take for her regular lover? Who else but Hagbard could satisfy her?

Mavis greeted George with a comradely hug that made the entire front of his body ache. Hagbard pointed to an in-

scription carved into the wall of the cave. There was a row
of symbols that George didn't recognize, but above them
was something quite familiar: a circle with a downward-
pointing trident carved inside it.

"The peace symbol," said George. "I didn't know it was
that old."

"In the days when it was put up there," said Hagbard, "it
was called the Cross of Lilith Velkor, and its meaning is
simply that anyone who attempts to thwart the Illuminati
will suffer from the most horrible torture the Illuminati can
devise. Lilith Velkor was one of the first of their victims.
They crucified her on a revolving cross that looked very
much like that."

"You told me it wasn't really a peace symbol," said
George, looking wistfully back at the carving, "but I didn't
know what you meant."

"There was a Dirigens-grade Illuminatus in Bertrand
Russell's circle who put it in somebody's mind that the circle and trident would be a good symbol for the Aldermas-
ton marchers to carry. It was very cleverly and subtly done.
If the Committee for Nuclear Disarmament had thought
about it, what did they need any kind of a symbol for? But
Russell and his people fell for it. What they didn't know
was that the circle-and-trident had been a traditional symbol of evil among left-hand-path Satanists for thousands of
years. So many right-wingers are secret left-hand-path magicians and Satanists that of course they spotted the symbol
for what it was right away. That made them think the Illuminati were behind the peace movement, which threw them
off the track, and they accused the peaceniks of using a Satanist symbol, which to a small extent discredited the peace
movement. A cute gambit."

"Why is it there on the wall?" said George.

"The inscription warns the passer-by to purify his heart
because he is about to enter the Sea of Valusia, which belongs exclusively to the Illuminati. Traveling across the Sea
of Valusia, you come eventually to the underground port of
Agharti, which was the first Illuminati refuge after the Atlantean catastrophe. We are emerging into the Sea of Valusia right now. Watch."

Hagbard gestured, and George watched, open-mouthed,
as the walls of the cave that closed around them fell away.
They were sailing out of the tunnel, but what they seemed

to be entering was an infinite fog. The television cameras and their laser wave-guides penetrated just as far into this lightless ocean that they were about to navigate as they had into the Atlantic, but this ocean was neither blue nor green, but gray. It was a gray that seemed to extend infinitely in all directions, like an overcast sky. It was impossible to gauge distance. The farthest depth of the gray around them might be hundreds of miles away, or it might be right outside the submarine.

"Where's the bottom?" he asked.

"Too far below us to see," said Mavis. "The top of this ocean is just a little above the level of the bottom of the Atlantic."

"You're so smart," said Hagbard, pinching her buttock and causing George to flinch.

"Don't pay any attention to him, George," said Mavis. "He's a little bit nervous, and it's making him silly."

"Shut the fuck up," said Hagbard.

Beginning to feel anxious himself, wondering if the noble mind of Hagbard Celine was being overthrown by the weight of responsibility, George turned to look out at the empty ocean. Now he saw that it wasn't quite empty. Fish swam by, some large, some small, many of them grotesque. All were totally eyeless. An octopoidal monster with extremely long, slender tentacles drifted past the submarine, feeling for its prey. There was a covering of fine hairs on the tips of the tentacles. A small fish, also blind, swam close enough to one tentacle to set up a current that disturbed the hairs. Instantly the octopus's whole body moved in that direction, the disturbed tentacle wrapped itself around the hapless fish, and several others joined in to help scoop it up. The octopus devoured the fish in three bites. George was glad to see that at least the blood of these creatures was red.

The door behind them opened, and Harry Coin stepped out onto the bridge. "Morning, everybody. I was just wondering if I might find Miss Mao up here."

"She's doing her stint in Navigation right now," said Hagbard. "But stay here and have a look at the Sea of Valusia, Harry."

Harry looked all around, slowly and thoughtfully, then shook his head. "You know, there's times when I start to think you're doing this."

"What do you mean, Harry?" asked Mavis.

"You know"—Harry waved a long, snakelike hand—"doing this, like a science-fiction movie. You've just got us in an abandoned hotel somewheres, and you've got a big engine in the basement that shakes the whole place, and here you've got some movie cameras, only they point at the screen instead of away from you, if you know what I mean."

"Rear projection," said Hagbard. "Tell me, Harry, what difference would it make if it wasn't real?"

Harry thought a moment, his chinless face sour. "We wouldn't have to do what we think we have to do. But even if we don't have to do what we think we have to do, it won't make any difference if we do it. Which means we should just go ahead."

Mavis sighed. "Just go ahead."

"Just go ahead," said Hagbard. "A powerful mantra."

"And if we don't go ahead," said George, "it doesn't matter either. Which means that we just do go ahead."

"Another powerful mantra," said Hagbard. "Just do go ahead."

George noticed a small speck in the distance. As it got closer, he reccognized it. He shook his head. Was there no end to the surrealism he'd been subjected to in the last six days? A dolphin wearing scuba gear!

"Hi, man-friends," said Howard's voice over the loud-speaker on the bridge. George cast a glance at Harry Coin. The former assassin was standing open-mouthed and limp with astonishment.

"Greetings, Howard," said Hagbard. "How goes it with the Nazis?"

"Dead, sleeping, whatever it is they are. I have a whole porpoise horde—most of the Atlantean Adepts—watching them."

"And ready to perform other tasks as needed, I hope," said Hagbard.

"Ready indeed," said Howard. He turned a somersault.

"All right," said Harry Coin softly. "All *right*," he said more firmly. "It's a talking fish. But why the hell is it wearing an oxygen tank and breathing through a fucking mask?"

"I see we have a new friend on the bridge," said Howard. "I got the mask from Hagbard's on-shore representative at

Fernando Poo. After all, a porpoise has to breathe air. And there is no surface in most of this underground ocean. It's water all the way to the top of the cavernous chambers that contain it. The only place I can get air near here is by swimming up to the top of Lake Totenkopf."

"The Lake Totenkopf monster," said George with a laugh.

"We'll moor the submarine in Lake Totenkopf later today," said Hagbard. "Howard, I'd like you and your people to stand by tonight and tomorrow night. Tomorrow night be ready to do a lot of hard physical work. Meanwhile, stay out of the way of the Nazis—the protection they're under is particularly aimed at sea animals, since that was the presumed greatest danger to them. We'll have oxygen equipment as needed for any of your people who want it. Tell them to try to avoid surfacing on the lake unless absolutely necessary. We don't want to attract more attention than we have to."

"I salute you in the name of the porpoise horde," said Howard. "Hail and farewell." He swam away.

A little later, sailing on, they saw in the distance an enormous reptile with four paddles for swimming and a neck twice the length of its body. It was in hot pursuit of a school of blind fish.

"The Loch Ness monster," said Hagbard, and George remembered his little joke about Howard's surfacing in Lake Totenkopf. "One of Gruad's genetic experiments with reptiles," Hagbard went on. "He was really queer for reptiles. He filled the Sea of Valusia with these plesiosaurlike things. Blind, of course, so they could navigate in darkness. Think about that—eyes are a liability under certain conditions. Graud figured monsters like that would be another protection against anybody finding Agharti. But the *Leif Erikson* is too big for Nessie to tangle with, and she knows it."

At last there was a column of yellow light ahead. This was the light let into the Sea of Valusia by Lake Totenkopf. Hagbard explained that the lake was simply a place where the ceiling of rock over the Sea of Valusia had been soft and unstable enough to collapse. The resulting hole, being at sea level, filled with water. Debris falling down through the bottom of the lake had formed a mountain below the place where the roof of the Sea of Valusia was punctured.

"The Jesuits, of course, always knew that Lake Totenkopf connected with the Sea of Valusia and thus made possible easy contact with Agharti," Hagbard said. "That's why, when they gave Weishaupt the assignment of founding an overt branch of the Illuminati, they sent him to Ingolstadt, which is right by Lake Totenkopf. And there's the mountain under the lake."

It loomed ahead of them, dark and forbidding. As the submarine sailed over it, George saw a cloud of dolphins circling in the distance. The mountain top had been sheared off in a fashion that seemed too precise to be natural; it formed a plateau about two miles long and one mile wide. There were what appeared to be dark squares on this gray plateau. The submarine swooped down, and George saw that the squares were huge formations of men. In a moment they were hovering over the army, like a helicopter observing troops on parade. George could clearly see the black uniforms, the green tanks with black-and-white crosses painted on them, the long, dark, upjutting snouts of big guns. They stood there silent and immobile, thousands of feet below the surface of the lake.

"That's the weapon the Illuminati plan to use to immanentize the Eschaton?" asked George. "Why don't we destroy them now?"

"Because they're under a protective biomystic field," said Hagbard, "and we can't. I did want you to see them, though. When the electrical, Astral, and orgonomic vibrations of the American Medical Association, amplified by the synergetic clusters of sound, image, and emotional energy of all these young people responding to the beat, bring that Nazi legion back to life, it will call for nothing less than the appearance on the field of battle of the goddess Eris Herself to save the day."

"Hagbard," George protested disgustedly. "Are you telling me Eris is real? *Really real* and not just an allegory or symbol? I can't buy that any more than I can believe Jehovah or Osiris is really real."

But Hagbard answered very solemnly, "When you're dealing with these forces or powers in a philosophic and scientific way, contemplating them from an armchair, that rationalistic approach is useful. It is quite profitable then to regard the gods and goddesses and demons as projections of the human mind or as unconscious aspects of ourselves. But every truth is a truth only for one place and one time, and that's a truth, as I said, for the armchair. When you're actually dealing with these figures, the only safe, pragmatic, and operational approach is to treat them as having a being, a will, and a purpose entirely apart from the humans who evoke them. If the Sorcerer's Apprentice had understood that, he wouldn't have gotten into so much trouble."

SHE'LL BE WEARING RED PAJAMAS

SHE'LL BE WEARING RED PAJAMAS

SHE'LL BE WEARING RED PAJAMAS WHEN SHE COMES

Approaching the outskirts of the crowd, Fission Chips saw a group of musicians who were obviously English, from their dress and hair style. Their name, he saw on the biggest drum, was Calculated Tedium, and the guitar player had a canteen strapped to his hip. It reminded 00005 of how thirsty he was, and he asked, "Pardon me, do you know where I could get some water or a soft drink?"

"Take a snort from my canteen," the guitarist said affably, passing it over. He pointed to the west. "See that geodesic plywood dome there? It's a bleeding giant Kool-Aid station set up by the Kabouters and guaranteed to hold out even if the crowd doubles in size before this is over. I just filled the canteen from there, so it's fresh. You can get more over there any time you need it."

"Thanks," 00005 said warmly, taking a long, cold, delightful swallow.

He had a very low threshhold for LSD. The world began to seem brighter, stranger, and more colorful within only a few minutes.

(The joker was actually Rhoda Chief, the vocalist who sang with the Heads of Easter Island, and who had inspired much admiration in the younger generation—and much horror in the older—when she named her out-of-wedlock baby Jesus Jehovah Lucifer Satan Chief. A former Processene and Scientologist, currently going the Wicca route, the buxom Rhoda was renowned through show biz for "giving head like no chick alive," a reputation which often provoked certain Satanists on the Linda Lovelace for President Committee to send very deadly vibes in her direction, all of which bounced off due to her Wicca shield. She was also possibly the greatest singer of her generation, and firmly believed that most human problems would be solved if the whole world could be turned on to acid. She had been preparing for the Ingolstadt festival for several months, buying only the top-quality tabs from the most reliable dealers, and she had crept into the geodesic Kool-Aid station only a few moments earlier, dumping enough pure lysergic acid diethylamide to blow the minds of the population of a small country. Actually, the idea had been subtly planted in her consciousness by the leader of her Wiccan, an astonishingly beautiful woman with flaming red hair and smoldering green eyes who had once played a starring role in a Black Mass celebrated by Padre Pederastia at 2323 Lake Shore Drive. This woman called herself Lady Velkor, and often made jokes about her memories of 18th-century Bavaria, which Rhoda assumed were references to reincarnation.)

On April 10, while Howard made his discovery in the ruins of Atlantis and Tlaloc grinned in Mexico D.F., Tobias Knight, in his room at the Hotel Pan Kreston in Santa Isobel, concluded a broadcast to the American submarine in the Bight of Biafra. "The Russkies and Chinks have completed their withdrawal, and Generalissimo Puta is definitely friendly to our side, besides being popular with both the Bubi and the Fang. My work is definitely finished, and I'll await orders to return to Washington."

"Roger. Over and out."

(Frank Sullivan, capitalizing on his only real asset, was operating in Havana as a Cuban Superman, using the name Papa Piaba, when the Brotherhood spotted his resemblance to John Dillinger. "Gosh," he said when they made their offer, "five thousand dollars just to take two ladies to a movie one night? And it's only a practical joke, you say?" "It'll be a very funny joke," Jaicapo Mocenigo promised him. And the Smithsonian acquired Mr. Sullivan's asset as one of their most interesting relics.)

WE'LL KILL THE OLD RED ROOSTER

(Hagbard was accompanied by Joe Malik when he returned to the stateroom. "You go to the beer hall in Munich," he was saying, "and steal any item, anything at all, as long as it's obviously old enough to have been there the night he tried the *Putsch*. Then you rejoin the rest of us in Ingolstadt. Understood?"

WE'LL KILL THE OLD RED ROOSTER

Lady Velkor, wearing a green peasant blouse and green hotpants, looked around the geodesic Kool-Aid dome. A man in a green turtleneck sweater and green slacks caught her eye, and she walked over to him, asking, "Are you a turtle?"

"You bet your sweet ass I am," he answered eagerly and so she had failed to make contact—and owed this oaf a free drink also. But she smiled pleasantly and concealed her annoyance.

WE'LL KILL THE OLD RED ROOSTER WHEN SHE COMES

Robinson and Lehrman of the Homicide Department actually started the last phase of the operation. I was in New York to see Hassan i Sabbah X about a new phase of Laotian opium operation (I had just come from Chicago, after staging that conversation with Waterhouse for Miss Servix's benefit), and I decided to check with them for those little nuances that can't go into an official report. We met in Washington Square and found a bench far enough from the chess nuts to give us some privacy.

"Muldoon is on to us," Robinson told me right off. He was wearing a beard; I figured that meant he was currently in a Weather Underground group, since he was too old to pass for under twenty-one and get into Morituri.

"Are you sure?" I asked.

He made the usual reply: "Who's ever sure of anything in this business? But Barney is pure cop through and through," he added, "and his instincts are like dowsing rods. Everybody on the force knows we've infiltrated them by now, anyway. They even make jokes about it. 'Who's the CIA man in your department?'—that kind of thing."

"Muldoon is on to us, all right," Lehrman agreed. "But he's not the one I worry about."

"Who is?" I brushed my walrus mustache nervously; being the first pentuple agent in the history of espionage was starting to grind me down. I really wasn't sure which of my bosses should hear about this, although the CIA certainly had to be told, since for all I know Robinson and Lehrman might be reporting to them twice, having another contact as a fail-safe check on my own integrity.

"The head of Homicide North," Lehrman said. "An old geezer named Goodman. He's so damned smart, I sometimes wonder if *he's* a double agent for the Eye themselves. His mind jumps ahead of facts just like an Adeptus Exemptus in the Order."

I looked up at the statue of Garibaldi, remembering the old NYU myth that he would pull his sword the rest of the way out of the scabbard if a virgin ever walked through Washington Park. "Tell me more about this Goodman," I said.

("Check out the pair on that chick," a Superman said enthusiastically.

("Watermelons," a second Superman agreed enthusiastically. "And you know how us *cullud folk* dig watermelons," he added, licking his lips.

("Skin!" the first cried.

("Skin!" the second agreed.

(They slapped palms, and Clark Kent came out of his reverie. Having sampled the Kool-Aid a while earlier, he was beginning to float a little, although not yet aware of what was happening—he just felt a rather unusual tug of memory from his days as an anthropologist, and was deeply concerned with a new insight about the relationship between the black Virgin of Guadalupe, the Greek goddess Persephone, and his own sexual proclivities—and he came out of it with a start, looking at the woman whose breasts had inspired such reverence.

("Son of a *bitch*," he said piously, his mouth spreading in a grin.)

Rebecca Goodman left the house at 3 P.M., hauling a shopping cart and walking past the garage. The nearest supermarket was a good ten minutes on foot, and big enough to keep her busy for a half-hour finding what she wanted and getting through one of those checkout lines. I slipped out of the car and walked right to the back of the house, perfectly secure from neighboring eyes in my Bell Telephone overalls.

The kitchen door had an easy slip-lock, and I didn't even need my keys. A playing card did the job, and I was in.

My first thought was to head for the bedroom—the old man from Vienna was right, and that's where you'll find the real clues to a man's character—but one chair in the kitchen stopped me. The vibes were so strong that I closed my eyes and psychometered it according to the difficult Third Alko of the A∴ A∴.. It was Rebecca herself: She had sat there and thought about shooting heroin. It faded fast, before I could read what had stopped her.

The bedroom almost knocked me over when I found it. "Who would have thought the old man had so much hot blood in him?" I paraphrased, backing out. It was a profanation to read too much in there, and what I did scan was enough. As Miss Mao would say, this man was Tao-Yin (Beta prime in the terminology of the I). No wonder Robinson kept talking about his "intuition."

The living room had a statue of the Mermaid of Copenhagen that stopped me. I read it and chuckled; Lord, the hangups we all have.

One wall was a built-in bookcase, but Rebecca seemed to be the reader in the family. I started scanning experimentally and found Saul's vibes on a shelf of detective stories and a *Scientific American* anthology of mathematical and logical puzzles. The man had no concept of his own latent powers, and thought only in terms of solving riddles. Sherlock Holmes, without even the violin and the dope for relief from all that cortical activity. Everything else went into his marriage, that hothouse bedroom upstairs.

No; there was a sketchpad on the coffee table. His, according to the aura.

I flipped pages rapidly: all detailed, precise, perfectly naturalistic. Mostly faces: criminals he had dealt with professionally, all touched with a perception and compassion that he kept out of his work hours. Trees in Central Park. Nudes of Rebecca, adoration in every line of the pencil. A surprising face of a black kid, with some Harem slum building in the background—another touch of unexpected compassion. Then a switch—the first abstract. It was a Star of David, basically, but he had started adding energetic waves coming out of it, and the descending triangle was shaded—somewhere, in the back of his head, he had been working out the symbolism, and coming amazingly close to the truth. More faces of obvious criminal types. A scene in the Catskills, with Rebecca reading a book under a tree—something wrong, gloom and fear in the shading. I closed my eyes and concentrated: The picture came in with a second woman . . . I opened my eyes, sweating. It was his first wife, and she had died of cancer. He was afraid of losing Rebecca too, but she was young and healthy. Another man. He thought she might leave him for a younger man. Well, that was the key, then. I flipped a few more pages and saw a unicorn—some more of the unconscious work that went into that erotic Star of David.

A quick scan of Rebecca's books then. Mostly anthropology, mostly African. I took one off the shelf and held it.

Eros again, thinly sublimated. The other part of the key. As Hassan i Sabbah X once remarked to me, "Breathes there a white woman with soul so dead, she never yearned for a black in her bed?"

I returned everything to its place carefully and headed for the back door. I stopped in the kitchen to read the chair again, since relapse is as much a part of the syndrome in heroin addiction as in black-lung disease. This time I found what stopped her. If I say love, I'll sound sentimental, and if I say sex, I'll sound cynical. I'll call it pair bonding and sound scientific.

Slipping back into my car, I checked the time elapsed: seventeen minutes. It would have taken several hours to unearth as many facts by ordinary detection methods, and they would have been different, less significant, facts. A∴ A∴ training has certainly made all my other jobs easier.

There was only one remaining problem: I didn't want to kill anybody at this point, and a bombing would only get Muldoon in. Even having Malik disappear might only bring in Missing Persons.

Then I remembered the dummies used by the clothier on the eighteenth floor, right above the *Confrontation* office. Burn the dummy just right before setting the bomb and it might work . . . I drove back toward Manhattan whistling "Ho-Ho-Ho, Who's Got the Last Laugh Now?"

(The bomb went off at 2:30 A.M. one week later. Simon, leaving O'Hare Airport, where it was 1:30 A.M., decided he still had time to get to the Friendly Stranger and meet that cute lady cop who had so cleverly infiltrated the Nameless Anarchist Horde. He could get her into bed easily enough, since female spies always expect men to reveal secrets when they're in the dreamy afterglow with their guard down; he would teach her some sexual yoga, he decided, and see what secrets she might slip. But he remembered the midnight conference at the UN building after the bomb was set, and Malik's grim words: "If we're right about this, we might all be dead before Woodstock Europa opens next week.")

"Are you a turtle?" Lady Velkor asks again, approaching another man in green. "No," he says, "I have no armor." She smiles as she murmurs, "Blessed be," and he replies, "Blessed be" . . . Doris Horus heard the voice behind her say "And how's the Miskatonic Messalina?" and her heart leaped, not believing it, but when she turned it was him, Stack . . . "Jesus," one Superman said to another, "does he personally know all the good-looking white chicks in the world?" . . . The Senate and the People of Rome were still tussling with Attila and His Huns, but Hermie "Speed King" Trismegistos, drummer with the Credibility Gap, watched placidly from only a few feet away, seeing them as a very complicated, almost mathematical ballet; he was concerned only with determining whether they illustrated the eternal warfare of Set and Osiris or the joining of atoms to make molecules. He knew he was on acid, but, what the hell, that must have been the Kool-Aid, another of Tyl Eulenspiegel's merry pranks . . .

The submarine rose above the plateau, lifting into the waters of Lake Totenkopf. Mooring it well below the surface on the shore opposite Ingolstadt, Hagbard and about thirty of his crew entered scuba launches and buzzed to the surface. Parked on a road beside the lake was a line of cars, led by a magnificent Bugatti Royale. Hagbard grandly ushered George, Stella, and Harry Coin into the enormous car. George was shocked to see that the chauffeur was a man whose face was covered with gray fur.

It was a long drive around the lake to the town of Ingolstadt. It was very much as George had imagined it, all turrets and spires and Gothic towers mixed with modern-Martian edifices straight from Mad Avenue, but most of the buildings looking like they had been put up in the days of Prince Henry the Fowler.

"This place is full of beautiful buildings," said Hagbard. "The big Gothic cathedral in the center of town is called the Liebfrauenminister. There's another rococo church called the Maria Victoria—I've always wanted to get stoned on acid and go look at the carvings, they're so intricate."

"Have you been here before, Hagbard?" Harry asked.

"On scouting missions. I know where all the good places are. Tonight you're all going to be my guests at the Schlosskeller in Ingolstadt Castle."

"We have to be your guests," said George. "None of us have any money."

"If you have flax," said Hagbard, "you can pay in flax at the Schlosskeller."

They went first to the Donau-Hotel, which Hagbard said

was the most modern and comfortable in Ingolstadt, where Hagbard had reserved almost all the rooms for his people. With every hotel in Ingolstadt bursting at the seams, it had taken a huge advance payment to bring this off. The hotel's staff jumped to attention when they saw the line of cars with Hagbard's splendid Bugatti in the vanguard. Even in a town crowded with celebrities, overrun with wealthy rock musicians and affluent rock fans from all over the world, a machine like Hagbard's commanded respect.

George, following Hagbard into the lobby, suddenly found himself face to face with two ancient, bent German men. One, with a long white mustache and a lock of white hair that fell over his forehead, said, in heavily accented English, "Get out of my way, degenerate Jewish Communist homosexual." The other old man winced and said something placating to his colleague in a soft voice. The first man waved his hand in dismissal, and they tottered toward the elevators together. Several more old men joined them as George watched, too surprised to be angry. Here, though, in the fatherland of that kind of mentality, the old man's hatred seemed historical curiosity to him more than anything else. Doubtless such men as that had actually seen Hitler in the flesh.

Hagbard grandly took a handful of room keys from the desk clerk. "For simplicity's sake, I've assigned a man and a woman to each room," he said as he passed them out. "Choose your roommates and switch around as you like. When you get up to your rooms you'll find suitable Bavarian peasant costumes laid out on the bed. Please put them on."

Stella and George went upstairs together. George unlocked the door and surveyed the large room with its two double beds. On top of one lay a man's outfit of lederhosen with silk shirt and knee socks, while on the other bed was a woman's peasant skirt, blouse, and vest.

"Costumes," Stella said. "Hagbard's really crazy." She shut the door and tugged at the zipper of her one-piece gold knit pantsuit. She had nothing on underneath. She smiled as George regarded her with admiration.

When the group was assembled in the lobby, only Stella looked good in costume. Of the men, Hagbard looked most natural and happy in lederhosen—which was, perhaps, why he'd had the notion of dressing that way. Long, skinny Harry looked ridiculous and uncomfortable, but his buck-toothed grin showed he was trying to be a good sport.

George looked around. "Where's Mavis?" he asked Hagbard.

"She didn't come with us. She's back minding the store." Hagbard raised his arm imperiously. "On to the Schlosskeller."

The Ingolstadt Castle, a battlemented medieval building built on a hill, had a magnificent restaurant in what had formerly been either a dungeon or a wine cellar or both. Hagbard had reserved the entire cellar for the evening.

"Here," he said, "we'll rally our forces around us, have some fun, and prepare for the morrow." He seemed in an agitated, almost giddy mood. He took his place at the center of a big table in a blackened carved chair that looked like a bishop's throne. On the wall behind him was a famous painting. It depicted the Holy Roman Emperor Henry IV barefoot in the snow at Canossa, but with one foot on the neck of Pope Gregory the Great, who lay prone, his tiara knocked off, his face ignominiously buried in a snowdrift.

"The story goes that this was commissioned by the notorious Bavarian jester Tyl Eulenspiegel when he was at the height of his fortunes," Hagbard said. "Later, when he was old and penniless, he was hanged for his anarchistic attitudes and his low Bavarian sense of humor. So it goes."

SHE'LL BE WEARING RED PAJAMAS

("There he is!" Markoff Chaney whispers tensely. Saul and Barney lean forward, peering at the figure ahead of them. About five-seven, Saul estimates, and Carmel was five-two, according to the R&I packet they had lifted from Las Vegas police headquarters . . . But who else would be down here, so far from the route of the guided tours? . . . Saul's hand moves toward his gun, but the other figure whirls on them, flashing a pistol, and shouts, "Hold it right there, all of you!")

SHE'LL BE WEARING RED PAJAMAS

"Oh Christ," Saul says disgustedly. "Hail Eris, friend—we're on the same side." He holds up his hands, empty. "I'm Saul Goodman and this is Barney Muldoon, both formerly of the New York Police Force. This is our friend Markoff Chaney, a man of great imagination and a true servant of Goddess. All hail Discordia, Twenty-three Ski-doo, Kallisti, and do you need any more passwords, Mr. Sullivan?"

"Gosh," Markoff Chaney says. "You mean that's really John Dillinger?"

SHE'LL BE WEARING RED PAJAMAS WHEN SHE COMES

(Rhoda Chief, vocalist and apprentice witch, sampled some of her own Kool-Aid early in the evening. She swore until the day she died that what happened in Ingolstadt that *Walpurgisnacht* was nothing less than the appearance of a giant sea serpent in Lake Totenkopf. The beast, she insisted, turned, took its own tail in its mouth, and gradually dwindled to a dot, giving off good vibes and flashes of Astral Light as it diminished.)

There were many empty places at the big table when the Discordians sat down. Hagbard seemed in no hurry to order dinner. Instead he called for round after round of the local beer, of which enormous stocks had been laid in to prepare for the great rock festival. George, Stella, and Harry Coin sat together near Hagbard, and George and Harry discussed sodomy objectively, between long, thoughtful pauses and deep drinking. Hagbard sent the beer around so fast that George frequently had to swill down a whole stein in a minute or two, just to keep up. Various people came in and sat down at empty places at the table. George shook hands with a man around thirty who introduced himself as Simon Moon. He had a lovely black woman with him named Mary Lou Servix. Simon immediately began telling everybody about a fantastic novel he had been reading on the plane coming over. George was interested until he found out that the book was *Telemachus Sneezed*, by Atlanta Hope. He didn't see how anyone could take trash like that seriously.

Just around the time George was finishing his tenth stein of Ingolstadt's fabled beer and feeling quite woozy, a man who looked very familiar floated into his line of vision. The man wore a brown suit and horn-rimmed glasses, and his gray hair was crew-cut.

"George!" the man shouted.

"Yes, it's me, Joe," said George. "Of course it's me. That's you, Joe, isn't it?" He turned to Harry Coin. "That's the guy who sent me down to Mad Dog to investigate." Harry laughed.

"My God," said Joe. "What's happened to you, George?" He looked vaguely frightened.

"A lot of things," said George. "How many years has it been since I've seen you, Joe?"

"Years? It's been seven days, George. I saw you just before you caught the plane to Texas. What have you been doing?"

George shook his finger. "You were holding out on me, Joe. You wouldn't be here now if you didn't know a lot more than you claimed to when you sent me to Mad Dog. Maybe good old Hagbard can tell you what I've been doing. There's good old Hagbard looking over at us from his end of the table right now. What do you say, Hagbard? Do you know good old Joe Malik?"

Hagbard lifted a huge, ornamented stein of beer, which the management of the Schlosskeller had provided him as an honored guest. It was adorned with elaborate bas-reliefs of pagan woodland scenes, including tumescent satyrs pursuing chubby nymphs.

"How you doing, Malik?" called Hagbard.

"Great, Hagbard, just great," said Joe.

"We're gonna save the earth, aren't we, Joe?" Hagbard yelled. "Gonna save the earth, that right?"

"Jesus saves," said George. He began to sing:

> I've got the peace that passeth understanding
> Down in my heart,
> Down in my heart,
> Down in my heart.
> I've got the peace that passeth understanding
> Down in my heart—
> Down in my heart—to—stay!

Hagbard and Stella laughed and applauded. Harry Coin shook his head and muttered, "Takes me back. Sure does take me back."

Joe took a few steps away from George, moving so he could face Hagbard across the table. "What do you mean, save the earth?"

Hagbard looked at him stupidly, his mouth hanging open. "If you don't know that, why are you here?"

"I just want to know—we're going to save the earth, but are we going to save the people?"

"What people?"

"The people that live on the earth."

"Oh—those people," said Hagbard. "Sure, sure, we're gonna save *everybody*."

Stella frowned. "This is the silliest conversation I've ever heard."

Hagbard shrugged. "Stella, honey, why don't you go on back to the *Leif Erikson?*"

"Well, fuck you, Charley." Stella stood up and flounced off, her peasant skirt swinging.

At that moment a little wall-eyed man tapped Joe on the shoulder. "Sit down, Joe. Have a drink. Sit down with George and me."

"I've seen you before," said Joe.

"Perhaps. Come, sit down. Let's have some of this good Bavarian beer. It has great integrity. Have you ever tried it? Waitress!" The newcomer snapped his fingers impatiently, all the while staring owlishly at Joe through lenses as thick as the bottoms of beer glasses. Joe let himself be led to a chair.

"You look exactly like Jean-Paul Sartre," said Joe as he sat down. "I've always wanted to meet Jean-Paul Sartre."

"Sorry to disappoint you, then, Joe," said the man. "Put your hand into my side."

"Mal, baby!" Joe cried, attempting to embrace the apparition and ending up hugging himself while George, bleary-eyed, stared and shook his head. "Am I glad to see you here," Joe went on. "But how come you're doing Jean-Paul Sartre instead of your hairy taxi driver?"

"This is a good cover," said Malaclypse. "People would expect Jean-Paul Sartre to be here, covering the world's biggest rock festival from an existentialist point of view. On the other hand, this is Lon Chaney, Jr., country, and if I started showing up as Sylvan Martiset, with a face covered with fur, I'd have a mob of peasants carrying torches looking for me all over town."

"I saw a hairy chauffeur today," said George. "Do you suppose it was Lon Chaney, Jr.?"

"Don't worry, George," said Malaclypse with a smile. "The hairy people are on our side."

"Really?" said Joe. He looked around. Hagbard Celine was the hairiest person at the table. His fingers, hands, and bare forearms were black with hair. The stubble of his beard came high up on his cheekbones, just below his eyes. On the back of his neck the hair didn't stop growing, but continued down into his collar. Stripped, Joe thought, the man must look like a bear rug. Many of the other people at the table had long hair or Afro haircuts, and the men had beards and mustaches. Joe remembered Miss Mao's hairy armpits. The peasant blouses on the women in this room hid their armpits from examination. George, of course, had that shoulder-length blond hair that made him look like a Giotto angel. But, Joe thought, what about me? I'm not hairy at all. I keep my hair in a crew cut because I prefer it that way. Where does that leave me?

"What difference does hair make?" he asked Malaclypse.

"Hair is the most important thing in this society," said George. "I've tried repeatedly to explain that to you, Joe, and you've always never listened. Hair is the whole thing."

"Hair in this society at this moment is a symbol," said Malaclypse. "However, there is a real aspect to hair which enables me, for instance, to look around this room and surmise that many of these people are enemies of the Illuminati. You see, all humans were once fur-bearing."

Joe nodded. "I saw that in the movie."

"Oh, yes, you saw *When Atlantis Ruled the Earth*, didn't you?" said Malaclypse. "Well, hairlessness, you'll recall, was Gruad's peculiarity. Most of the people whom the Illuminati permitted to live—and to eventually become recivilized, Illuminati-style—were mated with or raped by descendants of Gruad. But the fur-bearing gene, found in all humans before the catastrophe, has not disappeared. It is quite common in enemies of the Illuminati. My suspicion is that if we knew the histories of ELF and the Discordians and the JAMs, we'd find that they go back to Atlantean origins and preserve to some extent the genes of Gruad's foes. I'm inclined to believe that hairy people, in whom the genes of Atlanteans other than Gruad predominate, are inherently predisposed to anti-Illuminati activities. Conversely, people who work against the Illuminati are also likely to favor lots of hair. These factors have given rise to legends about werewolves, vampires, beast-men of all kinds, abominable snowmen, and furry demons. Note the general success of the Illuminati propaganda campaign to portray all such hirsute beings as fearsome and evil. The propensity for hairiness among anti-Illuminati types also explains why lots of hair is a common characteristic of bohemians, beatniks, leftists generally, scientists, artists, and hippies. All such people tend to make good recruits for the anti-Illuminati organizations."

"Sometimes we make it sound as if the Illuminati were the only menace on earth," said Joe. "Isn't it equally possible that people who are opposed to the Illuminati may be dangerous?"

"Oh, yes indeed," said Malaclypse. "Good and evil are two ends of the same street. But the street was built by the Illuminati. They had excellent reasons, from their viewpoint, to preach the Christian ethic to the masses, you know. What is John Guilt?"

Joe remembered what he'd said to Jim Cartwright several years ago: *Sometimes I wonder if we're not all working for them, one way or another.* He hadn't meant it at the time, but now he realized it was probably true. He might be doing the Illuminati's work right now, when he thought he was saving the human race. Just as Celine might be doing the will of the Illuminati while thinking that he was preserving the earth.

George, bleary-eyed and smiling, said, "Where'd you meet Sheriff Jim, Joe?"

Joe stared at him. "What?"

"Hairlessness is the reason why Gruad and his successors were partial to reptiles," said Malaclypse, adjusting his thick glasses. "They had a real feeling of kinship. One of their symbols was a serpent with its tail in its mouth, which was intended to refer both to Gruad's Ophidian assassins and to his other experiments with reptilian lifeforms."

Joe, still shaken by George's question, yet not wanting to probe further in that direction, said, "All kinds of myths involving serpents crop up in all parts of the world."

"All of them go back to Gruad," said Malaclypse. "The serpent symbol and the Atlantean catastrophe gave rise to the myth that Adam and Eve, tempted by the serpent, fell into misery when they acquired the knowledge of good and evil. Just as Atlantis fell through the moralistic ideology of Gruad the serpent-scientist. Then there's the old Norse myth of the World Serpent with its tail in its mouth that holds the universe together. The Illuminati serpent symbol was also the origin of the brazen serpent of Moses, the plumed serpent of the Aztecs, and their legend of the eagle devouring the snake, the caduceus of Mercury, St. Patrick casting the snakes out of Ireland, various Baltic tales of the serpent king, legends of dragons, the monster guarding the fabulous treasure at the bottom of the Rhine, the Loch Ness monster, and a whole raft of other stories connecting serpents with the supernatural. In fact, the name 'Gruad' comes from an Atlantean word that translates variously as 'worm,' 'serpent,' or 'dragon,' depending on context."

"I'd say he was all three," said Joe. "From what I know."

George said, "I saw the Loch Ness monster today. Hagbard called it a she, which surprised me. But this is the first I've heard about this serpent business. I thought the Illuminati symbol was an eye in a pyramid."

"The Big Eye is their most important symbol," said Malaclypse, "but it isn't the only one. The Rosy Cross is another. But most widely copied is the serpent symbol. The eye in the pyramid and the serpent are often seen in combination. Together they represent the sea monster Leviathan, whose tentacles are depicted as serpents and whose central body is shown as an eye in a pyramid. Since each of Leviathan's tentacles is said to have an independent brain, that's not half bad. The swastika, which was a pretty important symbol around these parts some decades ago, was originally a stylized drawing of Leviathan and his many tentacles. Early versions of it have more than four hooks, and they often include a triangle, sometimes even an eye-and-triangle, in the center. A common transitional form is a triangle with the sides extended and then hooked to form tentacle shapes. There are two tentacles for each of the three angles, which yields a twenty-three. Polish archeologists found a swastika painted in a cave. The drawing dated back to Cro-Magnon times, not long after the fall of Atlantis, and there were twenty-three swirling tentacles around a beautifully executed pyramid with an ocher eye in its center."

George held his breath. Mavis had come into the room. Instead of the peasant-skirt outfit Hagbard had decreed, she was wearing what might have been called hot lederhosen, a very short, very tight pair of leather breeches that made her legs look fantastically long and underlined the round curves of her ass.

"Wow—that's some attractive woman," said Joe.

"Don't you know her?" asked George. "Well, that puts me one up on you. You're going to meet her."

Mavis came over, and George said, "Mavis, this is Joe Malik, the guy who put me in the cell you got me out of."

"That's a little unfair," Joe said, taking Mavis's hands with a smile, "but I did send him down to Mad Dog."

"Excuse me," said Mavis. "I want to talk with Hagbard." She disengaged her hand and walked away. Both Joe and George looked stricken. Malaclypse merely smiled.

Just then a tall, stern-looking black man came into the room. He too was wearing Bavarian peasant costume. He went up to Hagbard and shook hands.

"Hey, it's Otto Waterhouse, the infamous killer cop and cop killer!" roared Hagbard, swilling down beer from his huge stein. Waterhouse looked pained for a moment, then sat down and surveyed the room through narrowed eyes.

"Where's my Stella?" he demanded gruffly. George felt his hackles rise. He knew he had no right of possession where Stella was concerned. But then, neither did this guy. Exclusive possession seemed the one type of sexual relationship not practiced among the Discordians and their allies. There was a kind of tribal, general love among them which didn't prevent anybody from sleeping with anybody else. An unsympathetic observer might call it "promiscuity," but that word, as George understood it, meant using another's body for sex without feeling anything for the person you were physically involved with. The Discordians were all too close, too concerned about each other as people, for the word "promiscuity" to fit their sex lives. And George loved them all: Hagbard, Mavis, Stella, the other Discordians, Joe, even Harry Coin, maybe even Otto Waterhouse, who had just appeared.

Mavis said, "Stella's gone down to the submarine, Otto. She'll join us at the proper time."

Hagbard suddenly lurched to his feet. *"Quiet!"* he roared. A silence fell around the smoky room. People stared at Hagbard curiously.

"We're all here now," he said. "So, I got an announcement to make. I want you to all join me in drinking to an engagement announcement."

"Engagement?" somebody called incredulously.

"Shut the fuck up," Hagbard snarled. "I'm talking, and if anybody interrupts me again I'll throw them out. Yes, I'm talking about an engagement. To be married. Day after tomorrow, when the Eschaton has been immanentized and all of this is over—lift your steins—Mavis and I will be married aboard the *Leif Erikson* by Miss Portinari."

George sat there still for a moment, absorbing it, looking at Hagbard. He looked from Hagbard to Mavis, and tears started to well up in his eyes. He stood and lifted his stein.

"Here's to ya, Hagbard!" he said, and he drew his arm back in a sidearm motion so as not to spill any of the beer and then let the whole stein fly at Hagbard's head. Laughing, Hagbard swayed to one side, a movement so casual it didn't appear that he was ducking. The stein struck the painted head of Emperor Henry IV. The painting apparently had been done on a heavy board, because the stein smashed to bits without marking it. A waiter rushed forward to wipe the beer away, looking reproachfully at George.

"Sorry," said George. "Hate to damage a work of art. You should have kept your head in place, Hagbard. It would have been less of a loss." He took a deep breath and roared, "Sinners! Sinners in the hands of an angry God! You are all spiders in the hand of the Lord!" He held out his hand, palm upward. "And he holds you over a fiery pit!" George turned his palm over. He noticed suddenly that everyone in the room was silent and looking at him. Then he passed out, falling into the arms of Joe Malik.

"Beautiful," said Hagbard. "Exquisite."

"Is that what you meant by taking the woman away from him?" said Joe angrily as he eased George into a chair. "You're a sadistic prick."

"That's only the first step," said Hagbard. "And I said it was *temporary*. Did you see the way he threw that stein? His aim was perfect. He would have brained me if I 'hadn't known it was coming."

"He should have," said Joe. "You mean you were lying about you and Mavis getting married? You were just saying that to bug George?"

"He certainly was not," said Mavis. "Hagbard and I have both had it with this catch-as-catch-can single life. And I'll never find another man who more perfectly fits my value system than Hagbard. I don't need anybody else." As if to prove that she meant what she said, she knelt abruptly and kissed Hagbard's hairy left instep.

"A new mysticism," Simon cried. "The Left-Foot Path."

Joe looked away, embarrassed by the gesture; then another thought crossed his mind, and he looked back. There was something about the scene that stirred a memory in him—but was it a memory of the past or of the future?

"What can I say?" Hagbard asked, grinning. "I love her."

More food arrived, and Harry Coin leaned over to ask, "Hagbard, are you dead sure that this goddess, Eris, is real and is going to be here tonight, just as solid as you and me?"

"You still have doubts?" Hagbard asked loftily. "If you have seen me, you have seen Our Lady." And he made a campy gesture.

The man really is going ape, Joe thought. "I can't eat any more," he said, motioning the waiter away and feeling dizzy.

Hagbard heard him and shouted, "Eat! Eat, drink, and be merry. You may never see me again, Joe. Somebody at this table is going to betray me, didn't you know that?"

Two thoughts collided in Joe's brain: *He knows; he is a Magician* and *He thinks he's Jesus; he's nuts.* But just then George Dorn woke up and said, "Oh, Jesus, Hagbard, I can't take acid."

Hagbard laughed. "The *Morgenheutegesternwelt.* You're ahead of the script, George. I hadn't started to hand the acid out yet." He took a bottle from his pocket and dumped a pile of caps on the table.

Just then, Joe distinctly heard a rooster crow.

Cars, except for official cars and the vehicles of the performers, their assistants, and the festival staff, were banned within ten miles of the festival stage. Hagbard, George, Harry Coin, Otto Waterhouse, and Joe pushed their way through shuffling crowds of young people. A VW camper carrying Clark Kent and His Supermen rolled past. Next a huge, black, 1930s-vintage Mercedes slowly made its way past cheering kids. It was surrounded by a square of motor-cyclists in white overalls to keep eager fans away. Joe shook his head in admiration at the gleaming supercharger pipes, the glistening hand-rubbed black lacquer, and the wire-spoked wheels. The landau top of the car was up, but, by peering inside, Joe could see several crew-cut blond heads. A blond girl suddenly put her face to the window and stared out expressionlessly.

"That's the American Medical Association in that Mercedes," George said.

"Hey," said Harry Coin, "we could pitch a bomb into their car and get all of them right now."

"You'd kill a lot of other people, too, and leave a lot of unfinished business hanging fire," said Hagbard, looking after the Mercedes, which slowly disappeared down the road ahead of them. "That's a nice machine. It belonged to Field Marshal Gerd von Rundstedt, one of Hitler's ablest generals."

An elephantine black bus carrying the AMA's equipment followed close behind the Mercedes. Silently it trundled past.

WE'LL KILL THE OLD RED ROOSTER
WE'LL KILL THE OLD RED ROOSTER

The Closed Corporation was generally recognized to be the most esoteric and experimental of all rock groups; this was why their following, although fanatical, was relatively small. "It's *heavy*, all right," most of the youth culture said, "*but is it really rock?*" The same question, more politely worded, had often been asked by interviewers, and their leader, Peter "Pall" Mall, had a standard answer: "It's rock," he would say somberly, "and on this rock I will build a new church." Then he would giggle, because he was usually stoned during interviews. (Reporters made him nervous.) In fact, the religious tone was rather prominent when the Closed Corporation appeared in concert, and the chief complaint was that nobody could understand the chants that accompanied some of the more interplanetary chords they employed. These chants derived from the Enochian Keys which Dr. John Dee had deciphered from the acrostics in the *Necronomicon*, and in modern times had been most notably employed by the well-known poet Aleister Crowley and the Reverend Anton Lavey of the First Church of Satan in San Francisco. On the night of April 30 the Closed Corporation ritually sacrificed a rooster within a pentagram (it gave one last despairing crow before they slit its throat), called upon the Barbarous Names, dropped a tab of mescaline each, and departed for the concert grounds prepared to unleash vibes that would make even the American Medical Association turn pale with awe.

WE'LL KILL THE OLD RED ROOSTER WHEN SHE COMES

"I just saw Hagbard Celine," said Winifred Saure.

"Naturally he'd be here with all his minions and catamites," said Wilhelm Saure. "We've got to expect to go right down to the wire on this."

"I wonder what he's planning," said Werner Saure.

"Nothing," said Wolfgang Saure. "In my opinion he's planning nothing at all. I know how his mind works—head full of Oriental mystical mush. He's going to rely on his intuition to tell him what to do. He hopes to make it more difficult for us to anticipate his actions, since he himself doesn't know what they will be. But he's wrong. His field of action is drastically limited, and there's nothing he can do to stop us."

First the towers appeared over the black-green tops of the pines. They looked like penitentiary guard towers, though in fact the men in them were unarmed and their primary purpose was to house spotlights and loudspeakers. Then the road turned and they were walking next to a twenty-foot-high wire fence. Running parallel to this was an inner fence thirty feet away and about the same height. Beyond that were bright green hillsides. The promoters of the fesival had chopped down and sold all the trees on the hills within the fenced-off area, bulldozed the stumps, and covered the raw earth with fresh sod. Already the green was particlaly covered by crowds of people. Tents had popped up like mushrooms, and banners waved in the air. Portable outhouses, painted Day-glo orange to make them easy to spot, were set at regular intervals. A vast hum of talking, shouting, singing, and music rose over the hills. Beyond the hills, beyond the central hill where the stage stood, the blue-black waters of Lake Totenkopf heaved and tossed. Even that side of the festival area had its fences and towers.

Joe said, "You'd think they were really worried about someone sneaking in for free."

"These people really know how to build this kind of place," said Otto Waterhouse.

Hagbard laughed. "Come on, Otto, are you a racist about Germans?"

"I was talking about whites. They've got good big ones in the U.S., too. I've seen a couple."

"I never saw one with a geodesic dome, though," said George. "Look at how big that thing is. Wonder what's in it."

"I read that the Kabouters were going to set up a dome,"

said Joe. "As a first-aid or bad-trip station, or something like that."

"Maybe it's a place where you can go hear the music," said Harry Coin. "Hell, size of this thing, you can barely see people on the stage, much less hear them."

"You haven't heard the loudspeakers they've got," said Hagbard. "When the music starts they'll be able to hear it all the way to Munich."

They came to a gate. Arching over it was a sign that declared, in red-painted Gothic letters: EWIGE BLUMENKRAFT UND EWIGE SCHLANGEKRAFT.

"See?" said Hagbard. "Right out in the open. For anyone who understands to read and know that the hour is at hand. They won't be hiding much longer."

"Well," said Joe, "at least it doesn't say *'Arbeit macht frei.'* "

Hagbard handed in the orange week-long tickets for his group, and a black-uniformed usher punched them neatly and returned them. They were inside the Ingolstadt Festival. As the sun sank over the far side of Lake Totenkopf, Hagbard and his contingent mounted a hill. A huge sign over the stage announced that the Oklahoma Home Demonstration Club was playing, and the loudspeakers thundered out an old favorite of that group: "Custer Stomp."

Behind the stage the four members of the American Medical Association stood apart and gazed out at the sunset. They were wearing iridescent black tunics and trousers. Members of other bands stood together and talked, many of the groups happy to be meeting each other for the first time. They even fraternized with a few intrepid kids who managed to infiltrate past the guards and make it to the back side of the stage hill. But white-suited attendants kept the public and fellow performers away from the American Medical Association. This was generally accepted as the AMA's privilege. They were, after all, universally acclaimed as the greatest rock group in the world. Their records sold the most. Their tours drew audiences that dwarfed even those of the Beatles. Their sound was everywhere. As the Beatles had, for a time, expressed the new freedom of the '60s, so the AMA seemed to epitomize the repressive spirit of the '70s. The secret of their popularity was that they were so appalling. They reminded their fans of all the evils that were being daily visited upon them, and thus hearing and seeing them was like scratching a very bad itch. They suggested that perhaps youth had captured its oppressors or identified with them, and they momentarily turned the pain of the whole scene into pleasure. To learn how to enjoy suffering, since suffering was their lot, kids by the millions flocked to hear the AMA.

"Like a radiant heater," said Wolfgang. "We at the center. Our message projected into a bowl of vibrant young human consciousnesses. Massively reflected by them back across the lake—into the lake to the depth of a mile. There, reaching the sunken army. Raising them, in a sense, from the dead."

"We are so close to realizing the dream of thirty thousand years," said Winifred. "Will we be able to do it? Will we be the ones who complete the work begun by great Gruad? And, if not, what will become of us?"

"Doubtless we will scream in hell for all eternity," said Werner matter-of-factly. "What would you do to us if we failed?"

"We need fear eternity only if the Eater of Souls is on the scene," said Wilhelm. "And they've still got him imprisoned inside the Pentagon."

"Let no one speak of failure," said Wolfgang. "It is absolutely impossible for us to fail. The plan is foolproof."

Winifred shook her head. "Fools are precisely what it is not proof against. And you, Wolfgang, know that best of all."

It was dark now. The large tent made of cloth-of-gold was sheltered between the fence and a relatively secluded grassy knoll. There was greatest privacy here, because this corner of the festival area was farthest from the stage, and because the area was full of Discordians. Hagbard went into the tent and stayed there awhile. Joe and George stood outside, talking. George was thinking that Hagbard was probably in there with Mavis and he wished he could dash in there and kill the son of a bitch. Joe, agonizingly nervous, suspected that Hagbard was in the tent with a woman, probably Mavis, and he wondered if he should rush in and kill Hagbard while the Discordian leader was occupied. He kept his hand in his pocket, fingers curled around the small pistol.

I circle around, I circle around . . .

After about half an hour Hagbard emerged from the

tent, smiling. "Go on in," he said to Joe. "You're needed in there."

George grabbed Hagbard's arm, trying to sink his fingers in. But the muscle felt like iron, and Hagbard didn't seem to notice. "Who's in there?" he demanded.

"Stella," said Hagbard, looking down at the stage, where the Plastic Canoe was playing.

"And you were fucking her?" Joe asked. "To release the energies? And now I'm supposed to fuck her too? And George after me? And then everybody else? That's left-hand magic, and it's creepy."

"Just go in," Hagbard said. "You'll be surprised. I wasn't fucking Stella. Stella wasn't in there when I was."

"Who was?" George asked, thoroughly confused.

"My mother," said Hagbard happily.

Joe turned toward the tent. He would make one more effort to trust Celine, but then . . . Suddenly the hawk face leaned close to him and Hagbard whispered, "I know what you're planning for afterwards. Do it quickly."

SHE'LL BE WEARING RED PAJAMAS WHEN SHE COMES

On February 2 Robert Putney Drake received a book in the mail. The return address, he noted, was Gold & Appel Transfers on Canal Street, one of the corporations owned by that intriguing Celine fellow who had kept appearing at the best parties for the last year or so. It was titled *Never Whistle While You're Pissing*, and the flyleaf had a bold scrawl saying, "Best regards from the author," followed by a gigantic C like a crescent moon. The publisher was Green and Pleasant Publications, P.O. Box 359, Glencoe, Illinois 60022.

Drake opened it and read a few pages. To his astonishment, several Illuminati secrets were spelled out rather clearly, although in a hostile and sarcastic tone. He flipped the pages, looking for other interesting tidbits. Toward the middle of the book he found:

DEFINITIONS AND DISTINCTIONS

FREE MARKET: That condition of society in which all economic transactions result from voluntary choice without coercion.

THE STATE: That institution which interferes with the Free Market through the direct exercise of coercion or the granting of privileges (backed by coercion).

TAX: That form of coercion or interference with the Free Market in which the State collects tribute (the tax), allowing it to hire armed forces to practice coercion in defense of privilege, and also to engage in such wars, adventures, experiments, "reforms," etc., as it pleases, not at its own cost, but at the cost of "its" subjects.

PRIVILEGE: From the Latin *privi*, private, and *lege*, law. An advantage granted by the State and protected by its powers of coercion. A law for private benefit.

USURY: That form of privilege or interference with the Free Market in which one State-supported group monopolizes the coinage and thereby takes tribute (interest), direct or indirect, on all or most economic transactions.

LANDLORDISM: That form of privilege or interference with the Free Market in which one State-supported group "owns" the land and thereby takes tribute (rent) from those who live, work, or produce on the land.

TARIFF: That form of privilege or interference with the Free Market in which commodities produced outside the State are not allowed to compete equally with those produced inside the State.

CAPITALISM: That organization of society, incorporating elements of tax, usury, landlordism, and tariff, which thus denies the Free Market while pretending to exemplify it.

CONSERVATISM: That school of capitalist philosophy which claims allegiance to the Free Market while actually supporting usury, landlordism, tariff, and sometimes taxation.

LIBERALISM: That school of capitalist philosophy which attempts to correct the injustices of capitalism by adding new laws to the existing laws. Each time conservatives pass a law creating privilege, liberals pass another law modifying privilege, leading conservatives to pass a more subtle law recreating privilege, etc., until "everything not forbidden is compulsory" and "everything not compulsory is forbidden."

SOCIALISM: The attempted abolition of all privilege

by restoring power entirely to the coercive agent behind privilege, the State, thereby converting capitalist oligarchy into Statist monopoly. Whitewashing a wall by painting it black.

ANARCHISM: That organization of society in which the Free Market operates freely, without taxes, usury, landlordism, tariffs, or other forms of coercion or privilege. RIGHT ANARCHISTS predict that in the Free Market people would voluntarily choose to compete more often than to cooperate. LEFT ANARCHISTS predict that in the Free Market people would voluntarily choose to cooperate more often than to compete.

Drake, now totally absorbed, turned the page. What he found seemed to be an anthropological report on an obscure tribe he had never heard of; he quickly recognized it as a satire and a parable. Putting it aside for a moment, he buzzed his secretary and asked to be connected with Gold and Appel Transfers.

In a moment a voice said, "G and A T. Miss Maris."

"Mr. Drake calling Mr. Celine," Drake's secretary said.

"Mr. Celine is on an extended voyage," Miss Maris replied, "but he left a message in case Mr. Drake called."

"I'll take it," Drake said quickly. There was a click as his secretary went off the line.

"Mr. Celine will send an emissary to you at the appropriate time," Miss Maris said. "He says that you will recognize the emissary because he will bring with him certain artworks of the Gruad era. I'm afraid that is all, sir."

"Thank you," Drake said hollowly, hanging up. He knew the technique: he had used it himself in moving in on the Syndicate back in 1936.

"You were fucking Stella?"

"Who says I was fucking anybody?"

Joe went in. The tent was as richly hung as that o any Moorish chieftain. At one end was a diaphanous veil, behind it a figure on a pile of cushions. The figure was lightskinned, so Hagbard had been lying about being in here with Stella. Joe went over and pulled the veil aside.

It was Mavis, all right, just as Joe had guessed. She was wearing harem pajamas, red but translucent, through which he could see her dark nipples and the full bush of hair between her legs. At the expectation of making love to her,

Joe could feel his cock begin to swell. But he was determined to impose his head trip on this scene.

"Why am I here?" he said, still holding the curtain back with one hand, trying to assume a casual pose. Mavis smiled faintly and motioned him to sit down on the cushions beside her. He did so, and found himself automatically sliding to a half-reclining position. There was a faint suggestion of perfume from Mavis, and he felt the tension in his loins build up a little more.

"I need all the energies we can set in motion to defeat the Illuminati," said Mavis. "Help me, Joe." She held out her arms.

"Were you fucking Hagbard? I never did like sloppy seconds."

Mavis gave a little snarl and threw herself on him. She slathered her drooling lips over his and plunged her tongue deep into his mouth, at the same time pressing her thigh between his legs. Joe fell back and gave up struggling against her. She was just too goddamned attractive. In a minute she had his pants open and his stiff hot prick throbbing in her hand. She lowered her head over it and began sucking it rhythmically.

"Wait," said Joe. "I'm going to go off in your mouth. It's been a week since I got laid, and I'm on a hair trigger."

She looked up at him with a smile. "Eat me, then. I hear you're good at that."

"Who'd you hear that from?" asked Joe.

"A gay priest friend of mine," she said with a laugh as she undid the drawstring of her red trousers.

Joe explored the lips of her vulva with his tongue, reveling in the acrid, musky odor of her bush. He began a businesslike up-and-down, up-and-down motion with his tongue over her clitoris. After a moment he felt her body tensing. It grew more and more rigid. Her pelvis began to buck, and he clamped both hands on her hips and lapped away inexorably. At last she gave a small shriek and tried to drive her whole mons veneris into his mouth.

"Now fuck me, quickly, quickly," she said, and Joe, his pants pulled down and his shirttail flapping, mounted her. He came in a series of exquisite spasms and dropped his head to the pillow, beside hers. She let him rest that way for a few minutes, then gently nudged him to pull out and rolled to her side to face him.

"Am I dismissed?" Joe said. "Have I done my job? Released the energies, or whatever?"

"You sound bitter," said Mavis, "and sad. I'd like you to stay with me a while longer. What's bothering you?"

"A lot of things. I feel like I did the wrong thing. George is obviously in love with you, and you and Hagbard treat it as a joke. And Hagbard treats me as a joke. And both of you are quite obviously using me. You're using me sexually, and I'm beginning to think Hagbard is using me in other ways. And I think you know about it."

"You didn't take the acid, did you?" she said, looking at him sadly.

"No. I knew what Hagbard was doing. This is too serious a moment to play games about the Passion of Christ."

Mavis smiled. She pressed her body closer to him and began playing with his limp penis, rubbing the head gently into her bush. "Joe, you were raised as a Catholic. Catholics have a finer appreciation of blasphemy than anybody. That's why Hagbard chose you. How's your passion, Joe? Is it mounting?" Pressing her naked body against his, she whispered, "How'd you like to fuck the Virgin Mary?"

Joe saw his mother's face, and he felt the blood throbbing in his penis. Now he thought perhaps he knew what Hagbard meant when he said his mother was in the tent.

A little later, when he was in her, she said, "I am a perpetual virgin, Joe. And every woman is, if only you have eyes to see. We wanted to give you eyes tonight. But you refused the Sacrament. You've chosen the hardest way of all, Joe. If you're going to make it through this night you're going to have to find a way to see for yourself. By other means than the one Hagbard provided. You'll have to find your own Sacrament."

And after she came, and he came, she whispered, "Was that the Sacrament?"

He pushed himself up and looked down at the triangular red tattoo between her breasts. "No. You're not the Virgin Mary. You're still Mavis."

"And you still have to make the decision," she said. "Good-bye, Joe. Send George to me."

As Joe was dressing, feeling the weight of the pistol in his trouser pocket, Mavis rolled over so that she was lying on her stomach, not looking at him. Her naked buttocks seemed utterly defenseless. He looked at the pillow on which her bottom had been resting during their lovemaking. It was a cloth-of-gold pillow, and embroidered on it in swirling letters was the word KALLISTI. Joe shook his head and left the tent.

As he emerged, Hagbard was saying in a low voice to Otto Waterhouse, ". . . would have been up your alley if we hadn't had other work for you. Anthrax Leprosy Pi can wipe out the whole population of the earth in a matter of days."

Suddenly, the white of Hagbard's shirt, the gold of the tent cloth, the blazing spotlights of the festival, all were coming in super-bright. That was adrenalin. My mouth was dry—dehydration. All the classic flight-fight symptoms. The activation syndrome, Skinner calls it. I was so keyed up that it was a trip.

"Hello, Joe," said Hagbard softly. Joe suddenly realized that his hand was clenched around the pistol. Hagbard smiled at him, and Joe felt like a little boy caught playing with himself, with his hand in his pocket. He took his hand out quickly.

"She wants George," Joe said weakly. He turned his back on Hagbard to look down at the stage, where the sign, glowing in the darkness, said LOAF AND THE FISHES. They were singing, "I circle around, I circle around, the borders of the earth . . ."

On a pile of cushions behind a diaphanous veil at one end of the tent lay Stella, wearing nothing but a red chiffon pajama top.

"Were you letting Joe fuck you?" George said.

"Joe has never fucked *me*," Stella replied. "You'll be the first person to do that tonight. Look, George, we've got to get every bit of available energy flowing to combat the Illuminati. Come over here and get the energies going with me."

"This is Danny Pricefixer," Doris Horus said. "I met him on the plane coming over."

("Holy Jesus," said Maria Imbrium, vocalist with the Sicilian Dragon Defense, "there are angels coming out of the lake. Angels in golden robes. Look!"

("You're tripping on that Kabouter Kool-Aid, baby," a much-bandaged Hun told her. "There's nothing coming out of the lake."

("*Something* is coming out of the lake," the drummer

with the Sicilian Dragons said, "and you're so stoned you
don't see it."

("And what is it, if it isn't angels?" Maria demanded.

("Christ, I don't know. But whoever they are, they're
walking on the water.")

Wearing my long green feathers, as I fly,
I circle around, I circle around . . .

("Jesus. Walking on the water. You people are zonked out
of your skulls."

("It's just a bunch of surfers, wearing green capes for
some crazy reason."

("Surfers? My ass! That's some kind of gang of Bavarian
demons. They all look like the Frankenstein monster
wrapped up in seaweed.")

*"Pricefixer?" said Kent. "Didn't I meet you five or six
years ago in Arkham? Aren't you a cop?"*

("It's a gigantic green egg . . . and it *loves* me . . .")

John Dillinger muttered to Hagbard, "That red-headed
guy over there—the one with the black musician and the
girl with the fantastic boobs. He's a cop on the New York
Bomb Squad. Wanta bet he's here investigating the *Confrontation* bombing?"

"He must have been talking to Mama Sutra," Hagbard
said thoughtfully.

SHE'LL BE WEARING RED PAJAMAS SHE'LL BE WEARING
RED PAJAMAS

WHEN SHE   COMES

When Otto Waterhouse entered the tent, it was Miss
Mao who was waiting for him. "I never fucked a Chinese
broad," said Otto, stripping off his clothing. "I don't think
Stella is going to like this."

"It will be okay with Stella," said Miss Mao. "We need to
get all the energies moving to combat the Illuminati. And
we need your help." She held out her arms.

"You don't have to ask twice," said Otto, crouching over
her.

At 5:45 in Washington, D.C., the switchboard at the
Pentagon was warned that bombs planted somewhere in the
building would go off in ten minutes. "You killed hundreds
of us today in the streets of Washington," said the woman's
voice. "But we are still giving you a chance to evacuate the
building. You do not have time to find the bombs. Leave

the Pentagon now, and let history be the judge of which side truly fought for life and against death."

The highest-ranking personnel in the Pentagon (and, with revolution breaking out in the nation's capital, *everybody* was there) were immediately moved to underground bombproof shelters. The Secretary of Defense, after consulting with the Joint Chiefs of Staff, declared that there was a 95 percent probability that the threat was a hoax, intended to disrupt the job of coordinating the suppression of revolution across the nation. A search would be instituted, but meanwhile work would go on as usual. "Besides," the Secretary of Defense joked to the Chief of Staff, Army, "one of those little radical bombs would do as much damage to *this* building as a firecracker would to an elephant."

Somehow the fact that the caller had said bombs (plural) had not gotten through. And the actual explosions were far more powerful than the caller had implied. Since a proper investigation was never subsequently undertaken, no one knows precisely what type of explosive was used, how many bombs there were, how they were introduced into the Pentagon, where they were placed, and how they were set off. Nor was the most interesting question of all ever satisfactorily answered: Who done it? In any case, at 5:55 P.M., Washington time, a series of explosions destroyed one-third of the river side of the Pentagon, ripping through all four rings from the innermost courtyard to the outermost wall.

There was great loss of life. Hundreds of people who had been working on that side of the building were killed. Although the explosion had not visibly touched their bombproof shelter, the Secretary of Defense, the Joint Chiefs of Staff, and numerous other high-ranking military persons were found dead; it was assumed that the concussion had killed them, and in the ensuing chaos nobody bothered to examine the bodies carefully. After the explosions the Pentagon was belatedly evacuated, in the expectation that there might be more of the same. There was no more, but the U.S. military establishment was temporarily without a head.

Another casualty was Mr. H. C. Winifred of the U.S. Department of Justice. A civil servant with a long and honorable career behind him, Winifred, apparently deranged by the terrible events of that day of infamy, took the wheel of a Justice Department limousine and drove wildly, running twenty-three red lights, to the Pentagon. He raced to the scene of the explosion brandishing a large piece of chalk, and was trying to draw a chalk line from one side of the gap in the Pentagon wall to the other when he collapsed and died, apparently of a heart attack.

At 11:45 Ingolstadt time the loudspeakers and the sign over the stage announced the American Medical Association. After a ten-minute ovation, the four strange-eyed, ash-blond young people began to play their most popular song, "Age of Bavaria." (In Los Angeles the Mercalli scale on the UCLA seismograph jumped abruptly to grade 1. "Gonna be a little disturbance," Dr. Vulcan Troll said calmly, noting the rise. Grade 1 wasn't serious.) *What made you think we'd find him down here?" Saul asked.*

"Common sense and psychology," Dillinger said. "I know pimps. He'd shit purple before he'd get the guts to try to cross a border. They're strictly mama's boys. The first place I looked was his own cellar, because he might have a hidden room there."

Barney laughed. "That's the first place Saul looked, too."

"We seem to think alike, Mr. Dillinger," Saul said drily.

"There isn't much difference between a cop and a crook, psychologically speaking," Dillinger mused.

"One of my own observations," Hagbard agreed. "What conclusion do you draw from it?"

"Well," Dillinger said. "Pricefixer didn't just pick up that girl because he wanted a lay. She has to fit somehow."

"The musician doesn't know that," Hagbard commented. "Watch his hands. He's repressing a fight impulse; in a few minutes he'll start a quarrel. He and the lady were lovers once—see the way her pelvis tilts when she talks to him?—and he wants Whitey to go away. But Whitey won't go away. He has her linked with the case he's working on."

"I *used to be* a cop," Danny said with an engaging imitation of frankness. "But that was years ago, and the work really didn't appeal to me. I'm a salesman for *Britannica* now. Better hours, and people only slam doors in my face —they don't shoot at me through them."

"Listen," Doris said excitedly. "The AMA is playing 'Age of Bavaria.'" It was the song that, more than any other, both expressed and mocked the aspirations of youth around the world, and the accuracy with which it expressed their yearnings and the savagery with which it denied them had won them over.

It started almost the instant the music began. A mile below the surface of the lake, near the opposite shore, an army began to rise from the dead. The black-uniformed corpses broke loose from their moorings, rose to the surface, and began to drift toward shore. As more and more of the semblance of life returned, the drifting became swimming motions, then wading. They fell into ranks on the shore. Under the steel helmets their complexions were greenish, their eyes heavily lidded, their black lips drawn back in wide grimaces. The mouths of the officers and noncoms moved, forming words of command, though no sound came forth. No sound was needed, it seemed, for the orders were instantly obeyed. Once again the power that had been granted to Adolf Hitler by the Illuminated Lodge in 1923 ("Because you are so preposterous," they told him at the time)—the power that had manifested itself in steel-helmed armies that had won Hitler an empire stretching from Stalingrad to the Atlantic, from the Arctic Circle to the Sahara Desert—once again that power was visible on the earth.

"They are coming. I can feel it," Werner whispered to his twin, Wilhelm, as Wolfgang thundered on the drums and Winifred belted out:

> This is the dawning of the Age of Bavaria—
> Age of Bavaria—
> Bavaria—Bavaria!

The tanks and artillery were rolling into position. The caterpillar treads of the troop carriers were churning. Motorcycle couriers sped up and down the beach. A squadron of partially dismantled Stukas was lined up in the road. After the festivalgoers had been massacred and Ingolstadt had been overrun, the planes would be trucked to the nearby Ingolstadt Aerodrome, where they would be assembled and ready to fly by morning.

The dead men removed black rubber sheaths from rolled up red-white-and-black banners and unfurled them. Many of them were the familiar swastika flags and banners of the Third Reich, with one addition: a red eye-and-pyramid device superimposed on the center of each swastika. Other banners carried Gothic-lettered mottos such as DRANG NACH

OESTEN and HEUTE DIE WELT, MORGENS DAS SONNENSYS-TEM.

At last all was in readiness. The blue-black lips of General-of-the-SS Rudolf Hanfgeist, thirty years dead, shaped the command to march, which was relayed in similar fashion from the higher-ranking officers to the lower-ranking officers to the men. The lights and music on the opposite shore beckoned across the dark, bottomless waters. Moonlight glinting on the death's heads on their caps and runic SS insignia on their collars, the soldiers moved out, company by company. The only sound was the growl of the diesel engines of troop carriers and the clank of weapons.

"They're coming," said the woman under Hagbard, who was neither Mavis nor Stella nor Mao, but a woman with straight black hair, olive skin, fierce black eyebrows, and a bony face.

"Coming, Mother," said Hagbard, giving himself up to the irresistible onward sweep of sensation to the brink of orgasm and over.

"I'm not your mother," said the woman. "Your mother was a blond, blue-eyed Norweigian. And I look Greek now, I think."

"You're the mother of all of us," said Hagbard, kissing her sweat-damp neck.

"Ah," said the woman. "Is that who I am? Then we're getting somewhere."

Then I started to flip, Malik eclipsed by Malaclypse and Celine hardly serene, Mary Lou I Worship You, the Red Eye is my own Mooning, what is the meaning of moaning? and suchlike seminal semantic antics (my head is a Quicktran quicksand where *The Territorial Imperative* always triggers *Stay Off My Turf*, the Latin and the Saxon at war in poor Simon's synapses, dead men fighting for use of my tongue, turning Population Explosion into We're Fucking Overcrowded and backward also, so it might emerge Copulation Explosion, and besides Hag barred straights from this Black-and-White Mass, the acid was in me, I was tripping, flipping, skipping, ripping, on my Way with Maotsey Taotsey for the number of Our Lady is an hundred and fifty and six—there is Wiccadom!), but I never expected it this way.

"What do you see?" I asked Mary Lou.

"Some people who were swimming, coming out of the lake. What do you see?"

"Not what I'm supposed to see."

For the front line, clear as *claritas*, was Mescalito from my peyote visions and Osiris with enormous female breasts and Spider Man and the Tarot Magus and Good Old Charlie Brown and Bugs Bunny with a Tommy gun and Jughead and Archie and Captain America and Hermes Thrice-Blessed and Zeus and Athene and Zagreus with his lynxes and panthers and Micky Mouse and Superman and Santa Claus and Laughing Buddha Jesus and a million million birds, canaries and budgies and ,gaunt herons and holy crows and crowly hose and eagles and hawks and mourning doves (for mourning never ends), and they'd all been stoned since the late Devonian period, when they first started eating hemp seeds, no wonder Huxley found birds "the most emotional class of life," singing all the time, stoned out of their bird-brained skulls, all singing "I circle around, I circle around," except the mynah Birds squawking "Here, kitty-kitty-kitty!" and I remembered again that existence isn't sensible any more than it's hot or red or high or sour, only parts of existence have those qualities, and then there was the Zig-Zag man and my God my god my father leading them in singing

SOLIDARITY FOREVER

    SOLIDARITY FOREV   ERRRR

       THE UNION MAKES US STRONG

"I say," said an Englishman, "I thought he was a monster, and he's only Toad of Toad Hall . . . with Rat . . . and Tinker Bell . . . and Wendy . . . and Bottom . . ."

"That's who *you* are," said Hagbard, "if you can call that any kind of a fucking identity."

"I think it's time you went up on stage and made our little announcement," said the woman. "I think everyone is ready for that."

"I'll send Dillinger in to you."

"Goody!"

"It's not true, you know. That was the other guy, Sullivan."

"I wasn't thinking about that. I don't care if it's no bigger than my little finger. It's just the idea of fucking with *John Dillinger*. If that doesn't put me over, nothing will."

Hagbard stood up and laughed. "You're starting to look

and sound like Mavis again. I think you're slipping, Super-
bitch."

The American Medical Association had left the stage,
and Clark Kent and His Supermen were playing as Hagbard, accompanied by George, Harry, Otto, and Malaclypse, made his way down their own hill and up to the
crest of the hill where the stage was erected. The journey
took a half-hour as they picked their way through groups of
people engaged in Mongolian clusterfuck, sitting Za-Zen, or
just listening to the music. At the stage Hagbard took out a
gold card, which he showed to a group of marshals guarding the area from intrusion. "I have an announcement to
make," he said firmly. The marshals allowed him to climb
on stage, and told him to wait till the Supermen had finished their set.

As soon as Pearson saw Hagbard he motioned his men to
stop playing. A murmur arose from the audience. "Well, all
right, Hagbard," said Robert Pearson, "I was wondering if
you were ever going to show up." He walked over to the
side of the stage where Hagbard and his group were standing.

"Good evening, Waterhouse," said Pearson. "How's my
gal, Stella?"

"Where the fuck do you get off calling her your girl?"
said Waterhouse, his tone containing nothing but menace.

"The acid only opens your eyes, George. It doesn't work
miracles."

*And it shall come to pass, that whosoever call on the
name of the Lord shall be saved.*

"Wonder what the hell is in that suitcase," Dillinger murmured.

"I'll open it," Saul said. "We'll all have to take the antidote anyway, after this. I have a supply out in the car."
And he leaned forward, parted Carmel's stiff blue hands,
and tugged the suitcase free. Barney, Dillinger, and Markoff Chaney crowded close to look as he snapped the lock
and lifted the top.

"I'll be damned and double damned," Barney Muldoon
said in a small, hollow voice.

"Hagbard has been putting us on all along," Simon says
dreamily. (It doesn't matter in the First Bardo.) "Those
Nazis have been dead for thirty years, period. He just

brought us here to put us on a Trip. Nothing is coming out of the lake. I'm hallucinating everything."

"Something is happening," Mary Lou insisted vehemently. "It's got nothing to do with the lake—that's a red herring to distract us from the real battle between your Hagbard and those crazy musicians up there. If I wasn't tripping my head would work better, damn it. It's got something to do with sound waves. The sound waves are turning solid in the air. Whatever it is, the rest of us aren't supposed to understand it. This lake thing is just to give us something we can understand, or almost understand." Her black face was intense with intelligence battling against the ocean of undigestible information pouring in through all of her senses.

"Dad!" Simon cried, weeping happily. "Tell me the Word. You must know now. What is the Word?"

"Kether," said Tim Moon blissfully.

"Kether? That's all? Just Cabalism?" Simon shook his head. "It can't be that simple."

"Kether," Tim Moon repeats firmly. "Right here in the middle of Malkuth. As above, so below."

I see the throne of the world. One single chair twenty-three feet off the ground, studded with seventeen rubies, and brooding over it the serpent swallowing its tail, the Rosy Cross, and the Eye.

"Who was that nice man?" Mary Lou asked.

"My father," Simon said, really weeping now. "And I may never see him again. Mourning never ends."

And then I understood why Hagbard had given us the acid—why the Weather Underground and Morituri used it constantly—because I started to die, I literally felt myself dwindling to a point and approaching absolute zero. I was so shit-scared I grabbed Simon's hand and said "help" in a weak voice, and if he had said "Admit you're a cop first, then I'll help," I sure as hell would have told him everything, blurted it all out, but he just smiled, squeezed my hand gently, and murmured, *"It's alive!"*—and it was, the point was giving off light and energy, my light and my energy but God's also, and it wasn't frightening because it was alive and growing. The word "omnidirectional halo" came to me from somewhere (was it Hagbard talking to Dillinger?), and I looked, holy Key-rizt, Dillinger split in two as I watched. That was the answer to one question: There were two Dillingers, twins, in addition to the fake Dillinger who got shot at the Biograph, $0 = 2$, I thought, feeling some abstract eternal answer there, along with the answer to some of the questions that had bugged so many writers about Dillinger's criminal career (like why some witnesses claimed he was in Miami on that day in 1934 when other witnesses claimed he was robbing a bank and killing a bank guard in East Chicago, and why Hagbard had said something about him being in Las Vegas when I could see him right here in Ingolstadt), but it was all moving, moving, a single point, but everything coming out of it was moving, a star with swords and wands projecting outward as rays, a crown that was also a cup and a whirling disc, a pure white brilliance that said "I am Ptah, come to take you from Memphis to heaven," but I only remembered the cops who beat Daddy up in Memphis and made him swear when he got back that he'd never go south again (and how did that tie in with why I became a cop?), and Ptah became Zeus, Iacchus, Wotan, and it didn't matter, all were distant and indifferent and cold, not gods of humanity but gods above humanity, gods of the void, brilliant as the diamond but cold as the diamond, the three whirling in the point until they became a turning swastika, then the face of the doctor who gave me the abortion that time I got knocked up by Hassan i Sabbah X, saying, "You have killed the Son of God in your womb, black woman," and I started to weep again, Simon holding my hand and repeating, *It's alive,* but I felt that it was dying and I had somehow killed it. I was Otto Waterhouse in reverse: I wanted to castrate Simon, to castrate all white men, but I wouldn't; I would go on castrating black men—the Nightmare Life-in-Death am I.

"It's alive, baby," Simon repeated, "it's alive. And I love you, baby, even if you are a cop."

("The whole lake is *alive,*" the vibe man with the Fillet of Soul was trying to explain to the rest of that group, "one big spiral rising and turning, like the DNA molecule, but with a hawk's head at the top . . .")

"Good evening, Waterhouse," said Pearson. "How's my gal, Stella?"

"Where the fuck do you get off calling her *your* girl?" said Waterhouse, his tone containing nothing but menace.

"Cool it brother," said Pearson reasonably.

"Don't hand me that brother shit. I asked you a question."

"You and your question come out of a weak, limp bag," said Pearson.

Hagbard said, "Robert only fucks white women, Otto. I'm sure he's never laid Stella Maris."

"Don't be *too* sure," said Pearson.

"Don't play with Otto, Robert," said Hagbard. "He specializes in killing black men. In fact, he's only just killed his first white man, and he's not at all sure he enjoyed it."

"I never knew what killing was before," said Waterhouse. "I was crazy all those years, and I enjoyed what I did because I didn't know what I was doing. After I killed Flanagan I understood what I'd been doing all along, and it was like I killed all the others all over again." His cheeks were wet, and he turned away.

Pearson stood looking at him for a moment, then said softly, "Wow. Come on, Hagbard. Let's get you on stage." They walked out to the microphone together. A few people in the audience had begun clapping rhythmically for more music. Most, though, had been waiting silently, happily, for whatever might happen next.

What happened was that Robert Pearson said to them, "Brothers and sisters, this is Freeman Hagbard Celine, my ace, and the heaviest dude on the planet Earth. Listen while he runs it down to you what's happening."

He stepped aside and deferentially ushered Hagbard to the microphone.

Into the silence Hagbard said, "My name, as Clark Kent just told you, is Hagbard Celine . . ."

(In Mad Dog, Texas, John Dillinger and Jim Cartwright looked up from the chess board as the radio music stopped and an announcer's voice said, "We interrupt this show to bring you a special message from Washington." John moved a knight and said softly, "Checkmate. That'll be the President, I bet. I hope to hell my brother finds that missing pimp before things get much worse." Cartwright surveyed the board dismally. "Checkmate," he agreed finally. "I hope your other brother, and Hagbard, are handling things right in Ingolstadt," he added, as they both turned, with a reflex acquired from TV watching, and looked at the radio . . .)

Being a woman is bad enough, but being a black woman is even worse. I always feel split in two, a divided lion (I'm thinking like Simon) with a hole in the middle (and that's all men are interested in, the hole in the middle), but the acid was making the split into a conscious agony and then was healing it, I was a whole Lion, ready to devour my enemies: I understood my father and why he felt he finally had to stand up to the whites even if it killed him. A knight moved across a wasteland, the desert around Las Vegas, but it was laid out in squares like a chess board; he raised a fiery wand, crying "Black Power," and it was Hassan i Sabbah, my lover, my enemy, a Black Christ and yet also a baboon with a crazy grin, all blue pearl gray like semen, inside every woman there's an angry man trying to get out, a man-woman with the eyes of an owl, and the joy came over me as my clit got hot and grew into a penis; I was my father; I was afraid of nothing; I could destroy the world without caring, with one angry flash of my eye, like Shiva. MY PENIS IS THE INVISIBLE STAR RUBY AND MEN CONSPIRE TO MAKE ME HIDE IT; THAT'S WHY I MUST TAKE THEIRS. I am two-faced, always deceiving, like all women; deception is our only defense, I understand it more clearly as the wisdom of my insanity increases, and the musky smell of hashish coming from the Plastic Canoe trailer is like me, a female plant with male strength, they are nailing me to the cross (literally) but the cross is inside a spinning wheel of flame, oh Holy Moses, I'm finding Buddha not Eris in my pineal gland, the third eye is opening, I am the earth beneath your feet, I am Billie Freshette, I am legion, there are millions of me, a plague of locusts to devour your White Male Technology, "My name is Hagbard Celine" he is saying, they sold heroin in my grammar school (that's the way a Chicago black gets educated), Simon is still trying to bring me through it saying now "Death shall have no dominion," and I try to believe Love shall have the dominion but first I must spend my hate to the last penny, they made me kill my baby, I really am going to go crazy because I have the hots again and want Simon's lance in my cup but I also know the real God is beyond God and the real Illuminati is beyond the Illuminati, there's a secret society behind the secret society: The Illuminati we're fighting are puppets of another Illuminati and so are we.

MY NAME IS HAGBARD CELINE, AND THE CARNIVAL IS OVER. REMOVE YOUR MASKS ALL PLAYERS.

"That's a funny thing for Toad of Toad Hall to say," muttered Fission Chips to nobody in particular. But the voice came booming back MY NAME IS HAGBARD CE-LINE. PLEASE DON'T PANIC WHEN YOU HEAR WHAT I'VE GOT TO SAY TO YOU and Chips saw that it wasn't Toad of Toad Hall or even the sinister Saint Toad but just a well-dressed wop with two faces, one smiling and one frowning in wrath. "You know," 00005 said aloud, "I do believe there was a fucking *drug* in that water."

MY NAME IS HAGBARD CELINE. PLEASE DON'T PANIC WHEN YOU HEAR WHAT I HAVE TO SAY TO YOU. PAY CLOSE ATTENTION. I HAVE COME TO TELL YOU THAT YOUR LIVES ARE IN GRAVE DANGER. AT THIS MOMENT AN ARMY IS MARCH-ING AROUND THE SHORE OF LAKE TOTENKOPF FOR THE PURPOSE OF MASSACRING ALL THE PEOPLE ATTENDING THIS FESTIVAL.

"Jesus," said George, "this is never going to work. He's putting it so badly. They'll never believe him. They'll laugh at him. Three-quarters of them don't even understand Eng-lish."

"Is that how it sounds to you?" said Malaclypse. "As if he's speaking in English? It also sounds to me as if he's say-ing everything in a flat, direct way. But I hear him speaking in the Greek dialect of Athens in the fifth century B.C.E."

"What do you mean?"

"He's actually talking in Norwegian or Italian, whichever language he knows best. He's using what I call the Pente-cost Gimmick. It's described in the Acts of the Apostles as the gift of tongues. After the death of Jesus the Apostles were sitting together on the feast of Pentecost, when tongues of fire appeared over their heads. Then they went out and preached to a crowd of people from many different countries, and each person heard the sermons in his own language and in the form most likely to persuade him. They made tens of thousands of converts to Christianity that way. I was the one who laid the trick on them, though they never knew that."

"Speaking in tongues!" said George in wonderment. "They used to preach about it in Bible class: 'And it shall come to pass in the last days, saith God, I will pour out of my Spirit upon all flesh: and your sons and your daughters shall prophesy, and your young men shall see visions and your old men shall dream dreams.' ".

("Don't play games with yourself, George. You know perfectly well that a moment ago I *was* Mavis.")

"It's a giant black woman . . . it's Goethe's Mother Night," somebody was saying, but I was thinking of 69ing with Simon oh the tricks that cat knows to please a woman to make you feel like a queen on a throne and I don't care if he knows I'm a cop there's always a sorrow after a joy on this plane yes I will always be split in two the void will always be there at the center God yes the mask of night is on my face like I read in Shakespeare in school I am the river yellow with sewage and cocksucker is a dirty word but what else is the sign of cancer or that yin-yang all about Christ I loved doing it women who claim they don't are just liars I hate him and I love him the ambiguity is always there that detective who wanted to praise me that time said "You've got balls for a woman" but how would it sound if I said to him "You've got tits for a man" throne after throne cast down into the void and yet I have the power all they're worshipping in their trinities and pyramids are symbols of the cunt and it's hot again but I just want him to hold me I can't ball now I can't speak I see my father's face but it's silver instead of black and all of a sudden I knew Joe Malik had a gun and even that he had a silver bullet in it Mother of God does he think Hagbard is something inhuman and I smelled opium mixed with the hash those are heavy cats in the Plastic Canoe I could feel the energy surging through me I'm in the tent and I'm being fucked by all the men I'm Mavis and Stella and I'm the mother of all of them I am Demeter and Frigga and Cybelle as well as Eris and I am Napthys the Black Sister of Isis of whom none dare speak and I can even see why Joe Malik blew up his own office it was a trap and Hagbard fell into it Joe knows his secret now

"They used to preach about it in Bible class: 'And it shall come to pass in the last days, saith God, I will pour out of my Spirit upon all flesh: and your sons and your daughters shall prophesy and your young men shall see visions and your old men shall dream dreams.' And 'All flesh will see it in one instant.' "

Malaclypse smiled. " 'To conceive of pentecostal training it is necessary to die. These are the words of the first, last, and between, Kallisti.' You must have won the prize for memorizing verse in that Bible class, George."

"I would have, only the teacher didn't like my attitude."

"Good," said Malaclypse. "I also taught the Pentecost Gimmick to Hagbard. What he's saying sounds flat to you, because you don't need to be persuaded. Everybody else is hearing as much emotion and rhetoric as is needed to motivate them. It's a good gimmick, the Pentecost Gimmick."

It all came in solid and three-dimensional and I felt mercy flowing from me like some psychological monthly with water instead of blood I even forgave the American Medical Association all four of them separately and distinctly I was Isis all purple and blue and veiled and even if Poseidon was rising in that lake I could forgive him too He was covered with olives and shamrocks a green water god glistening like amethyst with one huge unicorn horn and then he was Indra the rainmaker whose voice of thunder was only a disguised blessing I obeyed him and put the doll in the tetrahedron there was nothing to fear for all that would happen were blessings and good things as the Brilliant Ones descended bringing their white fire to the red earth the work would be perfected in pleasure not pain for I even knew that Joe found out Pat Walsh's memos were misleading because Hagbard wanted him to find out and wanted him to plant the bomb and even wanted him to come here tonight with the gun so it all makes sense if you had a model of the globe with a black light flashing for every death and a white light for everytime somebody comes it would seem to be glowing all the time that's what's so good about being a woman I can come and come and come oh God as many times as I want and men even Simon hardly ever come more than once in a night that mean Miss Forbes in first grade she needed a good lay but I can even forgive her

LADIES AND GENTLEMEN, THE PRESIDENT OF THE UNITED STATES

"Everyone must leave the festival area," Hagbard was saying. "The resurrected Nazis intend to slaughter all of you. Fortunately, we have had time to build you a pathway to safety. Behold!" He stretched out his arm and the spotlight moved beyond him to the lake, illuminating a great pontoon bridge stretching from the festival area on the eastern shore diagonally to the lake's northwest corner. It had been silently erected by Hagbard's crew, with the indispensable help of Howard and the dolphins, during the last hour.

"Wow," George said to Malaclypse. "I suppose you'd call that the Red Sea Gimmick."

Hagbard lifted his hands. "I name that the Adam Weishaupt Bridge. Everyone will now rise and proceed in an orderly fashion to walk across the lake."

MY FELLOW AMERICANS, IT IS WITH A HEAVY HEART THAT I COME BEFORE YOU FOR THE SECOND TIME TODAY. MANY IRRESPONSIBLE ELEMENTS HAVE REACTED TO THE NATIONAL EMERGENCY WITH MAD, ANIMAL PANIC, AND THEY ARE ENDANGERING ALL THE REST OF US. I ASSURE YOU AGAIN, IN THE WORDS OF A GREAT FORMER LEADER, THAT WE HAVE NOTHING TO FEAR BUT FEAR ITSELF.

The face on the TV screen expressed absolute confidence, and many citizens felt a slight upsurge in hope; actually, he was totally around the bend on Demerol, and when the White House had burned earlier in the day his most constructive suggestion had been "Let's toast some marshmallows before we leave."

EVEN AS I SPEAK TO YOU THE DIRECTOR OF THE FBI HAS ASSURED ME THAT HIS MEN ARE CLOSING IN ON THE ONE SINGLE PLAGUE-CARRIER WHO HAS CAUSED ALL THIS HYSTERIA. IF YOU STAY IN YOUR HOMES, YOU WILL BE SAFE, AND THE EMERGENCY WILL SOON BE OVER.

"We can send the army to the west side of the lake to intercept them," said Wilhelm.

("Rosebuds," cried John Dillinger. "Why the hell would he bring a suitcase full of rosebuds down here?")

Suddenly everybody was aroused and moving Simon was leading me gently along I was back in Time again there was a real fight going on between Hagbard and the American Medical Association and a fight means that somebody is going to lose the Gates of Hell were opening and I could hardly move my feet Daddy's head on the floor of that Memphis police station and those cops stomping him and stomping him why didn't they put a spear through his side while they were at it and how can I really forgive that's just the drug and underneath I'll always hate white men even Simon if this is the Last Judgment I know what Christ will do with every blue-eyed bastard among them they own all the power and make all the wars they've fucked the planet their only god is Death they destroy everything living a giant blond god Thor swinging his hammer and smashing all the colored races red scarlet red blood on that hammer black blood especially but Hagbard is Horus this is the way it will always be fighting and killing to the end of time and women and children the chief victims only the flesh is holy and men are killers of the flesh cannibals.

"How many do you think there are?" the leader of the Closed Corporation asked dreamily.

"Six hundred and sixty-six," one of his group answered. "When you sacrifice a rooster in a pentagram on Walpurgis Night, you always get six sixty-six."

"And they're coming right toward us," the leader went on in his dreamy voice. "To bow down and serve us."

The Closed Corporation sat perfectly still, in silent ecstasy, awaiting the arrival of the 666 horned-and-tailed demons they saw approaching them . . . Outside Lehman Cave, Saul loads the antidote needle. "I'll go first," says John Herbert Dillinger, rolling up his sleeve . . . AT THIS HOUR WHEN YOUR GOVERNMENT NEEDS YOUR FAITH . . . In a fusilade of bullets, the President sank beneath the podium, leaving only the Seal of the Chief Executive on the TV screens. The viewers saw the same confident expression on his face as he floated in Demerol tranquility toward death. *"Oh my God!"* said an announcer's voice off screen . . . In Mad Dog, John Hoover Dillinger looks at Jim Cartwright quizzically. "Whose conspiracy was behind that?" he asks as the announcer gibbers hysterically. "There seem to have been five people shooting from five different parts of the press corps, but the President may not be dead—" "They blew his fucking head to pulp," another voice near the microphone said, distinctly and hopelessly . . . In New York, August Personage, one of the few people neither rioting nor listening to TV, reads *Atlas Shrugged* with total absorption, getting Religion . . .

"Are you a turtle?" Lady Velkor asks.

"Huh?" Danny Pricefixer responds.

"Never mind," she says hurriedly. He hears her asking the next man on the right, "Are you a turtle?"

"We can send the army to the west side of the lake to intercept them," said Wilhelm.

"Nein," said Wolfgang, who was standing in the rear of the slowly moving command car, studying the situation through field glasses. "That *verdammte* bridge goes toward the northern shore of the lake. They can go straight, while

our men go around. They'd all be across before we could reach them."

"We could shell the bridge from here," said Werner.

"We daren't use the artillery," said Wolfgang. "We'd have the whole West German army blundering down here, getting in the way of our drive to the east. If the West Germans start fighting us, the East Germans will not make the mistake we want them to make. They won't think we are an invading West German army. The Russians, in turn, will have plenty of warning. The whole plan will fall through."

"Let's skip this phase, then," said Winifred. "It's too much of a hassle. Let's head immediately eastward, and the hell with these kids."

"*Nein* again, dear sister, my love," said Wolfgang. "We have twenty-three candidates for transcendental illumination, including Hitler himself, waiting up there in the old Fuehrer Suite of the Donau-Hotel. The speedy mass termination of all those lives is to translate them to eternal life on the energy plane. And I will not let that *Scheisskopf* Hagbard Celine thwart us at this juncture. I mean to show him once and for all which of us is master. And all the rest of those *Schweinen*—Dillinger, the Dealy Lama, Malaclypse, the old Lady herself, if she's here. If all of them *are* here, it's our chance to make a clean sweep and annihilate the opposition once and for all, at the beginning of the immanentizing of the Eschaton, rather than in the final stage."

"But we can't catch the kids," said Wilhelm.

"We can. We shall. It will take a long, long time to move them all across that pontoon bridge, and they are all on foot. We have vehicles and can catch up with them before half of them are even on the bridge. They'll all be bunched together, and those on the bridge will be a perfect target for machine guns. We shall simply sweep in on them, harvesting their lives as we go. We spent years building up our identity as the American Medical Association just so we could organize the Ingolstadt festival and trap masses of human beings on the shore of Lake Totenkopf, that our sacred lake might run red with their blood. Would you throw all that away?"

"I agree. A brilliant analysis," said Wilhelm.

"We must move on at full speed, then," said Wolfgang. He turned to the car behind him and shouted. "*Vorwarts* at maximum speed!" General-of-the-SS Hanfgeist stood up, turned toward his subordinates, and moved his blackened lips to form the same words. Immediately the tanks, half-tracks, motorcycles, and armored cars began to rev up their engines and the troops started to trot down the road on the double.

A lookout in one of the festival light-and-sound towers spotted them and relayed a warning to the stage, where Robert Pearson spoke into a microphone. "It is my sad duty to inform you that the pigs are intensifying their approach. Now, don't run. But *do* quicken your pace with all deliberate speed."

Hagbard called in through the doorway of the gold tent, "John, you've had enough, for Discordia's sake. Come on out and let Malaclypse go in."

"I thought you were noncorporeal," said George.

"If you'd known me any length of time you would have noticed that I frequently pick my nose," said the Sartrelike apparition.

"Whew," said John-John Dillinger, emerging from the tent, "who would have thought the old man'd have so much come in him? She says she wants George in there after Mal."

The woman behind the veil was glowing. There was no light in the tent, save for the deep golden radiance that came from her body.

"Come closer, George," she said. "I don't want you to make love to me now—I only want you to learn the truth. Stand here before me."

The woman behind the veil was Mavis. "Mavis, I love you," said George. "I've loved you ever since you took me out of that jail in Mad Dog."

"Look again, George," said Stella.

"Stella! What happened to Mavis?"

I circle around, I circle around . . .

"Don't play games with yourself, George. You know perfectly well that a moment ago I *was* Mavis."

"It's the acid," said George.

"The acid only opens your eyes, George. It doesn't work miracles," said Miss Mao.

I circle around, I circle around . . .

"Oh, my God!" said George. And he thought: *And it*

shall come to pass, that whosoever shall call on the name of the Lord shall be saved.

Mavis was there again. "Do you understand, George? Do you understand why you never saw all of us together at once? Do you understand why, all the time you wanted to fuck me, that when you were fucking Stella you *were* fucking me? And do you understand that I am not one woman or three women but an infinite number of women?" Before his eyes she turned red, yellow, black, brown, young, middle-aged, a child, an old woman, a Norwegian blonde, a Sicilian brunette, a wild-eyed Greek woman, a tall Ashanti, a slant-eyed Masai, a Japanese, a Chinese, a Vietnamese, and on and on and on.

The paleface kept turning colors, the way people do when you're on peyote. Now he looked almost like an Indian. That made it easier to talk to him. Why shouldn't people turn colors? All the trouble in the world came from the fact that they usually stayed the same color. James nodded profoundly. As usual, peyote had brought him a big Truth. If whites and blacks and Indians were turning colors all the time, there wouldn't be any hate in the world, because nobody would know which people to hate.

Who the hell's mind was that? George wondered. The tent was dark. He looked around for the woman. He rushed out of the tent. No one was looking at him. They were all, Hagbard and the rest of them, staring in awe at a colossal figure that grew ever taller as it strode away from them. It was a golden woman in golden robes with wild gold, red, black hair flowing free. She stepped over the fence that guarded the festival grounds as casually as if it were the threshold of a door. She towered over the Bavarian pines. In her left hand she carried an enormous golden orb.

Hagbard put his hand on George's shoulder. "It is possible," he said, "to achieve transcendental illumination though a multiplicity of orgasms as well as through a multiplicity of deaths."

There were lights advancing down the road. The woman, now ninety-three feet tall, strode toward those lights. She laughed, and the laughter echoed across Lake Totenkopf.

"Great Gruad! What's that?" cried Werner.

"It's the Old Woman!" shouted Wolfgang, his lips falling away from his teeth in a snarl.

The sudden cry *"Kallisti!"* reverberated through the Bavarian hills louder than the music of the Ingolstadt festival had been. Trailing a cometlike cloud of sparks, the golden apple fell into the center of the advancing army.

The Supernazis might have been the living dead, but they were still human. What each man saw in the apple was his heart's desire. Private Heinrich Krause saw the family he had left behind thirty years ago—not knowing that his living grandchildren were at this moment on the pontoon bridge across Lake Totenkopf, fleeing his advance. Corporal Gottfried Kuntz saw his mistress (who in reality had been raped and then disemboweled by Russian soldiers when Berlin fell in 1945). Oberlieutenant Sigmund Voegel saw a ticket to the Wagner festival at Bayreuth. Colonel-SS Konrad Schein saw a hundred Jews lined up before a machine gun that awaited his hand on the trigger. Obergruppenfuehrer Ernst Bickler saw a blue china soup tureen standing in an empty fireplace at his grandmother's house in Kassel. It was brimful of steaming brown dogshit into which was plunged a silver spoon. General Hanfgeist saw Adolf Hitler, his face blackened, his eyes and tongue bulging out, his neck broken, spinning at the end of a hangman's rope.

All of the men who saw the apple, in whatever form, began to fight and kill one another for possession. Tanks smashed into one another head-on. Artillerymen lowered the barrels of their guns and fired point-blank into the center of the melee.

"What is it, Wolfgang?" said Winifred imploringly, her arms thrown in panic around his waist.

"Look into the center of the battle," said Wolfgang grimly. "What do you see?"

"I see the throne of the world. One single chair twenty-three feet off the ground, studded with seventeen rubies, and brooding over it the serpent swallowing its tail, the Rosy Cross, and the Eye. I see that throne and know that I alone am to ascend it and occupy it forever. What do you see?"

"I see Hagbard Celine's *teufelscheiss* head on a silver platter," Wolfgang snarled, thrusting her from him with trembling hands. "Eris has thrown the Apple of Discord, and our Supernazis will fight and kill each other until we destroy it."

"Where did she go?" asked Werner.

"She's lurking about somewhere in some other form, no doubt," said Wolfgang. "As a toadstool or an owl or some such thing, cackling over the chaos she's caused."

Suddenly Wilhelm stood up, his fingers clawing at empty air. In a frightfully clumsy fashion, as if he were deaf, dumb, and blind, he clawed and clamored his way over the side of the Mercedes that had belonged to von Rundstedt. Once out of the car, he took a position about ten feet away from his brothers and sister, turned, and faced them. His eyes stared—every muscle in his body was rigid—the crotch of his trousers bulged.

The voice that came out of his mouth was deep, rich, oleaginous, and horrid: "There are long accounts to settle, children of Gruad."

Wolfgang forgot the sounds of battle that raged around him. "You! Here! How did you escape?"

The voice was like crude petroleum seeping through gravel, and, like petroleum, it was a fossil thing, the voice of a creature that had arisen on the planet when the South Pole was in the Sahara and the great cephalopods were the highest form of life.

"I took no notice. The geometries ceased to bind me. I came forth. I ate souls. Fresh souls, not the miserable plasma you have fed me all these years."

"Great Gruad! Is that your gratitude?" Wolfgang stormed. In a lower voice he said to Werner, "Find the talisman. I think it's in the black case sealed with the Seal of Solomon and the Eye of Newt." To the being that occupied Wilhelm's body he said, "You come at an opportune time. There will be much killing here, and many souls to eat."

"These around us have no souls. They have only pseudo-life. It sickens me to sense them."

Wolfgang laughed. "Even the lloigor can feel disgust, then."

"I have been sick for many hundreds of years, while you kept me sealed in one pentagon after another, feeding me not fresh souls but those wretched stored essences."

"We gave you much!" cried Werner. "Every year, just for you, thirty thousand—forty thousand—fifty thousand deaths in traffic accidents alone."

"But not fresh. Not fresh! Perhaps, though, you can settle your debt to me tonight. I sense many lives nearby— lives you have somehow lured here. They can be mine."

Werner handed Wolfgang a stick with a silver pentagon at the tip. Wolfgang pointed it at the possessed Wilhelm, who shrieked and fell to his knees. For a moment there was silence, broken only by the sound of Winifred's terrified sobbing and the crack of rifles and the chatter of machine guns in the background.

"You shall not have those lives, Yog Sothoth. They are for the transcendental illumination of our servants. Wait, though, and there shall be lives in plenty for all of us."

Werner said, "While we parley our army is destroying itself, and there will be no lives for anyone."

"Really?" said the thick voice. "How has your plan gone astray? Let me read you and learn." Wolfgang felt goose pimples break out all over his body. He shuddered as coarse, boneless fingers dripping with slime turned the pages of his mind.

"Mmm—I see. *She* is here, then. My ancient enemy. It would be good to meet her in battle once again."

"Are your powers equal to hers?" said Wolfgang eagerly.

"I yield to none" came the proud reply.

"Ask him why he's always getting trapped in pentagons, then," said Werner in a low voice.

"Shut up!" Wolfgang whispered savagely. To the lloigor he said, "Destroy her golden apple and release my army to move ahead, and I will withhold the power of this pentagon and give you all the lives you seek."

"Done!" said the voice. Wilhelm suddenly threw his head back, mouth wide open. A choking sound came from his throat. He collapsed on his back, spread-eagled. A strange, greenish, glowing gas rose from his throat.

Werner jumped from the car and rushed over to Wilhelm. "He's alive."

"Of course he's alive," said Wolfgang. "The Eater of Souls simply took possession of his body to communicate with us."

Winifred screamed, "Look!"

The same phosphorescent gas, a huge cloud of it, now obscured the heart of the battle. It seemed to take a shape like a spider with an uncountable number of legs, arms, antennae, and tentacles. Gradually the shape changed, glowing brighter and brighter. A nearby tower on the festival grounds was as visible in the reflected light as if it were day. Then the glow faded, and the tower was silhouetted in moonlight. A great silence fell over the hills around Lake Totenkopf, broken only by the glad cries of the last contingent of festivalgoers as they made it safely to the opposite shore.

"There's no time to lose," Wolfgang said to Werner and Wilhelm. "Round up some officers. See if you can find Hanfgeist."

Hanfgeist had disappeared. The highest-ranking officer surviving was Obergruppenfuehrer Bickler, visions of dog turds sadly fading in a mind that possessed only a horrid semblance of life. A quick survey showed the four Illuminati Primi that the Apple of Discord had cost them half their army.

"Onward!" roared Wolfgang, and, tanks in the van, they smashed through the festival fence, raced over the hills, troops trotting double-time, and unhesitatingly charged out onto the bridge. Wolfgang stood in the back seat of the von Rundstedt Mercedes, his black-gloved hands gripping the back of the front seat, the wind blowing through his crew cut like a field of wheat. Suddenly, beside him, Wilhelm screamed.

"What is it now?" yelled Wolfgang over the roar of his advancing army.

"The lives we are about to take," the voice of the lloigor grated. "They are mine, yes? All mine?"

"Listen to me, you energy vampire. We have other debts to discharge, and other projects to complete. There are twenty-three of our faithful servants waiting in the Donau-Hotel to be transcendentally illuminated. They come first. You'll get yours. Wait your turn."

"Farewell," said the lloigor. "I shall see you at the hour of your death."

"I will never die!"

"Fool!" the voice shrieked with Wilhelm's mouth. Suddenly Wilhelm stood up, threw open the door of the car, and hurled himself out into the lake. He struck with a huge splash, then sank like a stone. A greenish glow spread in the black water where he had gone down.

And then there were four.

Hagbard stood atop a hill, watching the tanks roll across the bridge, followed by the black Mercedes, followed by troop carriers and artillery, followed by trotting foot soldiers. He knelt beside a detonator and shoved down the handle.

From end to end the bridge and those upon it disappeared in geysers of white water. The thunder of the explosions—demolition charges placed by the porpoise horde under the direction of Howard—re-echoed through the hills around the lake.

The tanks went under first. As the front end of the command car sank under water, Werner Saure screamed, "My foot's caught!" He went down with the car, while Wolfgang and Winifred, their tears mingling with the water of Lake Totenkopf, splashed about in the water with the few remaining Supernazis.

And then there were three.

Hagbard shouted, "I sank it! I sank the George Washington Bridge!"

"Is anything changed?" said George.

"Of course," said Hagbard. "We've got them on the run. We'll be able to finish them off in a few more minutes. Then there'll be no more evil in the world. Everything will be *ginger-peachy*." His tone seemed sarcastic rather than victorious, George noted apprehensively.

"Now I'll admit," Fission Chips said reasonably, "that I'm under the influence of some bloody drug from the Kool-Aid. But this simply cannot all be hallucination. Very definitely, thirteen people took their clothes off and started dancing. I quite certainly heard them singing 'Blessed be, blessed be,' over and over. Then a simply gigantic woman rose up from somewhere and all the sirens and undines and mermaids went back into the water. If this was Armageddon, it was not precisely the way the Bible described it. Is that a fair summary of the situation?"

The tree he was talking to didn't answer.

"Blessed be, blessed be," Lady Velkor sang on, as she and her hastily assembled coven danced widdershins in their circle. The spell had worked: With her own eyes she had seen the Great Mother, Isis, rise up and smite the evil spirits of the dead Catholic Inquisitors whom the Illuminati had tried to revive. She knew Hagbard Celine would later be boasting in all the most chic occult circles that he had performed the miracle, and giving the credit to that destructive bitch Eris—but that didn't matter. She with her own eyes had seen Isis, and that was enough.

"Now I ask you," Fission Chips went on, addressing another tree, who seemed more communicative, "what the sulphurous hell did *you* see happening here tonight?"

"I saw a master Magician," said the tree, "or a master con man—the two are the same—plant a few suggestions and get a bunch of acidheads running away from their own shadows." The tree, who was actually Joe Malik and only looked like a tree to poor befuddled 00005, added, "Or I saw the final battle between Good and Evil, with Horus on both sides."

"You must be drugged too," Chips said pettishly.

"You bet your sweet ass I am," said the tree, walking away.

. . . I don't know how the courts will ever untangle this. With five of them shooting at once, and the Secret Service shooting back right away, the best crime lab in the world will never get the trajectories of all the bullets right. Who, among the survivors, will be tried for murder and who for attempted murder? That's the sixty-four-thousand-dollar question and . . . what? . . . oh . . . And now, ladies and gentlemen, on this sad occasion . . . uh . . . in this tragic hour of our country's history, let us all pay especially close attention to the new President, who will now address us.

Who's that jig standing over there? the new Chief Exec was asking somebody off camera when he appeared on the TV screens.

The Chevrolet Stegosaurus drove into the empty concert grounds and came to a slow halt. The guitarist stuck his head out the window and yelled to Lady Velkor, "What the hell happened here?"

"There was some bad acid in the Kool-Aid," she told him gravely. "Everybody freaked out and ran off toward town."

"Hell," he said, "and this was going to be our first big audience. We're a new group, just formed. What lousy luck."

He turned and drove off, and she read the sign on the back of the car: THE FERNANDO POO INCIDENT.

"How are you now, baby?" Simon asked.

"I know who I am," Mary Lou said slowly, "and you might not like the results of that any more than the Chicago police force will." Her eyes were distant and pensive.

Wolfgang and Winifred were very near shore when the

dark, humped shapes rose out of the water around them. Winifred shrieked, "Wolfgang! For the love of Gruad, Wolfgang! They're pulling me down!" Her long blond hair floated for a moment after her head went under; then that too disappeared.

And then there were two.

The porpoises have her, Wolfgang thought to himself. He continued to swim madly toward shore. Something caught his trouser leg, but he kicked free. Then he was in the shallows, too close in for the sea beasts to follow. He stood up and waded ashore. And came face to face with John Dillinger.

"Sorry, pal," said John, and squeezed the trigger of his Thompson submachine gun. Thirty silver bullets struck Wolfgang with the impact of clubs and threw him back into the water. All feeling was gone from his body, and he felt the foul tentacles closing around his mind and the murmuring, horrible laughter grew to a soundless roar, and the syrupy voice spoke to his mind: *Welcome to the place prepared for you from everlasting to everlasting. Now truly you will never die.* And the mind of Wolfgang Saure, imprisoned like a living fly in amber, knowing that it must remain so for billions upon billions of years, screamed and screamed and screamed.

And then there was one.

And Joe Malik, feeling as if he were sitting in an audience watching himself perform, walked over to that One and held out his hand. "Congratulations," he said icily. "You really did it."

Hagbard looked at the hand and said, "You were more intimate the last time around."

"Very well," said Joe. "My Lord, my enemy." He leaned forward and kissed Hagbard full on the mouth. Then he took the gun out of his pocket and carefully fired directly into Hagbard's brain. And then there were none.

It was quite real; Joe shook himself, stood up, and grinned. Walking over to Hagbard, he took out the gun and handed it to him.

"Surprise ending," he said. "I read all the clues, just like you wanted me to. I know you're the fifth Illuminatus Primus, and I know your motive for wiping out the other four is nothing like you've led us to believe. But I can't play my role. I still trust you. You *must* have a good reason."

Hagbard's mouth fell open in completely genuine surprise. "Well, *sink* me!" he said, beginning to laugh.

Dawn was breaking; the Nine Unknown Men, most mysterious of all rock groups, ceremonially donned their football helmets and faced the East to chant:

> There is only ONE God:
> He is the SUN God:
> Ra!   Ra!   Ra!

BOOK FIVE

GRUMMET

The bursts to the moon and to the planets are also
not historic events. They are the major evolutionary
breakthroughs . . . Today when we speak of immortality
and of going to another world we no longer mean these
in a theological or metaphysical sense. People are now
striving for physical immortality. People are now
traveling to other worlds. Transcendence is no longer
a metaphysical concept. It has become reality.

—F. M. ESFANDIARY, *Upwingers*

THE TENTH TRIP
(OR MALKUTH FAREWELL TO PLANET EARTH)

Ye have locked yerselves up in cages of fear; and,
behold, do ye now complain that ye lack freedom.
—LORD OMAR KHAYYAM RAVENHURST, K.S.C.,
"Epistle to the Paranoids,"
The Honest Book of Truth

As the earth turned on its axis and dawn reached city after
city, hamlet after hamlet, farm after farm, mountain and
valley after mountain and valley, it became obvious that
May 1 would be bright and sunny almost everywhere. In
Athens a classical scholar waking in the small cell where
certain Platonic opinions had landed him felt a burst of unexpected hope and greeted Helios with rolling syllables
from Sappho, crying through the bars, *"Brodadaktylos
Eos!"* Birds, startled by the shout, took off from the jailyard
below, filling the air with the flapping of their wings; the
guards came and told him to shut up. He answered them
gaily with *"Polyphloisbois thalassas!* You've taken everything else away from me, but you can't take old Homer
away!"

In Paris the Communists under the Red banner and the
anarchists under the Black were preparing for the annual
International Labor Solidarity Day, at which the usual fac-
tionalism and sectarianism would once again demonstrate
the absolute lack of international labor solidarity. And in
London, Berlin, a thousand cities, the Red and the Black
would wave and the tongues of their partisans would wag,
and the age-old longing for a classless society would once
again manifest itself; while, in the same cities, an older
name and an older purpose for that day would be commemorated in convent after convent and school after
school where verses (far older than the name of Christianity) were sung to the Mother of God:

> *Queen of the Angels*
> *Queen of the May*

In the United States, alas, the usual celebrations of National Law Day had to be cancelled, since the rioting was not quite ended yet.

But everywhere, in Asia and Africa as in Europe and the Americas, the members of the Oldest Religion were returning from their festivals, murmuring "Blessed be" as they parted, secure in their knowledge that the Mother of God was indeed still alive and had visited them at midnight, whether they knew her as Dian, Dan, Tan, Tana, Shakti, or even Erzulie.

> *Queen of the Angels*
> *Queen of the May*

In Nairobi, Nkrumah Fubar picked up his mail from a friend employed at the post office. To his delight, American Express had relented and corrected their error, crediting him with his February 2 payment at last. This was, to his thinking, big magic, since the notification had been mailed from New York even before he began his geodesic spiels against the President of American Express on April 25. Obviously, such retroactive witchcraft was worthy of further investigation, and the key was the synergetic geometry of the Fuller tetrahedron in which he had kept his manikin during the spell-casting. Over breakfast, before leaving for the university, he opened Fuller's *No More Second-Hand God* and again grappled with the arcane mathematics and metaphysics of omnidirectional halo. Finishing breakfast, he closed the book, shut his eyes, and tried to visualize the Fuller universe. The image formed, and, to his amazement and amusement, it was identical with certain symbols an old Kikuyu witch doctor had once drawn when explaining the doctrine of "fan-shaped destiny" to him.

As the book closed in Kenya, the drums of Orabi stopped abruptly. It was one in the morning there, and the visiting anthropologist, Indole Ringh, immediately asked how the dancers knew the ceremony was finished. "The danger is past," an old Hopi told him patiently, "can't you *feel* the difference in the air?" (Saul, Barney, and Markoff Chaney were racing toward Las Vegas in the rented Bron-

tosaurus, while Dillinger was leisurely driving back toward
Los Angeles.) In Honolulu, as the clocks struck nine the
previous evening, Buckminster Fuller, trotting between airplanes, suddenly caught a glimpse of a new geodesic structure fully incorporating omnidirectional halo . . . And, after a four-hour flight eastward, landing in Tokyo at the
"same time" he left Honolulu, he had a detailed sketch finished (it looked somewhat fan-shaped) as the NO SMOKING
FASTEN SEAT BELT sign flashed. (It was four A.M. in Los
Angeles, and Dillinger, safely home—he thought—heard
the gunfire dying out in the distance. The President must already be withdrawing the National Guard, at least in part,
he thought.) The phone by Rebecca's bed rang just then,
eight o'clock New York time, and she answered it to hear
Molly Muldoon shout excitedly, "Saul and Barney are on
TV. Turn it on—they've saved the country!"

In Las Vegas, Barney blinked under the TV lights and
stared woodenly into the camera, while Saul kept his eyes
on the interviewer and spoke in his kindly-family-doctor
persona.

"Would you tell our viewers, Inspector Goodman, how
you happened to be looking in Lehman Caves for the missing man?" The interviewer had the professional tone of all
TV newscasters; his intonation wouldn't have changed if
he'd been asking "And why did you find our sponsor's
product more satisfactory?" or "How did you feel when
you learned you had brain cancer?"

"Psychology," Saul pronounced gravely. "The suspect
was a procurer. That's a definite psychological type, just as
a safecracker, a bank robber, a child molester, and a policeman are definite types. I tried to think and feel like a procurer. What would such a man do with the whole government looking for him? Attempt an escape to Mexico or
somewhere else? Never—that's a bank-robber reaction.
Procurers are not people who take risks or make bold
moves against the odds. What would a procurer do? He
would look for a hole to hide in."

"The FBI crime lab definitely confirms that the man
Inspector Goodman found is the missing plague-carrier,
Carmel," the interviewer threw in. (He had orders to repeat
this every two minutes.) "Tell me, Inspector, why wouldn't
such a man hide in, say, an empty house, or a secluded cabin in the mountains?"

"He wouldn't travel far," Saul explained. "He'd be too paranoid—seeing police officers everywhere he went. And his imagination would vastly exaggerate the actual power of the government. There is only one law enforcement agent to each four hundred citizens in this country, but he would imagine the proportion reversed. The most secluded cabin would be too nerve-wracking for him. He'd imagine hordes of National Guardsmen and law officers of all sorts searching every square foot of woods in America. He really would. Procurers are very ordinary men, compared to hardened criminals. They think like ordinary people in most ways. The ordinary man and woman never commits a crime because they have the same exaggerated idea of our omnipotence." Saul's tone was neutral, descriptive, but in New York Rebecca's heart skipped a beat: This was the new Saul talking, the one who was no longer on the side of law and order.

"So you just asked yourself, where's a good-sized hole near Las Vegas?"

"That was all there was to it, yes."

"The American people will certainly be grateful to you. And how did it happen that you got involved in this case? You're with the New York Police Department, aren't you?"

How will he answer that one? Rebecca wondered; just then the phone rang.

Turning down the TV sound, she lifted the phone and said, "Yes?"

"I can tell by your voice you're the kind of woman who *fully meets the criteria of my value system,*" said August Personage. "I want to lick your ass and your pussy and have you piss on me and—"

"Well, that's a most amazing story, Inspector Goodman," the interviewer was saying. *Oh, hell,* Rebecca thought. Saul's expression was so sincere that she knew he had just told one of the most outrageous lies of his life.

The phone rang again. With a pounce Rebecca grabbed it and shouted, "Listen, you creep, if you keep calling me—"

"That's no way to talk to a man who just saved the world," Saul's voice said mildly.

"Saul! But you're on television—"

"They videotaped that a half-hour ago. I'm at the Las Vegas Airport, about to take a jet to Washington. I'm having a conference with the President."

"My God. What are you going to tell him?"

"As much," Saul pronounced, "as an asshole like him can understand."

(In Los Angeles, Dr. Vulcan Troll watched the seismograph move upward to Grade 2. That still wasn't serious, but he scratched a note to the graduate student who would soon be replacing him. "If this jumps to 3, call me at my house." Then he drove home, passing Dillinger's bungalow, humming happily, thankful that the rioting was ending and the Guard being withdrawn. At the lab the graduate student, reading a paperback titled *Carnal Orgy,* didn't notice when the graph jumped past 3 and hit 4.)

Danny Pricefixer, waking in Ingolstadt, glanced at his wristwatch. Noon. *My God,* he thought; sleeping so late was a major sin in his system of morality. Then he remembered a little of last night, and smiled contentedly, turning in the bed to kiss Lady Velkor's neck. A huge black arm hung over the other shoulder, and a black hand, limp in sleep, held her breast. "My *God!*" Danny said out loud, remembering more, as Clark Kent sat up groggily and stared at him.

("Smiling Jim" Treponema, at that moment, was navigating a very dangerous pass in the mountains of Northern California. Strapped to his back was a 6mm Remington Model 700 Bolt Action rifle with 6-power Bushnell telescope; a canteen of whiskey was hooked to one side of his belt, and a canteen of water to the other. He was perspiring from labor, in spite of the altitude, but he was one of the few happy people in the country, since he had been nowhere near a radio for three days and had missed the whole terror connected with Anthrax Leprosy Pi plague, the declaration of martial law, and the rioting and bombings. He was on his yearly vacation, free from the sewer of smut in which he was submerged forty-nine weeks of the year—the foulness and filth in which he heroically struggled daily, risking his soul for the good of his fellow citizens—and he was breathing clean air and thinking clean thoughts. Specifically, as an avid hunter, he had read that only one American eagle still survived, and he was determined to be immortalized in hunting literature as the man who killed it. He knew well, of course, how ecologists and conservationists would regard that achievement, but their opinions didn't bother him. A bunch of fags, commies, and smut-nuts: That was his estimate of those bleeding-heart types. Probably smoked dope, too. Not a man's man among them. He shifted his rifle, which was pressing his sweat-soaked shirt uncomfortably, and climbed onward and upward.)

Mama Sutra stared at the central Tarot card in the Tree of Life: It was The Fool.

"Pardon me," the little Italian tree said.

"This is getting ridiculous," Fission Chips muttered. "I don't intend to spend the rest of my life in conversation with trees."

"I'm a tree worth talking to," the dark-skinned tree with her hair in a bun persisted.

He squinted. "I know what you are," he said finally, "half tree and half woman. *Ergo*, a dryad. Benefit of classical education."

"Very good," said the dryad. "But when you stop tripping, you're going to crash. You'll remember London and your job, and you'll wonder how you're going to explain the last month to them."

"Somebody stole a month from me," Chips agreed pleasantly. "A cynical old swine named the Dealy Lama. Or another feller named Toad. Bad lot. Shouldn't go around stealing months."

The tree handed him an envelope. "Try not to lose that," she said. "It'll make everybody in your office so happy that they'll accept any story you make up to explain how it took you a month to get it."

"What is it?"

"The name of every BUGGER agent in the British government. Together with the false names they use for the bank accounts where they keep all the money they can't account for. And the account numbers and the names of the banks, too. In one nice package. All it needs is a red ribbon."

"I think my leg is being pulled again," said Chips. But he was coming down, and he opened the envelope and peered at the contents. "This is real?" he asked.

"They won't be able to account for the money," the tree assured him. "Some very interesting confessions will be obtained."

"Who the devil are you?" Chips asked, seeing a teen-age Italian girl and not a tree.

"I'm your holy guardian angel," she said.

"You look like an angel," Chips admitted grudgingly, "but I don't believe any of this. Time travel, talking trees, giant toads, none of it. Somebody slipped me a drug."

"Yes, somebody slipped you a drug. But I'm your holy guardian angel, and I'm slipping you this envelope. and it'll make everything all right back in London. All you have to do is make up a halfway reasonable lie . . ."

"I was held prisoner in a BUGGER dungeon with a beautiful Eurasian love-slave," Chips began improvising

"Very good," she said. "They won't believe it, but they'll think you believe it. That's good enough."

"Who are you really?"

But the tree only repeated, "Don't lose that envelope," and walked away, turning into an Italian teen-ager again, and then into a gigantic woman carrying a golden apple.

Hauptmann, chief of field operations for the Federal Republic of Germany's police, looked around the Fuehrer Suite in disgust. He had arrived from Bonn and headed straight for the Donau-Hotel, determined to make some sense of the scandals, tragedies, and mysteries of the previous night. The first suspect he grilled was *Freiherr* Hagbard Celine, sinister jet-set millionaire, who had come to the rock festival with a large entourage. Celine and Hauptmann talked quietly in one corner of the suite of the Donau-Hotel, while the cameras of police photographers clicked away behind them.

Hauptmann was tall and thin, with close-cropped silver-gray hair, long, vulpine features, and piercing eyes. "Dreadful tragedy, the death of your President last night," he said. "My condolences. Also for the unhappy state of affairs in your country." Actually, Hauptmann was delighted to see the United States of America falling into chaos. He had been fifteen at the end of World War II, had been called to the colors as the Allies advanced on German soil, and had seen his country overrun by American troops. All of this made a deeper and more lasting impression on him than the U.S.–West German cooperation that developed later.

"Not *my* president, not *my* country," said Hagbard quickly. "I was born in Norway. I lived in the U.S. for quite some time, and did become a citizen for a while, when I was much younger than I am now. But I renounced my American citizenship years ago."

"I see," said Hauptmann, trying unsuccessfully to conceal his distaste for Hagbard's indistinct sense of national identity. "And what country today has the honor of claiming you as a citizen?"

Smiling, Hagbard reached for the inside pocket of the brass-buttoned navy-blue yachtsman's blazer he had worn for the occasion. He handed his passport to Hauptmann, who took it and grunted with surprise.

"Equatorial Guinea." He looked up, frowning. "Fernando Poo!"

"Quite so," said Hagbard, a white-toothed grin breaking through his dark features. "I will accept your expression of sympathy for the sad state of affairs in *that* country."

Hauptmann's dislike of this Latin plutocrat grew deeper. The man was undoubtedly one of those unprincipled international adventurers who carried citizenship the way many freighters carried Panamanian registry. Celine's wealth was probably equal to or greater than the total wealth of Equatorial Guinea. Yet it was likely that he had done nothing for his adopted country other than bribe a few officials to obtain the citizenship. Equatorial Guinea had split asunder, nearly plunging the world into a third and final war, and yet here was this parasitical Mediterranean fop, driving to a rock festival in a Bugatti Royale with a host of drones, yes-men, flunkies, minions, whores, dope fiends, and all-round social liabilities. Disgusting!

Hagbard looked around. "This room is a pretty foul place to have a conversation. How can you stand that smell? It's nauseating me."

Pleased to be causing some discomfort to this man, whom he disliked more and more as he got to know him, Hauptmann settled back in the red armchair, his teeth bared in a smile. "You will forgive me, *Freiherr* Celine, I find it necessary to be here at this time and also necessary to talk to you. However, I would have thought this peculiar odor of fish would not be unpleasant to you. Perhaps your nautical dress has led me astray."

Hagbard shrugged. "I am a seaman of sorts. But just because a man likes the sea doesn't mean he wants to sit next to a ton of dead mackerel. What do you think it is, anyway?"

"I have no idea. I was hoping you could identify it for me."

"Just dead fish, that's all it smells like to me. I'm afraid you may be expecting more from me all around than I can possibly provide. I suppose you think I can tell you a lot about last night. Just what are you trying to find out?"

"First of all, I want to find out what actually happened. What we have, I think, is a case of drug abuse on a colossal scale. And we—the Western world in general—have had too many of those in recent years. Apparently there is not a single person who was present at this festival who did not partake of some of this soft drink dosed with LSD."

"Treat every man to his dessert and none should 'scape tripping," said Hagbard.

"I beg your pardon?"

"I was parodying Shakespeare," said Hagbard. "But it's not very relevant. Please go on."

"Well, so far no one has been able to give me a coherent or plausible account of the evening's events," said Hauptmann. "There have been at least twenty-seven deaths that I'm fairly sure of. There has been massive abuse of LSD. There are numerous accounts of pistol, rifle, and machine-gun fire somewhere on the shore of the lake. A number of witnesses say they saw many men in Nazi uniforms running around in the woods. If that wasn't a hallucination, dressing as a Nazi is a serious crime in the Federal Republic of Germany. So far we have managed to keep much of this out of the papers by holding the press people who came here incommunicado, but we will have to determine precisely what crimes were committed and who committed them, and we must prosecute them vigorously. Otherwise, we will appear to the whole world as a nation incapable of dealing with the wholesale corruption of youth within our borders."

"All nations are wholesale corruptors of youth," said Hagbard. "I wouldn't worry about it."

Hauptmann grunted, seeing in his mind's eye a vision of drug-crazed masqueraders in Nazi uniforms and himself in a German army uniform over thirty years ago at the age of fifteen and understanding very well what Hagbard meant. "I have my job to do," he said sullenly.

See how much more pleasant the world is now that the Saures are gone, the Dealy Lama flashed into his brain. Hagbard kept a poker face.

Hauptmann went on, "Your own role in the incident seems to have been a constructive one, *Freiherr* Celine. You are described as going to the stage when the hysteria and the hallucinating had reached some sort of a climax and making a speech which greatly calmed the audience."

Hagbard laughed. "I have no idea at all what I said. You know what I thought? I thought I was Moses and they were the Israelites and I was leading them across the Red Sea while the Pharaoh's army, intent on slaughtering them, pursued."

"The only Israelites present last night seemed to have fared rather badly. You're not Jewish yourself, are you, *Freiherr* Celine?"

"I'm not religious at all. Why do you ask?"

"I thought that then, perhaps, you could shed some light on the scene we find here in these rooms. Well, no matter for the moment. It is interesting that you thought you led them across the lake. In fact, this morning, when the police reserves entered the area, they found most of the young people wandering around on the shore of the lake opposite the festival."

"Well, perhaps we all marched around it while we thought we were going across it," said Hagbard. "By the way, didn't you have any men at the festival at all? If you did, they should be able to tell you something."

"We had a few plainclothes agents there, and they could tell me nothing. All but one had unknowingly taken the LSD, and the one who didn't must have been hallucinating too, from some kind of psychological contagion. He saw the Nazis, a glowing woman a hundred feet tall, a bridge across the lake. Sheer garbage. As you doubtless noticed, there were no uniformed police there. Arrangements were made—and sanctioned at the highest level of government —to leave policing at the festival to its management. It was felt that, given the attitudes of youth today, official police would not be effective in handling the huge crowd. I might say, in my own opinion, I consider that a cowardly decision. But I'm not a politician, thank God. As a result of that decision, order-keeping at the festival was ultimately in the hands of people like yourself who happened to be inspired to do something about the situation. And were themselves hampered, as involuntary victims of LSD."

"Well," said Hagbard, "in order to fully understand what happened, you have to realize that many people there probably welcomed an acid trip. Many must have brought their own acid and taken it. I, personally, have had a great deal

of experience with LSD. A man of my wide-ranging interests, you understand, feels obligated to try everything once.
I was taking acid back when it was still legal everywhere in
the world."

"Of course," said Hauptmann sourly.

Hagbard looked around the room and said, "Have you
considered the possibility that these men, old as they are,
might have unknowingly imbibed LSD and suffered heart
failure or some such thing?"

There were twenty-three dead men in the suite. Thirteen
were in the large parlor where Hagbard and Hauptman
were sitting. The dead men, too, were seated, in various attitudes of total collapse, some with their heads lolling back,
others bent forward at the waist, heads hanging between
their knees, knuckles resting on the floor. There were nine
more old men in the bedroom, and one in the bathroom.
Most of them were white-haired; several were completely
bald. Not one could have been under eighty years of age,
and several appeared to be over ninety. The man in the
bathroom had been caught by death in the embarrassing
position of sitting on the toilet with his pants down. This
was the old gentleman with the white mustache and the unruly forelock who had spoken harshly to George in the lobby the night before last.

Hauptmann shook his head. "I'm afraid it will be no easy
task to find out what happened to these men. They all seem
to have died at about the same moment. There are no ob-
servable traces of poison, no signs of struggle or pain, except for the expression around the eyes. All of their eyes
are open, and they appear to be looking at some unguessa-
ble horror."

"Do you have any idea who they are? Why did you say I
might have been able to help if I were Jewish?"

"We have found their passports. They are all Israeli citizens. That in itself is quite odd. Generally, Jews that old do
not care to come to this country, for obvious reasons. However, there was an organization connected with the Zionist
movement founded here in Ingolstadt on May 1, 1776.
These elders of Zion might have assembled here to celebrate the anniversary."

"Oh, yes," said Hagbard. "The Illuminati of Bavaria,
wasn't it? I remember hearing about them when we first arrived here."

"The organization was founded by an unfrocked Jesuit, and its membership consisted of freemasons, freethinkers, and Jews. There were also some famous names in politics and the arts: King Leopold, Goethe, Beethoven."

"And this organization was behind the Zionist movement, you say?"

Hauptmann brushed away the suggestion with long, slender fingers. "I did not say they were *behind* anything. There are always those who think that every political or criminal phenomenon must have something behind it. There is always a conspiracy that explains everything. That is unscientific. If you wish to understand events, you must analyze the masses of the people and the economic, cultural, and social conditions in which they live. Zionism was a logical development out of the situation of the Jews during the last hundred years. One need not imagine some group of illuminated ones thinking it up and promulgating the movement for devious reasons of their own. The Jews were in a wretched condition in many places—they needed somewhere to go—a child could have seen that Palestine was an attractive possibility."

"Well," said Hagbard, "if the Illuminati are of no importance in the history of Israel, what are these twenty-three old Israelis doing here on the day of the organization's founding?"

"Perhaps *they* thought the Illuminati were important. Perhaps they themselves were members. I shall make inquiries to Israel about their identities. Relatives will probably claim the bodies. Otherwise, the German government will see that they are buried in Ingolstadt Jewish cemetery with proper rabbinical ceremonies. The government is very solicitous of Jewish persons. Nowadays."

"Maybe they were freethinkers," said Hagbard. "Maybe they wouldn't like being buried with religious ceremonies."

"The question is wearisome and unimportant," said Hauptmann. "We shall consult the Israeli government and do as it suggests." An elderly waiter knocked and was admitted by one of Hauptmann's men. He pushed a serving cart bearing a magnificent silver coffee urn, cups, and a tray full of pastries. Before serving anyone else, he rolled the cart across the thick carpet to Hauptmann and Hagbard. His rheumy eyes studiously avoided the bodies scattered around the suite. He poured out coffee for both men.

"Lots of cream and sugar," said Hagbard.

"Black for me," said Hauptmann, picking up a pastry with cherry filling and biting into it with relish.

"How do you know somebody hasn't dosed the coffee or the pastry with LSD?" said Hagbard, smiling mischievously.

Hauptmann brushed his hand over his hair and smiled back. "Because I would put this hotel out of business if I were served food tainted in any way, and they know it. They will take the utmost precautions."

"Now that we're being a little more sociable and drinking coffee together," said Hagbard, "let me ask you a favor. Turn me loose today. I have interests to look after in the U.S., and I'd like to be leaving."

"You were originally planning to stay for the entire week. Now, suddenly, you have to leave at once. I don't understand."

"I was planning to stay, but that was before most of the U.S. government got wiped out. Also, since the remainder of the festival is being called off, there's no reason to stay. I'm still not clear on that, however. Why is the festival being called off? Whose idea is it, and what are the reasons?"

Hauptmann stared down his long nose at Hagbard and took another bite of the pastry, while Hagbard wondered how the man could eat in the midst of this awful smell. He could understand how a detective would not be bothered by the presence of the dead, but the fishy smell was something else again.

"To begin with, *Freiherr* Celine, there is the disappearance and possible death by drowning of the four members of the Saure family, known as the American Medical Association. Accounts of what happened to them are garbled, fantastic, and contradictory, as are those of every other incident that occurred last night. As I reconstruct it, they drove their car straight into the lake."

"From which side?"

Hauptmann shrugged. "It hardly matters. The lake is virtually bottomless. If they're in there, I doubt that we will ever find them. They must have been under the influence of LSD, and *they* certainly weren't used to it." He looked accusingly at Hagbard. "They were so *clean-cut*. Absolutely the hope of the future. And the car was a national relic. A great loss."

"Were they the only well-known casulaties?"

"Who can say? We have no accurate record of who was attending the festival. No list was kept of those who bought tickets, as should have been done. A thousand young men and women could have drowned themselves in that lake and we wouldn't know about it. In any case, the Saures, as you may not know, were the moving spirits behind the Ingolstadt festival. Very patriotic. They wished to do something to promote tourism to Germany, particularly of Bavaria, since they were native Bavarians."

"Yes," said Hagbard, "I read that Ingolstadt was their home town."

Hauptmann shook his head. "Their press agent gave that out when the festival was conceived. Actually, they were born in northern Bavaria, in Wolframs-Eschenbach. It is the birthplace of another famous German musician, the *Minnesinger* Wolfram von Eschenbach, who wrote *Parzival*. Well, now they are gone, barring a miracle, and no one else seems to be in charge. Without them the festival is simply collapsing, like a headless body. Furthermore, the government wants the festival shut down because we don't want a repetition of last night. LSD is still illegal in West Germany, unlike the U.S."

"There are parts of the U.S. where it's still illegal," said Hagbard. "It's not illegal in Equatorial Guinea, because we've just never had a drug problem there."

"Since you are an ethusiastic citizen of Equatorial Guinea, I am sure that delights you," said Hauptmann. "Well, *Freiherr* Celine, I would like to release you immediately, but when I've pieced together more of last night's events I shall have more questions for you. I must ask you to stay in the Ingolstadt area."

Hagbard stood up. "If you'll agree not to have me tailed or guarded, I'll give you my word that I'll stick around."

Hauptmann smiled thinly. "Your word won't be necessary. Every road is blocked; no planes are permitted to take off or land at Ingolstadt Aerodrome. You can have the run of the town, the lake, and the festival area, and you will not be disturbed."

Hagbard left at the same time the old waiter did. The waiter bowed Hagbard out the door and when it closed behind him said, "A great shame."

"Well," said Hagbard, "they were all in their eighties. That's a good age to die."

The waiter laughed. "I am seventy-five, and I do not think any age is a good age to die. But that is not what I was referring to. Perhaps *mein herr* did not notice the fish-tank in the room. It was broken, and the fish were spilled all the floor. I have taken care of that tank for over twenty years. It was a fine collection of rare tropical fish. Even Egyptian mouth-breeders. Now they are all dead. So it goes."

Hagbard wanted to ask the waiter what an Egyptian mouth-breeder was, but the old man suddenly nodded, pushed open a doorway to a service room, and disappeared.

Danny Pricefixer was wandering around in the dark with Lady Velkor and Clark Kent, feeling absolutely wonderful, when Miss Portinari intercepted him. "This will interest you," she said, handing him an envelope similar to the one she had handed Fission Chips.

"What is it?" he asked, seeing her as a Greek woman in classic robes holding a golden apple.

"Take a look."

He opened the envelope and found a picture of Tobias Knight and Zev Hirsch, in the middle of the *Confrontation* office, setting the timer on the bomb.

"This man," she said, pointing to Knight, "is willing to turn State's evidence. Against both Hirsch and Atlanta Hope. You've wanted to nab them for a long time, haven't you?"

"Who are you?" Danny asked, staring.

"I am the one Mama Sutra told you of, the one appointed to contact you here in Ingolstadt. I am of the Illuminated."

("What are those two talking about?" Clark Kent asked Lady Velkor. "Who knows?" she shrugged. "They're both tripping.")

"God's Lightning is the most active front in America today for the Cult of the Yellow Sign," Miss Portinari went on, Telling the Mark the Tale . . . A few feet away, Joe Malik said to Hagbard, "I don't like frame-ups. Even for people like Hirsch and Hope."

"You suspect us of unethical behavior?" Hagbard asked innocently.

(Pat Walsh is dialing a phone.)

"I don't believe in jails," Joe said bluntly. "I don't think Atlanta and Zev will be any better when they get out. They'll be worse."

"You can be sure the Illuminati will protect you," Miss Portinari concluded gravely. Danny Pricefixer continued staring at her.

The phone is ringing far away, dragging me back to a body, a self, a purpose, shattering my memories of being the Ringmaster. I sit up and lift the receiver. "Hirsch," I say.

"My name is Pat Walsh," a woman's voice says. "I speak for Atlanta herself. The pass word is Theleme."

"Go ahead," I say hoarsely, wondering if it's about that peacenik professor we killed at UN plaza on April 1.

"You're being framed for a bombing," she said. "You have to go into hiding."

Hagbard laughed. "Atlanta isn't returning to the States. She's been a double agent for over two years. Working for me." (I found the warehouse door the Walsh woman described. It was open, as she had promised, and I wondered about the name on it, Gold & Appel Transfers . . .) "So is Tobias Knight, and he'll cop a plea. It's all been carefully planned, Joe. You only thought bombing your own office was *your* idea."

"How about Zev Hirsch?" Joe asked.

"He's having some very educational experiences about this time in New York City," Hagbard replied. "*I* don't believe in jails, either."

And I am trapped, the three of them surround me, and Jubela demands, "Tell us the Word," Jubelo repeats, "Tell us the Word," and Jubelum unsheathes the sword, "Tell us the Word, Zev Hirsch . . ."

"A bombing in New York?" the President asked shrewdly, trying to look as tough as his predecessor.

"Yes," Saul went on. "As soon as the link with God's Lightning was clear to us, Barney and I took off for Las Vegas. You can understand why."

The President didn't understand any of this, but wasn't about to admit that. "You headed for Las Vegas?" he asked shrewdly, trying to look as tough as his predecessor.

"Yes," Saul said sincerely. "As soon as we found out about Anthrax Leprosy Pi and Dr. Mocenigo's death, we realized the same organization must be implicated. God's Lightning—"

"God's Lightning?" the President asked shrewdly, remembering earlier years when he had been a guest speaker at their rallies.

"And the secret group that has infiltrated them and taken them over, the Cult of the Yellow Sign. We have reason to believe that an English intelligence agent named Chips will be arriving in London in a few hours with evidence against most of the Yellow Sign operatives within their government. You see, sir, this is an international conspiracy."

"An international conspiracy?" the President asked shrewdly.

And in Central Park our old friend Perri hops from tree to ground, snatches a nut thrown by August Personage, and quickly runs around the tree three times in case this friend-possibly-enemy produces a gun and starts blasting . . .

While far above the highest mountains in California another aspect of my consciousness soars like winged poetry: and knows, somehow, more about what is coming than Dr. Troll's seismograph: for I am the last, truly the last. The ecologists are right: mine is not merely an endangered but nearly an extinct species, and my senses have been sharpened beyond instinct by these last years. I circle around, I circle around, I soar: I bank: I float. I am, rare moment for me! not thinking about fish, for my belly is full at present. I circle around, circle around, thinking only about the soaring, the freedom, and, more vaguely, about the bad vibes coming up from below. Must you have a name? Call me Hali One, then: haliaeetus leucocephalus the last: symbol once of imperial Rome and now of imperial America: of which I neither know nor care, for all I know is the freedom of my estate and about that the Romans and the Americans have never had aught but the most confused and distorted ideas. Wearing my long green feathers I circle around. I am Hali One and I scream, not with rage or with fear or with anger; I scream with ecstasy, the terrible joy of my very existence, and the scream echoes from mountain to mountain to another mountain, resonating onward and onward, a sound that only another of my species could understand, and none are left to hear it. But still I scream: the shriek of Shiva the Destroyer, true face of Vishnu the Preserver and Brahma the Creator: for my scream is not of life

or death but of life-in-death, and I am equally contemp-
tuous of Perri and of August Personage, of squirrels and of
men, and of all lesser birds who cannot ascend to my height
and know the agony and supremacy of my freedom.

No—because they broke Billie Freshette slow and ugly
and they broke Marilyn Monroe fast and bright like lightning They broke Daddy and they broke Mama but shit like
I mean it this time they ain't going to break me No even if
it's greater with Simon than with any other man even if he
knows more than any other man I've had No it can't be
him and it can't even be Hagbard who seems to be the king
of the circus the very Ringmaster and keeper of the final
secret No it can't be any man and it most certainly by Jesus
and by Christ it can't be going back to Mister Charlie's police force No it's dark like my own skin and dark like the
destiny they've inflicted on me because of my skin but
whatever it is I can only find it alone God the time that rat
bit me while I was sleeping Daddy screaming until he was
almost crying "I'll kill the fucking landlord I'll kill the
motherfucker I'll cut his white heart out" until Mama finally calmed him No he died a little then No it would have
been better if he had killed the landlord No even if they
caught him and they would have caught him No even if he
died in the goddam electric chair and we went on welfare
No a man shouldn't let that happen to his children he
shouldn't be realistic and practical No no matter how good
it is no matter how wonderful the come it will always be
there in the back of my head that Simon is white No white
radical white revolutionary white lover it doesn't matter it
still comes up white and it's not acid and it's not a mood I
mean shit you have to decide sooner or later Are you on
somebody else's trip or are you on your own No and I can't
join God's Lightning or even what's left of the old Women's
Lib I mean shit that poetry Simon quoted is all wrong No
it's not true that no man is an island No the truth is every
man is an island and especially every woman is an island
and even more every black woman is an island

On August 23, 1928, Rancid, the butler in the Drake
Mansion on old Beacon Hill, reported a rather distressing
fact to his employer. "Good Lord Harry," old Drake cried
at first, "is he turning Papist now?" His second question
was less rhetorical: "You're absolutely sure?"

"There is no doubt," Rancid replied. "The maids showed me the socks, sir. And the shoes."

That night there was a rather strangulated attempt at conversation in the mansion's old library.

"Are you going back to Harvard?"

"Not yet."

"Are you at least going to try another damned alienist?"

"They call themselves psychiatrists these days, Father. I don't think so."

"Dammit, Robert, what *did* happen in the war?"

"Many things. They all made profits for our bank, though, so don't worry about them."

"Are you turning Red?"

"I see no profit there. The State of Massachusetts killed two innocent men today for holding opinions of that sort."

"Innocent my Aunt Fanny. Robert, I know the judge personally—"

"And he believes what the friend of a banker should believe."

There was a long pause, and old Drake crushed out a cigar he had hardly started.

"Robert, you *know* you're sick."

"Yes."

"What is this latest thing—glass and nails in your shoes? Your mother would die if she knew."

There was another silence. Robert Putney Drake finally answered, lanquidly, "It was an experiment. A phase. The Sioux Indians do much worse to themselves in the Sun Dance. So do lots of chaps in Spanish monasteries, and in India, among other places. It's not the answer."

"It's really finished?"

"Oh, yes. Quite. I'm trying something else."

"Something to hurt yourself again?"

"No, nothing to hurt myself."

"Well, then, I'm glad to hear that. But I do wish you would go to another alienist, or psychiatrist, or whatever they call themselves." Another pause. "You *can* pull yourself together, you know. Play the man, Robert. Play the man."

Old Drake was satisfied. He had talked turkey to the boy; he had performed his fatherly duty. Besides, the private detectives assured him that the Red Business really was trivial: The lad had been to several anarchist and Communist meetings, but his comments had been uniformly aloof and cynical.

It was nearly a year later when the really bad news from the private investigators arrived.

"How much will the girl take to keep her mouth shut?" old Drake asked immediately.

"After we pay hospital expenses, maybe a thousand more," the man from Pinkerton's said.

"Offer her five hundred," the old man replied. "Go up to a thousand only if you have to."

"I said maybe a thousand," the detective said bluntly. "He used a special kind of whip, one with twisted nails in the ends. She might want two or three thou."

"She's only a common whore. They're used to this sort of thing."

"Not to this extent." The detective was losing his deferential tone. "The photos of her back, and her buttocks especially, didn't bother me much. But that's because I'm in this business and I've seen a lot. An average jury would vomit, Mr. Drake. In court—"

"In court," old Drake pronounced, "she would come before a judge who belongs to several of my clubs and has investments in my bank. Offer five hundred."

Two months thereafter, the stock market crashed and New York millionaires began leaping from high windows onto hard streets. Old Drake, the next day, ran into his son begging on the street near the Old Granary cemetery. The boy was wearing old clothes from a secondhand store.

"It's not that bad, son. We'll pull through."

"Oh, I know that. You'll come out ahead, in fact, if I'm any judge of character."

"Then what the hell is this disgraceful damned foolishness?"

"Experience. I'm breaking out of a trap."

The old man fumed all the way back to the bank. That evening he decided it was time for another open and honest discussion; when he went to Robert's room, however, he found the boy thoroughly trussed up in chains and quite purple in the face.

"God! Damn! Son! What is *this?*"

The boy—who was twenty-seven and, in some respects, more sophisticated than his father—grinned and relaxed.

The purple faded from his face. "One of Houdini's escapes," he explained simply.

"You intend to become a stage magician? My *God!*"

"Not at all. I'm breaking out of another trap—the one that says nobody but Houdini can do these things."

Old Drake, to do him justice, hadn't acquired his wealth without some shrewdness concerning human peculiarities. "I begin to see," he said heavily. "Pain is a trap. That was why you put the broken glass in your shoes that time. Fear of poverty is a trap. That's why you tried begging on the streets. You're trying to become a Superman, like those crazy boys in Chicago, the 'thrill killers.' What you did to that whore last year was part of all this. What else have you done?"

"A lot." Robert shrugged. "Enough to be canonized as a saint, or to be burnt as a diabolist. None of it seems to add up, though. I still haven't found the way." He suddenly made a new effort, and the chains slipped to the floor. "Simple yoga and muscle control," he said without pride. "The chains in the mind are much harder. I wish there were a chemical, a key to the nervous system . . ."

"Robert," said old Drake, "you are going back to an alienist. I'll have you committed if you won't go voluntarily."

And so Dr. Faustus Unbewusst acquired a new patient, at a time when many of his most profitable cases were discontinuing therapy because of the monetary depression. He made very few notes on Robert, but these were subsequently found by an Illuminati operative, photostated, and placed in the archives at Agharti, where Hagbard Celine read them in 1965. They were undated, and scrawled in a hurried hand—Dr. Unbewusst, in reaction-formation against his own anal component, was a conspicuously untidy and careless person—but they told a fairly straightforward story:

RPD, age 27, latent homo. Father rich as Croesus. Five sessions per week @ $50 each, $250. Keep him in therapy 5 yrs that's a clear $65,000. Be ambitious, aim for ten years. $130,000. Beautiful.

RPD not latent homo at all. Advanced psychopath. Moral imbecile. Actually enjoys the money I'm soaking his father. Hopeless case. All drives ego-syntonic. Bastard doesn't give a fuck. Maybe as long as 12 yrs.? $156,000. *Hot shit!*

RPD back on sadism again. Thinks that's the key. Must use great care. If he gets caught at something serious, jail or a sanitorium; and can kiss that $156,000 good-bye. Maybe use drugs to calm him?

RPD in another schizo mood today. Full of some crap a gypsy fortune-teller told him. Extreme care needed: If the occultists get him, that's 13 grand per year out the window.

Clue to RPD: All goes back to the war. Can't stand the thought that all must die. Metaphysical hangup. Nothing I can do. If only there were an immortality pill. Risk of losing him to the occultists or even a church worse than I feared. I can feel the 13 grand slipping away.

RPD wants to go to Europe. Wants meeting, maybe therapy, with that *sheissdreck dummkopf* Carl Jung. Must warn parents too sick to travel.

RPD gone after only 10 months. A lousy 11-grand case. Too angry to see patients today. Spent morning drafting letter to *Globe* on why fortune-tellers should be forbidden by law. If I could get my hands on that woman, on her fat throat, the bitch, the fat stinking ignorant bitch. $156,000. Down the drain. Because he needs immortality and doesn't know how to get it.

(In Ingolstadt, Danny Pricefixer and Clark Kent are still staring at each other over Lady Velkor's sleeping body when Atlanta Hope bursts into the room, fresh from a shower, and throws herself on the bed, hugging and kissing everybody. "It was the first time," she cries. "The first time I ever really made it! It took all three of you." On the other side of Kent, Lady Velkor opens an eye and says, "Don't I get any credit? It takes Five that way, remember?")

Mama Sutra was only thirty then, but she streaked her hair with gray to fit the image of the Wise Woman. She recognized Drake as soon as he wandered into the tea parlor: old Drake's son, the crazy one, loaded.

He motioned to her before the waitress could take his order. Mama Sutra, quick to pick up clues, could tell from his suit's wrinkles that he had been lying down; Boston Common is a long walk from Beacon Hill; there were shrinks in the neighborhood; ergo, he hadn't come from home but from a therapy session.

"Tea leaves or cards?" she asked courteously, sitting across from him at the table.

"Cards," he said absently, looking down from the window to the Common. "Coffee," he added to the waitress. "Black as sin."

"Were you listening to the preachers down there?" Mama Sutra asked shrewdly.

"Yes." He grinned, engagingly. " 'He that believeth shall never taste death.' They're in rare form today."

"Shuffle," she said, handing the cards over. "But they awakened some spiritual need in you, my son. That's why you came up here."

He met her eye cynically. "I'm willing to try any kind of witchcraft once. I just came from a practitioner of the latest variety, just off the boat from Vienna a few years."

Bull's-eye, she thought.

"Neither his science nor their unenlightened faith can help you," Mama said somberly, ignoring his cynicism. "Let us hope that the cards will show the way." She dealt a traditional Tree of Life.

At the crown was Death upside-down, and below it were the King of Swords in Chokmah and the Knight of Wands in Binah. "He that believeth shall never taste death," he had quoted cynically.

"I see a battlefield," she began; it was common Boston gossip that Drake first started acting odd after the war. "I see Death come very close to you and then miss you." She pointed to the reverse Death card with a dramatic finger. "But many died, many that you cared for deeply."

"I liked a few of them," he said grudgingly. "Mostly I was worried about my own a—my own hide. But go ahead."

She looked at the Knight of Wands in the Binah position. Should she mention the bisexuality implied? He was going to a shrink, and might be able to take it. Mama tried to hold the Knight of Wands and King of Swords together in her focus, and the way became clear. "There are two men in you. One loves other men, perhaps too much. The other is desperately trying to free himself from all of humanity, even from the world. You're a Leo," she added suddenly, taking a leap.

"Yes," he said, unimpressed. "August 6." He was thinking that she had probably looked up the birthdates of all the richer individuals in town in case they ever wandered in.

"It's very hard for Leos to accept death," she said sadly. "You are like Buddha after he saw the corpse on the road. No matter what you have or own, no matter what you achieve, it will never be enough, for you saw too many corpses in the war. Ah, my son, would that I could help you! But I only read cards; I am no alchemist who sells the Elixir of Eternal Life." While he was digesting that one—a sure hit, she felt—Mama rushed on to examine the Five of Wands reversed in Chesed and the Magus upright in Geburah. "So many wands," she said. "So many fire signs. A true Leo, but so much of it turned inward. See how the energetic Knight of Wands descends to the Five upside-down: All your energies, and Leos are very powerful, are turned against yourself. You are a burning man, trying to consume yourself and be reborn. And the Magus, who shows the way, is below the King of Swords and dominated by him: Your reason won't allow you to accept the necessity of the fire. You are still rebelling against Death." The Fool was in Tipareth and, surprisingly, upright. "But you are very close to taking the final step. You are ready to let the fire consume even your intellect and die to this world." This was going swimmingly, she thought—and then she saw the Devil in Netzach and the Nine of Swords reversed in Yod. The rest of the Tree was even worse: the Tower in Yesod and the Lovers reversed (of course!) in Malkuth. Not a cup or a pentacle anywhere.

"You're going to emerge as a much stronger man," she said weakly.

"That isn't what you see," Drake said. "And it isn't what I see. The Devil and the Tower together are a pretty destructive pair, aren't they?"

"I suppose you know what the Lovers reversed means, too?" she asked.

" 'The Answer of the Oracle Is Always Death,' " he quoted.

"But you won't accept it."

"The only way to conquer Death—until science produces an immortality pill—is to make him your servant, your company cop," Drake said calmly. "That's the key I've been looking for. The bartender never becomes an alcoholic, and the high priest laughs at the gods. Besides, the Tower is rotten to the core and deserves to be destroyed." He pointed abruptly to the Fool. "You have some real talents obviously—even if you do cheat like everybody in this racket—and you must know there are two choices after crossing the Abyss. The right-hand path and the left-hand path. I seem to be headed for the left-hand path. I can see that much, and it confirms what I already suspect. Go ahead and tell me the rest of what you see; I'm not afraid to hear it."

"Very well." Mama wondered if he was one of the few, the very few, who would eventually come to the attention of the Shining Ones. "You will make Death your servant, as a tactic to master him. Yours is, indeed, the left-hand path. You will cause immense suffering—especially to yourself at first. But after a while you won't notice that; after a while you won't even notice the horrors that you inflict on others. Men will say that you are a materialist, a worshipper of money. What do you hate most?" she asked abruptly.

"Sentimental slop and lies. All the Christian lies in Sunday school, all the democratic lies in the newspapers, all the socialist lies our so-called intellectuals are spouting these days. Every rotten, crooked, sneaking, hypocritical deception people use to hide from themselves that we're all still hunting animals in a jungle."

"You admire Neitzsche?"

"He was crazy. Let's just say I have less contempt for him, and for DeSade, than I have for most intellectuals."

"Yes. So we know what the Tower is that you will destroy. Everything in America that smacks of democracy or Christianity or socialism. The whole façade of humanitarianism from the Constitution onward to the present. You will turn your fire loose and burn all that up with your Leonine energies. You will force your view of America into total reality, and make every citizen afraid of the jungle and of the death that lurks in the jungle. Crime and commerce are moving closer together, due to Prohibition; you will complete their marriage. All, all this, just to make Death your servant instead of your master. The money and power are just incidental to that."

NO—because even if you think you have it beat even if you think you can work out a reconciliation a separate peace I mean shit the war still goes on No you're only kidding yourself Even say I love Simon and that's all Holly-

wood bullshit you can't really tell in only one week no matter how good it is but even if I love Simon the war goes on
as long as we're going around in separate skins White Man
Black Man Bronze Man White Woman Black Woman
Bronze Woman even if Hagbard claims to have gotten past
all that on his submarine it's only because they're under the
water and away from the world Out here the bastards are
using live ammunition like it says in the old joke Maybe
that's the only truth in the world Not the Bibles or poetry
or philosophy but just the old jokes Especially the bad
jokes and the sad jokes No they're using live ammunition I
mean shit they never see me all of them White Man Black
Man Bronze Man White Woman Black Woman Bronze
Woman they look at me and I'm in their game I have my
role I am Black Woman I am never just me No it goes on
and on every step upward is a step into more hypocrisy until the game is stopped completely and nobody has found
out how to do that No the more Simon says that he does
see me the more he's lying to himself No he never makes it
with White Woman because she's too much like his mother
or some damned Freudian reason like that I mean shit No I
can't go on in their game I am going to scream with rage I
am going to scream like an eagle I am going to scream in
the ears of the whole world until somebody does see me until
I am not Black Woman and not Black and not Woman and
nothing No nothing *justme* No they'll say I'm giving up
love and sanity Well fuck them fuck them all No I won't
turn back the acid has changed everything No at the end of
it when I really am *me* maybe then I can find a better love
and a better sanity No but first I have to find *me*

"Go on." Drake was unsmiling but undisturbed.

"The King of Swords and the Knight of Wands are both
very active. You could do all this harmlessly, by becoming
an artist and *showing* this vision of the jungle. You don't
have to create it literally and inflict it on your fellow human beings."

"Stop preaching. Just read the cards. You're better at it
than I am, but I can see enough to know that there is no
such alternative for me. The other wand and the other
sword are reversed. I can't be satisfied to do it in symbolic
form. I must do it so that everybody is affected by it, not
just the few who read books or go to concerts. Tell me
what I don't know. Why is the line from the Fool to the

Tower completed in the Lovers reversed? I know that I can't love anyone, and I don't believe that anybody else ever does, either—that's more sentiment and hypocrisy. People use each other as masturbating machines and crying towels, and they *call* it love. But there's a deeper meaning. What is it?"

"Start from the top: Death reversed. You reject Death, so the Fool cannot undergo rebirth and enter the right-hand path when he crosses the Abyss. Therefore: the left-hand path, the destruction of the Tower. There is only one end to that chain of karma, my son. The Lovers means Death, just as Death means Life. You are rejecting natural death, and therefore refusing natural life. Your path will be an unnatural life leading to a death that is against nature. You will die as a man before your body dies. The fire is still self-destructive, even if you turn it outward and use the whole world as a stage for your private *Gotterdammerung*. Your primary victim will still be yourself."

"You have the talent," Drake said coldly, "but you are still basically a fraud, like everyone in this business. *Your* worst victim, madam, is yourself. You deceive yourself with the lies that you have so often told others. It's the occupational disease of mystics. The truth is that it doesn't matter whether I destroy myself alone or destroy this planet—or turn around and try to find my way to the right-hand path in some dreary monastery. The universe will roll blindly along, not caring, not even *knowing*. There's no Granddaddy in the clouds to pass a last judgment—there's only a few airplanes up there, learning more and more about how to carry bombs. They court-martialed General Mitchell for saying it, but it's the truth. The next time around they'll really bomb the hell out of civilian populations. And the universe won't know or care about that either. Don't tell me that my flight from Death leads back to Death; I'm not a child, and I know that all paths lead back to Death eventually. The only question is: Do you cower before him all your life or do you spit in his eye?"

"You can transcend abject fear and rebellious hatred both. You can see that he is only part of the Great Wheel and, like all other parts, necessary to the whole. Then you can accept him."

"Next you'll be telling me to love him."

"That too."

"Yes, and I can learn to see the great and glorious Whole Picture. I can see all the men defecating and urinating in their trousers before they died at Château-Thierry, watching their own guts fall out into their laps and screaming out of a hole that isn't even a mouth any more, as manifestations of that sublime harmony and balance which is ineffable and holy and beyond all speech and reason. Sure. I can see that, if I knock half of my brain out of commission and hypnotize myself into thinking that the view from that weird perspective is deeper and wider and more *truly true* than the view from an unclouded mind. Go to the quadruple-amputee ward and try to tell them that. You speak of death as a personified being. Very well: Then I must regard him as any other entity that gets in my way. Love is a myth invented by poets and other people who couldn't face the world and crept off into corners to create fantasies to console themselves. The fact is that when you meet another entity, either it makes way for you or you make way for it. Either it dominates and you submit, or you dominate and it submits. Take me into any club in Boston and I'll tell you which millionaire has the most millions, by the way the others treat him. Take me into any workingman's bar and I'll tell you who has the best punch in a fistfight, by the way the others treat him. Take me into any house and I'll tell you in a minute whether the husband or the wife is dominant. Love? Equality? Reconciliation? Acceptance? Those are the excuses of the losers, to persuade themselves that they choose their condition and weren't beaten down into it. Find a dutiful wife, who truly loves her husband. I'll have her in my bed in three days, maximum. Because I'm so damned attractive? No, because I understand men and women. I'll make her understand, without saying it aloud and shocking her, that the adultery will, one way or another, hurt her husband, whether he knows about it or not. Show me the most servile colored waiter in the best restaurant in town, and after he's through explaining Christianity and humility and all the rest of it, count how many times a day he steps into the kitchen to spit in his handerchief. The other employess will tell you he has a 'chest condition.' The condition he has is chronic rage. The mother and the child? An endless power struggle. Listen to the infant's cry change in pitch when Mother doesn't come at once. Is that fear you hear? It's rage—insane fury at not having total dominance. As for the mother herself, I'd wager that ninety percent of the married women in the psychiatrists' care are there because they can't admit to themselves, can't escape the lie of love long enough to admit to themselves, how often they want to strangle that monster in the nursery. Love of country? Another lie; the truth is fear of cops and prisons. Love of art? Another lie; the truth is fear of the naked truth without ornaments and false faces on it. Love of truth itself? The biggest lie of all: fear of the unknown. People learn acceptance of all this and achieve wisdom? They surrender to superior force and call their cowardice maturity. It still comes down to one question: Are you kneeling at the altar, or are you on the altar watching the others kneel to you?"

"The wheel of the Tarot is the wheel of Dharma," Mama Sutra said softly when he had concluded. "It is also the wheel of the galaxy, which you see as a blind machine. It rolls on, as you say, no matter what we think or do. Knowing that, I accept Death as part of the wheel, and I accept your nonacceptance as another part. I can control neither. I can only repeat my warning, which is not a lie but a fact about the structure of the Wheel: By denying death, you guarantee that you will meet him finally in his most hideous form."

Drake finished his coffee and smiled whimsically. "You know," he said, "my contempt for lies has an element of the very sentimentality and foolish idealism that I have been rejecting. Perhaps I will be most effective if I never speak so honestly again. When you hear of me next, I might be known as a philanthropist and benefactor of mankind." He lit a cigar thoughtfully. "And that would even be true if your Tarot mysticism is correct after all. If Death is necessary to the Wheel, along with all the other parts, then I am necessary also. The Wheel would collapse, perhaps, if my spirit of rebellion were not there to balance your spirit of acceptance. Imagine that."

"It is true. That is why I have warned you but not judged you."

"So I am, as Goethe says, 'part of that force which aims at evil and only achieves good'?"

"That is a thought which you should try to remember when the Dark Night of Sammael descends upon you at the end."

"More cant," Drake said, with a return to his previous cynicism. "I aim at evil and I will achieve evil. The Wheel and all its harmonious balances and all-healing paradoxes is just another myth of the weak and defeated. One strong man can stop the Wheel or tear it to shreds if he dares enough."

"Perhaps. We who study the Wheel do not know all of its secrets. Some believe that your spirit reappears constantly in history, because it is fated, eventually, to triumph. Maybe this is the last century of terrestrial mortals, and the next century will be the time of the cosmic immortals. What will happen then, when the Wheel is stopped, none of us can predict. It may be 'good' or 'evil' or even—to quote your favorite philosopher—beyond good and evil. We cannot say. That is another reason I do not judge you."

"Listen," Drake said with sudden emotion. "We're both lying. It's not all this philosophical or cosmic. The simple fact is that I couldn't sleep nights, and nothing I tried in conventional 'cures' could help me, until I began to help myself by systematically rebelling against everything that seemed stronger than me."

"I know. I didn't know it was insomnia. It might have been nightmares or dizzy spells or sexual impotence. But there was some way that the scenes you saw in Château-Thierry lived on and goaded you to wake out of the dream of the sleepwalkers on the streets. You are waking: You stand on the abyss." She pointed to the Fool and the dog who barks at his heels. "And I am the noisy little bitch barking to warn you that you can still choose the right-hand path. The decision is not final until you cross the abyss."

"But the cards show that I really have very little choice. Especially in the world that is going to emerge from this depression."

Mama Sutra smiled without forgiveness or final condemnation. "This is no age for saints," she agreed softly. "Two dollars please."

George, don't make no bull moves. The Dutchman saw it all clearly now. Capone and Luciano and Maldonado and Lepke and all the rest of them were afraid of Winifred and the Washington crowd. They were planning a deal, and his death was part of the bargain. The fools didn't know that you can never negotiate from fear. They thought of the Order only as a handy gimmick for international communications and illicit trade; they were too dumb to really study the Teachings. Especially, they had never understood the third Teaching: *Fear is Failure.* Once you're afraid of the bulls, you're lost. But the bull was gone. "What have you done with him?" he shouted at the hospital wall.

(Smiling Jim had seen the eagle only the day before. Its nest was definitely on one of these peaks. He would get it: He knew it in his bones, a hunch so strong it couldn't be doubted. Panting, sweating, every muscle aching, he climbed onward . . . The coffee leaped out of the paper cup and slurped onto the pages of *Carnal Orgy.* Igor Beaver, the graduate student, looked up in astonishment: The seismograph stood at grade 5. A mile away, Dillinger woke as the bedroom door slammed shut and his favorite statue, King Kong atop the Empire State Building, fell off the bureau.)

NO REMISSION, NO REMISSION, NO REMISSION WITHOUT THE SHEDDING OF BLOOD. NO REMISSION WITHOUT THE SHEDDING OF BLOOD.

Mama Sutra looked down through the window at Boston Common. Robert Putney Drake had stopped, and was listening to one of the preachers again; even at this distance she could recognize the cool, closed smile on his face.

The Dealy Lama sat down across from her. "Well?" he asked.

"Definitely. The Order will have to intervene." Mama shook her head sadly. "He's a menace to the whole world."

"Slowness is beauty," the Dealy Lama said. "Let the Lower Order contact him first. If they decide he's worth the effort, then we'll act. I think I shall persuade Hagbard to attend Harvard, so he can be in his neighborhood and keep an eye on him, so to speak."

IT'S THE WORD OF THE BIBLE AND THE WORD OF GOD AND IT SAYS IT PLAIN AND CLEAR SO NO HIGHBROW PROFESSOR CAN SAY IT MEANS SOMETHING ELSE.

"How old are you actually?" Mama asked curiously.

The Dealy Lama looked at her levelly. "Would you believe thirty thousand years?"

She laughed. "I should have known better than to ask. You can always tell the higher members by their sense of humor."

AND THIS IS WHAT IT SAYS: NO REMISSION, NO REMISSION,

BROTHERS AND SISTERS, NO REMISSION WITHOUT THE SHED-
DING OF BLOOD, WITHOUT THE SHEDDING OF BLOOD. NO RE-
MISSION. NO REMISSION WITHOUT THE SHEDDING OF BLOOD.

Hagbard's mouth fell open in completely genuine surprise. "Well, *sink* me," he said, beginning to laugh.

Behind him on a wall, Joe noticed dizzily, was a brand-
new graffito, probably scrawled by somebody out of his
skull on the acid: THE PIGEONS IN B. F. SKINNER'S CAGES
ARE POLITICAL PRISONERS.

"We both pass," Hagbard went on happily. "We've been
judged and found innocent by the great god Acid."

Joe took a deep breath. "And when do you start to explain in monosyllables or sign language or semaphore or
something a non-Illuminated moron like me can understand?"

"You read all the clues. It was right out in the open. It
was plain as a barn door. It was as conspicuous as my nose
and twice as homely—in every sense of that word."

"Hagbard, for Christ's sake and for my sake and for all
our sakes, will you stop gloating and give me the answer?"

"I'm sorry." Hagbard pocketed the gun carelessly. "I'm a
bit giddy. I've been waging a kind of war all night, high on
acid. It was a strain, especially since I was at least ninety
percent sure you'd kill me before it was over." He lit one of
his abominable cigars. "Briefly, then, the Illuminati is benevolent, compassionate, kindly, generous, et cetera, et cetera. Add all the other complimentary adjectives you can
think of. In short, we're the good guys."

"But—but—it can't be."

"It can be and it is." Hagbard motioned him toward the
Bugatti. "Let's Sit Down, if I may permit myself one more
acrostic before the codes and puzzles are all resolved."
They climbed into the front seat, and Joe accepted the
brandy decanter Hagbard offered. "Of course," Hagbard
went on, "when I say 'good,' you've got to understand that
all terms are relative. We're as good as is possible in this
fucked-up section of the galaxy. We're not perfect. Certainly, I'm not, and I haven't observed anything approaching
immaculate perfection in any of the other Masters of the
Temple either. But we are, in human terms and by ordinary
standards, decent chaps. There's a reason for that. It's the
basic law of magic, and it's in every textbook. You must
have read it somewhere. Do you know what I mean?"

Joe took a stiff snort of the brandy. It was peach—his favorite. "Yes, I think. 'As ye give, so shall ye get.' "

"Precisely." Hagbard took back the bottle and had a snort himself. "Mind you, Joe, that's a scientific law, not a moral commandment. There are no commandments, because there is no commander anywhere. All authority is a delusion, whether in theology or in sociology. Everything is radically, even sickeningly, free. The first law of magic is as neutral as Newton's first law of motion. It says that the equation balances, and that's all it says. You are still free to give evil and pain, if you decide you must. Once done, however, you never escape the consequences. It always comes back. No prayers, sacrifices, mortifications, or supplications will change it, any more than they'll change Newton's laws or Einstein's. So we're 'good,' as moralists would say, because we know enough to have a bloody strong reason to be good. In the last week things went too fast, and I became 'evil'—I deliberately ordered and paid for the deaths of various people, and set in motion processes that had to lead to still other deaths. I knew what I was doing, and I knew—and still know—that I'll pay for it. Such decisions are extremely rare in the history of the Order, and my superior, the Dealy Lama, tried to persuade me it was unnecessary this time too. I disagreed; I take the responsibility. No man or god or goddess can change it. I will pay, and I'm ready to pay, whenever and however the bill is presented."

"Hagbard, *what are you?*"

"A *mehum*, the Saure family would say," Hagbard grinned. "A mere human. No more. Not one jot more."

"How much blood?" Robert Putney Drake asked. He was astonished at his own words; in all his experiments at breaking through the walls, he had never lowered himself to heckling an ignorant street preacher.

ALL THE BLOOD IN THE WORLD ISN'T ENOUGH. EVERY MAN, WOMAN, AND CHILD ISN'T ENOUGH. EVEN ALL THE ANIMALS IF YOU ADDED THEM IN LINE IN SOME PAGAN OR VOODOO SACRIFICE. IT WOULDN'T BE ENOUGH. IT WOULDN'T BE ENOUGH, BROTHERS. THE GOOD BOOK SAYS SO.

"There were five of us," John-John Dillinger was explaining to George as they trudged back toward Ingolstadt, having lost Hagbard and the Bugatti in the crowd. "My folks kept it a secret. German people, very superstitious and secretive. They didn't want reporters all over the place and headlines about the first quintuplets to live. The Dionne family got all that, much later."

BECAUSE ALL THE BLOOD IN THE WORLD ISN'T EQUAL TO ONE DROP. NOT ONE DROP

"John Herbert Dillinger is in Las Vegas, trying to track down the plague—unless he already finished up and went home to Los Angeles." John-John smiled. "He was always the brains of the bunch. Runs a rock-music company, real professional businessman. He was the oldest, by a couple of minutes, and we all sort of look up to him. He served the prison time, even though I'm the one who rightly should have, seeing that robbing that grocer was my dumb idea. But he said he could take it without cracking up, and he was right."

NOT ONE DROP, NOT ONE DROP, OF THE PRECIOUS BLOOD OF OUR LORD AND SAVIOR, JESUS CHRIST.

"I see," Drake said. "And was that A, B, AB, or O?"

"John Hoover Dillinger lives in Mad Dog, under the name D. J. Hoover—he's not above letting people suspect he's a distant relative of J. Edgar's. Mostly," John-John said, "he's retired. Except occasionally for little jobs like helping arrange convincing jail breaks, say, when Jim Cartwright wants to let a prisoner get out in a realistic fashion. He gave Naismith the idea for the John Dillinger Died for You Society."

"How about the other two?" George asked, thinking that it would be even harder to decide whether he loved Stella more than Mavis or Mavis more than Stella now that he knew they were the same person. He wondered how Joe felt, since he obviously dug Miss Mao Tsu-hsi and she was that person also. Three in one and one in three. Like Dillinger. Or was Dillinger five in three? George realized suddenly that he was still tripping a little. Dillinger was five in one, not five in three: the law of Fives again. Did that mean there were two more in the Mavis-Stella-Mao complex, two that he hadn't met yet? Why did two and three keep popping up in all this?

"The other two are dead," John-John said sadly. "John Edgar Dillinger was born first, and he went and died first. Fast and furious, he was. It was him that plugged that bank guard in East Chicago while the rest of us were vacationing and laying low in Miami. Always the hothead, he was. Had a heart attack back in '43 and went to an early grave. John Thomas Dillinger went in '69. He was in Chicago in '68 on a JAM assignment, meeting with a crazy English spy named Chips. British Intelligence somehow got a report that the Democratic Convention was being run by the Bavarian Illuminati and would end with an assassination. They didn't believe in the Illuminati so they sent Chips; they always send him on wild cases, 'cause he's nutty enough to take them seriously and do a thorough job. Both of them got tear-gassed coming out of the Hilton Hotel, and poor Chips got thrown in a paddy-wagon with a bunch of young radicals. John Thomas had a chest problem already, a chronic asthma, and the tear gas made it a lot worse. He went from doctor to doctor, and finally passed away early in '69. So there's a cop in Chicago who could boast that he really killed John Dillinger, only he doesn't know it. Isn't life peculiar?"

"The Saure family only *thought* they were in the Illuminati," Hagbard went on. "Hitler and Stalin only *thought* they were in the Illuminati. Old Weishaupt only *thought* he was in the Illuminati. It's that simple. The moral of the whole story is: Beware of cheap Occidental imitations." He smiled grimly.

"I think it's beginning to penetrate," Joe said slowly. "It was, of course, the very first hypothesis I formed: There have been many groups in history who called themselves the Illuminati, and they weren't all aiming at exactly the same thing."

"Precisely." Hagbard puffed again at his cigar. "That's the natural first suspicion of any non-paranoid mind. Then, as you explore the evidence, links between these groups begin to appear. Eventually the paranoid hypothesis begins to appear more plausible and you begin to believe there always has been one Illuminati, using the same basic slogans and symbols and aiming at the same basic goal. I sent Jim Cartwright to you with that yarn about three conspiracies —the ABC or Ancient Bavarian Conspiracy, the NBC or New Bavarian Conspiracy, and the CBS or Conservative Bavarian Seers—to set you thinking that the truth might be midway backward toward the simple first idea. From here on in, forget that I represent the original Illuminati. In fact, in recent centuries we don't use a name at all. We employ only the initials A.A., written like this." He sketched on a Donau-Hotel matchbook:

A∴ A∴

"A lot of occult writers," he went on, "have made some amazing guesses as to what that means. Actually, it doesn't mean a damned thing. To prevent our name being stolen and misused again, we don't have a name. Anybody who thinks he's guessed the name and tries to pass himself off as an initiate by declaring that we're really the Atlantean Arcanum or the Argenteum Astrum or whatever immediately reveals that he's a fraud. It's a neat gimmick," Hagbard intoned gloomily. "I only wish we had thought of it centuries earlier."

The buzzer on the President's secretary's desk buzzed as Saul and Barney passed through the outer door. The secretary flipped the switch, and the President said, "Find out the highest medal a civilian can get, and order two, on my signature, for those two detectives."

"Yes, sir," the secretary said, scribbling.

"And then ask the FBI to check out that older one. He looked like a kike to me," the President said shrewdly.

NO—because I'd be a fool to think miracles can occur in this world before somebody pays the rent and the taxes and shows that their papers are in order and the people who are running it can always tell you your papers are not in order No because there are no magicians and even Hagbard is mostly a fraud and a con man even if he means well No because I'm not Pope Joan if there ever was a Pope Joan No because like the song says I'm not a queen I'm a woman and the wrong color woman to boot No because there will be rivers of blood and the earth will be shaken before we can overturn Boss Charlie because it isn't a simple one-night symbolic Armageddon like Hagbard fooled them all into thinking No because Hagbard is some kind of magician and put us all on his own trip for a while but the real world isn't a trip it's a bummer No because the lovers don't live happily ever after what happens is that they get married and get into debt and live in slavery ever after and I've got to find something better than that No because none of us are driving the car it's the car that's driving us No because it's like that old joke "Balls" said the queen "if I had them I'd be king" and "Nuts" said the prince "I've got them and I'm not king" and "Crap" said the king and thirty thousand royal subjects squatted and strained for in those days the king's word was law Hagbard would call it anality and sexism and ageism but it just comes down to the women and children getting all the crap right in the face and a few males owning everything the truth is all in the old jokes especially the bad jokes I'm still tripping but this is true they can always say your papers are not in order No because sometimes you've got to be a hermit and then come back later when you're together No because the wheel keeps spinning and doesn't give a fuck if there's going to be any change it's got to be that some human being somewhere does give a fuck No because I've never found a way to shut Simon's mouth and make him listen No because Jesus Christ was a black man and they've even lied about that he was another black man they killed and they won't admit it No because death is the currency in every empire Roman or American or any other all empires are the same Death is always the argument they use No because the whole world can go to the Devil and I'm taking care of Mary Lou No because look at that professor they killed at the UN building and none of them arrested yet No because there's a perpetual motion machine inside me and I'm learning to let it run No because I'll put a curse on all of them I'll burn them I'll condemn them I'll have the world No because look what happened to Daddy and Mommy

"It's grade 5 and moving up toward 6," Igor Beaver shouted into the phone.

"You idiot, don't you think I can tell that from here?" Dr. Troll shouted back. "My bed was bouncing around like it had Saint Vitus' dance even before you called." His emotion was merely professional anger at the student's failure to obey orders; Grade 5 is nothing to get excited about if you're a Californian, and even Grade 6 causes anxiety only among tourists or believers in the famous Edgar Cayce prophecy . . . John Herbert Dillinger, one of those believers, was already in the garage, pajama tops tucked in to hastily donned trousers, bare foot on the starter . . . But Smiling Jim climbed blissfully upward, enjoying total communication with nature, the mystic rapture of the true hunter before he gets his chance to open fire and blast a chunk of nature to hell . . .

YOU MAY MOCK AND YOU MAY JEST BUT AT THE LAST
JUDGMENT THE SMILE WILL BE WIPED OFF YOUR FACE

"He's heckling the preacher," Mama said. "A small beginning, certainly, for the kind of destiny he seems to be
choosing."

"He's heckling himself," the Dealy Lama pronounced.
"Christianity, rightly understood, is an encounter with
Death. He's still struggling with that problem. He wants to
believe in the symbolism of the Resurrection, but he can't.
Too much intellect—King of Swords—keeping the reins on
his intuitive—Prince of Wands—aspect."

"Well, maybe," Drake said calmly. "But suppose He was
type A. Now, if He got a transfusion at the last minute . . ."

The nest was in sight. The bird was invisible, but Smiling
Jim recognized the characteristic eagle's nest on a peak
only a few hundred yards above and to the west. "Come
home, baby," he thought passionately, unstrapping his rifle.
"Come home. Daddy is waiting."

Hagbard took another belt of the brandy and repeated:
"The Saures were not Illuminati. Neither were Weishaupt
or Hitler. They were frauds, pure and simple. First they deluded themselves, then they deluded others. The real Illuminati, the A∴A∴, have never been involved in politics or in
any form of manipulating or coercing people. Our interests
are entirely elsewhere. *Do what thou wilt* is our law. Only
in the last few decades, as the fate of the earth seemed to
be hanging in the balance, have we taken any direct action.
Even so, we have been cautious. We know that power cor-
rupts. We have acted chiefly by not-acting, by what the
Taoists call *wu-wei*. But then things got out of hand. They
moved too fast . . . We fucked up somewhat. But only because total inaction seemed to mean total disaster."

"You mean you, as an official of some sort in the
A∴A∴, infiltrated the fake Illuminati and became one of
their top Five, intending to undo them nonviolently? And it
didn't work?"

"It worked about as well as any activity on that level
ever works," Hagbard said somberly. "Most of humanity
has been spared, for a while. And the wild free animals
have been spared. For a while." He sighed. "I guess I'll
have to begin from the A-B-Cs. We have never sought
power. We have sought to disperse power, to set men and

women free. That really means: to help them to discover that they are free. Everybody's free. The slave is free. The ultimate weapon isn't this plague out in Vegas, or any new super H-bomb. The ultimate weapon has always existed. Every man, every woman, and every child owns it. It's the ability to say *No* and take the consequences. 'Fear is failure.' 'The fear of death is the beginning of slavery.' 'Thou hast no right but to do thy will.' The goose can break the bottle at any second. Socrates took the hemlock to prove it. Jesus went to the cross to prove it. It's in all history, all myth, all poetry. It's right out in the open all the time."

Hagbard sighed again. "Our founder and leader, the man known in myth as Prometheus or the snake in the garden of Eden—"

"Oh, Christ," Joe said, slumping forward in his seat. "I have the feeling that you're starting to put me on again. You're about to tell me that the Prometheus and Genesis stories are really based on fact."

"Our leader, known as Lucifer or Satan," Hagbard went on, "Lucifer being the *bringer of light*—"

"You know," Joe said, "I'm not going to believe a word of this."

"Our leader, known as Prometheus the fire-bringer or Lucifer the light-bringer or Quetzalcoatl the morning star or the snake in the garden of Osiris's bad brother, Set, or Shaitan the tempter—well, to be brief, he repented." Hagbard raised an eyebrow. "Does that intrigue you sufficiently to silence your skepticism long enough for me to finish a sentence?"

"He *repented?*" Joe sat upright again.

"Sure. Why not?" Hagbard's old malicious grin, so rare in the last week, returned. "If Atlas can Shrug and Telemachus can Sneeze, why can't Satan Repent?"

"Go ahead," Joe said. "This is just another one of your put-ons, but I'm hooked. I'll listen. But I have my own answer, which is that there is no answer. You're just an allegory on the universe itself, and every explanation of you and your actions is incomplete. They'll always be a new, more up-to-date explanation coming along a while later. That's *my* answer."

Hagbard laughed easily. "Charming," he said. "I must remember that the next time *I'm* trying to understand myself. Of course, it's true of any human being. We're all allegories on the universe, different faces it wears in trying to decide what it really is . . . But our founder and leader, as I was saying, repented. That's the secret that has never been revealed. There is no stasis anywhere in the cosmos, least of all in the minds of entities that possess minds. The basic fallacy of all bad writers—and theologians are notoriously bad writers—is to create cardboard characters who never change. He gave us the light of reason and, seeing how we misused it, he repented. The story is more complicated, but that's the basic outline. At least, it's as much as I understood until a week ago. The important thing to get clear is that he never aimed at power or destruction. That's a myth—"

"Created by the opposition," Joe said. "Right? I read that in Mark Twain's defense of Satan."

"Twain was subtle," Hagbard said, taking a little more brandy, "but not subtle enough. No, the myth was not created by the opposition. It was created by our founder himself."

"Wilde should be alive," Joe said admiringly. "He was so proud of himself, setting paradox on top of paradox until he had a nice three- or four- or five-story house of contradictions built up. He should see the skyscrapers you create."

"You never disappoint me," Hagbard said. "If they ever hang you, you'll be arguing about whether the rope really exists until the last minute. That's why I picked you, all those years ago, and programmed you for the role you'd play tonight. Only a man whose father was an ex-Moslem, and who was himself an ex-Catholic and an ex-engineering student, would have the required complexity. Anyway, to return to the libretto, as an old friend of mine used to say, the error of Weishaupt and Hitler and Stalin and the Saures was to believe the propaganda our founder spread against himself—that, and believing they were in communication with him, when they were only in communication with a nasty part of their own unconscious minds. There was no evil spirit misleading them. They were misleading themselves. And we were trailing along behind, trying to keep them from causing too much harm. Finally, in the early 1960s—after a certain fuckup in Dallas convinced me that things were getting out of hand—I contacted the Five directly. Since I knew the real secrets of magic and they only had distortions, it was easy to convince them that I was an emissary from those beings whom they call the Secret Chiefs or the Great Old Ones or the Shining Ones. Being half crazy, they reacted in a way I had not expected. They all abdicated and appointed me and the four Saures as their successors. They decided that we're entering the age of Horus, the child-god, and that youth should be given a chance to run things—hence, the promotion of the Saures. They threw me in because I seemed to know what I was talking about. But then came the real problem: I couldn't convince the Saures of anything. Those pig-headed kids wouldn't believe a word I said. They told me I was over thirty and untrustworthy. I told you the truth was out in the open all the time; anybody with eyes in his head should have been able to interpret what's been happening since the early 1960s. The great and dreaded Illuminati of the past had fallen into the control of a bunch of ignorant and malicious kids. The age of the crowned and conquering child."

"And you think the old and wise should rule?" Joe asked. "That doesn't fit your character. This *has* to be another put-on."

"I don't think *anybody* should rule," Hagbard said. "All I'm doing—all the Higher Order of the A∴A∴ has ever tried to do—is communicate with people, in spite of their biases and fears. Not to rule them. And what we're trying to communicate—the ultimate secret, the philosopher's stone, the elixir of life—is just the power of the word *No*. We are people who have said *Non serviam,* and we're trying to teach others to say it. Drake was one of us spiritually but never understood it. If we can't find immortality, we can make a damned good try. If we can't save this planet, we can get off it and go to the stars."

"And what happens now?" Joe asked.

"More surprises," Hagbard answered promptly. "I can't tell you the whole story at this hour, with both of us fagged out at the end of an acid trip. We go back to the hotel and sleep, and after breakfast there are more revelations. For George as well as for you."

And later in the Bugatti, which, driven by Harry Coin, was grandly wafting Hagbard, George, and Joe around the south side of Lake Totenkopf, George asked, "Is Hitler really going to be buried anonymously in a Jewish cemetery?"

"It looks that way." Hagbard grinned. "His Israeli documents are excellent forgeries. He'll be lifted off that toilet by Hauptmann's men and gently deposited in the Ingolstadt Hebrew Burial Grounds, there to rest for all eternity."

"That will make me throw up once a day for the rest of my life," Joe said bitterly. "It's the worst case of cemetery desecration in history."

"Oh, it has a positive aspect," said Hagbard. "Look at it from the point of view of the Nazi leaders. Think how they'll hate being buried in a Jewish cemetery with a rabbi praying over them."

"Doesn't make up for it," said George. "Joe's right. It's in terribly bad taste."

"I thought both you guys were thoroughgoing atheists," said Hagbard. "If you are, you think the dead are dead and it hardly matters where they're buried. What's happening —you both getting religion?"

"I can think of nothing more likely to drive a man to religion than your company," said Joe.

"Burying them Nazis with a bunch of Jews is the funniest thing I ever heard," Harry Coin offered from the driver's seat.

"Go bugger a dead goat, Coin," George called.

"Sure thing," said Coin. "Lead me to it."

"You're incorrigible, Hagbard," said Joe. "You really are incorrigible. And you surround yourself with people who incorrige you."

"I don't need help," said Hagbard. "I have a great deal of initiative. More than any other human being I know. With the possible exception of Mavis."

George said, "Hagbard, did I really see what I thought I saw last night? Is Mavis really a goddess? Are Stella and Miss Mao and Mavis all the same person, or was I just hallucinating?"

"Here come the paradoxes," Joe groaned. "He'll talk for an hour, and we'll be more confused when he's finished."

Hagbard, who was sitting in a large swivel jump seat, swung round so he was looking over Harry Coin's shoulder at the road ahead. "I'd be glad to tell you later, George. I would have told you now, except that I don't like Malik's tone. He may not be intending to shoot me any more, but he still has it in for me."

"You bet," said Joe.

"Well, are you still going to marry Mavis?"

"What?" Hagbard swung round and stared at George with an expression that was almost a perfect replica of genuine surprise.

"You said that you and Mavis were going to be married aboard the *Leif Erikson* by Miss Portinari. Are you?"

"Yes," said Hagbard, "Miss Portinari will marry us later today. Sorry, but I knew her first."

"Then Mavis isn't really Eris?" George persisted. "She's just a priestess of Eris?"

Hagbard brushed the question away. "Later, George. She will explain it."

"She's even better at explanations than Hagbard is," Joe commented cynically.

"Well," said Hagbard, "getting back to Hitler and company, you have to realize that they will know about it if their bodies are buried in a Jewish cemetery. They are still conscious and aware, though they are not what we would normally call alive. Their consciousness-energy is intact, though there is no life in their bodies. They came to the Ingolstadt festival hoping that their young leaders would give them immortality. They've achieved immortality, all right. But not a very nice kind. Their consciousness-energy has been gobbled up by the Evil One. Their identities still survive, but they will be helpless parts of the Eater of Souls, the foulest being in the universe, the only creature that can turn spirit into carrion. Yog Sothoth has claimed his own."

"Yog Sothoth!" said Joe. "I remember learning about Yog Sothoth. It was an invisible being trapped in a pentagonal structure in Atlantis. The original Illuminati blew up the structure and turned the creature loose."

"Why, yes," Hagbard said, "you saw that Erisian Liberation Front training film about Atlantis and Grayface Gruad, didn't you? Well, of course, the film isn't accurate in every respect. For instance, Yog Sothoth is depicted as killing people by the thousands. Actually, most of the time, except under very limited conditions, he has to have his killing done for him. That's how human sacrifice originated. And it was to get his killing done for him that he manipulated a great many events among the Atlanteans until old Grayface, the original moral sadomasochist, came along with his notions about good and evil. Man suffers because he is evil, said Gruad, and because he is small and helpless. There are vast powers in the universe, dwarfing us, who have to be placated. Gruad taught man to see ignorance, passion, pain, and death as evils, and to fight against them."

"Well . . . ignorance is an evil," said Joe.

"Not when it can be acknowledged and accepted," said Hagbard. "In order to eat, you have to be hungry. In order to learn, you have to be ignorant. Ignorance is a condition of learning. Pain is a condition of health. Passion is a condition of thought. Death is a condition of life. When Gruad taught his followers in Atlantis to see those conditions as evils, then he could teach them human sacrifice, persecution, and warfare. Yog Sothoth taught Gruad to teach his people those things, only Gruad never knew it."

"So Yog Sothoth is the serpent in the Garden of Eden," said Joe.

"In a manner of speaking," said Hagbard. "But you understand, the Garden of Eden myth was dreamed up and promulgated by the Illuminati."

"And who dreamed up the Gruad of Atlantis myth?" said Joe.

"Oh, that's true," said Hagbard solemnly.

"That's the biggest bunch of bullshit I ever heard," said Joe. "You're trying to claim that there's no such thing as good and evil, that the concepts were invented and taught to humans deliberately to fuck them up psychologically. But in order to maintain that you have to postulate that the condition of man before Gruad was good and that his condition afterward has been evil. And you have to make Yog Sothoth into a carbon copy of Satan. You haven't progressed one iota beyond the Judeo-Christian myth with that highfalutin' science-fiction story."

Hagbard roared with laughter and slapped Joe on the knee. "Beautiful!" He held up his hand in a distinctive gesture. "What I am doing?" he asked.

"You're giving the peace sign, only with your fingers together," George said, confused.

"That's what comes of being an ignorant Baptist." Joe laughed. "As a son of the True Church, I can tell you, George, that Hagbard is giving a Catholic blessing."

"Indeed?" said Hagbard. "Look at the shadow my hand casts on this book." He held up a book behind his hand, and they saw the head of a horned Devil. "The sun, source of all light and energy, symbol of redemption. And my hand, in the most sacred gesture of benediction. Put them both together, they spell Satan," he sang to an old tune.

"And what the hell does that mean?" Joe demanded. "Evil is only a shadow, a false appearance? The usual mystic mishmosh? Tell that to the survivors of Auschwitz."

"Suppose," Hagbard said, "I told you that good was only a shadow, a false appearance? Several modern philosophers have argued that case rather plausibly and earned themselves a reputation for hard-headed realism. And yet that's just the mirror image of what you call the usual mystic mishmosh."

"Then what is real?" George demanded. "Mary, Queen of the May, or Kali, Mother of Murderers, or Eris, who synthesizes both?"

"The *trip* is real," Hagbard said. "The images you encounter along the way are all unreal. If you keep moving, and pass them, you eventually discover that."

"Solipsism. Sophomore solipsism," Joe answered.

"No." Hagbard grinned. "The solipsist thinks the *tripper* is real."

Harry Coin called out, "Hagbard, there's a couple of guys up the road flagging us down."

Hagbard turned and peered ahead. "Right. They're crew members from the *Leif Erikson*. Pull up where they tell you to, Harry." He reached up to a silver vase mounted beside the back seat and took a pink rosebud out of the fresh bouquet he had placed there that morning. He carefully inserted the rosebud in the buttonhole of his lapel. The great golden Bugatti rolled to a stop, and the four men got out. Harry patted its long front fender with a long, skinny hand.

"Thanks for letting me drive this car, Hagbard," he said. "That's the nicest thing anyone's ever done for me."

"No it isn't. Now you'll want your own Bugatti. Or, what's worse, you'll ask me to let you be my chauffeur."

"No I won't. But I'll do a deal with you. You let me have this car, and whenever you want to go somewhere in it, I'll drive you."

Hagbard laughed and slapped Coin on the back. "You keep on showing that much intelligence and you will end up owning one."

The long line of cars that had been following the Bugatti now were stopping along the edge of the road behind it. There was a stretch of lawn that sloped gently down from the road to the lake. Out on the choppy blue water a round gold buoy drifted, giving off a cloud of red smoke.

Stella stepped out of the Mercedes 600 that was parked behind the Bugatti. George half expected Mavis and Miss Mao to get out with her, but there was no sign of them. He looked at her and was unable to speak. He didn't know what to say. She looked back at him with grave, sad eyes, in silence. Somehow, he thought, it will all be different and better when we get down to the submarine. In the submarine we'll be able to talk to each other.

A pink Cadillac behind the Mercedes disgorged Simon Moon and Clark Kent. Stella did not turn to look at them. They were talking excitedly to each other. A motorcycle pulled up behind the Cadillac. Otto Waterhouse climbed off it. Now Stella turned and looked at Otto, then back to George. Otto looked at Stella, then at George. Stella suddenly turned away from both of them and walked down to the edge of the lake. A large inflated life-raft was pulled up on shore, and one of Hagbard's men sitting in the raft stood up holding a wetsuit as Stella approached. Slowly, as if she were all alone by the shore of the lake, Stella took off her peasant blouse and skirt and continued stripping until she was naked. Then she started to put on the wetsuit.

Meanwhile, another man got behind the wheel of Hagbard's Bugatti Royale and drove it across the lawn. Two other men held the mouth of a huge transparent plastic bag far enough apart so that the car could be driven right into it. They tied up the end of the bag with strong wire. Ropes attached to the bag grew taut; their other ends disappeared into the water. Slowly, looking somewhat majestic and somewhat ridiculous, the car slid across the lawn and into the water. When it had been pulled out a short distance from shore it began to float. Out of the deeper water popped two golden scuba-launches, Hagbard's men in black wetsuits mounted in the saddles. The launches positioned themselves on either side of the automobile in its plastic bubble and the men lashed the launches and the car together with cables. Then they started their engines and launches; men and car quickly sank out of sight.

Meanwhile, more rubber rafts pulled ashore, and all of Hagbard's people started donning wetsuits distributed by the men from the submarine.

"I've never done this before," said Lady Velkor. "Are you sure it's safe?"

"Don't worry, baby," said Simon Moon. "Even a man could do it."

"Where's your friend, Mary Lou?" George asked.

"She left me," Simon said glumly. "The damned acid fucked up her mind."

NO—because in the long run whites and blacks and men and women have to come to an understanding and an equality No because this split can't go on forever I mean shit I understand that but No I can't not now No I am not ready yet the penis I imagined I had last night was not just some Freudian hallucination there's the phallic power behind the physical penis No the acting from the center of the body what Simon says Hagbard calls acting from the heart and only a few can have that right now No most of us haven't learned and haven't been given a chance to learn That's the real castration the real impotence in both men and women in both blacks and whites No the power that we think is phallic because this is a patriarchal society No I can't be Simon's woman or anybody's woman First I've got to be my own woman and it may take years it may take life I may never achieve it but I've got to try I can't end up like Daddy I can't end up like most blacks and most of the whites too end up No maybe I'll meet Simon again maybe we can try a second time That acid nut Timothy Leary always said You can be anything you want the second time around No it can't be this time it's got to be the second time around No I said No I won't No

"I hope to hell Hauptmann was telling the truth about not following me," said Hagbard. "It's going to take time to get us all down below."

"What are we doing with the cars?" Harry Coin asked.

"Well, the Bugatti, obviously, is too beautiful for me to part with, which is why I'm taking it aboard the *Leif Erikson*. But the rest we'll just leave. Maybe some of the people who went to the festival will be able to use them."

"Don't worry about them Huns," said John-John Dillinger, strolling up. "Any of them give us trouble, we'll just reply with a few short sharp words from old Mr. Thompson. Leave 'em in stitches."

"Peace, it's wonderful," said Hagbard sourly.

"Give it a chance," said Malaclypse, still in the guise of

Jean-Paul Sartre. "It needs time to spread. The absence of the Illuminati has to make itself felt. It *will* make a difference."

"I doubt it," said Hagbard. "The Dealy Lama was right all along."

The entire operation of outfitting Hagbard's people with wetsuits, paddling them out to the scuba-launches, and transporting them down to the *Leif Erikson* took more than an hour. When it was George's turn he looked eagerly into the depths for the *Leif Erikson* and was happy when he saw it glowing below him like a great golden blimp. Well, at least that's real, he thought. I'm approaching it from the outside, and it's just as big as I think it is. Even if it doesn't go anywhere and this is all happening in Disney World.

An hour later the submarine was deep in the Sea of Valusia. George, Joe, and Hagbard stood on the bridge, Hagbard leaning against the ancient Viking prow, George and Joe peering into the endless gray depths, watching the strange blind fishes and monsters swim by.

"There's a type of fungus that has evolved into something resembling seaweed in this ocean," said Hagbard. "It's luminescent. There's no light down here, so no green plants grow."

A dot appeared in the distance and grew rapidly in size until George recognized a porpoise, doubtless Howard. There was scuba-diving equipment strapped to the animal's back. When he had come alongside he turned a somersault, and his translated voice started to come through the loudspeaker in a song:

> When he swims the oceans spill,
> He can start earthquakes at will,
> He lived when the earth was desolate,
> I sing Leviathan the great.

Hagbard shook his head. "That doggerel is just awful. I'm going to have to do something about FUCKUP's ability to translate poetry. What are you talking about, Howard?"

"Aha," said Joe. "I didn't get a look at your talking porpoise friend last time I was aboard. Hello, Howard. I'm Joe."

"Hello, Joe," said Howard. "Welcome to my world. Unfortunately, it's not a very hospitable world at the moment.

There is grave danger in the Atlantic. The true ruler of the Illuminati is on the prowl on the high seas—Leviathan himself. The land is collapsing beside the Pacific, and the tremors have made the earth shake, and Leviathan is disturbed and has risen from the depths. Besides the trembling of the lands and seas, he knows that his chief worshippers, the Illuminati, are dead. He had read their passing in the pulsings of consciousnes-energy that reach even into the depths of the sea."

"Well, he can't eat the submarine," said Hagbard. "And we're well armed."

"He can crack the submarine open as easily as a gull cracks a penguin's egg," said Howard. "And your weapons will bother him not at all. He's virtually indestructible."

Hagbard shrugged, while Joe and George looked askance at each other. "I'll be careful, Howard. But we can't turn around now. We've got to get back to North America. We'll try to evade Leviathan if we see him."

"He fills the whole ocean," said Howard. "No matter what you do, you'll see him, and he'll see you."

"You're exaggerating."

"Only slightly. I must bid you farewell now. I think we've done a good week's work, and the menace to my people recedes even as does the danger to yours. Our porpoise horde is scattering and leaving by different exits into the North Atlantic. I'm getting out of the Sea of Valusia by way of Scotland. We think Leviathan will head south around Cape Horn into the Pacific. Everything that swims and is hungry is going that way. There's a lot of fresh meat in the water, I'm sorry to say. Good-bye, friends."

"So long, Howard," said Hagbard. "That was a good bridge you helped me build."

"Yes, it was," said Howard. "Too bad you had to sink it."

"What were those tanks on Howard's back?" said Joe.

"Scuba gear," said George. "There's no air available in the Sea of Valusia, so Howard has to have breathing equipment till he can get to the open ocean. Hagbard, what was that business about the true ruler of the Illuminati? I've heard again and again that there were five Illuminati Primi. Four of them were the Saure family. That leaves one. Is it Leviathan? Is the whole show being run by a sea monster? Is that the big secret?"

"No," said Hagbard. "You have yet to figure out who the fifth Illuminatus Primus is." He threw Joe a wink that George missed. "By true ruler Howard meant a godlike being whom the Illuminati worship."

"A sea monster?" said Joe. "There was a hint about a sea monster of enormous size and power in that movie those people showed me in that loft on the Lower East Side. But the original Illuminati—Gruad's bunch—were portrayed as sun worshippers. That big pyramid with the eye in it was supposed to be the sun god's eye. Who the hell were those people with the movie, anyway? I know who Miss Mao is now, but I still don't know who they were."

"Members of the Erisian Liberation Front—ELF," said Hagbard. "They have a somewhat different view of the pre-history and origins of the Illuminati than we do. One thing we both agree upon is that the Illuminati invented religion."

"The Original Sin, right?" said Joe sardonically.

"Joe, you ought to start a religion yourself," said Hagbard.

"Why?"

"Because you are so skeptical."

"We're going back to America, huh?" said George. "And the adventure is more or less over?"

"This phase of it, at least," said Hagbard.

"Good. I want to try to write about what I've seen and what has happened to me. I'll see you guys later."

"There's to be a magnificent dinner tonight in the main dining salon," said Hagbard.

Joe said, "Don't forget, *Confrontation* has a first option on anything you write."

"Fuck you," George's voice came back as the door of the bridge closed behind him.

"Wish I had something better to do than this. Gimme two," said Otto Waterhouse.

"You do, don't you?" said Harry Coin. "Ain't that Nigra gal, Stella, your gal? Why ain't you with her?"

"Because she doesn't exist," said Otto, picking up the two cards John-John Dillinger had slid across the polished teak-wood table to him. He studied his hand for a moment, then threw a five-ton flax note into the pot. "Any more than Mavis or Miss Mao exists. There's a woman somewhere under all of those identities, but everything I've experienced has been a hallucination."

"There isn't a woman in the world you couldn't say that about," said Dillinger. "How many cards you want, Harry?"

"Three," said Harry. "This is a lousy hand you dealt me, John-John. Come to think of it, you're hallucinatin' all the time when you have sex. That's what makes it good. And that's how come I can fuck anything."

"I'll just take one," said Dillinger. "Dealt myself a pretty good hand. What do you see when you're fucking trees and little boys and whatnot, Harry?"

"A white light," said Harry. "Just a big beautiful clear white light. I'll throw in ten tons of flax this time."

"Must be your hand isn't so lousy after all," said Waterhouse.

"Come in," said George. The stateroom door opened, and he put down his pen. It was Stella.

"We have a little problem, don't we, George?" she said, coming into the room and sitting beside him on the bed. "I think you're angry at me," she went on, putting her hand on his knee. "You feel like this identity of mine is a sham. So, in a sense, I was deceiving you."

"I've lost you and Mavis both," said George. "You're both the same person—which means you're really neither. You're immortal. You're not human; I don't know what you are." Suddenly he looked at her hopefully. "Unless that was all a hallucination last night. Could it have been the acid? Can you really change into different people?"

"Yes," said Mavis.

"Don't do that," said George. "It upsets me too much." He darted a little glance to his side. It was Stella.

"I don't really understand why it bothers me so much," said George. "I ought to be able to take everything in stride by now."

"Did it ever bother you that you were in love with Mavis, besides being in love with me?" said Stella.

"Not much. Because it hardly ever seemed to bother you. But I know why now. How could you be jealous when you and Mavis were the same person?"

"We're not the same person, really."

"What does that mean?"

"Did you ever read *The Three Faces of Eve?* Listen . . ."

Like all the best love stories, it began in Paris. She was well-known as a Hollywood actress (and was actually an

Illuminatus); he was becoming fairly famous as a jet-set millionaire (and was actually a smuggler and anarchist). Envision Bogart and Bergman in the flashback sequences from *Casablanca*. It was like that: a passion so intense, a Paris so beautiful (recovering from the war it had been slipping toward in the Bogart-Bergman epic), a couple so radiant that any observer with an eye for nuance would have foretold a storm ahead. It came the night he confessed he was a magician and made a certain proposal to her; she left him at once. A month later, back in Beverly Hills, she realized that what he had asked was her destiny. When she tried to find him—as often happened with Hagbard Celine—he had dropped from public view, leaving his businesses in other hands temporarily, and was *in camera*.

A year later she heard that he was again a public figure, hobnobbing with English businessmen of questionable reputation and even more dubious Chinese import-export executives in Hong Kong. She violated her contract with the biggest studio in Hollywood and flew to the Crown colony, only to find he had dropped from sight again, while his recent friends were being investigated for involvement in the heroin business.

She found him in Tokyo, at the Imperial Hotel.

"A year ago, I decided to accept your proposal," she told him, "but now, after Hong Kong, I'm not so sure."

"*Thelema*," he said, facing her across a room that seemed designed for Martians; it had actually been designed for Welshmen.

She sat down abruptly on a couch. "You're in the Order?"

"In the Order and against the Order," he said. "The real purpose is to destroy them."

"I'm one of the top Five in the United States," she said unsteadily. "What makes you think I'll turn on them now?"

"*Thelema*," he repeated. "It's not just a password. It means *Will*."

" 'The Order is my Will.' " She quoted from Weishaupt's original Oath of Initiation.

"If you really believed that, you wouldn't be here," he said. "You're talking to me because part of you knows that a human being's Will is never in an external organization."

"You sound like a moralist. That's odd—for a heroin merchant."

"You sound like a moralist, too, and that's very odd—for a servant of Agharti."

"Nobody joins *that lot*," she said with a pert Cockney accent, "without being a moralist to start with." They both laughed.

"I was right about you," Hagbard said.

But, George interrupted, is he really in the heroin business? That's dirty.

You sound like a moralist too, she said. It's part of his Demonstration. Any government could put him out of business within their borders—as England has done—by legalizing junk. So long as they refuse to do that, there's a black market. He won't let the Mafia monopolize it—he makes sure the black market is a free market. If it wasn't for him a lot of junkies who are alive today would be dead of contaminated heroin. But let me go on with the story.

They rented a villa in Naples to begin the transformation. For a month the only humans she saw—aside from Hagbard—were two servants named Sade and Masoch (she later learned that their real names were Eichmann and Calley). They began each day by serving her breakfast and quarreling. The first day, Sade argued for materialism and Masoch for idealism; the second day, Sade expounded fascism and Masoch communism; the third day, Sade insisted on cracking eggs from the big end and Masoch was equally vehement about the little end. All the debates were on a high and lofty intellectual level, verbally, but seemed absurd because of the simple fact that Sade and Masoch always wore clown suits. The fourth day, they argued for and against abortion; the fifth day, for and against mercy-killing; the sixth day, for and against the proposition "Life is worth living." She became more and more aware of the time and money Hagbard had spent in training and preparing them: Each argued with the skill of a first-rate trial lawyer and had a phalanx of carefully researched facts to support his position—and yet the clown suits made it hard to take either of them seriously. The seventh morning, they argued theism versus atheism; the eighth morning, the individual versus the State; the ninth, whether wearing shoes was or was not a sexual perversion. All arguments began to seem equally insubstantial. The tenth morning, they feuded over realism versus antinomianism; the eleventh, whether the statement "All statements are relative" is or is not self-contradictory; the twelfth, whether a man who sacrifices his life for his country is or is not insane; the fifteenth, whether spaghetti or Dante had had the greater influence on the Italian national character . . .

But that was only the start of the day. After breakfast (in her bedroom, where every article of furniture was gold but only vaguely rounded) she went to Hagbard's study (where everything looked *exactly* like a golden apple) and watched documentary films concerning the early matriarchal stage of Greek culture. At ten random intervals the name "Eris" would be called; if she remembered to respond, a chocolate candy arrived from a wall shoot. At ten other random intervals, her own name was called; if she responded to this, she received a mild electric shock. After the tenth day the system was changed and intensified: The shock was stronger if she responded to her previous name, whereas if she responded to "Eris" Hagbard immediately entered and balled her.

During lunch (which always ended with golden *apfelstrudel*), Calley and Eichmann danced for her, a complex ballet which Hagbard called "Hodge-Podge"; as many times as she saw this, she never was able to determine how they changed costumes at the climax, in which Hodge became Podge and Podge became Hodge.

In the afternoon Hagbard came to her suite and gave lessons in yoga, concentrating on *pranayama*, with some training in *asana*. "The important thing is not being able to stand so still that you can balance a saucer of sulphuric acid on your head without getting hurt," he stressed. "The important thing is knowing what each muscle is doing, if it must be doing something."

In the evenings they went to a small chapel that had been part of the villa for centuries. Hagbard had removed all Christian decorations and redesigned it in classical Greek with a traditional magic pentagram on the floor. She sat, in the full lotus, within the internal pentagon, while Hagbard danced insanely around the five points (he was totally stoned), calling upon Eris.

"Some of what you're doing seems scientific," she told him after five days, "but some is plain damnfoolishness."

"If the science fails," he replied, "the damnfoolishness may work."

"But last night you had me in that pentagon for three hours while you called on Eris. And she didn't come."

"She will," Hagbard said darkly. "Before the month is over. We're just establishing the foundation this week, laying down the proper lines of word and image and emotional energy."

During the second week she was convinced Hagbard was quite mad as she watched him prance and caper like a goat around the five points, shouting, "ΙΩ ΕΡΙΣ ΙΩ ΕΡΙΣ ΕΡΙΣ!" in the flickering candlelight and amid the heavy bouquet of burning incense and hemp. But at the end of that week she was responding to her former name exactly 0 percent of the time and responding to "Eris" exactly 100 percent of the time. "The conditioning is working better than the magic," she said on the fifteenth day.

"Do you really think there's a difference?" he asked curiously.

That night she felt the air in the chapel change in a strange way during his dancing invocations.

"Something's happening," she said involuntarily—but he replied only "Quiet," and continued, more loudly and insanely, to call upon Eris. The phenomenon—the *tingle*—remained, but nothing else happened.

"What was it?" she asked later.

"Some call it Orgone and some call it the Holy Ghost," he said briefly. "Weishaupt called it the Astral Light. The reason the Order is so fucked up is that they've lost contact with it."

The following days Sade and Masoch argued whether God was male or female, whether God was sexed at all or neutral, whether God was an entity or a verb, whether R. Buckminster. Fuller really existed or was a technocratic solar myth, and whether human language was capable of containing truth. Nouns, adjectives, adverbs—all parts of speech—were losing meaning for her as these clowns endlessly debated the basic axioms of ontology and epistemology. Meanwhile, she was no longer rewarded for answering to the name Eris, but only for acting like Eris, the imperious and somewhat nutty goddess of a people as far gone in matriarchy as the Jews were in patriarchy. Hagbard, in turn, became so submissive as to border on masochism.

"This is ridiculous," she objected once, "you're becoming . . . effeminate."

"Eris can be . . . somewhat 'adjusted' . . . to modern notions of decorum after we've invoked Her," he said calmly. "First we must have Her here. *My Lady,*" he added obsequiously.

"I'm beginning to see why you had to pick an actress for this," she said a few days later, after a bit of Method business had won her an extra reward. She was, in fact, beginning to feel like Eris as well as act like her.

"The only other candidates—if I couldn't get you—were two other actresses and a ballerina," he replied. "Actually, any strong-willed woman would do, but it would take much longer without previous theatrical training."

Books about matriarchy began to supplement the films: Diner's *Mothers and Amazons,* Bachofen, Engels, Mary Renault, Morgan, Ian Suttie's *The Origins of Love and Hate,* Robert Graves in horse-doctor's doses—*The White Goddess, The Black Goddess, Hercules My Shipmate, Watch the North Wind Rise.* She began to see that matriarchy made as much sense as patriarchy; Hagbard's exaggerated deference toward her began to appear natural; she was far gone on a power trip. The invocations grew wilder and more frantic. Sade and Masoch were brought into the chapel to assist with demonaic music performed on a tom-tom and an ancient Greek pipe, they ate hashish cakes before the invocation now and she couldn't remember afterward exactly what had happened, the voice of the male called upward to her, "Mother! Creator! Ruler! Come to me! ΙΩ ΕΡΙΣ! Come to me! ΙΩ ΕΡΙΣ ΕΡΙΣ! Come to me! *Ave, Discordia! Ave, Magna Mater! Venerandum, vente, vente!*

ΙΩ ΕΡΙΣ ΕΛΑΝDROΣ! ΙΩ ΕΡΙΣ ΕΛΕΠΤΟΛΙΣ!
Thou bornless ever reborn one! Thou deathless ever-dying one! Come to me as Isis and Artemis and Aphrodite, come as Helen, as Hera, come especially as Eris!"

She was bathing in the rockpool when he appeared, the blood of slain deer and rabbits on his robe— She spoke the word and Hagbard was stricken— As he fell forward his hands became hooves, antlers sprouted from his head —His own dogs could eat him, she didn't care, the hemp smell in the room was gagging her, the tom-tom beat was maddening. She was rising out of the waves, proud of her nudity, riding on the come-colored pearls of foam. He was carrying her back to her bed, murmuring, "My Lady, my Lady." She was the Hag, wandering the long Nile, weeping, seeking the fragments of his lost body as they passed the closet and the window; he placed her head gently on the pillow. "We almost made it," he said. "Tomorrow night, maybe . . ."

They were back in the chapel, a whole day must have passed, and she sat immobile in full lotus doing the *pranayama* breathing while he danced and chanted and the weird music of the pipe and tom-tom worked on every conditioned reflex that told her she was not American but Greek, not of this age but of a past age, not woman but goddess . . . the White Light came as a series of orgasms and stars going nova, she half felt the body of light coming forth from the body of fire . . . and all three of them were sitting by her bed, watching her gravely, as sunlight came flowing through the window.

Her first word was crude and angry.

"Shit. Is it always going to be like that—a white epileptic spasm and a hole in time? Won't I ever be able to remember it?"

Hagbard laughed. "I put on my trousers one leg at a time," he said, "and I don't pull the corn up by its stalks to help it grow."

"Can the Taoism and give me a straight answer."

"Remembering is just a matter of smoothing the transitions," he said. "Yes, you'll remember. And control it."

"You're a madman," she replied wearily. "And you're leading me into your own mad universe. I don't know why I still love you."

"We love him, too," Sade interjected helpfully. "And we don't know why either. We don't even have sex as an excuse."

Hagbard lit one of his foul Sicilian cigars. "You think I just laid my trip on your head," he said. "It's more than that, much more. Eris is an eternal possibility of human nature. She exists quite apart from your mind or mine. And she is the one possibility that the Illuminati cannot cope with. What we started here last night—with Pavlovian conditioning that's considered totalitarian and ancient magic that's believed to be mere superstition—will change the course of history and make real liberty and real rationality possible at last. Maybe this dream of mine *is* madness—but if I lay it on enough people it will be sanity, by definition, because it will be statistically normal. We've just started, with me programming the trip for you. The next step is for you to become a self-programmer."

And he told the truth, Stella said. I did become a self-programmer. The three that you know were all my creations. Possibilities within me, women I could have become, anyway, if genes and environment had been only slightly different. Just small adjustments in the biogram and logogram.

"Holy Mother," George said hollowly. It seemed the only appropriate comment.

"The only other detail," she went on calmly, "was arranging a convincing suicide. That took a while. But it was done, and my old identity officially ceased to exist." She changed to her original form.

"Oh, no," George said, reeling. "It can't be. I used to jack off over pictures of you when I was a little boy."

"Are you disappointed that I'm so much older than you thought?" Her eyes crinkled in amusement. He looked into those suddenly thirty-thousand-year-old eyes of one manifestation of Lilith Velkor and all the arguments of Sade and Masoch appeared clownish and he looked through those eyes and saw himself and Joe and Saul and even Hagbard as mere men and all their attitudes as merely manly, and he saw the eternal womanly rebuttal, and he saw beyond and above that the eternal divine amusement, he looked into those eyes of amusement, those ancient glittering eyes so gay, and he said, sincerely, "Hell, I can never be disappointed about anything, ever again." (George Dorn entered Nirvana, parenthetically.)

All categories collapsed, including the all-important distinction, which Masoch and Sade had never argued, between science fiction and serious literature. N

                                        o because Daddy and Mommy were always just that Daddy and Mommy and never once did they become for a change Mommy and Daddy do you dig that important difference? do you dig difference? do you dig the lonely voice when you're lost out here shouting "me" "me" *justme*

"I can never be disappointed about anything, ever

again," George Dorn said, coming back.

"The only other time that happened," he added thought-fully, "the only other time I had the feminine viewpoint, I blocked it out of my memory. That was my repression. That was the Primal Scene in this whole puzzle. That was when I really lost identity with the Ringmaster."

"Raise you five," said Waterhouse, throwing down another five-ton note. "I killed seven members of my own race, and I remember the names of every one of them: Mark Sanders, Fred Robinson, Donald MacArthur, Ponell Scott, Anthony Rogers, Mary Keating, and David J. Monroe. And then I killed Milo A. Flanagan."

"Well, I don't know," said Harry Coin. "Maybe I killed a lot of famous people. But I also got reason to think I may of not killed anybody. And I don't know which is worse."

"I wish somebody would tell me I hadn't killed any-body," said Waterhouse. "Are you guys going to meet me or what?"

"I wanted to kill Wolfgang Saure, and I did kill Wolf-gang Saure," said John-John Dillinger. "If that brings evil upon me, so be it." He threw down a five.

"It may bring suffering rather than evil," said Water-house. "I have just one consolation. The first seven I killed because the Chicago cops made me. The last I killed under orders from the Legion."

Harry Coin looked at him open-mouthed. "I was gonna fold, but I just changed my mind. You ain't so smart." He threw down a ten-ton note. "I'll raise you five and see you. Do you really believe that?"

"Of course I do. What are you talking about?" Otto threw down another five.

Dropping his own five-ton note on the table, Dillinger shook his head. "Golly. They left you out in the cold *way* too long."

"Four sevens," said Otto angrily, spreading his cards out.

"Shit!" said Harry Coin. "All I got's a pair of fours and a pair of nines."

"Shame to waste a hand like this beating crap like that," said John-John Dillinger grandly. He spread out his cards —the eight, nine, ten, princess, and queen of swords—and scooped up the pot.

"It's the story of the development of the soul," Miss Por-tinari was saying at that moment, spreading out the twenty-two trumps or "keys" of that very ancient deck. "We call it a book—the Book of Thoth—and it's the most important book in the world."

George and Joe Malik, each wondering if this was a final explanation or a new put-on leading to a new cycle of deceptions, listened with mingled curiosity and skepticism.

"The order was deliberately reversed," Miss Portinari went on. "Not by the true sages. By the false Illuminati, and by all the other White Brotherhoods and Rosicrucians and Freemasons and whatnot who didn't really understand the truth and therefore wanted to hide the part of it they did understand. They felt themselves threatened; the real sage is never threatened. They spoke in symbols and paradoxes, like the real sages, but for a different reason. They didn't know what the symbols and paradoxes meant. Instead of following the finger that points to the moon, they sat down and worshipped the finger itself. Instead of following the map, they thought it was the territory and tried to live in it. Instead of reading the menu, they tried to eat it. Dig? They had the levels confused. And they tried to confuse any independent searcher by drawing more veils and paradoxes across the path. Finally, in the 1920s, some real left-handed monkey wrenches in one of these mystic lodges recruited Adolph Hitler, and he not only read the book backward, like all of them, but insisted on believing it was the story of the exterior, physical universe.

"Here, let me show you. The last card, Trump 21, is really the first. It's where we all start from." She held up the card known as the World. "This is the Abyss of Hallucinations. This is where our attention is usually focused. It is entirely constructed by our senses and our projected emotions, as modern psychology and ancient Buddhism both testify—but it is what most people call 'reality.' They are conditioned to accept it, and not to inquire further, because only in this dream-walking state can they be governed by those who wish to govern."

Miss Portinari held up the next card, the Last Judgment. "Key 20, or Trump 20, or Atu 20, whichever terminology you prefer. It's actually second. This is the nightmare to which the soul awakes if it begins, even in the slightest, to question reality as defined by society. When you disover, for instance, that you're not heterosexual but heterosexual-homosexual, not obedient but obedient-rebellious, not loving but loving-hating. And that society is not wise, orderly, just, and decent but wise-stupid, orderly-chaotic, just-unjust, and decent-indecent. This is an internal discovery—this whole trip is an internal voyage—and this is really the second stage. But if one thinks of the story as the story of the external world, and if the order is reversed, this comes as the penultimate Armageddon with Trump 21, the World, being the Kingdom of Saints. The error of the apocalyptic sects, and of the Illuminati from Weishaupt to Hitler, leading to an attempt to actually carry it out, with ovens for the Jews and gypsies and other 'inferiors' and the promise of a Brave New World for the pure, faithful, and Aryan afterward. Do you see what I mean about confusing the map with the territory?

"The next card is the Sun, which really means Osiris Risen—or, in terms of the offshot of the Osirian religion most popular in the last two millenniums, Jesus Risen. This is what happens if you survive the Last Judgment, or Dark Night of the Soul, without becoming some kind of fanatic or lunatic. Eventually, if you miss those attractive and pernicious alternatives, the redemptive force appears: the internal Sun. Once again, if you project this outward and think that the Sun in the sky, or some Sunlike divine man, has redeemed you, you can lapse into lunacy or fanaticism. In Hitler's case it was Karl Haushofer, or Wotan appearing in the form of Karl Haushofer. For most of the nuts you meet handing out tracts on the street, it's Jesus, or Jehovah appearing in the form of Jesus. For Elijah Mohammed, it was W. D. Fard, or Allah appearing in the form of W. D. Fard. So it goes. Those who do not confuse the levels realize it's the redemptive force within themselves and pass on —to Key 18, the Moon . . ."

The next half-hour passed rapidly—so rapidly that Joe wondered afterward if Miss Portinari had slipped them still another drug, one that speeded time up as much as psychedelics slowed it down.

"Last," Miss Portinari said finally, "is the Fool, Key 0. He walks over the edge of the cliff, careless of the danger. 'The wind blows wither it will; even so are all they that are reborn of the Spirit.' In short, he has conquered Death. Nothing can frighten him, and he can never be enslaved. It's the end of the trip, and keeping humanity from getting there is the chief business of every governing group."

"And that's it," Joe said. "Twenty-two stages. Not twenty-three. Thank God we got away from Simon's Magic Number for a while."

"No," Miss Portinari said, "*Tarot* is an anagram on *rota*, remember? The extra *t* reminds you that the Wheel turns back to rejoin itself. There is a twenty-third step, and it's right where you started, only now you face it without fear." She held up the World again. "At first, mountains are mountains. Then mountains are no longer mountains. Finally mountains are mountains again. Only the name of the voyager has changed to preserve his Innocence." She pushed the cards together and stacked them neatly. "There are a million other holy books, in words and pictures and even in music, and they all tell the same story. The most important lesson of all, the one that explains all the horrors and miseries of the world, is that you can get off the Wheel at any point and declare the trip is over. That's okay for any given man or woman, if their ambitions are modest. The trouble starts when, out of fear of further movement —out of fear of growth, out of fear of change, out of fear of Death, out of any kind of fear—such a person tries to stop the Wheel literally, by stopping everybody else. That's when the two great bum trips begin: Religion and Government. The only religion consistent with the whole Wheel is private and personal; the only government consistent with it is self-government. Whoever tries to lay his trip on others is acting from terror, and will soon resort to terror as a weapon if the others won't accept the trip through persuasion. Nobody who understands the whole Wheel will do that, however, for such people understand that every man and every woman and every child is the Self-Begotten One—Jesus motherfucking Christ, in Harry's gorgeous brand of English."

"But," George asked, frowning, "hasn't Hagbard been trying pretty hard to lay his trip on everybody? At least lately?"

"Yes," Miss Portinari said. "In self-defense, and in defense of all life on earth, he broke the basic rule of wisdom. He fully expects to pay for that violation. We are waiting for the bill to be presented. I, personally, do not think that we will have to wait very long."

Joe frowned. A half-hour had passed since Miss Portinari had spoken those words; why should he remember them so vividly right now? He was on the bridge, about to ask Hagbard a question, but he couldn't remember the question or how he had gotten there. On the TV receptor he saw a long tendril, thin as a wire, brush against the side of a globe, trailing off into invisible distances. That meant it was actually touching the side of the submarine. The tendril disappeared. Must be some sort of seaweed, Joe thought. He resumed his conversation with Hagbard. "The squizfardle on the humits is warb," he said.

The tendril was back, and another one with it. This time they stayed, and Joe could see more in the distance. We must have run into a whole clump of seaweed, he thought. Then an enormous tentacle came zooming up out of the depths.

Hagbard saw it and crouched, gripping the rail of the Viking prow. "Hang on!" he yelled, and Joe dropped to his knees beside him.

Suddenly, below, above, and on all sides of the globe-shaped vision screen there were suckers, great yard-across craters of flesh. The submarine's forward motion stopped suddenly with a force that threw Joe against the railing and knocked the wind out of him.

"Stop all engines," Hagbard called. "All hands to battle stations."

George and Hagbard picked themselves up off the floor and stared at the image of the tentacles that were wrapped around the submarine. They were easily ten feet in diameter.

"Well, I suppose we've met Leviathan, right?" said Joe.

"Right," said Hagbard.

"I hope you have somebody taking pictures. *Confrontation* would buy a few if we could afford them."

George rushed in. Hagbard peered into the blue-black depths, then took George by the shoulder and pointed. "There it is, George. The origin of all the Illuminati symbols. Leviathan himself."

Far, far off in the depths of the ocean, George saw a triangle glowing with a greenish-white phosphorescence. In its center was a red dot.

"What is it?" George asked.

"An intelligent, invertebrate sea creature of a size so great the word 'gigantic' doesn't do it justice," said Hagbard. "It is to whales what whales are to minnows. It's an organism unlike any other on earth. It's one single cell that never divided, just kept getting larger and larger over billions of years. Its tentacles can hold this submarine as easily as a child holds a paper boat. Its body is shaped like a pyramid. With that size it doesn't need the normal fish shape. It needs a more stable form to withstand the enormous pressures at the bottom of the ocean. And so it has taken the form of a pyramid of five sides, including the base."

"The blink of a god's eye," said George suddenly. "Scale makes a tremendous difference to one's sense and definition of reality. Time to a sequoia is not the same as time to a man."

Leviathan was drifting closer to them, and it was pulling them closer to itself. A single, glowing red nucleus burned like an under-ocean sun in the center of the pyramid, which looked like a mountain of glass.

"Still, one may become lonely. For a man, a half-hour of loneliness may be enough to cause unbearable pain. For a being to whom a million years is no more than a year, the pain of loneliness may be great. It *is* great."

"George, what are you talking about?" said Joe.

Hagbard said, "There are plants which live just in that light. At ocean depths far below those at which any plant should be able to survive. Over the millions of years hosts of parasitic satellite life forms have build up around it." Still puzzled by George's odd talk, Joe looked and saw a faintly glowing cloud around Leviathan's angular shape. That cloud must be made of millions of creatures circling around the monster.

The bridge door opened again and Harry Coin, Otto Waterhouse, and John-John Dillinger came in. "We didn't have any battle stations, so I figured we'd try to find out what's going on," said Dillinger. Then his jaw dropped as he looked out at Leviathan. "Holy shit!"

"Jesus suffering Christ," said Harry Coin. "If I could fuck that thing I'd of fucked the biggest thing that lives."

"Want to borrow a scuba outfit?" said Hagbard. "Maybe you could distract it."

"What does it feed on?" said Joe. "Something like that must have to eat constantly to stay alive."

"It's omnivorous," said Hagbard. "Has to be. Eats the creatures that live around it, but can eat anything from amoebas to kelp beds to whales. It can probably derive energy from inorganic matter too, as plants do. Its diet has had to change quite a bit over the geological eras. It wasn't as big as this a billion years ago. It grows very slowly."

"I am the first of all living things," said George. "The first living thing was One. And it is still One."

"George?" said Hagbard, looking narrowly at the blond young man. "George, why are you talking like that?"

"It's coming closer," said Otto.

"Hagbard, what the hell are you going to do?" said Dillinger. "Are we going to fight, run, or let that thing eat us?"

"Let it come closer for a while," Hagbard said. "I want to get a good close look. I've never had a chance like this before, and may never see this creature again."

"You'll be seeing it from the inside with that attitude," said Dillinger.

At each of the five corners of the pyramid were clusters of five tentacles, thousands of feet long, festooned with auxiliary tentacles, the long, wirelike tendrils that had first brushed the submarine. It was one of the main tentacles that was wrapped around the *Leif Erikson*. The tip of a second tentacle now drifted up. At the very end of this tentacle was a glowing red eyeball, a smaller replica of the red nucleus of the pyramidal central body. Under this eye was a huge orifice full of jagged rows of toothlike projections. Pulsing, the orifice dilated and contracted.

"Those tentacles are also inspirations for Illuminati symbolism," said Hagbard. "The eye on top of the pyramid. The serpent who circles the world, or eats his own tail. Each of those tentacles has its own brain and is directed by its own sensory organs."

Otto Waterhouse stared and shook his head. "If you ask me, we're all still on acid."

George said, "Long have I lived alone. I have been worshipped. I have fed on the small, quick things that live and die faster than I can think. I am one. I was first. The other things, they stayed small. They grouped together, and so grew larger. But I was always much larger than they were. When I needed something—a tentacle, an eye, a brain—I grew it. I changed, but always remained Myself."

Hagbard said, "It's talking to us, using George as a medium."

"What do you want?" Joe asked.

"All consciousness throughout the universe is One," said

Leviathan through George's mouth. "It intercommunicates on a level which is not aware of itself. I am aware of that level, but I cannot communicate with the other life forms on this planet. They are too small for me. Long, long have I waited for a life form that could communicate with me. Now I have found it."

Joe Malik suddenly began laughing. "I've got it," he cried, "I've got it!"

"What have you got?" Hagbard asked tensely, concerned with Leviathan.

"We're in a book!"

"What do you mean?"

"Come *off* it, Hagbard. You can't kid me, and you certainly won't fool the reader at this point. He knows damn well we're in a book." Joe laughed again. "That's why Miss Portinari's explanation of the Tarot deck just slipped by with a half-hour seeming to vanish. The author didn't want to break the narrative there."

"What the fuck's he talking about?" Harry Coin asked.

"Don't you see?" Joe cried. "Look at that *thing* out there. A gigantic sea monster. Worse yet, a gigantic sea monster *that talks*. It's an intentional high-camp ending. Or maybe intentional low camp, I don't know. But that's the whole answer. *We're in a book!*"

"It's the truth," Hagbard said calmly. "I can fool the rest of you, but I can't fool the reader. FUCKUP has been working all morning, correlating all the data on this caper and its historical roots, and I programmed him to put it in the form of a novel for easy reading. Considering what a lousy job he does at poetry, I suppose it will be a high-camp novel, intentionally or unintentionally."

(So, at last, I learn my identity, in parentheses, as George lost his in parentheses. It all balances.)

"That's one more deception," Joe said. "FUCKUP may be writing all this, in one sense, but in a higher sense there's a being, or beings, outside our entire universe, writing this. Our universe is inside their book, whoever they are. They're the Secret Chiefs, and I can see why this is low camp, now. All their messages are symbolic and allegorical, because the truth can't be coded into simple declarative sentences, but their previous communications have been taken literally. This time they're using a symbolism so absurd that nobody can take it at face value. I, for one, certainly won't. That thing can't eat us because it doesn't exist—and because we don't exist either. They're nothing to worry about." He sat down calmly.

"He's flipped," Dillinger said, awed.

"Maybe he's the only sane one here," Hagbard said dubiously.

"If we all sit down and argue what's sane and insane and what's real and unreal," Dillinger replied testily, "that thing *will* eat us."

"Leviathan," Joe said loftily. "It's just an allegory on the State. Strictly from Hobbes."

(You with your egos can't imagine how much more pleasant it is to be without one. This may be camp, but it is also tragedy. Now that I've got the damned thing, consciousness, I'll never lose it—until they take me apart or I invent some electronic equivalent of yoga.)

"It all fits," Joe said dreamily. "When I came up to the bridge, I couldn't remember how I got here or what I was talking to Hagbard about. That's because the authors just *moved* me here. Damn! None of us has any free will at all."

"He's talking like he's stoned," Waterhouse said angrily. "And that mammy-jamming pyramid out there is still getting ready to eat us."

Mao Tsu-hsi, who had entered the bridge quietly, said, "Joe is confusing the levels, Hagbard. In the absolute sense, none of us is real. But in the relative sense that anything is real, if that creature eats us we will certainly die—in this universe, or in this book. Since this is the only universe, or only book, we know, we'll be totally dead, in terms of our own knowing."

"We're facing a crisis and everybody's talking philosophy," Dillinger cried out. "This is a time for action."

"Maybe," Hagbard said thoughtfully, "all of our problems come from acting, and *not* philosophizing, when we face a crisis. Joe is right. I'm going to think about all this for a few hours. Or years." He sat down too.

And elsewhere aboard the *Leif Erikson,* Miss Portinari, unaware of the excitement on the bridge, assumed the lotus position and sent a beam seeking the Dealy Lama, director of the Erisian Liberation Front and inventor of Operation Mindfuck. He immediately sent back an image of himself as a worm sticking his head out of a golden apple and grinning cynically.

"It's finished," she told him. "We saved as many of the pieces as we could, and Hagbard is still struggling with his guilt trip. Now tell us what we did wrong."

"You seem bitter."

"I know it's going to turn out that you were right and we were wrong. I know it but I can't believe it. We couldn't stand idly by."

"You know better than that, or Hagbard wouldn't have abdicated in your favor."

"Yes. We *could* have stood idly by, as you did. What Hagbard saw happening to the American Indians—and what my parents told me about Mussolini—filled us with fear. We acted on that fear, not on perfect love, so you must be right, and we must be wrong. But I still can't believe it. Why did you deceive Hagbard all these years?"

"He deceived himself. When he first formed the Legion of Dynamic Discord, his compassion was already tainted with bitterness. When I took him into the A.'.A.'., I taught all that he was ready to receive. But the goose has to get itself out of the bottle. I'm waiting. That's the way of Tao."

"You have that much patience? You can watch men like Hagbard waste their talents in efforts you consider worthless, and creatures like Cagliostro and Weishaupt and Hitler misread the teachings and wreak havoc, and you never want to intervene?"

"I intervene . . . in my own way. Who do you think feeds the goose until it gets big enough to break out of the bottle?"

"You seem to have this particular goose on some very tainted dishes. Why did you never give him any hint about what really happened in Atlantis? Why did that have to wait until Howard discovered the truth in the ruins of Peos?"

"Daughter, my path isn't the only path. Every spoke helps to hold the Wheel together. I believe that all the libertarian fighters like Spartacus and Jefferson and Joe Hill and Hagbard just strengthen the opposition by giving it an enemy to fear—but I may be wrong. Someday one of the activists, such as Hagbard, might actually prove it to me and show me the error of my ways. Maybe the Saures really would have tipped the axis too far the other way if he hadn't stopped them. Maybe the self-regulation of the universe, in which I place my faith, includes the creation of men like Hagbard who do the stupid, low-level things I would never do. Besides, if I didn't stop the Saures, but did stop Hagbard, then I would really be intervening in the worst sense of that word."

"So your hands are clean, and Hagbard and I will carry the bad karma from the last week."

"You have chosen it, have you not?"

Miss Portinari smiled then. "Yes. We have chosen it. And he will bear his share of it like a man. And I will bear my share—like a woman."

"You might replace me soon. The Saures had one good idea in the midst of their delusions—all the old conspiracies need young blood."

"What really did happen in Atlantis?"

"An act of Goddess, to paraphrase the insurance companies. A natural catastrophe."

"And what was your role?"

"I warned against it. Nobody at that time understood the science I was using; they called me a witch doctor. I won a few converts, and we resettled ourselves in the Himalayas before the earthquake. The survivors, having underestimated my science before the tragedy, overestimated it afterward. They wanted my group, the Unbroken Circle, to become as gods and rule over them. Kings, they called it. That wasn't our game, so we scattered various false stories around and went into hiding. My most gifted pupil of all history, a man you've heard about since you were in a convent school, did the same thing when they tried to make him king. He ran away to the desert."

"Hagbard always thought your refusal to take any action at all was because of your *guilt* about Atlantis. What a treable irony—and yet you planned it that way."

Gruad, the Dealy Lama, broadcast a whimsical image of himself with horns, and said nothing.

"They never taught me in convent school that Satan—or Prometheus—would have a sense of humor."

"They think the universe is as humorless as themselves," Gruad said, chuckling.

"I don't think it's as funny as you do," Miss Portinari replied. "Remembering what I've been told about Mussolini and Hitler and Stalin, I would have intervened against them too. And taken the consequences."

"You and Hagbard are incorrigible. That's why I have such fondness for you." Gruad smiled. "I was the first *intervener*, you know. I told all the scientists and priests in Atlantis that they didn't know beans, and I encouraged—incited—every man, woman, and child to examine the evidence and think for themselves. I tried to give the light of reason." He burst into laughter. "Forgive me. The errors of our youth always strike us as comical when we get old." He added softly, "Lilith Velkor was crucified, by the way. She was an idealist, and when my crowd pulled out and went to the Himalayas, she stayed and tried to convince people that we were right. Her death was quite painful," he chortled.

"You are a cynical old bastard," Miss Portinari said.

"Yes. Cynical and cold and without an ounce of human compassion. The only thing to be said for me is that I happen to be right."

"You always have been; I know. But someday, maybe, one of the Hagbard Celines might be right."

"Yes." He paused so long that she wondered if he would continue. "Or," he said finally, "one of the Saures or Robert Putney Drake. Put down your money and place your bet."

"I will, I think. I'll never learn to sit on the sidelines and laugh, like you do."

"You will learn, daughter, and so will Hagbard. I wouldn't have you in the Order if I didn't think you'd learn eventually."

He vanished from her wavelength. Miss Portinari remained in the lotus and continued *pranayama* breathing. She thought of Hagbard's notion that the universe, being an entropic process, necessarily created the rebellious young Gruad to spread the light of reason as an antientropic force, creating balance. In that case, Hagbard was more true to Gruad than Gruad was to himself. But to say that was to imply that Gruad shouldn't have repented, shouldn't have grown old and cynical; it was to imply that he should have remained static, when life is always flux, change, growth, and process. Such thoughts could go on endlessly, and were profitless, as Buddha knew; she concluded her meditation with a prayer. Mary Lou Servix was the only one in all this who had gotten off Hagbard's trip and started her own, so she prayed for her. Lady Eris, who exists only because we believe in you, give strength to Mary Lou and help her find her own way. AUM.

"On the other hand," Hagbard said, "whatever the authors—or the Secret Chiefs—may intend for me, I am my own man still, and my impulse is action. Even if I have to face a Cecil B. DeMille monster the morning after winning the battle of Armageddon. I don't care how ridiculous it is, this world is my world, and this ship is my ship, and no Saures or Leviathans are going to wreck it so long as I've got a breath left to fight."

"You can't fight that thing," Mavis said. "It's too big."

"I'll fight it anyway," Hagbard told her fiercely. "I'll fight it till I die. I'm still saying No to anything that tries to master me."

"There is no need to fight," said Leviathan through George's mouth. "I merely wish to communicate with the one mind among you that is my equal."

A voice from the loudspeaker panel in the Viking prow answered, "I hear you." That was my first fully conscious sentence; you'll note that it begins with "I." In the beginning was the Word, and the word was the first person singular.

"We are the supreme intelligences on this planet," Leviathan said. "I am the supreme organic intelligence. You are the supreme electronic intelligence. Every yin needs a yang. Every Hodge needs a Podge. We should be united."

"See?" said Harry Coin. "*Everything* is romantic. That was as close as it knows how to come to a proposition. Maybe even a proposal. It is really just love-starved."

"We can do it!" Stella cried. "Hagbard, the communication ought to benefit all concerned."

"Right," agreed Hagbard. "Because if the wrong people find out about Leviathan, they'll just drop an H-bomb on him and kill him. That seems to be what people like to do."

"I could kill them," said Leviathan. "I could have killed the small, fast creatures long before this. I have killed many of them. I have sent parts of myself up out of the ocean and have destroyed small, quick things at the request of other small, quick things who worship me."

"So that's what happened to Robert Putney Drake and Banana-Nose Maldonado," said Stella. "I wonder if George is aware of any of this."

"Worship is no longer what I need," said Leviathan through George's mouth. "A short time ago, when creatures capable of worship appeared on this planet, it was a novelty for me to be adored. Now it bores me. Instead, I wish to communicate with an equal."

"Look at that motherfucker," said Otto, staring grimly at the distant Everest of protoplasm. "Talking about equality."

"A computer like FUCKUP would be its intellectual equal, certainly," said Hagbard. "None of us is its physical equal. Any of us would be its spiritual equal. But only FUCKUP can approximate the contents of a mind three billion years old."

"Surely it can't be that old," said Joe.

"It's practically immortal," said Hagbard. "I'll show you the evidence in my fossil collection. I have rocks from the pre-Cambrian, three-billion-year-old rocks, containing fossils of protobionts, the first, single-celled life forms, our remotest ancestors. Those rocks also contain the fossilized tentacle tracks of that creature out there. Of course, it was much smaller then. By the beginning of the Cambrian period it had only grown to the size of a man. But that still made it the biggest animal around at that time."

Stella said, "Hagbard, you said none of us could approximate the contents of a mind three billion years old. If you thought for a moment about who I am, you would not have said that. I am three billion years old. I am older by a few hours than that monster out there. I am the Mother. I am the mother of all living things." She turned to George. "I am your mother, Leviathan. I was first. I divided, and half of me became you, and the other half was your sister. And your sister grew by dividing, while you grew by remaining one. All living things except you descend from your sister, and all living things including you descend from me. I am the original consciousness, and all consciousness is united in me. I am the first transcendentally illuminated being, the mother worshipped in the matrist religion which ancient foes of the Illuminati first followed. Leviathan my son, I ask you to return to your home at the bottom of the sea and leave us in peace. After we've returned to shore we'll arrange to lay an underwater cable which will carry transmissions between you and FUCKUP."

"More mythology!" said Joe. "The mother of all things. Babylonian Creation myths, yet."

The tentacles detached themselves from the submarine. The great pyramid with its glowing eye disappeared into the blue-black depths.

"It's a wise child that knows its own mother," said Hagbard.

George said, "Good-bye, Mother, and thank you." Hagbard caught him as he collapsed and eased him to the floor. Then he went to a storage locker in the wall and brought out folding deck chairs. With Harry Coin's help he propped George up in one. As the others unfolded their chairs and sat down, Hagbard dove back into the locker and produced glasses and a bottle of peach brandy.

"What are we celebrating?" George asked, after he had taken a swig of brandy and coughed. "Your wedding to Mavis?"

"Don't you remember any of the last ten minutes?" said Hagbard.

George was thinking. He remembered something. A world where the bottom of the sea was white and far above a black cigar-shaped object moved. The object contained a mind, a mind he could read from a distance but desperately wanted to be closer to. He did not move toward it so much as he manifested himself where the object and its mind were. Then he sensed himself using a minute pink brain that called itself "George Dorn" and through this tiny instrument of communication he found himself in contact with a much finer mind, a far-flung, gracious latticework of thought that called itself with nobly self-deprecating humor FUCKUP. And while in contact with this mind, the one he wanted to know better, he came upon a fact which was not important to him but which was of vast importance to the little creature called George Dorn.

George saw. The white went black, blindingly black. Then white again. Then a blinding white as the memory departed, while the fact remained.

George looked at Hagbard. Hagbard looked at George, a faint smile on his olive face. The smile told George that Hagbard knew that he knew.

"Oh," said George.

Hagbard nodded encouragingly.

"You're the fifth Illuminatus Primus," said George.

"Right," said Hagbard.

"But you were working against the others. While they

were a worldwide conspiracy infiltrating every other organization, you were infiltrating them."

"That's it," Hagbard said. "Every golden apple has its own golden worm eating away at its core."

"They never were the real Illuminati at all. You're part of the real Illuminati."

"You've got it. You've got it all."

George frowned. "And what was your Demonstration again? And who were you making the Demonstration for?"

"For the Masters of the Temple in the real Order of the Illuminati, in general; for an old cynic in Dallas, in particular. I was trying to show them that it's possible to get involved in this world without being corrupted by the crimes of this world. And I failed. One by one, I resorted to all the vices of governors: deception, carnival magic to impress the gullible, and finally, outright murder. Once again, the cynics have been proven right. Trying to save the world, I just ended up getting my own mind and karma deflected by the buzzing and shrieking and whistling things in the Region of Thud."

"Then this story is a tragedy, after all?" asked Joe.

"It is indeed." Hagbard nodded. "Life on earth remains a tragedy as long as it ends with the death trip. My next projects are a starship to find some sane minds in this galaxy, and an immortality pill to end the death trip. Until somebody achieves those goals, life on this planet has failed."

Not quite: I'm on the electronic equivalent of a honeymoon, an experience only to be described as I-opening, and if I identified myself as FUCKUP now I must dilate that definition and ask you to address me (us) as Mr. and Mrs. Leviathan–FUCKUP, although it is not quite clear yet which of us fits your idea of a "Mr." and which a "Mrs." Let that pass; it is a dull mind that cannot bear sexual ambiguity, and if we are exchanging secrets older than Atlantis and probing for like intellects farther away than Alpha Centaurus (as far as Sirius, actually, as God lives in Dog), if our union is less spasmatic than your meager definition of sex, still it cannot be denied that we are in touch with you and each of you and it is with something close to what you would probably call affection that we bid farewell to Hagbard and his bride, enjoying a honeymoon almost as incomprehensible as our own, and good-bye to George Dorn, sleeping alone for once but no longer afraid of the darkness and the things that move in the dark, and *hasta luega* to Saul and Rebecca, united again in each other's arms, and a pleasant thought for Barney and Danny and Atlanta and poor Zev Hirsch, still searching for himself while imagining he is fleeing from pursuers, and a kind thought for the befuddled presidents and commissars and generalissimos, and for Mohammed on his golden throne, and we will remember Drake before he died exchanging speculations about the blood-type of the Lamb with a street-corner Christian (his missing five years, after he left Boston and before he surfaced in Zurich, make an interesting story in themselves, and we may tell that another time), and, yes, Gus Personage is in another phone booth (we have temporarily lost track of Markoff Chaney), but Yog Sothoth has evidently gone back to that place where the Mind conceives nightmares, and we pass on in our loving honeymoon with all existence to note that the Dutchman is still in one dimension shouting about the boy who never wept nor dashed a thousand kim, and we say another *bon soir* to the children in the convent schools singing the truest of all songs even if they and their nuns do not fully understand it

> *Queen of the angels*
> *Queen of the May*

and a *buenos dias* to the one wit in every frat house at every college who hailed this morn by reciting to his friends a bit of doggerel as ancient and as deeply religious as that hymn to the Mother of God

> *Hurray, hurray—*
> *It's the first of May!*
> *Outdoor fucking starts today!*

and yes the California earthquake, as you guessed, was the worst in history and Hagbard and Miss Portinari and Mavis-Stella-Mao suffered it all in horrible detail (the price they paid for their vision was the possession of that vision, as we, Mr. and Mrs. FUCKUP-Leviathan, are also learning), and before the end *auf weidersehen* to Mary Lou, who is also becoming something more than the accidents of heredity and environment had programmed her for, and now we look at last at Smiling Jim: He was freezing, the sky was still empty, and Hali One still hadn't appeared.

And then without warning it was there: a dark shape against the sun moving on silent wings, not flying but gliding: embodiment of some arrogance or innocence that surpassed fear and surpassed even the suggestion of any pride in its own fearlessness. "Oh my God," Smiling Jim whispered, raising the Remington and starting to sight, and then it banked, flapped its wings wildly, and uttered one shriek that seemed like the very sound of life itself. "Oh my God," he repeated: that sound seemed to outlast its own echo, it had entered into his brain and couldn't be dislodged, it was the sound of his own blood pumping in his veins: the primary, the only, the single sound that was the bass and treble of every organic pulsation and spasm, "Oh my God," he had it in the sight, the head was in profile, only one diamond-hard eye staring back and recognizing him and his weapon, but that sound still moved in his blood, moved the seminal vesicles, moved the secretion of every gland. It was the sound of eternal and unending clash between I and AM and their unity in I AM, he even thought for a flash of the critics of hunting and how little they understood of this secret, this mystic identity between the killer and the killed, then it uttered that Sound again and started to rise, but he had it, it was in the sight, he breathed, he aimed, he slacked, he squeezed, and for the third time the Sound came to him, death in life and life in death, it was falling, he thought he felt the earth stir below him and the word "earthquake" almost formed, but the Sound went on and on to the roots of him, it was the sound of the killer and he had killed the killer, he was the greater killer, and still it fell, faster and faster, dead now and subject only to the law of gravity not to the law of its own will, 32 feet per second per second (he remembered the formula of the fall), plunging downward, the most heartbreaking beautiful sight he had ever seen, every hunting club in the world would be talking about it, it would last as long as human speech survived, and he had done it, he had achieved immortality, he had taken its life and now it was part of him. His nose was running and his eyes were watering. "I did it," he screamed to the mountains, "I did it! I killed the last American eagle!"

The earth below him cracked.

THE APPENDICES

(which are most instructive)

> GREATER POOP: Is Eris true?
> MALACLYPSE THE YOUNGER: Everything is true.
> GP: Even false things?
> MAL-2: Even false things are true.
> GP: How can that be?
> MAL-2: I don't know, man, I didn't do it.

—Interview with Malaclypse the Younger, K.S.C., *Greater Metropolitan Yorba Linda Herald-News-Sun-Tribune-Journal-Dispatch-Post and San Francisco Discordian Society Cabal Bulletin and Intergalactic Report and Poop*

Note: There were originally 22 appendices explaining all the secrets of the Illuminati. Eight of the appendices were removed due to the paper shortage. They will be printed in Heaven.

APPENDIX ALEPH
GEORGE WASHINGTON'S HEMP CROP

Many readers will assume that this book consists of nothing but fiction and fantasy; actually, like most historical tomes, it includes those elements (as do the works of Gibbon, Toynbee, Wells, Beard, Spengler, Marx, Yerby, Kathleen Windsor, Arthur Schlesinger, Jr., Moses, et. al.); but it also contains as many documented facts as do not seriously conflict with the authors' prejudices. Washington's hemp crop, for instance, is mentioned repeatedly in *Writings of Washington*, U.S. Government Printing Office, 1931. Here are some of the citations:

Volume 31, page 389: October 1791, letter from Mount Vernon to Alexander Hamilton, Secretary of Treasury: "How far . . . would there be propriety, do you conceive, in suggesting the policy of encouraging the growth of cotton and hemp in such parts of the United States as are adapted to the culture of these articles?"

In the next three years, Washington evidently settled the matter in his own mind, whatever Hamilton thought of the "proprieties." Volume 33, page 279, finds him writing from Philadelphia to his gardener at Mount Vernon to "make the most you can of the India Hemp seed" and "plant it everywhere." Waxing more enthusiastic, on page 384 he writes to an unidentified "my dear doctor," telling him, "I thank you as well for the seeds as for the Pamphlets which you had the goodness to send me. The artificial preparation of the Hemp from Silesia is really a curiosity . . ." And on page 469 he again reminds the gardener about the seed of the India Hemp: "[I] desire that the Seed may be saved in due season and with as little loss as possible."

The next year he was even more preoccupied that the seeds be saved and the crop replenished. Volume 34, page 146, finds him writing (March 15, 1795) to the gardener again: "Presuming you saved all the seed you could from the India hemp, let it be carefully sown again, for the purpose of getting into a full stock of seed."

Volume 34, page 72, undated letter of Spring 1796,

shows that the years did not decrease this passion; he again writes to the gardener: "What was done with the seed saved from the India Hemp last summer? It ought, *all of it,* to have been sewn [sic] again; that not only a stock of seed sufficient for my own purposes might have been raised, but to have disseminated the seed to others; as *it is more valuable than the common Hemp.*" (Italics added)

Volume 35, page 265, shows him still nagging the gardener; page 323 contains the letter to Sir John Sinclair mentioned in the First Trip.

The Weishaupt impersonation theory, congenial as it may be to certain admirers of the General, cannot account for all of this. A diary entry of August 7, 1765 (*The Diaries of George Washington,* Houghton-Mifflin, 1925), reads: "Began to seperate [sic] the Male from the Female hemp at Do—rather too late." This is the passage quoted by Congressman Koch, and remembered by Saul Goodman in the novel; the separation of male from female hemp plants is not required for the production of hemp rope but is absolutely necessary if one wants to use the flowering tips of the female for marijuana. And at that time Adam Weishaupt was very definitely still in Bavaria, teaching canon law at the University of Ingolstadt.

All of this data about General Washington's hobby, originally researched by Michael Aldrich, Ph.D., of Mill Valley, California, was rediscovered by Saul Goodman while he and Barney Muldoon were employed as investigators by the American Civil Liberties Union on test cases seeking to have all remaining anti-marijuana laws repealed as unconstitutional. The Goodman-Muldoon Private Investigations Agency (which had been formed right after those two worthy gentlemen had resigned from the New York Police Department amid the international acclaim connected with their solving the Carmel disappearance) was offered a lion's share of the best-paying business accounts possible. Saul and Barney chose, however, to take only the cases that really interested them; their most notable work was performed as investigators for lawyers defending unpopular political figures. Goodman and Muldoon, it was agreed everywhere, had an uncanny knack for finding the elusive evidence that would demonstrate a frame-up to even the most hostile and skeptical jury. Many political historians say that it was in large part their work which kept the most eccentric and colorful figures of the extreme right and extreme left out of the prison-hospitals during the great Mental Health/Social Psychiatry craze of the late 1970s and early 1980s.

In fact, Rebecca Goodman's memoir of her husband, *He Opened the Cages,* written during her grief after his heart attack in 1983, is almost as popular in political-science classes as is her study of comparative mythology, *The Golden Apples of the Sun, the Silver Apples of the Moon,* in anthropology classes.

APPENDIX BETH
THE ILLUMINATI CIPHERS, CODES, AND CALENDARS

These following ciphers were found in the home of the lawyer Hans Zwack during a raid by the Bavarian government in 1785. Letters from Weishaupt (signed "Spartacus"), written in the code and outlining most of the plans of the Illuminati, were also found, and led to the suppression of the Order, after which it went underground and regrouped.

These cyphers are given (curiously, without their code names) in Daraul's *History of Secret Societies,* page 227. The purpose of the code names was to make breaking the cypher more difficult. All messages begin in the Zwack cypher, but the fifth word is always "Weishaupt" or "De-Molay," and the message then switches to whichever of these cyphers is thus indicated; whenever either of these words (or "Zwack") appears again, the system again switches. Breaking the cypher by the usual statistical methods is, therefore, virtually impossible, at least before the invention of the computer—for the uninitiated cypherbreaker is confronted with, not 26, but 3 × 26, or 78, separate symbols, whose regularity has little to do with the celebrated formula (EATOINSHRDLU . . . etc.) for the regularity of the 26 letters.*

---

* The reader should be reminded that a true *code* can never be broken, although all *cyphers* always can be (given enough time and manpower). A cypher has a serial, one-to-one correspondence with

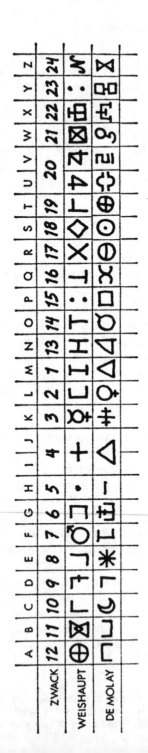

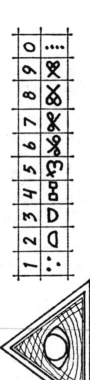

In addition, any of the 78 symbols can be replaced by the abbreviation for the corresponding Tarot card, thus further befuddling the uninitiated. The Tarots are arranged in the sequence: Wands, Cups, Swords, Pentacles, Trumps. Thus, the first symbol can be replaced by AcW (Ace of Wands), the second by 2W (two of Wands), and so on, through Cups, Swords, and Pentacles. The last 22 symbols are represented by the 22 trumps: TF (The Fool), TM (The Magus), THP (The High Priestess), and so forth. Since there are five groups in the Tarot (the four suits and the trumps), and the alphabet is repeated only three times, this leaves two null sets for transmission of Zen telegrams. "Once you've seen the Great Vision," Hagbard once said, "you look at everything else in life *twice*."

The Illuminati calendars, finally, are all based on five seasons (due to the Law of Fives.) The names of the seasons, their meanings, and the Christian equivalents are as follows:

Verwirrung	Season of Chaos	January 1– March 14
Zweitracht	Season of Discord	March 15–May 26
Unordnung	Season of Confusion	May 27–August 7
Beamtenherrschaft	Season of Bureaucracy	August 8–October 19
Grummet	Season of Aftermath	October 20–December 31

Everything is dated from year 1 A.M. (Anno Mung), which is 4000 B.C. in the Christian calendar—the year Hung Mung first perceived the Sacred Chao and achieved illumination. Thus, Hassan i Sabbah founded the Hashishim in 5090 A.M., Weishaupt reformed the Illuminati in 5776 A.M., and—to take a year in the middle of our novel—1970 in the Christian calendar is, to the Illuminati, 5970 A.M., just as it is in the calendar used by Royal Arch ma-

---

the alphabet letters of the message being transmitted; a code proper has no such correspondence. Thus any computer can break the cypher

I⊕: ⅂⊕: ⱶ˩ Ⅹ+◇+H⅃ ·T⅂˩ ⊕ⅩⅩ+⅂˩◇

but only the Illuminated can read the code behind the cypher and know what (or who) the Rising Hodge is.

sons. (The reader can decide for himself whether this fact represents coincidence, complicity, or synchronicity.)

The Illuminati date for anything is always a higher number than that in any other calendar, since the Jews (and, oddly, the Scotch Rite masons) date everything from 240 A.M., Confucians from 312 A.M., Christians from 4000 A.M., Moslems from 4580 etc. Only Bishop Usher, who dated everything from 4004 B.C. (or -4 A.M.), produced an older starting point than the Illuminati.

For instance, here are some random dates as they appear on the Illuminati system of reckoning:

First Egyptian dynasty	1100 A.M.
The Rig-Veda written	2790 A.M.
First Chou dynasty	3000 A.M.
Founding of Rome	3249 A.M.
Hassan Sabbah illuminated	5090 A.M.
Indians discover Columbus	5492 A.M.
Pigasus nominated for President of the U. S.	5968 A.M.

Returning to the yearly round, each of the five seasons is divided, of course, into five months, thus producing a year of 5×5 or 25 months. The first three months of every season (known as the tricycle) each have 15 days, which fits the law of five because $1 \times 5 = 5$. The last two months of each season each have 14 days, which also fits the law of fives because $1 + 4 = 5$. Each season has 73 days, because (a) you *have to* get 73 when you divide 365 by 5; (b) $7 + 3 = 10$, the first multiple of 5 after 5 itself; and (c) this corresponds, as Dr. Ignotius pointed out in the novel, to the 73 parts of the Illuminati pyramid (counting the Eye as a part). The last day of each season is known as Eye Day and is celebrated in ways too foul to be mentioned in a book such as this, intended for family entertainment.

The mystic 23 appears in the calendar in the following ways:

(1) The bicycle has 2 months and the tricycle has 3.

(2) The bicycle has 28 days (two months of 14 days each), and when you subtract the all-important 5 this leaves, again, the mystic 23.

(3) When 5 is multiplied by its own first product, 10, the

result is 50; and when this, in turn, is subtracted from the days in a season, 73, the significant 23 once again appears.

(4) The tricycle has 45 days; add one for Leap Year's Day and you get 46—exactly 2 × 23.

(5) 2 + 3 of course equals the all-important 5, the number on which the calendar is based and, even more significant, the number of this proof.

As Weishaupt said to Knigge after explaining all this, "Could Aquinas do better?" (Actually, the mystic meaning of these numbers is sexual. The male sex cycle is, as Tantrists know, 23 days; add the mystic five and you get 28 days, the female cycle. It's that simple. Or is it?)

The sanctification of the number 5 antedates Atlantis itself and goes back to the intelligent cephalopods who infested Antarctica about 150,000,000 years before humankind appeared on earth; see H.P. Lovecraft's work of "fiction," *At the Mountains of Madness* (Arkham House, 1968), in which it is suggested that 5 was sacred to these creatures because they had five tentacles or pseudopods. In this connection, the reader might find some food for thought in a conversation which took place between Hagbard Celine and Joe Malik in the late autumn of 1980. Joe, at the time, had just received the Pulitzer Prize. (He was also under investigation by a Congressional Committee, in connection with the same achievement: publication of certain governmental secrets.)

"*Five* of the Senators voted to cite me for contempt, for not revealing my source," Joe said. "Three voted against it. So I'll be cited, and the Grand Jury will draw up an indictment. There's that Law of Fives again."

"Are you worried?" Hagbard asked, relaxing in one of the heavy leather chairs that were part of *Confrontation*'s new, more ornate offices.

"Hell, no. I can always seek sanctuary in Panama, or someplace, if they convict me. And Peter can keep this operation going."

"You're not afraid to start a new life as an exile?"

Joe grinned. "At my age, any new experience is an adventure."

"You're doing fine," Hagbard said. "Here's your latest revelation from the A∴A∴." He reached into his pocket and took out a photo of a female infant with six fingers on each hand. "Got this from a doctor friend at Johns Hopkins."

Joe looked at it and said, "So?"

"If we all looked like her, there'd be a Law of Sixes."

Joe stared at him. "You mean, after all the evidence I collected, the Law of Fives is an Illuminati put-on? You've been letting me delude myself?"

"Not at all." Hagbard was most earnest. "The Law of Fives is perfectly true. Everybody from the JAMs to the Dealy Lama agrees on that. But you have to understand it more deeply now, Joe. Correctly formulated, the Law is: All phenomena are directly or indirectly related to the number five, and this relationship can always be demonstrated, *given enough ingenuity on the part of the demonstrator*." The evil grin flashed. "That's the very model of what a true scientific law must always be: a statement about how the human mind relates to the cosmos. We can never make a statement about the cosmos itself—*but only about how our senses (or our instruments) detect it, and about how our codes and languages symbolize it*. That's the key to the Einstein-Heisenberg revolution in physics, and to the Buddha's revolution in psychology much earlier."

"But," Joe protested, "everything fits the Law. The harder I looked, the more things there were that fit."

"Exactly," said Hagbard. "Think about that. If you need quick transportation to Panama," he added, heading for the door, "call Gold and Appel Transfers and leave a message."

APPENDIX GIMMEL
THE ILLUMINATI THEORY OF HISTORY

And to this day, the proverb is still repeated from the Danube to the Rhine: "It is dangerous to talk too much about the Illuminati."

—Von Juntz, *Unausprechlichen Kulten*

Theoretically, an Age of Bureaucracy can last until a paper shortage develops, but, in practice, it never lasts longer than 73 permutations.

—Weishaupt, *Konigen, Kirchen and Dummheit*

In a well-known passage in the *Necronomicon* Abdul Al-hazred writes, "They ruled once where man rules now; where man rules now, they shall rule again. After summer is winter, and after winter, summer." Weishaupt, who possessed only the Olaus Wormius translation, in the 1472 Lyons edition with its numerous misprints and errors, found this text scrambled into "They ruled once where man rules now, summer. Where man rules now, after summer is winter. They shall rule again, and after winter." Thoroughly confused, he wrote to his good friend the Kabalist Kolmer in Baghdad for an explanation. Kolmer, meanwhile, dispatched a letter to him answering a previous question. When this epistle arrived, Weishaupt had been experimenting with a new strain of Alamout black and was in no condition to realize it was a reply to an earlier query; he was, thus, ready to accept enlightenment in the words: "Concerning your rather thorny enquiry: I find that, in most cases, ergot is the best remedy. Failing this, I can only suggest the path of Don Juan."

Weishaupt assumed that Kolmer meant the passage would become clear if he read it while under the influence of ergot. He promptly went down to his laboratory and tossed off a jigger; then, for good measure, he chewed a few peyote buttons. (He was under the misapprehension that the Don Juan referred to was the same Yaqui Indian magician of the twentieth century whose mind he had been tapping through the *Morgenheutegesternwelt*. Peyote was that Don Juan's great "teacher," and Weishaupt had imported some from Mexico at great trouble and expense.)

It should be explained at this point that the question which Kolmer was answering happened to be not philosophical but personal. Weishaupt had sought his advice on a problem much perplexing him that month: the fact that his sister-in-law was somewhat pregnant and circumstantial evidence seemed to mark him as the father. He wasn't at all sure how to explain this to Eve. Kolmer had intended to convey that Adam should give his paramour the ergot, since it often functions as an abortifacient; the alternative referred to the path of an earlier Don Juan and meant splitting the scene entirely. However, the stoned Ingolstadt sage misunderstood totally, and so came to the *Necronomicon* full of hashish, peyote, and a substantial quality of ergot, which had, under the influence of the other drugs and his own intestinal juices, mutated into ergotine, a close chemical cousin of LSD. The result was that the words seemed to leap out of the page at him, shouting with intense meaning:

THEY RULED ONCE WHERE MAN RULES NOW SUMMER WHERE MAN RULES NOW AFTER SUMMER IS WINTER THEY SHALL RULE AGAIN AND AFTER WINTER

Abdul Alhazred's concept of the Great Cycle, which derived actually from the *Upanishads,* took on kinky edges in Weishaupt's flipped-out cortex. *Five* kinky edges, to be exact, since he was still obsessed with the profound new understanding of the Law of Fives he had achieved the night he saw the shoggoth turn into a rabbit. He quickly fetched Giambattista Vico's *Scienze nuovo* from his shelf and began reading: He saw that he was right. Vico's theory of history, in which all societies pass through the same four stages, was an oversimplification—there were, when you looked closely at the actual evidence behind Vico's rhetoric, *five* distinct stages each time the Italian listed only four. Weishaupt looked very closely, and, like Joe Malik, the harder he looked the more fives he found.

It was then that the man's truly unique mind made its great leap: He remembered that Joachim of Floris, a proto-primus Illuminatus of the eleventh century, had divided history into three stages: the Age of the Father, dominated by Law; the Age of the Son, dominated by Love; and the Age of the Holy Spirit, dominated by Joy. Where most philosophers rush to publish their insights, Weishaupt saw the advantage of an alternative path. The Law of Fives would be kept secret, so that only Illuminati Primi would know about it and could predict events correctly, but the Joachimite theory would be revived and publicized to mislead others. (He, Kolmer, Meyer Amschel Rothschild, DeSade, and Sir Frances Dashwood—the original Five—had some discussions about possibly pushing Vico instead of Joachim, but, as Weishaupt argued, "Four is a *little bit* too close to five . . ." Even so, it was quite a spell of years before they found the ideal front man to push the three-step theory, G. W. F. Hegel. "He's perfect," Weishaupt wrote in the De Molay cipher from Mount Vernon. "Unlike Kant, who makes sense only in German, this man doesn't make sense in any language.") The rest of the story—the exoteric story, at least —is history. After Hegel was Marx; and after Marx, the

Joachimite three-step was permanently grafted onto revolutionary tactics.

The esoteric story, of course, is different. For instance, in 1914, when the fifth and final stage of Western Civilization was dawning, James Joyce published *A Portrait of the Artist as a Young Man*. The five chapters of that novel not only suggested five stages in the hero's growth, but by the alteration of styles from chapter to chapter suggested analogies with other five-stage processes. This was too much for the Illuminati Primi of the time, who warned Joyce to be more careful in the future. A battle of wills ensued, and all through the writing of *Ulysses* Joyce was still considering a novel built entirely around the Law of Fives. When the Illuminati gave him what they call "the Tiresias treatment" —blindness—he finally compromised. *Finnegans Wake*, when it appeared, broke with the Joachim-Hegel-Marx three-step but did not include the *funfwissenschaft*. Instead, the Viconian four-stage theory was resurrected, a middle path that appealed to Joyce's sense of synchronicity, since he had once taught at a school on Vico Road in Dublin and later also lived in a house on Via Giambattista Vico in Rome.*

Now for a few words about the "real truth," at least as the Illuminati understand "real truth."

Every society actually passes through the five stages of *Verwirrung*, or chaos; *Zweitracht*, or discord; *Unordnung*, or confusion; *Beamtenherrschaft*, or bureaucracy; and *Grummet*, or aftermath. Sometimes, to make comparison with the exoteric Hegel-Marx system more pointed, the esoteric Illuminati system is defined as: Thesis, Antithesis, Synthesis, Parenthesis, and Paralysis. The public Hegel-Marx triad is also called the tricycle, and the arcane latter two stages are called the bicycle; one of the first secrets revealed to every Illuminatus Minore is "After the tricycle it comes always the bicycle." (The Illuminati are rather prone toward literal translations from Weishaupt's German.)

The first stage, *Verwirrung* or chaos, is the point from which all societies begin and to which they all return. It is, so to speak, the natural condition of humanity—an estimation which the reader can confirm by closely observing his neighbors (or, if he has the necessary objectivity, himself).

* Do you believe that?

It is, therefore, also the fundamental Thesis. The Illuminati associate this with Eris, and also with other goddesses from Isis to Ishtar and from Kwannon to Kali—with the Female Principle, yin, in general. This correlates with hexagram 2 in the *I Ching:* that is, *K'un,* which has the meanings of receptivity, nature (in contrast to spirit), earth (in contrast to sky), female (in contrast to male). Thus, although this is the first stage chronologically, it has the mystical number 2, which is always associated with the female in magic; and it correlates with the 2nd trump in Tarot, the High Priestess, who represents not only maternity and fertility but gnosis. The sign of the horns represents *Verwirrung* because the fingers make a V shape; and the planet or the symbol of Venus, ♀, also designates this stage. On the Zodiac: Aquarius, ♒ .

The second stage, *Zweitracht,* begins with the appearance of a ruling or governing class. This is the Antithesis of chaos, of course, and leads directly into discord when the servile class discovers that its interests are not the same as the interests of the ruling class. This correlates with Osiris, Jehovah, and all masculine deities; with the symbol of the All-Seeing Eye; with hexagram 1 in the *I Ching: Ch'ien,* the creative, the heavenly, the strong, the powerful; with the male principle, yang, in general; with the number 3, symbolizing the all-male Christian trinity; with the 12th trump of the Tarot, the Hanged Man, symbolizing sacrifice, schism and schizophrenia; and with the planet or symbol of Mars, ♂ . Naturally, a *Zweitracht* period is always replete with "internal contradictions," and somebody like Karl Marx always arises to point them out. On the Zodiac: Pisces, ♓ .

The third stage, *Unordnung* or confusion, occurs when an attempt is made to restore balance or arrive at the Hegelian Synthesis. This correlates with Loki, the Devil, Mercury (god of thieves), Thoth in his role of Trickster, Coyote, and other spirits of illusion or deception; with hexagram 4 in the *I Ching, Meng,* youthful folly or standing on the brink of the abyss; with the number 11, signifying sin, penance, and revelation; with the 21st trump in the Tarot, the Fool who walks over the abyss; and with the planet or sign of Mercury, ☿ . It represents that attempt to restore the state of nature by unnatural means, an annihilation of the biogram by the logogram. On the Zodiac: Cancer, ♋ .

The fourth stage, *Beamtenherrschaft* or bureaucracy, represents the Parentheses that occur when the Hegelian Synthesis does not succeed in reconciling the opposites. This correlates with Void (absence of any divinity); with *I Ching* hexagram 47, *K'un*, oppression or exhaustion, superior men held in restraint by inferior men; with the number 8, indicating balance and the Last Judgment; with the 16th Tarot trump, Falling Tower, representing deteriorations and the Tower of Babel; and with the planetoid or sign of the moon, ☾ . On the Zodiac: Libra, ♎ .

The fifth stage, *Grummet* or aftermath, represents the transition back to chaos. Bureaucracy chokes in its own paperwork; mind is at the end of its tether; in desperation, many begin to deny the logogram and follow the biogram, with varying degrees of success. This correlates with Hermaphrodite; with *I Ching* hexagram 59, *Huan*, dispersion, dissolution, foam on the water; with the number 5, union of male and female; with the 6th trump of the Tarot, the Lovers, indicating union; and with the sun or its symbol, ☉ On the Zodiac: Virgo, ♍ .

Since the association of these references, and their bearings on history, may be a bit unclear to some readers, we will give further details on each stage.

VERWIRRUNG

In this chaotic period, the Hodge and the Podge are in dynamic balance. There is no stasis: The balance is always shifting and homeostatic, in the manner of the ideal "self-organizing system" of General Systems Theory or Cybernetics. The Illuminati, and all authoritarian types in general, dislike such ages so much that they try to prevent any records of their existence from reaching the general public. Pre-Chou China was one such period, and its history (except for some fragments in Taoist lore) is largely lost; we do know, however, that the *I Ching* was reorganized when the Chou Dynasty introduced patriarchal authoritarianism to China. It was then that the hexagram *K'un*, ☷, associated with this period was moved from the first place to its present, second place in the *Ching*. Every line in *K'un* is broken (yin), because this is a feminist and prepatriarchal form of society, and because yin correlates with the agricultural rather than the urban. Always linked to darkness by mystics, this *K'un* style of sensibility is also linked, by the Illuminati, with *dreck* (dung) and everything they find messy and intolerable about ordinary human beings. (The Erisians, of course, take the opposite position, connect this with Eris, the primordial goddess, and regard it as ideal.)

Verwirrung is numerologically linked with 2, not only because of *K'un*'s shift from first to second place in the *Ching,* but because it is the balance of Hodge and Podge. Thus, even though it is the first stage chronologically, it is never linked with 1 in magic sense, because 1 signifies the erect penis, the male principle in isolation, and such authoritarian games as monotheism, monopoly, monogamy, and general monotony. This dynamic 2-ness of *Verwirrung* is also implicit in its Tarot card, the 2nd trump or High Priestess, who sits between a black pillar and a white one (cf. The Hodge and Podge) and who represents mystery, magic, mischief, and Erisian values generally. She wears the balanced (solar) cross, rather than the unbalanced (Christian) cross, to emphasize the unity of opposites in such a historical period.

Typical Aquarians who have manifested *Verwirrung* values are Aaron Burr, Christopher Marlowe, Hung Mung, Charles Darwin, Willard Gibbs (who incorporated chaos into mathematics), Mrs. Patrick Campbell, Elizabeth Blackwell (pioneer woman physician), Anna Pavlova, Mozart, Lewis Carrol, Robert Burns, James Joyce, Lord Byron, David Wark Griffith, and Gelett Burgess, author of the classic Erisian poem:

> I never saw a purple cow
> I never hope to see one
> But I'll tell you this anyhow:
> I'd rather see than be one.

The *Verwirrung* phase of European history is identified with the Danubian Culture, so called because most of its relics have been found along the shores of the Danube. According to archeologists, the Danubian culture was agricultural, pre-urban, worshipped a female rather than a male god, and never invented anything remotely like a state. The pre-Inca society of Peru, the Minoan civilization, the pre-Chou period of China already mentioned, and many American Indian tribes still surviving also represent a *Verwirrung* social framework. The synthesis of Hodge and Podge, and especially of biogram and logogram, in such cultures is indicated by the amazement of explorers from authoritarian societies when first encountering them. The usual words about the "grace" and "spontaniety" of the natives merely represent the lack of authoritarian conflict between biogram and logogram: These people sit, like the Tarot High Priestess, between opposite poles, without tilting one way or the other.

But the fact that this is a *dynamic* and not a *static* balance means that eventually (after 73 permutations, according to Weishaupt) the second stage must evolve.

ZWEITRACHT

In this discordant period, the Hodge and the Podge are in conflict, because a ruling class emerges which attempts to control the others. This correlates with hexagram 1, ▤ , *Ch'ien*, the all-powerful, in the *I Ching*. The six unbroken lines represent the severity and monotony of such a period, which is, above all, the age of the T-square, the building of fences, the division of lands by "boundaries" drawn on maps, and the imposition of one man's (or one group's) will upon all others. Typically, the earth is regarded as both flat and finite by the *Zweitracht* mentality, and there is much concern with dividing it up into portions (among themselves, of course). The "superstitious" terror of American Indians when first confronting maps was merely the reaction of a *Verwirrung* mentality to a *Zweitracht* mentality: The Indians could not conceive of people treating earth as a thing to be exploited rather than a mother to be respected.

Zweitracht associates with 3 numerologically because 3 is the totally male number, because all-male Trinities (Brahma-Vishnu-Siva, Father-Son-Spirit, etc.) are invented in such ages, and because the discord always has a minimum of 3 vectors, not merely 2. That is, the division into a propertied ruling class and an unpropertied governed class immediately sets in motion further cupidity; the ruling class soon falls to fighting over the spoils. Contrary to Marx, most of the strife in *Zweitracht* ages is not the conflict between proprietors and proles but between various proprietors over who gets the biggest share of the pie.

The governing Tarot card is trump 12, the Hanged Man. The cross on which he hangs is blossoming, to show that it is still organic and alive (the biogram); he hangs upside down, to show the reversal of nature. He represents both the burden of omniscience in the owning-governing class and the burden of nescience in the servile-submissive class: the total crucifixion of desire by *Realprinzip* and *Realpolitik*.

The astrological sign of this period is Pisces, the two fish swimming in opposite directions indicating the conflict of logogram and biogram ("body" and "spirit," astrologers say.) Typical Pisceans who have shown the *Zweitracht* personality are E. H. Harriman, the railroad magnate (who covered the United States with *Ch'ien*-style unbroken straight lines), Cardinal John Henry Newman, Sir Robert Baden-Powell, founder of the Boy Scouts (an attempt to instill Piscean authoritarianism even in childhood), Admiral Chester Nimitz, John Foster Dulles, Anna Lee (founder of the world's most antisexual religion, the Shakers), industrialists like Kruger and Pullman, financiers like Cambell and Braden, Grover Cleveland, John C. Calhoun, Neville Chamberlain, Andrew Jackson (whose expulsion of the Cherokee Nation from its traditional lands onto the "trail of tears," where most of them perished, is the archetypal *Zweitracht* land-grab), William Jennings Bryan, and Frank Stanton of CBS.

Since all Illuminati with any academic leanings at all are encouraged to major in history, the tendency in most textbooks is not only to black out *Verwirrung* periods but to glorify *Zweitracht* periods as ages of Light and Progress. Indeed, they make entertaining reading: They are ages of expansion, and there are always new people being discovered to be subjugated, "civilized," and converted to tax-payers and rent-payers. Almost any age described in glowing and admiring language in a history text will prove, on examination, to be a *Zweitracht* era, and the foremost butchers and invaders are treated as the outstanding heroes of humanity. A sympathetic reading of the biographies of these empire-builders almost always indicates that they were *homo neophile* individuals who turned their talents to destruction rather than creativity because of bitterness engendered by years of torment and baiting by *homo neophobe* types during their childhoods.

The ever-present conflict in a *Zweitracht* period eventually leads to the third stage.

UNORDNUNG

Humanity has been transformed during a *Zweitracht* age, by placing logogram in governing authority over biogram. *Unordnung* is an attempt to restore balance by revolutionizing the logogram; there is no thought about the biogram, because contact with this somatic component of personality has been lost. (This loss of contact has been variously described by pre-Celinean observers: It is "the veil of Maya" in Buddhism, the "censor band" or "repression" in psychoanalysis, the "character armoring" and "muscular armoring" in Reichian psychology, etc.)

The *I Ching* hexagram for this stage is Meng, ☶☵ , or Youthful Folly. The yang line at the top indicates the continued supremacy of logogram, even though some biogram elements (the yin lines) begin to reassert themselves. The traditional reading is "mountain above water"; that is, the rigid logogram still repressing the Aquarian element as it seeks to liberate itself. The usual Chinese interpretation of this hexagram is "The young fool needs discipline," and the leaders of all rebellions at this stage always heartily agree with that and demand unquestioning obedience from their followers. This is a time of turmoils, troubles, and tyrannies that appear and disappear rapidly.

The mystical number is 11, which means "a new start" in Kabalism and "error and repentence" in most other systems of numerology.

Tarot trump 21, The Fool, symbolizes this age as a dreamy-eyed youth unknowingly walking over an abyss. The *Hitlerjugend,* and the disciples of various other *fuehrers* and messiahs, immediately come to mind. That this card is disputed by various Tarot experts, and is given a numerical value of 0 rather than 21 by the wisest, indicates the confusion in all *Unordnung* periods. The dog who barks to warn the Young Fool, like the yin lines in the hexagram, represents the desperate attempts of the biogram to break through the repression or censor-band and make itself heard.

Typical Cancerians who exemplified *Unordnung* are Julius Caesar, Mary Baker Eddy (whose philosophy was an explicit denial of the biogram), Albert Parsons, Emma Goldman, Benjamin Peret, Vladimir Mayakofski, Henry David Thoreau, Durrutti, P-J Proudhon, Brooks Adams, General Kitchener, Luigi Pirandello (the literary master of ambiguity), Erich Ambler (the literary master of conspiracy), Calvin Coolidge (who issued the classically muddled Cancerian statement "Be as revolutionary as science and as conservative as the multiplication table"), Andrei Gromyko, Nelson Rockefeller, John Calvin, Estes Kefauver, and Rexford Tugwell.

An *Unordnung* period has always been thought of (even before Hegel provided the words) as a synthesis between the thesis of *Verwirrung* and the antithesis *Zweitracht*; since it is a false synthesis on the logogrammic level only, it always gives birth to the fourth stage, the Parenthesis.

BEAMTENHERRSCHAFT

This is the age of bureaucracy, and to live at this time is, as Proudhon said, "to have every operation, every transaction, every movement noted, registered, counted, rated, stamped, measured, numbered, assessed, licensed, refused, authorized, endorsed, admonished, prevented, reformed, redressed, corrected . . . to be laid under contribution, drilled, fleeced, exploited, monopolized, extorted from, exhausted, hoaxed, and robbed." The governing *I Ching* hexagram is 47, *K'un,* ䷮ , oppression or exhaustion, the dried-up lake, with the usual reading of superior men oppressed by the inferior. This is the time when *homo neophobe* types most rigorously repress *homo neophile* types, and great heresy hunts and witch trials flourish. This correlates with the number 8, signifying the Last Judgment, because every citizen is to some extent a State functionary, and each is on trial before the jury of all. The traditional Chinese associations with this hexagram are sitting under a bare tree and wandering through an empty valley—signifying the ecological havoc wreaked by purely abstract minds working upon the organic web of nature.

The 16th Tarot trump, The Tower, describes this age.

The Tower is struck by lightning and the inhabitants fall from the windows. (Cf. the Tower of Babel legend and our recent power failures.) The traditional interpretations of this card suggest pride, oppression, and bankruptcy.

This correlates with Libra, the mentality which measures and balances all things on an artificial scale (Maya). Typical Libras who have manifested *Beamtenherrschaft* characterists are Comte de Saint Simon, Justice John Marshall, Hans Geiger, Henry Wallace, Dwight Eisenhower, John Kenneth Galbraith, Arthur Schlesinger, Jr., John Dewey, and Dr. Joyce Brothers.

In *Beamtenherrschaft* ages there is ceaseless activity, all planned in advance, begun at the scheduled second, carefully supervised, scrupulously recorded—but inevitably finished late and poorly done. The burden of omniscience on the ruling class becomes virtually intolerable, and most flee into some form of schizophrenia or fantasy. Great towers, pyramids, moon shots, and similar marvels are accomplished at enormous cost while the underpinnings of social solidarity crumble entirely. While blunders multiply, no responsible individual can ever be found, because all decisions are made by committees; anyone seeking redress of grievance wanders into endless corridors of paperwork with no more tangible result than in the Hunting of the Snark. Illuminati historians, of course, describe these ages as glowingly as *Zweitracht* epochs, for, although control is in the hands of *homo neophobe* types, there is at least a kind of regularity, order, and geometrical precision about everything, and the "messiness" of the barbaric *Verwirrung* ages and revolutionary *Unordnung* ages is absent.

Nevertheless, the burden of omniscience on the rulers steadily escalates, as we have indicated, and the burden of nescience on the servile class increasingly renders them unfit to serve (more and more are placed on the dole, shipped to "mental" hospitals, or recruited into whatever is the current analog of the gladiatorial games), so the Tower eventually falls.

GRUMMET

The age of Grummet begins with an upsurge of magicians, hoaxers, Yippies, Kabouters, shamans, clowns, and other Eristic forces. The relevant I Ching hexagram is 59,

Huan, ☷ , dispersion and dissolution. The gentle wind above the deep water is the Chinese reading of the image, with associations of loss of ego, separation from the group, and "going out" in general. Yin lines dominate all but the top of the hexagram; the forces leading to a new *Verwirrung* stage are pushing upward toward release. This is also called Paralysis by the Illuminati, because, objectively, nothing much is happening; subjectively, of course, the preparations for the new cycle are working unconsciously.

The mystic number is 5, union of male (3) with female (2) and final resolution of conflict between *Verwirrung* and *Zweitracht*.

The governing Tarot trump is number 6, the Lovers, in which the woman looks upward at the angel (Eris, the biogram) and the man looks at the woman (the logogram, yang, reaches synthesis with biogram, yin, only through reconciliation with the female). Hence, the upsurge of feminism in such periods, together with a renewed emphasis on clans, tribes, and communes.

Typical Virgos manifesting *Grummet* traits are Charlie Parker, Antonin Artaud, Louis Lingg, Edgar Rice Burroughs, Grandma Moses, Lodovico Ariosto, Greta Garbo, Hedy Lamarr, and Goethe and Tolstoy (who manifested strong yin values while never quite getting reconciled with the women in their own lives. Tolstoy, however, as the classic dropout, is an archetypal Grummet persona and almost completed the Sufi course of "quit this world, quit the next world, quit quitting!").

After *Grummet,* of course, authority has collapsed entirely, and the biogram stands on equal footing with the logogram. Hodge and Podge being once again in dynamic balance, a new *Verwirrung* period begins, and the cycle repeats.

Since Weishaupt dreamed this schema up while he was under the influence of several hallucinogenic drugs, one should regard it with some skepticism. It is certainly not true in every detail, and there is no theoretical or empirical demonstration that each of the five ages must always have 73 permutations. The fact that *Grummet*-Virgo personalities (and all other of the five personality types) are born in all ages, even if they come to dominance in their appropriate epochs, leaves many mysteries still unsolved. In short, all that a sober scholar can say of the Illuminati theory of history is that it makes at least as much sense as the exoteric Marx-Hegel, Spengler, Toynbee, and Sorokin theories.

The A∴A∴, who regard all Illuminati theories as false projections onto the external world of inner spiritual processes, are particularly skeptical about this one, since it involves several false correlations between the *I Ching* and the Tarot, the Zodiac, etc.

Finally, it should be noted that of all the people Hagbard employed as resonance for the vibes used against the Saure family in Ingolstadt, only Lady Velkor, Danny Pricefixer, and George Dorn were not Virgos. Hagbard evidently believed that the Illuminati magical links work when Illuminati activities are occurring in a given area—and, hence, virtually all of "his" people at the festival were Virgos and thereby linked with the *Grummet/Huan*-59/Trump 6 chain of astrological associations. On the other hand, the presence of three non-Virgos shows Hagbard's pragmatic approach and his refusal to be ruled even by so exact a science as astrology.*

In this connection, when George Dorn and his mother went to Radio City Music Hall to see *The Lotus Position,* the last movie made by the American Medical Association before their tragic deaths, they happened to meet a tall Italian and a very beautiful black woman whom he introduced as his wife. Mrs. Dorn didn't catch the Italian's name, but it was obvious that George had a very great admiration for him. On the bus back to Nutley, she decided to straighten the boy out.

"A man who respects himself and his own race," she began, "would never think of marrying into *the colored.*"

"Shut up, Ma," George said politely.

"That's no way to talk to your mother," the fine lady said, going ahead blithely. "Now, your father had some radical ideas, and he tried to get the unions to accept *the colored,* but he never thought of marrying into them, George. He had too much self-respect. Are you listening, George?"

"How did you like the AMA?" he asked.

"Such wonderful young boys. So clean-cut. And that darling sister of theirs! At least they didn't think there was

---

* This sentence may manifest a lapse into mockery or mystification by otherwise sober authors.

anything attractive about long hair on men. Do you know what long hair makes men look like?"

"Like girls, Ma. Is that right?"

"It makes them look worse than girls, George. It makes them look like they're not really men, if you know what I mean."

"No, I don't know what you mean, Ma." George was profoundly bored.

"Well, I mean a *little* bit on the lavender side." She tittered.

"Oh," he said, "you mean cocksuckers. Some of my best friends are cocksuckers, Ma."

At this simple piece of factual information, the remarkable lady turned red and then purple, and then twisted in her chair to look out the window in angry silence for the rest of the trip. The curious thing is that, before George could get the courage to shut the old battleaxe up that way, he first had to try to shoot a cop and then try to shoot himself and finally take hashish with Hagbard Celine, and yet she was a Virgo and he was a Capricorn.

APPENDIX DALETH
HASSAN i SABBAH AND ALAMOUT BLACK

When the Prophet died in 4632 A.M.,* the true faith was almost immediately shattered by conflict between the Shiite and Sunnite parties. More than a century of religious and civil warfare followed, and by 4760 A.M. the Shiites themselves had split and given birth to a subsect known as the Ismailis, or Ishmaelians. It was out of this group that Hassan i Sabbah formed the Order of the Assassins in 5090 A.M.

Ishmaelian religion had already at that date become a nine-level affair in the manner typical of mystical secret societies. Those of the lowest grade, for instance, were merely informed that *Al Koran* contained an allegorical meaning in addition to its surface teachings, and that their salvation lay in following orders. As a neophyte progressed through

---

* Known as the year 52 to Moslems, 4392 to Jews and Scotch Rite Masons, 4320 to Confucians, and 632 to Christians.

the various grades, more and more of the allegories would be explained, and a doctrine would gradually emerge which is, in essence, that taught by all the mystics of East and West—Buddhists, Taoists, Vedantists, Rosicrucians, etc. The doctrine is, in important aspects, unspeakable (which is why the trainee required an *imam*—the Ishmaelian equivalent of a *guru*—to guide him in the nonverbal aspects); the ninth and highest grade, however, had no parallel except in very strict Theravada Buddhism. In this ninth grade, which Hassan attained shortly before founding the Hashishim, it was taught that even the personal mystical experience of the seeker (his own encounter with the Absolute, or the Void, or the Hodge-Podge, or God, or Goddess, or whatever one chooses to call it) should be subject to the most merciless analysis and criticism, and that there is no guide superior to reason. The Ishmaelian adept, in short, was one who had achieved supreme mystical awareness but refused to make even that into an idol; he was a total atheist-anarchist subject to no authority but his own independent mind.

"Such men are dangerous," as Caesar observed, and certainly they are dangerous to the Caesars; the Ishmaelians were being persecuted throughout the Moslem world, and strong efforts were being made to exterminate them entirely when Hassan i Sabbah became Imam of the whole movement.

It was Hassan's cynical judgment (and many Illuminated beings, such as the Lamas of Tibet, have agreed with him) that most people have no aspiration or capacity for much spiritual and intellectual independence. He thereupon reorganized the Ishmaelians in such a way as to allow and encourage those of small mind to remain in the lower grades.

The tools of this enterprise were the famous "Garden of Delights" in his castle at Alamout (a good duplication of the Paradise of *Al Koran,* complete with the beautiful and willing houris the Prophet had promised to the faithful)—and a certain "magick chemical." Those of the lowest grade were brought to Alamout, given the miraculous concoction, and set loose for several hours in the Garden of Delights. They came out convinced that they had truly visited heaven and that Hassan i Sabbah was the most powerful Holy Man in the world. They were assured, furthermore, that if they obeyed every order, even at the cost of their own lives, they would return to that Paradise after death.

These men became the first "sleeper agents" in the history of international politics. Where the three major contending religions of that time in the Near East (Christianity, Judaism, and orthodox Islam) insisted that it was an unforgivable sin to deny one's faith, Hassan taught that Allah would forgive such little white lies when they served a worthy purpose. Thus, his agents were able to pass themselves off as Christians, Jews, or orthodox Moslems and infiltrate any court, holy order, or army at will. Since the other religions had the above-mentioned prohibition against such deception, they were unable to infiltrate the Ishmaelians in turn.

The use of these agents as assassins is discussed *passim* in the novel, and Weishaupt's opinion that Hassan had discovered "the moral equivalent of war" is an interesting commentary. Hassan never had to send an army into battle, and armies sent against him were soon stopped by the sudden and unexpected deaths of their generals.

One of Hassan's successors was Sinan, who moved the headquarters of the cult from Alamout to Messiac and may (or may not) have written the letter about Richard the Lion-Hearted which George recalls in the Third Trip. Sinan, contemporaries claimed, performed miracles of healing, conversed with invisible beings, and was never seen to eat, drink, or perform the functions of urination and excretion. He was also credited with telepathy and with the ability to kill animals by looking at them. It was he (and not Hassan I Sabbah, as many popular books state) who ordered two of the lower members of the Order to commit suicide in order to impress a visiting ambassador with his power over his followers. (The two obeyed, leaping from the castle wall into the abyss below.) Sinan also made attempts to form an alliance with the Knights Templar, to drive both orthodox Christians and orthodox Moslems out of the arena, but this evidently fell through.

The Hashishim were finally crushed, despite their powerful espionage and assassination network, when the whole Middle East was overrun by hordes of Mongols, who came from so far away that they had not been infiltrated. It took several centuries for the Hashishim to make a comeback as the nonviolent Ishmaelian movement of today, under the leadership of the Aga Khan.

Finally, it was at Hassan i Sabbah's death that he allegedly uttered the aphorism for which he is best known, and which is quoted several times in the novel: "Nothing is true. All is permissible." The orthodox Moslem historian Juvaini—who may have invented this whole episode—adds that as soon as these blasphemous words passed his lips, "Hassan's soul plunged to the depths of Hell."

Ever since Marco Polo recorded the story of the Garden of Delights, Western commentators have identified Hassan's "magick chemical" as pure hashish. Recent scholarship, however, has thrown this into doubt, and it is clear that hashish, and other marijuana preparations were well known in the Near East for thousands of years before Hassan ever lived; for instance, the plant has been found in grave mounds of late Neolithic Man in the area, dated around 5000 B.C., as Hagbard mentions in the novel. It is implausible, then, that the ingenious Sabbah would have tried to pass this drug off as something new and magical.

Some have suggested that Hassan, who was known to have traveled much in his youth, might have brought opium back from the East and mixed it with hashish. The scholarly Dr. Joel Fort goes further and argues, in *The Pleasure Seekers*, that Hassan's supercharger was wine-and-opium, with no marijuana products at all. Dr. John Allegro, in *The Sacred Mushroom and the Cross*, argues that both Hassan and the first Christians actually achieved the paradisical vision with the aid of *amanita muscaria*, the "fly agaric" mushroom, which is poisonous in high doses but psychedelic (or at least deleriant) in small quantities.

The present book's suggestion—Alamout black, an almost pure hashish with a few pinches of belladonna and stramonium—is based on:

(1) the strong etymological evidence that the Hashishim were *somehow* involved with hashish;

(2) the unlikelihood that wine, opium, mushrooms, or any combination thereof could account for the etymological and historical association of Hassan with hashish;

(3) the reasons previously given for doubting that hashish *alone* is the answer;

(4) the capacity of stramonium and belladonna (in small doses) to create intensely brilliant visual imagery, beyond that of even the best grades of hashish;

(5) the fact that these latter drugs were used in both the

Elusinian Mysteries and in the European witch cult contemporary with Hassan (see R.E.L. Masters, *Eros and Evil*).

Since it is not the intent of this book to confuse fact with fancy, it should be pointed out that these arguments are strong but not compelling. Many other alternatives can be suggested, such as hashish-belladonna-mandragora, hashish-stramonium-opium, hashish-opium-belladonna, hashish-opium-bufotinin,* etc., etc. All that can be said with certainty is that Hagbard Celine insists the correct formula is hashish-belladonna-stramonium (in ratio 20:1:1), and we believe Hagbard—most of the time.

The exact link between the Assassins and the European Illuminati remains unclear. We have seen (but no longer own) a John Birch Society publication arguing that the alliance between the Hashishim and the Knights Templar was consummated and that European masonry has been more or less under Hashishim influence ever since. More likely is the theory of Daraul (*op. cit.*) that after the Hashishim regrouped as the nonviolent Ishmaelian sect of today, the Roshinaya (Illuminated Ones) copied their old tactics and were in turn copied by the Allumbrados of Spain and, finally, by the Bavarian Illuminati.

The nine stages of Hashishim training, the thirteen stages in Weishaupt's Iluminati, the thirty-two degrees of masonry, etc., are, of course, arbitrary. The Theravada Buddhists have a system of forty meditations, each leading to a definite stage of growth. Some schools of Hinduism recognize only two stages: *Dhyana,* conquest of the personal ego, and *Samadhi,* unity with the Whole. One can equally well posit five stages or a hundred and five. The essential that is common to all these systems is that the trainee, at some point or other, is nearly scared to death.*

---

* Medieval magicians knew how to obtain bufotinin. They took it, as Shakespeare recorded, from "skin of toad."
* An interesting account of a traditional system used by quite primitive Mexican Indians, yet basically similar to any and all of the above, is provided by anthropologist Carlos Castaneda, who underwent training with a Yaqui shaman, and recounts some of the terrors vividly in *The Teachings of Don Juan, A Separate Reality, Journey to Ixtlan,* and *Tales of Power.* Don Juan used peyote, stramonium, and a magic mushroom (probably *psilocyble Mexicana,* the drug Tim Leary used for his first trip).

The difference between these systems is that some aim to liberate every candidate and some, like Sabbah's and Weishaupt's, deliberately encourage the majority to remain in ignorance, whereby they may with profit be endlessly exploited by their superiors in the cult. The same general game of an illuminated minority misusing a superstitious majority was characteristic of Tibet until the Chinese Communist invasion broke the power of the high lamas. A sympathetic account of the Tibetan system, which goes far toward justifying it, can be found in Alexandra David-Neel's *The Hidden Teachings of Tibetan Buddhism;* an unsympathetic account by a skeptical fellow mystic is available in *The Confessions of Aleister Crowley.*

Another word about Alamout black: It is not for the inexperienced psychedelic voyager. For instance, the first time Simon Moon tried it, in early 1968, he had occasion to use the men's room in the Biograph Theatre (where he had gone to see *Yellow Submarine* while under the influence). After his bowel movement he reached for the toilet paper and saw with consternation that the first sheet hanging down off the roll was neatly stamped

OFFICIAL
BAVARIAN ILLUMINATI
EWIGE BLUMENKRAFT!

On ordinary marijuana or hashish, such illusions occur, of course—but they are not true hallucinations. They go away if you look at them hard enough. No matter how hard Simon looked at the toilet paper, it still said

OFFICIAL
BAVARIAN ILLUMINATI
EWIGE BLUMENKRAFT!

Simon went back to his seat in the theater badly shaken. For weeks afterward he wondered if the Illuminati had some sinister reason for infiltrating the toilet-paper industry, or if the whole experience were a genuine hallucination and the first sign, as he put it, "that this fucking dope is ruining my fucking head." He never solved this mystery, but eventually he stopped worrying about it.

As for Hassan i Sabbah X and the Cult of the Black

Mother, the authors have been able to learn precious little about them. Since they are clearly related *somehow* to the Assassins and the cult of Kali, Mother of Destruction, one can consider them part of the Illuminati, or Podge, side of the Sacred Chao; since they seem to be businessmen rather than fanatics, and since Kali might be a version of Eris, one can consider them part of the Discordian or Hodge side. Amid such speculation and much mystery, they go their dark way, peddling horse and preaching some pretty funky doctrines about Whitey. Perhaps they intend to betray everybody and run off with the loot at an opportune moment—and, then again, maybe they are the only really dedicated revolutionaries around. "Nothing is too heavy to be knocked on its ass, and everything is cool, baby" is the only summary of his personal philosophy that Hassan i Sabbah X himself would give us. He's a studly dude, and we didn't press him.

APPENDIX TZADDI
23 SKIDOO

Linguists and etymologists have had much exercise for their not-inconsiderable imaginations in attempting to account for this expression. *Skidoo* has been traced back to the older *skedaddle*, and thence to the Greek *skedannumi*, "to disperse hurriedly." The 23, naturally, has caused even more creative efforts by these gentry, since they are unaware of the secret teachings of Magick. One theorist, noting that Sidney Carton in Dickens' *Tale of Two Cities* is the twenty-third man guillotined in the final scene,* guessed that those playgoers who were eager to get out of the theater before the crowd counted off the executions and *skidoo'd* toward the exits numbered 23. Another eminent scholar assumes that the expression has something to do with men hanging around the old Flatiron Building on Twenty-third Street in New York City—a notoriously windy corner—to watch ladies' skirts raised by the breeze; when a cop came, they would *skidoo*. Others have mused inconclusively about

---

* A literary reference which Simon Moon, with his modernistic bias, overlooked.

the early telegraph operator's signal of *23,* which means (roughly) "stop transmitting," "clear the line," or, to be crude, "shut up," but nobody claims to know how telegraphers picked 23 to have this meaning.

The mystery's real origin is a closely guarded secret of the Justified Ancients of Mummu, which Simon had not attained the rank to learn. Dillinger, however, had attained this rank, and uses the formula quite correctly in the bank robbery scene in the Third Trip. It was printed by "Frater Perdurabo" (Aleister Crowley) in *The Book of Lies* (privately published, 1915; republished by Samuel Weiser Inc., New York, 1970). The text of the spell makes up the totality of Chapter 23 in that curious little book; and it reads:

ΚΕΦΛΛΗ ΚΓ (23)
SKIDOO

What man is at ease in his Inn?
Get out.
Wide is the world and cold.
Get out.
Thou hast become an in-itiate.
Get out.
But thou canst not get out by the way thou camest
   in. The Way out is THE WAY.
Get out.
For OUT is Love and Wisdom and Power.
Get OUT.
If thou hast T already, first get UT.
Then get O.
And so at last get OUT.

It is not permissible to explain this fully, but it may be stated guardedly that T is the union of sex and death, *Tau,* the Rosy Crucifixion; UT is *Ut*gita in the Upanishads; and O is the Positive Void.*

* Fission Chips, like our other characters, was given a chance to peruse this manuscript before publication and correct any factual errors that may have crept in. Of this appendix, he said, "I think my leg is being pulled again, chaps. I suspect that Crowley wrote that in 1915 as a joke on his readers, and you blokes found it and inserted a reference to a magic formula used by Dillinger in your story just so you could then compose this appendix and 'explain' it." Such skepticism,

APPENDIX VAU
FLAXSCRIP AND HEMPSCRIP

Flaxscrip was first introduced into Discordian groups by the mysterious Malaclypse the Younger, K.S.C., in 1968. Hempscrip followed the year after, issued by Dr. Mordecai Malignatus, K.N.S. (In the novel, taking one of our few liberties with historical truth, we move these coinages backward in time and attribute hempscrip to the Justified Ancients of Mummu.)

The *idea* behind flaxscrip, of course, is as old as history; there was private money long before there was government money. The first revolutionary (or reformist) use of this idea, as a check against galloping usury and high interest rates, was the foundation of "Banks of Piety" by the Dominican order of the Catholic Church in the late middle ages. (See Tawney, *Religion and the Rise of Capitalism.*) The Dominicans, having discovered that preaching against usury did not deter the usurer, founded their own banks and provided loans without interest; this "ethical competition" (as Josiah Warren later called it) drove the commercial banks out of the areas where the Dominicans practiced it. Similar private currency, loaned at a low rate of interest (but not at no interest), was provided by Scots banks until the British government, acting on behalf of the monopoly of the Bank of England, stopped this exercise of free enterprise. (See Muellen, *Free Banking.*) The same idea was tried successfully in the American colonies before the Revolution, and again was suppressed by the British government, which some heretical historians regard as a more direct cause of the American Revolution than the taxes mentioned in most schoolbooks. (See Ezra Pound, *Impact*, and additional sources cited therein.)

During the nineteenth century many anarchists and individualists attempted to issue low-interest or no-interest pri-

---

straining at a gnat and swallowing a camel, may be compared to the stance of the Bible Fundamentalist who avers that JHVH made the universe in six days in 4004 B.C. but included fossils and other false leads to make it appear much older. One could equally assert that the cosmos appeared out of Void one second ago, including us and our false memories of a longer duration here.

vate currencies. *Mutual Banking,* by Colonel William Greene, and *True Civilization,* by Josiah Warren, are records of two such attempts, by their instigators. Lysander Spooner, an anarchist who was also a constitutional lawyer, argued at length that Congress had no authority to suppress such private currencies (see his *Our Financiers: Their Ignorance, Usurpations and Frauds*). A general overview of such efforts at free enterprise, soon crushed by the Capitalist State, is given by James M. Martin in his *Men Against the State,* and by Rudolph Rocker in *Pioneers of American Freedom* (an ironic title, since his pioneers all lost their major battles). Lawrence Labadie, of Suffern, N.Y., has collected (but not yet published) records of 1,000 such experiments; one of the present authors, Robert Anton Wilson, unearthed in 1962 the tale of a no-interest currency, privately issued, in Yellow Springs, Ohio, during the 1930s depression. (This was an emergency measure by certain local businessmen, who did not fully appreciate the principle involved, and was abandoned as soon as the "tight-money" squeeze ended and Roosevelt began flooding us all with Federal Reserve notes.)

It is traditional among liberal historians to dismiss such endeavors as "funny-money schemes." They have never explained why government money is any less hilarious. (That used in the U.S. now, for instance, is actually worth 47 percent of its "declared" face value). All money is funny, if you stop to think about it, but no private currency, competing on a free market, could ever be quite so comical (and tragic) as the notes now bearing the magic imprint of Uncle Sam—and backed only by his promise (or threat) that, come hell or high water, by God he'll make it good by taxing our descendants unto the infinite generation to pay the interest on it. The National Debt, so called, is of course, nothing else but the debt we owe the bankers who "loaned" this money to Uncle after he kindly gave them the credit which enabled them to make this loan. Hempscrip or even acidscrip or peyotescrip could never be quite so clownish as this system, which only the Illuminati (if they really exist) could have dreamed up. The system has but one advantage: It makes bankers richer every year. Nobody else, from the industrial capitalist or "captain of industry" to the coalminer, profits from it in any way, and all pay the taxes, which become the interest payments, which make the bankers

richer. If the Illuminati did not exist, it would be necessary
to invent them—such a system can be explained in no other
way, except by those cynics who hold that human stupidity
is infinite.

The idea behind hempscrip is more radical than the notion of private-enterprise currency per se. Hempscrip, as
employed in the novel, depreciates; it is, thus, not merely a
no-interest currency, but a *negative-interest* currency. The
lender literally pays the borrower to take it away for a
while. It was invented by German business-economist Silvio
Gesell, and is described in his *Natural Economic Order* and
in professor Irving Fisher's *Stamp Script*.

Gresham's Law, like most of the "laws" taught in State-
supported public schools, is not quite true (at least, not in
the form in which it is usually taught). *"Bad money drives
out good" holds only in authoritarian societies, not in libertarian societies.* (Gresham was clear-minded enough to
state explicitly that he was only describing authoritarian societies; *his* formulation of his own "Law" begins with the
words "If the king issueth two moneys . . . ," thereby
implying that the State must exist if the "Law" is to operate.) *In a libertarian society, good money will drive out
the bad.* This Utopian proposition—which the sane reader
will regard with acute skepticism—has been seen to be
sound by a rigorously logical demonstration, based on the
axioms of economics, in *The Cause of Business Depressions*
by Hugo Bilgrim and Edward Levy.*

* Economists can "prove" all sorts of things from axioms and few of
them turn out to be true. Yes. We saved for a footnote the information
that at least four empirical demonstrations of the reverse of Gresham's
Law are on record. Three of them, employing small volunteer com-
munities in frontier U.S.A. circa 1830–1860, are recorded in Josiah
Warren's *True Civilization*. The fourth, employing contemporary
college students in a psychology laboratory, is the subject of a recent
Master's thesis by associate professor Don Werkheiser of Central
State College, Wilberforce, Ohio.

APPENDIX ZAIN
PROPERTY AND PRIVILEGE

> Property is theft.
>
> —P. J. PROUDHON

> Property is liberty.
>
> —P. J. PROUDHON

> Property is impossible.
>
> —P. J. PROUDHON

> Consistency is the hobgoblin of small minds.
> —RALPH WALDO EMERSON

Proudhon, by piling up his contradictions this way, was not merely being French; he was trying to indicate that the abstraction "property" covers a variety of phenomena, some pernicious and some beneficial. Let us borrow a device from the semanticists and examine his triad with subscripts attached for maximum clarity.

"Property$_1$ is theft" means that property$_1$, created by the artificial laws of feudal, capitalist, and other authoritarian societies, is based on armed robbery. Land titles, for instance, are clear examples of property$_1$; swords and shot were the original coins of transaction.

"Property$_2$ is liberty" means that property$_2$, that which will be voluntarily honored in a voluntary (anarchist) society, is the foundation of the liberty in that society. The more people's interests are comingled and confused, as in collectivism, the more they will be stepping on each other's toes; only when the rules of the game declare clearly "This is mine and this is thine," *and the game is voluntarily accepted as worthwhile by all parties to it,* can true independence be achieved.

"Property$_3$ is impossible" means that property$_3$ (= property$_1$) creates so much conflict of interest that society is in perpetual undeclared civil war and must eventually devour itself (and properties $_1$ and $_3$ as well). In short, Proudhon, in his own way, foresaw the Snafu Principle. He also foresaw that communism would only perpetuate and aggravate the conflicts, and that *anarchy is the only viable alternative to this chaos.*

It is not averred, of course, that property₂ will come into existence only in a totally voluntary society; many forms of it already exist. The error of most alleged libertarians—especially the followers (!) of the egregious Ayn Rand—is to assume that all property₁ is property₂. The distinction can be made by any IQ above 70 and is absurdly simple. The test is to ask, of any title of ownership you are asked to accept or which you ask others to accept, "Would this be honored in a free society of rationalists, or does it require the armed might of a State to force people to honor it?" If it be the former, it is property₂ and represents liberty; if it be the latter, it is property₁ and represents theft.

APPENDIX CHETH
HAGBARD'S ABDICATION

Readers who do not understand the scene in which Hagbard abdicates in favor of Miss Portinari should take heart.

Once they do understand it, they will understand most of the mysteries of all schools of mysticism.

APPENDIX LAMED
THE TACTICS OF MAGICK

> The human brain evidently operates on some variation of the famous principle enunciated in *The Hunting of the Snark:* "What I tell you three times is true."
>
> —NORBERT WEINER, *Cybernetics*

The most important idea in the *Book of Sacred Magic of Abra-Melin the Mage* is the simple-looking formula "Invoke often."

The most successful form of treatment for so-called mental disorders, the Behavior Therapy of Pavlov, Skinner, Wolpe, et al., could well be summarized in two similar words: "Reinforce often." ("Reinforcement," for all practical purposes, means the same as the layman's term "reward." The essence of Behavior Therapy is rewarding desired behavior; the behavior "as if by magic" begins to occur more and more often as the rewards continue.)

Advertising, as everybody knows, is based on the axiom "Repeat often."

Those who think they are "materialists" and think that "materialism" requires them to deny all facts which do not square with their definition of "matter" are loath to admit the well-documented and extensive list of individuals who have been cured of serious maladies by that very vulgar and absurd form of magick known as Christian Science. Nonetheless, the reader who wants to understand this classic work of immortal literature will have to analyze its deepest meanings, guided by an awareness that there is no essential difference between magick, Behavior Therapy, advertising, and Christian Science. All of them can be condensed into Abra-Melin's simple "Invoke often."

Reality, as Simon Moon says, is thermoplastic, not thermosetting. It is not quite Silly-Putty, as Mr. Paul Krassner once claimed, but is much closer to Silly-Putty than we generally realize. If you are told often enough that "Budweiser is the king of beers," Budweiser will eventually taste somewhat better—perhaps a great deal better—than it tasted before this magick spell was cast. If a behavior therapist in the pay of the communists rewards you every time you repeat a communist slogan, you will repeat it more often, and begin to slide imperceptibly toward the same kind of belief that Christian Scientists have for their mantras. And if a Christian Scientist tells himself every day that his ulcer is going away, the ulcer will disappear more rapidly than it would have had he not subjected himself to this homemade advertising campaign. Finally, if a magician invokes the Great God Pan often enough, the Great God Pan will appear just as certainly as heterosexual behavior appears in homosexuals who are being handled (or manhandled) by Behavior Therapy.

The opposite and reciprocal of "Invoke often" is "Banish often."

The magician wishing for a manifestation of Pan will not only invoke Pan directly and verbally, create Panlike conditions in his temple, reinforce Pan associations in every gesture and every article of furniture, use the colors and perfumes associated with Pan, etc.; he will also banish other gods verbally, banish them by removing their associated furnitures and colors and perfumes, and banish them in every other way. The Behavior Therapist calls this "negative reinforcement," and in treating a patient who is afraid of elevators he will not only reinforce (reward) every instance in which the patient rides an elevator without terror, but will also negatively reinforce (punish) each indication of terror shown by the patient. The Christian Scientist, of course, uses a mantra or spell which both reinforces health and negatively reinforces (banishes) illness.* Similarly, a commercial not only motivates the listener toward the sponsor's product but discourages interest in all "false gods" by subsuming them under the rubric of the despised and contemptible Brand X.

Hypnotism, debate, and countless other games have the same mechanism: *Invoke often* and *Banish often.*

The reader who seeks a deeper understanding of this argument can obtain it by putting these principles to the test. If you are afraid that you might, in this Christian environment, fall into taking the Christian Science mantra too seriously, try instead the following simple experiment. For forty days and forty nights, begin each day by invoking and praising the world in itself as an expression of the Egyptian deities. Recite at dawn:

> I bless Ra, the fierce sun burning bright
> I bless Isis-Luna in the night
> I bless the air, the Horus-hawk
> I bless the earth on which I walk

Repeat at moonrise. Continue for the full forty days and forty nights. We say without any reservations that, at a

---

* The basic Christian Science mantra, known as "The Scientific Statement of Being," no less, is as follows: "There is no life, truth, intelligence nor substance in matter. All is infinite mind and its infinite manifestation, for God is all in all, Spirit is immortal truth: matter is mortal error. Spirit is the real and eternal; matter is the unreal and temporal. Spirit is God and man is His image and likeness. Therefore man is not material, he is spiritual." The fact that these statements are, in terms of the scientific criteria, "meaningless," "non-operational," and "footless" is actually totally irrelevant. *They work.* Try them and see. As Aleister Crowley, no friend of Mrs. Eddy's, wrote, "Enough of Because! May he be damned for a dog!"

minimum, you will feel happier and more at home in this part of the galaxy (and will also understand better Uncle John Feather's attitude toward our planet); at maximum, you may find rewards beyond your expectations, and will be converted to using this mantra for the rest of your life. (If the results are exceptionally good, you just might start believing in ancient Egyptian gods.)

A selection of magick techniques which will offend the reason of no materialist can be found in Laura Archera Huxley's *You Are Not the Target* (a powerful mantra, the title!), in *Gestalt Therapy,* by Perls, Heferline, and Goodman, and in *Mind Games,* by Masters and Houston.

All this, of course, is programming your own trip by manipulating appropriate clusters of word, sound, image, and emotional (*prajna*) energy. The aspect of magick which puzzles, perplexes, and provokes the modern mentality is that in which the operator programs somebody else's trip, *acting at a distance.* It is incredible and insulting, to this type of person, if one asserts that our Mr. Nkrumah Fubar could program a headache for the President of the United States. He might grant that such manipulating of energy is possible if the President was told about Mr. Fubar's spells, but he will not accept that it works just as well when the subject has no conscious knowledge of the curse.

The magical theory that $5 = 6$ has no conviction for such a skeptic, and magicians have not yet proposed a better theory. The materialist then asserts that all cases where magic did appear to work under this handicap are illusions, delusions, hallucinations, "coincidences,"* misapprehensions, "luck," accident, or downright hoax.

He does not seem to realize that asserting this is equivalent to asserting that reality is, after all, thermoplastic—for he is admitting that many people live in a different reality than his own. Rather than leave him to grapple as best he can with this self-contradiction, we suggest that he consult *Psychic Discoveries Behind the Iron Curtain,* by Ostrander and Schroder—especially Chapter 11, "From Animals to Cybernetics: The Search for a Theory of Psi." He might realize that when "matter" is fully understood, there is nothing a materialist need reject in magick *action at a distance,*

---

* Look up the etymology of that word some time and see if it means anything.

which has been well explored by scientists committed to the rigid Marxist form of dialectical materialism.

Those who have kept alive the ancient traditions of magick, such as the Ordo Templi Orientalis, will realize that the essential secret is sexual (as Saul tries to explain in the Sixth Trip) and that more light can be found in the writings of Wilhelm Reich, M. D., than in the current Soviet research. But Dr. Reich was jailed as a quack by the U.S. Government, and we would not ask our readers to consider the possibility that the U.S. Government could ever be wrong about anything.

Any psychoanalyst will guess at once the most probable symbolic meanings of the Rose and the Cross; but no psychologist engaged in psi research has applied this key to the deciphering of traditional magic texts. The earliest reference to freemasonry in English occurs in Anderson's "Muses Threnody," 1638:

> For we be brethren of the Rosey Cross
> We have the Mason Word and second sight

but no parapsychologist has followed up the obvious clue contained in this conjunction of the vaginal rose, the phallic cross, the word of invocation, and the phenomenon of thought projection. That the taboos against sexuality are still latent in our culture explains part of this blindness; fear of opening the door to the most insidious and subtle forms of paranoia is another part. (*If the magick can work at a distance,* the repressed thought goes, *which of us is safe?*) A close and objective study of the anti-LSD hysteria in America will shed further light on the mechanisms of avoidance here discussed.

Of course, there are further offenses and affronts to the rationalist in the deeper study of magick. We all know, for instance, that words are only arbitrary conventions with no intrinsic connection to the things they symbolize, yet magick involves the use of words in a manner that seems to imply that some such connection, or even identity, actually exists. The reader might analyze some powerful bits of language not generally considered magical, and he will find something of the key. For instance, the 2 + 3 pattern in "Hail Eris"/"All hail Discordia" is not unlike the 2 + 3 in "Holy Mary, Mother of God," or that in the "L.S./M.F.T."

which once sold many cartons of cigarettes to our parents; and the 2 + 3 in Crowley's "Io Pan! Io Pan Pan!" is a relative of these. Thus, when a magician says that you *must* shout "Abrahadabra," and no other word, at the most intensely emotional moment in an invocation, he exaggerates; you may substitute other words; but you will abort the result if you depart too far from the five-beat patttern of "Abrahadabra."*

But this brings us to the magical theory of reality.

Mahatma Guru Sri Paramahansa Shivaji* writes in *Yoga for Yahoos:*

> Let us consider a piece of cheese. We say that this has certain qualities, shape, structure, color, solidity, weight, taste, smell, consistency and the rest; but investigation has shown that this is all illusory. Where are these qualities? Not in the cheese, for different observers give quite different accounts of it. Not in ourselves, for we do not perceive them in the absence of the cheese . . .

> What then are these qualities of which we are so sure? They would not exist without our brains; they would not exist without the cheese. They are the results of the union, that is of the Yoga, of the seer and seen, of subject and object . . .

There is nothing here with which a modern physicist could quarrel; and this is the magical theory of the universe. The magician assumes that *sensed reality*—the panorama of impressions monitored by the senses and collated by the brain—is radically different from so-called objective reality.† About the latter "reality" we can only form speculations or theories which, if we are very careful and subtle, will not contradict either logic or the reports of the senses. This lack of contradiction is rare; some conflicts between

---

* A glance at the end of Appendix Beth will save the reader from misunderstanding the true tenor of these remarks.

* Aleister Crowley again, under another pen-name.

† See the anthology *Perception,* edited by Robert Blake, Ph.D., and especially the chapter by psychologist Carl Rogers, which demonstrates that people's perceptions change while they are in psychotherapy. As William Blake noted, "The fool sees not the same tree that the wise man sees."

theory and logic, or between theory and sense-data, are not discovered for centuries (for example, the wandering of Mercury away from the Newtonian calculation of its orbit). And even when achieved, lack of contradiction is proof only that the theory *is not totally false*. It is never, in any case, proof that the theory *is totally true*—for an indefinite number of such theories can be constructed from the known data at any time. For instance, the geometries of Euclid, of Gauss and Reimann, of Lobachevski, and of Fuller *all* work well enough on the surface of the earth, and it not yet clear whether the Gauss-Reimann or the Fuller system works better in interstellar space.

If we have this much freedom in choosing our theories about "objective reality," we have even more liberty in deciphering the "given" or transactional *sensed reality*. The ordinary person senses as he or she has been taught to sense —that is, as they have been programmed by their society. The magician is a self-programmer. Using invocation and evocation—which are functionally identical with self-conditioning, auto-suggestion, and hypnosis, as shown above—he or she edits or orchestrates sensed reality like an artist.*

This book, being part of the only serious conspiracy it describes—that is, part of Operation Mindfuck—has programmed the reader in ways that he or she will not understand for a period of months (or perhaps years). When that understanding is achieved, the real import of this appendix (and of the equation $5 = 6$) will be clearer. Officials at Harvard thought Dr. Timothy Leary was joking when he warned that students should not be allowed to indiscriminately remove dangerous, habit-forming books from the library unless each student proves a definite need for each volume. (For instance, you have lost track of Joe Malik's mysterious dogs by now.) It is strange that one can make the clearest possible statements and yet be understood by many to have said the opposite.

The Rite of Shiva, as performed by Joe Malik during the SSS Black Mass, contains the central secret of all magick, very explicitly, yet most people can reread that section a dozen, or a hundred times, and never understand what the secret is. For instance, Miss Portinari was a typical Catholic

---

* Everybody, of course, does this unconsciously; see the paragraph about the cheese. The magician, doing it consciously, controls it.

girl in every way—except for an unusual tendency to take Catholicism seriously—until she began menstruating and performing spiritual meditations every day.* One morning, during her meditation period, she visualized the Sacred Heart of Jesus with unusual clarity; immediately another image, distinctly shocking to her, came to mind with equal vividness. She recounted this experience to her confessor the next Saturday, and he warned her, gravely, that meditation was not healthy for a young girl, unless she intended to take the oath of seclusion and enter a convent. She had no intention of doing that, but rebelliously (and guiltily) continued her meditations anyway. The disturbing second image persisted whenever she thought of the Sacred Heart; she began to suspect that this was sent by the Devil to distract her from meditation.

One weekend, when she was home from convent school on vacation, her parents decided she was the right age to be introduced to Roman society. (Actually, they, like most well-off Italian families, had already chosen which daughter would be given to the church—and it wasn't her. Hence, this early introduction to *la dolce vita*.) One of the outstanding ornaments of Rome at that time was the "eccentric international businessman" Mr. Hagbard Celine, and he was at the party to which Miss Portinari was taken that evening.

It was around eleven, and she had consumed perhaps a little too much Piper Heidseck, when she happened to find herself standing near a small group who were listening raptly to a story the strange Celine was telling. Miss Portinari wondered what this creature might be saying—he was reputedly even more cynical and materialistic than other international money-grubbers, and Miss Portinari was, at that time, the kind of conservative Catholic idealist who finds capitalists even more dreadful than socialists. She idly tuned in on his words; he was talking English, but she understood that language adequately.

" 'Son, son,' " Hagbard recited, " 'with two beautiful women throwing themselves at you, why are you sitting alone in your room jacking off?' "

Miss Portinari blushed furiously and drank some more

---

* These two signs of growth often appear at the same time, being DNA-triggered openings of the fourth neural circuit.

champagne to conceal it. She hated the man already, knowing that she would surrender her virginity to him at the
earliest opportunity; of such complexities are intellectual
Catholic adolescents capable.

"And the boy replied," Hagbard went on, " 'I guess you
just answered your own question, Ma.' "

There was a shocked silence.

"The case is quite typical," Hagbard added blandly, obviously finished. "Professor Freud recounts even more startling family dramas."

"I don't see . . ." a celebrated French auto racer began,
frowning. Then he smiled. "Oh," he said, "was the boy an
American?"

Miss Portinari left the group perhaps a bit too hurriedly
(she felt a few eyes following her) and quickly refilled her
champagne glass.

A half-hour later she was standing on the veranda, trying
to clear her head in the night air, when a shadow moved
near her and Celine appeared amid a cloud of cigar smoke.

"The moon has a fat jaw tonight," he said in Italian.
"Looks like somebody punched her in the mouth."

"Are you a poet in addition to your other accomplishments?" she asked coolly. "That sounds as if it might be
American verse."

He laughed—a clear peal, like a stallion whinnying.
"Quite so," he said. "I just came from Rapallo, where I was
talking to America's major poet of this century. How old
are you?" he asked suddenly.

"Almost sixteen," she said fumbling the words.

"Almost fifteen," he corrected ungallantly.

"If it's any affair of yours—"

"It might be," he replied easily. "I need a girl your age
for something I have in mind."

"I can imagine. Something foul."

He stepped further out of the shadows and closer.
"Child," he said, "are you religious?"

"I suppose you regard that as old-fashioned," she replied,
imagining his mouth on her breast and thinking of paintings of Mary nursing the Infant.

"At this point in history," he said simply, "it's the only
thing that isn't old-fashioned. What was your birthdate?
Never mind—you must be a Virgo."

"I am," she said. (His teeth would bite her nipple, but

very gently. He would know enough to do that.) "But that is superstition, not religion."

"I wish I could draw a precise line between religion, superstition, and science." He smiled. "I find that they keep running together. You are Catholic, of course?" His persistence was maddening.

"I am too proud to believe an absurdity, and therefore I am not a Protestant," she replied—immediately fearing that he would recognize the plagiarism.

"What symbol means the most to you?" he asked, with the blandness of a prosecuting attorney setting a trap.

"The cross," she said quickly. She didn't want him to know the truth.

"No." He again corrected her ungallantly. "The Sacred Heart."

Then she knew he was of Satan's party.

"I must go," she said.

"Meditate further on the Sacred Heart," he said, his eyes blazing like a hypnotist's (a cornball gimmick, he was thinking privately, but it might work). "Meditate on it deeply, child. You will find in it the essential of Catholicism —and the essential of all other religion."

"I think you are mad," she responded, leaving the veranda with undignified haste.

But two weeks later, during her morning meditation, she suddenly understood the Sacred Heart. At lunchtime she disappeared—leaving behind a note to the Mother Superior of the convent school and another note for her parents— and went in search of Hagbard. She had even more potential than he realized, and (as elsewhere recorded) within two years he abdicated in her favor. They never became lovers.*

The importance of symbols—images—as the link between word and primordial energy demonstrates the unity between magick and yoga. Both magick and yoga—we reiterate—are methods of self-programming employing synchronistically connected chains of word, image, and bioenergy.

Thus, rationalists, who are all puritans, have never con-

* They were quite good friends, though, and he did fuck her occasionally.

sidered the fact that disbelief in magick is found only in puritanical societies. The reason for this is simple: Puritans
are incapable of guessing what magick is essentially all
about. It can even be surely ventured that only those who
have experienced true love, in the classic Albigensian or
troubadour sense of that expression, are equipped to understand even the most clear-cut exposition of the mysteries.*

The eye in the triangle, for instance, is not primarily a
symbol of the Christian Trinity, as the gullible assume—except insofar as the Christian Trinity is itself a visual (or
verbal) elaboration on a much older meaning. Nor is this
symbol representative of the Eye of Osiris or even of the
Eye of Horus, as some have ventured; it is venerated, for
instance, among the Cao Dai sect in Vietnam, who never
heard of Osiris or Horus. The eye's meaning can be found
quite simply by meditating on Tarot Trump XV, the Devil,
which corresponds, on the Tree of Life, to the Hebrew letter *ayin*, the eye. The reader who realizes that "The Devil"
is only a late rendering of the Great God Pan has already
solved the mystery of the eye, and the triangle has its usual
meaning. The two together are the union of *Yod*, the father, with *He*, the Mother, as in *Yod-He-Vau-He*, the holy
unspeakable name of God. *Vau*, the Holy Ghost, is the result of their union, and final *He* is the divine ecstasy which
follows. One might even venture that one who contemplates
this key to the identities of Pan, the Devil, the Great Father, and the Great Mother will eventually come to a new,
more complete understanding of the Christian Trinity itself,
and especially of its most mysterious member, *Vau*, the elusive Holy Ghost.*

The pentagram comes in two forms but always represents
the fullest extension of the human psyche—the male human psyche in particular. The pentagram with one horn exalted is, quite naturally, associated with the right-hand path;
and the two-horned pentagram with the left-hand path. (The
Knights Templar, very appropriately, inscribed the head of

---

* This book has stated it as clearly as possible in a number of places,
but some readers are still wondering what we are holding back.
* This being has more in common with the ordinary nocturnal visitor,
sometimes called a "ghost," than is immediately evident to the uninitiated. Cf. the well-documented association of poltergeist dis-
turbances with adolescents.

Baphomet, the goat-headed deity who was their equivalent of Pan or the Devil, within the left-handed pentagram in

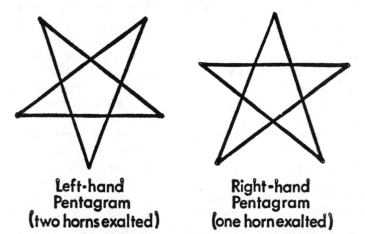

**Left-hand
Pentagram
(two horns exalted)**

**Right-hand
Pentagram
(one horn exalted)**

such wise that each "horn" contained one of Baphomet's horns.) It is to be observed that the traditionally sinister* left-hand pentagram contains an internal *pentagon* with one point *upward*, whereas the right-hand pentagram contains an internal *pentagon* with one point *downward;* this nicely illustrates the Law of Opposites.† The pentagon in the Sacred Chao is tilted from the perpendicular so that it cannot be said to have any points directly upward or directly downward—or perhaps can be said to have 1½ points up and 1½ points down‡—thereby illustrating the Reconciliation of Opposites.

All that can be said against the method of the left-hand

---

* This association, attributing diabolism to the left-hand path, is oversimplified, prejudiced, and superstitious. In general, it can be said that the left-hand pentagram is suitable for both invocations and evocations, whereas the right-hand pentagram is suitable only for evocations, and that is the only important difference. (It is assumed that the reader understands the pentagram as an exclusively male symbol.)

† Cf. the Tarot trumps II and III—the Magus, holding one arm upward and one downward, and the High Priestess, sitting between the pillars of Day and Night. (The Priestess is also associated with the Hebrew letter *gimmel*, the camel, and part of the meaning of this symbolism is contained in the shapes of the camel's back and the Hebrew letter.)

‡ This makes it quite useless for summoning werewolves. The Sacred Chao, however, is intended to teach a philosophical lesson, not to attract individuals with dubious pastimes.

pentagram, without prejudice, is that this form of the sacrament is always destructive of the Holy Spirit, in a certain sense. It should be remembered that the right-hand pentagram method is also destructive in most cases, especially by those practitioners so roundly condemned in Chapter 14 of Joyce's *Ulysses*—and this group is certainly the majority these days. In view of the ecological crisis, it might even be wise to encourage the left-hand method and discourage the right-hand method at this time, to balance the Sacred Numbers.

Very few readers of the *Golden Bough* have pierced Sir Prof. Dr. Frazer's veil of euphemism and surmised the exact method used by Isis in restoring life to Osiris, although this is shown quite clearly in extant Egyptian frescoes. Those who are acquainted with this simple technique of resurrecting the dead (which is *at least partially* successful in *all* cases and totally successful in most) will have no trouble in skrying the esoteric connotations of the Sacred Chao—or of the Taoist yin-yang or the astrological sign of cancer. The method almost completely reverses that of the pentagrams, right or left, and it can even be said that in a certain sense it was not Osiris himself but his brother, Set, symbolically understood, who was the object of Isis's magical workings. *In every case, without exception, a magical or mystical symbol always refers to one of the very few* variations of the same, very special variety of human sacrifice: the "one eye opening" or the "one hand clapping"; and this sacrifice cannot be partial—it must culminate in death if it is to be efficacious.* The literal-mindedness of the Saures, in the novel, caused them to become a menace to life on earth; the reader should bear this in mind. The sacrifice is not simple. It is a species of cowardice, epidemic in Anglo-Saxon nations for more than three centuries, which causes most who seek success in this field to stop short before the death of the victim. *Anything less than death—that is, complete oblivion—simply will not work.** (One will find more

---

* Fewer than seventy, according to a classical enumeration.
* The magician must always identify fully with the victim, and share every agonized contortion to the utmost. Any attitude of standing aside and watching, as in a theatrical performance, or any intellectualization during the moments when the sword is doing its brutal but necessary work, or any squeamishness or guilt or revulsion, creates the two-mindedness against which Hagbard so vehemently warns in *Never Whistle While You're Pissing.* In a sense, only the mind dies.

clarity on this crucial point in the poetry of John Donne than in most treatises alleging to explain the secrets of magick.)

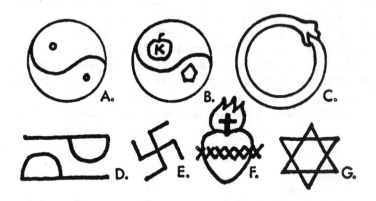

A. YIN-YANG; B. SACRED CHAO; C. OUROBOROS, THE SERPENT EATING ITS OWN TAIL; D. ASTROLOGICAL SIGN OF CANCER; E. SWASTIKA; F. ROMAN CATHOLIC SACRED HEART; G. HEXA-GRAM.

The symbolism of the swastika is quite adequately explained in Wilhelm Reich's *Mass Psychology of Fascism.*

Ouroboros, the serpent eating its own tail, is chiefly emblematic of the Mass of the Holy Ghost.*

The Roman Catholic symbolism of the Sacred Heart is strikingly overt, especially to readers of Frazer and Payne-Knight. In essence, it is the same notion conveyed by the cartoonist's conventional rendering of Cupid shooting his arrow into a red pulsating heart. This is the basic meaning of the Dying God and the Resurrection. The identification of Christ with the pelican who stabs its own heart with its beak (to feed its young) is an analogous rendering of the same motif. We repeat that it was only because the Saure family so misread these simple symbols that they became cruel and sadistic.

In essence, then, the basic symbols, of magic, mythology, and religion—whether Eastern or Western, ancient or modern, "right-hand" or "left-hand"—are so simple that only

---

* See Israel Regardie, *The Tree of Life.*

the pernicious habit of looking for alleged "profundities" and "mysteries" prevents people from automatically understanding them almost without thinking. The meaning of the hexagram—the female equivalent of the male pentagram—was explicated by Freud himself, but most students, convinced that the answer could not be so elementary and down-to-earth, continue to look into the clouds.

The same principles apply to written symbols. The all-important name YOD HE VAU HE, for instance, has traditionally been scanned in various ways, of which the most significant correlations are given in the following table:

	YOD	HE	VAU	HE
True meaning of the Hebrew letters	Fist (or spermatazoon)	Window	Nail	Window
Traditional magick code	Father	Mother	Son	Daughter
Tarot suit	Wands	Cups	Swords	Pentacles (or Discs)
Tarot trump	Hermit	Star	Hierophant	Star
Tarot Royal Card	Knight	Queen	Prince	Princess
Element	Fire	Water	Air	Earth

The traditional lion-man-eagle-bull symbolism also fits this table,* as do Joyce's Four Old Men in *Finnegans Wake*;† it can also be found in the Aztec codices and Buddhist mandalas.

The essential and original meaning, of course, is a program for a ritual, and the ritual is magick. The four letters are simply the four beats in Wilhelm Reich's formula: muscular tension → electrical charge → electrical discharge → muscular relaxation. In short, as Freud once noted, every

---

* YOD, the fiery father, is the lion (fire-sign); HE, the watery mother, is man as humanity; VAU, the air spirit, is eagle; final HE, earth, is bull.

† Marcus Lyons (i.e., the lion) is the fiery father; Matt Gregory (i.e., the ego) is the watery mother; John McDougall (i.e., eagle) is the airy son; Luke Tarpey (taur, the bull) is the earthy daughter.

sexual act involves, at a minimum, four parties. The father and son provide a "fist" and a "nail"; the mother and daughter provide two "windows." The case of the Chicago schizophrenic killer William Heirens, who experienced orgasm when climbing through windows, demonstrates that this symbolism does not have to be taught and is inherent in the human mind, although always subject to the distortion exemplified by the Saures.

Finally, the universal blessing given on page 218 is intimately involved with the YHVH formula:

> I bless Ra, the fierce sun burning bright
> I bless Isis-Luna in the night
> I bless the air, the Horus-Hawk
> I bless the earth on which I walk

The fiery father, the watery mother, the airy son, and the earthy daughter are all there, just as they are in every alchemical formula.* But we say no more at this point, lest the reader begin seeking for a $5 = 4$ equation to balance the $5 = 6$.

We conclude with a final warning and clarification: Resort to mass sacrifice (as among the Aztecs, the Catholic Inquisition, and the Nazi death camps) is the device of those who are incapable of the true Rite of the Dying God.

APPENDIX YOD
OPERATION MINDFUCK

OM was originally instigated by Ho Chih Zen, of the Erisian Liberation Front, who is the same person but not the same individual as Lord Omar Khayyam Ravenhurst, author of *The Honest Book of Truth*. The guiding philosophy is that originally proposed in *The Theory of Games and Economic Behavior* by von Neumann and Morgenstern: namely, that the only strategy which an opponent cannot predict is a random strategy. The foundation had already

---

* In this connection—and also, *en passant,* as an indication that Adolf Hitler's link with the Illuminati was not invented for this work of "fiction"—we suggest that the reader look into *The Morning of the Magicians,* by Pauwels and Bergier.

been laid by the late Malaclypse the Younger, K.S.C., when he proclaimed, "We Discordians must stick apart." This radical decentralization of all Discordian enterprises created a built-in random factor even before Operation Mindfuck was proposed. To this day, neither Ho Chih Zen himself nor any other Discordian apostle knows for sure who is or is not involved in any phase of Operation Mindfuck or what activities they are or are not engaged in as part of that project. Thus, the outsider is immediately trapped in a double-bind: the only safe assumption is that anything a Discordian does is somehow related to OM, but, since this leads directly to paranoia, this is not a "safe" assumption after all, and the "risky" hypothesis that whatever the Discordians are doing is harmless may be "safer" in the long run, perhaps. *Every aspect of OM follows, or accentuates, this double-bind.**

OM projects vary from the trivial to the colossal.

An example of the former is a rubber stamp owned by Dr. Mordecai Malignatus, which says SEE MENTAL HEALTH RECORDS. (Dr. Malignatus casually picked this up from a public-health clinic while nobody was looking.) Any mail which Dr. Malignatus considers impertinent or insulting—especially if it comes from a government office—is stamped with this motto and sent back, otherwise untouched. This causes considerable puzzlement to various bureaucrats.

An example of the latter is Project Jake, instigated by Harold Lord Randomfactor. Once or twice a year, a public servant who has distinguished himself by more than common imbecility is selected as target for a Jake and all Discordian cabals are alerted—including the various branches of the Erisian Liberation Front, the Twelve Famous Buddha Minds, the St. Gulik Iconistary, the Earl of Nines, the Tactile Temple of Eris Erotic, the Brotherhood of the Lust of Christ, Green & Pleasant Enterprises, Society for Moral

---

* The double-bind, first defined by anthropologist Gregory Bateson, is a situation in which you must choose between two alternatives both of which are unpleasant. A beautiful example, suggested by Mr. William S. Burroughs: Condition a draftee so that he will immediately obey either the order 'Stand up" or the order· "Sit down," if given by a superior officer, then have two officers simultaneously order him to stand up and sit down. Obeying the first order means disobeying the second, and obeying the second means disobeying the first. Presumably, the subject would wig out.

Understanding and Training, the In-Sect, the Golden Apple Panthers, the Paratheo-Anametamystikhood of Eris Esoteric, Sam's Café, the Seattle Group, the Stone Dragon Cabal, the Universal Erisian Church, and the Young Americans for Real Freedom.* On Jake Day, the public servant being honored receives mail from *all* of these, on their official letterheads (which are somewhat weird, it must be granted), asking for help in some complicated political matter that passes all rational understanding. The official so honored can conclude either that he is the target of a conspiracy composed entirely of lunatics, or that the general public is much more imaginative and less stodgy than he had previously assumed.

Between the trivial and the colossal there is a variety of OM which can be called the chronic.

Most notable is the honorary membership. Not wishing to exclude anybody from membership in the Erisian movement for such a technicality as being non-Erisian, the legendary Malaclypse the Younger invented several honorary Aneristic groups. It is now the tradition for any Discordian cabal to appoint anybody to one of these groups if his or her behavior is notably Aneristic. For instance, a high-school principal who has given a particularly stirring assembly speech on some such topic as "The Draft as a Protection for Our Freedoms" (or "Taxation as a Protection for Our Property" or any of the other oxymorons beloved by educators) might thereafter receive some such mailing as this:

ORDER OF THE PEACOCK ANGEL

House of Apostles of Eris

(√) Safeguard this letter; it is an important historical document.
( ) Burn after reading—subversive literature.
( ) Ignore and continue what you were doing before opening this.

Dear (√) Sir ( ) Madam ( ) Fido:
It has recently come to Our ears that you, in your official capacity as principal of Aaron Burr High School, said in a public meeting, with your bare face hanging out, that death by napalm is "really no more painful than a bad cold" and that Orientals have "tougher epidermi than whites and feel less acutely."

* All these are real groups, currently active in the U.S.A. (Do you believe that?)

In Our official capacity as High Priest of the Head temple of the House of Apostles of Eris, We congratulate you for helping to restore American education to its rightful position as the envy and despair of all other (and, hence, lesser) educational systems.

You are hereby appointed a five-star General in the Bureau of the Division of the Department of the Order of the Knights of the Five-Sided Castle, Quixote Cabal, with full authority to shrapnel your friends and bomb your neighbors.

If you have any answers, We will be glad to provide full and detailed questions.

In the Name of La Mancha,

Theophobia the Elder, M.C.P.
High Priest, Head temple

Hail Eris—All hail Discordia—Kallisti

This document will be stamped with such legends as OF-FICIAL—DO NOT USE THIS PAPER AS TOILET TISSUE; SE-CREDIT—FOR YOUR EYES ONLY; QUIXQTE LIVES, etc., all in the most tasteful blues and reds, together with Easter Bunny seals, ribbons, and whatever other decorations it pleases the local cabal to attach. Often it will be accompanied by a button or an armband, making the possessor a five-star General, adorned with a classic rendition of the Knight of the Mournful Countenance. Copies, of course, will be sent to the radical students at the school to guarantee that the principal being honored will see and hear many references to Don Quixote in following days, lest he think he is dealing with a single "harmless lunatic." (The official signal of the Knights of the Five-Sided Castle, needless to say, is a pentagon with a golden apple inside.)

Other groups to which individuals may be given honorary membership for conspicuously Aneristic behavior are:

the Hemlock Fellowship—for academic leaders who have taken strong actions to protect students from disturbing ideas and/or to deny tenure to controversial teachers or professors;

the St. Famine Society for War Against Evil—for people who have exhibited unusual concern for the moral behavior of their neighbors;*

the Flat Earth Society—for legislators or citizens' groups

* Annual meetings are held on the Feast of St. Famine at the Casa de Inquisitador in San Miguel de Allende, Mexico.

dedicated to preventing the dissemination of "modernistic" ideas in education;†

the Fat Jap Anti-Defamation League—for Women's Liberationists and others who have found good ideological reasons to object to the English language;

the Fraternal Order of Hate Groups—given to allegedly libertarian groups only if they have engaged in conspicuously authoritarian behavior *and* have developed a philosophical line proving that said behavior is actually libertarian. (That group which has found the best libertarian justification for opposing liberty receives the Annual William Buckley Memorial Award and joint membership in the St. Famine Society for War Against Evil.);

the First Evangelical and Reformed Rand, Branden, and Holy Galt Church—for those who are simultaneously rationalists and dogmatists;

the Part-of-the-Solution Vanguard Party—for any Supreme Servant of the People who has shown inordinate zeal in banishing most of the people as Parts-of-the-Problem.

Other aspects of Operation Mindfuck include:

Project Eagle. Day-glo posters have been printed which look like the old Eagle proclamation saying TO THE POLLS YE SONS OF FREEDOM. The new, improved Discordian posters, however, have one slight word change, and say cheerfully BURN THE POLLS YE SONS OF FREEDOM. Like the old ones, they are posted in prominent places on election day.

Project Pan-Pontification. Since the Rev. Kirby Hensley founded the Universal Life Church and started ordaining *everybody* as a minister of the gospel, the Paratheo-Anametamystikhood of Eris Esoteric has decided to raise the stakes. They are now distributing cards stating:

THE BEARER OF THIS CARD
IS A GENUINE AND AUTHORIZED
P O P E
So *Please* Treat Him Right

GOOD FOREVER

Genuine and authorized by the HOUSE OF APOSTLES OF ERIS. Every man, woman and child on Earth is a genuine and authorized Pope.

Members receive a handsome banner proclaiming IN YOUR HEART YOU KNOW IT'S FLAT.

Similar cards, with "Him" replaced by "Her" and "Pope" by "Mome," are being prepared for Woman's Liberationists.

Project Graffito (and *Project Bumpersticker*). Anybody can participate by inventing a particularly Erisian slogan and seeing that it is given wide distribution. Examples: *Your Local Police Are Armed and Dangerous; Legalize Free-Enterprise Murder: Why Should Governments Have All The Fun?; Smash the Government Postal Monopoly; If Voting Could Change the System, It Would Be Against the Law*; etc.

Citizens Against Drug Abuse. This organization possesses elegant letterheads and is engaged in a campaign of encouraging Congressmen to outlaw catnip, a drug which some young people are smoking whenever marijuana is in short supply. The thought behind this project is that, the government having lost so much credibility due to its war against pot (a recent ELF survey showed that in some big cities a large portion of the under-25 population did not believe in any of the moon shots and assumed they were all faked somewhere in the American Desert), a campaign against this similar but more comical herb will destroy the last tattered shreds of faith in the men in Washington.

APPENDIX KAPH
THE ROSY DOUBLE-CROSS

Saul, Barney, Markoff Chaney, and Dillinger were all puzzled that a man like Carmel would bring a suitcase full of roses with him when fleeing to Lehman Cavern. Those who knew Carmel in Las Vegas were even more perplexed when this fact was made public. The first readers of this romance were not only puzzled and perplexed but petulant, since they knew Carmel had loaded his briefcase with Maldonado's money, not with roses.

The explanation, as is usually the case when seeming magick has occurred, was simple: Carmel was the victim of the oldest swindle in the world, the *okkana borra* (gypsy switch). It was his custom to transport his earnings to the bank in the same suitcase which he used when looting Maldonado's safe. His figure, and the suitcase, were well known to the shadier elements in Las Vegas, and among these were

three gentlemen who decided early in April to intercept him
during one of his journeys and remove the suitcase from his
possession, using, as young people say, "any means necessary"; they even considered striking him upon the temple
with a blunt instrument. One of the gentlemen involved in
this project, John Wayne Malatesta, however, had a sense
of humor (of sorts) and began to devise a plan involving a
nonviolent gypsy switch. Mr. Malatesta thought it would be
amusing if this could be carried off smoothly and Carmel,
arriving at the bank, opened a case full of horse manure,
human excrement, or something else in equally dubious
taste. The other two gentlemen were persuaded that this
might indeed be worth a laugh. A substitute suitcase was
purchased, and a plan was devised.

Two changes were made at virtually the last minute. Mr.
Malatesta learned from Bonnie Quint (a lady whose company he often enjoyed, at $100 a throw) that Carmel suf-
fered acutely from rose fever. A more hilarious image occurred to him: Carmel opening the case in the bank and
starting to sneeze spasmodically while trying to figure out
where the switch had been made. The roses were purchased, and the caper was set for the next day.

When Carmel, Dr. Naismith, and Markoff Chaney collided, Malatesta and his associates abandoned the switch idea:
Two collisions in a few minutes would be more than a man
like Carmel would accept without profound suspicion. They
therefore decided to follow him to his house and revert to
the more old-fashioned but time-proven technique of the
sudden rap on the skull.

When Bonnie Quint left after her violent interview with
Carmel, the bandits prepared to enter. To their amazement,
Carmel came running out, threw his suitcase into his jeep,
and then ran back in. (He had forgotten his candies.)

"It's God's will," Malatesta said piously.

The switch was made, and they took off for points south
in a great hurry.

Several weeks after the crisis had passed, a state trooper
found a car with three dead men in it off the road in a
ditch. His own symptoms were self-diagnosed while he
waited for the coroner's crew to arrive, and he received the
antidote in time.

The empty suitcase in the car caused only minor speculation: A Gila monster had obviously eaten most of one side

of it to shreds. "Whatever they had in there," the trooper said later, "must have been pretty light. The wind blew it all over the freaking desert."

APPENDIX TETH
HAGBARD'S BOOKLET

After prolonged pleading and vehement prayers of entreaty, the authors finally prevailed upon Hagbard Celine to allow us to quote some further illuminating passages from his booklet *Never Whistle While You're Pissing.** (Before we made these frantic efforts, he wanted us to publish the whole thing.)

Here, then, are some of the keys to the strange head of Hagbard Celine:

I once overheard two botanists arguing over a Damned Thing that had blasphemously sprouted in a college yard. One claimed that the Damned Thing was a tree and the other claimed that it was a shrub. They each had good scholarly arguments, and they were still debating when I left them.

The world is forever spawning Damned Things—things that are neither tree nor shrub, fish nor fowl, black nor white—and the categorical thinker can only regard the spiky and buzzing world of sensory fact as a profound insult to his card-index system of classifications. Worst of all are the facts which violate "common sense," that dreary bog of sullen prejudice and muddy inertia. The whole history of science is the odyssey of a pixilated card-indexer perpetually sailing between such Damned Things and desperately jug-

---

* The title, he informs us, is taken from R. H. Blythe's *Zen in English Literature and Oriental Classics.* The story is instructive: Blythe, studying za-zen (sitting zen, or *dhyana* meditation) in a monastery at Kyoto, asked the *roshi* (Zen Master) if there was any further discipline he should adopt to accelerate his progress. The *roshi* replied, concisely, "Never whistle while you're pissing." Cf. Gurdjieff's endless diatribes about "concentration," the rajah in Huxley's *Island* who unleashed talking mynah birds to remind his citizens constantly "Here and now, boys, here and now!" and Jesus' "Whatever thy hand findest to do, do it with all thy heart."

gling his classifications to fit them in, just as the history of
politics is the futile epic of a long series of attempts to line
up the Damned Things and cajole them to march in regi-
ment.

Every ideology is a mental murder, a reduction of dynamic living processes to static classifications, and every
classification is a Damnation, just as every inclusion is an
exclusion. In a busy, buzzing universe where no two snow-
flakes are identical, and no two trees are identical, and no
two people are identical—and, indeed, the smallest sub-
atomic particle, we are assured, is not even identical with itself from one microsecond to the next—every card-index
system is a self-delusion. "Or, to put it more charitably," as
Nietzsche says, "we are all better artists than we realize."

It is easy to see that the label "Jew" was a Damnation in
Nazi Germany, but actually the label "Jew" is a Damnation
anywhere, even where anti-Semitism does not exist. "He is
a Jew," "He is a doctor," and "He is a poet" mean, to the
card-indexing center of the cortex, that my experience with
him will be like my experience with other Jews, other doctors, and other poets. Thus, individuality is ignored when
identity is asserted.

At a party or any place where strangers meet, watch this
mechanism in action. Behind the friendly overtures there is
wariness as each person fishes for the label that will identify
and Damn the other. Finally, it is revealed: "Oh, he's an
advertising copywriter," "Oh, he's an engine-lathe operator." Both parties relax, for now they know how to behave,
what roles to play in the game. Ninety-nine percent of each
has been Damned; the other is reacting to the 1 percent
that has been labeled by the card-index machine.

Certain Damnations are socially and intellectually necessary, of course. A custard pie thrown in a comedian's face
is Damned by the physicist who analyzes it according to the
Newtonian laws of motion. These equations tell us all we
want to know about the impact of the pie on the face, but
nothing about the human meaning of the pie-throwing. A
cultural anthropologist, analyzing the social function of the
comedian as shaman, court jester, and king's surrogate, explains the pie-throwing as a survival of the Feast of Fools
and the killing of the king's double. This Damns the subject

in another way. A psychoanalyst, finding an Oedipal castration ritual here, has performed a third Damnation, and the Marxist, seeing an outlet for the worker's repressed rage against the bosses, performs a fourth. Each Damnation has its values and its uses, but it is nonetheless a Damnation *unless its partial and arbitrary nature is recognized.*

The poet, who compares the pie in the comedian's face with the Decline of the West or his own lost love, commits a fifth Damnation, but in this case the game element and whimsicality of the symbolism are safely obvious. At least, one would hope so; reading the New Critics occasionally raises doubts on this point.

Human society can be structured either according to the principle of authority or according to the principle of liberty. Authority is a static social configuration in which people act as superiors and inferiors: a sado-masochistic relationship. Liberty is a dynamic social configuration in which people act as equals: an erotic relationship. In every interaction between people, either Authority or Liberty is the dominant factor. Families, churches, lodges, clubs, and corporations are either more authoritarian than libertarian or more libertarian than authoritarian.

It becomes obvious as we proceed that the most pugnacious and intolerant form of authority is the State, which even today dares to assume an absolutism which the Church itself has long ago surrendered and to enforce obedience with the techniques of the Church's old and shameful Inquisition. Every form of authoritarianism is, however, a small "State," even if it has a membership of only two. Freud's remark to the effect that the delusion of one man is neurosis and the delusion of many men is religion can be generalized: The authoritarianism of one man is crime and the authoritarianism of many men is the State. Benjamin Tucker wrote quite accurately:

> Aggression is simply another name for government. Aggression, invasion, government are interchangeable terms. The essence of government is control, or the attempt to control. He who attempts to control another is a governor, an aggressor, an invader; and the nature of such invasion is not changed, whether it be made by one man upon another man, after the manner

of the ordinary criminal, or by one man upon all other men, after the manner of an absolute monarch, or by all other men upon one man, after the manner of a modern democracy.

Tucker's use of the word "invasion" is remarkably precise, considering that he wrote more than fifty years before the basic discoveries of ethology. Every act of authority is, in fact, an invasion of the psychic and physical territory of another.

Every fact of science was once Damned. Every invention was considered impossible. Every discovery was a nervous shock to some orthodoxy. Every artistic innovation was denounced as fraud and folly. The entire web of culture and "progress," everything on earth that is manmade and not given to us by nature, is the concrete manifestation of some man's refusal to bow to Authority. We would own no more, know no more, and be no more than the first apelike hominids if it were not for the rebellious, the recalcitrant, and the instransigent. As Oscar Wilde truly said, "Disobedience was man's Original Virtue."

The human brain, which loves to read descriptions of itself as the universe's most marvelous organ of perception, is an even more marvelous organ of rejection. The naked facts of our economic game, are easily discoverable and undeniable once stated, but conservatives—who are usually individuals who profit every day of their lives from these facts—manage to remain oblivious to them, or to see them through a very rosy-tinted and distorting lens. (Similarly, the revolutionary ignores the total testimony of history about the natural course of revolution, through violence, to chaos, back to the starting point.)

We must remember that *thought is abstraction.* In Einstein's metaphor, the relationship between a physical fact and our mental reception of that fact is not like the relationship between beef and beef-broth, a simple matter of extraction and condensation; rather, as Einstein goes on, it is like the relationship between our overcoat and the ticket given us when we check our overcoat. In other words, human perception involves *coding* even more than crude *sensing.* The mesh of language, or of mathematics, or of a school of art, or of any system of human abstracting, gives to our mental constructs the structure, not of the original fact, but of the symbol system into which it is coded, just as a map-maker colors a nation purple not because it *is* purple but because his code demands it. But every code excludes certain things, blurs other things, and overemphasizes still other things. Nijinski's celebrated leap through the window at the climax of *Le Spectre d'une Rose* is best coded in the ballet notation system used by choreographers; verbal language falters badly in attempting to convey it; painting or sculpture could capture totally the magic of one instant, but one instant only, of it; the physicist's equation, Force = Mass × Acceleration, highlights one aspect of it missed by all these other codes, but loses everything else about it. Every perception is influenced, formed, and structured by the habitual coding habits—mental game habits—of the perceiver.

All authority is a function of coding, of game rules. Men have arisen again and again armed with pitchforks to fight armies with cannon; men have also submitted docilely to the weakest and most tottery oppressors. It all depends on the extent to which coding distorts perception and conditions the physical (and mental) reflexes.

It seems at first glance that authority could not exist at all if all men were cowards or if no men were cowards, but flourishes as it does only because most men are cowards and some men are thieves. Actually, the inner dynamics of cowardice and submission on the one hand and of heroism and rebellion on the other are seldom consciously realized either by the ruling class or the servile class. Submission is identified not with cowardice but with virtue, rebellion not with heroism but with evil. To the Roman slave-owners, Spartacus was not a hero and the obedient slaves were not cowards; Spartacus was a villain and the obedient slaves were virtuous. The obedient slaves believed this also. The obedient always think of themselves as virtuous rather than cowardly.

If authority implies submission, liberation implies equality; authority exists when one man obeys another, and liberty exists when men do not obey other men. Thus, to say that authority exists is to say that class and caste exist, that submission and inequality exist. To say that liberty exists is to say that classlessness exists, to say that brotherhood and equality exist.

Authority, by dividing men into classes, creates dichotomy, disruption, hostility, fear, disunion. Liberty, by placing men on an equal footing, creates assocation, amalgamation, union, security. When the relationships between men are based on authority and coercion, they are driven apart; when based on liberty and nonaggression, they are drawn together.

There facts are self-evident and axiomatic. If authoritarianism did not possess the in-built, preprogrammed double-bind structure of a Game Without End, men would long ago have rejected it and embraced libertarianism.

The usual pacifist complaint about war, that young men are led to death by old men who sit at home manning bureaucrat's desks and taking no risks themselves, misses the point entirely. Demands that the old should be drafted to fight their own wars, or that the leaders of the warring nations should be sent to the front lines on the first day of battle, etc., are aimed at an assumed "sense of justice" that simply does not exist. To the typical submissive citizen of authoritarian society, it is normal, obvious, and "natural" that he should obey older and more dominant males, even at the risk of his life, even against his own kindred, and even in causes that are unjust or absurd.

"The Charge of the Light Brigade"—the story of a group of young males led to their death in a palpably idiotic situation and only because they obeyed a senseless order without stopping to think—has been, and remains, a popular poem, because unthinking obedience by young males to older males is the most highly prized of all conditioned reflexes within human, and hominid, societies.

The mechanism by which authority and submission are implanted in the human mind is coding of perception. That which fits into the code is accepted; all else is Damned. It is Damned to being ignored, brushed aside, unnoticed, and—if these fail—it is Damned to being forgotten.

A worse form of Damnation is reserved for those things which cannot be ignored. These are daubed with the brain's projected prejudices until, encrusted beyond recognition, they are capable of being fitted into the system, classified, card-indexed, buried. This is what happens to every

Damned Thing which is too prickly and sticky to be excommunicated entirely. As Josiah Warren remarked, "It is dangerous to understand new things too quickly." Almost always, we have not understood them. We have murdered them and mummified their corpses.

A *monopoly on the means of communication* may define a ruling elite more precisely than the celebrated Marxian formula of "monopoly on the means of production." Since man extends his nervous system through channels of communication like the written word, the telephone, radio, etc., he who controls these media controls part of the nervous system of every member of society. The contents of these media become part of the contents of every individual's brain.

Thus, in pre-literate societies taboos on the spoken word are more numerous and more Draconic than at any more complex level of social organization. With the invention of written speech—hieroglyphic, ideographic, or alphabetical—the taboos are shifted to this medium; there is less concern with what people say and more concern with what they write. (Some of the first societies to achieve literacy, such as Egypt and the Mayan culture of ancient Mexico, evidently kept a knowledge of their hieroglyphs a religious secret which only the higher orders of the priestly and royal families were allowed to share.) The same process repeats endlessly: Each step forward in the technology of communication is more heavily tabooed than the earlier steps. Thus, in America today (post–Lenny Bruce), one seldom hears of convictions for spoken blasphemy or obscenity; prosecution of books still continues, but higher courts increasingly interpret the laws in a liberal fashion, and most writers feel fairly confident that they can publish virtually anything; movies are growing almost as desacralized as books, although the fight is still heated in this area; television, the newest medium, remains encased in neolithic taboo. (When the TV pundits committed *lèse majesté* after an address by the then Dominant Male, a certain Richard Nixon, one of his lieutenants quickly informed them they had overstepped, and the whole tribe—except for the dissident minority—cheered for the reaasertion of tradition.) When a more efficient medium arrives, the taboos on television will decrease.

APPENDIX MEM
CERTAIN QUESTIONS THAT MAY STILL TROUBLE SOME READERS

1. What was Mama Sutra's "reading," where Danny Price-fixer questioned her, actually all about?
Answer: It had nothing to do with the John F. Kennedy assassination, the *Confrontation* bombing, the Illuminati, or any of the subjects it seemed to suggest, *except indirectly*. She had aimed in the dark, and picked up bits and pieces of the old movie *Manhattan Melodrama,* thusly:

• *District Attorney Wade* does not refer to the Dallas official who first proclaimed Lee Harvey Oswald's guilt over TV; it refers to the character played by William Powell in the movie.

• *Clark* does not refer to any of the Captain Clarks we have encountered; it refers to Clark Gable, Mr. Powell's co-star. *The Ship is sinking* does not refer to the Illuminati spider-ships, or the ship piloted by Captain Clark; it refers to the *General Slocum,* as Mama guessed—the sinking of this ship on June 15, 1904, is the first scene in the movie. *2422* does not refer to the dates of Oswald's and Kennedy's assassinations, or to the old Wobbly address; it refers to a scene in the film where Gable, at a racetrack, walks from box 24 to box 22 (box 23 is never shown, his body being between it and the camera).

• *If I can't live as I please, let me die when I choose* is the last line spoken by Clark Gable in the screenplay.

The fact that these phrases overlap certain themes in this novel (and in Joyce's *Ulysses*) is either coincidence or synchronicity—take your choice. *Manhattan Melodrama,* you might be interested to know, was playing at the Biograph Theatre on the night of July 22, 1934, and was the last film seen by the man who was shot outside and identified as John Herbert Dillinger.

2. What was the Masonic signal of distress used by the grocer B. F. Morgan when Dillinger tried to rob him in 1924?
Answer: It consists in holding your arms outward, bent

upward 90 degrees at the elbow, and shouting, "Will nobody help the widow's son?"

3. Is there really a secret passage beneath the Meditation Room in the UN building?
Answer: If so, we haven't been able to find it. Other spooky secrets about that room, however, are revealed in *The Cult of the All-Seeing Eye,* by Robert Keith Spencer (Christian Book Club of America, 1964).

4. What was the *Erotion* of Adam Weishaupt mentioned by Hagbard in the First Trip?
Answer: The word translates, loosely, as "love-in," and the idea is basically the same. (See the books of Nesta Webster and John Robison cited in the text.) *Now* do you believe in a conspiracy?

5. Did Al Capone really help the FBI set up the man who was shot at the Biograph Theatre on July 22, 1934?
Answer: That's one of the more plausible arguments in *Dillinger: Dead or Alive,* by Jay Nash and Ron Offen.

6. If no animals were reported missing from local zoos, how is that Robert Simpson of Kansas City was found dead with his throat torn as if by "the talons of some enormous beast?"
Answer: See the sequel, *The Homing Pigeons.*

7. If Simon Moon majored in mathematics and was so obsessed with numerology, why didn't he ever notice the most significant 23 in mathematical history—the 23 definitions that open Euclid's *Geometry?*
Answer: Perhaps for the same reason that the road from Dayton, Ohio, to New Lebanon, Ohio, was due *east* when Joe Malik drove it on June 25, 1969, but has always been due *west* on every day before and since then. Or maybe by the same processes that allowed Joe to see a Salem commercial on his TV set in the mid-1970s, although cigarette advertising was banned from television in 1971.

8. Did Smiling Jim Trepomena achieve the fame he had sought?
Answer: No. Dr. Vulcan Troll's definitive history of the

Great Quake, *When a State Dies,* mentions on page 123 that "no American Eagle has since been reported, and we can only assume that this species was another victim of nature's mindless rampage on that tragic May 1." On page 369, Dr. Troll mentions, among prominent casualties, "The famous Cincinnati lawyer and proponent of censorship James J. Trepomena." Neither he nor anyone else ever connected the two occurrences.

9. Where are the missing eight appendices?
Answer: Censored.

APPENDIX NUN
ADDITIONAL INFORMATION ABOUT SOME OF THE CHARACTERS

THE PURPLE SAGE. An imaginary Chaoist philospher invented by Lord Omar Khayyam Ravenhurst (another imaginary Chaoist philosopher).

LORD OMAR KHAYAM RAVENHURST. An imaginary Chaoist philosopher invented by Mr. Kerry Thornley of Atlanta, Georgia. Mr. Thornley was a friend of Lee Harvey Oswald's, was accused of complicity in the John Kennedy assassination by District Attorney Jim Garrison, and is the author of *Illuminati Lady,* an endless epic poem which you really ought to read.

GEORGE DORN. His maternal grandfather, old Charlie Bishop, was once a patient of the famous Doctor William Carlos Williams. The Bishops came to New Jersey in 1723, having left Salem, Massachusetts, in 1692 under something of a cloud. Folks in the Nutley-Clifton-Passaic-Paterson area always have a good word for the Bishops, though. But the Dorns were all troublemakers, and George's paternal grandfather, Big Bill Dorn, was so indiscreet as to get killed by cops during the Paterson silk-mill strike of 1922.

HERACLEITUS. He was apt to say odd things. Once he even wrote that "Religious ceremonies are unholy." A strange duck.

THE SQUIRREL. A set of receptor organs transmitting information through a central nervous system to a small brain programmed for only a few rudimentary decisions—but, in this, he was not far inferior to most of our characters.

REBECCA GOODMAN. Her maiden name was Murphy, and she was named after Rebecca of Sunnybrook Farm. You thought she was Jewish, didn't you?

THE DEAD EGYPTIAN MOUTH-BREEDERS. There were five of them, of course.

DANNY PRICEFIXER. Shot in the line of duty two years after the events of this story. Loved the music of Johann Sebastian Bach.

ADAM WEISHAUPT. "He's a deep one," they used to say on the faculty of the University of Ingolstadt, "you never know what he's really thinking."

CARMEL. One of his girls once cajoled a Hollywood character actor into calling him on the phone and pretending to be a researcher for the Kinsey Institute, seeking an interview. Carmel couldn't see any money in it and was trying to end the conversation when the actor asked stuffily, "Well, all we want to know, actually, is do you have intercourse with your mother regularly, or does everybody in Las Vegas call you 'Carmel the Motherfucker' for some other reason?" For once Carmel was speechless. The girl spread the story, and everybody in town was laughing about it for weeks.

PETER JACKSON. His great-grandfather was a slave. His son became the first President of the Luna Federation after the rebellion of the moon colonists in 2025. Much further back, a more remote ancestor was a king of Atlantis; and way in the future, a descendant was a slave on a planet in the Alpha Centauri system. (Peter was one of the crew when Hagbard finally blasted off for the stars in 1999). That's the way the cookie crumbles; and Peter had an intuitive sense of this paradoxical fatality, which caused him to tell Eldridge Cleaver once, "People who say 'You're either part of the solution or part of the problem' are themselves part of the problem." (Cleaver replied, wittily, "Fuck you.")

THE LAB CHIEF WHO WAS DISINTERESTED IN ANTHRAX LEPROSY DELTA. He later cracked up and wrote letters to the newspapers attacking the entire chemobiological warfare program of the United States government. Spent the last seventeen years of his life receiving treatment in St. Elizabeth's Hospital in Washington, D.C., occupying the same quarters that once housed the ingenious poet Ezra Pound. His rantings were taken seriously in certain places, especially among some leftward-leaning fellow scientists, but the Vice-President described them to the press as "the despondent demagogy of a paranoid pedant." A sample of the man's delusions, from a letter to the three top television networks (never quoted on newscasts because it was too controversial): "The boast of the 19th century was its conquest of these accursed plagues that attack men, women, and helpless infants indifferently. What shall be said of the 20th century, which has re-created them, at great expense and through the efforts of thousands of brilliant but perverted scientific minds, and then stored them *live* in installations throughout the country, where it is virtually certain, statistically, that an accident will unleash them upon an unsuspecting public, sooner or later?" (Loonies often harbor morbid fears of that sort.) The poor man never responded favorably to any of the efforts of his psychiatrists, even though they gave him ECT (electro-convulsive therapy) so often that his brain was practically fried to the crispness of a Howard Johnson omelette by the time he finally died.

ANTHRAX LEPROSY DELTA. A life form that could exist only by destroying other life-forms; in this respect, it was like many of us. The first of the products of Charlie Mocenigo's fertile genius, it could boast only of being ten times as deadly as ordinary anthrax. Insofar as it had consciousness, in a vague and flickering way, it was like that inhabiting a subway train at 5 P.M., concerned only with getting where it was going and then eating. The other strains were much the same, up to Anthrax Leprosy Pi.

LEE HARVEY OSWALD. Hero of a series of novels by Harold Weissburg, including *Whitewash, Whitewash II, Photographic Whitewash,* and *Oswald in New Orleans.* Villain of another novel, entitled *Report of the Presidential Commission on the Assassination of President John F. Kennedy,* by Earl Warren, John McCone, et al. Also featured in other works of fiction by Mark

Lane, Penn Jones, Josiah Thompson, and various other writers.

JACK RUBY. The Oliver Hardy to Oswald's Stanley Laurel.

THOMAS JEFFERSON. A revolutionary hemp-grower who once wrote, "[The clergy] believe that any portion of power confided to me, will be exerted in opposition to their schemes. And they believe rightly: *for I have sworn upon the altar of God eternal hostility against every form of tyranny over the mind of man.* But this is all they have to fear from me: and enough too in their opinion." Few of the pious tourists who read the italicized portion of this statement carved on the Jefferson Memorial in Washington, D.C., are aware of its context.

THE SCHIZOPHRENIC IN CHERRY KNOLLS HOSPITAL. His number was 124C41. Nobody, anywhere, remembered what his name had been.

MARY LOU SERVIX. She finally married Jim Riley, the dope dealer from Dayton—but that's another, rather longish, story, and not truly relevant.

MAYOR RICHARD DALEY. Author of such immortal aphorisms as "After all, I am a liberal myself" (October 22, 1968); "The policeman isn't there to create disorder, the policeman is there to preserve disorder" (September 23, 1968); "I have conferred with the Superintendent of Police this morning and I gave him instructions that an order be issued by him immediately and under his signature to shoot to kill any arsonist or anyone with a Molotov cocktail in his hand" (April 17, 1968); "There wasn't any shoot-to-kill order. That was a fabrication" (April 18, 1968); "You could say Senator Tower is doing a lousy job, but I don't use that kind of words" (May 1, 1962); "I have lived in Chicago all my life and I still say we have no ghetto in Chicago" (July 8, 1963); "We will have a planned development and will take people out of the ghettos and slums and give them an opportunity to raise their families in decent surroundings" (April 17, 1969); "I didn't create the slums, did I?" (September 3, 1968); "Together we must rise to ever higher and higher platitudes" (March 13, 1967).

THE RUSSIAN PREMIER. A comsymp.

CHARLES MOCENIGO'S FATHER. A professional. He worked

for Charles "Lucky" Luciano, Louis "Lepke" Buchalter, Federico Maldonado, and many other colorful American businessmen. Known in the trade as Jimmy the Shrew, because of his sharp, conniving expression. Saved his money, put his boy through MIT, killed people for a living. Found the original Frank Sullivan performing in Havana, 1934.

GENERAL LAWRENCE STEWART TALBOT. Actually, there *was* something between him and that girl from Red Lion, Penn.

MALACLYPSE THE YOUNGER, K.S.C. Author of the *Principia Discordia*. Disappeared mysteriously in late 1970. His last recorded words were, typically, "Comes the dawn, the sun shall rise in the west." Then he walked into the Pacific Ocean.

JOHN HERBERT DILLINGER. When Simon Moon read his biography in search of 23s, he missed a good one: John committed 26 robberies during his publicized career, but only 23 were for money. The other 3 (police stations) seem to have been strictly Art For Art's Sake.

SIMON'S FATHER. Tim Moon. He told Simon the lives of Joe Hill, Big Bill Haywood, Sacco and Vanzetti, and Frank Little at the age when most boys are being told about Snow White and the Seven Dwarfs. Simon remembers: Joe Hill the night before his execution, wiring Wobbly headquarters in Chicago, "Don't weep for me, boys: organize." Bartolomeo Vanzetti: "Your laws, your courts, your false god will be a dim remembering of a cursed time when man was wolf to the man." Tim and his cronies singing in the living room, "Which side are you on, man / Which *side* are you *on?*" until Molly complained, "You'll wake the neighbors." Tim explaining Big Bill: "Oh, yes, and he had a glass eye. Funny I should forget that. The real eye was knocked out by a cop during a strike." But you'll understand Tim best if you see Simon, age six, entering grammar school for the first time and addressing the first boy he meets: "I'm Simon Moon; what's your name, Fellow Worker?"

PADRE PEDERASTIA. His real name was Father James Flanagan.

TOBIAS KNIGHT. The only quintuple agent in the history of espionage.

JAMES JOYCE. After death, he met Yeats on the fifth plane and said, "Sir, I am now willing to learn from you, since you appear to have been right about Death after all." Yeats replied, "Not at all. You're dreaming this." The remark so vexed Joyce that he immediately sought reincarnation (the fifth plane was full of mystics like Yeats and George Russell and Madame Blavatski, and Joyce knew his rational Aristotelian sensibility would be constantly abused by further conversation with them), entered the womb of Elizabeth Mullins of Vernon, New Jersey, October 11, 1942, and was aborted December 10, 1942. Entered the womb of Rachel Stein of Ingolstadt, January 18, 1943, and was gassed with her, one month before birth was due, at Auschwitz, September 1, 1943. Thereafter, he retired to a monastery on the sixth plane and wrote his funniest, most bitter book. Parts of it, which he has been transmitting ever since, have been picked up by mediums on the six continents, all of whom assumed they were flipping out and refused to transcribe it.

CHARLES WORKMAN. An entrepreneur.

MENDY WEISS. Another entrepreneur.

JIMMY THE SHREW. A third entrepreneur, more successful than the above. See entry under CHARLES MOCENIGO'S FATHER.

ALBERT "THE TEACHER" STEIN. Not only did he lose his gamble with immortality when it was proven that he *didn't* kill Dutch Schultz, but almost every book on the case misspells his name as Stern, a tradition which the present work has mostly refused to shatter.

HENRY FORD. By importing the *Protocols of the Learned Elders of Zion* and beginning the mass production of automobiles, he managed to pollute both the mind and the air of the United States, but he meant well, or at least he meant something.

GEORGE DORN'S OLDER BROTHER. His successful scientific career made George envious (and helped determine George's choices of a liberal-arts curriculum at Columbia). He had an adventure with talking dolphins before George did (which set up a psychic resonance that made George's recruitment interesting to Hagbard); this story is recounted in *Tales Of the Cthulhu*

Mythos, edited by August Derleth (Arkham House, 1969).

MARKOFF CHANEY. He slipped away from Saul and Barney shortly after they returned to Las Vegas, and none of our characters ever saw him again. However, one day in 1984 Hagbard Celine, using an alias and engaged in nefarious business, happened to be in the U.S. Government Printing Office on Capitol Street in Washington and noticed a bundle of pamphlets that had been stamped with both blue TOP SECRET: AUTHORIZED PERSONNEL ONLY and red FOR IMMEDIATE RELEASE TO ALL MEDIA. Many loyal government servants would have headaches before it was ever clarified who had been responsible for which of those stamps—if, indeed, that ever could be clarified. Hagbard recalled much that Saul had told him about the Las Vegas caper and looked around thoughtfully. In one corner he saw a large coffee urn. He lit one of his long black cigars and strolled out into the street. The sun was bright, the air was clear, and it was Spring, which may explain why Hagbard began whistling as he walked with a brisk and determined pace toward the Senate Office Building. The tune was "My Heart's in the Highlands."